THAT TERRIBLE
SHADOWIN

The Quest Across Time for Caravaggio's Killer

THAT TERRIBLE
SHADOWING

'In every way the new manner of that terrible style of shadowing, the truth of those nudes, the resounding lights without many reflections, stunned, not only the dilettantes, but most of the practitioners.'

Bernardo de Dominici

DAVID STEDMAN

Matador
5 Weir Road
Kibworth Beauchamp
Leicester LE8 0LQ, UK
Tel: (+44) 116 279 2299
Email: books@troubador.co.uk
Web: www.troubador.co.uk/matador

ISBN 978 1848761 315

British Library Cataloguing in Publication Data.
A catalogue record for this book is available from the British Library.

Typeset in 11.5pt Bembo by Troubador Publishing Ltd, Leicester, UK
Printed in the UK by TJ International, Padstow, Cornwall

Matador is an imprint of Troubador Publishing Ltd

To
Fiona Hamilton for the inspiration
and
Helen Langdon for the information

1

As with so many young men, before and since, it was lust and curiosity about female flesh that led to all my later tribulations. Curiosity, then as now, has been my redemption and my ruin, and lured me into the dark orbit of a man whose overweening genius reverberates down the centuries. How I wish I had never been introduced to his poignant and capricious soul, yet how spiritually undernourished my life, and the life of all humanity, would have been without him.

One cold November day in 1965, when I was sixteen years old and when I had just left school but not yet embarked on the delights of working life, I was in London and engaged in the favourite teenage pastime of mooching about. I wandered aimlessly into Trafalgar Square and, simply because it was there, decided to visit the National Gallery. I had no particular interest in art and no particular desire to visit the National Gallery but it did possess one over-riding attraction for an impecunious adolescent visiting London . . . free admission. Also, there was the lure of naked women. In the mid-1960s, images of naked women were not so widely distributed in every tabloid newspaper, cinema film and television programme as they are in the early 21st century. The hormones coursing through my adolescent body took control and visions of pearly white women with rosy pink nipples beckoned me inside the gallery. None of the gallery staff took any notice of a gangly, stick-thin, nose-picking, acne-faced youth wearing a plastic imitation leather jacket, winkle-picker shoes and a greasy Mick Jagger hairstyle. We all looked like that in those days, except those poncey Mods.

After scrutinising the wallplan of the National Gallery I selected what I thought were the most promising galleries in my search for nipples or, if I was really lucky, pubic hair. I found myself in Italian art of the Renaissance and Baroque periods. Leonardo da Vinci's Virgin of the Rocks was impressive, even to a philistine adolescent like me, but the vacuous prettiness of Botticelli, the fervid chocolate-box stiffness of Raphael and the soft-focus piety of Correggio et al was really beginning to piss me off, despite the occasional nipple. Then I saw a painting that caught my interest as forcibly as if Britt Ekland had been standing there naked, despite the painting being devoid of any trace of nipples or pubic hair. The picture looked like a scene from a Martin Scorsese film that had been photographed on to a piece of canvas and then surrounded by a gold frame. What the hell was it? Surely it should be in a gallery of modern art, not stuck in here with all these dead, and dead boring, Italians? I read the picture notes attached to the wall beside the painting. It was called Supper at Emmaus (*Plate 2*) and had been painted by an artist known as Caravaggio in about 1601. That could not be right! It had to be a modern work! The dramatic immediacy of the scene was spellbinding. On the right of the picture, Saint James throws out his arms to protest about something. In the foreground, Cleophas is rising angrily from his chair and looks as if he is about to deck somebody. The innkeeper in the background is looking at Christ as if to say 'what the fuck is all this going on in my tavern?'. Christ Himself remains calm, an oasis of benediction, but He does not look like any Christ I have seen before. He is soft, androgynous, almost pudgy and pretty, but with a commanding air of authority. In front of them, on the dining table, are fruit, fowl, bread and a carafe of wine, all painted with an astonishing dew-fresh realism. The whole painting is as dew-fresh as the day it was completed. Here was not a prissy, nancy-boy, lisping vicar, village social type of art. Here was not the art of cosy curled-up cats or pretty vases of flowers or country lanes winding through lush meadows or false promises of a soft eternal life hereafter. Here was a punk anarchist, spit-in-yer-face, what-the-fuck-are-you-looking at, bovver boy type of art. Fascinated, I gazed at the painting for I don't know how long, forgetting all about rosy nipples and pubic hair.

Excited by my discovery, I took the train home to Bedfordshire and went directly to the local library just before it closed for the day. I found the most promising-looking volume of artist biographies and looked up the section on this man Caravaggio. He was everything that a sixteen-year-old yob, with testosterone raging through his bloodstream, could hope for. His real name was Michelangelo Merisi, he was called Caravaggio after his home town in Lombardy, and he lived from 1571 until 1610. The writer of the biography, with barely concealed distaste, stated that Michelangelo Merisi da Caravaggio was a notorious braggart, a violent bully, a drunken habitué of the brothels of Rome, an equally regular habitué of the prisons of Rome and, in the end, became a fugitive from justice after killing a rival in a duel. Oh, and by the way, he was an artist of genius whose original vision changed the course of Western art and still influences the way we see the world today. He really was the dog's bollocks. Imagine my surprise when, some forty years later, I found him sitting next to me in the National Gallery.

I had travelled to London to visit a client. Thankfully, considering my client's vodka-and-onion breath, our business had been concluded much sooner than I had anticipated. I left his office and even the London traffic fumes seemed tropically-scented after Mr. Halitosis-on-legs. I was within walking distance of Trafalgar Square. Just as it had been forty years before, it was a cold day but bright and bracing and, on a whim, I decided to stroll to the National Gallery and pay homage to the painting that I had discovered all those forty years ago but had not seen 'in the flesh' for several years. Just as I had done when I was a priapic teenager, I toured some of the galleries from other eras first, just to heighten my sense of anticipation. Finally, I could resist temptation no longer and made my way to the 1600-1700 gallery. When I saw my painting again, it was with that stomach-churning sense of excitement and nostalgia that you feel when you glimpse a long-lost love in the crowd. Caravaggio is now much more famous than he was forty years ago and the Supper at Emmaus always attracts a big audience. It was irritating to have to share my picture with hordes of gawping tourists but there it was, still frozen in time, and as compelling as the first time I saw it. The brown leather bench in front of the painting became vacant. I sat down. Someone sat down beside me, on my left. I studied my painting, having to glance at it in between the moving bodies of dozens of spectators, until I became aware that the same man had been sitting next to me for several minutes. He had moved uncomfortably close to me. I looked around at him, trying to be casual about it, and found that he was staring at me with an amused and interested expression.

'Hello, Steve,' he said, in a guttural, almost mechanical-sounding, foreign accent.

'Hello,' I replied, in that hesitant and startled way you do when someone catches you by surprise. 'I'm sorry, do I know you?'

The intruder ignored my question and, indicating the Supper at Emmaus, asked: 'What do you think of that painting?'

I answered cautiously. 'I like it very much. What do you think of it?'

'I like it very much too,' he replied, 'but then I should do because I painted it.'

You know the feeling . . . the dishevelled junkie boards the tube train, mumbling to himself, and you think 'please God, don't let him come and sit next to me'. This time, God had decided to play His little joke on me.

'You painted it?' I repeated.

'Yes,' the intruder confirmed, still with an amused look on his face.

'Well, you must give me the name of your embalmer because you're wearing very well for someone who died four hundred years ago.' I stood up and started to move away towards the exit, my enjoyment ruined by the gallery lunatic.

The lunatic stood up with me and blocked my escape. 'No, I didn't die, or so I've been told. I've been here waiting for you, Steve.'

'Look, how do you know my name?'

'The people who sent me here showed me what you look like, told me your name is Steve Maddan and told me all about you. You were on a television quiz show, whatever that is, answering questions about me.'

Reassured by this statement and beginning to understand - so I thought - what was going on, I decided to humour him. 'You mean Mastermind?'

'Yes, that's it. I've been waiting for you since then. I am Michelangelo Merisi, known as Caravaggio, but you can call me Michele.' He offered me his hand to shake. I did not take it.

I studied his appearance. I had to admit that, from what I could remember of the portrait drawing (*Plate 1*) by his friend and contemporary Ottavio Leoni, this man looked like Caravaggio. A lot like Caravaggio. He was tall, with a stocky, powerful physique. His hair was long, thick and black. His eyes were also black, with very long eyebrows which were bushy and rounded. His black moustache was full but his black beard was thinner and more wispy. He wore an ill-fitting black business suit, in which he looked awkward and uncomfortable, over a grubby open-necked white shirt. I glimpsed an ornate gold chain underneath his shirt. The most disturbing element of his appearance was the whitened and barely visible remains of scars that had once disfigured his face. Or so it had been made to appear. I was beginning to understand that this was some practical joke or television candid camera stunt. I decided to go along with it for the time being.

I asked: 'How did you know I would be here today?'

'We didn't, but there is a sensor hidden in the frame of my picture. It told us you were here.'

'Us?'

'Yes. Come and look at the frame if you don't believe me.' He grabbed my sleeve. I momentarily tried to pull away but then allowed him to drag me through the throng of spectators until we were uncomfortably close to the Supper at Emmaus. I looked around and saw the gallery attendant watching us intently, ready to intervene. He was a black guy and he was big and he looked as if he could handle himself.

'Look, there it is,' the lunatic said, pointing at a gold convex scallop among the many gold convex scallops that decorated the elaborate frame. The scallop he indicated was slightly larger than the rest. It certainly disturbed the symmetry of the frame but it could have been a defect in the manufacture of the frame and proved nothing. Wary of the gallery attendant, I decided not to argue and moved away from the picture.

'That is a sensor that told you I was here?' I asked, allowing an edge of sarcasm in my tone of voice.

'Yes, and I was automatically reactivated out of ChronoStasis and sent through time to meet you here. We knew you would one day return to look at my picture again. We didn't know how else to find you. You took your time.'

'Please accept my apologies for that,' I said, 'I've been busy helping Vincent Van Gogh look for his missing ear.' I looked around theatrically. 'Where are the hidden cameras?'

'I don't know what you mean?' the lunatic replied.

'Okay,' I said, in a louder voice, playing to the hidden microphones, 'you are an Italian artist who died four hundred years ago and you have travelled through time specifically to meet me.'

'Yes, that's right.'

'How come you speak English so well?'

'They gave me some sort of translator device so that I think in Italian but, when I speak, it comes out of my mouth in English.' He held up his hand to show me a thin gold ring around his left middle finger. 'This is it.'

'So that's why you sound like Chico Marx.'

'Who is Chico Marx?'

'Who are "they",' I asked.

'I'll explain everything when we get back to where you live and then I can . . .'

'Whoa, hold on,' I said, beginning to tire of this nonsense, 'you are not coming home with me.'

'Why not? You admire my work, don't you? We are friends already, aren't we? You are the only one who can help me.'

'Look, I wouldn't care if you were the Mona Lisa come back to tell me what the hell you were smiling at, you're not coming home with me. I'm sorry to ruin your carefully prepared stunt. I'm saying sorry to the film crew, wherever they are hidden. I'm saying sorry to the bouffant-haired egomaniac presenter or whoever is waiting to jump out and take the piss if I fall for this crap, but this has gone far enough. You are a good actor and you do look very like Caravaggio. I hope you've been well-paid for doing this but I'm leaving.' My voice had raised in volume without me being aware of it and I was now attracting some suspicious looks from the gallery visitors. I pushed past the lunatic and walked away quickly towards the exit.

To my surprise, 'Caravaggio' followed me and grabbed my arm again. 'Wait a minute, you English fucker,' he shouted angrily. 'How dare you talk to me like that? Me, the greatest fucking artist in Italy, has already waited four hundred years and then been put in ChronoStasis for another three years in this poxed-up museum waiting for you to show up and then you won't have anything to do with me? You arrogant cunt. You should think yourself lucky that I let you even look at my pictures, let alone talk to me.'

We were now attracting many more suspicious looks and my temper was beginning to flare up. Then I realised, with relief and almost with amusement, that this is just how the real Caravaggio would react and that this actor was staying in character in a last ditch effort to persuade me to remain in the show. Clever!

In a conciliatory and much softer voice, I said to him: 'Okay, you are a very good actor. You've performed your act very well, very cleverly, but I'm just not interested in being involved in this stunt, whatever it is. Go back to your producer, or whoever you are working for, and tell them I won't play along and that I'm sorry I'm not more of a good sport.' I began to walk away again.

'No, I'm coming with you,' Caravaggio said. 'You have to help me.' He now had an arm wrapped around my neck, holding me back. The gallery attendant stood up and began to move towards us. I broke free, ran out of the gallery and looked for the way out. Caravaggio was right behind me shouting: 'Stop. Steve, stop and wait for me.' I ignored him but he carried on following me. I pushed through a door and through a throng of tourists, knocking an elderly Japanese couple out of the way, mumbling hasty apologies as I did so. I burst through another door and then I was leaping down a flight of stairs towards the Trafalgar Square exit with Caravaggio right behind me trying to grab my jacket. The gallery visitors frantically parted to allow we two running fugitives through. Then Caravaggio really cut loose. He started screaming: 'Cunt, fucker, bastard, shithead, fucking English fucker.' This was really not funny anymore. I ran out of the building, turned left and down the steps into the throng of Trafalgar Square tourists. I hastily looked back to see if Caravaggio was following me. To my surprise and relief he had stopped at the top of the National Gallery steps. He appeared to be open-mouthed in shock and amazement as he stared at the crowds, the tall buildings, the fountains sparkling in the bright glare of the afternoon sun, the soaring stone column with Nelson perched on top, and the traffic of red buses, rumbling lorries and cars roaring past on the far side of the square.

I escaped into the crowd and away from the lunatic's line of sight. I turned left into St. Martin's Lane, past the statue of Edith Cavell, and zigzagged through the back streets to make sure he could not follow me. I did not know or care which way I was going. I was badly shaken by the whole experience. Whoever had set me up for this practical joke, whether it was a television company or sick-minded friends, they had carried the whole thing too far. I determined that, if I ever found out who they were, I would make them pay dearly for frightening me like that. I went into a pub and ordered a double scotch to calm my nerves. As I sat on the bar stool, calmed by Famous Grouse and comforted by Victorian burnished wood and gleaming brass, it occurred to me that nobody knew I was going to be in the National Gallery that day. Even I did not know until a few minutes before I actually decided to go. Nobody even knew I was travelling to London that day. Even if I was being followed and then seen going into the National Gallery, 'they' would have had only a few minutes to set-up hidden cameras and microphones and prepare the actor who was playing Caravaggio. Either that, or the film crew would have to be on permanent stand-by in case I dropped in to the gallery. Neither of those options was practical, feasible or sensible. No, the only explanation was that 'Caravaggio' was a mentally unbalanced individual who really did think he was the artist. He must have remembered my name and what I looked like from my appearance on the television quiz show Mastermind, when I had taken the life and work of Caravaggio as my specialist subject. By coincidence, this deluded individual had happened to be in the National Gallery at the same time as me. This encounter had been a very disturbing experience. I was relieved to think that I had recently moved away from where I had been living when I appeared on Mastermind. There was no possibility that the lunatic could know where I lived. With that reassuring thought, I drank up, found the nearest underground tube station to transport me to St. Pancras railway station and caught a mainline train that returned me, with relief, to the anonymous rural calm of Bedfordshire. I congratulated myself for extricating myself adroitly from a tricky situation. I would not have been so smug if I had known that the situation was about to become a whole lot trickier.

2

Thanks to the most painless and advantageous kind of death in the family, that of someone unloved but wealthy, and some labyrinthine legal manouevring to avoid the imposition of inheritance tax by the ever-grasping British Government, I had recently been able to afford to buy my dream home. It was a Victorian cottage in a village situated just outside the county town of Bedford. The cottage itself was modest but the garden was a delight, with a long front garden and a very long, albeit narrow, rear garden backing on to the River Ouse. I work from home in a sedentary job and it had always been my dream to have sufficient land to create a beautiful garden as a relaxing hobby and as a form of exercise to counteract my otherwise flab-inducing lifestyle. The cottage was detached but located within a row of similar cottages on either side. Upstairs, there were two large bedrooms and a bathroom which I had converted from a small third bedroom. Downstairs, there was a very spacious modernised kitchen and, outside, an old coal shed had been converted into a lavatory. I had converted the front room into an office and kept the larger back room as the living room. The living room looked out onto the back garden and there was a sliding door that gave access to a large patio outside. There were tall mature trees in the back garden, willows and alders down by the river, which I intended to keep. The rest of the garden was mainly grass, with an old dilapidated summerhouse halfway down the garden on the left. The summerhouse had been an elegant and ornately-decorated wooden structure when first built but it was now in such a sadly neglected state that it would have to be demolished as soon as I found the time.

Two days after my encounter with the lunatic in the National Gallery, I was working in my office when the telephone rang. I answered with my usual spiel: 'Steve Maddan Publishing, Steve speaking.'

'Ah, Mr. Maddan,' the caller said, 'this is P.C. George Chappell at West End Central police station in London. We have arrested an Italian national named Michelangelo Merisi. He claims he is staying with you. Can you confirm that?'

My heart sank. I decided that I had to nip this absurd situation in the bud, firmly and decisively. 'No,' I replied. 'I do not know a Mr. Merisi.'

'Are you the Mr. Maddan who appeared on the television show Mastermind last year and who won Brain of Britain a few years ago?'

'Yes, I am.'

'Then you are definitely the person that Mr. Merisi claims to know.'

'I do not know Mr. Merisi,' I said, emphatically. 'He is certainly not staying with me. He accosted me in the National Gallery, no doubt after recognising me from that television show, and made some extraordinary and, I have to say, almost violent claims to be a seventeenth century Baroque artist named Caravaggio. That artist was my specialist subject on Mastermind and this Merisi person has some sort of unbalanced delusion that he is Caravaggio. That is all I can tell you about him. I want nothing to do with him.' Then, out of the sheer stupid curiousity that has plagued me all my life, I asked: 'Why was he arrested?'

'Just a minute, sir,' P.C. Chappell said, and I heard him in brief muffled conversation with someone else. 'Er, Mr. Merisi was attempting to steal items from a delicatessen. He assaulted the officer who was trying to arrest him by knocking his hat off. Merisi then described an accompanying female officer as an Ortaccio whore, whatever that means. We think Merisi deliberately got himself arrested in order to obtain a meal and a bed for the night. He claims he was hungry and had no money to buy food because you had stolen it from him.'

'What!' I shouted. 'That is simply not true! I have not stolen anything from him. I have done nothing to injure him in any way. It was him who assaulted me . . . almost.' Then realisation dawned on me and I cursed my own slow stupidity. This was no police officer on the telephone. This was another attempt to drag me into some television stunt or practical joke. 'Look, you had me believing you there,' I said 'but I'm not going to get involved in whatever stunt you are trying to set-up and this continual harassment is becoming bloody irritating.'

P.C. Chappell, or whoever he was, carried on as if I had not said anything. 'Mr. Merisi also claims that you have stolen his identity papers. He has no form of identification on his person, no passport, no driving licence, no money, keys, credit cards, or anything that can confirm who he is. I'm sure there's been some sort of misunderstanding. Could you come down to the station so that we can sort all this out?'

'Absolutely not. I am not wasting a day travelling to London because of something that has nothing to do with me or just to help you make a television show. If all this is genuine, can't the Italian embassy help?'

'We've tried them, sir. They have no knowledge of anyone of this name. They have not been approached by Mr. Merisi and, without documentation, there is nothing they can do and they do not want to know.'

'Well, that makes two of us,' I said. I quickly thought of a cunning ploy to expose P.C. Chappell as a fraud. 'Listen, you have found out where I live and you have probably run a check on me to see if I have a criminal record. Am I right?'

P. C. Chappell did not answer for a few seconds. 'Yes, that's right,' he answered.

'Then you will have found out that I was convicted of grievous bodily harm in 1998.' It was a complete falsehood but would this television flunkey calling himself P.C. Chappell fall into the trap?

'One moment, sir.' There were sounds of a computer keyboard being tapped. Then: 'There is no record of such a conviction. As far as we are concerned you do not have a criminal record, that is why we wanted to give you the benefit of the doubt and sort all this out in a reasonable manner. There is obviously some disagreement between you and Mr. Merisi.'

'He certainly disagrees with me, like a bad curry,' I said heatedly, disappointed that my bluff had failed. 'Either you are trying to set me up for some television show or this Merisi person is a mentally unbalanced fantasist and is making up these accusations. For God's sake don't tell him where I live.'

'If you would come down and . . . .'

'No', I repeated. 'I am not coming down to London. It has nothing to do with me. I suggest that you let a doctor, preferably a psychiatrist, examine Merisi. I'm sure he would soon conclude that he is some sort of deluded fantasist.'

'That might be a possibility,' P. C. Chappell said. 'but if you just came down . . .'

'No.'

'You are making a mistake by not co-operating with us.'

'My only mistake was visiting the National Gallery when the local nutter was in residence. I am not getting involved any further. And don't tell him where I am. I don't want him stalking me.'

'Don't worry, Mr. Maddan, we will not give Mr. Merisi any information about your whereabouts without your permission.'

'Good.'

'Well, if you are adamant about refusing to co-operate then we will have to leave it there for the time being, but you will probably be hearing from us again . . . soon.'

It sounded like a threat but I let it go. 'You do what you have to do.'

'Oh, don't worry, sir, we will,' Chappell said, and abruptly put down the telephone.

I replaced my receiver and sat back to think about what had just happened.

This situation was spiralling out of control. If it was not a television set-up, I considered whether I had made the right move in refusing to go back down to London and sort things out. But, even if it was not a television set-up and P. C. Chappell was the genuine article, to have gone down to London would have seemed like an admission that I was somehow involved or responsible. I carried on working with the half-hearted hope that my latest refusal would deter the television practical jokers or a real brush with the law would frighten Merisi, or whoever he was, out of his fantasy world.

The hope lasted almost exactly one day. I saw, from my front room office window, a police car pull up at my front gate and a female police officer walking up to my front door. I got up, reluctantly, from my desk and went to open the front door.

'Good morning,' I said.

'Mr. Maddan?'

'I would dearly love to say no,' I replied. 'I bet you're not here to sell tickets for the police raffle.'

She looked at me blankly. 'I am Sergeant Caro of Bedfordshire police, sir. I've been sent to try to settle this dispute between you and a Mr. Merisi.'

Sergeant Caro looked too young and attractive to be a police sergeant. She wore her chequer-banded hat at an angle that was slightly too jaunty for the nature of her office. She had a kind face and irresistible brown eyes. She was a tad unsure of herself. I could see my neighbour, Mrs. Chowdry, standing in her front garden watching proceedings with a keen interest, as neighbours do when the police turn up.

'Before I ask you in, could I see your warrant card, please.' If this was another wind-up, I was determined to stop it before it started.

Sergeant Caro looked surprised. 'Of course, sir,' she replied, and fumbled in her uniform pockets before finding her warrant card and handing it to me. I looked at it as if I knew what I was looking at and then said: 'Excuse me while I shut the front door on you. I'm just going to check that you are who you say you are.'

I closed the front door on Sergeant Caro and walked back into my office. I found the telephone number of Bedford police station and dialled it. A female voice, probably a civilian helper, answered the telephone and I said: 'My name is Steven Maddan. I've got a Sergeant Caro waiting on my doorstep claiming to be a Bedfordshire police officer. Do you have an officer by that name on the force?'

'Yes, sir,' she said, 'I know Sergeant Caro.' Damn, I thought.

'Can you describe her to me?' I asked.

'Oh, gosh,' the civilian helper replied. 'She's fairly tall, about five feet six inches, but quite stocky. She wears her hair short, in a bob, but it works for her.

She's got a lovely complexion, like a permanent suntan. I think her mother was from Antigua and her father is Italian.'

'That's fine. You've been . . .'

'Oh, and she's got lovely big brown eyes . . . you know, the kind you can just melt into. Wish mine were the same!'

'Okay, you've been most helpful. Thank . . .'

'And she's got a mole on her left cheek. Her face, that is, not . . . you know, down below, if you pardon my French. Trust her to have a mole just where it looks like the cutest dimple. I remember we had a Chief Inspector once who . . .'

'Thank you,' I said, putting down the telephone and not regretting that I would never find out what happened with the Chief Inspector.

I thought for a moment. Sergeant Caro was the genuine article. I had truly hoped she was not. I went back and opened the front door. I checked the mole on Caro's left cheek. 'Would you mind taking your hat off?' I asked. I just wanted to be absolutely certain.

Sergeant Caro hesitated for a second and then removed her hat to reveal glossy black hair cut in a stylish and attractive short bob.

'You'll be very pleased to know that you are who you say you are, and that your big brown eyes are famous throughout the station.'

Sergeant Caro smiled, pleased with the compliment, then quickly remembered the dignity of her office and the smile was replaced with a serious demeanour. 'The Met police have dropped all charges against Mr. Merisi and have dumped, er, handed this problem over to us,' she said. 'I've got Mr. Merisi waiting in the car, with a colleague, and if we . . .'

'Hold on', I interrupted, panic rising. 'You've brought this Merisi here, to my home?'

'Yes, he's waiting in the car. He is being transferred to Yarl's Wood immigration detention centre which is just up the road. Could we bring him in and sort this out?'

'I specifically asked what's-his-name at West End Central, P.C. Chappell, not to let Merisi know where I live.'

'Mr. Merisi claims he lives with you, that you owe him money, but he is willing to withdraw any other complaints against you if you just pay him what you owe him, then he will move out and leave you alone in future.'

'Merisi does not live with me and I do not owe him money. But bring him in, if you must, and let's sort this out, once and for all.'

This charade was now beginning to seem like an elaborate scam to con money out of me. If that was the case and handing over money was the only way to get rid of this Merisi impersonator, then I was willing to consider it, even if that would be a craven cave-in. He had now seen where I lived so I might as well let him come in and try to talk sense into him. Sergeant Caro walked back down to the police car and, after a few moments, was escorting the maniac Merisi up to my front door with the assistance of a male constable who, I was relieved to see, towered above both Merisi and Sergeant Caro. I recognised the police constable as a former England rugby union international. He was literally almost seven feet tall and would certainly be able to restrain the Merisi madman if the need arose. Sergeant Caro introduced her colleague. 'This is P.C. Greenfield,' she said.

I nodded in acknowledgement and, holding the front door open, said: 'Duck. That's not a term of endearment, you understand.' Greenfield looked at me with a sour expression, wishing he had been given a five pound note for every time he had heard feeble remarks like that.

The three of them entered my hallway. Merisi looked at me accusingly but said nothing. To maintain a formal, business-like character to this encounter, I took them into my office, rather than the living room, and did not invite them to sit down.

Merisi spoke before anyone else could. 'I'm sorry I threatened you, Stefano. Give me what you owe me so that I can buy brushes and canvas and materials to make paints and I will not bother you again.' Then, unnoticed by the police officers, he winked at me. He actually winked at me!

I knew I was being incredibly stupid but I was psychologically disturbed by the recent chain of events and I just wanted this encounter to end, so I took Merisi's hint. 'Will one hundred pounds satisfy you?' I asked Merisi.

'That is approximately 150 Euros,' P.C. Greenfield told Merisi.

Merisi looked at him without comprehension and said: 'How much is that in scudi?'

'What are scudi?' Greenfield asked.

I said: 'One hundred pounds is about four hundred scudi.'

'That is very generous,' Merisi nodded. 'Is that enough to buy materials and something to eat and some wine in this country?'

'Better make it two hundred pounds,' I offered. 'Just to make sure.'

The two police officers, clearly bemused by this exchange and just as keen to resolve this situation as I was, looked at Merisi. Sergeant Caro said: 'Would that satisfy you, Mr. Merisi?'

'Yes,' he said. 'Stefano is most generous.'

'If I give you the cash now, do you promise, in front of these police officers, that you will never contact me or bother me again.'

Merisi nodded again. 'As a Knight of Magistral Obedience, I do so promise.'

The police officers shifted uncomfortably at this strange utterance but I knew what Merisi meant. 'Wait here, please,' I said to the officers, 'and don't let him touch anything.'

I went into the living room. I kept some cash in a hidden compartment in my bureau and found to my relief that I had just enough. I counted out £200. Merisi had concocted a ridiculously elaborate scam just to earn £200 but, like most blackmail victims, I knew in my heart of hearts that this would not be the end of it. I returned to my office and handed the £200 to Sergeant Caro. 'I want something in writing to prove that I have given Mr. Merisi his money and that he his now fully satisfied and promises not to make any more demands. Don't give him this money until he has signed it.'

'Very well,' Sergeant Caro said. 'We'll take Mr. Merisi back to the station, write up our report on what has occurred here, get Mr. Merisi to sign a disclaimer and send it you to be countersigned as well. We will have to consider if there are any other charges to be laid against you or Mr. Merisi.'

'Like what?' I asked, irritably. 'Entering the National Gallery without due care and attention? Looking at paintings with a loud and offensive nutcase?'

'Perhaps the Met will want to go ahead with a charge against Mr. Merisi for attempted theft and assaulting their officer. Or perhaps there will be a charge of wasting police time against both Mr. Merisi and yourself.' I opened my mouth to protest but Caro said: 'I don't think it will come to that. As you have both been sensible enough to sort this out in an amicable manner, with no real harm done, I think it likely that all charges will be dropped.'

No harm done, I thought, except to my bank balance. 'What is going to happen to Mr. Merisi,' I asked. 'Where will he go now? Will he be deported back to Italy?'

'We are all members of the European Union now, Mr. Maddan,' said Caro, in a prim school-marmish tone.

'Yes, I'd almost forgotten that the nation has been signed up to such joys. Three cheers for spaghetti and garlic and Guinness and wiener schnitzel.'

Caro said: 'Mr. Merisi will be taken to Yarl's Wood immigration detention centre where the immigration service will be asked to investigate his status.'

'So he'll be kept in custody for the time being?'

'Yes, until Yarl's Wood can properly establish Mr. Merisi's status and identity.'

It was a relief to know that Merisi was going to be kept in captivity for a while. 'Good,' I said. 'Is that it, then?'

'Yes, for now,' said Sergeant Caro. 'We'll be in touch if we need anything else from you.'

'Please do. It's been such a pleasure having you here. We must do this again some time.'

Caro and her colleague did not look pleased at my sarcasm. Merisi smiled, and winked at me again.

'Well, Mr. Merisi,' I said. 'What do you think of our English prison cells? So much more comfortable than the Tor di Nona prison in Rome where you were incarcerated for coarse language and carrying arms without a licence in, what was it, October 1604?'

'Very good, Stefano,' Merisi smiled. 'I was indeed imprisoned in the Tor di Nona in October 1604, but that was for throwing stones at the police in the Via dei Greci. For the other offences you mentioned, I was back inside again in November. One day soon, Stefano, you will believe that I am who I say I am.'

The police officers, puzzled and edgy, bustled Merisi out of my house before more trouble started. Mrs. Chowdry was still in her front garden watching these comings and goings with a bemused expression. I waved to her reassuringly and, caught out being the nosey parker, she waved back with a nervous and unsure half-smile. I closed the front door and headed for the living room bookcase. I selected the best biography of Michelangelo Merisi da Caravaggio that I owned, which is entitled Caravaggio: A Life by the educator and historian Helen Langdon. I flicked through the index and found the appropriate references. I turned to the appropriate page and found, to my dismay, that Merisi was right and I was wrong about the dates and reasons for his incarcerations in the prisons of Rome. I had not been trying to catch him out but he had caught me out! But if this madman truly believed he was Caravaggio then it was not surprising that he had such detailed knowledge of Caravaggio's life. Still, I was a little shaken.

Two days later, when Sergeant Caro rang me up, her news caused me no surprise. 'Hello, Mr. Maddan,' she said. 'I'm ringing to inform you that Michaelangelo Merisi has absconded from custody at Yarl's Wood immigration centre.'

I let out a theatrical sigh of exasperation. 'How did he do it? Caravaggio was always very good at escaping from custody.'

Caro pounced on my comment like a good detective. 'So you know Mr. Merisi better than you have admitted?'

'No, I do not,' I replied, 'but I know a lot about the man he deludedly thinks he is.'

'And who is that?'

'Michelangelo Merisi da Caravaggio, an Italian artist who died four hundred years ago.'

'Oh,' Sergeant Caro exclaimed, and then, unwilling to pursue such a bizarre premise any further, said: 'Well, this is just to warn you in case he tries to return to your house.'

'To which the police force so kindly showed him in the first place. Did you provide him with a map and a packed lunch this time?'

Caro either missed or chose to ignore my withering sarcasm. 'No, he somehow slipped out at night past the security guards. Just be careful, that's all.'

'Yes, I will,' I promised. 'Thank you for informing me.'

'Not at all. Please don't hesitate to contact us if you need help or if he causes any trouble.'

'Thank you. I'll bear that in mind when Signor Merisi is punching my lights out.'

I put down the telephone and immediately made a tour of the cottage to ensure that all the doors were locked and all the windows were closed and secured. It was early in the Spring and the weather was mild so it was irksome to have to shut myself in but I knew that Merisi would be heading back my way. I put the emergency services 999 number on speed dial on my mobile phone and determined to keep the mobile with me at all times. From my tennis playing days, many years before, I had kept a selection of graphite-framed rackets which would make handy defensive weapons. I strategically placed one each at the front and back doors, near the patio sliding door and up in my bedroom.

Several days passed without incident and I was mentally beginning to relax and hope that Merisi had learned his lesson and was staying away from me. At 8.30 one evening, while I was watching television in the living room, there was a loud knocking at the front door. Okay, here we go, I thought to myself. I knew it had to be Merisi. There was an electric bell on the front door but, to stay in character, the Caravaggio impersonator would not use it because a seventeenth century Italian would not understand how to use such things. I tried to see out of the front room office window but it was too dark outside and the porch of the cottage obscured the view to the front door. Never mind, I thought, let's sort this maniac out once and for all. Brandishing my trusty Slazenger graphite above my head, I crept to the front door and suddenly pulled it open. Mrs. Chowdry stepped back with a startled exclamation of fear and surprise.

'Oh, Mr. Maddan,' she exclaimed. 'You frightened me to death.'

'I'm so sorry, Mrs. Chowdry,' I said, lowering the racket. 'I was just practising my top spin lob. Wimbledon beckons again this year, strawberries and cream and lashings of rain. I thought you were someone else.'

She gave me a peculiar look and then said: 'In that case you probably already know that you've got a tramp living in your summerhouse.'

It took me a few seconds to comprehend what she had said. 'A tramp?' I repeated.

'Yes, I've noticed a man going in and out once or twice during the day but I thought you had hired a gardener or something. But he is in there now. I can see a light flickering in your summerhouse from my bedroom window.'

I bet you can, I thought, through those 20 x 50 binoculars you keep up there. Mrs. Chowdry was a good-hearted soul. She was about 65 years old and had lived in her cottage for nigh on forty years and, like many people who have lived in the same house for many years and are then faced with a new neighbour, they seem to think that their long tenure gives them some sort of proprietorial interest over the new neighbour's property as well. Mrs. Chowdry had recently retired from running her own business in Bedford but she retained a seat on the town council and she was also a Justice of the Peace. Her three children had all married and moved away and her husband was often abroad on business in the Indian sub-continent, so Mrs. Chowdry was on her own for much of the time. The daily comings and goings of her neighbours had become her prime social interest and had assumed a disproportionately large part in her life. She was always well-dressed and well-groomed and believed in keeping up standards. I knew she was a genuinely kind and caring person beneath her prim and proper demeanour. I could have fared much worse as neighbours go, so I was anxious to reassure her.

'Thank you for telling me, Mrs. Chowdry. I'm letting a friend of mine do a little work for me on the summerhouse. He's probably just finishing something off tonight.'

'Oh, I see,' Mrs. Chowdry said. 'I thought I had better tell you. I hope you don't think I'm being nosey, Mr. Maddan. After seeing the police here the other day, I thought you might need to know.' She looked at me expectantly, hoping to glean more gossip about my visit from the police.

'It's very kind of you to be concerned,' I said, refusing to feed her curiosity.

Not deterred, Mrs. Chowdry went on: 'I know that the lady at the end of the row had a problem with travellers not so long ago. I thought they might have broken into your . . . .'

'No, no. Please don't concern yourself,' I interrupted, adopting a reassuringly brisk and jocular tone. 'I was just going out to see my friend. I'll tell him it's time to clock off.'

'Oh, well, sorry to have disturbed you, Mr. Maddan.'

'Not at all. Goodnight, Mrs. Chowdry.'

Mrs. Chowdry scuttled off down my front garden path and I closed the front door pensively. What should I do? Would it be best to call the police? Whether it was Merisi out there, or whether it was a tramp or a traveller, the police could deal with it without any risk to myself. In the end, it was a desire not to get entangled with officaldom, and – I have to admit – that cursed sheer curiosity, that made me decide to confront the intruder myself. I was not afraid of Merisi. He was a big man but so am I and, despite his temper and coarse language, I had not sensed any real intention on his part to harm me physically.

I went back into the living room, found a powerful torch in my bureau, switched off the living room lights and peered out through the window into my back garden. If there had been a light flickering in the summerhouse before,

I could not see one now. I unlocked the patio door, slid it back, and stepped out into the darkness. Clutching the Slazenger graphite racket tightly, I walked quietly up to the summerhouse and looked through the windows. It was too dark to see anything and I did not want to warn whoever was in there by shining the torch through the glass. Still clutching the tennis racket in my left hand, I lifted the latch of the summerhouse door with a spare finger, pulled open the door and immediately switched on the torch in my right hand. A pile of what looked like old rags suddenly rose from the floor on my right and a face, wild-eyed with fright, looked round at me.

'Who the fuck is it?' Merisi cried. 'Who are you?'

I switched off the torch and said: 'It's me . . . Steve.'

Merisi sat up and then sank back to rest his back on the wall of the summerhouse. He was breathing heavily and sweating profusely despite the cool April night air. He looked badly frightened.

'Steve,' he mumbled distractedly. 'I was having a bad dream.'

'I'm sorry,' I said. 'I didn't know you were asleep. I didn't know who you were.' Why do we English apologise for everything, even when it is not our fault?

Merisi pointed over to my right. 'There's a bottle of wine over there. Give me the wine.'

I switched on the torch and saw the half-empty bottle standing on an upturned wooden packing crate. There were also the remains of a meal. Breadcrumbs, a piece of cheese, and what looked like chicken bones, all eaten off an old paint can lid. I handed the wine bottle to Merisi and he took several gulps. There was a Calor gas lamp on a shelf above the remains of his meal. I took it down and switched it on. The summerhouse was illuminated with a weak and pale bluish light. I could see that Merisi had been sleeping under some old hessian sacks and a paint-stained white dust sheet, with more hessian sacks folded up to make a pillow. He was still wearing the same black suit and white shirt that he had worn at the National Gallery. He looked at me, bleary-eyed, still half-drunk.

I asked: 'What are you doing here?'

'I'm living here. Working here.'

'Well, you can't,' I said.

'Why not? I've lived in worse places.' He belched and I could smell his foul breath even from this distance.

'That's not what I mean. You cannot live here. Haven't you got a home of your own.'

'No, never had. Always had to beg from other people.'

'What do you want from me? Why have you come back here?' I asked, more exasperated than apprehensive.

Merisi looked at me appraisingly. 'Perhaps I will paint your portrait one day. You have an interesting face. Your nose is too big and your chin is weak but you have a pleasant smile. I came back here because if you don't believe what I say, you might believe my skill.'

'How do you mean?' I asked.

Merisi started to get to his feet. 'Don't bloody try anything,' I warned, showing him the tennis racket.

Merisi laughed. 'You play tennis, Stefano! We must have a game for a small wager one day. Mind you, as you know, I got into a lot of trouble on a tennis court once. An awful lot of trouble. Hope you are a better player than that fucker Tomassoni. Got to piss.' Merisi stood up and walked past me out of the door. Instead of seeking a secluded spot, he stood just outside the door and relieved himself on the grass. I prayed that Mrs. Chowdry was no longer looking out of her bedroom window.

He came back in and with sudden enthusiasm said: 'Look what I've found, over here!'

I held up the Calor gas lamp. On the left of the summerhouse I could see oil painting materials strewn on the floor. There were brushes stuck in an old jam jar, a bottle of linseed oil, a mahlstick, and many tubes of oil paints, one of which Merisi picked up and held up as if he had discovered a prized treasure. 'Look,' he cried. 'Paint held in these silvery tubes, ready to use, in all sorts of colours. Of all the wonders I have seen in this age, this is the best yet! I don't have to spend hours making my paints. I just squeeze and out it comes!'

I hung the gas lamp on an old nail above our heads. 'You can cut out this nonsense about pretending to be Caravaggio,' I said. 'All this play acting won't work. He has been dead for four hundred years and nothing can change that fact. If you really believe you are Caravaggio, you need to seek professional psychiatric help. I'll help you get it, if you like, but you must stop behaving like this.'

The light from the gas lamp cast a pale glow on Merisi's face and caused his features to throw deep shadows across his face. He was looking at my face, seeing a similar effect. 'Yes, you have an interesting face,' he said. 'A big nose and tired eyes but you have a merry smile, when you choose to bestow it. And I like the way the light reflects off your bald head.'

Despite my scepticism, I felt a disturbing emotion. This impostor would know that this was the sort of slanting deep-shadow lighting effect that Caravaggio employed so often in his paintings. I knew that this man must be acting and yet all this felt so real. I shook myself out of the mood and asked: 'You've been working in here? Have you been painting?'

In reply, Merisi just pointed to an old piece of sacking that had been hung to form a canopy over a couple of lengths of old wood. I could see the legs of an easel under the canopy.

'Have a look,' Merisi said. 'Lift the sacking. But please be careful. The painting is still wet.'

If anything was going to prove that this was not Caravaggio returned to life, it was going to be this painting. I knew that underneath the sacking would be a sad daub or, at best, a poor imitation of the style of the master. I gently folded back the sacking and then took it away completely to reveal the painting beneath. I knew Merisi was watching me with a look of amusement.

I was looking at a double portrait, about four feet high by three feet wide, of two men. I did not recognise either of them. The man on the left was stern-looking, appeared to be dressed as the pope, and his hand was raised in a blessing. The man on the right had a more worldy, relaxed and humorous look about him, although he was dressed as a cardinal. On the wall behind them and between them, hung a large crucifix with Christ, head down, dying on the Cross. The man on the right had his arms stretched out in front of him, inviting the viewer to inspect an array of objects on a table in front of him. The table was covered in musical instruments, scientific instruments, a geographical globe, books, artefacts, fruit, flowers and an abundance of food.

Merisi asked. 'Does it remind you of any other painting in that gallery where you first met me?'

'Yes, it does,' I replied. 'It remains me of a painting called The Ambassadors by a German artist named Hans Holbein.' (*Plate 3*).

'Very good, Stefano. We had heard talk of this man Holbein, even while I was still an apprentice. When I saw that painting of his, superb as it is, I knew I could match it. Do you think I have succeeded?'

I had switched on my torch and was examining the canvas in better light. My heart was pounding with excitement and yet I knew this was not possible. Only a master of the very highest degree could have accomplished such a work. The faces, the figures, the texture of the men's robes, and the array of goods in front of them were rendered with exquisite skill. The colours were luminous and the play of light on the whole scene was as striking as anything Vermeer had ever achieved.

'Well?' Merisi said.

'You could not have painted this.'

'Why not?' he asked, with a hint of annoyance.

'Is it still wet? Let me touch it.'

'Touch it then, if you must.'

I looked for an area of the canvas where a fingerprint blemish could easily be remedied. I touched it. My finger came away smeared with deep red oil paint.

Merisi said: 'It feels deeply satisfying to pick up the brushes again after four hundred years. And these modern paints and paint brushes are very good, much better than we had back then.'

His comment shook me back to reality. 'I accept that this picture is still wet, has just been painted, but you did not paint it.'

'Who else could have painted it?' Merisi replied, with real anger this time. 'Who else has the skill to paint like this? What the fuck do I have to do to convince you?'

'Who are these men in the picture?' I said, ignoring his anger but reassured by the feel of the tennis racket in my hand.

Merisi took a breath to calm himself down and then said: 'On the left of the picture is Camillo Borghese, who is . . . was Pope Paul. On the right of the picture is Camillo's nephew, Cardinal Scipione Borghese, indicating to us all the benefits that the two of them will bring during their benign tenure of the papal office.' There was a trace of irony in Merisi's voice.

'Pope Paul eventually pardoned Caravaggio for murdering Ranuccio Tomassoni,' I said. 'Why did you pick these two as a subject?'

'Yes, Pope Paul pardoned me and the reason for this picture will be made clear to you soon. But you do not believe that I painted it?'

'You probably know, as well as I do, the story of Han Van Meegeren. He forged the paintings of Vermeer and Pieter de Hooch and fooled all the experts. Either you are a forger as good as Van Meegeren or you have found someone else who is as skilled as he was. You are not Caravaggio. This is just part of your elaborate hoax.'

'I have never heard of these people you talk about. Why don't you come and watch me finish the painting tomorrow. I still have to complete some of the foreground objects.'

'That would prove that you painted this picture. It would prove that you are an artist of the highest skill. It would not prove that you are Caravaggio.'

'Take it to one of those experts, then. Someone who knows my work well.'

'As I just said, Van Meegeren fooled the experts. They might verify this picture as the work of Caravaggio but it would not prove that you are Caravaggio because such things cannot be. People cannot return from the dead after four hundred years.'

'Christ returned from the dead.'

'Do you compare yourself with Him?'

'Of course not. He is the Son of God. But it sets a precedent.' Merisi was thoughtful for a few seconds. 'Very well,' he said. 'I am an impatient and ill-tempered man. I understand that this must be very difficult for you to accept. I thought I could convince you of my true identity through my skill as an artist but you will not accept that proof either. There are people who have spent an enormous amount of effort, centuries of effort as I understand it, to bring me here. One of them has sacrificed all he has known and loved, for many years, to enable me to be here. Will you listen to a message from them?'

'When? Now?'

'No,' Merisi said. 'It is not appropriate now. Will you allow me into your house tomorrow? We will sleep now and then, tomorrow, let me into your house. What you have to see will not take more than an hour. If what I have to show you tomorrow cannot convince you, I swear I will leave you alone and not trouble you ever again.'

'Who are you . . . really?' I said.

'I am Michelangelo Merisi da Caravaggio. You are the only person in this world who can help me.'

It was hopeless. His delusion was too strong. 'I will allow you into the house tomorrow,' I said. 'I will give you your hour, but only if you tell me now, right now, what you want from me.'

Merisi looked at me intently through the pale light from the gas lamp. 'I want you to find out who murdered me, and why.'

3

In the morning, Merisi sat at my kitchen table looking around. He commented: 'You people now live like cardinals, or even popes and princes. What are all these big white boxes for?'

'You can drop the act, Mr. Merisi,' I said. 'You know perfectly well what all these "big white boxes" are for.'

Merisi shrugged and showed no annoyance. I had made him a mug of coffee and I put it on the table in front of him. He looked at it suspiciously. 'What is this?' he asked. He poked a finger into the liquid and immediately withdrew it with a gasp. 'It's hot! How did you make it so hot so quickly?'

'One of the wonders of the 21st century,' I said. 'I wish I could do the same to women.'

'What is it?' he repeated.

'It's coffee,' I said. 'You know very well . . .'

'Are you trying to poison me?' Merisi looked at me with a dark scowl.

'It might make you feel light-headed if you haven't drunk it before but it's a very popular beverage here in the 21st century. It comes from South America.'

'Where?'

'Oh, the Spanish vice-royalty of New Granada,' I said.

'Ah, I see,' Merisi said and, despite myself, I had to inwardly smile at his performance.

Merisi lifted the mug to his lips and gingerly took a sip. 'Oh, that is excellent,' he exclaimed. 'It is sweet and warming. Thank you, Stefano.'

'Are you hungry?' I asked.

'Yes. Some food would be most welcome.'

I popped some three-minute porridge into the microwave oven. Merisi watched it go round and round on the turntable with feigned fascination. I took it out and placed it in front of him.

'Be careful. It's very hot,' I warned.

'What is it?'

'It's a Scottish dish called porridge, flavoured with apple and blueberry,' I replied. 'It's made from oats. It's a very popular breakfast in Scotland but here in England we usually feed it to the horses.'

'Are you saying I am only fit to be given horse fodder?' Merisi scowled.

'I was forgetting, of course, that you have never heard of Doctor Samuel Johnson.'

'You talk in riddles, Stefano. Let me taste this.' Merisi tasted a small spoonful of the porridge. He grimaced. 'That is disgusting. You are trying to poison me!'

'If you think that is disgusting, you should try haggis. It's all you are going to get, so let's stop this nonsense and get down to business. I want you out of here and out of my life. What's the deal?'

Merisi wolfed down the porridge, despite his misgivings, and took another sip of coffee. From the right-hand pocket of his jacket he took out a flat disc which looked like a DVD except it was a dull bronze colour. He handed it to me and then, out of the same pocket, he took a piece of paper. He silently read some instructions written on the paper. 'Do you have something called a computer?' he asked me.

'Yes, in my office,' I said, cautiously.

'You play that disc just like a . . . DVD.' He pronounced the three letters slowly and distinctly. 'Does that make sense to you?'

'Yes, of course,' I replied.

'Very well. I am instructed to ask you to play this disc. It will take about an hour. Be completely sure that you are alone and cannot be interrupted under any circumstances. The disc will explain everything.'

I looked at the dull bronze disc and turned it over in my hands.

Merisi continued: 'I am instructed to tell you that it does not play like any DVD you will know. Do not be afraid. You will see amazing things but, all the time, you will not leave your office and you will be completely safe. The images you will see are like a hologram. Do you know what a hologram is?'

'Yes. I watch Star Trek: Voyager. I'm not going to stick this thing in my computer,' I protested. 'I have enough trouble with spam and viruses. I cannot run my business without that computer. This thing looks as if it will fuck it up completely.'

Merisi shrugged. 'You talk to me in riddles again. I can only tell you what the people who sent me have instructed me to say.'

'I'll think about running it,' I said, with no intention of doing so. 'Why don't you go back out and finish your painting? I'll let you know when I've decided what to do.'

'Very well,' Merisi said, standing up. 'I cannot force you or persuade you because I do not understand how any of these miracles work. But if you do not use that disc, then you will never know what miracle you have missed. Ciao, Stefano.' He opened the back door and stepped out.

I stood up and called after him. 'Merisi! Are you familiar with the word "toilet" or "lavatory"?'

He around looked at me. 'Yes, of course.'

'Well,' I said. 'That door on the right is a lavatory. If you need to piss, or anything else, could you please do so in there and not on my lawn.'

Merisi shook his head. 'All so clean now,' he muttered, and stalked off.

I took the disc into my office, sat down, and pondered what to do. My hand hovered over the telephone for a few seconds. I was ready to ring the police and have Merisi removed off my property. There was no way that I was going to risk the precious business information contained in my computer by playing that disc. At worst, it might trash all my vital files. At best, it might simply block the DVD player drawer. Then I found myself preparing to back-up all my computer files and knew that, subconsciously, I had made the decision and that damned troublesome curiosity had again won the argument. When the back-up had been completed, I locked the office door, went back to my desk, sat down, and slid the dull bronze disc into the computer processor. For a second, nothing happened. And then, without me having touched anything, the computer screen lit up brilliantly and I ducked in surprise and fright as multi-coloured pixels started pouring out of the screen. Not on the screen but out of it, in a dazzling swirl of rainbow colours, a multi-coloured whirlwind that seemed to be filling up and then opening up the room. The pixels very swiftly reformed themselves into what seemed to be a host of figures seated within an auditorium of huge dimensions. I found myself sitting in the midst of this enormous amphitheatre, with literally thousands of spectators applauding me, whistling and cheering, and calling my name. I was badly frightened and, remembering what Merisi had said, I groped forward. With intense relief, I felt the objects on my desk such as the telephone and fax machine, so I knew that I was really still in my office. The illusion formed by the pixels was real and overwhelming. I wanted to switch it off but I didn't know how. And then, as quickly as it had formed, the illusion dissolved and I was back in my office. Everything was normal, except there was a figure of a man standing in front of my desk and smiling at me.

The figure was tall, slim and elegant. He was dressed like an Edwardian gentleman, with a heavy Harris tweed suit and waistcoat, complete with silver watch chain, a riding stock at his throat and a bowler hat on his head. He also sported a fine set of mutton-chop whiskers.

'Greetings, Mr. Maddan,' he announced. 'I am President Azumah of the planet Tralfamadore and what you have just witnessed are greetings and salutations from the people of Tralfamadore to a much-loved and revered personage.'

'Who is that?' I croaked, hardly able to speak.

'Why, you, sir,' Azumah said. 'Mr. Steven Maddan.' Azumah was now speaking to me but he was no longer looking at me. 'I should hasten to reassure you, Mr. Maddan, that I am not here in person. I am real on the planet Tralfamadore but what you are seeing, and have just seen, is what we call a Chronogram, similar to what you know as a hologram but much more sophisticated.'

'You can say that again,' I said, finding that I was still gripping the edge of my desk so hard that my knuckles had turned white.

'Because you have played the Chronogram, it tells me that you have been in contact with Mr. Michelangelo Merisi, known as the artist Caravaggio. You will find everything that has occurred since you met him very hard to accept, perhaps even beyond your comprehension, and I have been sent in this Chronographic form to answer any questions that you might have. I have been programmed to answer any conceivable question that you might ask but you may have a question that I cannot answer, in which case I will say: "Information unavailable".'

'Here is your first question, President Azumah. Am I going fucking mad?'

The Chronographic figure went into a loop for a second or two by repeating the same slight bodily gestures over and over again. It then answered: 'Information unavailable. Perhaps you will allow me to explain the background to all this and why you have been selected and then you can ask me any question you like.'

'Selected,' I repeated. 'Selected for what?'

Again the figure went into a loop. 'Perhaps you will allow me to explain the background to all this and why . . . .'

'Yes, all right,' I interrupted. 'Would you like to sit down?'

'Information unavailable,' Azumah said.

'Very well, say what you have to say. I'm already on three types of blood pressure medication and this little stunt of yours is not helping my treatment one little bit.' I sat back in my chair and tried to relax and steady my breathing and heart rate.

President Azumah began: 'In the year 2441, the Former United Kingdom, thanks to the aggressive and expansionist policies of the Liberal Democrat government, which had been in power for the past 83 years, is the world's only remaining superpower. In this year the first inter-stellar . . .'

'Hold on,' I interrupted Azumah. 'What do you mean "Former United Kingdom"? And what happened to the other superpowers?'

'When parliament was abolished in favour of computer referendums and the royal family were imprisoned for treason, the countries once known as England, Scotland, Wales and Northern Ireland were collectively renamed as the Former

United Kingdom and designated as the regions FUK One, FUK Two, etc. This led to . . .'

'Hold on again,' I said. 'I don't really want to know. But what about the other superpowers, the United States of America and so on.'

'The U.S.A. was taken over by a combined invasion from north and south and is now known as Mexinada, although some prefer to call it Canxico. The capital was moved to Des Moines and . . .'

'Never mind', I said. 'Start again from where you said "first inter-stellar" something or other.'

Azumah looped back jerkily and continued: 'In the year 2441, the first inter-stellar time travel mission was launched by the FUK. The time travel craft was named ChronoCruiser One. For reasons that are still not fully understood, the mission went disastrously wrong and the ChronoCruiser crash landed on a planet in what you will know as the Helix Nebula, or Aquarius NGC 7293. This nebula is approximately 300 light years from Earth and contains the nearest planetary system to the Earth's Sun. By great good fortune, the planet we crashed on has an atmosphere similar to Earth and is capable of sustaining human life. Unfortunately, the malfunction caused us to go back in time and, in Earth time, it was the year 1906 when we crashed. The crash also destroyed the computer memory banks and left us with little knowledge of Earth, the home planet. There were 328 people in the crew and they had no alternative but to settle on Tralfamadore and make a new life. In the following years . . . .'

'Can I stop you there again?' I said. 'Why didn't the crew repair the spaceship and travel back to Earth?'

'The crew did not have the knowledge or the equipment to make such repairs. The ChronoCruiser was such an advanced concept that nobody thought anything could go wrong with it.'

'Yes, everybody thought the same about an ocean liner here on Earth once.'

'Not long after we crashed!' Azumah exclaimed. 'It was named the Titanic, wasn't it?'

'Yes it was.'

'Well, it is a good analogy because we hit what you might call an iceberg in time. And the one positive result of this catastrophe was that we discovered the secret of travelling through time, and across immense stellar distances, by the manipulation of parallel dimensions.'

'Couldn't you all use that technique to get back to Earth?' I asked.

'The process is extremely difficult, very costly and time consuming, in both senses of that phrase, and we only have the resources to send one, or at most, a few people through the ChronoGate every few years or so. The 328 members of that original crew of the ChronoCruiser have adapted well to life on Tralfamadore and there are now approximately eleven million of us.'

'That's an impressive population growth. I don't suppose there was much else to do when you first arrived.'

'Exactly!' Azumah cried. 'And the planet Tralfamadore is approximately two-and-a-half times bigger than Earth, so there is plenty of room for everyone!'

'Who chose the name Tralfamadore,' I asked.

'Why, it was the captain of the original ChronoCruiser. It's from a book that he was very fond of by some 20th century author. He said it means "beautiful haven". Is that correct?'

'If the captain of any vessel says that it is so,' I replied, 'then it makes it so. Please carry on.' Despite my scepticism, I was beginning to believe that all I was experiencing must be real. I had never heard or read of a DVD or hologram capable of creating the effect I had just witnessed. It was not conceiveable that Merisi could have created such an advanced technological effect all by himself. It was all so astonishingly real that either it was real or I had gone completely insane. I found myself reciting the eight-times table and the soliloquy from 'Hamlet' just to reassure myself that my brain was still functioning normally.

The Azumah ChronoGram had started speaking again: 'The new population of Tralfamadore had to accept that they were marooned on their new home planet but they did have enough knowledge, materials and equipment to be able to make and erect radio receiving devices. They hoped to one day contact Earth or other civilisations that may have been able to help them. They were sadly disappointed until over three hundred years later when the first radio signals were intercepted. It became increasingly obvious that these signals emanated from Earth itself. These signals, as we now know, were the first radio transmissions by the great Marconi. They had been travelling for three hundred light years to reach us. After three hundred years the technological capabilities of the Tralfamadorians had increased exponentially and we were able to start recording and analysing these signals and thus building up our knowledge of Mother Earth and its inhabitants. Soon, the radio broadcasts became the prime form of entertainment on Tralfamadore. Then, about thirty years later, the first television pictures began to arrive and the whole planet went into paroxysms of delight. We had teams recording, analysing and sifting knowledge from every transmission we could find. The whole population of Tralfamadore were glued to their television screens every day.'

'Yes, they must be human,' I said.

'We became particularly fond of quiz shows because of the amount of knowledge contained in them that we could process and catalogue very easily. Quiz show hosts and, more especially, quiz show winners have become superstars on Tralfamadore. You are a popular favourite,' Azumah said.

'Who, me!?' I exclaimed. 'Why me?'

'Mr. Maddan,' Azumah said, 'the whole planet followed your progress on that quiz show Fifteen-to-One, presented by the godlike William G. Stewart, and when you actually won the grand final, the celebrations went on for days.'

'You,' I said, 'are taking the piss.'

Azumah went into a loop for a second and then said: 'If I understand your remark correctly, you think that I am making some joke at your expense but I can assure you that I am perfectly serious. We on Tralfamadore are not as keen on sport as you Earth folk. We much prefer quiz contests. Sporting stars like this David Beckham that your women seem to rate so highly are not considered attractive to Tralfamadorian women, whereas you, Mr. Maddan, are a pin-up poster idol in every teenage girl's bedroom. No less that 1,482 Tralfamadorian women asked me to bring proposals of marriage with me but there is not time.'

'Oh, couldn't we find time?' I said. 'Tell me, could I make money on your planet?'

'My dear sir, you would be what the ever-popular Del Boy calls a mill-yon-aire on Tralfamadore.' The Azumah Chronogram actually smiled at its own humorous remark.

'Great,' I sighed. 'Out there is a planet of millions of inhabitants on which I am the object of lust for thousands of teenage girls, on which I could be mega-rich, and there is no way to get there. I've won first prize in the Universal Lottery and there is no way of collecting my prize. Please carry on, Mr. Azumah.'

'Well, a few months later, the planet was again plunged into days of celebration when you won the title of Brain of Britain on the radio. Then we were disappointed not to see or hear anything of you for three years until you popped up on the greatest quiz show of them all, Mastermind. Imagine our added delight when your specialist subject was announced as the life and work of Caravaggio.'

'Why should that have caused added delight?' I asked.

'Because, to Trafamaldorians, Caravaggio is considered to be one of the five all-time greatest artists that Earth has produced.'

'Really?' I said. 'Who are the other four?'

Azumah looped and then said: 'The others are Michelangelo Buonarotti, Rembrandt van Rijn, Vincent van Gogh and Tracy Emin.'

I pondered this astounding revelation for a moment and then asked: 'Tell me, Prime Minister, apart from we quiz personalities, what other shows or entertainment personalities are popular on Tralfamadore at the moment.'

Azumah searched his memory for a second and then replied: 'Ant and Dec are revered, as is Keith Chegwin. The Krankies and the Chuckle Brothers are comedy giants, and shows like Dixon of Dock Green are very exciting. The Black and White Minstrel Show is considered to have been a major contributor to good race relations on Earth. As you can see from my appearance, there were as many black people as white on the ChronoCruiser. Davina McCall and Graham Norton are . . .'

'Thank you,' I interrupted. 'I now have a much better idea of the standard of popular taste on Tralfamadore. I am no longer surprised that I am a superstar. Please continue.'

'After seeing you winning all these quiz shows, including Brain of Britain, we decided that you must be just about the most intelligent man on Earth. When we watched you answering questions on the life and work of the great Caravaggio, we all agreed that you were the perfect person to investigate his death.'

For a few seconds I was stumped by this last statement. 'Why does his death need investigating?'

'You must admit,' countered Azumah, 'that there were many unexplained mysteries in the last few months of his life.'

'I agree, but like most mysteries they are only mysterious because of our lack of proper facts and knowledge.'

'Yes, and we are asking you to find out those facts and that knowledge.'

'Why me?' I pleaded, beginning to feel anxious at what was being suggested to me. 'I am not an investigator, a policeman, a private eye or whatever. I'm not even an art historian. I'm just a small publisher of specialist magazines and books. I have no special knowledge of Caravaggio. I merely studied a few reference books in order to win a quiz game. You'll have to find someone else.'

'There is no-one else. Or no-one we know of. This investigation has been waiting for centuries for the right person to undertake it. You are that person, Mr. Maddan. It is now or never. Now that Mr. Merisi has been brought back to life, there will be no other opportunity.'

Azumah's comment shook me back to my logical senses again. 'Yes,' I said. 'That is a good point. Just how and why is Mr. Merisi back to life. How did you lot perform that little resurrection trick?'

'It is not a little trick at all, it has taken years of planning and centuries of waiting,' Azumah said. Irony was obviously not big in Tralfamadorian conversation. 'Using our ChronoConverter technology to its utmost limits, a three-person team was sent back to Porto Ercole to July 1610, to the time and place where Caravaggio supposedly died. Just before he expired, the team spirited away his body. They remedied his fever, repaired his terrible scars and other infirmities and, ever since then, he has been kept alive but unconscious in ChronoStasis at a secret location until the time came to revive him and use his help in investigating the circumstances of his own near demise.'

It was true, I had to admit, that Caravaggio's body had disappeared immediately after his death and had never been found, despite the fact that he was the most famous artist in Italy at the time. I posed the obvious question. 'If your time travel team could transport themselves back to the exact time when Caravaggio was murdered, why couldn't they simply prevent the murderer from performing the foul deed or, if they could not prevent it, simply identify who the murderer was?'

'We knew you would ask this very obvious question,' Azumah replied. 'The universal laws of time travel, and the limitations of our ChronoTechnology, prevent any persons from the future materialising in the past in the presence of any persons from that past. Therefore, our Chrono rescue team had to materialise out of sight away from where Caravaggio was being done away with and they arrived at his sick room just after the murderer had fled. They were just too late to be able to identify Caravaggio's killer.'

'Well, couldn't they travel back again and set up a video camera in the sick room to film whoever it was trying to murder Caravaggio?'

'Firstly, it had taken years of intense effort to prepare the mission to rescue Caravaggio and such a mission could only be repeated with extreme difficulty in terms of resources, money, manpower and political will. Not every inhabitant of Tralfamadore approved of the planetary resources being spent on this project. Secondly, the universal laws of time travel prevent any incongruous object, such as a video camera, being introduced into a past time such as the seventeenth century, unless it is very carefully disguised as an object which would naturally be present in that time. So you see, now that Caravaggio has been brought back to consciousness, the only possible and cost-effective way of completing this mission is for the investigation into Caravaggio's murder to be carried out now, and it must be conducted by you.'

'Must,' I shouted. 'Must, must, must! I have no obligation whatsoever to take part in this insane scheme. People die every day, thousands of them. Why should I, or anybody else, give a flying fuck why some artist died four hundred years ago.'

'Because, if you do not, you will disappoint millions on Tralfamadore, render years of intense effort fruitless, and you will fail in your duty to posterity here on Earth.'

'Fuck posterity. Listen, this team you sent back to rescue Caravaggio, why can't they conduct this investigation?'

'Because they are long dead, except one.'

'Another team then?'

'No-one on Tralfamadore has the knowledge that you have and there is no time to teach them. They do not know enough about Earth or about

Caravaggio. When we saw you on Mastermind, we knew you were the one for the job and that we had to seize this opportunity.'

'Hold on,' I said. 'You just said "except one".'

Azumah went into that familiar loop and then said: 'I do not understand. Please repeat the question.'

'You said, about the team who saved Caravaggio, they are long dead, except one. Who is that one?'

'He is the team leader. He volunteered to remain in the year 1610, with Caravaggio's body, for however long it would take us to launch this mission. He has been awarded the Joe Pasquale Hero of the Planet award for his devotion to knowledge. His life will have been sacrificed for nothing if you refuse to help us.'

I thought about all this for quite a long time. Eventually Azumah asked: 'Well, Mr. Maddan. Will you help us?'

'What is his name, this team leader?'

'His name, where he is now, is Guglielmo Pellegrino.'

'Where is he now?'

'He is waiting in Rome in the year 1611.'

'What is he waiting for?'

'For a signal from us that the matter of Caravaggio's supposed death is being investigated.'

'And can he ever return to Tralfamadore?'

'It might be possible, depending on how the mission goes, but he will probably have to remain on Earth for the rest of his life. The ChronoConverter technology becomes unstable when going backwards and forwards more than about four hundred years. We are not sure exactly how long and we don't know why it becomes unstable. The original team took a great risk in travelling back in time so far.'

'Did they return to Tralfamadore safely?'

Azumah took a while to reply. 'No, they were lost,' he said. 'On the return journey.'

'You mean dead?'

'We do not know. They may be dead. They may have disappeared into another dimension. As I said, the ChronoConverter becomes very unstable after more than four hundred years. They have been honoured with a memorial in the Barbara Windsor quiz stadium.'

'Very comforting for them, I'm sure. How do you know that Pellegrino is still alive?'

'We are able to contact him without the necessity of time travel. It was Pellegrino who came back to plant the detector device in the frame of the Supper at Emmaus. That is the only way we could think of finding you. After what you said on Mastermind about the painting, that comment about admiring it since you were sixteen years old, we knew that one day you would return to look at it again.'

'Why didn't Pellegrino just look in the phone book or on the internet? Or just ask the first person he met? Hasn't he heard of six degrees of separation?'

'I do not understand what you are saying. And Pellegrino does not have the knowledge of your world to know what to do or how to find you.'

'What about Merisi?' I asked. 'Wasn't he mildly surprised to wake up in a completely different world four hundred years after he died.'

'It was, of course, very difficult for him to comprehend, but you must remember that people from his time had a much stronger belief in things spiritual, much more faith that miracles and resurrection can actually happen. He is also an exceptionally intelligent and strong-willed individual . . . and we have certain drugs. He has adjusted well, although we are still unable to curb that vile temper of his.'

'I've noticed,' I said. 'If I do this, what happens if I fail.'

'Nothing,' Azumah replied. 'If you do your best and fail, then you fail.'

'You won't zap me with a death ray or something?'

Azumah went into a loop and said: 'Information unavailable.'

'That's reassuring', I said. 'What do I have to do? Where do I start?'

'From this point,' President Azumah said, 'Mr. Merisi can answer any more questions you may have. He has been thoroughly trained. This Chronographic demonstration has been to persuade you that what we say, and what you are experiencing, is completely true and genuine. Do you accept that?'

After a long pause, I said: 'Yes, I have to. It's better than thinking myself insane.'

'In that case, I will bid you farewell, Mr. Maddan. It has been an honour to meet you. On behalf of the people of Tralfamadore, we wish you the best of luck on your quest for Caravaggio's killer.'

The ChronoGram image of President Azumah disappeared instantly. I felt stunned and disorientated. I ejected the dull bronze DVD and looked at it, in the completely irrational hope that it would give me more answers, but it did not. I cannot remember how long I sat there, but it was a very long time. The telephone rang several times but I let the answerphone pick up the calls. I knew I would have to go and speak to Merisi or, as I now accepted, Michelangelo Merisi da Caravaggio, a Baroque artist who had risen from the dead after four hundred years and who was now living and working in my summerhouse. Eventually I left the office, went to the living room and, from the drinks cabinet, picked up a bottle of bourbon. It was an unwanted Christmas present. Unwanted until now. I took out two whisky glasses. I stepped out through the patio door into my back garden and walked quietly up to the summerhouse. I peeked in through the window. Merisi had his back to me as he worked on his painting. There was a palpable intensity and sense of concentration about him as he worked. He worked rapidly. He was finishing the musical instruments in the foreground of the picture. I watched him for a long time. There could be no doubt of his skill, no doubt that he had painted this masterpiece.

I knocked on the summerhouse door lightly and went in. Merisi turned to look at me with an intense dark stare. 'Well?' he asked, expecting to be rejected again.

'I understand,' I replied, 'that many people, including cardinals and nobles, used to visit your studio just to watch you work. Is that true?'

'That is true,' Merisi nodded.

'Then, will you accord me that same privilege for a few minutes?'

'Do you accept that I truly am the artist Michelangelo Merisi, known as Caravaggio?'

'Yes,' I said. 'I have to.'

'Good,' Merisi answered, and then asked: 'What is in that bottle?'

'It's a drink called bourbon.'

'Is it wine?'

'No, it's a type of drink called whisky that you will not have heard of.'

'Is it good?'

'I think you will like it.'

'Good. Pour me some. Let's drink.'

'Believe me, Michele, this drink is much stronger than wine. After a few glasses of this you will not be capable of working. Let me watch you work then we will stop and drink . . . and talk.'

Merisi smiled at me and, for the first time, I glimpsed the charm of the man behind the dark saturnine looks. 'You called me Michele. This is good. You now believe who I am. We are friends?'

'Perhaps,' I replied cautiously.

His smile vanished and he asked: 'Where is your woman?'

'What woman?' I asked.

'Your wife, your mistress, your girl, whatever. Get her to bring us food. I am getting hungry again after all this work.' He looked back at his painting with an expression of deep satisfaction.

'I have no woman,' I said. 'If you want food, I'll have to get it.'

'No woman?' Merisi repeated, with astonishment. 'No wife, no mistress?'

'No.'

'You must have a servant, a maid. You are a rich man. Who does your cooking, your washing?'

'I do. Or rather, the big white boxes do. And I am not a rich man.'

'But the way you live!' Merisi exclaimed. 'You must be rich!'

'Everybody lives like me. Well, most people. Most people in England. Many people in other countries do not live so well.'

'What about my beloved Italy?' Merisi asked. 'How do they live now?'

I could not help laughing. 'Michele, they live better than we English do. The sun is warm, the food is good, the women are beautiful, the scenery is grand, their magnificent cities have not been ruined with ugly modern buildings, as we have ruined ours. The Italians know how to live, and they still love life.'

Merisi was pensive. 'That is good to hear, Stefano. I would love to see Rome again. Can we go?'

'Perhaps. I don't know. Why don't you carry on painting, then we'll talk?'

'Very well,' he said, and turned back to his canvas. But he stopped and turned back to me, with a suspicious look. 'You're not a bardassa, are you?' he asked.

'What the hell is a bardassa?'

'A bumboy, a sodomite.'

'What makes you think that?'

'You have no woman. Perhaps you prefer pretty boys.' Merisi grinned lasciviously.

'Would it bother you if I did?' I asked. 'Or perhaps you would prefer it. Many experts today believe you were a bardassa yourself.'

Merisi hurled his palette on to the floor. 'Who are they?' he demanded angrily. 'I'll slit their throats for them. Why do they think that?'

'Calm down, Michele. You must admit that many of your earlier paintings featured many pretty boys. It's a logical conclusion that you must have fancied the hairy peach yourself.'

'Shit!' he exclaimed. 'I painted what I was paid to paint in those early days. All those fancy cardinals with all their money surrounded themselves with pretty boy musicians and poets and pretended it was all in the cause of art. I gave them what they wanted. It was not what I wanted.'

'I'm glad to hear it, Michele. It is not what I am either. I had a woman, a wife. She walked out on me years ago. Can't blame her. I was lousy in bed and I had no money back then.'

'You're too fucking soft. It's a woman's duty to stand by her man. I used to tell that bitch Fillide the same thing but she never listened to me. She duped me. Walked out on me. I know how it feels. She was a great fuck though. What do you do now?' Merisi waggled his hand up and down in front of his crotch. 'Stick to the handjobs, Stefano. Your right hand never lets you down.' He laughed loudly.

'Pick up your palette and work, Michele. Then we have lots to talk about.'

Merisi gave me a mock bow. 'Of course, your eminence,' he said. 'Four hundred years later and there's still some rich cunt ordering me about.'

But he did pick up his palette and for the next two hours I watched him work. The speed of his brushwork and the deftness of his touch was extraordinary. Even if I still had a doubt that he really was Caravaggio, I could not doubt that he was a supremely accomplished artist in his own right. At last he stepped back, considered the canvas and, throwing aside the palette again, announced: 'There. It's done.' He moved aside and gestured to the painting with a silent invitation to comment. It was an extraordinary sensation to be sitting in my summerhouse, with a man who had been dead for four hundred years, gazing at a painting that dazzled me with its colour, its composition, and the breathtaking skill with which it had been painted. But, for some reason I could not fathom, I decided not to give him the satisfaction of saying so.

'It's worth a drink,' I shrugged, and I opened the bourbon and poured out two glasses. I handed one to Merisi and watched his reaction as he sipped it.

'That is wonderful,' he pronounced. 'Did you make this?'

'No,' I laughed. 'It comes all the way from America, from the New World.'

'Then I'll go there next,' Merisi chuckled, taking another gulp.

'Take it easy, Michele. It's much stronger than wine or ale. Let's go and get some food and we'll talk.'

Merisi followed me back into the kitchen and we sat at the table and had a simple lunch of soup, cheese, bread and grapes. Merisi ate heartily.

'Yesterday,' I began, 'you told me that you had been murdered. What reasons do you have for believing that?'

'Because the murderer told me as he was doing it,' Merisi answered.

'Okay,' I said. 'Let's get this straight. According to our history, the last we know of you is that you were desperately ill of a fever in Porto Ercole. Is that correct?'

'Yes,' Merisi confirmed.

'Where were you? Was it a hospital or a monastery or what?'

'It was in a small infirmary run by the brothers of San Sebastiano.'

'And was it in this infirmary that someone tried to murder you?'

'Yes it was. I was in a bad way and some bastard came in to my room and finished me off.'

'Are you sure? If you were feverish you may have been hallucinating or imagining things.'

'I am certain. I was very ill but my mind was surprisingly clear. I remember it all. These grapes are very good.' Merisi spat out a pip on to his plate. He did not seem in the least perturbed by the memory of his final minutes.

'You were in a room, on a bed, on your own?'

'Yes, and then a man came into the room. He had a monk's cowl pulled down to cover his face. The room was dark anyway.'

'You don't know who he was? You didn't recognise him?'

'If I had I wouldn't need you to help me find out, would I?'

I ignored his tart jibe and asked: 'What did he do? You said he talked to you?'

'At first I thought he was one of the brothers. He lifted up my head and gave me something to drink from a cup. He said: "This will ease all your problems. It is something you have always coveted, as all you artists do." That is exactly what he said. I clearly remember what he said, even in the state I was in, because it seemed such an odd thing to say and I couldn't understand what he meant. I drank whatever was in the cup, and then he laughed. He was mocking me. He said: "Now you will die, you bastard". I began to foam at the mouth. My limbs felt out of my control. I was shaking. I felt sick, and then vomited. An intense weariness overcame me, but I managed to say: "Who are you? Why have you done this?" This bastard was cooing at me, like a dove. "For love, Michele! It is done for love! You know very well who I am, and the why is in the paintings, but you will never know! You should have been more careful!" And that is the last thing I remember.'

'Hold on,' I said. I fetched a notepad from my office and noted down exactly what Merisi had told me.

'The answer is somewhere in my paintings,' Merisi continued. 'But I cannot think what it is.'

'With respect, Michele, this man did not say *your* paintings. He said in *the* paintings.'

'Very well, but he must have meant my paintings, surely. We will have to go to Rome and look at as many of my works as we can find and try to work out what he meant.'

'No need for that, Michele.' I went into the living room and, from the bookcase, took out the complete works of Caravaggio, a very large full-colour volume that had cost me a lot of money. I took it into the kitchen and placed it, unopened, on the table in front of Merisi.

'What is this?' Merisi asked, suspiciously.

'It's a book. You know what a book is. There are all your known paintings inside. Go on, open it.'

Merisi did not move, just looked at the book. 'Is this another of your modern wonders to frighten me with?'

'Listen, Michele, the art of printing was well-known in your day, is that not so?'

'Yes'.

'Well, this book is printed but now we know how to transfer pictures from place to place by a process known as photography and then print those pictures in colour. Inside are pictures of all your paintings. Look at them.'

'All my paintings?' Merisi repeated, still unwilling to believe me.

'Not the actual paintings but reproductions of your paintings. You will enjoy looking at them.' Still Merisi did not move so I took back the book. 'Let me show you,' I said. 'Let me show you that self-portrait you did, the one with the green face, where you are holding the grapes. We call it the Sick Bacchus.' (*Plate 4*). I found the picture and replaced the opened book in front of Merisi. His eyes opened wide in astonishment and he gazed at the portrait of his young self for several seconds. I was surprised by the emotion betrayed in his expression. Merisi touched the page lightly. 'I had been so ill,' he said softly. Then he began to turn the pages. He gazed at each of his paintings in turn. If he was not Caravaggio then it was the finest piece of acting I had ever witnessed. I decided to leave him alone with his memories. I picked up my glass of bourbon and went out into the garden. I strolled down to the river and looked at the slowly flowing water. The myriad difficulties of the task I had been landed with multiplied as I thought about it. In fact, I soon came to the conclusion that it was impossible. I would have to right away confront Merisi with my reservations and the inherent problems so that he would understand what we were up against. I walked back to the kitchen. Merisi had closed the book. He had composed himself but he did not speak and he sipped his bourbon thoughtfully.

'This,' I began, 'is an impossible task.'

'Why?' Merisi asked, distractedly.

'How can I put this point delicately, without hurting your feelings, Michele? You were . . . are a rotten, bad-tempered arrogant bastard and most people who got to know you well seemed to have ended up hating your guts.'

I expected an explosion of temper but he just smiled wearily. 'It is well you did not choose to become a diplomat. What is your point?'

'The point is that we have a list of dozens, if not hundreds, of possible culprits. Many people would have liked to have murdered you.'

'Not many would have dared,' he replied.

'And then if, as the putative murderer claimed, the answer is in your pictures, then we are still in real trouble.'

'Why?'

'You have just looked at your complete known works. Emphasise complete *known* works. You must have noticed that many of your paintings are missing.'

'Yes. Some of my best work is not in there.'

I sat down and opened the book at the index of lost works by Caravaggio. 'At a quick count, Michele, there are over thirty of your paintings missing, lost or destroyed. And they are just the ones we know to be missing. For instance, your portrtait of Fillide Melandroni was destroyed in a terrible war we suffered over sixty years ago.'

'Yes,' he said. 'She is in that wonderful book but in black and white only. That woman was black and white in everything she did.'

'If the answer to the mystery of who attempted to murder you is in your paintings, it may be in one that is now lost, and so it will be impossible to find, unless you can remember in detail every picture you ever painted.'

'That's impossible,' Merisi said, irritably.

'Exactly,' I said. 'Anyway, you can't keep on living in the summerhouse. Go and get your things. You will have to move in here with me.'

'I am comfortable enough in your summerhouse.'

'Well, my neighbour is not. Go and get your things.'

This time Merisi meekly complied. He returned with his few meagre belongings, all except his painting materials.

I said: 'You had better bring the painting into the house. It will be safer in here.'

'A good idea,' Merisi agreed, and went to bring back the painting. As he carried the painting into the house, he said: 'We need the paint to dry off as soon as it can. Is there anywhere warm we can store it?'

'Why does it need to dry quickly,' I asked.

'We will discuss that later,' Merisi replied.

'Okay. I have a warm airing cupboard upstairs. Follow me.'

With Merisi carrying his painting and me carrying his other belongings, Merisi followed me up the stairs. I showed him into the back bedroom, which was fairly spacious but shabby. I had not found the time to redecorate. It contained 1930s-style oak furniture, a threadbare Wilton carpet, and the wallpaper was a hideous pink colour and covered with tiny red rose motifs. Merisi looked it over and, completely without irony, said: 'It's a palazzo. Thank you, Stefano.' I dumped his belongings on the bed and we carefully stored the painting in the airing cupboard, which was situated outside on the landing.

'I'll get you some sheets and blankets,' I said, as we returned to Merisi's room. 'And I'll also get you some of my old clothes. Some clean clothes.'

'What is wrong with these?' Merisi asked, eyes wide in enquiry. As he plucked at his shirt I again caught a glimpse of the ornate gold chain around his neck.

'Let me explain something about the 21st century, Michele. We set great importance on cleanliness and personal hygiene. We wash all over, every day. We change our clothes, especially our underwear, every day. Sometimes twice, or even three times a day. We wash our dirty clothes every week, or as often as they need washing, in one of those big white boxes. I understand that you were in the habit of buying a fine suit of clothes and not taking them off until they rotted away. Is that true?'

'Yes,' Merisi scowled. 'Everybody did that. I was very proud of those fine clothes. What is the point of putting them on and taking them off all the time?'

'Trust me, Michele. If you are going to fit into 21st century society, you must bathe and change your clothes every day. Your clothes stink. And you stink. Come with me.'

Merisi followed me out of the room, muttering curses at me. I led him into the bathroom. Firstly, I unwrapped a new toothbrush, showed him a tube of toothpaste, and demonstrated how to use them. 'You must brush your teeth every morning after breakfast and after meals. That will stop your breath smelling like a Bactrian camel, as it does at the moment.' Then I showed him how to use the wash basin and the shower. He was fascinated by the taps. He kept turning them on and off and laughing as if it were a game of peek-a-boo. 'You can truly get water, all the time, every time, through these things?' he asked, with child-like delight.

'Yes, both hot and cold.' I handed him a bar of soap. 'Now, get under that shower, wash yourself thoroughly, hair included, then dry yourself on that towel. I'll find you some fresh clothes. I'll leave them in your room. Put them on and, when you're ready, come back down. We'll talk again.'

Merisi looked at me pleadingly, like a helpless child, as I left him to it. I looked out some of my old clothes and left them in Merisi's room. I was amused to hear him singing in the shower as I passed the bathroom door. About an hour later, he came back downstairs. I was in the living room. I gestured for him to sit down in the armchair opposite me on the other side of the big fireplace. I had poured him another bourbon. Merisi had put on a sweater. It was another ghastly unwanted Christmas present. Merisi had put it on back-to-front but I said nothing.

'Thank you, Stefano,' he said, lifting his glass and taking a swig. 'That shower is very refreshing. I now feel very relaxed.'

'That's good,' I said. 'I've been thinking about our project.'

Merisi did not reply but just looked at me, waiting for my comments.

'I am now forced to believe,' I began, 'that sitting opposite me is an artist who was virtually forgotten for centuries but who has miraculously come back to life and whose previous life now fascinates many people here on Earth and millions of people on another world called Tralfamadore.'

'Forgotten?' Merisi interjected. 'I was forgotten?'

'Yes, but mainly thanks to an art historian named Roberto Longhi, you have now taken your rightful place in the history of art.'

'Longhi!' Merisi cried. 'Onorio Longhi was my friend. We used to go drinking and fighting and whoring together! Could this Roberto Longhi be a descendant of Onorio?'

'I don't know, Michele,' I replied, gesturing for him to calm down. 'We'll go into all that later. Now, if we are going to conduct this investigation into your murder, I want to make something out of it. Does that sound fair to you?'

'You mean money, Stefano?'

'Yes. I want lots of money. I do not like being poor.'

Merisi laughed heartily. 'I think you are a cardinal in disguise!' he said. 'I can paint you a few pictures. How much could you get for one of my paintings now? The most I was ever paid was 1,000 scudi. Could you get that now?'

'Let me see,' I said, thinking quickly. 'If I am correct then 1,000 scudi is roughly the equivalent of £250 today, in our English money. So, if I sold an authenticated picture by Michelangelo Merisi da Caravaggio on the open market, even if it was one of your poorest works, I would not accept less than 40 million scudi.'

Merisi sat forward and pointed an accusing finger at me. 'You are a liar,' he said angrily. 'There is not that much money in the whole world. You mock me. Why should anyone pay a king's ransom for one of my paintings. The most I was ever offered was 6,000 scudi, to fresco Prince Doria's villa.'

'Yes, and you turned it down, didn't you? Please calm down, Michele. I swear by almighty God that I am not lying to you. One of your best works, such as the Supper at Emmaus, would be almost literally priceless. Many works by many great artists now sell for millions of scudi.'

'You imperil your soul by saying such things.'

'That was imperilled many years ago. I swear it is the truth.'

'These are strange times,' Merisi said in wonderment. Then he smiled broadly: 'We will be rich . . . richer than any cardinal, richer than any king, richer than any . . . pope!'

'Don't get too excited. It's not quite as simple as you might think.'

'When it comes to making money, there is always a snag,' Merisi said, gloomily.

'Not only do I want to make lots of money,' I continued, 'but I want to know much more about your life and your work. We will study all your known paintings and, as we look for clues as to who tried to murder you, I want you to tell me more about them.'

'In what way do you mean?' Merisi asked, warily.

'Well, who commissioned them, how much you were paid, how you devised the composition, what you were intending to say, things like that. Are you willing to do that?'

'Yes, of course,' Merisi replied. 'I love talking about my paintings. I was the greatest artist in Rome. The greatest artist in all Italy. We will solve all mysteries together.'

'Good. You will also have to tell me all about your life, especially the people you have known who might have wished you harm.'

Merisi laughed heartily. 'Stefano, you said it yourself, most of the people I ever knew ended up hating my guts!'

'Doesn't that bother you?' I asked.

'Not at all! Most of them were small creatures. Most of them were painters, poets and sculptors of little talent. They were amazed by my skill. Compared to me, they were little better than street scum, and I told them so.'

I shook my head in disgust. 'You didn't upset the cardinals and princes with such arrogance, did you?' I accused him.

'Of course not! They were the ones with the power and the money. I sucked up to them. I painted their pretty boys and suffered their pious devotions and their ostentatious displays of wealth. They weren't fit to lick my arse and they disgusted me but I was not stupid enough to show it.'

'Do you know what the word "hypocrite" means?' I asked.

Merisi became very agitated. 'Don't fucking patronise me, you fat English cunt,' he roared. 'Look at all this.' He waved his hand to encompass the room. 'You have never starved, or seen your loved ones carried off by plague, or watched the beggars dying in the streets, or had to bow to a scented churchman just to get a roof over your head! Don't fucking criticise me!'

I knew I had to defuse Merisi's temper or we would never finish the conversation. 'I apologise, Michele. These are the things I want to find out about.'

'Why?' he challenged, still upset. 'Why does anyone give a fuck about such things now?'

'Because you are considered one of the most important artists in history. We want to know more about you. If you tell me what it was like, I will become acknowledged as an expert on your life and work. I am a publisher. I could publish a book about you. There is money to be made from that.'

'You are just as big a "hypocrite" as I am,' Merisi sneered.

'Perhaps you are right,' I agreed. 'We must work together closely, if we are to solve the mystery of your murder. I have to interrogate you because I cannot interrogate the people you once knew, the people who might have wanted to murder you.'

To my surprise, a sly grin replaced Merisi's dark scowl. 'Tell me, Stefano,' he asked, 'that picture upstairs, why do you think I chose that particular subject after four hundred years of inactivity?'

'Pope Paul and Cardinal Borghese? I don't know? Why?'

Merisi answered by pulling off his sweater and unbuttoning his shirt. He took off the ornate gold chain from around his neck and laid it across his knees. Then he rebuttoned his shirt and put the sweater back on, this time the right way around. Then he held up the gold chain. The chain itself was very elaborate and it was much longer than it seemed because it had been clasped halfway along its length so that half its length hung down Merisi's back and half down his front. Hanging from the chain was a hexagonal pendant about the width of a cigarette packet and about ten centimetres across. Still holding up the chain, Merisi said: 'Even if you could interview the people who knew me, they would not talk to you. Why should they? And they would certainly not admit to murder. The only way they could be made to talk truthfully is if they knew that their immortal soul was in peril if they did not. And the only way to do that is if the pope orders them to talk to you truthfully on pain of excommunication and eternal damnation. And, like most popes, Pope Paul was susceptible to a bribe. His nephew, Scipione Borghese, was certainly susceptible to a bribe. Dear Scipione would do anything to get his hands on one of my paintings, especially one showing how close he is to his beloved uncle, the most powerful man in Christendom. If Scipione persuades his uncle to issue a papal warrant ordering people to tell you the truth, in peril of eternal damnation if they do not, then they will tell you the truth. This chain is called a ChronoConverter. You are going to travel back in time to present my painting to Pope Paul and Scipione Borghese in exchange for that papal warrant.'

Merisi laid the chain back across his knees and watched for my reaction.

'Oh, no,' I exclaimed, stunned by the realisation of what I had let myself in for. It was my turn to become angry and agitated. 'President Azumah didn't mention anything about me travelling back in time. I'm not fucking Doctor Who or Marty McFly. Oh, no, no, no. That is one thing I will not do!'

4

Merisi had opened out the gold ChronoConverter chain and arranged it, in a circular fashion, on the floor of the living room. 'Do you have a tape measure?' he asked me.

'A tape measure? Yes, I think my ex-wife may have left one in the drawer under the bookcase. It's about the only thing she did leave me.'

Merisi opened the drawer, fumbled around, and found the tape measure. Turning back to me, he said: 'Stand up, please.'

'What for?' I asked.

'If you are going to meet His Holiness, you have to be dressed correctly, as men were when he occupied the papal throne. Stand up, please.'

I stood up, and said: 'Look, is time travel really necessary. Couldn't we just stay here and study your paintings. You can tell me all about your life and maybe we can identify the murderer that way?'

'I *am* staying here. *You* are going to meet the pope. I painted his portrait once, so he knows what I look like. It would be a bit of a shock for His Holiness to see a dead man who is not Jesus Christ walking through his chambers.'

'You're not coming with me?' I asked, becoming more agitated.

'Look, studying my paintings and talking about my life might lead us in the right direction but it will not conclusively prove who the murderer was. The only way to find out is by interrogating the people who knew me and they will not talk to you unless ordered to do so by the pope himself. Before we do anything else, we have to know if we can secure that papal warrant or the whole project is pointless. Hold up your arms.' Merisi wrapped the tape measure around my chest. 'No, I cannot go with you. Even if I would not be recognised, the laws of time travel forbid me to go. It would be too dangerous. What manner of measures are these?'

'They are called centimetres. Why is it dangerous?'

Merisi wrapped the tape measure around my waist. 'I do not fully understand these things but, because I have been alive since 1610, I cannot go back because, wherever I return to, then there would be two of me and that would do something to the fabric of time and space that might cause catastrophic consequences. Something about matter and anti-matter and parallel dimensions. There are very strict rules about time travel. If I go back, I could destroy the universe and I would not want to be blamed for that by posterity, not that there would be any posterity left. You, however, are going back to a time long before you were born so there is no danger. You are like many people I have seen in this modern world, your waist is bigger than your chest.'

Merisi knelt down but I twisted away. 'You are not measuring my inside leg. You can measure the outside and guess the rest.'

Merisi chuckled. 'Afraid I might touch your little love gun?' he chortled. 'Or afraid you might enjoy it? I could just give it a little kiss while I'm down here.'

'Fuck off,' I said but, as he spoke, a horrifying realisation occurred to me, other than his lascivious suggestion, and I pushed Merisi away. 'The Azumah ChronoGram told me that the ChronoConverter technology becomes very unstable after about four hundred years of time travel. That's almost exactly the number of years you want me to go back to. No. I am not going, and that's the end of it.'

Merisi, still kneeling, looked up at me. 'I made the four hundred year journey forward without harm. Do you want to be rich?'

'Yes.'

'If you do this for me, I will paint you my best work. It will make you rich, you said so yourself. If you do not do this, you will get nothing. I will go away. You will not find out any more about my paintings or my life. Even if you tell anyone what has happened here, nobody will believe you. You will carry on being the pathetic little nobody that you are now.'

'Now you even sound like my ex-wife,' I said.

Merisi, still kneeling, turned to the ChronoConverter. The hexagonal pendant was fitted with an ingeniously disguised hinged lid, which Merisi opened. He pressed something in the centre of the pendant and a circle of tiny alternating red, green and yellow lights began revolving around the inside. Merisi talked into the pendant, quoted my bodily measurements and then closed the lid.

'What happens now?' I asked.

'We wait,' Merisi replied. He sat back in his armchair and we waited in silence.

'What are we waiting for?' I asked.

'Why should you care?' Merisi said, petulantly. 'You said you are not going to help me.'

'Why should I risk my life just to find out who murdered you?'

'For riches, and for fame,' Merisi replied.

We lapsed into an uneasy silence again for several minutes. I said: 'I can't speak your language. How do I ask for what I want if they cannot understand me? I'm sure they won't understand English, especially modern English.'

Merisi did not reply, but once again knelt down beside the ChronoConverter chain. He began to carefully feel around the edge of the intricate gold chain. He found what he was looking for and detached something that had been artfully concealed within the decoration of the chain. It looked like a very plain and thin gold finger ring. He handed it to me. On the inside of the ring was the same dull bronze colour of the material from which the ChronoGram DVD had been made.

'Put it on,' Merisi invited.

'Which finger?'

'Any finger. Whichever one it fits.'

It fitted best on the little finger of my right hand.

'What is the time?' Merisi asked.

I looked at my watch. 'Dieci e tre quarti' I was startled to hear myself say in Italian, and yet I know I had said it in English.

'A quarter to eleven,' Merisi repeated in English, and grinned at me. 'It takes a bit of getting used to. All the while you are wearing that ring, whatever you say will be translated into Italian. You will think in English. You can understand Italian if it is spoken to you. You can understand English if someone speaks to you, but your spoken or written reply will be in Italian. If you want to speak English again, you have to take off the ring.' Merisi held up his hand to show me that he was wearing the same type of ring, on the middle finger of his left hand. He took off the ring and (in Italian) said: 'Whatever I say now is in Italian. I cannot speak English even if I try, but you understand me, no?'

'Yes,' I replied, except it came out as 'Si'. (For the purposes of this narrative, I will carry on entirely in English from here, or else it gets very confusing!)

'Keep the ring on,' Merisi suggested, returning to his armchair. 'Get used to it.'

'Okay,' I said. 'I can speak Italian, but what do I say? What do I ask? I'm bound to put my foot in it with some gaffe or impoliteness or some breach of etiquette.'

'Listen to my accent as I speak English,' Merisi replied. 'It is good English but it is clear that I speak it with a foreign accent, an Italian accent. If I first say to English people: "forgive me if I do or say the wrong thing, I am an ignorant foreigner, I need your help" then they will forgive any gaffes I make. Knowing the English, they will enjoy seeing a funny little foreigner make a fool of himself. My people will be the same. But you had better not say you are English. If pressed, say you are a Hollander. They are ruled by Spain and they are looked upon as rustic northern clodhoppers. It will be safer. In my time the English are considered dangerous heretics and looked on with deep suspicion, especially after that excommunicate she-devil Elizabeth defeated the fleet that Philip of Spain sent against her.'

'Our present queen would not be pleased to hear you talk like that,' I replied.

'You still have a queen?' Merisi said. 'What is her name?'

'Elizabeth,' I said.

'My God,' Merisi said, sitting forward in his chair. 'Is she still alive?'

'After four hundred years? Not likely,' I said.

'Why not? I am here alive after four hundred years. I remember the rejoicing in Rome when we heard that the she-devil Elizabeth had died. She was an enemy of the Faith for what seems like forever. How long did she reign? Over forty years, wasn't it?'

'Indeed it was,' I said, 'and her successor, the second Elizabeth, has reigned for well over fifty years and is as loved by her people as the first one was.'

Merisi considered this information. 'Truly, you English are a race of devils. Does the pope still rule in Italy?'

'Only in an ecclesiastical sense,' I answered, 'and over Roman Catholics only, although he does have considerable influence throughout the world. He no longer has any military power.'

Merisi pondered the implications of this. 'It is just as well,' he said. 'Who is the pope today?'

'His papal name is Benedict.'

'Which great family is he part of?'

'No great family. A humble family.'

'Well, which part of Italy is he from?'

'He is not from Italy. He is a German.'

'A German?' Merisi spat. 'The country of that foul heretic Luther. A German now occupies the papal throne?'

'Yes, and the one before him was Polish.'

Merisi buried his head in his hands. 'All is so different now,' he muttered. Then, looking up, he asked: 'What about Lombardy, where I come from? Do the Spanish still rule? What about Milan? Which great prince or duke rules in my home now.'

I realised that, although Merisi talked about Italy as an overall entity, he did not know that it had been unified. I broke the news gently. 'Michele,' I said. 'There are no great princes or dukes ruling Italy now. Your country has been unified into one state. That means that Lombardy, Rome, Lazio, Florence, Tuscany, Umbria, Venezia, Sicily . . . they are all one country. And it is all ruled by the people, not by great men.'

'The people?' Merisi repeated, blankly.

'Yes. It's known as democracy. Every adult has a say in how the country is governed. Everyone votes for who is going to be their leader. Not ruler, but leader.'

'But you English still have your queen,' he protested.

'Yes, but we are the same. The queen has no real power, except that she has ultimate power if it is ever needed. The country is ruled by a parliament, or – for the past few years – a clique of Scotsmen headed by an egomaniac fantasist.'

'But all English people have voted to elect this Queen Elizabeth?'

'No. She is a hereditary monarch.'

'Then when she dies, all English people will vote to elect her successor?'

'No. She will be succeeded by her eldest son or whoever is next in line to the throne. The English people, or rather the British people, have no say in the process.'

'But you say that this queen has no real power. Who does have the power?'

'In theory, the parliament in London.'

'Why do you say "in theory"?'

'Because there are over six hundred members of our British parliament but only a very few of them have any real influence on decisions that affect the country.'

Merisi was beginning to look bewildered. 'Then who does have the authority to make decisions?'

'What we call the Cabinet, a group of twenty or so of the most able members of parliament. But, in recent years, they usually do what the Prime Minister tells them to do because they are all appointed by the Prime Minister.'

'Who is this Prime Minister?'

'Although, in theory, he is meant to be the first among equals, he is the most powerful man or woman in the land. At the moment, he is a Scotsman named Gordon Brown.'

'I thought Scotland was a separate country?'

'No, they joined with England and Wales to form the United Kingdom, although Scotland has its own parliament. So does Wales.'

'And where is the English parliament?'

'The English do not have their own parliament.'

'But this man Brown is a Scotsman. Was he elected by the people of England?'

'No. He was elected as a member of parliament by a handful of the people in his own constituency in Scotland and then served for many years as the Chancellor of the Exchequer of the United Kingdom. When the previous Prime Minister resigned, Gordon Brown took over, because the two men had made a secret agreement over lunch many years before.'

'So this man Brown can just do what he likes?'

'Oh, no, no. He is subject to scrutiny by the House of Commons, which is what we call our parliament, and by the upper house, which is known as the House of Lords.'

'Ah, so this House of Lords was elected by the people of England?'

'No. Most of them are aristocrats, hereditary members who were born into the job. Others are nominated and given the job by the Prime Minister.'

'So, these people who scrutinise the actions of the Prime Minister were either not chosen by the people or they were put in place by the man who they are supposed to be scrutinising.'

'Well,' I said, 'you could put it that way. If you have enough money, you can also buy a seat in the House of Lords from the Prime Minister.'

'Then who do you English vote for?'

'I told you. The members of our parliament.'

'You said the English do not have a parliament. If this man Brown is Scottish, can the English vote for members of the Scottish parliament?'

'No.'

'But the Scots can vote for members of this British parliament which controls England.'

'Yes, that's right.'

'Umm. You said that most of the members of this British parliament have little or no influence. What if they all disagree with what this Prime Minister is doing?'

'The Prime Minister is the head of the political party which has the most members in our parliament. If the members of his own party disagree with what the Prime Minister is doing, they can vote against him, but if they do so, they will be disciplined by the party whips and probably never again get a political job that is worth more than a bucket of warm spit.'

'You said "party whips". This Prime Minister can order his opponents to be whipped, like slaves?'

'No, not in the literal sense, although many of them pay for that service in private.'

'Are there any members of this parliament who can disagree with this Prime Minister?'

'Yes, of course.'

'Thank goodness for that! Who are they?'

'They are the members of the largest political party other than the Prime Minister's party. They are Her Majesty's Opposition.'

'They are appointed by Her Majesty the Queen?'

'No, they are elected by the people.'

'And they oppose everything that the Prime Minister does?'

'No. Not these days. They oppose some things but if the ruling party has a majority of members of parliament then the Opposition can do very little to control the Prime Minister.'

'It still sounds like this Prime Minister person can just do what he likes. He can have his opponents killed or imprisoned, or start an illegal war, and nobody can stop him.'

'No, he cannot . . . well, the previous one did start an illegal war but we are protected by the rule of law in England . . . in Britain. All the judges and law officers are under the command of an officer called the Lord Chancellor who then appoints the Attorney General and the Solicitor General.'

'Ah, now I understand, Stefano. This Lord Chancellor is elected by the people of England to control the power of this Prime Minister.'

'No. The Lord Chancellor is appointed by the Prime Minister.'

'Then just what does prevent this Prime Minister doing what he likes?'

'That's a very good question, Michele. Now I think about it, it's called a free press. Without that, we would really be stuffed.'

'Forgive me, Stefano, but I am having considerable trouble in understanding in what way England is a democracy.'

'Believe me, my friend, you are not alone in that. It's all academic anyway, because most of our laws are now imposed upon us by the European Parliament.'

'Really,' Merisi said, intrigued. 'So the whole of Europe now has a parliament? And are the members of this parliament voted for by all the people of Europe?'

'Yes, they are.'

'That is exciting news, Stefano. All the people of Europe now have control over their own lives and affairs?'

'Err, no. Most of the rules are made by the European Commission.'

'And they are elected by the people?'

'No, not exactly.'

'You are talking in riddles again,' Merisi said.

'Let's get back to our project,' I suggested, still desperately trying to think of good reasons why I should not have to travel back in time. 'Even if I meet the pope, why should he give me what I want. Why should he issue a papal warrant for me?'

'We bribe him. In exchange for that papal warrant, he gets that wondrous double portrait that is drying upstairs in your airing cupboard. Or, rather, if Pope Paul can resist my picture, his nephew Cardinal Scipione Borghese will not be able to, believe me. And Scipione can talk the pope into anything. When you go back to see the pope, we will make sure that Scipione is with him.'

'How can you do that?'

'Our agent, Pellegrino, will provide the correct ChronoCo-ordinates to take you back to exactly the right time and place. You will take my painting back with you. In exchange for the picture, you will get the papal warrant.'

'What if they don't agree? What if they just take the picture and kill me?'

'Do you think we were savages in my time?' Merisi said angrily. 'Calm yourself and trust me. I know these men. I spent nearly twenty years sucking up to such men in order to survive.'

At this moment, without warning and instantaneously, a large square box, which looked to be made of some opaque black plastic material, appeared within the circumference of the gold chain. I jumped with fright as it appeared. 'Jesus Christ,' I breathed. 'What the hell is that?'

'It should be your new suit of clothes, fit to meet a pope in.' Merisi prised open the lid of the box. First, he took out a hat, like something that D'Artagnan would wear in a film version of The Three Musketeers. Next out was a fine lace-up linen shirt with a large floppy collar trimmed with fancy lace. 'Very elegant,' Merisi commented. Then he took out a short cloak, which looked to be made of deep blue velvet, again with a fancy embroidered edging. 'Ah,' Merisi said, as he withdrew the next item and held it open for me to examine. It looked like a padded doublet which laced up at the front. It was made of black silk and richly embroidered in gold. 'This will mark you out as a man of substance, a man of wealth, not to be trifled with.' Next came a pair of thick black tights, which laced up at the waist and looked very uncomfortable, and then came some elegant boots made out of a tan leather which looked something like suede. Merisi next produced a smaller plastic-looking box and opened it. 'Your wig,' he announced, holding up a hairpiece, similar in appearance to Merisi's own long hair. He said: 'Fortunately you are bald on top and the rest of your hair, what little remains, is short. The wig should fit comfortably.'

'Why do I have to wear a wig?' I asked.

'Nobody had short hair like yours in my day, except for the monks, and then it could not be cut as short and evenly as you have it. You must look like a gentleman of substance. And here is your moustache and beard.' He held them up with a look of satisfaction.

'I won't look like a gentleman. I'll look like a complete prat.' The ChronoTranslator ring device had trouble with the word 'prat' because it come out of my mouth in English as 'brat'.

Merisi rummaged inside the big box. There were more clothes, which he took out, and then found what he was looking for. It was an ornately tooled leather belt and, hanging from the belt in a leather sheath, was a long dagger with a silver gilt handle. The handle was studded with small jewels. Merisi looked at it longingly, as if it was an alluring woman, and lovingly withdrew the dagger from its sheath. The keen steel blade glinted. 'This will keep you safe,' he breathed. 'You can swagger through the streets of Rome with this by your side.'

'Unlike you,' I said, 'I won't be looking for trouble.'

'I didn't look for trouble, but when it found me, I was ready,' Merisi said.

'Like you were ready for Tomassoni?' I asked. Merisi shot me a glance of pure malice and brandished the dagger at me. 'Hold your tongue, Englishman,' he hissed, 'or you might end up the same way.'

Hurrying to change the subject, I protested: 'I can't wear that dagger when I meet the pope.'

'No, you can't,' Merisi agreed, replacing the blade into its sheath. 'But you are certainly going to need it when you meet some of my other "friends".' From the large plastic box, he picked out a small brown bottle filled with tablets and held it up to show me. 'You will also need to take one of these tablets before you travel back to my time.'

'What for? What are they?'

'The Tralfamadorians consider that you will have very little natural bodily resistance against some of the diseases that were prevalent in my time. I don't know what that means but they assured me that if you take one of these before you go you will not return covered with suppurating pustules or vomiting black bile.'

My stomach turned over. The possibility of catching foul medieval diseases had not occurred to me. What other lethal possibilities had not occurred to me?

Merisi looked at me intently. 'Do you agree to travel back in time, to do this?'

'Yes,' I replied. 'But when I have completed this assignment, I intend to retire to a golden beach where the weather is hot and be fanned by a bevy of nubile young women while subservient waiters bring me endless tasty snacks and glasses of pina colada on a silver tray, so don't forget to paint my picture. Promise me?'

'I am a man of my word. I promise.' Merisi picked up the hexagonal pendant on the ChronoConverter. He opened the lid. The lights inside flashed alternately but this time Merisi did not press anything. He simply said: 'Camillo Borghese, known as Pope Paul, and Cardinal Scipione Borghese. Must be together. Eleven o'clock, Thursday, April 20th, 2008,' and closed the lid. 'All is prepared. Tomorrow you travel back to my time.'

5

In between frequent visits to the lavatory to ease my nervously melting bowels, I spent the rest of the day and most of the next morning contacting my clients, friends and family to tell them that, for the next few weeks, I might not be available. I concocted a story that I was working on a big project and would be travelling backwards and forwards overseas. It was not a complete lie. It would do my publishing business no good to be out of contact but, as I was gambling with my life, I could chance whether my miniscule business survived the Merisi project. I would not need to worry about my livelihood if Merisi stuck to his promise about painting me his best work yet.

At about 11.20, after a light brunch, I stood in the living room while Merisi examined my costume. The shirt and doublet were surprisingly comfortable. The hose was a little tight around the crotch but the boots were light and comfortable. The wig was comfortable but wearing it made me feel silly and self-conscious, like an ageing celebrity trying to convince his public that he is still young.

'The costume is convincing,' Merisi pronounced. 'It will do.'

Logically, I still had a feeling that all this was a huge practical joke and that Merisi would suddenly announce himself as a television presenter or something. But the things I had already experienced could not be faked. I had to accept that this was really happening.

The gold ChronoConverter chain was hanging around my neck, concealed under my shirt. Whatever metal or substance it was made of, it was not actual gold because it was much too light.

'Remember, Stefano,' Merisi said. 'Without that chain you cannot travel through time. Guard it with your life. Remember also that it will not work within sight of any human being who is not recognised by the ChronoSensor. You must be alone and out of sight before it will bring you back to this time. To return to this time, you simply open the lid of the hexagonal pendant and press the centre. Do you understand that?'

'Yes, but what if someone does get hold of the chain and looks inside that pendant with all those little flashing lights.'

'If anyone not authorised to use the ChronoConverter looks inside, nothing will happen. Those lights will not flash. They will simply look like tiny jewels. If you do lose the chain or get into serious trouble, try to find Guglielmo Pellegrino.' Merisi took out a piece of paper from his trouser pocket. 'There are these passwords so that you will recognise each other. You will raise your right hand and spread your fingers into this 'V' shape and say: "Live long and prosper" and Pellegrino will reply: "The needs of the many outweigh the needs of the few". I don't know what all that means but apparently you know where it comes from.'

'Yes, I understand, T'Pau.'

Merisi looked at my right hand. 'You are wearing your ChronoTranslator ring. Good. Here is the painting.' The unframed canvas had been fastened on to a light stretcher so that I could easily carry it with one hand. 'Remember that this picture is supposed to have been painted just a year or two before the time of this encounter with Pope Paul, so you must carry it under the ChronoConverter chain. If you hold it outside the molecular protection of the chain, whatever that means, it will age four hundred years.' I nodded in acknowledgement. 'The time has arrived, Stefano, literally. When you are ready, depress the centre of the pendant.'

I felt incredibly frightened and I hesitated for several seconds. Merisi gave me encouraging looks. Eventually I felt under my shirt. The lid of the pendant had been left slightly open. I felt inside with my finger and pressed the centre. The living room around me disappeared and for two or three seconds I felt a pleasant floating sensation. Then another room materialised around me but I felt myself toppling forward and just managed to fall clear of the painting, which flew out of my grasp and clattered loudly on to a tiled floor. Dazed from the fall rather than the time travel, I looked up to see two men staring at me. I had just had time to see that they both had their backs towards me before I pitched forward. They had been standing in front of a table examining some papers or documents. Now they had turned around and were staring at me. Both were dressed in clerical robes. The shorter man, on the left, wore a white robe buttoned to the neck. He was in his early fifties, with a puffy face, a pointed beard and small piggy eyes. They were the sort of deeply intelligent eyes that pierced into your soul and missed nothing. The man on the right was dressed in a voluminous red vestment with the red box-like hat of a cardinal on his head. His face was also fleshy with narrow eyes and a wispy beard and moustache. I recognised him as Cardinal Scipione Borghese. He looked exactly like the portrait bust by Gian Lorenzo Bernini. His companion was his uncle, Pope Paul V.

'Guards!' the Pope was shouting and, as I struggled to my feet, I was knocked over again as three Swiss Guards brandishing pikes burst through the door. They seized me and dragged me to my feet.

'Your Holiness, I am not an assassin,' I cried in panic. 'I am not armed.'

One of the Swiss Guards gave me a body search and, in doing so, ripped open my doublet and shirt to reveal the gold chain. 'He is not armed, Your Holiness,' the guard announced. 'There is just this chain.'

'How did you get in here?' Scipione Borghese asked me. He seemed calm, in contrast to his uncle, who was very agitated.

'I am not sure, Your Eminence. I got lost. I was trying to find my way out.' I knew I had to say something quickly. 'I have brought Your Holiness a gift from Michelangelo Merisi da Caravaggio.'

That statement made them pause. 'Caravaggio is dead,' Pope Paul said.

Scipione pointed at the picture, which had fallen face down. He asked: 'Is that it?'

'Yes, Your Eminence,' I replied. I knew I had to establish my credentials as soon as possible before I was thrown out on to the street or, worse, into prison. 'Please look at it, Your Eminence.'

'Keep hold of him tightly,' Scipione ordered the guards, and walked over to the picture. He lifted it up and looked at it. His eyebrows rose in surprise and delight. Then he looked at me keenly.

'Your Eminence,' I blathered, 'I swear by Almighty God that I mean no harm. I bring this gift and a message from my friend Michelangelo Merisi da Caravaggio. Forgive my rude intrusion. Will you please grant me a few minutes of your time?'

Scipione did not reply but carried the picture over to his uncle and showed it to him. Pope Paul did not look so impressed by it. Scipione talked to him quietly for a few minutes. Eventually the Pope shrugged and seemed to comply with whatever Scipione was suggesting.

Scipione turned back and pointed to one of the guards. 'You remain in this chamber with us.' Then he pointed at me. 'Watch this man carefully,' he said to the guard. 'Draw your sword and if he makes any move towards His Holiness, cut him down. The rest of you, let him go and leave, but remain outside the door.'

The Swiss Guards did as they were told. Scipione looked at me and said: 'What is your name?'

'In your language my name is Stefano Maddano.'

'It is clear from your accent that you are a foreigner.'

'Indeed, Your Eminence, and I beg your forgiveness in advance for any inadvertant lack of courtesy or respect that might be caused by my ignorant . . . foreign-ness.'

Scipione considered this awkward statement and it seemed to mollify him. 'You look distressed,' he commented. 'Would you like a glass of wine?'

'That is very kind, Your Eminence. A glass of wine would be most welcome.' The way I felt, preferably a magnum. I did not want to dull my wits but I equally did not want to offend the cardinal by refusing his hospitality. Scipione turned back to the table and poured red wine into a gold goblet from a gold decanter that was standing on a gold tray. Merisi had been correct about the Borghese love of luxury and ostentation. The large room was lavishly decorated. The ceiling was ornately stuccoed, with a gold chandelier hanging from it, and the walls were hung with tapestries of the finest quality. There was a massive fireplace, fire unlit. Intricately carved furniture made of dark wood, including chairs, a bookcase, a desk and the table that the two men were working on, was arrayed around the room. The table was standing on a carpet woven with an elaborate pattern but the carpet did not cover all of the floor. Around the edges of the floor were plain tiles, the ones that I had fallen face down on.

Scipione walked over and handed me the goblet of wine. 'Thank you,' I said, and took a sip. It tasted sour and disgusting, worse than grappa. 'Excellent wine,' I lied. 'Most refreshing.'

Pope Paul had seemingly lost interest in these proceedings and had turned back to the documents on the table. 'Now,' Scipione said, 'you say you were a friend of Caravaggio. I notice that you wear a gold chain around your neck. Are you an artist?'

It was as good a cover story as anything. 'Yes,' I replied. 'Albeit a poor one in comparison with my friend Michelangelo.'

'You cannot be so poor an artist if you have been awarded the gold chain,' Scipione said drily. 'But then, as you rightly say, most artists are poor in comparison with Caravaggio. How did you get to know him?'

Shit, I thought, I wasn't expecting the Spanish Inquisition. I mentally reviewed the life of Caravaggio and hit on what I hoped would be the right approach. 'I only met him towards the end of his life, Your Eminence, while he and I were both working in Naples. I helped him with his work and we became friends.'

'You are honoured,' the cardinal smiled wryly. 'Very few human beings were befriended by Merisi. Mostly the opposite.'

As I suspected, the Pope missed nothing, and he said: 'Caravaggio's life was a disgrace and many of his paintings are a disgrace.' He looked round accusingly, but affectionately, at his nephew. 'I cannot remember how you talked me into giving him a pardon.'

'Your Holiness,' Scipione said, 'there were many doubts about the death of the man Tomassoni. It was not clear that Caravaggio deliberately killed him. Some witnesses claimed it was an accident.'

I decided to push my luck. 'If I may make so bold, Your Holiness, that is precisely why I am here, at the request of my friend Michelangelo.'

Pope Paul looked at me and said: 'Explain yourself.'

'Michelangelo was aware that by causing the death of Tomassoni he had committed a grievous offence against God.' The Pope nodded in agreement. 'Before Michelangelo died, he knew that Your Holiness had granted him a pardon and he asked me, if I ever had the opportunity, to express his deep appreciation for your Christian forgiveness.' The Pope grunted sceptically. 'Michelangelo felt, however, that he was being pursued by persons unknown who wished him grave harm, even wished for his death. You may remember the terrible injuries he received after that attack outside a tavern in Naples.' Both men nodded. 'Michelangelo requested that, if he was ever killed in suspicious circumstances, I would take it upon myself to try to find who had harmed him and bring them to justice, for the peace of his immortal soul.'

Scipione and the Pope looked at each other. 'Do you believe Merisi's death was suspicious?' Scipione asked. 'I thought he had died of a fever?'

'That is the generally held opinion, Your Eminence, but I have good reasons to believe that Caravaggio was murdered.'

'What reasons are they?' Scipione asked.

'Caravaggio believed that the attack outside the Osteria de Cerriglia in Naples was meant to finish him off but the attackers were disturbed before they could complete their grisly task. After Caravaggio's death, someone spirited away his body and it has never been found, as if someone did not want the real cause of his death investigated.'

'Why did Caravaggio choose you to be his post-mortem guardian angel?' Scipione asked.

'I suppose I am one of the few people he trusted. I am a foreigner with no vested interests in Italian society. I am impartial.'

'Are you saying that Italians are not capable of administering justice fairly and impartially?' the Pope interjected.

'No, not at all,' I replied, flustered. 'I did not mean to offend Your . . .'

Scipione held up his hand to stop me. 'What do you want from His Holiness?' he said. 'I take it that this painting is meant to sweeten his judgement?'

'If it pleases His Holiness,' I replied.

Pope Paul picked up Caravaggio's painting and studied it. 'It is rendered with miraculous skill,' he commented. 'The colours are a tribute to God's light. How did Caravaggio achieve such colours?'

Winsor and Newton, £3.29 a tube, I thought, but said: 'Michele had been experimenting with new colour mixes, Your Holiness. He considered that some of his later work had been too . . . sombre.'

'Sombre is correct,' the Pope agreed. 'Sombre, dark and occasionally obscene and blasphemous.'

'But more often intensely moving,' I said. I should not have said that, I thought, as the Pope regarded me with disdain. I should not have contradicted the most powerful man in this world. Scipione observed his uncle's disapproval but, gagging to own Merisi's painting, tried to ease the atmosphere by saying: 'His Holiness is correct. Caravaggio's work was often unacceptable. But this work makes adequate compensation for his many transgressions. Do you not think so, Your Holiness?'

'Do you not think it rather too . . . boastful and worldly?' the Pope asked Scipione.

'If I may make so bold,' I interjected, before Scipione could answer, 'Michele told me that he intended this picture as a tribute to the enlightened and beneficent rule of Your Holiness, very ably supported by Your Eminence, and that your pose is intended to show that the fruit and flowers, the musical and scientific instruments, and so on, are your gifts of enlightenment, wisdom and plenty to your flock.' The American word 'baloney' came to mind as I waffled, and Pope Paul thought the same, as did Scipione, but the cardinal was willing to go along with the pretence in order to get his hands on the painting.

'A handsome apology by the late lamented Caravaggio,' Scipione said.

The Pope looked at him sceptically and then beckoned me forward. The guard moved with me but the Pope signalled to him to remain where he was. 'Follow me, Signor Maddano,' Pope Paul said, and he led me over to the far side of the room. He indicated a portrait that was hanging there. It was a portrait of the Pope himself and with a thrill of excitement I saw that it had been painted by Caravaggio, one of his works that has been lost four hundred years later in my time. 'This was painted by your friend,' he said. 'My nephew over there, Cardinal Borghese, introduced Caravaggio to me just after God granted that I became pontiff. What do you think of this portrait?'

I glanced behind me. Scipione and the guard were watching us intently. I turned back and said: 'I think it is superb, Your Holiness.' Caravaggio, with deft artfulness, had reduced the effect of the pope's piggy eyes and fleshy face, and had made him appear more noble, kindly and pious than he actually was.

'It is very flattering, is it not?' Pope Paul asked, looking at me shrewdly.

'It seems to me that my friend has captured your essential character, Your Holiness.'

The pope replied, in a soft tone that could not be heard across the room:

'You know nothing of my character. You are as practised a flatterer as Caravaggio was. Like him, there is something strange about you. There are at least ten armed guards in the corridor which leads to this apartment. They have all taken a sacred oath to defend me with their own lives. You could not have bribed them all in order to allow you to enter this room, although they will be interrogated later to ascertain if they did.'

'Your Holiness, I swear the guards are innocent of any collusion. I simply blundered my way in here by accident.'

Pope Paul ignored my protestation. 'There is no possibility that you could have approached anywhere near this room without being stopped and yet you suddenly appeared in here. Perhaps you were sent here by a divine hand.'

I could feel myself going red in the face and opened my mouth to speak but the pope held up his hand to stop me. 'My nephew aches to own that painting over there and I have a sentimental weakness for my family. I want him to have it. It is a masterpiece but I care nothing for it. What do you want from me?'

'Your Holiness, I had hoped that you could grant me papal authority to investigate the death of my friend Caravaggio. I am a stranger, a foreigner in this land. I have no authority to make people tell me the truth, or even to speak to me at all. But you have such authority. I am asking you to help me obtain justice for my friend and to grant him your mercy and peace for his troubled immortal soul.'

Pope Paul regarded me for a few seconds, weighing his decision. 'You have spoken well enough,' he answered. 'I will give you my warrant. It will require any witnesses to tell you the truth and I will issue a papal bull to that effect. If anyone refuses to talk to you, they will have me to answer to. That should loosen their tongues. To take someone's life is not only unlawful but it is a sin against God. Caravaggio committed such a sin but no-one has the right to commit the sin of murder against him, for whatever reason. Only God has the right of life or death over Man.'

I wondered what the thousands of people who have died on the orders of popes throughout the ages would think of that statement, but I said: 'Everything that I have heard about your wisdom and justice is true, Your Holiness.'

Although Pope Paul was aware of when he was being flattered, he also enjoyed it. He held out his white gloved hand to me and, stupidly, I did not know what to do. 'You may kiss my ring,' the pope said. Trying not to think of modern slang connotations, I took his hand and kissed the papal ring. Then the pope briskly went about business. 'Please send for my secretary,' he said to Scipione, who did as he was asked. The pope explained to him about the papal warrant that he had agreed to give me. Scipione looked at me sharply. 'Be careful, Signor Maddano,' he warned. 'You will be plunging into very murky waters. Even the pope's blessing and protection may not safeguard you against some of the black-hearted characters who inhabited Caravaggio's world.'

'Thank you for the warning, Your Eminence,' I replied.

'Thank you for this painting,' he smiled.

'I know that Michele will be very pleased that you approve of it. Would have been very pleased,' I corrected myself quickly. 'I still find it hard to accept that Michele has left us.'

At that opportune moment to help cover my gaffe, the pope's secretary entered the chamber. He was carrying a large, square, flat wooden box which contained the tools of his trade.

The pope looked at me and said: 'Please wait outside. My secretary here will bring out the warrant as soon as we have prepared it. Blessings and goodbye to you.' He turned back to the table where the papal secretary had sat down and was preparing his inks and vellum.

The guard opened the door for me and I walked out into a long carpeted corridor. I stopped to look out of a window while I waited for the warrant. The guards standing further along the corridor regarded me suspiciously. They knew that, later, there would be serious questions asked of them because of my sudden appearance in the pope's chamber. I looked around. I guessed I was in a palazzo, perhaps the Palazzo Borghese. I was on the second floor. There were the walls of another palazzo across the street but the activity in the narrow street below, and the noise coming from it, was staggering. Throngs of beggars and soldiers were wandering around, horses and riders clip-clopped past, carts filled with goods and produce rumbled up and down, and tradesman carrying baskets of goods on their heads shouted and cursed as they pushed their way through the crowd. The noise was far more cacophonous than that produced in any 21st century street. I watched this street scene with fascination and then, glancing along the street to my left, was thrilled to see the dome of St. Peter's thrusting above the buildings at the end of the street. I knew that the dome had been designed by Michelangelo Buonarotti but that the design had been altered after the great man's death by Giacomo della Porta and Domenico Fontana, who had made the dome taller and steeper than Michelangelo's original design. I also knew that the building of the dome had been completed not many years before this year I had travelled to and thus I was seeing it in its pristine newness. The ribbed dome glowed with dazzling whiteness and the elegant finial above it, which was decorated with gold leaf, lit up like a light bulb under the bright sun. For the first time, I felt an exhilaration about what the ChronoConverter was allowing me to see and do, rather than the natural apprehension about being landed in such a strange situation.

The papal secretary came out of the papal chamber, interrupted my reverie and handed me a rolled-up sheet of vellum tied up with a white ribbon. He turned to the guard and said: 'Escort this man outside,' and went back into the pope's chamber.

'Follow me,' the guard ordered. He led me along the corridor, down a flight of stairs and ushered me out into the street through a pair of huge wooden doors, which were guarded by two men carrying wicked-looking halberds. I walked out into bright sunlight and an almost overpowering stench. Despite the assurance of the protective tablet that the Tralfamadorians had given me, I wanted to get away and get back home before I caught bubonic plague or something. I nimbly made my way through the throng and found a narrow alleyway which looked deserted. I entered the alleyway and ducked into a doorway, out of sight of anyone. I fumbled inside my shirt to open the lid of the ChronoConverter and pressed the centre. The alleyway vanished, I felt the pleasant floating sensation and then, to my intense relief, I was standing in my own living room.

The relief lasted about ten seconds. I was gathering my wits when an explosion flung open the living room door. Terrified, and without thinking, I ducked down to kneel on the living room floor. I could hear glass crashing and I looked up to see steam and smoke billowing into the room. I crawled over to the door on my hands and knees and looked through into the kitchen, fearful that I might see flames engulfing my house. There were no flames, so I stood up and edged my way into the kitchen to see the face of Michelangelo Merisi peering, with a horrified expression, from the outside into the kitchen. All the panes of window glass had been blown out by the explosion. The outer kitchen door was lying, flattened and smashed, on the ground outside. Some sort of brown grunge had been flung all over the kitchen walls and some of it was dripping off. One of the overhead kitchen cupboards had been torn off its fastenings and was hanging drunkenly from the wall. All the contents of that cupboard had been emptied on to the kitchen floor and had been smashed, either by the explosion or by the fall. There were broken glasses, mugs, jars of coffee and condiments all over the floor. Black scorch marks had ruined the kitchen ceiling. The flourescent light tube had been smashed and the light fitting was hanging off. Merisi noticed me edging into the kitchen. 'Stefano, you're back!' he exclaimed. 'Are you injured?'

'No', I shouted back. 'Are you?'

'Merciful Mother of God, no, I am not,' he answered. 'Is it safe to come back in?'

'Wait a minute,' I said. 'Let me see what's happened.' I walked gingerly into the kitchen, avoiding the many shards of broken glass littering the floor. I looked around and saw what had caused the explosion. The microwave oven had blown up and the metal sides had burst open to make it look like some monstrous spiked flower.

Merisi looked on anxiously.

'It's safe now,' I said, beckoning him back inside. 'What did you do?'

'I was hungry,' he replied, stepping carefully back into the kitchen. 'You left me without food. I didn't know how long you would be gone in Rome. I found a container with the words "Italian style meatballs". I wanted to eat them hot, so I put them in that device I have seen you use, turned those knob things and pressed that button thing.'

'Had you opened the container?'

'No. Was I supposed to?'

'You put an unopened metal container, in a microwave oven, on full power?'

Merisi didn't reply. He just looked at me.

'Okay,' I said. 'Never mind. You weren't to know. It's a miracle you were not killed. Lucky you were outside. Why were you outside?'

'I was scared when that other thing exploded.'

'Other thing?' I exclaimed. 'What other thing?'

'I wanted some of that coffee drink. I pressed the switch on that device that makes hot water. A few minutes later, it went "bang" and I ran outside. That's when the other thing exploded.'

'The hot water device is called an electric kettle,' I said. 'Did you put any water in it before you switched it on?'

'No,' Merisi said. 'I thought it made the water in there.'

'No, you have to fill . . .' At that moment, there was a frantic knocking on the front door. I could hear my neighbour, Mrs. Chowdry shouting: 'Mr. Maddan! Are you alright?'

'Just a minute,' I said to Merisi. 'Wait here and don't touch anything.'

I went through to the front door and opened it. Mrs. Chowdry opened her mouth to speak but just gaped at me for a few seconds. Then she pulled herself together and said: 'Are you alright, Mr. Maddan. I heard such a bang that I was worried that you might be hurt.'

'Signora Chowdry! Come stai. Voi sembrare preoccupato. . .' Mrs. Chowdry looked completely nonplussed and then I realised that I was dressed like D'Artagnan and, thanks to the ChronoTranslator ring, I was gabbling away in Italian. I slipped the ring off my finger. 'I'm so sorry, Mrs. Chowdry,' I said. 'We're rehearsing for a play. I'm in the Bedford Amateur Dramatic Society production of Hamlet. I'm playing Laertes.'

'Oh, really,' she said. 'It sounded like you were speaking Italian.'

'Yes, I was,' I replied. 'We are doing an Italian language version for the Italian community in Bedford.'

'I didn't realise you were so talented,' Mrs. Chowdry said.

'Oh, actor, linguist, Brain of Britain. It all comes so easily to me.'

'But what about that bang? What was that?'

'I'm afraid I had a little accident with the microwave oven. Or rather, my friend did. He's from Italy. He is staying with me while we rehearse our Hamlet. He's playing Polonius. He's a fine Polonius but he isn't so good at microwave ovens. Apparently they work differently in Italy. They are not so used to them. Knives and forks are the height of technology where he lives.'

'Is he the man I've seen lurking in your garden?'

'Yes, that's right,' I said, brightly. 'He's staying with me. Working in the summerhouse, you know, helping me out.'

'Well, I don't like to mention it, but I have to tell you that I have seen that man relieving himself in the garden. I don't know what they get up to in Italy but this is a respectable village.'

'I'm so sorry about that, Mrs. Chowdry. He's from peasant stock. They do that sort of thing in the wilds of Umbria. You know, feed their relatives to the pigs and blow their nose on the table cloth. I've had a word with him. It won't happen again.'

'Well, as long as you're sure you're all right.'

'Perfectly,' I said. 'Thank you for enquiring. Good day to you.'

Mrs. Chowdry gave me a brief uncertain half-smile and said goodbye. I closed the front door. I suddenly felt exhausted. In the immortal words of John Lennon: 'Nobody told me there'd be days like these, strange days indeed'.

6

The next morning, Merisi and I began our research work in my office in order to stay out of the way of the workmen who were repairing the kitchen. Merisi had studied the papal warrant granted to me by Pope Paul and had given it his approval. Yesterday, after I had thought about the events of the day, I had become increasingly angry that the ChronoConverter had dumped me directly into the pope's chamber and straight into a potentially very dangerous situation. Merisi explained that, because of the number of guards surrounding the pope, it had been the only way to get me past them and that the Tralfamadore ChronoCouncil had approved the risk but decided not to warn me in case I backed out of the whole project. That explanation had made me even more angry. Surveying the wreckage of my kitchen had not improved my mood. So, today, I was all business. Using Helen Langdon's superb biography, and the copious study notes I had made in my attempt to win the television quiz Mastermind, I began to further probe the life and work of my troublesome houseguest.

'Very well, Michele,' I began, 'let's get down to some serious work. You were born Michelangelo Merisi in the small town of Caravaggio, near Milan, in 1571. Is that correct?'

'Yes.'

'Your exact date of birth is not known but the belief has been that you were born on September 29th, which is the feast day of the Archangel Saint Michael, and that is why you were named Michelangelo. Can you confirm that?'

Merisi said: 'Yes, that is right.'

'Good,' I said. 'That's the first unconfirmed fact about your life confirmed. You were born into fairly comfortable circumstances, we believe. Your father Fermo worked as magister to the Sforza family. What did he do?'

'He supervised the construction and decoration of their buildings and their palazzo in Milan. He was not actually an architect but he was a skilled mason. He was an overseer, checking that the work was being carried out correctly. When I was very young, he often used to take me to the places where he was working. That's how I became interested in painting. I was particularly fascinated by the fresco painters. They would let me help them prepare paints and other materials, or at least pretend to let me help. They also showed me many tricks of their trade. And, of course, I saw many easel paintings in the Sforza houses.'

'That's good,' I said encouragingly. 'What about your mother?'

'What about her?' Merisi replied, in a prickly tone.

'Her name was Lucia, wasn't it? Maiden name Aratori?'

'Yes. She was my father's second wife. My father had two daughters, my step-sisters, from his first marriage. My father and mother were married in 1571, the year I was born.'

'We know that Francesco Sforza was a witness at their wedding. That was a very great honour, wasn't it? The head of a noble family like the Sforzas attending the wedding of an employee?'

Merisi shifted in his chair, uncomfortable with these questions. 'My father was an important, valued and highly trusted employee. Why shouldn't Francesco attend his wedding?'

'Don't get angry,' I said. 'It was not my intention to demean your father. I was considering things in relation to English nobility. In the English class system, people like your father, tradesmen or artisans, were once scarcely considered to be human beings by the aristocracy. That mealy-mouthed toffee-nosed languid strata of English society would not demean themselves by attending the wedding of such a common person.'

'I understand,' Merisi conceded. 'It was an honour that Francesco attended, but not unusual. My father was on very good terms with Francesco's wife, Costanza Colonna Sforza. She was the daughter of Marcantonio Colonna who, later that year, became a hero when he commanded the papal galleys at the sea battle of Lepanto, in which the wicked heathen Turks were destroyed, praise be to God. Costanza and the whole Colonna family supported and protected me throughout my life, mainly thanks to my father. Costanza had married Francesco Sforza a few years before I was born. They were both very young when they married. Francesco was, I think, seventeen and Costanza was just eleven or twelve . . . much too young. At first, Costanza was very unhappy in the marriage. She threatened to kill herself, which is a sin against God, and she was so distraught that there were plans being made to send her to a convent. My father was a kind man and, having had two daughters himself, I think he took pity on Costanza and helped her as much as he was able. My father had lost one of his daughters, Caterina, before I was born, so I think he was very sympathetic and understanding of the young girl's plight. Far from being resentful, I think Francesco welcomed my father's efforts to reassure Costanza. Costanza must have reconciled herself to the marriage because her son Muzio was born a couple of years before me. My father even escorted Costanza to Paris in the December of the year before I was born. They were well to be away from Milan because God punished us with a terrible winter. It was bitterly cold and there was a famine that drove hundreds of peasants to seek refuge in the city. Costanza had asked to go to Paris to attend some big royal wedding and my father wanted to go to Paris to find suitable furniture and decorations for the Sforza palace. So, as you can see, the relationship between the Sforzas and my father was a lot more than just master and servant.'

'That's very interesting, Michele,' I said. 'Let's go back to your mother, Lucia. What was she like?'

'She was devoted to all her children. She worked very hard.'

'Her family, the Aratoris, were quite well-off, weren't they?'

'Yes. They were certainly not poor.'

'They might even have been descended from nobility. Is that true?'

'Oh, there was some gossip within the family,' Merisi said airily, 'but I don't know whether it is true or not.'

'According to our records, you had five siblings. Your older step-sister Caterina had died before you were born, you had another older step-sister named Margarita, and you had a younger full sister, also named Caterina, and two younger brothers, Giovan Battista and Giovanni Pietro. Is that right?'

'Yes, that is correct.'

'At this point, Michele, with your permission, I wish to ask you about events that must be very painful for you to remember.'

'I suppose you mean the plague?'

'Yes. We understand that it carried off both your grandfather and father within hours of each other.'

'Yes. I must have been about six years old. The plague broke out in Milan and spread to my home town of Caravaggio. I woke up one morning and was told that my father and grandfather, Bernardino, had gone. As with any small child, I don't suppose I understood what had happened, just that my father never came back. I missed him very much. Of course, the tragedy left my poor mother to look after five children without any husband to support her. Her father and my uncle Francesco helped out. We were better off than many but it was a very hard time for her. She always did her duty and took care of us. She didn't deserve to be treated like that by God.' Merisi was visibly upset by these memories. I didn't know what to say to comfort him, so I said nothing. With a conscious effort, Merisi regained his composure and said bitterly: 'I don't know how God can be so cruel, to send such pestilence to carry off my father and grandfather. What had they done to Him? People say I am cruel and arrogant, but I am not as cruel and arrogant as God.'

'Michele,' I said gently. 'We now know that the plague is not sent by God. It has nothing to do with God. Let me show you something . . .'

Merisi was sitting on the other side of my office desk. I turned the computer screen towards him. 'This is called a computer. It's a device that, thanks to the selfless generosity of an Englishman named Tim Berners-Lee, contains most of the knowledge of the world for free, or virtually free. Let me show you what I mean about the plague.' I tapped the words "bubonic plague causes" into Google and selected one of the many websites that appeared.

Merisi was fascinated by this demonstration. 'Are you serious, Stefano? You can find any knowledge through this box?'

'Yes, truly. It's like having every library in the world at your disposal.' I showed Merisi the text on the screen. 'There it is. Plague is a disease of rodents, like rats, caused by the bacillus Yersinia pestis. A bacillus is a very tiny living thing that you cannot see with the naked eye. We had to invent very powerful lenses in order to see them. Do you understand me?' Merisi nodded. I went on: 'The bacillus invades the rats, fleas feed on the rats, catch the plague, and pass the plague on to humans. It very rarely happens now because we know what causes it and how to stop it. That is why I said to you when you first arrived that cleanliness and hygiene are very important. Many, many diseases are caused by these invisible living things.'

Merisi sat back and looked troubled. 'If this is true, then it makes it worse.'

'How do you mean?' I asked.

'Well, if God had been punishing my father and grandfather, then perhaps there was a reason for their death. But now you tell me that they died simply because some tiny creature invaded their bodies.'

'I'm afraid so.'

Merisi stood up. 'No,' he said. 'This makes no sense. Perhaps God did send these tiny things. Perhaps He ordered the fleas to carry them to my father as a punishment.'

'A punishment for what, Michele? Everything you have told me about him suggests he was a good man, a kind man. A good husband and a loving father. What reason would God have to destroy him?'

'I don't know,' Merisi said. He was becoming very agitated.

'Look,' I said, 'about two hundred years before you were born, the plague invaded Europe and about one quarter of Europe, that's millions of souls, perished because of it. In some parts of Europe the plague killed most of the inhabitants. Was God punishing all of them? Were they all evil men and women? Were the young children so evil that God had to punish them? Believe me, Michele, God has nothing to do with the plague.'

Merisi, somewhat persuaded by my argument, sat down again. 'It's a good thing that your friend Pope Paul cannot hear you.' He gave me a wan smile.

'How did you get on with your brothers and sisters?' I asked, in an attempt to change the subject.

Merisi shrugged. 'The same as most families, I suppose. We had our fights, but nothing serious, or nothing serious that I can recall.'

'Your half-sister Margarita was quite a bit older than you and Giovanni Pietro was quite a bit younger. I would imagine that you were closest to either Caterina or Giovan Battista? Would that be right?'

'Yes, I suppose so. Giovan Battista was born only a year after me and we went to school together.'

'What was your education like? Was it in Caravaggio or Milan, and was it a good education?'

'Yes, it was a very good education. We started at the infant school called the Scuola di Leggere e Scrivere in Caravaggio and then went on to the grammar school in Caravaggio. We were taught to read and write and we were given a good grounding in classical literature. You know, the ancient Roman authors like Virgil and Ovid.'

'Were you a good scholar, would you say?'

'I would say very good, because I have always enjoyed books and learning new things. I know that my education was an invaluable help when it came to planning my paintings, especially those with a Biblical or classical theme.'

'Our records suggest that your brother Giovan Battista was an even better scholar. Is that true?'

Merisi pursed his lips. His expression was sceptical. 'Academically, yes, I would have to say that Giovan was a better scholar than me. But from a very early age he was set on a career in the Church and he was clever enough to be able to secure a place in the Jesuit College in Rome.'

'So you would say that your relations with your brothers and sisters were amicable and normal?'

'Yes.'

'And that you got on very well with Giovan Battista?'

'Yes, very well.'

'In that case, Michele, why, many years later in Rome when you were living in Cardinal Del Monte's palazzo, did you bluntly refuse to acknowledge Giovan when he visited you?' I watched Merisi's face for his reaction to this question. It was an angry reaction.

'That is a lie!' he exclaimed.

'Not according to your friend and biographer Giulio Mancini.'

'Mancini was not a man to be trusted.'

'You trusted him as a doctor to treat you when you were ill. But that is beside the point. Do you deny Mancini's story about your brother?'

'I did not think that anyone would know about that incident after all this time. You are tricking me!'

'I am not trying to trick you, Michele. I am trying to demonstrate that you must tell me the truth. You do not know how much we have found out about your life, so you must not tell me lies. What is the point of concealing the truth after four hundred years? We are trying to find out who murdered you or wanted you murdered. If you won't tell me the truth or give me all the facts I need, my task is impossible.'

'Are you suggesting that my own brother might have wanted me murdered?'

'Yes, why not? In Britain today, most murders involve family members. We must consider every possibility.'

Merisi sulked and said nothing, so I continued. 'Your biographer Mancini says that Giovan Battista, who was a priest by then, had heard of your growing fame as a painter and came to visit you at Cardinal Del Monte's palace. The cardinal sent for you but, when you saw Giovan standing there, you said that you did not know him and that he was not your brother. That is a curious phrase, Michele, to say that Giovan was not your brother.'

'It's just one of those things that people say,' Merisi protested. 'You know, like "I could kill you for that" but you don't actually mean it.'

'But there must have been some bad blood between you two?'

'It is family business,' Merisi said. 'It is not to be discussed with strangers, especially not nosey English fuckers.'

I threw up my arms in despair. 'I didn't ask for this job, Michele. You came to me, remember? You must tell me everything, family business or not, or we may miss some vital clue.'

Merisi was sulkily silent for several seconds. Finally, he said: 'We fell out over the sale of our mother's property.'

'Very well,' I said. 'We will be examining that period of your life soon, so we will come back to the issue of your mother's property. After you left your home town to become an artist in Rome, we have no other record, apart from this incident with Giovan, that you ever went back to Caravaggio to see your family or had any contact with your brothers and sisters again. Is that true?'

'Look,' Merisi said tetchily, 'travel was much more difficult in those days. We couldn't whizz about in these metal boxes you call cars.'

'That is not the reason, is it?' I challenged him.

'Well, fuck you, what do you want me to say?'

'You never married, did you? There is not any record of your ever having a really close and loving relationship with a woman, or a man. You alienated most of your friends. You are a cold-hearted, arrogant, self-centred, over-bearing prick who's only concern in life was being a famous artist. I don't think you ever really gave a fuck for anyone else.'

To my surprise, Merisi laughed. 'You have summed me up perfectly, Stefano. Except that there were women I loved. But you are right, all I ever really cared about was being acknowledged as a great artist.'

'Will you promise to tell me the truth from now on? Will you tell me about these women you loved? We know a lot about Fillide, so be careful.'

'Ah, beautiful Fillide. Do you not think that, in my portraits of her, I captured the heartless bitch behind that beautiful face?'

'Was that your intention?'

Merisi gave my question serious consideration but eventually said: 'No.'

'We have made good progress,' I announced. 'Let's have a coffee break.'

Merisi rubbed his hands together in glee. I had created a caffeine addict. I checked on the progress of my kitchen and made mugs of tea for the builders. Then I made coffee for Merisi and me and carried it back to my office. Merisi had moved into my office chair and was looking at something on the computer screen. He had typed the word 'Caravaggio' into the Google search engine but did not know what to do next. I showed him the mouse and showed how to click on it or tap the return key. The web pages flashed up and I showed him how to open one. He looked startled as his own face appeared on the computer screen.

'What is that?' he asked, pointing at the image.

I looked to see what he was pointing at. 'That's your portrait,' I said. 'By your friend Ottavio Leoni.'

'Yes, I know,' Merisi said, impatiently. 'What is that thing it's drawn on?'

'It's called a banknote,' I said. 'In Italy, they stopped using scudi and started using money called the lire. Large amounts of money can now be printed on paper, like the £200 I gave you, with the head of our Queen Elizabeth on it, to show it is genuine.'

'You mean, everyone uses this money?'

'Yes, everyone.'

'But this has got my face on it?' Merisi said, trying to grasp this novel concept.

'Yes, it's a banknote worth 100,000 lire. The Italians no longer use them but a few years ago they printed your face on them, to show they are genuine.'

'But I am not a king or a prince or a pope,' Merisi protested. 'Why should they put my face on these valuable things?'

'Because the Italians revere you as one of their greatest artists. So you were honoured in this way.'

Merisi gazed at the banknote, and then said: 'How much is it worth?'

'One hundred thousand lire? Probably about fifty pounds. Two hundred scudi.' I had no idea whether I had estimated these values correctly but I did not want to waste too much time on feeding Merisi's ego.

'And how many were made?'

'Thousands of them, I should imagine.'

'All with Leoni's portrait of me on them?'

'Yes.'

Merisi threw back his head and laughed gleefully. 'I have made that wanker Leoni more famous than he could ever have imagined.'

'I suppose you have,' I agreed. 'Let's drink our coffee, Michele, then when we have finished our work, you can play with the computer.'

'Very well, Stefano,' Merisi said, and moved back over to the opposite chair, overjoyed with the knowledge that he had become so famous in his native land.

While we drank our coffee, I answered Merisi's questions about modern Italy as well as I could, which was not very well, never having been there, and then we resumed our work. 'Let's move on to your apprenticeship with Peterzano,' I said. 'You must have shown artistic talent for him to have accepted you as an apprentice. Did you paint and draw before you started your apprenticehip?'

'Oh, yes, all the time, whenever I could. Caravaggio was a boring and undistinguished little town. The streets were straight and narrow, laid out on the ancient Roman model. There was not much architecture of any interest. In the church of Saints Fermo and Rustico, however, was the chapel of Corpus Domini which had been frescoed by Bernardino Campi. I studied and copied those frescoes assiduously. And, throughout my childhood, the church of San Giovanni Battista was being built. The Virgin Mary had appeared to a peasant girl about 150 years before, and the church was being built to honour that visitation. Luckily, my uncle Bernardino was the site architect, so I had access to its art works whenever I wanted. My uncle encouraged my artistic efforts.'

'What about Milan? Your father worked for the Sforza family so he must have been visiting Milan all the time.'

'Yes. Milan was an important city . . .'

'It still is,' I interrupted. 'With two very good football teams.'

'Football?' Merisi said. 'What is that?'

'Oh, it's a modern sport in which inarticulate and foul-mouthed competitors are paid enormous amounts of money to spit, trip over their own feet, pretend to be injured, be sick as parrots, abuse their opponents, blame the referee if they lose and perform wildly over-the-top celebrations when they actually manage to do anything skilful. Tell me about Milan.'

Merisi looked at me, baffled by my tirade, but then shrugged and said: 'As you know, Lombardy was ruled by the Spanish and, of course, their influence was everywhere. The city was dominated by the cathedral and by the Castello Sforzesco, from where the Spanish ruled Milan. The city was a strange mixture. It was built on a fertile plain and yet it was frequently racked by famine. And, before I was born, it had been badly affected by war. It was a rich city, with fine houses and beautiful gardens. A city of rich businessmen and well-off artisans. There was a huge demand for luxury goods and yet there were hundreds of beggars and destitutes on the streets who had moved into the city to escape war or famine. The Milanese were the best swordsmen in Italy. Milanese armourers were unrivalled and made the best swords and daggers in Italy.'

I was aware of Merisi's fascination with swords and daggers. His love of such weapons was a theme that ran through his life and his paintings but I decided not to press him on the subject at this point.

'Tell me about the Archbishop of Milan, Carlo Borromeo,' I said. 'I believe he had a great influence on the city and on art?'

'Yes, he was an austere and saintly man. He worked tirelessly to promote the Faith and to aid the poor. He was forever praying. He had close ties with the Colonna family, so I saw him a few times before he died, which was when I was about fourteen years old. I went to his funeral, God rest his soul. They say he saved the city in the terrible famine that struck in the months before I was born. My uncle Ludovico, who was a priest, was in Borromeo's service and lived in the Archbishop's palace.'

'Borromeo also influenced the art of your master, Peterzano, didn't he?'

'Yes. My master drummed it into me. I can still recite Borromeo's teachings on artistic style. Borromeo had contributed a chapter called, I think, "Sacred Images and Paintings" to some treatise on art and architecture. It said something like: "religious art should be decorous . . . it should, above all, incite to piety and avoid novelty, shunning whatever is profane, base or obscene, dishonest or provocative." Nothing about telling the truth, you notice. All bullshit from a man who never lifted a brush in his life.' For a moment I thought Merisi was going to spit on my office floor in disgust.

I said: 'Very well, let's move on to your master, Simone Peterzano. Why did you choose him as your master?'

Merisi shrugged indifferently. 'I didn't choose him,' he replied, 'but he was the best of a bad bunch. Costanza Colonna chose him for me. Or, at least, she recommended him to my mother. Costanza had been very kind to me after my father died. She encouraged my artistic talents and allowed me to visit the Palazzo Colonna in Milan any time I wished. Often, she would watch me draw and paint, and make suggestions, usually sensible ones. The palazzo was filled with paintings, frescoes and sculpture for me to copy and learn from. Also, as I we have just been saying, Peterzano was in the circle of Archbishop Borromeo, a close friend of the Colonna family, so they probably thought that Peterzano would treat me well. My mother also encouraged me and thought that being a painter would be a good secure trade for me. I know that my father would have been pleased with my choice as well.'

'You said that Peterzano was the best of a bad bunch. I would have thought that Milan would be filled with excellent artists?'

'Most of them were just poor imitators of an artist named Leonardo da Vinci,' Merisi replied. 'Have you heard of him?'

'Heard of him!' I exclaimed. 'He is considered to be perhaps the most sublime and versatile genius that humanity has yet produced. In the National Gallery, where you first met me, there is his painting called the Virgin of the Rocks. It's exquisite.'

Merisi's eyes lit with pleasure. 'That painting is here in England now? That is good to know. It used to be in San Francesco Grande in Milan. I studied that painting assiduously. All Milanese painters studied it, as well as Leonardo's fresco of the Last Supper in the refectory of Santa Maria della Grazie. Leonardo also improved the method of preparing oil paints by adding beeswax. There was a story that Leonardo, while he was an apprentice, painted an angel so perfectly that his master, Verrocchio, broke his own brushes in two and gave up painting forever in acknowledgement of Leonardo's genius. You know that I have nothing but contempt for most of my fellow artists, but even I bow down before the genius of Leonardo.'

'Steady on, Michele. The shock of hearing an admission of humility from your lips might be too much for my nervous system to bear.'

'Don't worry, Stefano, it does not happen very often.'

'Let's return to less talented painters,' I said. 'You entered your apprenticeship with Simone Peterzano when you were thirteen years old, didn't you?'

'Yes, that is correct. In 1584. It was a four year apprenticeship and I had to pay him twenty four scudi for the privilege. He overcharged me.'

'His studio was in Milan. Is it true that you had to go and live in his house?'

'Yes. He lived with his wife, Angelica, and other relatives, in a big house at the Porta Orientale. I had to live there for four years.'

'You talk as if you didn't have much respect for Peterzano's ability?' I said.

'No, that is not strictly true,' Merisi replied. 'Peterzano was very proud that he had been a pupil of an artist named Tiziano Vecelli in Venice. Vecelli was a famous artist at that time.'

'Known as Titian,' I interjected.

'Yes, that's right. Is he still famous today?'

'Very much so,' I replied. 'He is still considered to be one of the very greatest artists. He has never been forgotten or gone out of fashion.'

'Yet you told me that I was forgotten for centuries?'

'I'm afraid so, Michele. There is little justice in this world. I think that you upset too many people, before and after your death. They wanted you forgotten.'

Merisi looked at me keenly, to see if I was mocking him. 'Do you think that is the reason?'

'Yes. A French artist named Poussin, who came to Rome about fifteen years after your death, said that you had "come to destroy painting".'

'Bastard,' Merisi breathed. 'I wish I could have met him in one of the back alleys around the Piazza Navona. I would have changed his opinion with my fists. Was he any good as a painter?'

'If you like soft pretty cherubs and plump pink maidens dancing around naked fauns, yes, he was good. Personally, his work makes me want to vomit.'

Merisi laughed heartily. 'Then he was a putana. Let's ignore him.'

'You were saying that Peterzano was proud of being a pupil of Titian?'

'Yes. He used to sign his paintings as "a pupil of Titian". He had a high reputation in Milan. Over-inflated if you ask me. But, technically, he was very good at his trade. Just before I joined his studio, he had completed some big frescoes at a church in Garegnano. I have to say they were very accomplished and I studied them closely. I also stole a few of his ideas later in my career.'

'What sort of skills were you trained in?' I asked. 'What did you actually do?'

'To start with, it was the normal training that every apprentice painter had to undergo. I began with the lowliest of tasks, sweeping the floor, running errands, preparing wooden panels for painting. I had to learn how to prepare colours. They were not made ready to use, as they are today. We had to learn how to mix them to get exactly the right shades and consistency. Some of those colours were made from very expensive materials . . .'

'Like lapis lazuli?' I suggested.

'Exactly! That was the most expensive of them all, to get that beautiful blue colour. Heaven help us if we wasted any.'

'Was your master allowed to punish you physically? Anything like that?'

'He could have done but he knew I was sponsored by the Colonna family so he never laid a hand on me. Also, he feared my temper, which was fierce, even at that age. The worst that happened was a stern lecture, and Angelica might not give me as much food that day, although she would often give me an extra piece of sausage or bread or cheese later on without Simone knowing. The worst punishment for wasting colour was from the other apprentices "taking the piss", as you English say. I usually found the opportunity to get my own back.'

'I'll bet you did. What else did you have to learn?'

'On the technical side, we had to learn brush control, how to use the mahlstick, preparing varnishes, priming canvases and wooden boards. We had lessons in drawing, in perspective, in anatomy and figure work, in draperies, and so on. We had to copy one of the master's paintings to compare our progress against his finished article. I quickly showed an aptitude for painting fruit and flowers. Skill in painting those subjects was a Milanese speciality anyway, but that aspect of my progress pleased my master the most. He was not so proficient in that respect himself. Later, I became adept at portraiture and I executed many commissions that my master passed off as his own.'

I considered all that Merisi had told me. 'Were you happy during your apprenticeship? Were you happy living with Peterzano and his family?'

'It was strange at first, but I found the work so interesting that I quickly reconciled myself.'

'Were you homesick or anything like that?'

'No, not at all. My family lived close by in Caravaggio and, as you have so delicately pointed out, Stefano, I am a self-centred bastard, absorbed in my own affairs. There was always company. Peterzano and his family, the other apprentices, Costanza's sons.'

'You were friendly with Costanza's sons?'

'Yes. Their father, Francesco, died when the boys were still young, as my father had, so there was a mutual bond of understanding between us in that respect. Muzio was a couple of years older than me, so I was not so close to him, but Fabrizio and I were alike in temperament, always getting up to pranks together. I had visited the Palazzo Colonna so often during my life that I was like one of the family. If I needed company, I was always welcome there.'

'How did you get on with the other apprentices? Did they bully you, or you bully them?'

'No. There was a lot of teasing and piss-taking but my master would never have allowed any bullying or horse-play to get out of hand. Painting was not the leisurely dilettante pursuit that it seems to have become in this modern age. Peterzano ran a busy studio and he needed to make money to provide for us all.'

'Is there anyone from these days, master or apprentice, who might have borne a grudge against you and wished you dead many years later?'

'I think it is highly unlikely, Stefano. As for the other apprentices, I cannot even remember their names. As for my master, I think he may have become jealous of my talent but I did not see him again after I left his studio and he must have been an old man by the time I "died" in Porto Ercole.'

'Okay, what about outside of work? Was there anybody you might have upset or offended? What about girls?'

'When I was older I used to go into town in Milan with the other apprentices. We would get drunk, try to talk the girls into giving us a fuck, or pay for it if we had to. But I cannot recall doing anything to anybody, at that time, that might have caused them to want to kill me.'

I felt a surge of helplessness. 'And none of your paintings, from that time, are known today. Your murderer said that the answer was in the paintings. It could be a painting from that time. How can we know?'

Merisi shrugged. 'Most of my work was simply helping my master Peterzano on his commissions, filling in backgrounds, painting small figures, background landscapes, and so on. I cannot remember all the work that I did solely by myself. It is impossible.'

'Umm. Perhaps I ought to visit your master,' I said.

'Why? What good would that do?' Merisi protested.

'Perhaps he still has some of your work in store. Perhaps he can tell me more about your apprenticeship than you can remember . . . or are willing to tell me.'

'I have told you everything relevant. You will be wasting your time.'

'The Tralfamadorians have conquered time, Michele. Anyway, I am curious to meet your master.'

'Remember, it is forbidden to travel back to before the day I died. I don't even know if Peterzano was still alive at that time. If he was, he was an old man.'

'In that case, I shall return in a matter of seconds. You seem eager to find reasons why I should not go, Michele?'

Merisi waved his hand at me dismissively. 'Go then, and waste your time. But leave me some food this time so that I don't have to wreck your kitchen again!'

7

I materialised behind the thick trunk of a gnarled old tree and in front of a high wall constructed of stone blocks. I was hoping that it was the defensive wall surrounding the city of Milan. Because my ChronoCo-ordinator, Guglielmo Pellegrino, was in Rome and not Milan, he had experienced difficulty in calculating the correct ChronoCo-ordinates to transport me to Milan. I would have to find the exact location of Simone Peterzano's studio myself.

I was surprised to find the weather was cold. I was dressed in gentlemanly finery in order to impress the natives and, as I moved out of the shelter of the tree, I wrapped my velvet cloak around myself. Further along the wall, about one hundred metres in the distance, I could see a rickety wooden bridge crossing a narrow fetid stream and a road leading through a large gate into the city. There were a few horses, pedestrians and wagons moving in and out of the gate. If Pellegrino had worked out the ChronoCo-ordinates accurately, that gate should be the Porta Orientale. I walked along and entered the city. There was a ramshackle parade of shops, taverns and houses in front of me but surprisingly little activity on the street. I could see some larger stone buildings in the distance, which I guessed were nearer the city centre itself. There was a group of soldiers or watchmen just inside the gate. They were sitting on the ground eating their lunch. They looked unconcerned and uninterested as I approached them. 'Excuse me,' I said, 'I'm sorry to interrupt your meal but I wonder if you could direct me to the house of Simone Peterzano, the distinguished artist.' I thought to myself, I must stop sounding so apologetically English. They looked at me but none of the watchmen spoke. They just went on chewing. I had decided to move away when one of them, the youngest judging by his appearance, said: 'At the end of the street is another street on the right, where the Tavern of the Black Bull stands. Go down there and halfway down is a big house where Signore Peterzano lives.'

'Thank you, signor,' I said.

Before I could walk away, the young man said: 'He does not paint any more. Another artist, his nephew, now works there but he allows Signore Peterzano to live in the house, out of respect. I should hurry, if I were you.'

'Why do you say that?' I asked.

'They say Signore Peterzano is dying, so if you want him to paint your portrait, you'd better hurry.'

The young man's companions found his remark highly amusing. I thanked them again and walked off. I found the Tavern of the Black Bull and easily found Peterzano's studio because a very large canvas, secured on a stretcher, was being carried inside by two apprentices. The studio was within a very large two-storey house. I studied the house with interest. This was where Michelangelo Merisi da Caravaggio had served his four-year apprenticeship and learned the trade at which he had become such a brilliant practitioner. The exterior, which was in a dilapidated condition, was plain and was covered with hideous tan-coloured plaster. The downstairs windows were rounded at the top while the upstairs windows were rectangular, in typical Italian Renaissance style. The hipped roof, supported by decorative brackets, overhung the lower part of the house. A crude wooden structure had been built on the side of the house but the front entrance was adorned with an elegant portico. The apprentices were carrying the canvas through this portico. I followed them into the studio. There was a bustle of activity and a not unpleasant smell of paint, wood and canvas. The tiled floor was covered with straw. The painters stopped working and looked at me as I entered. One of the painters, who was the oldest, was directing where the huge canvas should be placed, so I decided to speak to him. I adopted my most confident and authoritarian pose and said: 'I wish to speak to the distinguished artist Simone Peterzano.'

The painter glanced around, hardly taking any notice of me, absorbed in giving his instructions about the positioning of the canvas. 'I am his nephew,' the man replied. 'My uncle can no longer work. If you want to commission a portrait or other work, I will be pleased to help you . . . sir.'

I was encouraged that he had decided to add on the 'sir'. It suggested I looked sufficiently imposing for him to consider that I might be someone of importance. I decided to reinforce that impression. 'I am not here to commission any work,' I said, more loudly that necessary. 'I am here, on the authority of Pope Paul himself, to interview Signore Peterzano.' That statement gained everyone's attention.

'May I ask your name?' the nephew said.

'My name is Stefano Maddano.'

'Why do you wish to see my uncle? Is he in any trouble?'

'No. I simply wish to ask him a few questions. I am investigating the death of his former pupil, Michelangelo Merisi, known as Caravaggio.'

There was an audible gasp from the onlooking apprentices and it made me realise, for the first time, the magic power that the name Caravaggio engendered in his fellow artists, even just after his own lifetime.

'Have you any proof of who you are and what you are doing?' the nephew asked.

With a flourish, I produced the papal warrant from inside my doublet and handed it to him. He examined the document and gave it back to me. 'Please wait here,' he said.

The assistants and apprentices, seven of them, stood and stared at me. One of the apprentices, wide-eyed with curiosity, asked: 'Did you know Caravaggio?'

'Yes,' I replied.

'Was he as great an artist as they say he was?'

Another, older, assistant said: 'He was the devil. He sold his soul to the devil so he could paint like he did.'

'Gentlemen,' I announced. 'I knew Caravaggio as well as any man. He had many faults but he was not the devil. After all, he was trained in this very studio so, if you learn your trade properly, you could become as skilful as him. He was a very great painter. If you ever get the chance, go to Rome and see for yourselves.'

The apprentices did not return to their tasks but just stood there gawping at me and asking me more questions about Caravaggio. I answered them as well as I could and I was pleased with the impression I had made. Then Peterzano's nephew returned. 'My uncle is very frail. He is dying. Please do not tax his strength with too many questions. My aunt Angelica is also willing to speak to you. Is that satisfactory?'

'Yes. I shall not be long. I have much respect for your uncle and will try not to take any longer than is necessary.'

'Good,' the nephew said. 'Please follow me.' I followed the nephew through the studio while the awestruck apprentices still gawped at me. 'Get on with your work!' the nephew shouted, and they snapped out of their trance. I followed the nephew up a flight of stairs on to a landing with several doors leading off. He led me down to the door on the extreme right. He opened it gently, looked in, and said: 'Signor Maddano is here.' He ushered me into the room. An elderly woman, plump and dressed simply, rose from a plain wooden chair, and gave me a small curtsey. I bowed back. 'This is my aunt Angelica,' the nephew said. 'And this is my uncle Simone.' He indicated to a plain wooden bed in the corner of the room. The old man was asleep. His wispy white hair was spread out on the pillow and he was snoring lightly. A fire roared in the grate and made the room very warm despite the cold outside. 'Call me if you need me, aunt,' the nephew said, and backed out of the room.

I said to Angelica: 'I am sorry to disturb you. I am investigating the death of Michelangelo Merisi, known as Caravaggio, who was once your husband's apprentice. Do you remember him?'

'Yes, of course I do,' Angelica replied. 'Please sit down, Signor Maddano.' She indicated some chairs arranged around a wooden table on the opposite side of the room. I pulled out one of the chairs and placed it opposite Angelica, closer to the old man's bed, and sat down.

I said: 'There is reason to believe that Michele may not have died of natural causes. In fact, he may have been murdered.'

Angelica clutched her throat in dismay, her plump face flushing red and her kindly blue eyes betraying genuine repugnance at the thought of murder. 'Oh, the poor boy,' she said.

'I am trying to find out if anyone from the time he was an apprentice might have been involved in his death. You know, one of the other apprentices, or someone else that Michele may have upset.'

Despite herself, Angelica managed a wan smile. 'Michele was always very good at upsetting people,' she said. 'He was a strange boy, but he was not a bad boy, not when we knew him. We have heard the stories about him. He never came back to see us, so I don't know what he was like later in his life. I liked him, despite his odd manners. He would look at me with those big black eyes of his and usually get what he wanted out of me. Once, when I was angry with him and threatened to punish him, he said that God had already taken his father, his grandfather and his uncle, so what more could I do to him? That melted my anger. How could it not? I wanted to give him a hug instead of a beating but, even then, there was something about his demeanour that thrust people away. Forgive me, Signor Maddano, I am rambling.'

'Not at all, signora. All that is very interesting. Did Michele ever get into any real trouble?'

'Not that I recall. He would get drunk and sometimes be unable to work. That made my husband cross. Michele would occasionally get into a fight and would come home with cuts and bruises. But many of the other apprentices behaved in the same way. Michele was a young man with all the passion and energy of a young man. They say he murdered someone before he died. I tell you, Signor Maddano, if Michele did kill someone, it was not deliberate. He was an angry, confused, mixed-up boy, but I always thought it was mostly bravado. I never sensed real evil in him.'

'I agree,' I said. 'Now what about his . . .'

Angelica interrupted me before I could ask the next question. 'Did you know Michele?' she asked.

'Yes, very well,' I replied.

'Did he ever speak of us, of his apprenticeship?' she asked eagerly, eyes bright with desire for a favourable answer. Perhaps I was wrong but, with her husband fading before her eyes, how could I deny her such comfort?

'Yes,' I lied. 'Michele always regretted that he did not return to see you. He remembered your kindness with affection and was very appreciative of the excellent training that your husband had given him'.

'That is most gratifying,' Angelica sighed.

'Whereabouts in the house did Michele sleep?'

'Downstairs,' Angelica said, 'where all the apprentices sleep. The upstairs here is where the family live and downstairs there is a dormitory next to the studio where the apprentices sleep and spend their leisure time, what little there is. Would you like to see it?'

'No, that won't be necessary, thank you. What about Michele's attitude to his work?' I asked. 'Was he a good pupil? Did he work hard?'

Angelica smiled. 'The trouble with Michele was getting him to stop work. He worked and worked and when he stopped, he would go crazy, go off drinking and causing trouble. But not serious trouble, just adolescent pranks.'

'You cannot think of anyone who would have wished him real harm, or that he wished real harm to? Remember, signora, that the pope has commanded the truth from all who speak to me on this matter.'

'I do speak the truth, Signor Maddano, and I curse anyone who caused such harm to my Michele.'

'Are there any examples of Michele's work still stored here?' I asked, more in hope than expectation.

'No,' Angelica replied. 'If there were, I could sell them to some rich cardinal and make my husband's last days more comfortable.'

At that moment, Angelica's husband stirred and woke up. He looked at me with watery eyes. 'Who are you?' he croaked.

I stood up and bowed. Before I could speak, Angelica said: 'This man is Stefano Maddano. He has been sent by the pope to ask us about Michelangelo Merisi, your old apprentice.'

Peterzano turned his thin face away from us and said: 'Give me some water.'

Angelica went to the table, poured water into a beaker, carried it back to the bed and gently helped her husband to take a few sips.

'Signore Peterzano,' I said. 'It is an honour for me to meet such a distinguished artist and pupil of the great Titian.' That statement seemed to liven Peterzano up a little and I guessed that, like most of us, he was susceptible to flattery.

'Simone,' his wife said, 'you remember that we heard that poor Michele had died in Porto Ercole. Signor Maddano thinks that he may have been murdered. He has been sent here by the pope to ask us if we knew anyone who might be responsible for his death. I cannot remember anyone. Can you?'

'Help me to sit up, woman,' Peterzano said. Angelica put her hands under his armpits and hauled him into a more upright position. Peterzano looked at me, his features gaunt, his shock of white hair standing out, and his face as pallid as parchment. 'Merisi murdered you say? I should like to have murdered him myself, the ungrateful wretch.'

'Simone!' his wife chided. 'Be careful what you say.' She turned to me. 'He does not mean that.'

'Of course I don't, woman. But why should I care what I say? My life's work is over. My life is almost over. I will be forgotten. All that will be remembered of me is that Michelangelo Merisi da Caravaggio was my apprentice.' He coughed lightly and Angelica gave him another sip of water. 'He was the best apprentice I ever had but, when he left my studio, he was not that good a painter. Lift me up some more, woman.'

'Please do not agitate yourself, Signore Peterzano,' I said, as his wife was helping him to find a comfortable position. I had already come to the conclusion that these two could not tell me anything of any significance about the attempt on Merisi's life.

'No, I want to tell you this,' Peterzano said, 'and if the pope has sent you, I want him to know, as God is my witness. When Merisi left my studio he was an accomplished but quite ordinary painter. Then, many years later, his fame grew. We kept hearing stories of how this new artist, Caravaggio, had taken the Roman art world by storm, didn't we, Angelica.' His wife nodded in agreement. 'When I heard that his name was Merisi, I could not believe it was my old apprentice. I travelled to Rome to see for myself. I toured the churches of Rome where his pictures hung. I could see some compositions and poses that he had copied from my works, and I was pleased. I decided to go and visit him. He was living and working at a great palazzo. I was told that Merisi was too busy to see me, but I knew that he simply did not wish to see me.'

'Were you upset and offended by that?' I asked.

'Of course I was. Merisi had always regarded me with contempt. He took care to conceal his true opinion from me, but I knew it. I'm not surprised he ended up murdering someone, and being murdered himself. I don't know who might have wanted to kill him. But I tell you this, signor, I stood in the Contarelli chapel in front of Merisi's Execution of St. Matthew and I knew that such a work was far beyond my powers to create. I taught Merisi well but something inside him must have been waiting to burst forth, something that I could never have taught him, something that could only have been placed there by God. Merisi's paintings were the best that I have ever seen, apart from the works of my master, Titian. I don't know how young Merisi did it, but there it is. I spent a lifetime trying to create work one-tenth as good as Merisi, and I failed. That's why I would have liked to murder him. Tell that to your pope . . .' The dying Peterzano was exhausted by the effort of speaking so passionately. His head sank back on to his pillow.

Angelica was anxious to mollify me, in case I had been offended by her husband's remarks. 'Take no notice of him, Signor Maddano. He didn't mean that.'

'I think he did, Signora Peterzano. I think it was very honest statement but I also think your husband is very hard on himself. I'm grateful for your time. I will take my leave.'

8

I floated back to my own time, materialised in my bedroom and checked myself in the full-length mirror to make sure I was still in one piece. I changed into modern dress before I went downstairs. I checked on how the builders were progressing in redecorating my kitchen and then went to my front room office. Merisi was sitting in my office chair gazing at the computer screen. 'Stefano, Stefano!' he cried. 'Come and see what I have found!'

I looked at the computer screen to find out what Merisi was getting excited about. It was an image of two women and a man performing sex acts on each other. 'For Christ's sake, how did you find that?' I asked.

'I don't know,' Merisi replied, entranced by his discovery. 'I tapped some words into that box and somehow this appeared. I've always wanted to do that, haven't you, Stefano? And look, they are such beautiful women. What are those marks on their bodies for?'

'Decoration,' I said. 'They are called tattoos.'

'They are so beautiful that they must be rich or noble women.'

'Yes, they go by the aristocratic title of crack cocaine whore.'

'And why have they got metal studs through their . . . down there.' He pointed at a part of the screen I really did not want to look at. I said nothing.

'And look,' he said, clicking on the mouse, 'here are two pretty boys doing things to each other. The cardinals back home would have paid big money for such pictures.'

I quickly pressed the home key and the images disappeared, much to Merisi's chagrin. 'Bastard,' he said. 'I wanted to look at more. I have never seen, or even imagined such things.'

'It's called pornography,' I said. 'There's plenty more where that came from. I don't want you twanging your wire in my office. Don't you want to know how your old master is?'

'You were not gone long. How is he?'

'He is dying,' I said.

Merisi pursed his lips but said nothing.

'Doesn't that mean anything to you?' I asked.

'He has been dead for four hundred years, as I should have been. He was an overbearing, pious and miserable old bastard. He served my purpose well enough. He taught me adequately.'

'You really are full of the milk of human kindness, aren't you?' I said.

'Don't try to make me say things I don't feel, Englishman,' Merisi said. 'You live here in your cosy little English house, protected from everything by all these modern marvels. Where I come from, death was an everyday fact of life.'

'Angelica spoke well of you. I think she was fond of you but a little frightened of you.'

'She wanted me to fuck her but she was too fat. What is she like now?'

'Even fatter,' I said. 'There, now I am becoming as callous as you are.'

'Fuck you,' Merisi sneered.

'Let's get back to work,' I said. 'You go back and sit over there, away from this computer screen and these refined and genteel ladies. Or should that be genital?'

Merisi reluctantly moved back to the other side of the desk and sat down.

'Did you know that Peterzano came to see you in Rome?'

'So what?'

'Why didn't you receive him?'

'I was busy. I had a lot of commissions to complete.'

'You lived in his house for four years,' I said. 'Weren't you at all interested in him?'

'No,' Merisi stated bluntly.

'He had come to Rome specifically to see your paintings. He admired them very much.'

'So he should. I am a far better artist than he ever was.'

I consulted my notes and, unable to control a sarcastic tone, said: 'With great reluctance then, and with eternal gratitude, you left the studio of Simone Peterzano in 1588. That was the year that the great Queen Elizabeth sent her tiny English fleet to destroy the mighty Spanish Armada.' I grinned at Merisi. I had an uncontrollable urge to puncture his arrogant complacency.

'May that woman rot in hell,' he said. 'All Europe hated that heathen bitch.'

'Oh, I don't know. We in England were quite fond of her.'

'A red-haired, white-faced hellcat, rightly excommunicated by His Holiness.'

'Quite a good description, Michele. But what were you doing in that year, after you left Peterzano?'

I was pleased to see that I had needled Merisi. He was very sulky. Finally he said: 'I tried to find some work in Milan. I went to my uncle Ludovico, the priest, to see if he could get me any commissions from his clerical friends but he was useless. I was forced to go back and live in my mother's house at Porta Folceria in Caravaggio.'

'None of your paintings survive from this period between leaving Peterzano and moving to Rome. Did you find any work?'

'A few small commissions. There was hardly enough money in them to buy bread and wine. I knew I had it in me to be a great painter but I knew I needed to learn more than Peterzano had been able to teach me, so I decided to travel and study some of the masters. My mother lent me some money. Costanza Colonna was still taking an interest in my career and was very generous to me.'

'Where did you go? Who influenced you the most?'

'During my apprenticeship I had been much influenced by the work of the Campi brothers, who had worked in Milan before my time. For a few weeks I travelled around all the towns near to Caravaggio. Towns like Brescia, Lodi, Cremona and Bergamo. The work of Lorenzo Lotto was much admired in Bergamo. I liked the work of Moretto, who had worked in Brescia. And the frescoes by Pordenone in Cremona were most impressive. Also in Cremona, I had the privilege of meeting the woman artist Sofonisba Anguisciola. She was, I should estimate, about sixty years old at that time. She had known Leonardo da Vinci personally and she was always pleased to relate her stories of the great man to eager young painters such as myself. She showed me one of her drawings. It was of her son Asdrubale being bitten by a crayfish when he was a little boy. I liked the subject so much that I did a version of the same theme in oils, a boy being bitten by a lizard. You may have noticed that painting in your National Gallery, where you first met me, hung next to the Supper at Emmaus.'

'Indeed,' I said. 'I know it well. The carafe of water is painted most skilfully.'

'As is the rest of the picture, but thank you anyway, Stefano.' (*Plate 5*).

'You may be interested to know,' I continued, 'that Sofonisba Anguisciola lived until 1625, until she was well over ninety years of age.'

'Good for her,' Merisi said, genuinely pleased. 'She was a great lady.'

'Well, it makes a refreshing change to hear you speak well of somebody,' I said tartly. Merisi simply regarded me with distaste, so I changed the subject. 'Art critics conjecture that the lighting effects of Girolamo Savoldo may have influenced your style.' I said. 'Can you confirm that?'

'Yes,' Merisi said. 'He gave me many ideas.'

'Any other local artists that influenced you?'

'Much of my early work contained influences from my master, Peterzano. It is only natural. But I wanted to travel further afield. I knew my paintings were still too provincial. Travelling around Italy in those days could be dangerous. It was better to travel in large groups, preferably with an armed escort. I eventually managed to see most of what I wanted to see.'

'What did you get to see?'

'I travelled to Vicenza where the work of Mantegna gave me many ideas about the use of perspective. In Bologna, my friend Annibale and his brother were already doing good work.'

'That's Annibale Carracci?' I asked.

'Yes, that's right.'

'I suspect he will re-enter your story after you have moved to Rome?'

'Oh, I have many stories to tell you about my strange friend Annibale Carracci. But, as you say, we will come to him later. The real revelation was in Venice. I was deeply impressed by most of the works I saw in that city. Titian we have already mentioned. His portraits were beyond compare. But the two artists I particularly admired were Giorgione and Giovanni Bellini. Particularly Bellini. He opened my eyes to what is possible in oil paints. A great master.'

'That is very interesting, Michele. I think that, today, Bellini is not regarded as highly as he should be. I'm pleased that you share my opinion of him.'

'You like my work,' Merisi smiled, 'which proves you have good taste.'

'Do you think,' I asked, 'that you would have become such an accomplished artist without these visits to study the work of these masters?'

'No, definitely not,' Merisi replied. 'As I have said, they opened my eyes to what was possible. Today, you can see all the works of the great artists in your wonderful coloured books or on that magical screen in front of you, but in my day we had no opportunity to see such works unless we travelled. If I had not travelled, I should have stayed in Milan and been little better than an artisan like Peterzano.'

I hesitated before I asked the next question. I guessed what Merisi's reaction would be and I phrased it carefully. 'Isn't it true,' I said. 'That there was another reason for all this travelling, apart from studying the works of your fellow artists.'

Merisi eyed me warily. 'What do you mean by that?'

'I mean, you were also running away from the law.'

'Why should I have been running away from the law?'

'One of your biographers, Bellori, states plainly that you had to flee after you killed a companion,' I replied.

Contrary to the reaction I expected, Merisi laughed. 'That is absurd,' he said. 'Bellori was making things up in order to make more money from his sensational jottings. Because I killed Tomassoni in Rome - an accident, by the way - and every time something is not known about me, people assume I must have been on the run after some terrible crime. Nonsense!'

'Possibly,' I answered, 'but your other biographer, Mancini, also states that you spent a year in prison in Milan after injuring someone in a street fight.'

'Mancini, Mancini,' Merisi scoffed. 'It is all nonsense.'

'You deny that you were ever in prison or in trouble with the law during this period?'

'Yes, I do deny it,' Merisi replied, but with less vehemence that I had come to expect from him.

'Very well,' I said. 'I have to accept your word. Let's move on to the period just before you left for Rome, when you were selling the land and property you had inherited. Was this the source of the disagreement between you and your brother Giovan Battista?'

Merisi looked at me thoughtfully, considering whether to deign to answer me.

'Look, I know you said it was family business,' I urged, 'but it was all long ago. Surely it cannot hurt to talk about it now? I must know everything if we are to find out who attempted to murder you.'

Merisi shrugged and accepted my argument. 'The family had fallen on hard times,' he began. 'Money was very short. My dear mother Lucia was struggling to make ends meet. I no longer had enough money to travel and to study. There was a piece of land that I owned jointly with Giovan. I wanted to sell it to help my mother and to provide me with enough money to move to Rome and support myself while I set up as an artist. Giovan refused to sell. We argued. As you know, I am angry and stubborn. Giovan is . . . was . . . placid and stubborn. I began to hate him. He might have felt the same about me. Eventually he gave in and we sold the land.'

'That was in 1589?'

'Yes, I was eighteen. I still did not have enough money to move to Rome, so I travelled some more, but soon afterwards our mother died suddenly.'

'Your mother's estate was divided between yourself, Giovan and your sister Caterina. Is that so?'

'Yes,' Merisi confirmed. 'Once again, I wanted to sell up and move to Rome but Giovan and Caterina were all for keeping the land and property.'

'Did things between you become bitter?'

'Yes, more than ever. My inheritance was the key to a new life in Rome. Without it I would be stuck in Milan or Caravaggio for the rest of my life.'

'Would that have been so bad?' I asked. 'Especially being stuck in Milan. It was a rich city. There must have been plenty of opportunity for a talented artist.'

Merisi stood up. 'No, no, no,' he said, agitated. 'Rome was the only place to be for an Italian artist. All the best painters were in Rome. I wanted to match myself against them. Rome was being rebuilt. There were many interesting and lucrative commissions to be won. Rome was the centre of the Christian universe. Yes, I could have made a living in Milan or Caravaggio or Bergamo, but I wanted more than a living. I wanted to be the greatest artist who ever lived. I had to go to Rome.' He slowly sat down again, distracted by his memories and emotions.

'Okay, I can understand that,' I said. 'It's just like Paris was the only place to be at the end of the nineteenth century or New York in the middle of the twentieth century.'

'Where is New York?' Merisi asked.

'In the New World, in America,' I replied. 'America has become a powerful and populous country and New York is its biggest city.'

'Why does this city have an English name? The Spanish and Italians discovered the New World?'

'Indeed they did, and the Spanish took possession of the southern part but we British nicked the northern part from the French. And then we were kicked out by the Americans about two hundred years after you died. The Americans have paid dearly for their folly. They tipped crates of tea into Boston harbour and now you can't get a decent cup of tea anywhere in that benighted country.'

Merisi looked puzzled but he simply nodded. 'Many things have changed,' he said, plaintively.

'Getting back to your property, it took over two years after your mother died before all of it was sold. Is that so?'

'Yes. Once again I had to battle with Cat and Giovan before they would consent to sell, but I was desperate to escape. In the end, they knew I would keep on causing them so much trouble that it was not worth fighting me. So they gave in.'

'And I suppose you never forgave them and they never forgave you?' I said.

'I don't know if Caterina ever did,' Merisi replied. 'I never saw her again after I moved to Rome. I think Giovan must have forgiven me, that is why he came to see me at the Palazzo Madama. He was a good Christian.'

'But you refused to see him?'

'I am not a good Christian,' Merisi said, dismissively. 'I am not a good man. But I am a great artist and that is all I care about.'

'So you took your inheritance, 393 imperial livre, according to our records, and moved to Rome?'

'That is so,' Merisi said. 'That was in the autumn of 1592.'

'We believe that you may have travelled to Rome in the entourage of Marchese Costanza Colonna. Is that so?'

'Yes,' Merisi said. 'The roads were very dangerous. There were many gangs of banditti roaming the countryside. I knew that the Marchese was travelling to Rome with an armed entourage and I asked if I could travel with her party. She kindly agreed.'

I considered what to do or say next. I was not entirely happy that Merisi was telling me the truth. I decided that a second opinion on these events was necessary before we started to examine Merisi's new life as an artist in Rome. 'Before we go any further,' I announced, 'I am going back to interview your brother.'

Merisi looked at me suspiciously. 'You do not trust my version of events?' he said, accusingly.

'Sometimes people involved in a certain event have different opinions, different perspectives, on what happened during that event. It is not that I don't trust your version. Giovan may shed some light on something you have forgotten, something our art historians have not discovered.'

'Go if you must.' Merisi said. 'You will probably find that he is glad that I am dead.'

'Not everyone, thank goodness, is as callous and cold-hearted as you are,' I said.

'Not everyone is as honest as I am. I say what I think. I paint what I feel. I don't utter pious platitudes, either through my mouth or on to canvas. Pious platitudes is all you'll get from Giovan Battista.'

9

I was ushered into a room which appeared to be a small library. The walls were lined with books and I knew that books were expensive objects in this century to which I had travelled. It was late evening but there was still a little light filtering through the high windows of the room. A fire had been lit and candles were burning in wall sconces. The room was panelled with wood and the atmosphere was suffused with a pleasing lightly incensed cedar smell. The man I had come to see, Giovan Battista Merisi, was sitting in a wooden armchair which was padded with cushions. Merisi had his left leg and foot, which was heavily bandaged, supported on a stool in front of him. A book lay open on his lap. The novice Jesuit priest who has escorted me to this room closed the door quietly behind him as he left. Merisi was looking at me with a smiling and reassuring expression. 'Forgive me for not rising to greet you,' he said. He indicated his bandaged foot. 'As you can see, I am somewhat discommoded at present. If you would like to sit with me, we can talk.'

The Jesuit novice had placed a wooden armchair in an appropriate position before he had left the room. I sat down by the fire, which was barely smouldering, opposite Merisi. Merisi was dressed simply in a black clerical gown with a large silver crucifix on a silver chain around his neck. He was clean shaven and his hair was fairly long. It was much lighter in colour than his brother Michelangelo's. I estimated that Giovan was tall, like his brother, although much lighter in build. He was almost willowy from what I could see of him. There was about him an air of genuine loving sweetness that, for some reason, I felt keenly. Without conscious reason, I immediately took a liking to him.

I said: 'Thank you for your hospitality and for consenting to see me, Signor Merisi. I am a foreigner in this land so please forgive me if, by any manner of speech or address, I happen to offend you. It will not be intentional. I'm afraid I have come to see you on a painful and delicate matter.'

'Yes, Signor Maddano,' Merisi sighed. 'I know why you have come. I have been expecting you ever since I heard that the Holy Father had granted you his papal warrant.' There was no tone of wariness or hostility in this statement, just weary resignation.

'Then you must know that His Holiness has commanded all who speak to me to tell me the truth.'

'I would not do otherwise, even if I thought it necessary,' Merisi replied. 'God sees everything in our hearts and in our minds. If I would lie to you, I could not lie to Him.'

'As you know, I am investigating the frankly mysterious circumstances surrounding the death of your brother, the famous painter.'

Giovan Merisi bowed his head and muttered something under his breath. I guessed it was a brief prayer for the soul of his brother and I did not interrupt. He looked up and said: 'I loved him dearly, you must know. But the Devil loved him more and stole him away from his family and from the grace of God. I have to confess that I was not surprised when I heard of his death. You think that he may have been murdered?'

'It is a possibility, yes,' I replied.

Merisi shuddered and crossed himself. His pain was palpable and I felt very uncomfortable.

'Can we talk about your childhood with Michele?' I asked. 'You grew up together, went to school together. Did you get on well with him?'

Merisi nodded. 'Michele was always a law unto himself. The world always had to revolve around him but, yes, we were friends. When we were at school, I hero-worshipped him. There are bullies at any school. I am not a big or strong person but Michele was. And the other boys feared that temper of his. Because of him, I was never bullied at school.' We talked about their childhood together for a long time. At times, Merisi's eyes shined with pleasure. He was enjoying to reminisce. I found it fascinating, how Michelangelo had discovered his artistic talent, how Giovan had been drawn to God and a life in the church, their different reactions to the sudden death of their father and grandfather. But his stories did not tell me anything I did not already know, or could infer from the historical records.

'How were relations with your sister, Caterina?' I asked.

'Cat and I were always very close,' Merisi replied. 'We still are. I think that Michele must have resented our closeness. But it was always in his temperament to push people away, so what can you expect? He and Cat were always wary of each other, always baiting each other. Perhaps Michele was resentful that we younger ones arrived and took our mother's attention away from him. Who knows, except God?'

'And how did Michele get on with your mother?'

'God forgive me for saying so, but our dear mother always seemed to be more fond of Cat and I than she was of Michele. She would hug and kiss we younger ones, spoil us with little treats when she could afford to, but I couldn't help but notice, even at that age, that she acted much more coolly towards Michele. Not that she didn't take care of him. She took good care of all of us, in very difficult circumstances. But Michele was always wilful and difficult to handle. Sometimes, I think she almost resented his existence.' Merisi bowed his head again. 'God forgive me.'

'I appreciate your candour, Signor Merisi. It is very helpful and illuminating. I knew Michele fairly well. He made it difficult to be kind to him.' Merisi smiled, accepting my point. I said: 'I am reluctant to remind you again of painful events but how did your mother's death affect you all?'

'It was shockingly sudden,' Merisi answered. 'Cat and I were very distraught.'

'And Michele . . .?'

Merisi took a deep breath. 'I don't know how the news affected him initially. Michele was in prison.'

'In prison!' I exclaimed, before I could stop myself. 'I didn't know that. Why was he in prison?'

Merisi made a gesture of helplessness and just shook his head.

I said: 'I regret having to pry into such painful and personal matters, Signor Merisi, but this circumstance, which I was unaware of, may be crucially relevant to my inquiry into Michele's death.'

'Of course,' Merisi replied. 'I am not blaming you at all. The simple truth is, I don't know why he was in prison. All I know, all anyone knows, is that Michele had been out on the town in Milan with some of his disreputable friends, no doubt getting drunk or playing cards, as was their habit. There was an argument and then an affray about something and Michele was arrested for wounding someone named Francois Dufre, a Frenchman who was working in Milan as a goldsmith.'

'In what way did Michele wound this man?' I asked.

'His favourite way,' Merisi said, 'with a dagger. Fortunately, the Frenchman was not killed, or even badly wounded, but the assault earned Michele several months in prison.'

'What about Michele's friends? Were they involved? What was the fight about?'

Once again, Merisi made a gesture of helplessness. 'Michele's friends had deserted him, as such people are wont to do in those circumstances. The police arrested Michele, who had been held down by some of Dufre's friends. Michele would not say what the argument was about and neither did Dufre. Dufre, oddly, was all for letting Michele go free or else Michele's prison sentence would have been much more severe. Michele would not say who his companions were. As far as I know, Michele has kept his silence over the matter ever since.'

'Do you know if this goldsmith, Dufre, is still working in Milan or anywhere in Italy?'

'I'm afraid he died of the plague several years ago, God rest his soul,' Merisi answered.

'If Michele was in prison when your mother died suddenly, was he allowed to attend the funeral?'

'No,' Merisi said. 'I went to the prison to talk to Michele about our mother's death. His reaction was strange. He was affected, then he was silent for a long time. Then he said: "Perhaps now I can get to Rome". I was very angry, God forgive me. Being so upset myself, I could not comprehend how Michele could seem so cold and self-centred in the matter. I upbraided him for his selfishness. But he just stared at me. I lost patience with him and left.'

'Forgive me again for intruding into the private affairs of your family but, after Michele had been released from prison, was there bad blood between you two over the disposal of your mother's estate?'

Merisi looked surprised. 'Did Michele tell you that?'

'In a manner of speaking,' I answered.

'Then you are honoured. Michele did not tell many people about our family differences during that painful period.'

'I believe there were arguments about whether to sell your mother's land and property or not,' I said, trying to draw him out a bit more.

'Yes,' Merisi sighed. 'There were bitter arguments, I am ashamed to say. Caterina and I strongly believed that we should keep hold of the land and property, that it was a valuable asset. All Michele cared about was cashing in, getting his share, and moving to Rome to become an independent artist. As usual, he got his way in the end.'

'I now have to ask . . . .' My sentence was interrupted by a commotion from outside the room. Someone was shouting: 'Get out of the way. I don't care if the pope's in there. I will see my patient now or not at all. I'm a busy man, I haven't got time to waste praying all day like you priests.' I looked at Merisi to see how he was reacting to all this shouting but, to my surprise, he was smiling indulgently. The door to the library burst open and a man, carrying a large candelabra, bustled into the room. 'Good God, it's as dark as a tomb in here,' he cried. 'I hope I'm not interrupting a conspiracy to steal God's light. Good evening, Giovanni.'

I stood up to confront the stranger, ready for trouble if he started anything.

'Good evening, Giulio,' Merisi said. 'May I introduce Signor Stefano Maddano. Signor Maddano, this is my friend and physician, Doctor Giulio Mancini.'

I was about to offer my hand but Mancini clapped me on the back like a long lost friend. 'Greetings, Signor Maddano,' Mancini said. 'I know why you are here, to interrogate Giovanni about his incorrigible brother. Isn't that so?'

'You are correct,' I replied. I was fascinated to meet Mancini although, of course, I had to pretend that I didn't know of him at all. He was one of Caravaggio's biographers, had treated him when he was ill, and knew him very well. Mancini was a doctor, a writer, an art dealer and collector, a serial philanderer and, most surprisingly of all, a self-confessed atheist when such a belief, or non-belief, could be very unhealthy indeed. I was very surprised that a pious priest like Giovan Battista Merisi would be on warm terms with such a man, let alone seem to be very fond of him. Mancini was a short man, dressed foppishly, but it suited his personality perfectly. There was an irresistible energy and vivacity about him. He was quite swarthy and his long black hair and short pointed beard made him seem like the god Pan. He was a man whose earthy appetites were far stronger than his spiritual ones.

'Don't let me interrupt the interrogation,' Mancini said. 'Let me look at your foot, my priestly friend. How does it feel now?' He had knelt down by the side of Merisi's chair and was busily unwrapping the bandage.

'It is still very painful, doctor.' To me, Merisi said: 'You will please forgive my friend Mancini. He has no manners and no shame. He has forgotten all about God and I should think that God, for once, is very relieved to be forgotten.'

'If God created me,' Mancini replied, 'shouldn't I have to forgive Him for creating my manifold faults in the first place.'

'We come into the world without sin, brother Giulio. If we end up as sinners, and with many faults, it's because we choose such a path, instead of the path of righteousness.'

'You mean like your brother,' Mancini shot back. The two friends enjoyed this sort of banter but mention of Michele made the smile fade from Merisi's face. Mancini had removed the bandage and was prodding Merisi's foot with his finger. Merisi winced. I could see that his big toe and his ankle were inflamed and swollen. 'There you are, Signor Maddano,' Mancini said to me, with a twinkle in his eye. 'As bad a case of gout as I have ever seen. These priests always pay for their rich diet and their fondness for the communion wine.'

Before I could bite my tongue, I said: 'Diet has nothing to do with it.'

Mancini looked at me keenly. 'Are you a doctor?' he asked.

'By no means,' I answered. 'I did not mean to interfere with your diagnosis. Please forgive me.'

'No, really, I am interested,' Mancini said, beginning to re-bandage Merisi's foot. 'You made that statement with such authority that I'm led to believe that you have some experience with this condition.'

'As you can tell from my accent, I am not from this country,' I blathered, annoyed with myself for my ill-advised comment. 'Where I come from, it is believed that gout is a hereditary condition.'

'Hereditary?' Mancini said, baffled.

'Err, passed from generation to generation. For instance, I would surmise that both Signor Merisi's father and grandfather suffered from the same condition.'

'Why, yes!' Merisi confirmed. 'As you know, they both died of the plague when I was very young but I can recall them with their feet up on a chair, just as I am doing now, complaining of the pain.'

'Yes, it's predominantly a male condition,' I said. 'I'll wager that Doctor Mancini has not treated many women with gout.'

'Now that you mention it, no, I have never known a woman to suffer from gout.' Mancini finished bandaging his friend's foot and stood up. He asked me: 'What would you prescribe for Brother Merisi's poor foot? You seem to have certain medical knowledge that I don't possess.'

'Where I come from, we find colchicine, taken as a medicine, very efficacious. Have you heard of it?' I asked.

'Yes, of course,' Mancini said. 'It is made from the autumn crocus, but I have never heard of it being used to treat gout.'

'Well, where I come from, it is a well-known cure.'

'Where do you come from, Signor Maddano?' Mancini inquired.

'Errm, from the Spanish Netherlands.'

Mancini regarded me critically and murmured, without malice: 'And I am the Man in the Moon. But Cardinal Del Monte dabbles in botany. I will ask him if he has any colchicine and we will try it on poor Merisi here.'

'Excellent,' I said, 'If you have completed your ministrations, I would like to resume my conversation with Signor Merisi.'

'Then I will take my leave,' Mancini said.

I suddenly realised that it might be useful if Mancini stayed with us. I said: 'From the comments you have made, doctor, you knew Michelangelo Merisi da Caravaggio very well.'

'Indeed I did. He was my patient and my friend.'

I turned to Giovan Battista. 'Signor Merisi, I still have some questions to ask that might be painful and personal but Doctor Mancini here may be able to shed some more light on Michele's personality and character and acquaintances. Would you object if he stayed with us?'

'Not at all,' Merisi said, without hesitation. 'Giulio is a Godless sinner but I trust him implicitly. I believe he was very fond of Michele. Can you stay, Giulio?'

'Yes, of course,' Mancini replied. 'Your brother was the most interesting painter I have ever known. He was a very flawed man but he was not evil. How well did you know him, Signor Maddano?'

'I only got to know him near the end of his life,' I said. 'I don't think I knew him nearly as well as you did.'

'I don't think anyone ever really knew Michele,' his brother said, mournfully.

Mancini asked. 'Are you a painter?'

'I used to be,' I replied, 'but I have little talent.'

'Did Michele give you any of his paintings?' Mancini asked eagerly. 'I would be willing to buy them from you.'

'No, I don't have any,' I said. 'I wish I did.'

'Oh,' Mancini said, with disappointment.

'Anyway, Signor Merisi was just telling me about Michele's time in prison, in Milan, before he moved to Rome. Did you know that Michele had been in prison then?'

Mancini said: 'Yes, I have heard of this regrettable incident but I can add nothing. Michele always resolutely refused to talk about what happened or why it happened. Is that not so, Giovanni?'

Merisi nodded. I turned my attention back to him. 'So, after Michele was released from prison, your mother's land and property were sold, in very acrimonious circumstances, and then Michele moved here to Rome?'

'Yes, that's right,' Merisi confirmed.

'And is it true to say that the next time you saw your brother, it was at the Palazzo Madama when he refused to acknowledge you as his brother?'

Merisi took a deep breath. 'You are well-informed, Signor Maddano. I did not think you would know about that.'

'Would you have told me?'

'Oh, yes. That was the last time I ever saw Michele. I still find the episode intensely painful. And very puzzling. I know we had had strong disagreements about the disposal of our mother's estate but I thought that the passage of time and his success as an artist would have mellowed his attitude towards me, but it only seemed to make him more bitter.'

Mancini said: 'That was a very curious aspect of Michele's personality, that the more success he had, the more bitter and aggressive he became.'

'Were you aware of this incident, Doctor Mancini?' I asked.

'Yes, it was well-known in Michele's circle of acquaintances. It was often cited to illustrate the perversity of his nature.'

'It was a strange thing to say,' I said, to both men. 'He saw his own brother standing there and said "I have no brother". Now, if Michele was still resentful towards you, Signor Merisi, I would fully expect him to tell you, forcefully, to go away, or even - God forgive me - strike you or even stab you. But he refused even to acknowledge you as a brother. Can either of you explain such a phrase?'

Merisi replied: 'I have turned this incident and that phrase over and over in my mind a thousand times and I still cannot make sense of it or understand it.'

I looked at Mancini. He said: 'It would take a better doctor, a better philosopher, than I to understand how Michele thought. I cannot explain it either.'

All three of us were silent for a few seconds. Then I said to Giovan Battista Merisi: 'I now have to ask you whether you caused the death of your brother Michelangelo or know of anyone who might have done so?'

Despite my attempt to ask such as question as diplomatically as I could, I could see that Merisi was upset. 'No, Signor Maddano,' he answered, 'the mark of Cain is not upon me. I know of many men, and women, who hated Michele with a passion, but I have no evidence or knowledge of anyone who might have caused my brother's death.'

'Thank you for your forebearance in such a painful matter,' I said. 'Doctor Mancini, I ask you the same question, and please be aware that the Holy Father has decreed that the truth be told to me, on threat of eternal damnation.' That statement sounded ludicrously theatrical to my modern ears but Mancini accepted it without any visible sign of demurring.

'I do not believe in eternal damnation but no, Signor Maddano, I didn't do it. Michele was under my care once or twice. If I had wanted to, I could have easily gotten rid of him, but I could not destroy a talent like that, much less a human life. And like Giovanni, I could give you a long list of people who probably whooped with joy when they heard of Michele's death, but I don't know of anyone who might have deliberately planned it.'

The three of us then spent nearly an hour reminiscing about Michelangelo Merisi da Caravaggio. My contributions were, of needs, vague and hesitant as I carefully made them up. It was fascinating and informative listening to Giovan Battista and Doctor Mancini but it added nothing to my quest for a possible murderer and I was relieved when I could escape into the Roman night and quickly float back to my own time and my own home.

10

While I was in my bedroom changing back into modern dress, I could hear a lot of noise and laughter emanating from the kitchen downstairs. A radio was on at full blast. I knew that British builders, painters and decorators love to work accompanied by one hundred decibels of earsplitting heavy metal but it was now late in the evening. Surely they should have finished for the day and gone home by now? I went downstairs and looked into the kitchen. Merisi and all five of the building workers were sitting around the kitchen table. The table was covered with opened boxes of pizza, along with several bottles of wine and cans of strong lager. It looked as if my kitchen had been repaired to a good standard but the workmen were pissed out of their brains.

Merisi turned around and saw me standing there and beckoned me forward. 'Stefano!' he cried, 'we're having a party to celebrate the opening of your new kitchen!' The builders thought this was a hilariously witty remark and guffawed loudly. 'These are my new friends,' Merisi continued. 'I told them that I am a painter too!' He winked at me. 'This is Ray, Gerry, Mike - Michael, like me -, Christopher, and Jerzy. I don't know what sort of name Jerzy is. He says he's Polish but I thought Jerzy was something you wore to keep warm in this freezing country.' Once again, Merisi's witticism was greeted as though he were Oscar Wilde. When the workmen saw the look on my face they realised that the party would soon be over and calmed down a degree. The one named Ray switched off the radio.

'Come on, Stefano,' Merisi urged me. 'Have some pizza and a glass of wine. Both Italian! Isn't that excellent!?'

'Where did you get all this pizza from?' I asked, not moving from where I stood.

'From this leaflet,' Merisi said, searching under the pizza boxes and producing a shiny colour printed flyer. 'Somebody pushed it through the door earlier today. Look, it's from Garibaldi's Pizza Place in Bedford and it says they deliver the best Italian-style pizza to your door. Isn't that a good idea? I ordered one of everything and asked my friends here to stay and enjoy it with me. I have never heard of pizza but it's very tasty. We Italians are clever, no?'

The carpenter, Gerry, who was only about twenty years old, thought this was hilarious. 'Never heard of pizza!' he snorted, 'and you're a fucking Italian!'

'Look, Ray has this miraculous device,' Merisi said. 'You can press a few buttons and then speak to somebody miles away. So I asked this Garibaldi to bring us some pizza. Go on, show him, Ray!' Ray took out his mobile phone from the top pocket of his overalls and, with a stupid and rueful grin on his face, waggled it at me.

This was too much for Gerry. 'Never heard of pizza and never seen a mobile phone.' The tears rolled down his cheeks. 'What part of fucking Italy are you from?'

Merisi slapped him on the back. 'You would be very surprised, my friend!'

I wanted to very quickly get them off the subject of where Merisi came from. 'Michele lives out in the country,' I said. 'They're a bit backward where he comes from. How did you pay for all this lot?'

'I found your credit card upstairs in your wallet. The boys told me what to look for and how to use it. Just read out a number and they bring you food and drink! What a fabulous country!'

Mike, who was the foreman and older and more sober than the rest, said: 'Was that all right, Mr. Maddan? Michele here said you had approved.'

I suddenly felt dispirited and weary, reluctant to cause a scene. 'Yes, that's okay,' I replied. 'How much did it all cost?'

'One hundred and thirty four pounds and sixty eight pennies,' Merisi announced proudly. 'Whatever they are.' Gerry literally fell off his chair and laid on the kitchen floor, gurgling in paroxysms of laughter at Merisi's latest pronouncement.

'Jesus fucking wept,' I said, surveying this madhouse. 'Give me a drink.' Merisi handed me a glass of white wine and I sat down on a kitchen stool.

'They have made an excellent job of restoring your kitchen, Stefano. Do you not think so?' Merisi waved his hand around, inviting me to inspect their handiwork.

'Very nice,' I said, wearily. 'I can't wait to see the bill. I like a bit of late night reading so I can cry myself to sleep.'

'You'll be able to claim it on your insurance,' Mike the foreman said. 'Michele told us how it happened but we'll back up whatever story you want to tell the insurance company.'

From somewhere down on the floor, Gerry gurgled: 'Microwave exploded . . . Italian meatballs . . . never heard of pizza . . .' Suddenly his head appeared above the table top, his face turned pale geen, he struggled to his feet, lurched to the back door, opened it and vomited copiously over the paving slabs outside. This was the piece-de-resistance of the evening's entertainment and the merriment at the sight of Gerry being sick outside my back door was unconfined.

'I think you had better get him home to his wife,' I suggested to Mike.

'Wife!' Ray exclaimed. 'He'll be lucky. Still living with his mum. Still pulling his pud!'

Gerry, who was outside breathing deeply trying to keep everything down, mustered the strength to say: 'I'd rather be pulling the pud than shagging your missus.'

Instead of being offended, Ray found this immensely funny. 'You got a point there, old son,' he chuckled. 'I'll tell her that. Perhaps she'll come and pull your pud for you.'

Mike got to his feet and finished off his glass of lager. 'Come on,' he said to his gang. 'Time to leave Mr. Maddan in peace.' Ray, Christopher and Jerzy rose unsteadily to their feet and went to assist Gerry, thanking Merisi with bleary comments of 'good party, mate' and 'thanks a lot.'

Merisi stood up and attempted to kiss them goodbye. 'Hey, fuck off,' Ray said, pushing him away. 'It wasn't that good a party.'

'We'll do it again sometime,' Merisi said. 'Stefano is going to be very rich soon.'

'Yeah, and I'm going to score the winning goal in the World Cup final,' Ray said.

Mike just nodded at me as they all stumbled out. I closed the door after them.

'Pour me another glass,' I said to Merisi.

'What am I, your fucking servant?' he said, but did as he was asked.

'What's left here?' I said, searching through the pizza boxes. 'I'll eat anything except olives and anchovies.' I found a ham and pineapple that hadn't been manhandled and pulled off a triangle.

'Are you mad at me?' Merisi asked.

'Yes, but not about this,' I replied, indicating the pizzas. I tucked into the ham and pineapple and then took a big slug of white wine. I said nothing else and Merisi regarded me cautiously. Finally, he could stand it no longer. 'What are you mad about?' he asked.

I belched and said simply: 'You're still lying to me.'

'I take it you saw my pious brother. What did you think of him?'

'Unlike you,' I answered, 'I found him courteous, charming, helpful, honest and there was something else that, again unlike you, I found very likeable about him.'

'What's that?'

'His obvious love and affection for you, despite your incredible callousness towards him.'

Merisi grunted. 'He calls himself a good Christian. It's his duty to love me, to love everyone.'

'I sensed his love for you is more than the duty of a good Christian. He told me you were in prison when your mother died. Is that true?'

'If he said it, of course it is.'

'Why didn't you tell me?'

'Because it has nothing to do with all this . . . all this shit that these people from another planet have stuck us with.'

I threw down my pizza crust. 'It might have everything to do with it!' I said, angrily. 'You attacked and wounded a Frenchman named Dufre. That act might have had all sorts of repercussions. What was it all about anyway?'

Merisi fixed me with a glance of pure malice. Whenever he was really angry, the residual white scar tissue from the attack in Naples stood out more prominently. The effect was, I have to admit, very intimidating. He said: 'Scream at me all you like, Englishman. I have never told anyone what that fight was all about. I will not tell you now, not even four hundred years later. It is nothing to do with you or those prying fuckers on the planet of Tralfamadore, or whatever it's called. I don't care that they have brought me back to life. I didn't ask to be resurrected and I will not reveal private things simply out of gratitiude. What happened with Dufre will go with me to my grave . . . again. Do you understand?'

I shrugged. 'Have it your way,' I said. 'But it means I'll have to check everything you tell me from now on. It will waste your time and mine.'

Merisi grunted. 'I've already wasted four hundred years. What will a few more weeks matter? I'll tell you the truth if and when I think it is relevant and necessary, but on some subjects I will keep silent. For eternity, if need be.'

I decided not to tell Merisi about meeting his biographer, Doctor Giulio Mancini. I considered that Mancini might be a useful card to keep up my sleeve. 'Tell me,' I said. 'Do you, or did you, suffer from gout?'

'Gout?' Merisi repeated, puzzled. 'No, not that I know of. How do you catch it?'

'From eating too much Italian pizza,' I replied, and took another slice of ham and pineapple.

11

The next day I slept late and, having consumed too much wine and pizza, woke up with a throbbing hangover and a stomach churning like the Anchor butter factory. I showered and dressed and staggered downstairs to the kitchen. Merisi had beaten me to it and was sitting at the kitchen table eating cold stale pizza. This disgusting spectacle turned my stomach even more and, for a few seconds, I thought I was going to emulate what Gerry had done out of the back door last night but, after a few deep breaths, the wave of nausea subsided. I searched in one of the brand new kitchen cupboards for some Alka-Seltzer. I am always careful to keep a good supply. I switched on the percolator and made some strong coffee. Neither Merisi or I had spoken, so I said: 'How do you feel this morning?'

'Terrible,' he replied. 'My brain thumps on the inside of my skull.'

'Then how the hell can you sit there eating that?'

'This?' he queried, examining a slice of pizza. 'What's wrong with it?'

'It's cold and stale.'

'It's delicious, and I dare not attempt to heat it up in case I wreck your kitchen again.'

'It's disgusting.'

'You should have tried working for Cardinal Salad,' Merisi said. 'You would have eaten this with relish after living on his food.'

'Yes,' I said, 'I hope we can talk about him later on today.'

Merisi shrugged. 'If we have to. When was this pizza stuff invented?' he asked.

'I'm not sure,' I answered.

'You are supposed to know everything,' Merisi said, scornfully. 'Pellegrino told me you are a genius who can answer any question. "Brain of Britain", my arse!'

I ignored his jibe. 'I think it was early in the 19th century,' I said. 'About 150 years ago. In Naples.'

Merisi was suddenly alert. 'Napoli?' he repeated. 'For me, in the end, a desolate place, but I did some good work there.'

'Here are some more modern miracles,' I said, placing a glass of fresh orange juice and a glass of tap water in front of him. 'It will help to clear your head.' I dropped two tablets of Alka-Seltzer into the water.

Merisi was startled and ducked away from the fizzing liquid. 'Witchcraft,' he said. 'You are a fucking witch. I'm not drinking that!'

'I will then,' I said, and drank the water in one gulp. I smacked my lips theatrically and said: 'Aahh, headache gone.'

'Very well,' Merisi said, 'give me some of this modern medicine. Does this cure all pain?' he asked.

'It will help,' I said. 'Do you have pain anywhere other than that thick head of yours?'

'I have been in constant pain ever since I was in hospital in Rome.'

'You were kicked by a horse, weren't you?' I asked.

'That was the story we put about, yes.'

'You mean you hadn't been kicked by a horse?'

Merisi did not answer my question. 'I had a fever. I was in a bad way.'

'I'll be very interested to hear more about your stay in hospital and the true reasons for it. I can understand you being grouchy if you are in constant pain. There are other modern medicines called paracetamol and ibuprofen which may be effective in relieving it. In the meantime, drink that and I'll pour us some coffee.'

Merisi drank the Alka-Seltzer and sat still, waiting for something to happen. 'My head still hurts. This is no good. You are a liar.'

'No,' I said. 'I just pretended that it works immediately. It will take an hour or two to work it's magic. It's based on a miraculous drug called aspirin.'

'As-pi-rin,' Merisi repeated, as if committing it to memory. He drank the orange juice and then the coffee. I prepared my favourite hangover cure, fried bacon and scrambled eggs, and forced it down. Neither of us spoke for several minutes, but then Merisi said: 'I feel much better. I approve of this aspirin. I am ready to work.'

It was a chilly late Spring day so I decided that we would work in the living room, in comfortable armchairs, either side of the large flame-effect gas fire, which fascinated Merisi. 'No wonder you don't need a maid or a servant or a wife,' he commented. 'These miraculous gadgets do everything for you just by touching them.'

'Let's just say they respond to my touch more enthusiastically than my wife ever did.' I opened my notebook and Helen Langdon's biography. 'You travelled to Rome in 1592, in the entourage of Marchese Costanza Colonna. How did you feel? Excited, or apprehensive?'

'Oh, excited,' Merisi answered. 'Elated. I felt free for the first time in my life.

I was not content to be a provincial artist. Rome, for an ambitious artist at that time, was the only place in Italy, the only place in the world. It was rising from the ashes, being rebuilt from the ruin it had been only a few short years before. It was the centre of Christendom, the centre of papal wealth and power. There were many artists working there but there were also many opportunities for work, for commissions. I was twenty one years old. I was set to conquer the world.'

Merisi's excitement at this memory communicated itself to me. It must have been a thrilling experience for a hot-blooded, passionate, talented young man like Merisi to be entering the most important city in Christendom for the first time. 'What was Rome like?' I asked.

Merisi grunted in an ironic fashion. 'Where do I start?' he said, rhetorically. 'Thanks to Pope Sixtus, the whole city was taking on a magnificence it had not seen since the days of the ancient Roman emperors. The cupola of St. Peter's had been finished only a year or two before I arrived. New churches were being built everywhere, and old churches renewed. The Vatican Library was being decorated by a team of fresco painters. I longed to be one of them but I was young and unknown and could not have obtained a place on that project. The palaces of the cardinals were magnificent. Behind those high protective walls was where the power and the patronage resided. I ached for an entrée, ached to make a name for myself.'

'But it wasn't all magnificence, was it? There was much poverty and violence as well, wasn't there?'

'Yes, that was the other side of the coin. As in Milan, the famines had forced many people to move into the city in search of relief, so the streets were teeming with beggars. There were many unemployed soldiers, paid off after war, inured to brutality and always spoiling for a fight. That's why I always carried a sword or a dagger, especially after dark.'

I doubted that was Merisi's real reason for carrying a weapon but I let it go. 'What about the political situation?' I asked. 'I believe there had been four new popes in little more than a year. What with the fear of the Protestant movement in the north, things must have felt very unsettled. Did that concern you?'

'Very much so,' Merisi replied. 'As an artist, this rapid succession of popes was a major concern. Who was it best to suck up to? Where was the work, the good commissions going to come from? A cardinal could support a pope, become powerful, then the pope died and that cardinal lost his power and influence overnight, even if not his money. And, as you say, there was much fear that the heretics in the north, in Germany and England, would taint and enfeeble the sacred Catholic religion. Forgive me for saying so, but we hated the Germans and you English.'

'No offence taken,' I smiled. 'The world is completely different now. For instance, the Turks are trying to become part of the European Union.'

'What!' Merisi exclaimed. 'We spent our lives in fear and loathing of the Turks! Costanza Colonna's father, Marcantonio, had become a hero fighting the Turks at Lepanto. The Knights of St. John in Malta, where I lived for a time, devoted their lives to fighting them off. And now they are asking to become part of Europe? It is insane. Are they going to be accepted?'

'It looks likely,' I said. 'They are a more secular, less aggressive nation now.'

'Truly, as you have said, the world is completely different.' Merisi shook his head in bafflement. 'What of France and the French?' he asked. 'What are they like now?'

'The French, as I suspect they have always done, put themselves first and go their own way. And who is to blame them? They are a unique and cultured nation, sometimes exasperating and baffling to the English way of thinking, but the world would be infinitely poorer without them. Many English people have now moved to live in France because they prefer the French way of life to their own.'

'Is that so?' Merisi said. 'That is very interesting. There was much suspicion of France in my time. Soon after I arrived in Rome, the French king Henry, who had been a supporter of the Protestant cause and who had killed many Catholics with his military skills, had announced his decision to return to the Catholic Church! It was, of course, a totally cynical move to strengthen his grip on his power and his kingdom. The Spanish king, as a good Catholic was duty-bound to do, tried to prevent this false conversion and Henry declared war on him! All this caused many massed fights in the streets of Rome between French and Spanish supporters. I, as a Lombard, Lombardy being ruled by Spain, supported the Spanish faction and spent many an hour knocking French heads together. Happy days!'

'I'm sure they were, for a belligerent brute like you,' I said, and was rewarded with an obscenity from Merisi. 'This King Henry of France you detested so much did a good job in restoring French wealth and prestige after his country had been torn apart by the wars between Catholics and Huguenots. He was a charismatic and forceful character. How can you blame him for trying to restore the fortunes of his country, even by such hypocritical tactics?'

'Hypocrite is the right description,' Merisi said. 'He was as much a hypocrite in his personal life, so I understand.'

'In what way?' I asked.

'From all accounts, he was a better swordsman in the bedroom than he was on the battlefield.' Merisi grinned and waggled his little finger in a lascivious way. 'As you have said, he was charming and charismatic, apparently, and had been a hero in battle. Together with one or two other small factors, such as dark good looks and being the king of France, the ladies found him irresistible. Even the Marchese Colonna, who met him once when she was a young girl, would not hear a bad word against him and went a delicate shade of pink whenever his name was mentioned. I was living in her house near Naples when the news came that he had been assassinated. It was only a month or two before I supposedly died. I was still recovering from my wounds and was in a bad way myself. Poor Costanza! She was already in a delicate state from all this violent upheaval and she became very distraught when she heard of King Henry's death. And she, as a member of the Colonna family, an ardent supporter of the Spanish cause! Good riddance to him, I thought. How to explain the workings of the female mind, eh, Stefano? It has perplexed us poor men for centuries.'

'And probably always will,' I agreed. 'But let's get back to Rome. Tell me about the art world in Rome when you first arrived.'

Merisi pondered this question for quite a long time. 'How can I explain it?' he said. 'It was a strange and difficult time, in some respects, to be an artist. Pope Clement was an austere and pious man who had taken a severe dislike to what he considered to be profane images in art, especially nudity. He ordered Cardinal Rusticucci to draw up an edict outlining many rules and regulations in the production of works of art, for builders and sculptors, as well as we painters. There were harsh penalties for transgressing these rules. Painters had to show preliminary drawings of their intended works to the authorities for their approval. Of course, none of this concerned me in the beginning. I was unknown. I had no reputation. But it was a lively subject of debate in the art world when I arrived in Rome. The powerful cardinals largely paid lip service to these new papal decrees about art, and about morality in general. The pope's nephew, Cardinal Pietro Aldobrandini, was a case in point. He was a strange little man, pockmarked and continually wheezing with asthma. He had a weakness for erotic art, and for married women, and for fucking all the courtesans in Rome that he could manage. And that was the very own nephew of such an austere pope!'

'Were all these cardinals such hypocrites?' I asked. 'Did any of them take their Christian office seriously?'

'Some of them took their Christian vows very seriously and did charitable work among the poor, distributing alms and so on. Rome was literally swarming with beggars, Jews, gypsies, vagrants and ne'er-do-wells. Some cardinals would provide shelter and food for these unfortunates. Some endowed hospitals for the sick and dying. A rare few actually worked among the poor. But they all retreated back to their rich palazzi and made very sure that they did not give away all their wealth, as Christ would surely have done. These were the people I had to beg work from! But, outside of the cardinalate, there were some truly holy men in Rome at that time. Men like Filippo Neri, whom even the pope revered and respected.'

'From what you have said, it sounds like Rome was a city of great contrasts in those days.'

'Yes,' Merisi confirmed. 'Behind the walls of the palazzi was wealth and luxury while outside on the streets there was hunger, violence and death. I, of course, was to live in both those worlds. Thanks to my skill as an artist, I was allowed into the rich world of Rome. There was selfless piety shoulder-to-shoulder with debauchery and vice. I only concerned myself with the debauchery and vice. I was never a pious man. But there was something else happening in Rome at that time. There was deep unease. The millennium was approaching. The Turks still menaced us. The northern heretics threatened all civilised values. But Rome was being rebuilt, along with the Catholic faith, and there was also a profound sense of excitement. Rome, we all felt, was the only place to be. The art world had become stultified and dull since the halcyon days of Raphael, Leonardo and my namesake Michelangelo Buonarotti. Art in Rome was primed to explode into life, and I was just the man to light the fuse.' Merisi smiled at me. 'Did I not do just that?' he asked.

'You certainly did,' I agreed. 'You not only lit the fuse but you poured petrol on the ensuing flames. But it took you a few years, didn't it?'

'Yes, it did. I felt I could see how painting needed to change. The desire burned inside of me that I had to tell the truth through my work. I had to bring back to life the reality of the faith, and of the human experience. The fashion in painting when I arrived in Rome was for the manera statuina, what you would call in English "in the manner of a statue". It was pallid, lifeless, posed, and deadening to the soul. I hated it. And then there was the new fashion for sweet, humble and pious art. Painters like that useless arsehole Pulzone became very popular. Naturally, the first thing I did when I arrived in Rome was to study all the works of the masters, such as Raphael and Michelangelo, that I could find. I admired some of them, but I knew that I could be a better painter than they were.'

'Modesty was never one of your more outstanding virtues, was it?' I commented.

'No, why should it have been, and fuck you,' Merisi shot back. 'I said what I felt, even then. It got me into a lot of fights. I was young and completely unknown. My fellow artists would say "who are you to talk like that, how can you criticise the masters when you have done fuck all yourself", but I was just waiting for my chance and I knew it would come one day.'

'How did you go about getting that chance?' I asked.

'The aim for most painters in those days was to get a position in the service of a prince or cardinal. In that way you could live in a luxurious palazzo, even if your own accommodation within it was not so luxurious, with regular food and servants to attend your needs. It was a pleasant life, mixing with other artists and creative people such as writers, poets and scientists. And, of course, it was the outlet for your work. You could gain a reputation through your patron's friends and family. But vacancies for such comfortable positions were rare and quite outside of my ability to secure when I first arrived in Rome. The more usual ambition was to obtain a place in a successful studio as an assistant to an established artist. This I did later on. It meant regular food, accommodation and payment but, to a man like me who burned with an ambition to paint great pictures in my own manner, it was soul destroying. Even this ambition eluded me when I first arrived in Rome, so I started among the lowest of the low, as a jobbing artist trying to sell my pictures through small dealers or small shops or even, with my friend Mario, selling them ourselves on the streets.'

'Do you mean Mario Minnitti?' I asked. 'He was this friend you mentioned?'

'Yes, that's right,' Merisi confirmed.

'That is interesting,' I said, 'because, according to what we know today, you did not make his acquaintance until later, when you joined the studio of Lorenzo Siciliano.'

'No. When I first arrived in Rome I found lodgings at a cheap rundown inn owned by a man named Tarquinio. Mario moved in there a day or two later, into the next room. Inevitably, we met up for a drink. I didn't like him, at first, but he seemed to like me and he was always seeking me out. I wondered at first if he was a bardassa, a poof, but he never made any move in that direction. He was an artist as well. I came to accept his company. I found out that he had an interesting past.'

'Yes,' I said. 'I'd like to talk more about Mario later on. We know he was your lifelong friend. But we believe you very soon found a place in the service of Cardinal Salad. Tell me about him.'

At the mention of Cardinal Salad, whose real name was Pandolfo Pucci, Merisi smiled but then frowned and made to spit into my fireplace until he remembered it was not a real fire. 'Excuse me, Stefano,' he said. 'Such are my mixed reactions when I hear that man's name.'

'How did you obtain a place in his service?'

'As with many things in my life, I have to thank the Colonna family. Pucci was the steward to Camilla Peretti, who was the sister of Pope Sixtus Peretti, and the Peretti family had close ties with the Colonna family. After Pope Sixtus died, Camilla Peretti retired and moved into a wing of the Palazzo Colonna, where Pucci lived with her and looked after her. No doubt the Colonna family thought they were doing me a favour placing me with Pandolfo Pucci, giving me a leg up into the Roman art world, but I couldn't stand it. My room and studio were comfortable enough but Pucci was a mean bastard. All we were given to eat, every evening, day after day, was salad. Salad after fucking salad. That's why we dubbed him Cardinal Salad, Monsignor Insalata in Italian. And the work he made me do was humiliating rubbish. All I was doing was copying devotional images onto canvas which he would then send to some church in Recanati. Day after day. Complete rubbish.'

'Unfortunately,' I said, 'none of those paintings survive, so we will not be able to tell whether there were any clues about your murderer in any of them.'

'Good,' Merisi said. 'They do not deserve to have survived. I am glad they have not survived.'

'Well, the fact that they have not survived does not help our murder inquiry. Can you remember if any of them might have contained a clue?'

'No,' Merisi said emphatically. 'I refuse to think about them. They were all copies of somebody else's work. Just hack work.'

'Very well,' I sighed. 'Is that why you left Pucci's employment?'

'Partly,' Merisi answered, 'but the main reason was that Pucci loved young boys. He would often visit me when I was working and, making it look like an absent-minded gesture, stroke my hair or my arse. That was the sort of sneaky and repulsive pervert he was. I would have liked to punch the little bastard but I knew I could not. I would not have cared about losing my food and lodging and wages but such an act would have deeply offended the Colonna family. Pucci knew that was the case, so I just had to stand there while that sweaty little cunt toyed with me. One day, I could stand it no longer. I just packed up my things and left. I went back to Tarquinio's inn.'

'What did you do next? To further your career, I mean.'

'There was only one thing that Mario and I could do. We had to try selling our pictures on the streets, or through a dealer, while looking for a place in an established studio.'

'Was Mario still lodging at Tarquinio's inn?'

'Yes. He had had no luck in finding a studio. We decided to share one room at Tarquinio's, to cut down on costs, you understand, not for any other reason. We would paint in that room or out in the courtyard on a clear day. We decided to work together. Not painting together but working together in hawking our pictures on the streets. We painted in quite different styles so if somebody did not like his pictures, they might like mine, and vice versa. That was the theory. It didn't help much but it did give us mutual moral support.'

'Let's talk about Mario Minnitti himself. You two had become friends. Good friends, would you say?'

'As good a friend as I ever had,' Merisi shrugged. 'Although, as you know, I'm a self-centred bastard, so I think he liked me more than I liked him.'

'What was he like?'

'He always looked a little strange to me. He was a Sicilian, you know, so his complexion was quite dark, with thick black hair that seemed to stand up on his head as if he could never manage to comb it flat. He was thin but his face was chubby, his eyes set wide apart, but his lips were like a small Cupid's bow and set very close to his big nose. It was a combination of features that was strange but interesting. That's why I often used him as a model.'

I said: 'We know that he had fled from Syracuse for some unknown reason and had travelled through Malta before he arrived in Rome. Do you know why he had to flee from Sicily?'

'Yes, he had killed a rival in a duel over some girl and, of course, the rival's family sought revenge. The Sicilians were relentless and vengeful bastards in those days.'

'They still are,' I said. 'One day, I will tell you about the Mafia.'

'Mafia?' Merisi repeated. 'I know the word mafie, meaning a private army. Is it the same?'

'Very similar,' I smiled. 'But let's not get sidetracked. I know this is a silly question but did it worry you that Mario was a killer?'

'Not in the least,' Merisi replied. 'I couldn't care less. Although, I will admit, that sometimes I found him creepy. Sometimes I caught him staring at me. Just staring, for no reason. I would ask him what he was looking at and he would just shrug. I had the feeling that, although we were friends on the surface, he would have stuck a dagger into my back without a qualm, if it had suited him to do so.'

I was excited by this revelation. 'Do you think he had anything to do with your murder?'

'No, not a chance. He always helped me out. Later on, in Sicily, when I was in big trouble, he helped me out a lot. No, it was not Mario.'

'Let's not dismiss this possibility too quickly,' I said. 'Your attempted murderer told you that the answer was in the pictures. Mario modelled for you, frequently. There may be some clue, some reason, for Mario to be involved in your attempted murder that you are not aware of. According to your biographer, Giulio Mancini, it might have been around this time that your earliest surviving paintings were completed, and that Mario modelled for them.'

'Which ones do you mean?' Merisi asked.

I fetched the large volume of Caravaggio's works from the bookcase. I showed Merisi his two paintings. 'There is this one of a boy peeling a fruit (*Plate 6*) and this one inspired by that drawing by Sofonisba Anguisciola of a boy being bitten by a lizard, the one that is hung next to the Supper at Emmaus in the National Gallery.'

'Yes,' Merisi smiled. 'I was delighted to see my lizard picture again when I materialised in your National Gallery. As you have said yourself, the carafe of water is painted with delicate skill. I was pleased with that one.'

'Did Mario model for both of these pictures?'

'Yes.'

'So could there be any hidden clues or messages in these two pictures? For instance, why is Mario wearing a rose behind his ear in the lizard picture?'

Merisi laughed. 'That was to attract the bardassas, the poofs, to make the picture more saleable. In Rome at that time, the rose behind the ear was a signal that the boy was available. You'll notice that I made Mario a lot prettier than he really was. He didn't know whether to be pleased because he looked better or annoyed that I had made him desirable to the bardassas! The lizard biting was a metaphor for the pain of love. I sold it eventually but I didn't get much for it. Not as much as I had hoped, anyway.'

'But you don't think there could be any clues about your murder in there?' I said.

'No, how could there be?' Merisi answered, tetchily. 'I painted it to sell it, not to send a message about anything. This is ridiculous!'

We lapsed into an uneasy silence for a few moments. I said: 'What about this boy peeling a fruit?'

'What about it?' Merisi said, still tetchy. 'It's just a boy peeling fruit. Such subjects were popular in those days. That one was painted earlier than the lizard picture. That was probably the first time I used Mario as a model. It is crude. I am not proud of it.'

'It was copied many times by other artists,' I said.

Merisi snorted. 'Just shows what poor taste they had,' he said. 'It's sentimental and commercial rubbish.'

'I'm sure that Her Majesty the Queen, who now owns it, would agree that it is commercial. Several million scudi commercial.'

'She is welcome to it,' Merisi said, dismissively.

'I think it's charming,' I said. 'The boy's hands and the fruit are painted skilfully and I'm intrigued by the smile that plays on the boy's face, as if he is thinking of something pleasant while he performs his chores. I wonder what he is thinking about.'

Merisi sneered at me. 'You sound like an old woman. I intended to give that effect. Knowing Mario, he was probably thinking of the whore he was going to fuck that night. That's why he was smiling.'

'Very well,' I sighed. 'I accept I am a tasteless old woman. What about this boy with a basket of fruit. (*Plate* 7). Before you say anything, and before you write it off, the basket and the fruit are superbly painted. You must agree with that?'

'I do agree,' Merisi nodded. 'Such work was what I was primarily trained to do in Peterzano's studio. There was a strong tradition of such still life painting where I came from in northern Italy. We Lombards were renowned for our facility in painting fruit and flowers. The boy peeling fruit picture had proved appealing and when I painted Mario as a bardassa in the lizard picture it was even more appealing, so I decided to combine the two elements in this basket of fruit picture. You will notice how sexually suggestive I made Mario, with those slightly parted red lips and that bare shoulder which is not, I have to say, painted well. I wanted to take this picture around the studios to show them what I could do. That's what we did. Mario took this picture to a fellow Sicilian artist, the one you now call Lorenzo Siciliano, together with one of his own paintings, and we both secured a place in Lorenzo's studio.'

'Okay, we'll talk about Lorenzo in a moment, but are you sure there are not any hidden messages or clues in these three pictures?'

'No,' Merisi answered, becoming more exasperated. 'Nothing that I can think of. They are simply portraits of Mario, dressed up to look like a pretty street boy, just to be saleable. What else can I say?'

'Very well. So you and Mario were given work in Lorenzo's studio. One of your biographers says that you were painting portraits, three a day, for a groat each. Is that true?'

'Yes, basically,' Merisi confirmed. 'Lorenzo was a bad artist, crude and clumsy. He worked for the tourist trade or small tradesmen with more money than taste who wanted a genuine portrait to adorn their houses and show off to their neighbours. I was knocking out copies of portraits of famous men. Such portraits were popular at that time. It was hack work but Mario and I were glad to get it. It put food in our bellies and allowed us to get drunk in the taverns. Although I hated doing such work at the time, it did improve my skills in portraiture. And, eventually, these pictures came to the notice of Grammatica, who offered me a place in his studio.'

'Let's have a coffee,' I suggested, 'and then we'll talk about this man Grammatica. One last question about Lorenzo Siciliano. Did you fall out with him in any way?'

'You mean, do you think he might have wished me dead? No, I don't think so. I didn't work at his studio for very long. He was a stupid man and he used to get annoyed at some of the things I said, especially about his work, but we parted on reasonably good terms. He is just another in a long list of people who simply didn't like me much.' Merisi twisted around in his armchair to look out of the window. It was a cold day but bright and clear, with a clear blue sky. 'Couldn't we go into the town in that contraption you call a car and get drunk?' he pleaded. 'I am bored with sitting here talking of these dead events.'

'No,' I insisted. 'We have to do this. When we have finished for the day I will show you how a car works and we'll go for a ride into town. That will be your reward for this work we are doing.'

Merisi gave me a look that said he didn't think much of his reward. I made us a mug of coffee each and we drank it in silence. Merisi gazed at the fake flames in the gas fire. I guessed that he was lost in thought about the old days in Rome but I couldn't be sure. Finally he said: 'I wonder if the flames of hell look like that? I have been granted a reprieve for four hundred years but I shall surely find out one day.'

'There is no such place, Michele,' I tried to reassure him. 'In fact, a very clever Frenchman once claimed that "hell is other people". I don't think he was far wrong.'

Merisi smiled. 'Well, the French have certainly made it hell for other people . . . on many occasions.'

'You don't know the half of it, Michele. I'll tell you about Napoleon Bonaparte one day, and garlic and French manners. But let's talk about this interesting character Antiveduto Grammatica. Antiveduto is a strange forename. It means "I told you so" or something like that. Do you know why he was called that?'

'Yes,' Merisi said, suddenly much more animated. 'He told me that his family had been travelling from Siena to Rome and that his mother had given birth on the road, an event that his father had evidently predicted, so he was given that strange forename. Antiveduto was about the same age as me. I liked him a lot and, what is more unusual, I carried on liking him. He was one of the few men in my life that I genuinely liked. He ran a very successful studio painting portraits. He was so skilled that he earned the epithet of "the great head painter". Anybody who was anybody in Rome, or who came visiting the city, made their way to his studio to have their portrait painted. He had been impressed by the heads that I had been painting for Lorenzo Siciliano and offered me a place, on much better terms, in his studio, so it was arrivederci Lorenzo for me. I learned a lot from Antiveduto, and not just about the technique of portrait painting. He was a wealthy man but he often invited me to dine with his family. I had a comfortable billet in his studio.'

'Sorry to interrupt, Michele, but did Mario move there with you?'

Merisi hesitated. 'No. I don't think Mario's work was of sufficient quality to attract Antiveduto.'

'Did you try to persuade Grammatica to give Mario a place?'

Merisi looked uneasy. 'No,' he replied.

'Even though Mario had obtained a place for you with Lorenzo?'

'Look, I lied,' Merisi said. 'I told Mario that I had tried to obtain him a place but it was a lie. The truth is, I didn't particularly want Mario with me. I cared nothing much for him. He was useful but he was like a devoted dog, always hanging around. Always . . . there!'

'Was he upset with you, or envious of your move?' I asked.

'That's the funny thing. Allowing for the fact that I had lied to him, so he was under the impression that I had fought for him when I had not, he seemed genuinely pleased for me. Relieved even. He always admitted that I had much more talent as a painter than he did, so I suppose he thought that it was inevitable that I would leave him behind one day. But Rome was not a particularly big city in those days and the world of the painters was mainly concentrated in one area. We would often meet up in a tavern or he would visit me at Antiveduto's studio. No, there was no jealousy or ill-feeling between us in that respect.'

'Very well,' I said. 'What was it about Antiveduto that you liked when most human beings seem to have enraged and repelled you?'

Merisi smiled ironically and said: 'That's a good question, and one I have never really thought about until this moment. First and foremost, he was an excellent painter. He was an ambitious man. He loved money – don't we all – but he loved art even more than money. We argued incessantly about painting but, instead of being irritating, as with most other artists, it was stimulating and instructive. He worked hard at his technique and, as I have said, I learned much from him. He had strong opinions about art, about everything really, but he was never didactic. He never gave the impression that he was the boss and that what he said was more important than what we others thought. Always there was humour and courtesy, consideration and kindness. I enjoyed his company, probably more than anyone I have ever known. I am considered to be a violent and aggressive man but that is mostly because I have refused to be browbeaten and belittled by others. I have given it back to them measure for measure, and more, and they learned to fear me, but with Antiveduto there was no necessity for that response. He was a cultured man and his studio was often filled with poets, musicians, princes, nobles, cardinals and men of learning. It was a most informative and stimulating atmosphere.'

'You are sure that Antiveduto Grammatica wished you no harm, either then or later,' I asked.

'Listen,' Merisi replied, emphatically. 'Antiveduto could no more inflict grievous harm on another human being than he could cut off his own painting hand. Look elsewhere for my murderer, Englishman.'

I was intrigued by a character such as Antiveduto Grammatica who could turn a snarling wolf like Merisi into a puppy waiting to have its stomach rubbed. I considered whether it would be worth going back to meet this man. I would have to give the matter some thought. I said: 'There are none of your paintings still in existence from your time in Grammatica's studio, except a portrait of Cardinal Cesare Baronio that has all the hallmarks of your early style and may have been done by you. Can you remember executing a portrait of Cardinal Baronio?'

'Indeed I can,' Merisi confirmed. 'Baronio was a distinguished churchman. His Annales Ecclesiastici, a history of the Catholic Church, had been written, at the suggestion of Filippo Neri, in order to correct some heresies about the Faith. For me, it was an honour to be given this commission to paint a portrait of such a distinguished figure, and a typically selfless gift by Antiveduto. I wanted to make a stir with that picture so I tried out one of my ideas about lighting effects. It was a success, attracted a lot of attention, and was an important step in my career. Antiveduto was as pleased as could be. He studied my portrait. He even said to me "one day, Michele, you will be a greater artist than I am. I think, perhaps, you already are". Later on, he began to copy my style.'

'Yes, we know that he did,' I said, 'and that such imitation usually enraged you, for some strange reason in that quirky brain of yours, but not when Antiveduto imitated your style.'

Merisi swallowed my jibe without comment and simply said: 'I don't know. When Antiveduto copied me, it was an honour, a compliment. When other, lesser, artists copied me, with their dark and thoughtless daubs, I felt it was endangering my reputation and the integrity of my technique.'

'We believe that it was in Grammatica's studio that you met Cherubino Alberti, another artist who supported you and stayed close to you. Is that correct?'

'Yes but, in his case, it was expedient for me to stay close to him.'

'Why's that?'

'Because he was at the centre of the Roman art world. He came from a distinguished family of artists, so he had a reputation right from the start of his career. He was a highly skilled engraver. He painted in an antique style. His painting style was so different from what I was doing that he posed no threat to me. His style pleased the popes, generally, and he had powerful friends within the art world as well as having considerable influence himself. He took to me in a friendly fashion. I would have been a fool to reject his friendship.'

'Even so, Michele,' I observed, with delicacy, 'you seem to have been more mellow at this stage of your career than you were later.'

'I would accept that,' he replied. 'I enjoyed working with Antiveduto, mixing with his cultured friends, and I felt that I was at last beginning to gain a certain reputation. But it was still a tiny reputation and no other artist was threatened by me. Yes, it was one of the few contented periods of my life.'

I thought about whether I should use the ChronoConverter to travel back in time to interview any of these people we had been talking about. I decided that it would probably be fruitless to interview Pandolfo Pucci, Lorenzo Siciliano, Cherubino Alberti or Antiveduto Grammatica, much as I was attracted to the idea of seeing what sort of man Grammatica was. The man who knew Merisi throughout the period we had been talking about was Mario Minnitti, but there might be a snag in going back to see him.

'Michele,' I said, 'I think it would be useful to travel back to interview your friend Mario Minnitti, but he is living in Syracuse in Sicily at the time I must interview him. Could our ChronoContact, Pellegrino, get the co-ordinates to transport me there to see him, do you think?'

'I think so,' Merisi replied. 'As I understand it, Pellegrino can travel around almost instantaneously as long as he has a good idea where he is going and where he is going to appear, so he can very quickly visit Syracuse and arrange it. Why don't we contact him?'

We sent Pellegrino a message saying where I wanted to be. There was no return confirmation, which meant that Pellegrino was in a situation in which he could not respond immediately. 'While we wait,' I said to Merisi, 'let's get some fresh air.'

'A good idea, Stefano,' he replied. 'I have noticed that the air in England is very fresh. You will no doubt find it a tad warmer in Syracuse.'

I said: 'I will show you how my beloved car works and we will go for a spin.'

The ChronoTranslator obviously had a problem translating the English slang word 'spin'. 'You mean our car only goes round and around,' Merisi asked, puzzled.

'Well, it can do,' I said, 'but mostly it goes in a straight line. "Spin" is English slang meaning a trip out in a car purely for pleasure. What should please you is that the Italians now make the sexiest cars in the world, and my car is . . . Italian.'

Merisi was delighted. 'I knew we had picked the right man for this project!' he cried, slapping me on the back. 'You have excellent taste. But how can one of these car things be "sexy". I don't understand.'

'Well, a car is primarily for travelling from place to place. But it can also display your taste or your wealth or your attractiveness to women. An expensive, beautifully made, shiny car is considered to be attractive to women and can be useful in convincing them to spend time with you. Such is the theory among men, at any rate. It is possible to make love to a woman in a car, although it can be uncomfortable. There is a theory that a car is seen, subliminally, by men as an extension of their penis. The bigger the car, the greater the need for a penis extension.'

'I'm not sure I understand,' Merisi said. 'What does "subliminally" mean? I have seen women steering these cars. Do they wish for a bigger penis?'

'No, no,' I said, beginning to flounder. 'It is like the clothes you wear. If you wear rags, you show you are poor and women will not want to be with you. Wear a fine suit of satin or velvet, with silver chains and gold rings, and both men and women will say "look, he is wealthy, he is powerful, I envy him, I want to know this man". Do you see what I mean? A car is just the same.'

Merisi nodded. 'It is clearer now. How big is your car?'

'It is big. Not the biggest, but big.'

'So this makes up for your small penis.'

'No, I don't have a small penis. Not that small, anyway.'

'And do women want to make love to you when you travel around in this car of yours?'

'Not noticeably,' I had to admit.

'Will they wish to make love to me when I am with you.'

'It is extremely unlikely,' I said.

'Then all you have told me is false. The pope was right about you English. You are a nation of liars and heretics.'

'Look, let's just go and look at the car.' I led Merisi out to the front garden drive where my beloved midnight blue Alfa Romeo GTV stood waiting for me. 'There,' I said proudly. 'It is called an Alfa Romeo and it was built in Italy. Isn't it a thing of beauty? It was styled by an Italian company named Pininfarina. It has a three litre V6 engine. In this we can travel at nearly one hundred and fifty miles per hour. A bit faster than horseback, eh, Michele.'

'Yes, but will it get us laid?' he said.

'Come on, get in, and we'll find out.'

12

The ChronoConverter landed me in a small grove of trees. I looked around cautiously to get my bearings and to see if anyone was around. It was difficult to see anything, so I strolled out of the grove, trying to look casual. To my surprise, I found I was on the top of a plateau. In front of me and far below me in the distance was a stretch of sparkling blue sea. The sky was also blue and clear of clouds. A pleasantly warm breeze fanned my face. After travelling from chilly England, it seemed delightful. Off to my left, and at least a mile below me, was an astonishing sight. It was, I hoped and assumed, the city of Syracuse. The city seemed to stand right on the sea. It was protected on all sides by towering defensive walls. The large harbour was filled with many ships, both merchant ships and warships, most of them gaily painted in bright colours and flying colourful bunting. A spit of land stretched out into the sea beyond the harbour and, right at the far point of the spit, was a massive fortress. I watched the activity in the harbour for many minutes, transfixed by a sight that time should never have allowed me to see. I looked behind to discover another astonishing sight. It looked like a gigantic disused quarry, with huge limestone cliffs towering behind it. The dip in the ground where the quarry had once been was now completely covered in grass. All around me, dotted over the grassy slopes, were tall trees, similar to the ones in the grove in which I had landed. The were spindly and cone-shaped, like unopened green umbrellas with their handles stuck in the ground. The whole effect of this scenery was breathtakingly lovely. Then I remembered why I had travelled to this place and wondered why the ChronoConverter had landed me so far away from the city. Perhaps it had been too dangerous to land me in Syracuse itself. I started walking down the slope towards the city. I had walked only a few yards when I heard somebody singing. I looked across to see a woman sitting beneath a tree, her back supported by the trunk, with her skirt pulled up to expose most of her legs. In her lap were apples, which she was peeling and placing in a small wooden pale which was filled with water. She was singing and humming to herself, a picture of blissful contentment. I was loathe to disturb her so I moved off to avoid her but she caught my movement out of the corner of her eye and shrieked with surprise. Her first concern was to pull her skirt back down over her legs. The remaining apples tumbled out of her lap and on to the grass. There was a low whitewashed cottage only a few yards beyond her and I guessed that is where she lived. Perhaps she was a shepherdess or goat herd. She was a woman of about forty years of age. A red headscarf tied back her long black hair. She had a full face, almost plumpish, with wide set dark eyes and a small mouth below a cute button nose. She had a voluptuously full figure. Her overall appearance was most pleasantly attractive. And there was something else . . . she looked familiar to me. I knew I had seen her before but I knew I could not have done. She was shocked to see a finely-dressed gentleman, as I purported to be, appear seemingly out of nowhere behind her. I held up my hands to reassure her and said: 'Please don't be alarmed, signora. I mean no harm. I am sorry I startled you.'

'Where have you come from?' she asked.

I made to move towards her but she shifted backwards and I stopped immediately. 'I came up from the city,' I said. 'It was such a beautiful day that I felt like taking a stroll. I am a stranger to this country. I am unfamiliar with your ways. I apologise if I am trespassing on your land.'

The woman considered this statement for a few seconds. 'I didn't see you walk up here,' she said. 'I've been sitting here for a long time.'

'No,' I said, bluffing desperately, 'I came up from the other side. I was trying to . . .' At that moment I felt a sharp pain in the middle of my back. A voice whispered: 'Don't move, or I will run you through. What do you want with my wife?'

The woman got to her feet and said: 'No, Mario, don't hurt him. I don't think he means any harm. He is a stranger here.'

Hearing the name Mario, I decided to take a chance that I had arrived at the right place. 'Your wife is right, Signor Minnitti. I did not mean to startle her. I mean no harm. It is you I have come to see.'

'Turn around,' Minnitti ordered. I did so, and saw that Minnitti was brandishing a wicked-looking rapier. His appearance was just as Merisi had described him. He was expensively dressed but in a casual style. He wore a fine linen shirt, open at the neck, with black velvet breeches and elegant brown leather boots. 'I do not recognise you,' he said, still pointing the sword towards me. 'Who are you and what do you want with me?'

With that thin deadly blade waving at my face, I decided to give Minnitti my credentials as rapidly as I could. 'My name is Stefano Maddano. I have travelled from Rome to see you under the blessing and protection of His Holiness Pope Paul, and at the request of your friend Michelangelo Merisi, known as Caravaggio.'

The reaction to this statement was not as I expected. Minnitti seemed unmoved but his wife gasped audibly and clutched at the folds in her skirt. 'Caravaggio is dead,' Minnitti said. 'How could he have sent you?'

'We became friends in Naples. He was in fear of his life. He asked me, if anything bad ever happened to him, to find out who had perpetrated the deed, for the peace of his immortal soul.'

Signora Minnitti said: 'He was a devil. He deserved to go where he has gone. He has gone to hell.'

Well, Bedfordshire's not that bad, I thought, but said: 'I have a warrant from the pope in my doublet. Will you allow me to take it out and show it to you without running me through with that sword?'

'Very well,' Minnitti said, 'but be careful.'

I took out the warrant and handed it to Minnitti. He gestured for his wife to move in and read it with him, all the while flicking glances at me to make sure I didn't move.

'Signor Minnitti,' I said. 'Before you decide what to do, could I talk to you in private, man-to-man, for a minute?'

'I keep no secrets from my wife,' Minnitti replied. 'Say what you have to say.'

'Very well. Michele told me that you had once killed a man, and I am aware of another incident in your life of a similar nature.' His wife looked unsurprised by this statement and Minnitti did not interrupt, so I carried on. 'Let me say that I am not at all interested in those incidents. I am only concerned about what happened to our mutual friend Michelangelo. I am not here to mete out punishment, whatever I find out, only to honour a promise I made to Michele. Michele always spoke very well of you, as a good friend, so I do not suspect you of any involvement in his murder.' I deliberately emphasised the word 'murder', but there was no visible reaction from either of them. 'You knew Michele very well during his early years in Rome. It may be that you have information that is useful to me in finding his killer.' Again there was no reaction at the use of the word 'killer', so I pushed my luck and said: 'You don't seemed surprised that your old friend may have been murdered?'

Minnitti made a contemptuous sound and said: 'Dear Michele made so many enemies that I would not have been surprised if he had been stoned to death by a crowd of them.' He looked at his wife and she nodded. They were obviously devoted to each other. Minnitti lowered the rapier and said: 'Come up to the cottage. We will take a glass of wine and talk. But don't try to trick me. I have a dagger as well.' He showed me a stiletto dagger tucked in a loop behind his back.

After seeing that dagger, and knowing that he had used it in earnest at least twice, I held up my hands and promised him: 'No tricks,' and meant it whole-heartedly.

As we walked towards the cottage, Minnitti was waving the rapier in a non-threatening but still alarming way as he talked. 'How well did you know Michele?' he asked.

'Not very well. I only met him at the end of his life.'

'A . . . strange and difficult man,' Minnitti said.

'Indeed he is . . .was,' I agreed. 'But a great artist. I can forgive him anything just for that.'

'You consider that the production of great works of art makes up for him being a worthless wretch as a human being?'

'Not completely,' I answered, 'but it goes a long way towards it.'

Minnitti's wife said: 'They should burn all of his pictures and never mention his name again.'

'As you can tell,' Minnitti said dryly, 'my wife does not share your high opinion of Michelangelo Merisi.'

I said: 'I suspect, signora, that even if all of Michele's pictures were burned, his reputation and achievement would live on in the minds of those who saw them and the memory handed down to the generations.'

'My name is Rafaella,' Signora Minnitti said. 'You may call me Rafaella. You seem like a gentleman, unlike your friend Merisi.'

'Thank you,' I replied. 'I am honoured. Tell me, I am surprised to find you living up here. Is there no danger from banditti here outside the town walls?'

'Not to us,' Minnitti answered. 'The Spanish garrison keeps them away from the town. And I am known to the local banditti. I painted a portrait of their leader. He was so pleased with it that he ordered me untouchable. That is why we can take our leisure up here in this beautiful place, while others cannot. That is why my wife was so surprised by your presence here.'

We had arrived at the cottage. Outside the cottage was a rough wooden table with rough wooden benches placed either side. Minnitti beckoned me to take the far bench so that my back was to the cottage wall. He sat down on the other bench so that he would be able to block my escape if I tried anything. He placed the rapier on the ground. It was out of my reach but easily within his. Rafaella went into the cottage and returned with a carafe of wine and three glasses. She poured the wine and I took a sip. It was just as sour as the wine that Pope Paul had given me but I wanted to retain their friendly favour by downing the glassful with every impression of having enjoyed it.

'Signor Minnitti,' I began, 'I have been trying to find out about Michele's early career in Rome, about his time with Cardinal Pucci, Lorenzo Siciliano and Antiveduto Grammatica. You met Michele as soon as he arrived in Rome, I believe, and became friends with him?'

'That's correct.'

'What did you think of Michele?'

'Not much,' Minnitti replied. 'I became a friend of Michele because I was paid to become his friend.'

For a moment, I thought I had not heard this bombshell statement correctly. Perhaps the ChronoTranslator had not translated it correctly? 'Excuse me, Signor Minnitti, but did you say that you had been paid to become his friend?'

'That is exactly what I said,' he confirmed. 'And you may call me Mario.'

'Signor Minnitti . . . Mario, I must confess that this information is a total surprise to me.'

'It would be, because nobody else in the world, except the person who paid me and my dear Rafaella here, knows about it.'

'Well, I thank you for your frankness.'

Minnitti said: 'The pope himself has ordered me to tell you the truth, so that is what I must do. I am a God-fearing man and God has been good to me. I have a wife I love, healthy children, a small talent as a painter which I have turned into a successful business, I am wealthy, and I live on this beautiful island. God has granted me all the happiness that was denied to Michele.'

'Because he was a Godless man. A devil,' Rafaella chipped in.

'From what I have heard about you, Mario, you are far too modest. Your fame as an artist has spread far and wide.'

He smiled. 'There is no need to butter me up, Signor Maddano. I have been successful as an artist, in monetary terms but, compared to Michele, I am a poor artisan. As are most other artists, I should add.'

'Please call me Stefano,' I said. 'And please tell me why you were paid to become a friend of Michele and who paid you.'

'The simple and honest truth is that I don't know, even to this day,' Minnitti replied. 'I am Sicilian by birth and in my youth I was as hot-blooded as only Sicilian youths can be. I was apprenticed as a painter here in Syracuse. I had nearly finished my apprenticeship when, one evening, I got into a drunken fight over a girl. I ended up killing my rival. I ran him through with this very dagger.' Minnitti pointed to the dagger stashed behind his back. 'I was imprisoned and charged with his murder. I had no defence. Many people had witnessed my deed. I was in grave danger from the boy's family, who were seeking revenge. For the time being I was safe in prison but I did not know whether I would end up being executed by the law or by my victim's family. I did not regret what I had done, although it was stupid. I had been cuckolded by that jeering bastard. He had dishonoured me and the girl I loved or, in my adolescent naïvety, thought I loved. I felt as vengeful as I would do if someone dishonoured Rafaella, although I love Rafaella infinitely more than I ever loved that girl.' The couple exchanged fond glances.

'How did you get out of this predicament?' I asked.

'One night, as I languished in prison, the cell door was opened and I was taken out and escorted to a small room within the prison. I was ushered into this room. There was a man sitting at a table. We were alone. I asked him who he was. He ignored me. On the table was a cloak with a hood. He told me that I was being released. He ordered me to put on the cloak. Of course, I was full of questions. He ignored them all. There was about him an air of authority. He was used to commanding men, to being obeyed. Finally, I did as I was told and put on the cloak. He ordered me to pull the hood up over my head. He told me to follow him and that if I tried to escape he would kill me without a qualm. I believed him. He led me out of the prison, through the town, and down to the harbour. He escorted me on to a felucca. He said it would set sail at dawn and take me to Malta and, in the meantime, not to show myself. I asked him: "What if I do not feel like going to Malta?". "Then you will die, without mercy, by my hand", he replied. I decided that Malta seemed the more desirable prospect. He gave me a small bagful of coins and told me that I would be met when I arrived in Malta.'

'You have no idea who this man was?' I asked.

'No, truly, to this day I have no idea,' Minnitti replied. 'We landed in Malta and, as I had been told, another man met me as I disembarked. Again, I asked him who he was and what was going on. Again, I was met with silence. He took me to a small hostelry and showed me into a small room where I was to stay the night. I sat down on the bed. This man remained standing. He told me that the next day I was going to sail for Rome. If I refused, I would be taken back to Syracuse and I would be executed. If I tried to escape the task that had been allotted to me, I would be found and executed without mercy. If, however, I dutifully performed my allotted task I would be well paid, on a regular basis, and all charges against me in Syracuse would disappear, and my victim's family would be prevented from ever seeking revenge against me. Obviously, I asked what my task was to be. I was to go to Rome to become an artist, I was told. Well, that was what I intended to do anyway, at some time. As soon as I arrived in Rome I was to find a fellow artist named Michelangelo Merisi, from the town of Caravaggio in Lombardy, and to become a friend to him. I was to stay as close to him as possible, to protect him from any harm, as far as I was able. They, whoever they were, knew that I was handy with a sword and a dagger and that I was not afraid to use them. I was to make a note of what this Merisi was doing and I was to make a regular report on his actions and movements. I asked, what if this Merisi does not wish to become my friend. I was told to make sure that he did or it was back to the gallows in Syracuse for me. I had no choice. I did as I was told. And, I have to admit, I was paid handsomely. The arrangement did me a lot of good financially. I was also to make sure that Merisi did not starve and that he had reasonable living conditions. On no account was he to ever find out that I was watching over him and protecting him. If he did, I was finished.'

'And you made regular reports about all this?' I asked. 'Was anything written down or was it all verbal?'

'All verbal,' Minnitti said. 'I would meet an agent about once a month, in a tavern, and report on what Merisi had been up to.'

'Was this agent the same man as released you from prison in Syracuse or met you in Malta?'

'No, it was a different man. I swear by Almighty God that I have no idea who any of them were, who they were working for, or why all this was being done. And I have never found out to this day. Now that Michele is dead, and the pope has ordered the truth, I see no harm in telling you all this.'

'I know that Michele had close ties with the Colonna family. They helped him in times of trouble throughout his life. Could it have been them who arranged all this?'

Minnitti shrugged, with an expression of helplessness. 'It is possible,' he admitted. 'I know that the Colonna family helped Michele to obtain a place with Cardinal Salad, and . . .'

Rafaella Minnitti giggled at the words 'Cardinal Salad'. I looked at her. She had a merry smile on her face. I suddenly realised, with a shock, where I had seen her before and I knew it was imperative that I could somehow arrange to talk to her on her own, but that would be very difficult. 'Cardinal Salad?' she giggled. 'There is no cardinal called Salad!'

Minnitti smiled indulgently at his wife's amusement. 'That is what Michele, and all the artists, called the mean and pompous Cardinal Pandolfo Pucci,' he explained. 'Praise God I did not have to work for him. I like my food and I do not like bardassas.'

Rafaella was intrigued, and was about to ask more questions about this character Pucci, but I did not want the conversation to go off track. I quickly said: 'Yes, I would like to ask you about Michele's time with Pucci later on, but I am still intrigued by this guardianship you were ordered to place on Michele. You obviously survived to tell the tale. Knowing how Michele was, it must have been very difficult for you. How did you cope with it?'

'It was very difficult. At times I disliked him intensely. At other times he could be charming and good company. In the early days, we roamed the streets hawking our pictures, or trying to persuade the dealers to put them in their windows. I modelled for him, frequently, which I hated.'

'Why was that?' I asked.

'He usually made me look like a bardassa. That was the fashionable thing in art at that time, to make boys look like girls and girls look like boys. That was what sold the picture. Of course, the gossip spread that I was a bardassa myself and that I was Michele's bum boy. The girls down on the Ortaccio, in the brothels, knew me differently.'

'Mario!' his wife scolded. 'Such talk is unseemly in front of this gentleman.'

'Hush, woman,' Minnitti responded. 'All that is in the past. If our friend Stefano here was friendly with Michele, he cannot be much of a gentleman.' This was said with gentle humour and I smiled to show that no offence was taken. 'And there was the drinking,' Minnitti continued. 'I like a glass of wine but many a thick head and a day away from my easel was caused by Michelangelo Merisi's fondness for the taverns of Rome. As the years rolled by I became increasingly tired of his company and his way of life. I wanted to concentrate on my own career. I had fallen in love with Rafaella here. She was living with relatives in Rome when we met but she is a good Sicilian girl. We both felt we wanted to get away from Rome and return to our homeland and start a family. In fact, Rafaella knew Michele before she knew me.'

To Rafaella, I said: 'It's clear that you have a low opinion of Michele. How did you get to know him?'

'I was living with my uncle and aunt in Rome. My uncle was a tailor and my aunt was a seamstress. They had a shop making fine clothes for the gentry, both men and women. I am a seamstress so I travelled to Rome to work for them. As a young girl it was exciting for me to be living and working in Rome and sometimes meeting these important people. Merisi came to the shop one day to order a fine suit of clothes. At that time he was just becoming a talked about painter in Rome. He took a shine to me but I would not countenance any relationship with him, and neither would my uncle and aunt. Then I met my Mario, a good Sicilian boy, the same way, when he came to the shop to order a suit of clothes. After that, I often met Merisi through his friendship with Mario. Of course, I did not know at that time that Mario was forced to be a friend to Merisi. He could not tell me. I hated the influence that Merisi had over Mario, the drinking and the fighting and the . . . other women. I was always trying to get Mario away from him, to come back to Sicily. I was puzzled and angry when Mario always refused. Eventually I left Mario and came back to Sicily alone. I thought Mario would follow me but he did not. Now I know why he could not follow me, why he had to stay with Merisi.'

I turned to Minnitti. 'How did you get out of this situation? Did these people release you from your obligation?'

'Not until I asked.' Minnitti replied. 'What had happened, and what nobody had expected, was how famous Michele had become and how out of control he became because of it. He had become the most famous painter in Rome, in all of Italy. Instead of being happy about it, he became increasingly jealous of other artists, increasingly violent and aggressive. In the end, even the people who were paying me realised that it was impossible for me to protect Michele. Events in his life had spiralled way beyond my power to do anything about, even on pain of death. One day, about a year after Rafaella had left me and returned to Sicily, I simply asked to be released from my obligation and, to my surprise, it was agreed. I was free to go, and I immediately came back to Syracuse to find my beloved Rafaella.'

At that point, the beloved Rafaella said to me: 'Do you need me to stay any longer, Signor Maddano?' Then to Mario: 'I should get back home and prepare our evening meal and see to the children.'

Minnitti nodded and said: 'Of course, my dear. I will stay here with Stefano and talk some more about our friend Michele. I will finish my drawings, if the light is good enough, when we have completed our talk.'

I wanted to stay and talk about Minnitti's early days in Rome but I wanted to talk to his wife, alone, even more. I considered that I might not get another chance, so I said: 'After what you have just told me, Mario, I don't think I need to ask you any more questions today. I have an appointment in the city and I would like to go back to consult my notes and ponder what you have told me. I would like to come and see you again sometime.'

'Anytime,' he replied. 'But, next time, come to my studio.'

There was a hint of a warning in Minnitti's last statement and I knew it was now or never to talk to his wife alone. I was about to suggest that I walk back with Rafaella when she beat me to it. She said: 'Perhaps Signor Maddano would be kind enough to escort me back to the city, with your permission, Mario.'

'I would be honoured,' I said quickly, but Minnitti was not keen on this idea. He said: 'Perhaps it is time I returned as well. My drawings can wait for another day.' He rose from the bench but Rafaella said gaily: 'Oh, Mario! I am sure I shall be quite safe with Signor Maddano. He is still young enough to protect me but he is clearly too old to have any designs upon my honour.' Thanks very much I thought, but I was pleased with her efforts to get us way from Mario. She wanted to talk to me alone as much as I wanted to talk to her. Minnitti still looked concerned, so Rafaella said: 'You should finish your drawings. We could do with the money. Signor Maddano is a foreigner, I grant you, but he has spoken to the pope and is here with the pope's blessing. I'm quite sure I will be safe with him.'

Minnitti sat down again but he gave me a look that did not need any accompanying words. It said: 'You mess with my woman and you're a dead man.'

'Let me go and collect my apples,' Rafaella said to me, 'and you can carry them down for me.'

I smiled as she walked away and then turned to Minnitti. 'Thank you for your hospitality,' I said, 'and for your frankness. I hope we will meet again soon.'

'Just make sure my wife arrives home safely,' he replied. I looked at the steely rapier lying on the grass and I was very relieved when Rafaella returned with her bucket of apples. I gallantly took them from her and we said farewell to her husband. He did not move and continued watching us as we walked away down the slope towards the city.

As soon as we were out of sight and earshot, Rafaella said: 'I must trust you with my life or imperil my immortal soul, but if my husband ever finds out the truth, he will kill me. Will you promise never to let him know what I am about to tell you?'

I said: 'If you are going to tell me that you and Michele were lovers, then I already know.' I did not already know but the effect on Rafaella was electric, as I hoped it would be. It made me look more prescient and knowledgeable than I actually was.

'Did Michele tell you?' Rafaella asked, tremulously. We were now well out of sight of Mario, hidden by the slope, and we had stopped walking and faced each other.

'In a way,' I replied, 'because you modelled for him, as the gypsy fortune teller. I recognised you from that painting.' (*Plate 8*).

'God forgive me,' Rafaella breathed and, for a moment, I thought she was about to faint. Beneath her Sicilian complexion, she had turned very pale.

'Let's sit down,' I suggested, and we sat down in the lush warm grass. 'Don't be afraid, Rafaella. I swear that nobody will know about your relationship with Michele until long after it ceases to matter. I am not here to incriminate anyone, or apportion blame, or to interfere in personal matters. Whatever you tell me, Mario will not hear of it, unless you give me permission. This I swear on my immortal soul.' Rafaella could not know that such an oath meant nothing to me and yet I felt a pang of guilt about my deception. She looked at me appraisingly and I attempted a Jimmy Stewart look of the utmost integrity.

'You have heard what my Mario is like,' she said. 'He has actually killed someone over a girl. You can imagine what he would do if he ever found out that Michele and I had been . . . lovers.'

'But you talked as if you hated Michele. Is that true?'

'Yes, I did hate him . . . in the end. He was using me, as he used everybody. When he came to our shop for his suit of clothes, I was fascinated by him. He was not quite the famous man, at that time, that he later became but I knew of his growing reputation as an artist. He was tall and good-looking and he had a swaggering confidence that was irresistible. He asked me to model for him, for a picture he had in mind. He said I had a perfect face for it, a beautiful face. He said the picture would make him rich and famous and it would also make me famous. I was an impressionable girl. I fell for it. I modelled for him and slept with him, God forgive me. My uncle and aunt never knew. Nobody ever knew. He was the first man I had ever had. The only man, apart from Mario, I have ever had. He took me whenever he fancied, until I met Mario. Michele was like the devil. I could not refuse him and, in the end, I feared him. I wanted to get away from him but I could not resist him. Then he became the most famous painter in Rome. When I met Mario and fell in love with him, I was horrified that he knew Michele so well. Michele, in that sadistic way of his, was amused by the whole situation. When all three of us were together, he used to tease me, to drop little hints about what had gone on between us in the past. But he was careful never to let Mario know the truth. Michele knew that Mario had killed over a girl and was quite capable of killing him because of me. I tried to get Mario away from him. I couldn't understand why Mario would not leave him but, as we have just been talking about, Mario had no choice. It was an awful situation. In the end, I could stand it no longer. I left them both and came back here to Syracuse.'

'What about the painting?' I asked. 'I recognised you from that picture. Weren't you afraid that Mario, or someone else, would recognise you from that picture?'

'Yes,' Rafaella said. 'I was terrified. Michele was selling it on the open market but luckily some cardinal very soon bought the picture and kept it in his palazzo, so Mario has never seen it. Is that where you saw it?'

'Err, yes, that's right,' I lied.

'Fortunately, none of the cardinal's friends would know a little shop girl like me. Nobody, except you, has recognised that the gypsy is me. When you suddenly turned up asking all these questions I was terrified that Mario might find out about Michele and me. That is why I decided to throw myself on your honour and beg you not to tell Mario. Oh, Signor Maddano, I truly love Mario. We have a fine life here. I have healthy children that I love more than life itself. We have food in our stomachs and wine on the table. Mario has been a violent man in the past but he has never given the children and I anything but love and protection. Please don't take all this away from me.'

'Rafaella,' I assured her. 'I can see why Mario loves you and, perhaps, why Michele may have loved you, in his own peculiar way. I swear again that I will do or say nothing that will cause you harm. But I have to ask you one final question and, remember, the Holy Father has enjoined you to tell me the truth.'

Rafaella looked at me with fear in her eyes. 'What is it?' she asked.

I said: 'Did you, or your husband, have anything to do with the death of Michele, or do you have any knowledge of anyone who did?'

'No,' Rafaella said emphatically and with relief. 'I know I hated Michele in the end but I could do nothing to harm him so grievously.'

'And Mario?' I asked.

'No. Despite of everything, he and Michele were friends, of a sort. I have no knowledge of anything Mario might have done to harm Michele.'

I stood up and helped Rafaella to her feet. 'Come along then, Signora Minnitti. I must get you home safely, to your children, and you can show me where Mario's studio is, in case I have to visit him again.'

To my surprise, she kissed me lightly on the cheek. 'You are an unusual man,' she said. 'You speak strangely, you act strangely, and yet I know I can trust you. I don't know why.'

'It must be the gypsy in your soul,' I said, and was rewarded with her delightful sparkling laughter. At her front door, in the bustling streets of Syracuse, I parted from Rafaella with real regret.

13

The ChronoConverter transported me back from Syracuse and landed me in my bedroom, which is at the front of my cottage. It was very dark so I shrewdly guessed it must be late at night. I was about to switch on the bedside lamp when I became aware of a blue light flashing through the fabric of my drawn bedroom curtains. There was also a very noisy commotion going on outside. People were shouting at each other and there was a graunching sound of metal being scraped along another surface. I pulled back the curtain and saw my beloved Alfa Romeo GTV hanging nose-down from a portable crane. The Alfa had all its doors open and there was water pouring out of it. I ran downstairs and out of the front door and gazed helplessly at my forlornly dangling car. The front of the car had been stoved in. The bonnet lid was open, making the car look like a gaping fish that had just been landed.

'Mr. Maddan!' screeched the outraged voice of my neighbour, Mrs. Chowdry, who was standing in her front garden. 'Your guest has just wrecked our garden fence, our plum tree and our ornamental pond!' She indicated the wreckage strewn in her garden. Her husband stood by her side, watching impassively as my car was lifted clear of their ornamental pond. He patted his wife on the arm to try to calm her down. 'There, there,' he said, as if she was a child. 'I'm sure it was just an accident.'

I became aware of two police officers looking at me warily. I realised that I had done it again and forgotten to change into modern dress. I was still dressed like an Elizabethan dandy. I recognised the police officers as Sergeant Caro and P.C. Greenfield, her very tall male colleague. They were the same two officers who had first brought Merisi to my home, which seemed a lifetime ago.

'Mr. Maddan!' Sergeant Caro exclaimed. 'We've been waiting for you to return home. Have you been at home all the time?'

I remembered to slip off the ChronoTranslator ring before I started gabbling away in Italian. 'What? No,' I replied. 'I've just got back from rehearsals. We're doing Hamlet in the village hall. For Christmas.'

'They're doing it in Italian as well,' Mrs. Chowdry added helpfully.

'I thought they were doing Babes In The Wood in the village hall for Christmas?' the giant police constable Greenfield said.

'No, that was last year,' Mr. Chowdry said. 'I thought it was Ali Baba and the Forty Thieves this year. I was approached to play Ali Baba, probably because of my colour.'

'Were you offended by such a racist approach?' Greenfield asked.

'Racist?' Mr. Chowdry said, puzzled. 'No, I was honoured, old chap. I was up for Aladdin one year but I wasn't yellow enough.'

'Be careful what you are saying, sir,' Greenfield warned. 'Such a remark could be deeply offensive to the Chinese community in Bedford.'

'But none of them are here to hear it?' Mr. Chowdry said.

'That's not the point,' Greenfield said. He turned his attention to me. 'Are you sure they are doing Hamlet this year? It seems an odd choice for a Christmas panto?'

'Look, never mind the Christmas panto, why is my car dangling from the end of a crane. What on earth has been going on here?' As if I needed to ask.

'When did you get back?' Sergeant Caro persisted.

'Well, just now,' I said.

'Which way did you come in?'

'Uhh, through the back way,' I said.

'What back way. The river runs along the back of these properties. How did you get across the river?'

'I didn't,' I said, 'I nipped over the garden fences.'

'Why? That's trespassing!' Caro said.

'Because I'd forgotten my ordinary clothes and I felt like a prat, so I came the back way so nobody would see me.'

'I'd advise you not to forget your street clothes again when going out to rehearse,' Greenfield said.

'Thank you for that sage advice, Inspector Clouseau. Can we forget about how I'm dressed and how I got home and would somebody please tell me what the hell has happened here?'

Sergeant Caro ignored my question and asked: 'Why didn't you inform us that Mr. Merisi was staying with you? I rang to warn you that he had absconded from Yarl's Wood immigration centre. You could have saved us a lot of work and trouble by letting us know. We have been looking for him.'

'I repeatedly asked the authorities to keep Mr. Merisi away from me and you failed, so I thought I might as well save myself all the anxiety and let him stay with me anyway. Perhaps you could bring him his pipe and slippers, if it's not too much trouble. Will you have to take him back to Yarl's Wood?'

'Not if he is staying with you and you are taking responsibility for him,' Sergeant Caro replied, keen to clear another problem off her desk.

Mrs. Chowdry, who had been listening to this conversation, said: 'Never mind Yarl's Wood. Broadmoor would be a more appropriate domicile for that man.'

'Okay, okay,' I said. 'Can you please tell me what has happened to my car?'

Sergeant Caro said: 'We were on patrol in the village, luckily, when we received an emergency call to these premises. It seems that your house guest, Mr. Merisi, tried to borrow your car. He's a bit confused about it all. I suspect that your car must have been in gear. He probably switched on the ignition and the car shot through the garden fence, knocked down your neighbour's plum tree and fell into their ornamental pond. The fountain is ruined.' The stoneware stork, which I detested, was also smashed to smithereens, so some good had come out of the evening after all.

'Where is Mr. Merisi?' I asked. 'Was he hurt?'

'No,' Caro replied. 'He's over there, helping them load your car on to the transporter.' My Alfa Romeo had now been manouevred on to the back of the crane transporter. It looked like a write-off.

I saw Merisi peeping warily around the side of the transporter. 'There he is,' I said.

The Jolly Greenfield Giant, as I was beginning to think of him, walked over to get Merisi. Greenfield led him by the arm back towards me. I realised that I must curb my temper until a more appropriate time. The last thing we wanted was all this fuss and attention, let alone for Merisi to be arrested.

'Hello, Michele,' I greeted him. 'I'm glad you are unhurt.'

Merisi nodded. From next door, Mrs. Chowdry shouted: 'How long is that dreadful man staying with you, Mr. Maddan? Urinating all over your garden was bad enough, but now he's wrecked our garden!'

'Why don't you shut up, woman!' Merisi shouted back. Then to Mr. Chowdry: 'Can't you control your wife, the screeching shrew. Act like a man!'

Mr. Chowdry looked completely bemused. His wife said: 'Screeching shrew? He called me a screeching shrew! How dare you!'

'Look here, old man,' Mr. Chowdry said. 'Steady on.'

Merisi bent down, picked up a lump of turf, and hurled it at the Chowdrys before I or the police officers could stop him. I roughly pulled Merisi to one side and whispered: 'For fuck's sake calm down. You'll get us both arrested and that'll ruin everything.' He was still fuming, but he did as he was told, especially when P.C. Greenfield moved towards him to prevent any more incidents.

I walked over to what was left of the garden fence and said to the Chowdrys: 'I'm most terribly sorry about all this. I will pay for all the damage that's been caused.'

'I'm sure it was an accident,' Mr. Chowdry said. 'No harm done.'

'No harm done!' his wife rounded on him. 'Our front garden has been destroyed!'

'We can put it right, dear,' Mr. Chowdry said.

'Not that dear little plum tree, we can't,' she said. 'We can't replace years of growth.'

I said: 'I'm sure my insurance company will buy you a new plum tree, Mrs. Chowdry.'

She glared at Merisi. 'When is that dreadful man going home to Italy where he belongs? This was a quiet and respectable neighbourhood before he arrived. He is a disgrace.'

'I agree,' I said, 'and I will make sure that he behaves himself in future.'

'Just see that he does,' Mrs. Chowdry warned.

At that point, one of the breakdown mechanics came up to me and said: 'We've loaded your car. We'll take it back to the garage but it looks like a write-off to me. We'll let you know in the morning. Sign here, please.' He handed me a clipboard with a filled out damage report and receipt attached to it. I signed and handed it back. Then, turning back to the police officers, I asked: 'What happens now? Will there be any charges against Mr. Merisi?'

The two police officers looked at each other. 'I don't think so,' Sergeant Caro said to her colleague. 'All this happened on private property, not on the highway. Mr. Merisi is unhurt. You have offered to pay for the damage. I don't see any real reason for taking it any further.' She looked at Merisi. 'You seem to have a great propensity for causing trouble, Mr. Merisi. We'll let this go without further action but the next time you do anything like this, you may not be so fortunate.'

Merisi made to move towards her and opened his mouth to speak. I grabbed his arm and said: 'Just shut up and stand still.'

'Thank you for being so reasonable about all this,' I said to the officers. I suspected they were equally relieved not to have to tackle all the paperwork involved in an arrest. I turned to the Chowdrys. 'I'll come and see you tomorrow and we can sort out what we can do to put this right,' I said.

They nodded and went back inside their house. I watched my car being driven away on the transporter. The police officers climbed in their patrol car and set off after the transporter. I went back inside my cottage. Merisi followed me in. I closed the front door. Unable to contain my fury any longer, I shouted at him: 'Just what in the name of fucking hell do you think you were doing?'

Merisi shoved me back against the wall. 'Fuck off,' he shouted back. One of the pictures hanging on the wall, a nineteenth century engraving of Margate pier, crashed to the floor as I fell back on to it.

I launched myself back at Merisi in a blind rage, rugby tackled him around the legs and brought him crashing down on to the carpet. Unfortunately, as I did so, I banged my head against the newel post of the staircase and nearly knocked myself out. Both Merisi, totally surprised by the ferocity of my response, and myself, dazed by the bang on my head, just sat on the floor and stared at each other. Merisi spoke first: 'I'm stuck in this fucking house all day while you travel backwards and forwards in time. I wanted to use your car to go into town, maybe get drunk, find a woman. You never take me. I've watched you drive that car. I thought it would be easy. I took that key and as soon as I turned it, the car shot forward before I could stop it.'

'First of all,' I said, still trying to get my breath and my senses back, 'you have to learn how to drive a car. They are very powerful. Especially mine. They can be deadly if they are not driven properly. You have to pass a test to get a licence to drive a car. You have no licence. What is more, you know nothing about road signs, rules of the road, or anything else. You can't just get in a car and drive it without any knowledge of what you are doing.'

Merisi got to his feet and came over to help me up. 'I am sorry,' he said. It was about as abject an apology as he was ever able to manage. 'Have you enough money to pay for all that damage?'

'Just about,' I said. 'The way you are going, I might as well have the insurance assessor move in with me. It'll save him time. And you had better do that painting you promised me. That'll pay for a thousand fences.'

'I have promised, haven't I,' Merisi said, as we staggered into the living room. 'Let me pour you some of that whisky. You look pale.'

'Pale!' I exclaimed. 'No wonder I'm pale! Your friend Mario Minnitti threatened to run me through with a rapier and then I come back to find you destroying half the neighbourhood. What is it with you Italians?'

I sat down in an armchair and Merisi handed me a glass of whisky. He grinned as he sat down with his glass. He took a big gulp. 'So you found my friend Mario?'

'Yes, I did.'

'Did you learn anything useful from him?'

I was not going to tell Merisi anything about the extraordinary 'guardian angel' arrangement that Minnitti had described to me, or about what Rafaella had told me about her relationship with Merisi. I decided to test the water to gauge Merisi's reaction, to see how honest he was being with me. 'He confirmed everything that you have told me and what historians have already found out. So, nothing particularly useful,' I said, 'except that he his very protective of that wife of his.'

For a brief moment, a look of concern crossed Merisi's face, but he said: 'You met Rafaella?'

'Yes'.

'What did you think of her?'

I shrugged, as if indifferent to her. 'Nothing much,' I replied. 'She serves lousy wine, but then so did the pope.'

Merisi laughed. Was there relief in that laugh? I couldn't be sure. I said: 'I know you've been cooped up in here for too long, Michele. We will go into town soon. We will take a taxi, then we can both get drunk. In fact, we'll have to take a taxi, because I no longer have a car.'

14

Later that evening, when my temper had cooled and my head had cleared, I took a hot shower and then went to bed, but I could not sleep. I lay in bed listening to the drunken snoring emanating from Merisi's room and mentally examined the astonishing revelations that I had been told by Minnitti and his wife Rafaella. I was already very much aware that my house guest, Merisi, was determined to keep many secrets from me, such as his time in prison in Milan, his relationship with his family, and now his relationship with Rafaella. I would have to overcome his reluctance to tell me everything, and that was in addition to all the other problems I faced in finding out the truth about his life and death. The most astonishing revelation, of course, was that Michele had had protection on a personal level through Minnitti. It was a matter of historical record that the Colonna family had protected Merisi during some difficult times but the extent of this guardianship was very surprising. I concluded that it must have been the Colonna family taking care of Merisi. Who else would be in the slightest degree interested in a struggling painter from Lombardy? I considered that, very soon, I would have to travel back in time to interview one of the Colonna clan, perhaps the Marchese Costanza Colonna, who had been very fond of Michele's father and had been fond of Merisi himself. Even so, it seemed unlikely that a noble and distinguished lady would go to such lengths to protect the son of an employee, however fond she was of him. It was troubling, and sleep came fitfully that night.

The next day, as was becoming our habit, Michele and I settled into our armchairs in front of the unlit gas fire, with a mug of coffee each, to continue the investigation into his life. I consulted Helen Langdon's biography and asked: 'You have said that you were happy working in the studio of Antiveduto Grammatica and yet you didn't stay with him for very long. Why was that?'

'Plain ambition,' Merisi replied. 'Yes, I was happy with Grammatica but, as I have told you before, I knew I had it in me to be a great painter and I was anxious to make a bigger reputation, to have more opportunities for big commissions. Through Cherubino Alberti, I started to put out feelers to some of the bigger, more successful, studios in Rome.'

'Who did you approach?'

'I tried Roncalli first.'

'That would be Cristofero Roncalli, the fresco painter?'

'Yes, that's right,' Merisi confirmed. 'He was a good artist and a learned man. He counted many cardinals and businessmen amongst his patrons. I thought it might be a good move, but he turned me down.'

'Do you know why?' I asked.

'I think he was intrigued by the work I had already done, especially the portrait of Cardinal Baronio, but Roncalli worked mainly in fresco, in which I was very inexperienced. He worked in a stuffy, mannered style. He thought my new bolder and dramatic approach would not suit his clients. That was the reason he gave, anyway.'

'Do you think there was another reason why he turned you down?'

'I had met him a few times. He was a very pious, virtuous and serious man. He had respect and love for his trade. I suspect that my temperamental ways, my drinking and whoring, would not have suited him at all. I think he was right. I bore him no resentment for his refusal.'

'Who did you approach next?' I asked.

Merisi smiled and shook his head with contempt. 'Next I tried the great Federico Zuccaro,' he said. 'I must have been mad! He was much older than me and he was the most wealthy and celebrated artist in Rome but his work was out of fashion. Even allowing for my well-known dismissive hostility to some of my fellow artists, I really did think his work was very poor. I couldn't understand why he had been so successful. It just shows how low the standard of art had become, before I arrived, that such a useless cunt had had so much fame and success. This pompous bastard would parade around in his finery pontificating about how painting should be. Do you know, he was also building his own palazzo! Just imagine! A lowly artist, just like me, trying to live like a prince or a cardinal! And he covered the walls of his palazzo with frescoes glorifying his own career! Was there ever such an arrogant pig!? I'll tell you truly, Stefano, many have called me arrogant but I am a model of modesty compared to Zuccaro. And do you know what he once said about my work? That it was nothing but a poor copy of Giorgione! That from a man who wouldn't know a Bellini from a pile of dog shit. Still, Bernardino and me taught him a lesson he didn't forget.'

'What do you mean "taught him a lesson", Michele? And who is Bernardino?'

Merisi was breathing heavily after his angry tirade against Zuccaro. 'It was nothing,' he said, realising he had admitted too much. 'Forget it.'

'Come on, Michele,' I urged. 'You must tell me the truth. It may be important.'

'Very well,' he said. 'Meeting Bernardino was a stroke of good fortune for me. He was a man after my own heart. He had been condemned to death for consorting with bandits. He had been forced to flee to Naples, just as I had to do later, but he had been pardoned and has just returned to Rome when I met him in a tavern. He had heard of me, and his adventures had been the talk of the art world for months. He was very entertaining company, always ready for a prank or a laugh, never out of sorts, even with a bastard like me baiting him, so we hit it off very well. Best of all, he was the brother of, and the chief assistant to . . .'

'Giuseppe Cesari, known as the Cavaliere d'Arpino.'

Merisi looked at me appreciatively. 'You know your stuff, Stefano. Yes, Bernardino was the brother of the new superstar of the Roman art world. Is "superstar" a proper word, or is my ChronoTranslator defective?'

'It is a proper modern word. The ChronoTranslator is working perfectly,' I said.

'Good. Well, as you know, Giuseppe Cesari, Cavaliere d'Arpino, was the most successful painter in Rome at that time. I had just become bosom buddies with his brother. Bosom buddies?' Merisi repeated. 'Another strange expression? I did not play with Bernardino's titties!'

'Don't worry,' I said, 'I know what it means. Carry on.'

'Cesari was only a couple of years older than me but he was way ahead of me in reputation. He had come to Rome with his mother, very quickly landed a job with a team of fresco painters at the Vatican and was hailed as a prodigy. His work was light and elegant. He painted in light, clear colours, very different to my approach. He also turned out beautifully finished easel paintings on mythological subjects. All his work had become highly fashionable. He worked for, and was friends with, many powerful and wealthy men, not least the pope himself. Giuseppe was an odd character, very different from Bernardino. But Bernardino persuaded his distinguished brother to find me a place in their studio.'

I asked: 'When you say that Giuseppe Cesari was odd, what do you mean?'

'Well, he had been blessed by God with everything that a man and an artist could wish for. As an artist, he was very talented and had been more successful, at an earlier age, than almost any other artist I can think of. As a man, he was tall, good-looking in a rather haughty, aristocratic way, with fine black hair, a clear complexion, strong teeth, and abundant energy. He never seemed to tire, or to become ill. He was intelligent, cultured . . . witty, even, when he had a mind to be. Tell me, Stefano, such a man should wake up every morning, say a prayer to God to thank Him for such a life, and walk around all day with a big smile on his face, is that not so?'

'Yes, it is,' I agreed.

'Not Giuseppe! He was the most miserable, the most pessimistic, the most ungrateful man I have ever known! Whatever he had achieved, however many honours and compliments he received, it was never enough and he felt slighted because there had not been more. However accomplished and popular his painting was, he felt dissatisfied because it was not good enough. And, if the slightest thing went wrong, he was convinced that the fates were conspiring to ruin him. I have known beggars in the gutter who were more grateful for their lot in life. Giuseppe had everything and yet thought himself hard done by. After I joined his studio, Bernardino and I had fun with him. Any little snag we could think of, any tiny little problem that occurred, we would turn into a major disaster and Giuseppe would fret about it all day. He never caught on what we were doing. How we laughed at him!'

'What sort of work did you do in Cesari's studio?'

'Oh, I got stuck with the usual hack work that I was so good at,' Merisi sighed. 'Mainly I worked adding decorative swags of fruit and flowers on Cesari's frescoes or adding such elements to his easel paintings. He ran a large studio and employed many artists. Cesari was also a dealer and, to give him his due, he was very aware of the latest trends and promoted some new trends himself. There were a few Dutch and Flemish painters in his studio. They brought with them a new skill and interest in painting landscape, still life and genre subjects. Their work was brightly coloured, often teeming with tiny figures, full of life. They made a refreshing change from the stuffy Roman art of the time and they gave me many new ideas for when I began to paint as an independent artist. Also, I told Cesari about the Milanese painter Archimboldo who constructed fanciful human heads out of various fruits and flowers. Clever stuff, but gimmicky crap as far as I was concerned, but my colleague Zucchi took up the idea and became very successful at it. Cesari occasionally trusted me with some individual pictures, some portraits and so on. And I assisted him on some big commissions such as the frescoes in the Olgiati chapel in Santa Prassede and the vault frescoes in the Contarelli chapel of San Luigi dei Francesi . . .'

'Where you were to very soon make a big name for yourself,' I interjected. 'We are not certain of any of your surviving pictures that were actually painted in Cesari's studio, except perhaps the boy with a basket of fruit or the sick bacchus.'

'As I have told you, I had completed the boy with basket of fruit long before I joined Cesari, as a presentation piece to show the studios what I could do. As for this sick bacchus you mention, I don't know which one you mean?' Merisi had already seen the reproduction of this work but I opened the complete works of Caravaggio and showed it to him again, his self-portrait with his face suffused with a sickly green tinge. Merisi laughed. 'Was I not handsome then?' he chuckled. 'No, that was done after I left Cesari, when I was recovering in hospital. It was a conceit, a frivolous comment on my own condition at that time. So, it is called Sick Bacchus now, is it?'

'Yes,' I confirmed.

'Well, as good a title as any, although Sick Hungover Satyr would be a better title.' Merisi chuckled again at his own humour.

'Okay, let's get back to Cesari,' I said. 'There are suggestions that a lot of enmity and jealousy developed between you and the Cavaliere. Is that true?'

'Yes, I suppose so. You know how bad-tempered I can be. Despite all of his success and wealth, Cesari was a mean bastard. His pessimistic nature convinced him he was on the verge of losing all his wealth, so he paid as little as possible and gave his employees as little as possible for our comfort. Some of his other assistants accepted this, simply pleased to be working for the great Cavaliere, but I resented this treatment and told him so. His food was lousy and he made me sleep on a straw mattress. Wouldn't even give me a proper bed to sleep on! Yes, my resentment festered.'

I said: 'You stayed with Cesari only for a few months and there are suggestions from your biographers that you left Cesari's studio under a cloud after being involved in some shady business. Was this the business with Federico Zuccaro you mentioned earlier? Some shady dealings involving your friend Bernardino?'

Merisi looked at me, considering whether to tell me everything.

'Come one, Michele,' I urged him, 'what does it matter after four hundred years? You cannot be arrested for it now, whatever it was.'

'It reflects badly on me,' Merisi said. 'I am not proud of what happened.'

'What happened?' I said. 'It might be important. Tell me.'

'Oh, very well,' Merisi shrugged. 'It was all because of what everyone in the art world was calling "the big commission". It was to redecorate one of the Farnese family palazzi. The Farnese family were arguably the wealthiest and most powerful family in Rome. It was to be an immensely lucrative commission. What is more, the young cardinal Odoardo Farnese, who had instigated the commission, was a lover of art and had exceptionally good taste. The winners of the commission would have had a free hand to do as they wished, without the constraints of Cardinal Rusticucci's strictures. It was an exciting prospect. Every studio in Rome was bidding to get it. It finally came down to two studios. Cesari's was one, but you know who won it? That useless cunt Zuccaro!'

'I thought you said that Cardinal Farnese had good taste?' I smiled.

'Well, like you, everyone else was amazed and disappointed. We all thought

Zuccaro was finished and God alone knows what strings he must have pulled to win the commission. The rumour going around was that Zuccaro had offered to do the work for nothing, simply for the prestige and in order to restore his place at the top of the Roman art world. Whether that was true or not, I don't know. Bernardino, Prosperino and me talked about it and decided that we could not allow Zuccaro to get away with it.'

'I take it that Prosperino was your friend Prospero Orsi?' I asked.

'Yes, that's right,' Merisi said. 'We called him Prosperino because he was a small man. He was a staunch friend of Cesari and sang the Cavaliere's praises throughout Rome as the best living artist, until he saw my work that is.' Merisi grinned with self-satisfaction, then went on: 'Prosperino was quite a talented fresco painter but his major talent, which endeared him to the Cavaliere, was as a painter of grotesques.'

'What do you mean by grotesques?' I asked. 'Do you mean ugly faces or something?'

'No, no,' Merisi corrected me. 'A grotesque was a type of fanciful wall decoration that used interlinked motifs, flowers and so on, together with animal or human figures, masks, and other similar elements. The word is derived from the name applied to certain ancient Roman buildings, called "grotte", in which such decoration is found.' The ChronoTranslator translated the word 'grotte' in the modern sense of 'grotty' but I understood what Merisi meant, so I did not interrupt. 'Such work was not to my taste, either doing it or looking at it,' he continued. 'I don't know how Prosperino stood the boredom. He became stuck with that work all the time because he was so good at it. We argued about the nature of art but he was a good friend. We got drunk together many times.'

Before Merisi went off track reminiscing about his friend, I said: 'Let's get back to the so-called "big commission". You mentioned there was a rumour that Zuccaro had offered to decorate the Palazzo Farnese for nothing. That seems an extravagant gesture, even for someone as hungry for glory as Zuccaro?'

'Well, as I have said, I don't know whether that rumour was true or not. Federico had been trained by his brother Taddeo, who had died many years before, and was devoted to Taddeo's memory. Taddeo had made a high reputation for himself when he painted the frescoes for the Farnese palace in Caprarola and the theory was that Federico Zuccaro was desperate to emulate his brother's achievement by winning and completing the Palazzo Farnese commission, and to honour his brother's memory at the same time. What convinced us that Zuccaro had pulled a fast one was the fact that my friend Prosperino's brother, Aurelio, was the secretary to the Farnese family, as well as being a distinguished poet. So, our employer Cesari, through Aurelio Orsi, actually had somebody very influential right at the heart of the Farnese family, and we still could not win the commission! You can well imagine that we brooded and complained and wondered and tried to figure out what had gone wrong. Cesari himself was in despair. To his pessimistic mind, this was the end of the world. So, his brother Bernardino, Prosperino and I decided to do something about it.'

'What could you do?' I asked. 'Short of murdering Zuccaro.'

Merisi looked at me archly. 'Not far wrong, my English friend. We decided that the only way we could stop Zuccaro was by making sure he could not work, for months if need be. We considered simply destroying his studio but that would not have achieved anything. With his wealth, he could have replaced all his equipment and found new premises overnight. No, if Zuccaro himself could not work and oversee his assistants and apply the finishing touches himself, then the Farnese family would have to give the commission to another studio. And which studio would that be? Why, almost certainly my esteemed employer, Giuseppe Cesari, the Cavaliere d'Arpino, who had been runner-up in the original contest.'

'Is violence your answer for everything?' I asked, in exasperation.

'Sometimes it can achieve one's objectives,' Merisi answered lightly, 'but you will be happy to hear that this adventure rebounded on me in a bad way. Naturally, there was a formidable amount of wine consumed while we formulated our strategy.'

'I hardly dare ask,' I said, 'but what was your strategy?'

'Rome was a dangerous city, full of violent men, full of desperate men. Would it be so strange if a group of armed desperadoes broke into a wealthy man's palazzo in search of booty? And if the owner of that palazzo, the distinguished artist Federico Zuccaro, tried to stop such men and he ended up badly injured, perhaps even dead, would there be any connection with a certain commission to decorate the Farnese palace? We thought, in our drunken enthusiasm, that such an assault would be well worth the risk.'

I shook my head in despair. 'It was a despicable plan,' I said. 'What about his wife and family? Didn't you consider the effect on them?'

'No,' Merisi said, bluntly.

'And did the Cavaliere know about this plan?'

'Certainly not. He would never have approved. Not for any moral reason but simply that the worry of it would have driven him crazy. In the end, that is what nearly happened.'

'Okay, so how did you put this plan into effect?' I asked.

'We simply waited and watched Zuccaro's palazzo, up on the Pincian hill, until we were sure that he was at home. The main entrance to his palazzo was surrounded by an archway made to look like a lion with an open mouth! Can you believe the ghastly bad taste of the man! Anyway, we climbed over the wall, which was only half-finished anyway, and climbed through a window into the kitchen of the palazzo. We had dressed ourselves in rags, as if we were beggars, and we wore cloaks with hoods that completely hid our faces. We were armed with cudgels, not swords or daggers. We went in search of Zuccaro. We had assumed that Zuccaro would be alone with his wife and family, perhaps with just a few maids or servants. One of the maids saw us first. She screamed in terror and dropped a jug of water on to the stone floor. This commotion ruined our plan. Before we had got any further, Zuccaro appeared. He was carrying a sword and a dagger. I have to give him credit, he was a big man and he was not a coward. As soon as he saw us, he came at us. Prosperino was already halfway back out of the window. I shouted to Bernardino to follow him while I held off Zuccaro. Remember, I only had a wooden cudgel against Zuccaro's sword and dagger. I managed to grab a metal frying pan, which helped to hold off Zuccaro's swinging sword. Of course, I was trying not to let him see my face. He had only met me briefly once or twice before this day, so he did not know me well, but he was shouting "I know who you are, you villain", or something like that. Luckily, I managed once to get under his guard, punched him in the stomach with the cudgel and caught him a blow to his shoulder with the frying pan. It gave me enough time to get halfway out of the window with my two accomplices trying to pull me out the rest of the way and Bernardino stupidly shouting, "come on, Michele". I almost got away with it but Zuccaro had come at me again and caught the top of my leg with his sword. Fortunately, he caught me more with the flat of the sword than with the edge of the blade, so it gave me a deep gash but didn't sever my leg, as a full-blooded strike might have done. I escaped out of the window, bleeding badly, with my two companions virtually carrying me along. Thankfully, Zuccaro thought that discretion was the better part of valour and did not pursue us, but he was shouting out of the window after us "I know you, you villain. I'll find you". We managed to get back to the studio without attracting the attention of the sbirri.'

'Of the what?' I asked, thinking Merisi's ChronoTranslator had malfunctioned. 'What is sbirri?'

'That was the Roman police force. It was more like a militia rather than the type of police force that you have in England now.'

'I see,' I said. 'You were all luckier than you deserved to be.'

'I admit it was a mad drunken scheme,' Merisi said, 'but if that maid had not seen us first, it might have worked. Anyway, I paid very dearly for this escapade.'

'Did the Cavaliere find out what you three had done?'

'Yes. The attack on Zuccaro swiftly became common knowledge. The Cavaliere knew that I had been wounded. I told him that I had been kicked by a horse but he was no fool. He knew from our behaviour, after we had returned to his studio that night, that we had been up to something. He put two and two together and Bernardino eventually told him what we had attempted to do. I don't think I have ever seen anyone so frantic or angry about anything. He cursed us as stupid idiots. He told us that, if anyone ever linked this attack to his studio, he would be ruined. He was terrified that I had been recognised by Zuccaro and would be exposed. Every time anyone knocked at the door of the studio, the Cavaliere would jump out of his skin.'

'How did you three react?' I asked.

'Bernardino had been under sentence of death for consorting with bandits not so many months before. He was almost as terrified of what might happen as his brother was. Cesari refused to let any of us go out of the studio. He cursed us incessantly for the fools we were. Prosperino, who had been a staunch friend and advocate of the Cavaliere, was particularly incensed by what he saw as the Cavaliere's ungrateful attitude. Prosperino argued that we had only been trying to help the Cavaliere win the big commission, but the Cavaliere was not to be placated. The atmosphere in that studio was very tense. The other assistants knew that something was going on but of course we could not tell them.'

'And how did you react?' I asked.

'Me?' Merisi replied. 'I couldn't care less. Despite what Zuccaro had been shouting, I didn't think he had recognised me at all. I was beginning to feel so ill that I didn't care anyway. The sword wound was beginning to fester but Cesari refused to let me out of the studio to consult a physician. He tried to treat it with some sort of herb concoction that he put a lot of faith in. It didn't work. I began to run a fever. I tried to carry on working. I was trying to finish a version of the death of Saint Joseph, but I collapsed unconscious while I was working. Even then, Cesari did not want me to leave his studio to go to the hospital. He would have preferred me to die rather than endanger his cosy life. Thankfully, my friend Mario Minnitti found out that I was ill. Mario barged his way into the studio and held a dagger to Cesari's throat and told him that if he didn't let him take me to the hospital, he would kill Cesari where he stood. Mario was not a man to be argued with when he had a dagger in his hand and Cesari knew that. Mario arranged a cart to take me to the Ospedale Santa Maria della Conzolazione. That was the end of my service with Giuseppe Cesari, the Cavaliere d'Arpino. After my recovery, he would not let me anywhere near his studio. I didn't want to go back anyway. But before all that, I had to cheat death . . . for the first time in my life.'

'Before we leave the Cavaliere d'Arpino's studio completely,' I said. 'Did you know a Dutch artist at the studio named Floris van Dyck?'

Merisi thought for a few seconds and then said: 'Yes, I did. He was quite an accomplished painter of small still life pictures. Almost as good as me.'

'You may be interested to know that Floris left us the first known biographical comment about you.'

'Really?' Merisi said. 'I can't say we were friends but we were on amiable terms.'

'Well, he seemed to think highly of you.' I found the appropriate page in Helen Langdon's biography and quoted Floris Van Dyck's description of the man sitting opposite me, Michelangelo Merisi da Caravaggio: '"He has climbed up from poverty through hard work and by taking on everything with foresight and courage, as some do who will not be held back by faint-heartedness or lack of courage, but who push themselves forward boldly and fearlessly and who everywhere seek their advantage boldly." What do you think of that?'

'A handsome statement,' Merisi said. 'The trouble is, I was about to sink back into poverty.'

'Before we go on to that, do you think Zuccaro ever found out that you were involved in the attack on his palazzo?'

'No, I'm sure he did not. There were never any repercussions after our stupid jape. I met Zuccaro a few times after that. He just ignored me, or treated me with contempt, as he did many fellow artists, but I'm sure the pompous prick didn't know what I had attempted to do. If you think he had anything to do with my attempted murder, I think it is extremely unlikely, especially as he died a year or two before I was supposed to have. I think the Cavaliere d'Arpino was a much more likely culprit, if you want my opinion.'

'Very well,' I said. 'It sounds safe enough to strike Zuccaro off the list of suspects. I might have to visit the good Cavaliere. But let's move on to your time in hospital.'

'Mario had taken me to the Ospedale Santa Maria della Conzolazione and left me in the care of the brothers. Mario told me afterwards that he had not expected to see me alive again. He had apparently become very agitated at the prospect of my demise. He was a good friend who cared for me deeply. Why are you smiling?' Merisi said. 'This is not funny.'

'No, of course not,' I said. 'Please forgive me, I was thinking of something else for a moment.' I was thinking of Mario Minnitti in mortal fear of retribution from the shadowy figures who had forced him to protect Michele if he had allowed Michele to die.

Merisi continued: 'I was unknown to the brothers of the hospital. Apparently, I was placed in a dark underground chamber, amongst the dying. Of course, I can remember nothing of this. Mario came to visit me and was horrified to find me in such a place. By happy coincidence, this underground chamber was connected to the Palazzo Colonna. Mario went to the palazzo to try to see Costanza, or anyone who could give him money, or help him to get me moved to a better place. Costanza was not in residence but, by good fortune, the prior of the hospital, a Spaniard named Contreras, was visiting the palazzo at that moment. He was a friend of Cardinal Salad and remembered me from my time working for the cardinal at the Palazzo Colonna. Mario showed him where I was, Contreras recognised me, and I was moved to a room on my own, in the continuous care of the sisters working at the hospital. The Colonna family paid generously for my care. Very slowly, the fever subsided, the leg wound healed cleanly and I recovered my health, although I was plagued with headaches and stomach aches for ever after. Prior Contreras could not have been kinder or more solicitous. When he felt I was strong enough, he allowed me to paint in my room. I completed several canvases, including the Sick Bacchus as you call it. I kept that one but the rest I gave to Contreras in gratitude for his care.'

'That's very interesting, Michele, and tallies closely with what we already know about your time in hospital. Prior Contreras sent your pictures back to his homeland in Spain.'

'Yes, I was aware of that,' Merisi said.

'None of them have survived to this day,' I said, 'but you may be interested to know that your pictures had a deep influence on a Spanish painter named Velazquez. He was born about ten years before you died.'

'Was he a good painter?' Merisi asked.

'He is accounted one of the greatest artists who ever lived. Let me show you some of his work.' I went to the bookcase and pulled out the History of World Art. I showed Merisi some of the Spanish artist's early works, such as An Old Woman Cooking Eggs and The Water Seller of Seville. 'I can see your influence, especially in his early pictures,' I said. 'Later on, he became the royal court painter and pursued fame and wealth rather than artistic achievement but he was a very accomplished painter.'

Merisi looked at the Rokeby Venus and Las Meninas. 'Yes, he was clearly very talented.' He looked at another early work by Velazquez, the Three Musicians. 'That is very much like my work.'

'Yes.' I agreed. 'Those pictures you gave to Contreras had a more profound impact on Western art than you could possibly have dreamed of. Not just Velazquez, but other Spanish painters such as Zurbaran and Murillo. And French artists like Georges de la Tour, and Dutch artists like Rembrandt Van Rijn, who was possibly better than you.'

I knew such a statement would engender a fierce reaction from Merisi. 'Impossible,' he cried. 'Show me his work. I must see whether you lie to me.'

I took the History of World Art away from Merisi and said: 'You can look at the work of Rembrandt later. I want to know what you did when you left the hospital.'

'The abortive adventure against Zuccaro with Prosperino Orsi had forged a closer bond between Orsi and me. I knew that he was becoming more and more enraptured with my new style of painting. He had been a tireless advocate of the Cavaliere d'Arpino's work, but the Cavaliere's pusillanimous and ungrateful attitude after the Zuccaro affair had enraged Orsi and, thereafter, he became a bitter enemy of the Cavaliere and gave all his allegiance to me. Orsi's brother, Aurelio, was secretary to the Farnese family and was very influential and admired in the Roman art world. Orsi urged Aurelio to promote my work. Prosperino believed in me and urged me to take the risk of setting up as an independent artist. I did not need much urging. I was sick and tired of being a hack in someone else's studio. But I had been very ill. I had no money. It was a very risky step to strike out on my own. Orsi lived with his mother in a poor part of the city. He could not take me in but, through his brother Aurelio, I found shelter with Asdrubale Mattei. He was the brother of Cardinal Mattei, who was later to buy my painting of the Supper at Emmaus that you admire so much. Very soon after I had moved into Asdrubale's part of the Palazzo Mattei, I received a fortuitous visitor.'

'Who was that?' I asked.

'It was an art dealer named Valentin. He lived with his wife and four children in the Piazza San Luigi dei Francesi, near the French church I was later to make famous. He was a strange man. He . . .'

'Forgive me for interrupting you, Michele, and I don't want to contradict you because you actually lived all this, but don't you mean Costantino Spata? Wasn't that the name of this dealer?'

Merisi smiled at me. 'You constantly surprise me, Stefano. Sometimes your knowledge of my life and works is abysmally lacking and sometimes you seem to know things which I would have thought would be totally forgotten by now.'

'It isn't me,' I corrected him, 'but very many clever and diligent historians such as Helen Langdon who have researched your life and times.'

'Well, bless them,' Merisi said, 'but you are correct, in a way, because Valentin and Costantino Spata were one and the same man. You see, Valentin was a Frenchman, married to an Italian girl named Caterina. He had moved to Rome, with his wife and children, about the same time that I did. Perhaps a little later. As I have told you, there was a lot of bad feeling between the French and Spanish factions in the city and, at that time, the French were especially unpopular because of the anti-Catholic activities of the French king, Henry. Valentin changed his name to an Italian name. He reasoned, with good sense I think, that if potential clients assumed he was Italian, they would not be prejudiced against buying his pictures. And his wife and children would not be harassed or bullied.'

'I agree that it sounds like a sensible move,' I said. 'You were saying that Valentin was a strange man?'

'Yes. Strange and secretive. He lived above his shop and, when he went out, he simply closed the shop. He did not have an assistant. Often clients would arrive to buy or sell something, only to find the shop closed. Nobody ever knew whether his shop would be closed or open. They would see a picture in his shop window, be interested in buying it and yet Valentin would be missing, sometimes for hours. Despite all this, he was successful. He had good taste and he knew what was popular. I got to know him through Orsi. We would often have a drink with Valentin in the taverns. Of course, he knew all the painters in Rome and cultivated their acquaintance. That was his job, to look out for new talent. You could never tell what he was thinking. You could ask what his opinion was of this artist or that artist, or this style or that style, and he would never tell you, except in the very vaguest terms, such as "he is not bad" or "not much talent" or, very rarely, "he is a good painter". He would never elaborate on these statements and he was careful never to become so drunk that he did not know what he was saying.'

'Did you offer him your pictures?' I asked.

'Yes! I had urged him to take my work many times but he never did. He simply shrugged his shoulders in that Gallic way of his and would not tell me why he did not like my work. The most he ever said was something like "won't sell". I gave up trying to persuade him and assumed that he did not like my style. Then, when I was staying at the Palazzo Mattei, he suddenly turned up and made me an offer. He commissioned me to paint two pictures. The first was to be a scene of a group of cardsharps fleecing a naïve victim. And the second was to be of a gypsy girl telling a young man's fortune but stealing the young man's gold ring off of his finger while she was doing so. Valentin warned me, quite rightly, that I must include some sort of moral or morally instructive element in the pictures in order to get them past the Vatican censors. That is why the two pictures were to contain such admonitory elements. Valentin said that if I painted them well, and if he liked them, he would pay me well. He said that he had a buyer in mind who would not be able to resist such pictures and would pay handsomely for them. Of course, Valentin would not tell me who this potential buyer was. He was afraid that I would cut him out of the deal, which I probably would have done!'

'Had anyone put Valentin up to this sudden change of heart?' I asked.

'That's exactly what I asked him,' Merisi replied, 'but he said no. He simply said he had been thinking about my work and that, if I painted something more popular, he thought it would sell.'

'Perhaps Orsi persuaded him,' I conjectured, 'or Mario Minnitti or the Colonna family or any of your friends and supporters.'

'I was very surprised by Valentin's sudden approach. I asked everyone I knew if they had persuaded Valentin to take my work but they all denied it. I assume it was a simple change of heart because my reputation was growing. I thought very hard about what he had said, about doing something popular and saleable. I thought back to what the Dutch and Flemish artists were doing at the Cavaliere's studio. They were painting genre pieces that were much lighter in tone than what Italian artists were painting. They were popular pieces and acceptable because they had not been painted by serious Italian artists but by frivolous foreigners. I decided that it was time an Italian artist tried the same approach.'

'Excellent,' I said. 'You will be pleased to know that both those paintings are well-known to us today. The Gypsy Fortune Teller is in an art gallery in Paris.'

'That is good news, Stefano. Valentin would be pleased that one of his sales has gone back to his homeland.'

'Tell me, Michele, weren't you prejudiced against Valentin, knowing that he was French? You told me that you were in the Spanish faction in the street fights, knocking French heads together.'

'No!' Merisi exclaimed. 'I don't really care a fig what nationality a man is, except for the Turks. I'm talking to you and you are a heretical Englishman but you buy me food and drinks and that is exactly what Valentin did, to butter up us poor painters. No, he was an amiable man, even if he was very deep and closed off.'

'Then let's talk about these two paintings of yours. Remember, we must look at them for clues to the identity of your attempted assassin, as well as going over their history. Why do you think Valentin considered that the subjects of these two paintings would be so popular?'

'Gambling with playing cards was a very popular pastime in Rome,' Merisi said. 'Gambling generally was looked on by the Church as an evil but that did not stop the populace gaming with dice and playing cards. A few years before I arrived in Rome, Pope Sixtus had issued an edict banning gaming with dice. But he was so desperate to improve his finances that he allowed gaming with playing cards, so he imposed a tax on card players.'

I could not help smiling and said: 'I'm not surprised to hear that the selfish hypocrisy of our rulers, masquerading as high-minded morality, has not changed over the years.'

Merisi continued: 'Many people were addicted to card playing. Even many of the cardinals and churchmen who preached against gambling could not resist the gaming table in private, playing against their like-minded friends. It used to be said that card playing was the whore's worst enemy because only card playing could arouse the same passion in a man as fucking. So, as a subject, the depiction of card players would be very attractive to many people, as long as the picture masqueraded as a moral warning. Do people still gamble with playing cards today?'

'Nothing much ever changes in the basics, Michele. Millions of people all around the world gamble, on cards, dice, horse races, football matches, lotteries, two flies climbing up a window. Many become so addicted that they cannot escape and lose all their money. As with your Pope Sixtus, our governments preach high-minded moral concern about gambling while raking in the tax money. But what of the gypsy fortune teller? Gypsies of a certain type are hated and feared today. Were they more popular in your day?'

'They were popular when they first arrived in Italy, which was about two hundred years before I was born.' Merisi said. 'They were welcomed as pilgrims but very soon this welcome turned to fear and hatred and they were condemned as thieves and beggars. They were looked on with a mixture of fear and fascination. They were exotic and mysterious. They were thought to have special knowledge of arcane magic and sexual techniques. Gypsy characters were very popular in the theatre. In a painting, an attractive gypsy girl and a handsome young man were sure to be popular subjects. Valentin chose well.'

'Were you pleased with his choice of subjects?' I asked.

'Yes, well pleased.' Merisi answered. 'At last I was free to paint pictures as I chose, not constrained by the head of a studio or by religious or mythological convention. I was tremendously excited by the project. As I have told you, I thought back to the lively genre paintings by the Dutch and Flemish artists that I had seen in the Cavaliere d'Arpino's studio. I knew I could do much better but in an Italian style that would be quite new in art. All the theories and ideas that had been swirling in my head since I first determined to be a great painter were about to be put into fruition. My pictures would amaze and delight the world.'

'That is certainly what they did, Michele. But let us search these pictures for clues to your murderer.'

'I don't think there will be much point in that,' Merisi protested. 'The subjects were provided by Valentin. I certainly did not include any hidden messages in these two pictures, apart from the moral message to get them past the censors.'

'Valentin did not force you to include any particular elements in these pictures?'

'No, certainly not. Apart from the basic subject matter, he gave me a completely free hand.'

'Very well, I can accept that,' I said. 'What about the people in the picture? Are any of them based on real people? Were the models known to you, or connected to you.' I was laying a neat trap to see if Merisi would tell me about Rafaella Minnitti modelling for the gypsy girl. I was almost certain he would not.

'They were only vaguely known to me,' Merisi replied. 'After I had planned what I was going to paint, I was forced to move lodgings again. An acquaintance of mine, Monsignor Fantin Petrignani, at the urging of Aurelio Orsi, gave me lodgings in his palazzo. For the cardsharps picture, I used some of the servants working in the palazzo as models.'

'What about the gypsy fortune teller?' I asked. 'Was she known to you?'

Merisi looked at me. I tried to keep a look of bland unconcern on my face. 'No,' he answered. 'She was just a maid at the palazzo. I cannot remember her name.'

'She was a pretty girl,' I commented.

Merisi shrugged. 'Yes, and she had a dark complexion like a gypsy. She suited my purpose very well.'

I had caught Merisi in another lie but I said nothing about it. 'Did Valentin pay you well for these pictures?' I asked.

'Yes, surprisingly well,' Merisi replied. 'I completed the cardsharps first. (*Plate 9*). Valentin was truly delighted with it. For the first time in months I had some real money to spend. I went out on a drinking spree, treated my friends, and bought a new suit of clothes.'

I did not tell Merisi that I knew where he had bought that suit of clothes, from the shop where he had met Rafaella Minnitti. I was attempting to give him enough rope to hang himself.

'And then you completed the gypsy picture?'

'Yes.'

'And Valentin paid well for that one?'

'Yes, equally well. He was just as pleased with that picture.'

'We know that both pictures caused a sensation in Rome,' I said. 'They were seen as an entirely new approach to art. They were fresh, dramatic, vivid, colourful, alive. The figures seem to leap out of the frame. There were even poems dedicated to them, poems written in admiration and wonder.'

'You have summed it up very well, Stefano,' Merisi said, with smug satisfaction. 'I had always wanted to paint the life of the street all around me, not portraits of stuffy cardinals or holy saints or long dead subjects from antiquity. I wanted to show life as it was, not as some romanticised fairy tale.'

I said: 'These pictures, almost overnight, helped to sweep away what we now call the Mannerist style of art that had held sway in Rome for so many years since the days of Michelangelo, Raphael and Leonardo.'

'Yes, they made me the talk of Rome. Valentin paid me well but he must have made a pretty penny himself because he sold both these pictures to the man who was to become my most important patron and supporter . . .'

'Cardinal Francesco Maria Del Monte,' I interjected. 'The man called Del Monte, he say "yes"!'

Merisi looked at me curiously. I did not bother to explain about a popular brand of tinned fruit. Instead I said: 'Let's leave the good cardinal until tomorrow. I think we have done enough work for today. Valentin, better known as Costantino Spata, had played an important part in your life and continued to do so. It may be an idea to go back and meet this man.'

'You won't get much out of him,' Merisi warned.

'Perhaps not,' I said.

'I thought we were going into town tonight,' Merisi said sulkily, 'to find a tavern and get drunk.'

'We'll leave that until another night,' I said. 'Tonight, while I am away, you are going to watch that large box standing in the corner.'

'This thing called television I have seen you gazing at?' Merisi asked.

'Yes. It's like looking at a book or a painting except everything is moving. It's like being at the theatre only it is transmitted into the box by methods which I cannot explain. Most of what is sent is puerile and juvenile crap, for which we have to pay a licence fee, but I think you will enjoy what is being performed tonight.'

'Why? What is it?'

'It is a film about your life, made by a man named Derek Jarman.'

15

I peered through the window of Valentin's shop. I could not see anybody inside. In fact, I could not see anything at all inside the shop. It looked empty. I had tried the door. It was locked. I felt annoyed. My ChronoContact, Guglielmo Pellegrino, must have calculated the ChronoCo-ordinates incorrectly. Valentin was supposed to be at home or working in his shop. I considered whether the ChronoConverter might have malfunctioned. There was a light rain falling but it was fairly warm. I watched the close-packed bustle of the Roman streets all around me and considered what to do. I decided that, to save wasting a time trip, I would seek out Giuseppe Cesari, the Cavaliere d'Arpino. Somebody suddenly tapped me on my shoulder. It made me jump with surprise and I looked round. It was Doctor Giulio Mancini. 'My apologies for startling you, Signor Maddano,' he said. 'I am pleased that I have bumped into you. I have a message from Giovan Battista Merisi.'

'What is it?' I asked, hoping that some priceless nugget of evidence was about to be presented to me.

'He thanks you very much and asks me to tell you that his gout has been very much eased by your suggested treatment.'

For a few moments I could not think what Mancini was talking about and then I remembered the gout treatment, using colchicine from the autumn crocus, that I had stupidly mentioned. 'It has proved very effective,' Mancini continued. 'I am using it on another patient of mine. In fact, I have been looking for you to see if you have any more remedies from your homeland. I could not find out where you are staying. Where are you staying?'

'Oh, I've been travelling around a fair bit,' I improvised. 'Moving around a lot.'

'I see,' Mancini said, not convinced. 'Who were you looking for at this shop?'

'The owner,' I replied. 'An art dealer named Valentin?'

'Valentin?' Mancini said, puzzled. Then: 'Oh, you mean the Frenchman who calls himself Spata?'

'Yes, that's right.'

'You won't find him in there.'

'Where is he?' I asked.

'Gone back home to Paris,' Mancini replied. 'Not long after our friend Michelangelo Merisi da Caravaggio fled from Rome for slaying poor Tomassoni.'

That had been about five years ago. My ChronoContact, Pellegrino, must have thought that Valentin was still in Rome and running this shop. 'In that case, doctor, I will visit the Cavaliere d'Arpino, if you would be good enough to direct me to his studio.'

'I can,' Mancini said, 'but you will not find him there today. He is working on the new frescoes at the church of Santa Maria della Grazia. It is not far from here. Follow me, I will take you there.'

I followed Mancini through the streets of seventeenth century Rome. I still found it a very peculiar experience, as if it was an enormous film set constructed solely for my benefit, but it was all real. The smells and the filth, the hundreds of extras, and the horrendously deformed or mutilated beggars that we passed could not have been reproduced for any film set. Mancini turned up some steps and led me into a large and imposing church. From the clean look of the stonework and the bustling activity inside, the church was newly constructed and was in the process of having the interior decorated. There had obviously not been a religious service conducted in the church yet. There was rickety-looking wooden scaffolding everywhere and a team of at least ten painters working. Mancini led me to a scaffold about halfway inside the church and looked up at a man working on a fresco high up on that wall. 'Hey, Cavaliere,' he shouted.

The man looked down and I recognised, from his portrait drawing by Ottavio Leoni, the thin haughty face of Giuseppe Cesari, the Cavaliere d'Arpino. 'Mancini!' he shouted back. 'What do you want?'

'There is a gentleman here to see you.'

'I can't see anyone. I am too busy. I must finish this fresco before the plaster dries.'

'He is here to talk to you about your friend Michelangelo Merisi da Caravaggio!' Mancini shouted. I noticed that all of the artists working within earshot of this exchange stopped what they were doing and looked at me keenly at the sound of that magic name 'Caravaggio'.

The Cavaliere shouted back: 'I especially don't want to waste time talking about that cunt.'

'I would advise you to talk to Signor Maddano, Cavaliere. He is a clever man and he is here with the blessing of the Holy Father.'

At the mention of the pope, the Cavaliere d'Arpino considered me with new interest. Before he could say anything, I shouted to him: 'Please carry on with your work until it is convenient for you to come down, sir. I do not wish to interrupt such important work by a most distinguished artist. I am in no hurry. I will wait here.'

The Cavaliere turned back to his work without another word. To a man like the Cavaliere, so keenly conscious of status and his own importance, it did no harm to try to gain his favourable opinion by buttering him up. If he refused to talk to me, I not only had the papal warrant but a secret weapon that he would not be able to ignore . . . my knowledge of the attack on Zuccaro. He would be desperate to keep that shameful episode a secret, so I was willing to wait for him in the knowledge that he would have to talk to me. It was, anyway, fascinating to watch the artists at work. I noticed that two of them working on the other side of the church were still watching me with interest. The younger men had gone back to work with the usual horseplay and banter that accompanies young men at work but these two watching me were older and clearly of higher status than assistants or apprentices. I said to Mancini: 'Who are those two men over there?'

Mancini looked across. 'They are Domenico Passignano and Ludovico Cigoli. They are both painters, with studios of there own, but the Cavaliere is under enormous pressure to finish these frescoes. He has hired them to help him out. They were friends of Michele. Would you like to talk to them while you are waiting for the great Cavaliere.'

'I was just about to ask if you would introduce me,' I said, 'but before you do, what is your opinion of them? Not as artists, I mean, but of their character. I have heard their names in connection with Caravaggio. Do you think they bore any ill will towards him?'

'They had every reason to,' Mancini replied, 'especially Passignano, but he will no doubt tell you his well-known story about Michele. They are both from Florence but they have worked in Rome for many years. Domenico Passignano is a sweet-tempered man, very easy going, a good tradesman but with not much talent. I used to regularly see him in the company of our friend Merisi. He was the butt of many jokes inflicted by Michele but he suffered them with patience and forbearance. I cannot believe that Domenico could hurt a fly, let alone plan a murder. The other one, Ludovico Cigoli is a man of much higher artistic stature. He is an architect as well as a considerable painter. He is a careful, patient and devout man. Many artists have been jealous of him, including Michele. He used to drink with Passignano and Michele. I have seen Michele bait him mercilessly but Cigoli would never respond. He kept his counsel. I can't say I know him very well but I would judge that he could be capable of planning murder, although I hesitate to accuse him. I will introduce you.' He looked over to the two artists and called out: 'Domenico, Ludovico! This gentleman wishes to make your acquaintance and pay his respects to two distinguished artists. Can you spare the time?'

Mancini turned back to me and winked. He was as much a shameful flatterer as I was. The two artists walked across and Mancini introduced me. He explained to them that I was looking into the mysterious circumstances surrounding the death of Michelangelo Merisi da Caravaggio and that my investigation had the pope's blessing. Having completed the introductions, Mancini turned to me and said: 'Will you excuse me now, Signor Maddano? I have a patient waiting for me.'

'Of course, doctor,' I said. 'You have been most helpful.'

'A pleasure,' he replied, and strode out of the church.

'A patient indeed,' Ludovico Cigoli said, watching Mancini walk away. 'I wonder what sort of treatment his mistress will be receiving from the doctor today.'

'It will no doubt bring her out in a sweat,' Domenico Passignano said, and the two men laughed.

'Thank you for agreeing to talk to me about Michelangelo Merisi,' I said to them. 'I understand from Doctor Mancini that you knew him well and used to drink with him. Let me come to the point immediately and please remember, as Doctor Mancini told you, that the pope himself has enjoined everyone to tell the truth in this matter on peril of their immortal souls. Did either of you do anything to cause the death of Michelangelo Merisi or know of anyone who did?'

The two men looked at each other but they did not seem at all perturbed by my blunt question. 'We thought poor Michele died of the plague?' Passignano said. 'Are you saying that somebody killed him?'

'It is a possibility,' I replied.

'Poor Michele!' Cigoli scoffed at his companion. 'You know as well as I do that if Merisi was murdered, he probably asked for it.'

Passignano nodded. 'It is true,' he confirmed. 'I never knew a man so difficult to get along with.'

'And yet you both went out drinking with Michele. If he was so difficult, why did you do that?'

Cigoli said: 'I usually did it to keep the peace. I didn't seek out his company but if you ran into him in a tavern or wherever, it was easier just to go along with his odd humours. If you tried to avoid him or stand up to him, you usually found yourself the victim of some cruel prank or vicious rumour. I was once accused of plagiarism and Merisi found that highly amusing. "Copycat Cigoli" he called me for a while, until the joke wore off. I simply kept my counsel and let him say it. With his temper, it was more healthy not to rise to his bait.'

Passignano nodded. 'Ludovico tells you the truth,' he confirmed. 'Cigoli here is a much better artist than I am and Michele feared and hated anyone who threatened to be as feted and successful as he was. I am a poor painter compared with Michele so he never felt threatened by me. He was a difficult man but he was also lively, passionate and funny. I liked him. I did not kill him, Signor Maddano, and if I knew of anyone who had done such a deed, I swear to God I would tell you.'

Cigoli said: 'I, too, swear to God I have no knowledge of any murder plot against Merisi. Despite what I thought of him personally, he was a very great painter. To destroy such talent would be a grave offence against God.' He looked across at the Cavaliere d'Arpino, who was slowly descending from the scaffolding. 'My friend, the Cavaliere over there, would give his right arm to have half the talent that Merisi had, despite his protests to the contrary. That's the real reason he ended up hating Merisi.'

Not the whole reason, I thought to myself, but I said to Passignano: 'Before the Cavaliere joins us, what is this well-known story that Doctor Mancini mentioned?'

'Oh, I was working on an altarpiece and had left an assistant to finish some minor detail. I had erected curtains around this workplace, to keep away the dust and any prying spectators. Michele crept up to the curtained enclosure, took out his sword, suddenly slashed open the curtain and stuck his head through the hole. My poor assistant nearly jumped out of his skin. Michele looked at my altarpiece and said to the assistant: "This is just as bad as I would have expected from a painter like him". Michele was delighted with himself and went around Rome telling everyone about his clever prank.'

'How did you react to that treatment?' I asked.

'As my friend Ludovico here has said, it was better to humour and ignore Michele when he was in such a mood. I chose to ignore it, and I went on drinking with him.' Cigoli looked at his fellow artist with pity and shook his head in disgust at the memory of Michele's disrespectful behaviour.

The Cavaliere d'Arpino walked up and said to me: 'We'll never get these damn frescoes done in time if you keep holding up my assistants. I'll be ruined. I'll never get another commission if we don't finish in time. Who are you and what do you want?'

I ignored d'Arpino's question and turned back to the other two artists. 'Thank you for your time, gentlemen. It has been most illuminating.' They nodded and returned to their workplace on the other side of the church. I turned back to d'Arpino and explained why I had come to see him.

'Yes, I heard there was someone snooping around asking questions about that bastard Merisi.'

'Can we talk somewhere in private?' I suggested.

'Say what you have to say here, Signor Maddano. I am not impressed by papal warrants and fancy foreign finery. I am an important and busy man myself. Everyone here knows what I thought of Merisi.'

It was time to take the pompous d'Arpino down a peg or two. I said, quietly: 'Perhaps they know what you thought of Merisi. But I doubt that they know what he and your brother tried to do to Zuccaro.'

The effect of this statement on d'Arpino was even better than I had anticipated. He turned ashen. For a moment, I thought he was going to faint. I reinforced my authority by saying: 'I am the only person, except those involved, who knows of this incident, and no-one else shall ever hear of it from my lips except if you do not talk to me fully and frankly about your relationship with Michelangelo Merisi da Caravaggio.' I looked around. 'Let's go and sit on the steps outside,' I suggested. 'You look as if you could do with some air.' I guided the dazed Cavaliere towards the door of the church. He made no resistance. We sat down on the steps just outside the door. Before I could say anything, the Cavaliere began to pour out his bile towards Merisi and it was difficult to stop him. We talked for a long time about Merisi's few months working for the Cavaliere, or plain Giuseppe Cesari as he had been before being knighted. I did not learn anything particularly new or useful but it was interesting to hear the Cavaliere's side of things.

'You see, Merisi was a maniac, Signor Maddano. What had I ever done to that man except give him food, wages, a place to live and an opportunity to enhance his reputation through working at my studio? Then, because of that mad escapade against Zuccaro, he led my brother astray and caused Prospero Orsi to turn against me after being my good friend. Both Orsi and Merisi hated and resented me ever afterwards. After I had been honoured by becoming a papal knight, Merisi's jealousy and resentment knew no bounds. He even challenged me to a duel. I was out riding when Merisi saw me. He confronted me and said: "This is the time to settle our quarrel, since we are both armed". I answered by telling him that, as a papal knight, I would not deign to fight with anyone of a lesser rank. My answer seemed to hurt and enrage him even more. I urged my horse past him and left him shouting curses at my back. I admit I was a little afraid of Merisi. He was mad, out of control. I felt he would have killed me with his sword without a qualm.'

'The question is, Cavaliere, did you take revenge on Merisi? Did you have anything to do with the death of Merisi in Porto Ercole? I rely on your honour as a papal knight, and the command from His Holiness, to tell me the truth. If you tell a lie, and I ever find out, the whole truth about the Zuccaro affair will be presented to the Holy Father.'

'No,' d'Arpino said, firmly. 'I had nothing to do with Merisi's death. He had fled from Rome and good riddance. I was free of him. I thought nothing more about him until you turned up today. I have told you the truth and I beg you to fulfil your promise and never mention the Zuccaro incident to anyone'.

'You have my promise,' I said, 'that no-one will know of it during your lifetime.'

16

The ChronoConverter transported me back to my own bedroom. It was late in the evening. I peered through the curtains, dreading what I might see going on outside, but all was quiet. I looked at my bedside clock. The time was 11.28 p.m. The television broadcast of Derek Jarman's film version of the life of Caravaggio was almost finished. I opened my bedroom door and listened. I could hear the sound from the television, so evidently my house guest, Michelangelo Merisi da Caravaggio, was still watching the film biography of his own life. I changed into modern casual clothes and walked out on to the landing. Just as I did so, there was an ear-splitting crash of glass from the living room, followed by a stream of the most filthy obscenities in both English and Italian. I guessed what had happened. I went downstairs and cautiously opened the living room door. I peered in. Merisi was stalking up and down the room with a murderous look on his face.

'Something wrong, Michele?' I asked, trying to suppress a smile.

He stopped and turned around. 'Something wrong? Something wrong?' he repeated furiously. 'I am ruined. This man Jarman has ruined me. I am going to seek him out and do to him what I did to Tomassoni.' He indicated the television. The screen had shattered and the shards were lying all over the carpet. In amongst the shards of the television screen were the shards of a whisky glass. Good malt whisky was dripping out of the remains of the television set and on to the carpet.

'You seem a little concerned about Mr. Jarman's portrayal of you,' I suggested.

'Concerned!' Merisi shouted. 'It is all lies! He has made me seem like a murderous maniac and a bardassa, a sodomite. He claims that Tomassoni modelled for me! He did no such thing. I wouldn't have allowed that arrogant bastard anywhere near my studio. He even showed me, God help me, kissing Tomassoni! I would sooner have kissed the crotch of the meanest beggar in Rome than do that!'

At that moment, the telephone rang. Merisi was startled by this sudden noise. I answered. It was Mrs. Chowdry from next door. 'We are in bed,' she said, 'trying to get to sleep. We heard a fearful crash and somebody shouting. Are you all right? Is everything okay?'

'Yes, yes,' I replied. 'I had a little accident with a tray of glasses and my friend Mr. Merisi turned up the volume of the television and didn't know how to turn it down. We do apologise for disturbing you.'

'As long as everything is all right,' Mrs. Chowdry said, with a hint of resignation in her voice.

'Yes, thank you,' I said, and put the phone down. I said to Merisi: 'Let's sit down, have another drink and talk about this film.'

'What's to talk about?' Merisi fumed. 'This man Jarman has dishonoured me. I will kill him.'

'I'm afraid you won't be able to do that,' I said.

'Why not?'

'Because he is already dead.'

'Oh,' Merisi said, and sat down in the armchair. He thought about this for a few seconds and said: 'Then I will kill the actors.'

'They've probably put up with some tough criticism over the years but killing the actors is not a possibility either.'

'Why not?'

'Because it is illegal. You would end up in prison again.'

'But don't you see, I will end up in prison anyway, if anyone else ever sees what was in that box. That is why I smashed it. You must buy another box that does not lie.'

For a few seconds, I was confused as to what Merisi meant, but then I realised that he had not grasped the concept of television. 'I'm afraid that thousands of people all around the country have just watched that same film. Well, dozens anyway.'

'What!' Merisi said, horrified. 'Then the police will be coming to arrest me at any minute.'

'Why should they do that?' I said, puzzled.

'Because sodomy is illegal,' Merisi replied. 'It carries the death sentence.'

'Michele, calm down,' I said. 'Sodomy, or homosexuality, might have been illegal in Rome in your century but is no long illegal today. Many think that it is well on the way to becoming compulsory. Couples of the same sex are allowed to marry each other. Homosexuality is even taught in schools as an acceptable alternative way of life for those so inclined. Believe me, Michele, in England today, you run more risk of ending up in prison for criticising homosexuality, for whatever reason, that you do for practising it.'

Merisi looked at me, considering whether to believe me or not. 'But what about the Church,' he protested, 'the cardinals and the clerics. Do they no longer condemn such practises?'

'The Roman Catholic Church still opposes it, but no longer has the power to forbid it. But the Church of England, or some segments of it, has embraced homosexuality with enthusiasm . . . literally.'

'It's just as I thought about you English. You are a profane, perverted and heretical nation.'

'In many ways, I have to agree with you,' I said. 'But you must admit that many art historians in England, and in other countries, had good reason to believe that you were a bardassa yourself.'

'Why?' Merisi demanded angrily. 'The penalty for such acts, in my day, was death. Such things went on but it was kept very quiet, very secret.'

'Many of your pictures are very homoerotic,' I said, 'like the first pictures you painted for your new sponsor, Cardinal Del Monte. But let's get off this subject, for now, and return to it tomorrow when we talk about Del Monte. Believe me, you are not about to be arrested.' To distract Merisi from his pique regarding Derek Jarman's film, I recounted the Cavaliere d'Arpino's shocked reaction to my knowledge about the attack on Federico Zuccaro. That cheered Merisi up considerably.

17

In the morning I cleaned up the broken glass, went over the carpet with Vanish cleaner, and rang an electrical retailer I knew to deliver and set-up a new television set and DVD recorder. Merisi's well-aimed glass of malt whisky had ruined the DVD player as well. I am incapable of understanding or setting up such devices myself. They are far too complicated, even for a former Brain of Britain. After I had finished cleaning up, Merisi and I settled into our customary armchairs and started work. I opened my notebook and Helen Langdon's biography of Caravaggio and began. 'We know that Cardinal Francesco Maria Del Monte was the most important and helpful figure in your entire artistic career. He had bought your two paintings, which are now known as The Cardsharps and The Gypsy Fortune Teller, and he had been so impressed by your work that he invited you to live and work in his palazzo, which was called the Palazzo Madama. We believe this was in about autumn 1595. Is that correct?'

'Yes, perfectly,' Merisi confirmed.

'What was Cardinal Del Monte like? How did you get on with him?'

'It would be no exaggeration to say that he became like a second father to me,' Merisi explained. 'He was a very cultured man, very learned, and he had deep knowledge of literature, poetry, history, archaeology, theatre, music and the natural sciences. Music, in particular, was his great love. He sponsored many young aspiring artists, not just myself, and took a genuine interest in our welfare, education and progress. He was about twenty years older than I was, so he was, I think, about fifty years old when I entered his service. He was born in Venice, into a grand family, and he seemed to know, and had known, anyone who was anyone in the Italian cultural world.'

'What was he like as a person?' I asked.

'He lived modestly and frugally, as befitted a cardinal and unlike most of the other cardinals. But unlike Cardinal Salad, he was generous to those in his service. I had a comfortable room, in the servant's quarters, and we had good food and he paid us reasonably well, although he was not a particularly wealthy man compared to most of the cardinals. I was allowed to set up my studio in the cellars of the Palazzo Madama and I had enough money to employ an apprentice.'

'Yes, but what was Del Monte like himself,' I persisted.

'He was a man of modesty, simplicity and charm,' Merisi replied. 'He was tall and elegant in appearance and he dressed simply and respectfully. His manners were impeccable. Although I was a lowly artist, in his service, he was never condescending. He never treated me as a servant but, equally, he never encouraged too much familiarity. He struck the right balance, usually with charm and good humour. He was a great joker, always ready with a quip. He was quick witted and insatiably curious about everything. He helped me out of many bad situations but he never scolded me, although he made plain his displeasure, and took pains to understand my nature. He was the sort of man who entered a room and cheered up everyone who was in it.'

'I can see why you liked this man,' I said, 'but he seems too good to be true. Is their anything bad you can say about this saintly man?'

'Why should there be?' Merisi asked, irritably. 'Can't you accept the concept of a thoroughly good and decent man? What right have you to criticise Del Monte? I knew him. You did not.'

'Don't get angry with me, Michele. You know why I have to ask these questions. When I say "bad" I don't mean evil or that he had anything to do with your death.'

'Then what do you mean?' Merisi challenged.

'There are suggestions from later historians, for instance, that Del Monte was fonder of the pleasures of the flesh than was openly known. Did you know anything about that?'

'There were rumours that Del Monte had enjoyed the company of women when he was a young man, before he became a cardinal. What is wrong with that? It is entirely natural.'

'I agree,' I said, 'but did his tastes, later in his life after he became a cardinal, turn to young boys?'

'I saw nothing to suggest that,' Merisi said tetchily.

'But there were many boys living and working at the Palazzo Madama. You, yourself, painted pictures of them; pictures I wish to ask you about later on.'

'I never saw the cardinal behave in an untoward manner with any boy at the palazzo. I never heard any rumours either.'

'But you did not live in, or visit, the cardinal's own chambers, did you? It is possible he may have indulged himself behind closed doors. You must admit that?'

'I admit nothing,' Merisi replied. 'You are trying to trick me into saying things that are not true.'

'Very well,' I said, changing tack. 'Cardinal Del Monte was a powerful man, in the service of the Medici family. Behind this mask of simple sincerity, was he a devious and subtle plotter who worked on behalf of his patron, Cardinal Ferdinando de Medici?'

'How would I know?' Merisi said, still perturbed. 'I was a painter, not a diplomat.'

'Did you hear any gossip to that effect?'

'No,' Merisi said, firmly. 'You never knew what the cardinal was thinking, in the political sense. I never heard him say anything that was strong in opinion, one way or another.'

'What about on a personal level?' I pressed.

'The cardinal told me the truth,' Merisi answered, 'when others, who were dearer to me, did not.'

'What do you mean?' I said. 'Told you the truth about what?'

Merisi shifted uncomfortably in his armchair. 'About my work, I mean. About my behaviour. He told me what others dare not.'

'That's because you had to accept whatever he said to you. You could not afford to upset him.'

'Fuck you,' Merisi spat. 'I will not besmirch that good man's name just because you cannot believe what I am telling you.'

'Okay, okay,' I said. I was not going to wheedle anything out of Merisi about Del Monte by this approach. 'I mentioned Del Monte's patron, Ferdinando de Medici. The two men were very close I believe.'

'Yes, very much so. Cardinal Ferdinando was the second son of Grand Duke Cosimo Medici. Ferdinando and Del Monte were friends and political allies for many years, so much so that they became indispensable to each other. Medici relied on Del Monte's political and diplomatic nous and Del Monte relied on Medici for advancement and financial gain. Then Ferdinando's elder brother Francesco, who was the Grand Duke, and Francesco's wife Bianca, died of a fever within a day of each other . . .'

'How convenient!' I interjected.

'There you go again,' Merisi shot back. 'Are you suggesting that there was something suspicious about a husband and wife dying within a day of each other? It was nothing extraordinary in those days, when the fever struck, for members of the same family to die within a short time of each other. My own father and grandfather had died within a day of each other when the plague struck.'

'A fair point,' I conceded. 'Please carry on.'

'Because of this unhappy tragedy, Ferdinando Medici became the new Grand Duke. He renounced his vows as a cardinal and hurried to Florence to take up his duties as Grand Duke. He took Del Monte with him to be his closest adviser. It was the making of both men. The new Grand Duke was greeted with jubilation by the people of Florence. His brother had been deeply unpopular. Ferdinando reversed the pro-Spanish policies pursued by his father and brother and courted the French faction. He lent a considerable sum of money to Henry of Navarre, who was fighting the Spanish. Ferdinando even married a French princess, Christine of Lorraine, a couple of years before I went to Rome. By that time, thanks to the new Grand Duke, Del Monte had been raised to the purple and made a cardinal. By the way, at the wedding of Ferdinando Medici and Christine of Lorraine, a comedy play called The Gypsies was performed. Del Monte was fascinated by the gypsy way of life. And Del Monte's vice, if you can call it that, was for playing cards. My friend Valentin knew that Del Monte would be tempted by two pictures on those subjects and he was right. Valentin was a very shrewd man.'

'Yes, it was a shame that I couldn't interview him yesterday,' I said.

'You wouldn't have wheedled much out of him anyway,' Merisi said. 'Ferdinando Medici was a keen card player as well. I believe that Del Monte gave him my picture of the cardsharps as a gift.'

'What was the Palazzo Madama like when you moved in there?' I asked. 'It still exists today but it was totally renovated many years after your supposed death and is now much bigger, grander and more palatial.'

'It was not a large palazzo, compared with some others in Rome, but the accommodation was a lot more luxurious that I had been used to, although nothing like these houses you live in today, where you only have to touch a switch to get heat, light and food. It was quite plain outside but there was a huge rendition of the Medici arms over the main doorway. As well as the main state rooms, where Del Monte lived, there were many rooms for courtiers and servants. There was a courtyard with stables and a coach house. As I have said, I worked in the cellars.'

'Was there enough light down there?' I asked.

'Oh, yes. Usually. Unless it was a dark day anyway. There were plenty of windows high up in the walls. That's where I perfected the idea of that slanting light effect that I included in many of my works.'

'What about the cardinal's state rooms? What were they like?'

'I was only allowed in them on certain occasions, when he wanted to show me off to his friends or if he wanted to discuss some project with me, then he would summon me to his quarters. Of course, they were very lavish compared with the way the rest of us lived. Ferdinando Medici had sent Del Monte many fine tapestries and carpets and grand furniture with which to decorate his rooms. Del Monte also had collections of books, scientific and musical instruments, sculptures and so on. He also owned an exquisitely delicate ancient Roman vase made of glass.'

'You will be interested to know that that vase still survives and is on display here in England. It's now called the Portland vase, after the Englishman who bought it many years later.'

'That is surprising,' Merisi commented. 'It was such a fragile thing that it could easily be smashed to pieces.'

'It was smashed to pieces once, by a madman, but it was cleverly put back together again.'

Merisi nodded in appreciation. 'Perhaps we could put your television screen back together again?' he said.

'Unfortunately, my television is not nearly as valuable as the Portland Vase.'

'What Del Monte owned that interested me the most, naturally, was his collection of paintings. He had hundreds of them, especially by the Venetian artists he was so fond of. He was building up an extensive collection of portraits of distinguished men and women of the time, portraits such as I had been employed to do by Lorenzo Siciliano and Grammatica. Portraits of kings, popes, emperors, cardinals, dukes and scholars.'

'I should like to see that,' I said.

'Well, you can go back and see it.'

'If it's necessary to our research, I will,' I said.

The front door bell rang and I went to answer it. It was my friend Joe, the electrical retailer. 'Morning, Steve,' he said. 'Brought your television.'

'That was quick,' I said. 'I didn't think you'd get here until this afternoon.'

'Had to deliver another one, not far from here, so I thought I'd kill two birds with one stone.'

'Okay, fine. Well, bring it in. Do you need a hand?'

'No,' Joe replied, as he went to the back of his van, which he had reversed up to my front door. He lifted out a brand new flat screen television and carried it into the house. He followed me into the living room.

When Merisi saw Joe carrying the television, he rose menacingly from his chair and said: 'Are you the man who sells the boxes that lie?'

Joe was completely unfazed by this odd statement. 'That's me, old son. Mostly they do lie. Same as the papers and all.'

'Take it easy, Michele,' I said. 'Joe has nothing to do with what is shown on these boxes.'

'Lucky for him,' Merisi said, 'otherwise he would have a taste of steel from me.'

Joe chuckled as he placed the television set on the floor.

'Michele,' I said, 'why don't you go and wait in my office. We'll carry on working in there.'

I made sure that I was standing between Joe and Merisi as Merisi stalked out of the room. Even so, Merisi could not resist an obscene gesture at Joe as he passed by.

'So that's the mad Eyetie you've got staying with you?' Joe said, completely unperturbed by Merisi's strange behaviour.

'You've heard about him?' I asked, surprised.

'He's becoming famous,' Joe said. 'I do a lot of work for Bedford nick. Sergeant Caro told me you'd taken in a barmy asylum seeker. She was asking me a lot of questions about you and him. Couldn't stop talking about him.'

'Yes, well, he won't be here for long,' I said. 'He's helping me with research on a book I'm publishing.'

'Nothing to do with me, Steve. Whatever you get up to in private is your affair.' Joe grinned at me, highly amused by this situation, clearly believing that Merisi was here for more than book research.

'I'll be in my office if you want me,' I said, picking up my books and backing out of the living room. I went into the office and sat down at my desk. Merisi, sitting opposite, glared at me, expecting me to say something about his rude behaviour, but I decided not to. It must have been utterly confusing for Merisi to come back to life, four hundred years after he last saw the world, and misunderstandings were inevitable.

'Let's get back to life in the Palazzo Madama with Cardinal Del Monte,' I said. 'There were many other artists, poets, musicians and scientists living and working at the palazzo. It must have been a stimulating intellectual atmosphere.'

'Yes, it was,' Merisi confirmed. 'Stimulating and companionable. I lived in one of the small rooms at the top of the palace. Mario had the room next to me, and . . .'

'That's Mario Minnitti?' I interrupted.

'Yes. The cardinal had offered him a place in his service at the same time as me.'

'At your suggestion?' I asked.

'No, not at all. The cardinal liked Mario's work. He knew we were friends, so it was a gesture of kindness to bring us together again. Opposite me, in another room, lived a French sculptor named Nicholas Cordier. I met other artists at the palazzo who either worked there or were frequent visitors, such as Ottavio Leoni, who drew that portrait of me, and Antonio Tempesta, who was a superb engraver and mapmaker. And I was well placed to meet the cardinal's wealthy and influential friends, many of whom liked my work. There were many palazzi in the same area, such as the Palazzo Giustiniani, just across the street, and the Palazzo Crescenzi a little further on. Being invited to live at the Palazzo Madama was a very important move and even an ingrate like me was immensely appreciative of Cardinal Del Monte for giving me such an opportunity.'

'It's interesting to hear that Mario Minnitti was also living at the Palazzo Madama at this time because we believe that he modelled for the first picture that you painted specifically for Cardinal Del Monte. We now call this picture The Musicians or The Concert Party.' (*Plate 10*). I showed Merisi his painting in the book of his complete works. 'To modern art historians, this picture is very homo-erotic. These luscious boys, with slightly parted lips, appear to be tempting the viewer. Was that the intention, Michele?'

Merisi smiled. 'I knew what would appeal to Cardinal Del Monte,' he said.

'But earlier you denied that the cardinal had any such inclinations.'

'No, I said that I had never seen or heard any definite proof that the cardinal acted on such inclinations. The cardinal was a lover of music. He was a lover of beauty as well, male and female. Such beautiful androgynous figures as in my painting were very popular in Rome at that time. In this picture, I wanted to please the cardinal and his friends, some of whom certainly did act upon their homosexual inclinations, and the whole Roman art world. I was trying to make a name for myself. I wanted to be talked about.'

'Fair enough,' I conceded. 'The figure with the lute looks like your beautified version of Mario. And the boy in the background looks like a self-portrait. Is that correct?'

'Yes, it is.'

'Who modelled as the Cupid figure in the background?' I asked.

'That was our friend, the French sculptor Nicholas Cordier,' Merisi said. 'He also modelled for the figure in the foreground, with his back to us. He was a fairly handsome boy but, as with Mario, I used artistic licence to improve his appearance. We were all three of us grateful to the cardinal for the opportunity he had given us and this was my way of saying thank you on behalf of all of us.'

'Did the cardinal like this picture?' I asked.

Merisi smiled broadly. 'The cardinal was enraptured by it. He whisked it away from me as soon as I had finished it, to gaze at it in private and to show it to his friends. I am a clever bastard, don't you think?'

There was a light knock on the office door, and Joe stuck his head round. 'I've set up the box that lies, and the DVD player that lies. I'll send you a bill that tells the painful truth.'

'Thanks, Joe,' I said.

'I'll see myself out,' Joe said. Then, with a smile and a hint of sarcasm, he said: 'Nice to have met you, Mr. Merisi.'

We heard the front door close. Then Merisi said: 'I do not like that man. He is, as you English say, "taking the piss".'

'It's a favourite English custom,' I agreed, 'but let's move on to your next work, which is now called The Lute Player. (*Plate 11*). Once again, Michele, this is a very sensuous work. There is evidence that it was commissioned by Cardinal Del Monte's rich neighbour Vincenzo Giustiniani, who lived across the street at the Palazzo Giustiniani. Is that true?'

'Yes, it is,' Merisi confirmed. 'Vincenzo had seen my painting of the musicians and commissioned me to create something in a similar style.'

'Did he give you the subject?'

'No, not exactly. He wanted something on a musical theme and he very much admired the skill with which I painted still life, so he asked me to include those elements, but left the exact details entirely to my discretion. For me, it was a perfect opportunity to send a message to the woman I was in love with.' Merisi smiled at the astonishment that showed on my face. 'Yes, Stefano, that surprises you, doesn't it?'

'Yes,' I replied. 'You haven't mentioned that you were in love.'

'You have not asked me such a question yet.'

'I just assumed that you were seeking out whatever you needed from the whores and the courtesans.'

'Many people seem to have assumed many things about me that are not true,' Merisi said primly. 'In this case, there could be no chance that this lady and I could be together openly. Our affair had to be a secret. I wanted to make my picture a token of my love for her, in the place where she lived, before we had to part forever.'

'I am intrigued, Michele,' I said. 'Who was this lady?'

'Is this fact not known to all these clever modern art historians who have delved into my life so assiduously?'

'No,' I said. 'We know that your painting of The Lute Player is packed with symbols of love. The lute, for instance, is a musical instrument associated with love. The fruit and the flowers, some decaying with ripeness, suggest the transcience of time and love. Most of all, of course, is the prominence you gave to the line from a madrigal by Jacques Arcadelt: "Voi sapete ch'io vi amo", which translates into English as "You know that I love you".'

'Very good, Stefano. All that is exactly what I intended.'

'Well, whoever this lady was, she was the recipient of one of the most beautiful love tokens ever given.'

'Thank you for the compliment,' Merisi said.

'Are you going to tell me her name?'

Merisi looked at me appraisingly, debating with himself whether to entrust me with such personal information, but then he said: 'She was Gerolama Giustiniani, the wife of Vincenzo's brother, Giuseppe.'

'Ah, I see. A married lady.'

'Yes,' Merisi confirmed. 'The wife of a noble, wealthy and powerful man.

That is why our affair could never last. She could not, or would not, divorce her husband to be with an impecunious and little known artist. Even if she had, we would both have been ruined, socially and professionally. Our love just could not be, which gave it an intensity and a piquancy that was painful but exciting and delightful. I had been introduced to Gerolama at one of Cardinal Del Monte's intellectual soirees. She was a woman of uncommon culture. She very much admired my work. We talked for a long time. We were both struck by the thunderbolt. Her husband Giuseppe was a dark, thin-lipped little man. Gerolama was a beautiful, sensual, full-lipped woman. She was highly intelligent, with a mind of her own. She had an aristocratic bearing, almost haughty, but that only inflamed my urge to possess her. And I knew she wanted me. We took incredible risks to be together, and it was for a few times only.'

'That sounds just like you,' I said. 'Every time you achieved success, you risked everything with some wild and ill-considered behaviour.'

'How could an Englishman with ice in his veins expect to understand,' Merisi shot back at me. 'It was a passion that swamped common sense, an almost unendurable longing.'

'How long did this affair last?'

'For a few months only. Then her husband began to suspect that she was up to something, although he never found out that it was me.'

'Are you sure, Michele?' I asked. 'Cuckolding a powerful man like Giuseppe Giustiniani would be a strong incentive for him to have you murdered.'

'If he did find out,' Merisi said, 'he waited a long time to take his revenge.'

'Some say that revenge is a dish best eaten cold,' I said. 'We must mark down this Giuseppe Giustiniani as a suspect.'

'Very well,' Merisi said, indifferently.

'It is clear, Michele, that you were always highly skilled as a painter of still life but your skill in these first two paintings at the Palazzo Madama is dazzling. There is only one pure still life by your hand that has survived, which is now considered one of the earliest masterpieces of the genre and now known simply as Basket of Fruit. It's housed in a gallery in your home city of Milan.' I showed Merisi the reproduction of the Basket of Fruit painting in his complete works. (*Plate 12*).

'Ah, yes,' Merisi said. 'That was commissioned by Cardinal Borromeo.'

'It's an unusual subject for the time, a pure still life. Can you remember why Cardinal Borromeo commissioned it?'

'As I remember, simply for the love of the subject and for the skill with which I painted such things. You see, both Borromeo and Cardinal Del Monte were fascinated by natural things, how they grew, how they lived, why they developed, and so on. Both Del Monte and his patron, Ferdinando de Medici, as well as

Borromeo, were fascinated by alchemy, botany and the natural sciences. Del Monte collected drawings and paintings of plants and animals. He experimented with cures for all sorts of ills by using ingredients made from herbs and flowers. He tried them out on his friends but, if they worked, he kept them secret. He once used an antidote to treat a painter who had been bitten by a viper. He supported and encouraged one of the Colonna family, Fabio, who was becoming a famous botanist not long before I "died". Also, Borromeo and Del Monte had extensive collections of optical instruments that they allowed me to use. Such instruments gave me many ideas about light effects for my pictures, such as light shining through glass and dew drops shining on leaves and flowers, and so on.'

'Yes,' I said, 'we know that Del Monte owned one of your paintings of a carafe of water with flowers in it. Unfortunately, it has disappeared but it was widely admired. Even your old rival Baglione was very complimentary about it, saying it was so lively and real. He claimed that you had said it was the best thing you had ever painted.'

'Well, I remember the painting but I don't remember saying that it was the best thing I had ever done. I am not surprised that Baglione was impressed by it since he was such a bad painter himself.'

'Talking of poor painters,' I said, 'there is a famous English artist, living today, named David Hockney, who has written a book claiming that the effects you achieved in your works, such as dramatic foreshortening effects, could only have been achieved by the use of the camera obscura. Would you care to comment on that?'

'Do you have any examples of this man's work?' Merisi asked me.

'Yes. Hold on.' I went out to my living room bookcase to get a volume on modern art which contained many examples of Hockney's work. I took it back to the office and Merisi examined them with interest.

'I'm not sure I understand this work,' Merisi said. 'He shows some facility as a painter but it is not outstanding. I have always found that it is those painters who cannot paint properly who accuse me of using such methods as the camera obscura. Why can't they just accept that I am a genius?'

I smiled. 'Many commentators have also found it hard to believe that you did not use preparatory drawings. A fine Flemish artist named Peter Paul Rubens, who was the painter Del Monte cured of a snake bite, admired your work but criticised you for not making preparatory drawings and thought your work would have been better if you had prepared more carefully.'

Merisi shrugged. 'I vaguely remember this man Rubens. I never found it necessary to make preparatory drawings. It was here in my head how the picture would look.' He tapped his temple with a finger. 'I sketched out the composition lightly in oils before I began. Why waste hours doing drawings when you can be painting? Later on, when I was on the run, I didn't have time for meticulous preparation. Perhaps some of my later works could have done with more thought and preparation but, tell me truly Stefano, would this painting of a lute player have been improved by preparatory drawings?'

I had to admit that it would not. 'By the way, Michele, how well did you know a Flemish painter named Jan Brueghel?'

Merisi's eyes lit up. 'Jan! I knew him very well. We were drinking buddies, always getting into scrapes together. Borromeo had to get him out of prison once. Is he still remembered today?'

'Very much so,' I said. 'He is nicknamed "Velvet Brueghel" because of the smoothness of his technique compared with his brothers and his father, who were also painters.'

'Yes, he was an exquisite painter. I learned much from him about the depiction of light. I am delighted that his reputation survives.'

I said: 'I'm intrigued by life in the Palazzo Madama. I think, this afternoon, I will pay a visit to your good friend Cardinal Del Monte.'

'This afternoon?' Merisi queried. 'Then what am I to do while you are gone?'

'I don't know,' I said. 'Watch the box that lies. Or go for a walk. It's a lovely afternoon.'

'Lovely!' Merisi exclaimed. 'It's freezing!'

'Nonsense,' I said. 'You can borrow my overcoat. It'll be most bracing for you.' Merisi adopted his sulky look. 'We'll have lunch soon,' I continued, 'but first I'd like to talk about two more of your most interesting works.'

'Very well,' Merisi sighed. 'Which ones?'

'Let's begin with this extraordinary image of the Medusa. (*Plate 13*). I assume that Cardinal Del Monte commissioned it. How did that come about?'

'Oh, that one,' Merisi said, almost dismissively. 'Del Monte wanted it as a gift for his patron Ferdinando Medici. He wanted to show Medici what his new pet artist could do. It was to be displayed in Medici's armoury, along with other displays of exotic arms and armour.'

'Today, it's one of your most famous works,' I said.

'Really?' Merisi said, surprised. 'It's nothing but a visual trick. It was painted on canvas and then fixed to a shield made of wood . . . poplar, if I remember rightly. It shows the moment that the Gorgon Medusa catches sight of herself in the shield of Perseus and knows she is doomed as Perseus slices off her head.'

'It's a terrifying image,' I said. 'Is there any hidden meaning in it?'

'In the context of our enquiry? No. Del Monte told me precisely what he wanted. All the elements are derived from classical mythology. As I have said, it was just a gift. It was, how you say, a "bagatelle".'

I had to smile to myself to hear such a powerful work described as a 'bagatelle' by the creator, but I said nothing more. 'Okay, let's talk about The Ecstasy of Saint Francis', (*Plate 14*) I continued. 'This is another of your works that has evoked widespread admiration. Some art historians have commented that this work is the beginning of what is now known as the Baroque style. It's a most moving work, tender and mystical. Who commissioned it?'

'I think it was Cardinal Borromeo, who had made a pilgrimage to where Saint Francis of Assissi had received the stigmata. I saw this picture as an opportunity to say something new about the subject and about art in general.'

'I think you succeeded brilliantly. The painting has an honesty, a simplicity and a beauty that is most compelling. It's suffused with love and tenderness. I find it hard to believe that someone as abrasive as you actually painted it.'

'You are a master of the backhanded compliment, but thank you,' Merisi said dryly. 'I am still pleased with this picture. I admit I have been a rough and vulgar man, a violent man. But in this picture I was inspired by the subject to reveal something of my own inner soul. I have to say it is a very personal work.'

'That doesn't surprise me, Michele. Who were the models?'

'My friend Cordier posed for the angel. Saint Francis was simply one of Del Monte's servants. He had a strong, interesting face and he was honoured to pose as Saint Francis. I used him again as a model, when I decorated a ceiling at Del Monte's new villa at the Porta Pinciana.'

'Ah, yes,' I said. 'This must be what is now known as the Villa Ludovisi.'

'It was situated in a lovely part of the city and Del Monte was very pleased with his new acquisition. He used this villa to entertain his guests to musical concerts. He set up a distillery and used the villa to perform his alchemical experiments and to formulate his experimental drugs and medicines. I frescoed the ceiling next to the distilllery. It was some mythological subject . . .'

'The gods Jupiter, Neptune and Pluto gathered around the sphere of the world,' I interjected.

'Yes, that's right, now that you refresh my memory. I found that work difficult. I was not experienced in working in fresco. I asked Mario Minnitti to help me. He was very valuable to me on that project. I think Del Monte was reasonably pleased with my work but he was shrewd enough to know that fresco was not my forte.'

I put my books to one side and said: 'A good morning's work, Michele. Let's stop for lunch. I'm getting hungry. What would you like to eat?'

'Anything you like,' Merisi said. 'I'm not fussy. I cannot understand where all this food comes from. You seem to have as much food as you want, all the time.'

'They had shops in your day, didn't they?'

'Of course. But there were only a few things to buy . . . meat, fish, bread, cheese, sausage. Now you go out in that car of yours and you come back half an hour later with bags made of some peculiar material and full of the most amazing things packed in metal, paper and some other peculiar material. You must be a very rich man.'

'Not at all,' I said. 'I have some very good friends named Tesco, Sainsbury and Morrison. They own huge shops which we now call supermarkets. Mr. Tesco owns one on the road between here and Bedford. He gives me all I want. Come on, let's go and eat.'

18

A manservant led me through the ground floor rooms of the palazzo but it was not, as I had told Merisi, the Palazzo Madama to interview Cardinal Del Monte. It was the Palazzo Giustiniani. The ChronoConverter had brought me back to interview Gerolama Giustiniani, the woman who Merisi claimed had been his lover. I was hoping that I could talk to her without her husband being present but that would be very difficult. It would not be decorous to be alone with a noble married lady and to have requested to see her alone would signal that there was some indiscreet or delicate matter that needed to be talked about in such privacy. I decided to play it by ear and see what I could find out about this alleged affair under the pretence of my inquiry about Merisi's murder, an inquiry which was common knowledge in Rome by now. I wanted to see Gerolama's husband Giuseppe as well. I wanted to gauge his mood regarding Caravaggio and try to ascertain whether he might have found out about his wife's affair with Caravaggio and whether he might have been implicated in any plot to kill Caravaggio. The manservant had told me that the couple were taking the air in their pleasance, a private garden in the enclosed courtyard of the palazzo. It was a lovely day in seventeenth century Rome. The sun was bright but it was not too hot and there was a pleasant cooling breeze. The manservant led me out into the garden. I was entranced by its beauty. The garden was enclosed by the elegant colonnades of the palazzo. A large fountain containing a huge sculture of some scene from classical mythology poured cool water rippling over pure white marble with an exquisite play of light and a soothing bubbling sound. Small trees mingled with antique statuary all around the garden. There were songbirds in golden cages, singing happily, and peacocks roamed loose on the lawns. I was led through a long pergola that was decorated with flowers. In the centre of the garden, seated on a marble bench positioned on an elaborate terrazzo base, were Giuseppe and Gerolama Giustiniani. They were talking and laughing animatedly and looked a picture of domestic contentment. Giuseppe stood up as he saw me approaching. He was, indeed, a short man, as Merisi had told me. He was elegantly dressed, as was only to be expected. His hair and neatly pointed beard were black. He was thin-lipped, again as Merisi had said, with a long thin nose. Instead of being unattractive, the combination of these features gave him a haughtily handsome appearance, like a compact bird of prey. I bowed to him, and then to Gerolama, as Merisi had instructed me to do in the presence of the nobility, but Merisi had thought that I was going to be bowing to Cardinal Del Monte. I said: 'Thank you for seeing me at such short notice. My apologies for interrupting your leisure on such a fine day.'

'Not at all,' Giuseppe said. 'I have, of course, heard about your mission regarding the artist Caravaggio. I have been curious to make your acquaintance and see what you might have learned about his mysterious demise. My wife has been equally curious.' Neither of them showed the slightest hesitancy or discomfort at the mention of the name Caravaggio. Giuseppe said: 'Perhaps we can show you around our garden while we talk. We're very proud of it.'

'With good reason,' I said. 'I would be delighted.'

'Come my dear,' Giuseppe invited, and held out his hand to assist his wife in rising from the marble bench. Gerolama stood up. She was at least six inches taller than her husband. She was a strikingly lovely and stately woman, with piercing blue eyes that complemented her blue brocaded dress and chestnut hair dressed in an elaborate but elegant style. Her eyes betrayed a fierce intelligence. I could see why Merisi, or any other man, would be smitten by her. The three of us strolled slowly around the garden exchanging small talk. I gave them a very abbreviated and censored version of what little I had found out about Merisi's death and then, finally, the conversation turned to their personal relationship with Caravaggio. I said to Gerolama: 'Your ladyship, I believe that you consented to model for Caravaggio in some of his pictures?'

Gerolama looked at her husband and they smiled at each other in that conspiratorial way that people do when they are sharing a private joke or a juicy secret. 'With my husband's permission, I did indeed consent to model for Caravaggio on two occasions.' Her voice was light but husky, a joy to listen to.

Giuseppe said: 'Caravaggio had told us that he needed a very beautiful woman to model for a picture he was planning, so I offered him my wife. I know of no more beautiful woman in the world.' Gerolama rewarded him with a smile filled with love and sweetness. If this was an act on her behalf, it was very convincing.

'I am a foreigner in this country,' I said, 'and not familiar with all its etiquette and manners, so I find it surprising that a lady of the nobility would sit as a model for an artist.'

'It amused my wife to do so,' Giuseppe said, 'and both pictures were of respectable subjects, so I saw no harm in it.'

'I admired Caravaggio's work very much,' Gerolama agreed, 'so I was interested to see how he worked. But my sitting for him was not very satisfactory.'

'Do you mind telling me why?' I asked.

'Because the poor man was so enamoured of me that he could hardly hold his brush.' Gerolama looked at Giuseppe and they both laughed heartily.

Giuseppe said: 'Here was this belligerent painter, a man who would swagger out on the town with a sword by his side, picking fights with whoever happened to upset him, consorting with the lowest sort of women by night, and yet he would stammer and blush whenever my wife spoke to him. It was a most comical sight.' The Giustiniani's could hardly contain their mirth at the memory of Merisi's discomfiture.

I had anticipated all sorts of reactions, but not this one. I asked Giuseppe: 'Did you see this yourself, my lord? Were you with your wife while she modelled for Caravaggio?'

'Oh, yes,' he said. 'I would not have left her alone with him. That would not have been decorous. As you can see, Caravaggio's discomfiture became our private amusement. Of course, we never betrayed that fact to him and it does us little credit to have laughed at him so, but we couldn't help it.'

'Do you consider, your ladyship, that Caravaggio had fallen in love with you?'

'I don't know about love,' Gerolama replied, 'but he was certainly most taken with me.'

'Let me be completely frank,' I said to Gerolama. 'Did you do or say anything to encourage this infatuation or to make him believe that you might have felt the same?'

'Of course not,' Gerolama said, gaily. 'It was all a fantasy in that poor crazy head of his.'

'I am going to be even more frank,' I persisted, anxious to find the truth. 'Caravaggio told me, when I knew him in Naples, that he had had a love affair with you. Do you deny that?'

Once again, the couple were not at all discomfited or offended by the question but laughed heartily at the mere thought of such a liaison. 'It is complete nonsense,' Gerolama replied, 'a figment of Caravaggio's wild imagination. Look around you, Signor Maddano. I have a beautiful home, a husband whom I love with all my heart, and an honoured and respected place in society. Do you think I would endanger all this to have an affair with an unstable painter who was, however talented, merely a lowly servant?'

At that moment I was not sure who to believe, Caravaggio or Gerolama, but Gerolama had made a convincing argument. But wasn't that exactly what she would say with her husband listening?

Giuseppe stopped and looked at me. 'This man Caravaggio touched on our lives only briefly,' he said. 'We thought it a little odd that you wished to see us on this matter of his death. Now that you have explained about Caravaggio's wild fantasy, we understand why you wished to do so. You suspected that my wife might have had an affair with Caravaggio, that I had found out about it and that I took my revenge on him. Is that not so?'

'Yes, it is,' I admitted.

Giuseppe said: 'I have heard that the Holy Father has enjoined us to tell you the truth, in fear of imperilling our immortal souls. I swear to you now, by Almighty God, that I had no reason and no cause to harm Caravaggio.'

Gerolama said: 'And I swear by Almighty God that I never betrayed my marital vows with Caravaggio. Besides,' she continued, smiling again, 'he was a smelly brute.'

'Do our answers satisfy your curiosity, Signor Maddano?' Giuseppe asked.

'Yes, certainly,' I answered. 'Thank you for your frankness. Before I leave you in peace, can I ask your ladyship which two of Caravaggio's pictures you modelled for?'

'The first one I modelled for was as Martha in his picture of the conversion of Mary Magdalen,' Gerolama said. 'He had me dress in humble clothing, like a servant. It was most amusing, wasn't it, husband.' Giuseppe nodded happily. (*Plate 15*).

'Did you model while the other woman in the picture was present?' I asked, knowing that the other woman had been Merisi's model and mistress, Fillide Melandroni.

'No,' Gerolama said. 'Caravaggio painted the two figures separately. I don't know who the other woman was.' Just as well, I thought to myself. 'And it was the same with the second picture,' Gerolama went on. 'I modelled as Judith beheading Holofernes. I was quite horrified when I saw the finished picture. It is very brutal.' (*Plate 16*).

'Do you regret having modelled for Caravaggio?' I asked.

'No, not at all,' Gerolama said. 'It was all most amusing and diverting and not many people know that it is was me who modelled for those pictures.' If you only knew, darling, I thought to myself.

I took my leave of the happy couple and their delightful pleasance and found myself outside again with the noisy, smelly, bustling commoners on the street. I had been convinced by the denials of Mr. and Mrs. Giustiniani, which meant that Merisi had lied to me yet again. Or, perhaps, because of his febrile imagination, he truly believed he had had an affair with Gerolama Giustiniani. Across the road stood the Palazzo Madama, clearly distinguishable by the large sculpted arms of the Medici family over the doorway. On an impulse, I decided to go and interview Cardinal Del Monte. I knew it was an injudicious decision, that I needed to prepare my approach before I saw him, but the meeting with the Giustiniani's had not taken long and I decided, as I was there, to take my chances. I crossed the street and knocked on the small auxiliary door that was set into the huge wooden double doors that served as the main entrance to the palazzo. A man opened the door but did not invite me in. He was dressed better than a servant but not as well as a noble. I guessed he was some sort of major-domo. I adopted my most imperious and pompous manner and said: 'I am here on papal business to see Cardinal Del Monte.'

'I'm sorry, sir,' the major-domo replied, 'but the cardinal is not in residence.'

'When will he be home?' I asked.

'He is travelling, sir, and will not return for several days.'

'Oh,' I said, completely deflated. I was about to take my leave when a voice behind me said: 'Signor Maddano! We meet again!'

I turned around to see Doctor Giulio Mancini smiling at me. This was beginning to seem more than a coincidence, the convenient way that Mancini kept 'accidentally' bumping into me. I would have to consider whether he was deliberately tailing me. It seemed unlikely, as I didn't know myself until a few minutes ago that I would be at the door of the Palazzo Madama. 'Doctor Mancini,' I said. 'A pleasant surprise to see you again. I had come to see Cardinal Del Monte but this man here informs me that he is not in residence.'

'That's correct,' Mancini confirmed. 'The good cardinal is off paying homage to his master, Grand Duke Ferdinando Medici. You will have to wait a few days.'

'Have you not come to visit the cardinal?' I asked.

'No, I am here to see the sculptor, Cordier. He is very ill.'

'Nicholas Cordier?' I asked. 'The Frenchman?'

'The very same,' Mancini replied. 'Would you like to see him? If you wish to interview him about our friend Caravaggio, it might be wise to seize your opportunity now. He may not last much longer.'

I knew from my research that Nicholas Cordier had not died until a few months later. I asked Mancini: 'What's wrong with him?'

'It's a very puzzling case,' Mancini said. 'You helped Caravaggio's brother with his gout problem. Perhaps you might have some ideas about what is wrong with Cordier. I have run out of ideas.'

'Very well,' I said, 'although I doubt whether I will be of any use on medical grounds.'

Mancini turned to the major-domo and said: 'Carlo . . . Signor Maddano here is known to me. He is an eminent physician in his own land and has kindly agreed to assist me with the treatment of the sculptor Cordier. I request that you admit him. I will take responsibility for him.'

Carlo nodded and held the door open so that we could step through. 'You know the way, Doctor Mancini,' Carlo said, indifferently. 'I'll leave you to it.'

Mancini slung his medical bag over his shoulder and beckoned me through a small door positioned a little way into the reception area. It led to a narrow stairway which was the backstairs of the palazzo, the stairs used by servants and other menials. We walked all the way up to the top floor and Mancini led me to a corridor that had been crudely divided by wooden panels into small rooms and cubicles. Cordier was lying in bed, asleep, in a small, sparsely furnished cubicle. Mancini went off and found a couple of stools for us to sit on. I looked at Cordier. He was snoring lightly. His face had a ghastly white pallor and he looked very thin, otherwise he seemed to be reasonably comfortable.

Mancini returned with the stools and whispered to me across the bed. 'It is a strange case. Cordier is losing control of his eyelids and, much more seriously, his ability to swallow anything. He has stopped taking solid food. He can just about swallow broth but he is losing weight because of his inability to eat properly.'

I looked at Cordier again. I knew that he was only in his mid-forties but he appeared much older. 'As you say, doctor, a most perplexing case. I cannot, offhand, think what malady could have caused these symptoms. I will give the problem some thought.' It sounded to me like Cordier might be suffering from muscular dystrophy but I was not prepared to raise Mancini's suspicions by parading any more of my medical knowledge in front of him.

Mancini put his hand on Cordier's brow and then took his wrist to feel his pulse. 'Much the same,' Mancini pronounced. 'He has been like this for several days now.' Mancini's attentions had stirred Cordier from his sleep. He opened his eyes and blinked at us both in turn.

'Nicholas,' Mancini said softly, indicating to me, 'this is Signor Stefano Maddano. He was a friend of Michelangelo Merisi da Caravaggio. He has been commanded by His Holiness to investigate the circumstances of Michele's death and he would like to ask you a few questions about Michele. Do you feel up to it?' Cordier nodded. Mancini went on: 'Before you talk, let me give you a drink of water and some of your medicine.' Mancini tenderly supported Cordier's head while the sculptor took several sips of water out of a wooden cup. There was a flask on a shelf beside Cordier's bed. Mancini measured several drops of some liquid contained in the flask into the wooden cup.

'What's that?' I asked.

'It is something that Cardinal Del Monte kindly prepared for Nicholas,'

Mancini said. 'The cardinal is highly knowledgeable about the medicinal effects of herbs and plants. I don't know what this is but it appears to ease the symptoms temporarily so that Nicholas can swallow and talk a little.' To Cordier he said: 'How do you feel today, Nicholas? Any better?'

'A little,' Cordier whispered huskily. 'Thank the cardinal for his medicine, would you?'

'Of course,' Mancini replied, not mentioning that Cardinal Del Monte was away on business.

'While you are here, doctor,' I said, 'permit me to ask you and Nicholas about something that Michele told me when we worked together in Naples.' I outlined Michele's claims that he had had an affair with Gerolama Giustiniani. Mancini chuckled, and even Cordier managed a wan smile.

'It is not possible,' Mancini said emphatically. 'It was just one of Michele's fantasies, like his being of noble birth.'

'Michele was like a lovelorn schoolboy with Gerolama,' Cordier croaked. 'He was completely besotted by her. But he never had an affair with her. Michele and I were very close at the time. I'd have known if he was up to something with her. She was just his fantasy while he was playing with himself.'

'I see,' I said. I did not think it was necessary to tell them that they had confirmed what Gerolama herself had just told me. 'Doctor, you said that Michele liked to claim that he was of noble birth. Do you think there was any truth in that?'

'No,' Mancini scoffed. 'Michele always thought he was better than everyone else, especially when he was in his cups.' I remembered from my researches that Michele's mother, Lucia Aratori, might have descended from a noble family. That was probably all there was to that fantasy. Mancini stood up and said: 'Can I leave you to talk to Nicholas, Signor Maddano? I have other patients to see and I'm sure that Nicholas will appreciate some cultured company.'

'Of course,' I said. 'I can find my own way out.' I was glad of the opportunity to talk to Cordier alone. 'He's a busy man,' I said to Cordier, as Mancini disappeared down the corridor.

'Busy in the bedroom,' Cordier whispered.

'I've heard other people say that about the good doctor.'

'That's just what he's not,' Cordier said.

'What?'

'A good doctor. He has no idea what is wrong with me.'

'He's working on it,' I said, trying to be a comfort. 'I'm sure he'll find the cure.' I knew that Cordier would die in this cubicle.

Cordier was not going to allow himself to be comforted. Before I could assist him, Cordier wriggled up the bed into a more upright position. 'I'll never see my lovely France again,' he said, out of breath from even such a small effort. 'I didn't want to come here in the first place and now I'll never get back.'

'You mean you didn't want to come to the Palazzo Madama?'

'I didn't want to come to Rome,' Cordier whispered. 'I didn't want to come to Italy.'

'Then why are you here?' I asked.

'I was very happy. I was in love with my wife. I was in love with my work as a sculptor. I was working in Nancy for Duke Charles of Lorraine. Then my whole world collapsed. My wife died of the plague. Then this Cardinal Del Monte invited me to come and live and work here in Rome. I was told that he admired my work and wanted to help and support me. Despite what had happened to my wife, I wanted to stay in Nancy. I wanted to carry on serving the Duke. He was a kind man, a humane man, but he ordered me to go to Rome. I asked him why he was sending me away. He said that he had no choice in the matter. He was almost as upset as I was. He paid all the expenses of my journey and gave me a very generous bonus. I arrived here to work for the cardinal and I have not been allowed to leave.'

'Why didn't you just stay in France? Find another patron?'

'It was made abundantly clear to me that there would be no further work for me in France. I either carried on my trade in Rome or I could not do it anywhere. I have requested to leave here several times but each time the message has been the same. If I return to France, or if I leave Rome, there will be no work for me anywhere.'

'Who ordered this to be?' I asked. I vaguely remembered, from my researches, that Cardinal Del Monte's master, Grand Duke Ferdinando de Medici, had married a princess named Christine of Lorraine. Was there a connection?

'I wish I knew who ordered my exile,' Cordier said, 'but each time I tried to get out of this imprisonment I was made aware, in no uncertain terms, that I could not.'

'How were you made aware?'

'By emissaries who would suddenly arrive and remind me of my duty and of the consequences if I did not follow orders. I love my work as a sculptor so I have made the best of it and got on with my work. But I yearn to see my homeland again.'

I was touched by this statement. I wished that I could help Cordier but I could not interfere in things that had already been and were yet to be. 'Let me ask you about our friend Michele,' I said, 'if you feel strong enough.'

'Yes, I am strong enough. I would like to talk about Michele. I was very sad when I heard of his death. As a human being, he was almost worthless. As a painter, he was the best. I cannot understand how such magnificence came out of that mixed-up mind and on to the canvas. Michele came here to the palazzo about two or three years after I had arrived. Cardinal Del Monte himself introduced me to him. The cardinal gave Michele a room next to mine and asked me, as a personal favour, to befriend Michele and keep an eye on him, to keep him out of trouble.'

'An impossible job,' I smiled.

'Certainly. But how could I refuse a great man like the cardinal?'

'How did you get on with Michele?'

'At first, not too badly. He was always a difficult man to understand but, as you know, he could be lively and charming company when he had a mind to be. I would go out drinking with Michele and Mario and other friends like Orsi and Longhi. I was never very keen on the Roman taverns but I had promised the cardinal that I would watch over Michele. It was a few months after Michele had moved into the palazzo that he started this foolish bragging about being of noble birth, of being of higher status than the rest of us. It was only when he was drunk that he would talk like that. Orsi and Longhi egged him on and Michele would get more and more furious with them. It usually ended up with a fight or an argument. I tried to keep the peace but it was impossible. In the morning, when he had sobered up, Michele would deny that he had ever said such things.'

'Do you believe he might have been of noble birth?'

Cordier tried to laugh but ended up coughing. I poured some water into his wooden cup and gave him a few sips. 'Merci,' he said. 'No, Michele was not of noble birth. It was just a ridiculous fantasy, just like his affair with Gerolama Giustiniani. Michele had a crazy brain. Who knows what imaginary lies inserted themselves into that brain, lies he came to believe himself. You understand what I mean?'

'Very much so,' I said. 'Where I come from, we had, for many years, a Prime Minister who thinks exactly like that.'

'Pardon,' Cordier said. 'What is "prime minister"?'

'Oh, a minor functionary,' I said. 'A warmonger who cares more about his own aggrandisement than about the legal and efficient performance of his duties.'

'Most princes behave in such a way,' Cordier agreed. 'Which country are you from, Signor Maddano?'

'Err, Scotland,' I lied.

'Ah, Scotland!' Cordier said. 'They have been friends of France against the English heretic barbarians for many centuries.'

'Yes, hoots mon and death to the English,' I said. The ChronoTranslator could not manage 'hoots mon' and it came out of my mouth as 'huge man'. Cordier did not seem to notice. 'Thank you for talking to me, Monseiur Cordier. I know that Michele admired your work.'

'Thank you for trying to comfort me, Signor Maddano, but I know that Michele was indifferent to my work, and to me.'

19

It was late afternoon when the ChronoConverter landed me back in my own bedroom. I changed into modern dress and went downstairs. Merisi was not in the house. My overcoat was missing from the coat rack in the hallway so I guessed that he had accepted my suggestion and gone out for a walk. I made myself a sandwich and a cup of coffee and then filled in my notebook with everything I had learned from the Giustinianis and from Nicholas Cordier. Then I carefully read back over my notes and tried to make sense of everything I had learned about Merisi and his life so far. It was all very puzzling. My main concern was why Merisi was lying to me or, at best, withholding the truth about so many aspects of his former life. It was very discouraging. Even if I confronted him with my discoveries and demanded that he tell me the exact truth in future, I doubted whether he would do so. He was such an obtuse bastard. With Merisi unco-operative, for whatever reason, with the problems of travelling back in time and choosing who to interview, with so many of Merisi's paintings lost forever, any one of which may have contained the clue or clues we were looking for, I was beginning to think that I would never uncover the reason why someone had tried to murder Merisi in Porto Ercole in 1610.

About two hours after I had travelled back from Rome, the front door bell rang. I thought it would be Merisi back from his walk. I opened the front door to see Sergeant Caro and the Jolly Greenfield Giant standing there. Sergeant Caro said: 'I think you had better come with us, Mr. Maddan.'

'Merisi?' I asked.

Caro nodded.

'I'll get my keys,' I said.

I climbed in the back of the police car. As we pulled out into the road, Sergeant Caro said to me: 'We've just had a call for back-up and it sounds like you could be useful to us. I know you haven't got a car after the previous incident involving Mr. Merisi, so we stopped to pick you up, just to save time.'

'Very considerate,' I said. Dusk was falling and the street lamps had just switched on. We turned on to the main road towards Bedford. The traffic was heavy but it was only five minutes later when the police car turned into the car park of the Tesco superstore. There was another police car already parked. Over by the main entrance, which was a large revolving door, there was some sort of commotion going on. There was a small crowd of onlookers and, beyond them, two policemen were standing outside the revolving door. Other shoppers were being shepherded in and out of a smaller swing door at the side of the building by Tesco staff. Sergeant Caro said: 'We had a report that Mr. Merisi had been drinking at the Riverside Tavern just outside Bedford. He was beginning to cause a bit of trouble but he did leave when the manager asked him to. Half an hour later we received reports about the commotion here.'

'Let's go and talk to him,' I sighed. We got out of the car and went over to the main entrance. Merisi was standing inside the revolving doors with a shopping trolley. The trolley was stacked to overflowing with goods. It was filled with boxes of pizzas, trays of cooked meats, sausages, cheeses, and dozens of bottles of wine and spirits. He had somehow used the shopping trolley to wedge himself inside the revolving door so that it could not turn and nobody could get to him. He was swigging out of a bottle of scotch. He was soaking wet. His hair, and my overcoat he was wearing, were caked with mud. He looked like the worst sort of down-and-out. The two police officers already on the scene were trying to coax him out. A Tesco security guard stood inside the store talking agitatedly into his mobile phone.

'This is my food,' Merisi was roaring. 'It belongs to me. Mister Tesco is a personal friend of my friend and he said I can have what I liked for nothing, so just fuck off and mind your own business.' I tapped on the glass and Merisi turned and looked at me with a befuddled glassy-eyed stare. Eventually he realised who I was and smiled broadly. 'Here he is!' he announced loudly to the crowd watching this scene. 'This is my friend Stefano. He is a personal friend of Mister Tesco. Tell them who you are, Stefano. Tell them that all this belongs to you.'

'Michele,' I shouted back through the glass, 'you've got the wrong idea. All these goods do not belong to you or me unless we have paid for them. They are not free.'

Merisi stared at me. 'But you told me you were a friend of Mister Tesco. And Mister Saints and Mister somebody or other. You said they give you everything you want.'

'I meant I can have as much as I want, but I still have to pay for it. I was being facetious. It was a joke. Why don't you come out before you get into any more trouble?'

'You have lied to me again,' Merisi said, angrily. 'Always you are lying to me.'

'Me lying to you!' I exclaimed, feeling embarassed and angry. 'That's rich!

You've been lying to me about most things since you moved in with me. You lied about being in prison. You said you had an affair with Gerolama when you didn't and didn't have an affair with Fillide when you did!' I heard a fat woman standing behind me say to the crowd: 'Oh, it sounds like a lover's tiff. That foreigner's been in prison and he's had an affair with Jeremy and Phil.' I shouted: 'Michele! I'm sorry I lied to you. Why are you wet?'

'I went for a swim in the river. Is that all right? Or do I have to pay for that to?'

There was a public footpath leading from the Riverside Tavern to the Tesco superstore, so I guessed that Merisi had slipped or fallen into the River Ouse after his drinking bout at the tavern. I said: 'Please put that bottle down and come out here. We can sort this out.'

Merisi looked at me accusingly, then took a large swig out of the scotch bottle but, to my relief, he shifted the shopping trolley so that the revolving door started to turn again. He pushed the trolley outside. He let go of the trolley and one of the policemen grabbed it and moved it out of the way. Merisi stood there swaying backwards and forwards. Sergeant Caro said: 'Mr. Merisi, I have to caution you that . . .' She had to stop mid-sentence as Merisi started pitching forward. I just managed to grab him before he fell full on his face. I broke his fall but his deadweight dragged me down and I ended up sprawled on top of him. I was rewarded with a round of applause from the onlookers.

'Why don't you two kiss and make up while you're down there?' the fat woman said.

I looked up at the Tesco security guard, who had come out to help defuse the situation, and said: 'I'll pay for the whisky and for any damage he might have caused.'

'That's all right, sir,' the security guard said. 'The goods are undamaged. The police know where you live. If the management decide to press charges, we'll let you know. I think it's best for all of us if you get him out of here and let us get back to trading normally.'

With the help of the Jolly Greenfield Giant, I staggered to my feet. Merisi was unconscious. 'Can we get him home?' I asked Sergeant Caro. She consulted with her fellow officers and they agreed. In Merisi's present condition there was no point arresting him or charging him.

'Yes, let's get him home so he can sleep it off,' Caro agreed. It took four of us to lift Merisi up and get him into the back of the police car. I climbed in beside him. His head fell on my shoulder and the greatest Italian Baroque artist of the seventeenth century began snoring loudly as we sped through the peaceful Bedfordshire countryside.

20

With the help of the police officers I managed to put Merisi to bed. We left him fully clothed except for taking off his mud-caked overcoat and sodden shoes. After the officers had left I strategically placed an empty bucket by the side of Merisi's bed and hoped that he would have sense enough to use it, if he desperately needed to. I looked in on him before I turned in. He was snoring heavily and was murmuring in a restless sleep. The bucket was still unused, so I left him to it. In the morning I looked in on him again. The bucket, thankfully, was still empty. He was snoring lightly and looked more peaceful. I studied his face while he slept. For some reason that I could not explain, I suddenly felt a strong sense of sadness and compassion on his behalf. He was a difficult man but he had faced and overcome many more terrible problems and tragedies in his life than I would ever have to. I was not alone in my sympathy with Merisi because, soon after I had finished my breakfast and was sitting in the kitchen reading the newspaper over a cup of coffee, the front doorbell rang. I went to open the door. The woman standing there looked familiar but, stupidly, I could not place who she was for a few seconds. Then it dawned on me. 'Sergeant Caro,' I said. 'I'm sorry, I didn't recognise you out of uniform.'

'I'm not on duty until later today,' she replied. 'I just called to see how Mr. Merisi is.'

I looked at Sergeant Caro's anxious face and knew why she had come. 'Come in and have a cup of coffee,' I said.

Caro smiled gratefully and I led her through to the kitchen and sat her in a chair. 'Michele is still asleep,' I said, while I poured a cup of coffee. 'I don't think he will be stirring very early today.'

'Michele.' Caro repeated the name, wistfully.

I placed the coffee on the table in front of her and sat down opposite her. 'He's okay,' I said, 'but I suspect he'll have the mother of all hangovers when he wakes up.' Caro gave me a wan smile and nodded. I said: 'You've been protecting him, haven't you?'

'No, not exactly,' Caro answered, but her hesitant tone and the slight pink tinge in her cheeks told me she was lying.

'I'm very grateful if you have been,' I said. 'I had expected him to be arrested or dragged back to an asylum centre long before this time.' Caro began to speak. 'No, you don't have to say anything,' I interrupted her. 'Whether you have or haven't been protecting him is nothing to do with me, and I won't say a word to anyone. But you cannot allow yourself to get emotionally attached to Michele.'

'Why?' she asked. 'Is he married?'

'No.'

'He's not gay, is he?'

'Certainly not.'

'Then why . . .'

I interrupted again. 'He has to return to where he comes from very soon and, for reasons he would not wish me to tell you, you could not go with him.'

'You mean, back to Italy?' Caro asked.

'Yes, but to a place where you could not go with him.'

'Oh, God, you mean prison, don't you?'

'Yes,' I lied, 'he is certainly a prisoner, of sorts. But tell me, what do you see in him? You've seen how he behaves, how unstable he is. If you think you could change him you'll be sadly mistaken.'

'I wouldn't want to change him,' Caro said. 'That's why he . . . fascinates me. I've always had a thing about Italian men, that's why I got a transfer to Bedford, because there is a large Italian community living here. My dad was Italian and my ex-husband was Italian, so Sigmund Freud would have enough material for an entire book with all that. But Michele seems different, even from other Italians. There is something strange, exotic, mysterious about him. It's like he doesn't quite belong in this world. Don't laugh, but he only has to look at me with those big black eyes of his and I forget that I'm a respectable officer in Bedfordshire constabulary. What is worse, I don't care.'

'I'm not laughing,' I said. 'I understand exactly what you mean, but you have to believe me that there is no future for you and him. Please don't throw away your life and career because of him. He is a worthless wretch who will just use you and then dump you.'

As often happens when you try to tell someone something bad about the person they are besotted with, Caro was not pleased by my bald statement. 'Then why do you let him live here?' she challenged, weakly.

'Because I am using him and in a few days, a few weeks at most, he will be gone back to where he came from and I will never see him again. Nor should you.'

Caro did not believe me and was struggling to control her emotions. She stood up and said: 'I shouldn't have come here today. Please don't tell Michele that I came to see him. I'd better go.'

I had no intention of telling Merisi how Sergeant Caro felt about him and I prayed that he would not stir until I had shifted her out of the front door. 'Just think about what he is like and what I have just told you,' I urged. 'I am not saying these things because of any hidden personal agenda but because they are true. Forget about him.' Caro looked at me, her eyes full of bitterness, and then hurried off down the drive to her car. I closed the door and let out a deep breath. The last thing I needed was Merisi to become personally involved with anyone else from this century, especially not a police officer, with all the attendant risks of the truth coming out about his most incredible presence in our modern world.

For the next two hours I sat at the kitchen table, trying to read the newspaper but all the time with my thoughts drifting off to my problems with Merisi, about this new emerging situation with Sergeant Caro, as well as my problems finding out the truth about his last hours back in 1610. Then the man himself staggered into the kitchen. He looked dreadful. His eyes were bloodshot, his face with a ghastly pallor, the remains of the white scars from the attack in Naples even more prominent than usual. He was unwashed and still dressed as he had been yesterday.

'Sit down,' I ordered. I poured him a glass of fresh orange juice, which he gulped greedily.

'Give me aspirin,' he croaked.

I gave him two aspirin and a couple of tabs of Alka-Seltzer for good measure. He swallowed the lot and sat with his head in his hands, groaning. I poured him a mug of strong, sweet coffee, then set about cooking him scrambled eggs with bacon. I placed the plate in front of him and he looked at it with horror. I hoped he was not going to throw up. 'Not hungry,' he said. 'Can't eat anything. Never had a headache like this before, not even when those bastards beat me up in Naples.'

'Just eat that,' I said. 'You'll feel much better a lot sooner if you do.' I had cut up the bacon and gave Merisi a spoon to eat it with. I doubted if he could manage a knife and fork. His hand trembled as he lifted the spoon to his mouth, but at least he was eating. I said: 'When you're ready, go and take a shower and change into clean clothes. Perhaps we can get some work done today. Do you remember what happened yesterday?'

'I went for a walk,' Merisi said. 'Found a place which said "tavern" outside, just like the Tavern of the Turk in Rome, where we used to drink. Had a few drinks. Walked back by a river. I think I slipped and fell in. Then I found this magical place, full of light, full of food, full of drink. I remember you saying that your friend owned it.'

'Mr. Tesco,' I smiled.

'Yes, that's right! I went in and I opened a bottle of whisky. Everything was free! Don't remember much after that. Did we have a fight? I seem to remember we were rolling about on the ground.'

'You tripped over, that's all.'

'Am I in any trouble?' Merisi asked, forlornly.

'No,' I replied. 'No more than usual. Some people seem to find your antics . . . attractive. Go and take a shower.'

When we finally settled down to work in the living room, quite late in the afternoon, I decided to needle Merisi while he was still in a fragile state. Underhand tactics, perhaps, but worth a try. 'Tell me,' I began, 'why is it that after you had been living with Cardinal Del Monte for two or three years, in comfortable circumstances in the Palazzo Madama, with your reputation as an artist of considerable skill growing all the time, that you became increasingly aggressive and sensitive to insults?' Merisi did, indeed, look suitably needled by my statement, so I verbally attacked him again. 'There you go,' I said. 'You look at me with disgust, as if I was a dog turd. Why were you, and are you, so sensitive?'

'Who says I was?'

'The criminal records from your time tell us you were,' I said. 'And the testimony of your friends and enemies. For instance, the first description we have of you from your time in Rome is from a barber named Luca. You, together with Prospero Orsi, were involved in some fracas involving a black cloak and . . .'

'It was me who returned the cloak to Luca!' Merisi protested. 'I returned his property and you accuse me of causing the trouble.'

'No,' I said, 'I am not accusing you. We know that you returned Luca's cloak after he had been assaulted in the street but Luca stated in court that you had previously been treated in his barber shop for a wound you had received in a fight. Your friend Costantino Spata, or Valentin, whichever you like to call him, appeared in court in your defence over this incident with the cloak. Valentin testified that you usually carried a sword, especially at night. Why did you habitually carry a sword?'

'We have already talked about this. Rome was a violent city at that time.'

'Other people, other artists, went out at night without a sword. Why did you think it was necessary?'

'I had a licence to carry a sword. Through my association with Cardinal Del Monte, I had the right to carry a weapon. If other people did not carry a sword, it was because they had no right, no licence to carry one.'

'Was Valentin covering up for you in court over this cloak incident?'

Merisi shrugged. 'He helped me out.'

'Why should he perjure himself to help you?'

'My pictures were selling well. He didn't want to lose a valuable source of income so he may have . . . bent the truth a little for me.' Merisi snorted at my look of moral indignation.

'This is what is so difficult for us to understand today,' I said. 'By day, you were living in the elegant and refined atmosphere of the palace of a cultured cardinal. You were painting the most exquisite works, full of beauty and gaiety on one hand, and intensely moving religious imagery on the other, then you would down your brushes, buckle on your sword and swagger out to the taverns and brothels of Rome, drinking, whoring, cursing, picking fights. It is such a dichotomy that we find it very difficult to reconcile the two sides of your nature.'

'What can I say? I am what I am. As I have said, Rome was a violent city. It was very much a male city. It was full of male churchmen, diplomats, ambassadors and so on, all with a retinue of male servants. It was full of artists and sculptors and builders. And soon after I arrived in Rome there was a huge influx of mercenary soldiers who had lost their employment after the wars ended. I wore a sword because it was sensible to try to protect oneself.'

'I can accept that,' I said, 'but, from all accounts, you went looking for trouble, not protecting yourself from it. We have accounts of you and your band of friends roaming from tavern to tavern, getting drunk, starting arguments, and always ready to defend your reputations and your honour with a violent response. "Nec spe, nec metu", wasn't that your motto?'

Merisi chuckled. 'That's right, Stefano. "Without hope, without fear". That summed up the attitude of most of us. What you need to understand, and what I cannot see in your browbeaten society today, is that a man's honour was of paramount importance in my time. What we were all hoping to achieve was status and respect. To be denigrated and insulted and to not respond to such insults was an open disgrace. We had to defend our honour and the weapon of choice for doing so was the sword or dagger. You could use your fists, if you had to, especially in a drunken street brawl, but for the gravest and most serious insults and slights, it was necessary to use the sword, to challenge your opponent to settle your differences man-to-man. To be a good swordsman was a universal ideal. Duelling had been deemed illegal but we ignored that law. And there was an elaborate ritual involved in answering slights against one's honour. It had to be done just so.'

'You're right,' I said, 'There is nothing like such codes of honour in England today. We are all so used to being trodden on by authority that we've gotten used to being insulted, abused, nannied and robbed by government and officialdom. Anyway, we know about most of your friends from that time. It seems that an architect named Onorio Longhi was the ringleader of your group of trouble makers. What was he like?'

'Onorio was a close friend,' Merisi said, smiling at the memory. 'He was just like me in temperament. What is it you English say . . . a man after my own heart. We both grew up around Milan so we had many mutual friends and acquaintances. He came from a family of architects and was the most talented of the lot. I didn't meet him until he came back to Rome in about 1598 or 1599. We took to each other immediately. We recognised each other as kindred spirits. He was much crazier than I was. He had a fierce temper. He was always starting fights in the taverns and the brothels. He would start a fight over anything . . . a tennis match, the way he was dressed, the quality of his work, anything. He was always in and out of court suing someone for libel or being sued himself. He always dressed very elegantly. He imagined himself an aristocrat and dressed himself in rich black velvet. He had a blond beard, so the contrast with the black velvet was striking. He was very attractive to the women. And he was very proud of the fact that he did not carry a sword himself but had a servant who carried a sword and followed Onorio around acting as his bodyguard. Onorio wanted to be a poet. He had some verse published but it wasn't very good. He had been educated at university, so he was cultured and very gifted as an architect. The best of him was that he was a very generous friend. I was in trouble many times, financially and physically, and Onorio was always there to help me out, without thought of gratitiude or repayment. I loved him like a brother.'

'Your old enemy, the biographer Baglione, said that, just like you, Longhi was a strange and difficult man and much hated by others . . .'

'That's because they did not understand him,' Merisi objected.

'But Baglione also commented on Longhi's generosity,' I said. 'When Longhi died, he did not leave much money. He had given most of it away.'

'Yes, that sounds just like Onorio,' Merisi chuckled. 'Do you know what happened to him after I supposedly died?'

'Yes, he died of a fever about ten years later,' I said. 'He was fifty years old.' Merisi made no further comment and was lost in thought for several seconds. I said: 'Did Longhi have any reason to wish you harm or to have plotted your death?'

Merisi snorted contemptuously. 'I told you, we were like brothers. We looked after each other.'

'I have to ask these questions,' I said. 'What about your other friends? We have already talked about Cherubino Alberti, who had helped you to find work and patrons. Did you remain friendly with him or fall out with him?'

To my surprise, Merisi laughed. 'Neither really,' he said. 'Cherubino was rich and successful as an engraver and artist. He came from an ancient and respected family. He had a wife and children, but he fell into a strange mood. He gave up his trade and started building catapults.'

'Catapults?' I repeated. 'What sort of catapults?'

'Siege catapults like mangonels and trebuchets and the like.'

'Do you mean full-size ones?' I asked.

'No, mainly large models. His house was full of these models. He would invite us to come and play with these models and test how they worked. He was crazy. We laughed at him behind his back. His poor wife was in despair. All he would do, all day, was play with these catapults.'

'What was the point?' I asked. 'Such weapons were obsolete. They had long been replaced by cannons. What did he think he was doing?'

Merisi pointed a finger at his temple and made the universal sign of craziness, but said no more about Alberti.

'Very well,' I said, 'let's talk about another friend of yours, Orazio Gentileschi.'

Merisi yawned. 'Do we have to?' he said. 'I'm very tired.'

'Let's just finish with Gentileschi, then you can go for a sleep. I'm sure you will find it interesting, especially about his daughter.'

'Artemisia?' Merisi said, suddenly alert. 'What about her?'

'We'll come to Artemisia in a moment,' I said, 'but let's deal with her father, Orazio, first. Of all the artists that were influenced by your new style during your life and just after your supposed death, Gentileschi became, for a time anyway, your closest follower.'

'Did he?' Merisi said, clearly intrigued.

'Yes, but the historical evidence suggests that Gentileschi was crazier than you or Alberti, or even Longhi!'

'In some ways, yes,' Merisi confirmed. 'I knew how to hold my tongue when in the presence of the rich and powerful. Orazio never did. He had no respect for anyone, high or low, who did not share his opinion. As you can imagine, we argued endlessly. Mostly I did it to annoy him, to . . . how you English say . . . wind him up! I knew that he was impressed by my innovations but I did not realise that he copied me so closely. That is quite a compliment from a man like him. But we were never close friends. We drifted apart after Baglione sued me for libel and Orazio had given evidence on my behalf.'

'Baglione tells us that Gentileschi acted "more like a beast than a human" and could have been much more successful in his career if he had held his tongue.'

'That's very true,' Merisi chuckled.

'And we know that the agent of Grand Duke Cosimo of Tuscany warned his master that Gentileschi was "a person of such strange manners and way of life and such temper that one can neither get on nor deal with him". Is that true?'

'Oh, yes,' Merisi confirmed. 'As I said, I took no notice of his whims and fancies. He was scared of me and my temper so he did not push me too far. He cared not a jot how he dressed or behaved or who he upset. I'm sure he would have told the pope himself to go to hell if he was in the mood to do so. He was quite a good artist, but Artemisia was much more talented.'

'Okay. Tell me about Artemisia.'

'She must have been about eleven or twelve years old when I first met her. We painters often exchanged props when we were working on a picture. I visited Orazio's studio to borrow a pair of angel wings that he owned. Orazio had just begun to properly instruct Artemisia in the painting trade and she was in the studio working on her drawing. My two pictures for Del Monte were the talk of Rome and had been copied many times. Orazio introduced me to her as the artist who had painted the originals. I asked her what she thought of my work. She just blushed in the most charming way and did not reply. She seemed to be overawed by me and just gazed at me with big sad eyes. I asked if I could see her charcoal drawing. For her age and sex, it was really very accomplished. I made a few suggestions and showed her how to make a couple of improvements. Orazio told me later that Artemisia thought I was wonderful. We sort of fell in love with each other, in the most innocent way of course. You know I am a cold and rough-mannered man but Artemisia melted my heart. Orazio allowed her to visit me at the Palazzo Madama, accompanied by her maid, and watch me working. She soon lost her shyness and we chatted away to each other. I enjoyed her company, her innocent charm, and I taught her a lot about the way I worked, techniques that I never revealed to anyone else. She must have been about thirteen or fourteen when I had to flee from Rome. Tell me, Stefano, do you know what happened to her?'

'Yes, I do,' I replied, 'but let's have a cup of coffee first.' I went out to the kitchen. I needed a few minutes to think what I should tell Merisi about Artemisia Gentileschi. He had been very fond of her and I could guess what his reaction was going to be if I told him the whole truth. In the end, I decided that I had to tell him truthfully what had happened to Artemisia because it could possibly have a bearing on what had happened to Merisi himself. I carried the two mugs of coffee back into the living room. 'Tell me, Michele,' I began, 'did you know a painter named Agostino Tassi?'

'Tassi? Tassi?' he repeated. 'That name sounds familiar. I can't quite place it.'

'Tassi was a pupil and a friend of Orazio Gentileschi.'

'Yes! That's right,' Merisi said. 'I remember him now.'

'Was he a friend of yours as well?'

'No, not at all. I had little to do with him, except when I visited Orazio's studio. I didn't care for him. He was a quiet and furtive sort of man. Not a good painter either. He painted landscapes of not much merit. What has he got to do with me?'

'Not you, Michele,' I said, 'but with Artemisia.'

'Go on,' Merisi said, sensing that what I was about to say would not be pleasant.

'About two years after you supposedly died, Artemisia Gentileschi was raped by Tassi.'

'What!' Merisi exploded. He thumped the side of his armchair and nearly spilt his coffee all over it. 'Tassi raped my Artemisia!?'

Merisi's reaction had been fiercer than I anticipated. I went on: 'Tassi then promised to marry Artemisia but reneged on that promise. Orazio took him to court for breach of promise. Artemisia herself had to give evidence . . . under torture.'

'Under torture?' Merisi repeated, shocked by this revelation. 'That is infamous. So Tassi raped my sweet Artemisia, then allowed her to be tortured to save his own skin.'

'That sums it up, as far as we know,' I said. 'Soon after this ordeal, Artemisia married someone else, a Florentine, and moved to Florence with him. She moved around quite often after that. We are not sure why. She came back to Rome for a time, then spent some time in Venice. From Venice she worked in Naples for a few years and, when she was about forty years old, she visited her father who was working in London as the court painter to King Charles. She became very successful in London, mainly through her portraits. Then she moved back to Naples and we know very little about her after that. You may or may not be pleased to know that Artemisia followed your style closely throughout her career.'

'Do you have any pictures of her work in one of your marvellous books?' Merisi asked.

'Yes,' I said, getting up and going to the bookcase. 'I think there is one example here somewhere. Yes, here it is.' I found the appropriate page in the History of World Art. 'It's a depiction of Judith beheading Holofernes. (*Plate 17*). It's now housed in a gallery in Naples.' I showed Merisi the book. He studied the reproduction of Artemisia's painting. He stroked it lightly as if such an action could put him back in touch with his young friend. 'It is an excellent work,' he pronounced. 'I should have been pleased to have painted such a work. The composition is dramatic and realistic. It is better than my version of the subject. I am pleased for Artemisia.'

'She painted this same subject many times,' I said. 'Many of her works contain violent themes, especially directed towards men. Modern art historians have speculated that what Tassi did to her gave her a lifelong fear and suspicion of men, but we don't know whether that is true or not.'

Merisi handed back the book and sat lost in thought for a long while. Finally he said: 'We have to stop it.'

'Stop what?' I asked.

'We have to stop Tassi raping Artemisia. We have the ability to go back in time and stop what he did to her.'

'Wait a minute,' I protested. 'First of all, you cannot go back in time. The ChronoConverter will not allow it.'

'Then you must do it.'

'Do what?' I asked.

'You have to kill Tassi,' Merisi said.

'I cannot,' I said. 'Unlike you, I am not capable of murdering another human being. And you know damn well that I am not allowed to interfere in events or take any action that would substantially change the course of history. What Tassi did to Artemisia is a matter of record. If I could have gone back and stopped it, then nothing would be known about it today because it would not have happened.'

'How do you know?' Merisi persisted. 'Perhaps if you go back and kill that bastard then everything changes in an instant. You have to save Artemisia.'

'It will not work,' I said. 'I cannot interfere. The Tralfamadorians were adamant about that aspect of time travel. I certainly could not kill Tassi in cold blood.'

'Then you could at least warn Artemisia or her father. That is the least you could do. The Tralfamadorians would never know.'

'I'm sorry, Michele, but no. I am not going back to interfere in things that have been and must be for all time.'

'Then fuck you and fuck the Tralfamadorians,' Merisi shouted angrily. 'You'll get no more help from me until you decide to help Artemisia. That's final.' He flung himself out of his armchair, opened the patio door into the garden and stalked out to the summerhouse. I heard the summerhouse door slam behind him. I had suspected that Merisi would react badly to the news about Artemisia but I had not anticipated that he would be this angry. He was deeply devoted to Artemisia. Perhaps she was like the child he never had. She adored Merisi and was in awe of his talent but, being a child when he knew her, she was not a threat to him like other 'Caravaggisti' painters who attempted to copy his chiaroscuro style. For once in his life, here was another person whom he could love without fear of betrayal, contempt, humiliation or loss. I felt sympathy for him. I decided it would not be a bad idea to travel back in time to interview Orazio Gentileschi. He had been a friend of Merisi and knew most of the characters in Merisi's drinking and trouble-making gang. I would have to lie to Merisi and say that I was making an attempt to warn Artemisia and prevent what happened to her but I knew that the ChronoConverter would not allow me to take any action that could change history. Yes, I would go back to see the Gentileschis. I was intrigued at the prospect of meeting Artemisia and seeing what manner of girl, or woman, she was to have had such an effect on a man like Merisi. But I let him stew in his own juice and calm down for a couple of hours, then I went out to the summerhouse and opened the door. Merisi was working at his easel. He was not painting but was working on what looked like a charcoal and chalk sketch. He turned round and looked at me. 'Fuck off,' he said.

'I've decided you are right, Michele. I will go back and try to save Artemisia. I need to interview Orazio Gentileschi anyway.'

'You are just saying that to mollify me,' Merisi said contemptuously.

'No, really. I will try do do something but you must accept that my powers are very limited by the restrictions imposed by the ChronoConverter.'

Merisi turned back to his easel and said nothing for a few minutes. Eventually he asked: 'What will you do?'

I said: 'I can warn Orazio that Tassi is up to no good and get him thrown out of the studio. I can try to get him away from Artemisia at least. Or I could warn Tassi not to lay a finger on Artemisia or I will come back and kill him. What do you think?' I had no intention of taking any such action.

'Orazio will not listen to you,' Merisi said. 'He never listens to anyone. But you could try. And you could warn Tassi. Tell him that if he harms Artemisia, the ghost of the great artist Caravaggio will come back and run him through with a rapier.' Merisi smiled faintly, as if he had accepted that there was little I could do. 'If you cannot save my Artemisia, at least you can give her my final gift.' Merisi took down the sketch from the easel and handed it to me. He said: 'That is Artemisia.'

I studied the charcoal and chalk sketch. It was on canvas and measured about twelve inches in width by about eighteen inches deep. Merisi had drawn Artemisia as she was when about twelve or thirteen years old. That was the age she had been the last time that Merisi ever saw her. Her hair was exquisitely rendered as raven black waves falling down over her shoulders. It could not be said that she was beautiful, but she was pretty in a slightly plump pre-pubescent way. It was possible that she would grow into beauty. As Merisi had mentioned earlier, her eyes were irresistible. Big dark sad eyes that looked out warily but with the unmistakeable eagerness of youth. What I held in my hands was the only known drawing by Michelangelo Merisi da Caravaggio. On the open market, it would be worth thousands, if not millions of pounds. My mind strayed to possible ways of keeping it but Merisi seemed to know what I was thinking. 'That,' he said firmly, 'is for Artemisia. You will get your reward before I take my leave of you.'

I could not help smiling. 'It takes a rogue to know a rogue,' I said. 'Art experts today do not think you did any drawings.'

'I didn't, not as preparatory drawings for my paintings, but I was, of course, taught to draw and sketch when I was an apprentice with Peterzano. I would sketch occasionally for my own pleasure or when I saw a subject that I wished to remember for one of my paintings. Anyway, I would have liked to have painted Artemisia's portrait but there isn't time. You must travel back and try to save her.'

21

Dressed in my seventeenth century finery and with a suitably authoritative bearing, I entered the studio of Orazio Gentileschi. The studio was a large dilapidated barn-like building. The roof and walls were supported by thick wooden pillars and there were several high windows and skylights that admitted plenty of light. Just inside the door, there was a long trestle table on which two young apprentices were mixing colours. 'I wish to see the artist Orazio Gentileschi,' I announced to the apprentices. One of them ran off to the far wall where a huge canvas depicting some mythological scene was being worked on by three artists. The apprentice tugged the sleeve of the artist on the right, who was standing on a wooden stool, and pointed at me. The artist stepped down, put down his palette, mahlstick and brush, and walked over to me. He was dressed in a skullcap and a smock which were both spotted with paint drips. He was a fairly small man with a red face and a wispy black beard and moustache. His eyes darted about restlessly and all his movements suggested quick nervous energy. 'Can I help you, sir?' he said, scenting a lucrative commission.

'Are you the distinguished artist Orazio Gentileschi?' I asked.

'Indeed I am, sir,' he replied.

'My name is Stefano Maddano. I am here, with papal authority, to interview you about the late artist Michelangelo Merisi da Caravaggio.'

Gentileschi's polite attitude, along with the possibility of a commission, vanished and turned into irritation. 'I've heard that you were snooping around asking about Merisi. Can you come back another time? I'm in the middle of an important piece of work.'

'So am I, Signor Gentileschi,' I replied. 'I cannot come back at another time. I have to talk to you now, otherwise the Holy Father will hear of this. It will not take long.' Of all the people I had interviewed about Merisi so far, Gentileschi was by far the most awkward and irritating. He did not invite me to sit down or offer me refreshment. I asked him many questions about the circle surrounding Merisi, people such as Prospero Orsi, Onorio Longhi and Cherubino Alberti. I also asked Gentileschi about many other characters that I had not fully discussed with Merisi as yet, people such as the painter Lionello Spada and the courtesan Fillide Melandroni. I soon realised I was wasting my time. Gentileschi was rambling, evasive, seemed incapable of sticking to the point, and was prejudiced and downright rude. In short, he was everything that his biographical information suggested he was. I was learning nothing useful from him. I completed my interrogation with the usual question about whether he knew who might have planned or executed the attempted murder of Merisi and was met with an irritable dismissal and denial of any knowledge. He was a very unlikeable character but I was more or less convinced that he had nothing to do with Merisi's murder or knew of anyone who might have done. As with most of the fellow artists I had interviewed about Merisi, Gentileschi admitted he had been very influenced by Merisi's radical new style but had found him a very difficult person to like. I could not imagine Gentileschi and Merisi working together. It would have been an explosive combination, to say the least. I concluded my questioning about Merisi and then said: 'Do you still employ an artist named Agostino Tassi?'

'Employ?' Gentileschi said, puzzled. 'We are partners. He used to be my pupil, now he is my friend and partner. He is an excellent landscape painter. We have worked on several canvases and frescoes together. He does the landscape and I do the figures. We are working on that one over there at the moment, the Bacchus and Ariadne. Why are you asking about him? He never had anything to do with Merisi.'

I pondered whether to say any more, then decided that it could do no harm and that I could tell Merisi, quite honestly, that I had tried. 'I would strongly recommend that you eject Tassi from your studio as soon as possible.'

'What!?' Gentileschi gasped. 'What are you talking about? Why should I do that?'

'I happen to know that he is a man of disreputable character who will cause you much harm if you retain his services.'

'You're mad!' Gentileschi cried, throwing his arms in the air. 'Get out of my studio!'

'I have told the truth about what I know. You should heed my advice.'

Gentileschi grabbed my arm and tried to hustle me to the studio door. The two apprentices, although they could not hear what we were saying, were watching this extraordinary scene with wide eyes. As I was resisting Gentileschi's attempt to get me out of the door, I saw a woman walk out from behind the back of the huge canvas. She was carrying a palette and a mahlstick and had come to see what the commotion was about. Even from a distance, I could see that she was Artemisia Gentileschi. 'Not so fast, Signor,' I said to Gentileschi, 'I wish to speak to your daughter.'

'You shall not,' Gentileschi replied emphatically. 'Get out of my studio.'

'Do I have to remind you, sir, that I am here with a papal warrant and under papal protection. Take your hands off of me or I will make sure that your career in Rome is at an end.'

Gentileschi kept hold of my arm. He asked: 'Why do you wish to speak to my daughter? She could not possibly have had anything to do with the death of Caravaggio. She was just a girl when he fled from Rome.'

'I know that very well,' I said, 'but Michele told me that he was very fond of Artemisia and she may have some information that is useful to me.'

Gentileschi let go of my arm and said: 'Very well. You can talk to her, but I will accompany you.'

'No,' I insisted. 'I must talk to her alone, in private. It is possible that she may be constrained by your presence, or that of anyone else, from telling me something that may be relevant to my inquiries.'

Gentileschi was still very angry but the threat of ruining his career in Rome had done the trick. 'Come with me,' he said. I followed him over to the huge canvas where Artemisia Gentileschi was still standing and watching us.

'Artemisia,' her father said, 'this man is inquiring into the death of Michele. You remember that we had heard such a man was going around asking questions. He wishes to talk to you about Michele. He wishes to talk to you alone. Are you willing to do that?'

Artemisia, who was taller than her father, looked at me. Her entrancing dark liquid eyes were just as Merisi had sketched them. They looked out on the world warily but with an eager intelligence. She was wearing a paint-spattered smock, just like her father was, but her hair was protected by a pretty lace-trimmed headscarf, which was tied under her chin. Her raven black hair tumbled down her back from beneath the headscarf. I looked across and saw one of the other painters watching us intently. I guessed it was Tassi but I had no intention of speaking to him. I turned back to Artemisia. 'I was a friend of Michele, in Naples,' I said, to reassure her.

'Are you an artist?' she asked, in an attractive lilting voice.

'Yes, a poor one,' I replied.

'Come and look at my picture. It's all right, father,' Artemisia said soothingly. 'I would be interested to talk to this gentleman about Michele.'

Her father looked at me contemptuously. 'Remember,' he warned, 'I will be just the other side of this canvas.'

'Please follow me, sir,' Artemisia said, and she led me to the back of the studio where her easel and equipment were set up. As she walked, she untied her headscarf and shook out her long black hair. She indicated the canvas she was working on. 'It is a scene of Susanna with the Elders,' she said. 'It is nearly finished. I am pleased with it. I think it is my best work yet. Do you like it?'

I studied the painting. The influence of our mutual friend Caravaggio was very evident. 'It is truly excellent,' I pronounced, with all sincerity. 'No wonder your father is so bad-tempered.' I looked at her and smiled, wondering how she would react to that remark. Artemisia suddenly understood what I meant and laughed merrily. She had lost some of her puppy fat since Michele knew her. Her face, shining with amusement, was very attractive. No wonder a wolf like Tassi could not resist her spell. I said: 'Our friend Michele would be proud of such a work. Would it be true to say that you learned a lot from him?'

'Yes, it would,' Artemisia said. 'He was very kind to me. I loved him dearly. I know what people say about him, and I have to accept that such things are true, but he was always kind and gentle with me. Did you like him?'

'Yes,' I said slowly, as if giving the question much thought. 'He was a strange man, difficult to get on with, but I could not help liking him, however much trouble he caused me. He somehow managed to get under my skin.'

Artemisia giggled. 'Get under your skin,' she repeated. 'That is an expression I have never heard before but I understand what it means. You are not Italian, are you?'

'No, I am not,' I replied, hoping that she would not ask me exactly where I was from.

'I cannot tell you anything about Michele's death,' she said, wistfully. 'I was only a girl when he had to leave Rome. I was very upset when I heard the news about what he had done and then all the rumours about where he had gone. I missed going to his studio and watching him work. It was fascinating. He was so quick, so facile. He was one of God's unique creatures.'

'He certainly was,' I agreed, 'but I did not wish to see you about Michele's death. I know that you, or your father, did not have anything to do with it. I came to give you a gift and a message from Michele.'

'A gift?' Artemisia repeated, suddenly tense.

From underneath my doublet, I took out the rolled-up sketch that Merisi had completed not many hours before. 'Michele always spoke of you with love and affection. He asked me to give you this, if anything should ever happen to him, in gratitude for all the happy memories he had of you.' I handed Artemisia the piece of canvas. She untied the ribbon and unrolled it. She gazed at the sketch of her younger self and whispered the words that Merisi had inscribed on it: 'With all my love, forever. Michele.'

Artemisia gazed at the sketch and was silent for several seconds. Eventually she said softly, as if finding it difficult to speak: 'Thank you. You have been very kind.'

I bowed to her and said: 'It has been a pleasure to meet you, signorina.' I walked out of the studio and found a suitably deserted place for the ChronoConverter to return me home. It was still early evening. I wondered what new disaster Merisi might have caused while I had been away but a light snoring from his bedroom told me that he had turned in early, exhausted by the debauchery of the day before.

22

After a long recuperating sleep, Merisi was much livelier in the morning. He chuckled when I related my encounter with Orazio Gentileschi and was pensive when I told him of my conversation with Artemisia Gentileschi. I exaggerated my attempt to persuade Gentileschi to get rid of the rapist Agostino Tassi but Merisi seemed to have accepted that there was nothing that could be done to expunge an event that took place four hundred years before. I was anxious to move on. I didn't feel we were getting very far in solving the mystery of Merisi's murder. I wanted to learn more about Merisi's personal relationships in Rome, the people who were much more likely to be involved in his murder and, in particular, the intriguing figure - in both senses of the word - of his courtesan lover, Fillide Melandroni. I decided to introduce the topic of Fillide Melandroni obliquely, through Merisi's painting of Judith and Holofernes, the subject so avidly copied in later years by Artemisia Gentileschi. I already knew that the woman who had modelled for Judith was Gerolama Giustiniani, not Fillide Melandroni. They were similar in looks, so it was another way of testing Merisi's veracity. When we were settled in our armchairs, I said: 'We've been talking about your work Judith and Holofernes, so let's get that one cleared up. Did Fillide Melandroni model for the figure of Judith? It looks like her.'

Merisi was immediately alert at the mention of Fillide's name. 'Yes, I suppose it was,' he replied guardedly. 'It was all such a long time ago. It must have been Fillide.'

'There is speculation that you yourself modelled for Holofernes as a self-portrait, perhaps the first time you included yourself in such a disturbing and violent work. Is that true?'

'No, definitely not,' Merisi denied. 'That is not a self-portrait. It looks a little like me but I'm sure I used one of Cardinal Del Monte's servants as the model. I cannot remember his name.'

'Can you remember who commissioned this painting?'

'Yes, it was for a banker named Costa. Ottavio Costa.'

'Was he pleased with it?'

'I think so. He looked pleased when he first saw it.'

'I can tell you that he was very pleased. In his will, Costa included a clause that his heirs should not part with any of your paintings, particularly not the Judith and Holofernes.'

Merisi smiled. 'Costa was a man of good taste. And very rich.'

'Okay, so tell me about Fillide,' I said. 'She is familiar to us today because of the many times she modelled for you, particularly a pure portrait of her that used to be housed in Germany but was unfortunately destroyed in a war about seventy years ago.'

'I made several portraits of Fillide,' Merisi said. 'Can you show me a picture of this one?' (*Plate 18*).

I had Caravaggio's complete works by the side of my chair so I passed the book over to him, opened at the page containing the Portrait of Fillide. 'Ah, yes,' Merisi said. 'I was commissioned to paint this portrait by her suitor, Giulio Strozzi. He was completed besotted by her. He wanted to marry her, despite knowing that she was a high-class whore.'

'Were you jealous of this relationship?' I asked.

'A little, I suppose,' Merisi said, unconvincingly.

'Were you in love with Fillide?' I persisted. 'She was a beguiling woman, judging from your portrait.'

'I was infatuated with her. Most men were, those who knew her well. She was about ten years younger than me. I got to know her a few years after I had moved to Rome. She was only about sixteen years old but she had already found a powerful client and protector, a man named Masetti, who was in the service of Cardinal Benedetto Giustiniani. That didn't stop her playing the field.'

'With you?' I asked.

'Sometimes,' Merisi said.

'And with Ranuccio Tomassoni?'

'Maybe,' Merisi said, unhappy with my line of questioning.

'Maybe nothing!' I shot back. 'We have it in her own words that she had "carnal knowledge" of Ranuccio Tomassoni. It seems he was popular with the women of the street.' Merisi shrugged. I asked: 'Were you jealous of Tomassoni?'

'I hated him, and all of his family. Ranuccio and I clashed on the street many times before I killed him. To think that a bastard like that was fucking a woman like Fillide made me angry.'

'Your hatred of the Tomassoni clan was not just over Fillide, was it?'

'No,' Merisi replied. 'They were a military family, skilled with arms, not afraid to use them, and bigger troublemakers than I was. They had returned from the wars at about the time I arrived in Rome. They were always in trouble with the sbirri, the Roman police, or the Corte, the Vatican police. My friends and I often clashed with all the Tomassonis. The head of the clan, a tough old soldier named Giovan Francesco Tomassoni, later became caporione, the chief lay official, in our neighbourhood, which made us resent them even more.'

I was encouraged and felt that we were now getting to the real deep-seated hatreds in Merisi's former life, but I wanted to stay on the subject of Fillide Melandroni. 'Tell me more about Fillide,' I said.

'What do you want to know?'

'Well, for my personal interest, what she was like as a woman, and for the purposes of our enquiry into your life, the pictures she modelled for and could there be any clues regarding your murderer in them.'

'What you should understand was that, in those days, whores or courtesans, whatever you want to call them, had a lot more freedom than most women. Today, here in your country, I see that women are totally free to do what they want . . . join the police like that Caro woman, work in shops, drive those car things, even run the country like that Thatcher woman you have mentioned, but back in my time ordinary women were under much tighter social constraint. They were dominated by the church and by their husbands and fathers. But the whores, because of the nature of their occupation, were largely free of these ties. Such freedom made their life attractive to some women. In Rome, where there were far more men than women, there was plenty of work for a whore and they could make a lot of money in a very short time. The objective of most of the courtesans was to find a wealthy, or at least well-off, husband or protector before their looks deteriorated. Most of the whores were confined to working in a part of the city known as the Ortaccio, down by the River Tiber, near the old Mausoleum of Augustus. All the houses were packed tightly in the narrow streets and the whores sat in the windows to advertise their "wares". I suppose this is where Fillide started working.'

I said: 'We know that Fillide must have been successful in her work because she very soon had the money to move herself and her mother to a more salubrious part of the city. For this man Strozzi, who was from the nobility, to want to marry her suggests that Fillide had risen way above being a mere Ortaccio whore.'

'All that is true,' Merisi confirmed. 'Fillide, as I hope my portrait shows, was the sort of woman who is always very attractive to men. She was very confident in herself. She was confident in her looks and her body and she enjoyed giving men, and herself, a good time, both in and out of bed. She was independent and fiery but good-natured and generous. Even so, if you tried to get out of paying her just dues, in any respect, she was a ferocious enemy. I always enjoyed using her as a model. She didn't care what I said or how I behaved, as long as I paid her, and we laughed a lot. Then, if we were both in the mood, we would make love, but I still had to pay her. It was worth it. I was infatuated with her but I knew she was not the sort of woman to fall in love with. She was a warm-hearted girl but with Fillide, it was always Fillide first and anyone else nowhere ... and who could blame her? Certainly not me. She was the sort of woman who blazes through your life, leaves a fire of warm and happy memories behind her, and then vanishes. I doubt, if I met her again, that she would even remember me.'

'Oh, I think she would, Michele,' I said. 'Thanks to you and your pictures, Fillide has become immortal.' Merisi nodded. In Caravaggio's complete works, I showed him the picture of the painting that we now call The Conversion of the Magdalen. I knew that Gerolama Giustiniani had modelled for the figure of Martha, on the left of the picture, but Merisi didn't know that I knew that. 'This is obviously Fillide modelling for Mary Magdalen here,' I said. 'This is an intriguing and mysterious picture, Michele. Fillide and her dress are beautifully painted. It's such a sensual image. What's the meaning of the mirror on which Fillide is resting her hand?'

'At the time I painted this picture, there was a lot of interest in the optical effects of mirrors and lenses. I remember that Cardinal Del Monte and his friends were experimenting with such things. The inclusion of the mirror served two purposes: to make the picture more attractive to any potential buyer who may have been interested in such things, and to suggest the process of looking yourself in the face and deciding to change your life, which the Magdalen is being persuaded to do by her sister Martha.'

'Who modelled for the Martha figure?' I asked.

Merisi hesitated, and then said: 'I cannot remember. Probably some other street girl or friend of Fillide.'

'Were the two women together like this when you painted this picture?'

'No, I preferred to paint Fillide when we were alone. It was more fun and it usually led to more sensual pleasures than daubing paint.' Only Merisi could describe the execution of such a masterpiece as 'daubing paint'!

'What's the meaning of the tiny flower that Fillide is holding?'

'It's a symbol of virginity. I remember that we laughed about that one. Fillide was the least virginal woman I ever knew. She wasn't at all prudish or self-conscious. The comb on the table, with a missing tooth, is also a symbol of lost innocence.'

'Who commissioned this picture?'

'I cannot remember. I'm sorry.'

'Never mind,' I said. I couldn't see any obvious clues as to the identity of Merisi's assassin in this picture, so I showed Merisi the next picture for which

Fillide certainly modelled, his vision of St. Catherine of Alexandria. (*Plate 19*). 'This is an extraordinary work, Michele. You have taken a saint, beloved for her refusal to renounce her faith and her virginity, and turned her into an erotic, almost pornographic image. Instead of the conventional pious image, you have given us a woman sensual and provocative, to say the least. Was this deliberate?'

'Not on my part,' Merisi replied. 'Cardinal Del Monte asked me to paint this subject, so I intended to paint a much more respectful image. Fillide was adamant that the cardinal would prefer this pose. She must have known the cardinal better than me, because she was right.'

'Del Monte liked the picture?'

'Very much. I remember being uneasy when I first showed it to him but he approved mightily. It became one of his most prized possessions.'

'Did Fillide usually have a say in how she posed and what you painted?'

'No. Normally she could not care less. She just did as I asked, as long as I paid her. But, for some reason, she took a keen interest in how I was composing this picture. As you know, Saint Catherine was of royal blood, so Fillide insisted that she wore her finest gown and then persuaded me to use my skills and imagination to decorate and embellish the dress even more richly.'

'The expression on her face is extraordinary,' I said. 'It's wary but at the same time intense and compelling. It's saying to us "look at me, look at who I am, look at what I'm doing". She is sending us a message, Michele. What is it?'

'I don't know what you mean?' Merisi said.

'Come one, Michele, you were there. Fillide must have said something or intended something!'

Merisi studied his picture again. 'I remember that her pose with the sword was her idea.'

'You mean the way she is laying her finger on the blade of the sword?'

'Yes. The double-meaning of "sword" is obvious. I thought the gesture was far too provocative, far too sexual, in a depiction of a saint such as Catherine.'

'But Fillide persuaded you to do it?'

'Yes. She had a very pleasant way of persuading me.'

'But why was she so adamant that you painted the picture in this way?'

'I don't know, Stefano. I really cannot remember.'

I scrutinised the look on Merisi's face but he looked genuinely perplexed. I said: 'Many of your works from this period are concerned with virginity and purity. Is there any reason for that?'

'Just coincidence,' Merisi answered, with a shrug. 'That is what the patrons wanted.'

'For instance,' I persisted, 'the charming picture we now call Penitent

Magdalen or Repentent Magdalen.' (*Plate 20*). I showed Merisi which painting I was talking about. 'This is another work expressing the conversion or repentance of a fallen woman. We don't know who commissioned this painting. Can you remember?'

'I don't know,' Merisi said. 'I seem to remember it was one of the cardinals in Del Monte's circle of friends, but I can't be sure.' He yawned and shifted restlessly. 'This is becoming boring, Stefano. Can't we go out and get drunk?'

'No, not now. When we've finished, we'll go into Bedford tonight and have a few drinks. Is that okay?'

'You are worse than my old schoolmaster in Caravaggio,' Merisi complained.

'Who did you use as the model for the Magdalen in this picture?' I asked, ignoring his grizzling.

Merisi looked at me and sighed wearily. 'I cannot remember,' he said.

'There are suggestions that it might have been a friend of Fillide's, another courtesan named Anna Bianchini. Could it be her?'

'Yes, yes,' Merisi said. 'Now I remember. Yes, Anna, with the lovely red hair.'

'You chose an unusual setting for this picture,' I said. 'Mary Magdalene was supposed to be rich, beautiful and sensual and yet you have set her in a bare room.'

Merisi replied with surprising animation and passion to defend his work. 'She is contemplating her former life and realising that she must repent and seek forgiveness for past sins. That is why she is crying. She is dressed in a fine dress but to have put her in a richly decorated room would have given the wrong impression. Mary is the patron saint of penitents and sinners. She is a consolation to women who have suffered. Here, this woman has realised that her past is filled with sin. She is, quite rightly, feeling guilty about the sins she has committed and the people she has betrayed. People who loved her.'

'Is there any meaning to the objects on the floor, the pearls, jewellery, clasps and jar of ointment?'

'Only to suggest that this woman has cast off the vanities and frivolities of her former life and must seek a simpler, purer life.'

'What about the unusual motif on the bottom of her dress? It looks like a vase or an urn or something. Does that mean anything?'

Merisi shrugged. 'I don't think so. It was just on the dress that Anna was wearing.'

'It's a very tender and affectionate portrayal,' I observed. 'Were you involved with Anna Bianchini as well as Fillide?'

'I took my pleasure wherever and whenever I could find it,' Merisi answered. 'Was that wrong?'

I ignored his question and handed him the book of his complete works. I said: 'You must have used Anna as the model for another picture from this period, the one we call The Rest on the Flight into Egypt. It is obviously the same woman.' (*Plate 21*).

'Yes, that is correct,' Merisi confirmed, studying his picture.

I waited for him to say more, but he didn't. 'It's an unusual composition,' I continued. 'The figure of the angel separates the Virgin Mary from her husband, Joseph. Joseph is depicted as an old man. Surely he must have been young, as Mary was young?'

'I was just keeping to tradition,' Merisi said. 'Joseph was often depicted as an old man in those days. More dignified, I suppose.'

'It seems odd to separate Mary from her loving husband. It divides the picture into two halves, seemingly unrelated. Was that deliberate?'

'I wanted the angel to have its back to the viewer. In that way I could keep the figure androgynous.'

I thought it was a weak and unconvincing reason but I didn't press him any further. Even geniuses have off days. 'What about that donkey, in the background behind Joseph, looking out with that huge eye? It's almost . . . disturbing.' Merisi just shrugged, so I carried on my analysis. 'I have to say that the Virgin Mary and her child are depicted with almost heart-breaking tenderness. It is a very sweet image.'

'Thank you,' Merisi said. 'That is why the angel's wing is covering Mary, as a promise that she will be protected from any harm.' His face lit up with poignant pleasure as he perused this section of his painting.

I decided to lay a trap for Merisi. 'What music is the angel playing?' I asked.

'I don't know,' Merisi replied. 'Just something I made up for the picture.'

'Liar,' I said. 'You know very well that it is a motet in honour of the Virgin Mary called How Beautiful Thou Art. It was written by some Flemish composer. Any cultured person from your time would know about this motet but you didn't think that we would now. Come on, Michele, admit it. This painting is a message to Anna Bianchini. You were in love with her, weren't you?'

'If you say so,' Merisi replied, uncomfortably.

'And that could have made someone else jealous,' I pressed, 'jealous enough to want to murder you. Who was it, Michele? This could be an important clue.'

'I don't know who it could have been,' Merisi protested. 'Anna was a courtesan. She had many lovers. It could have been anyone.'

I threw down my pen in disgust. 'What is the point of doing all this if you are going to lie to me and hide things from me.'

I expected Merisi to explode in temper but he just said, calmly and reasonably: 'I tell you, I don't know.'

'Well, who commissioned this painting. Was it the same person who commissioned the Penitent Magdalen?'

Merisi shrugged. 'It is very possible. I cannot remember.'

'This could be very important,' I said, vehemently. 'This could be the key to the whole . . .' At that moment, my mobile phone started to ring. I picked it up, still seething with annoyance, and said: 'Yes?'

A male voice, with an Italian accent said: 'Can I speak to Michele?'

With my mind still on Merisi's evasions, and before I could think sensibly, I said: 'It's for you' and handed the phone to Merisi. He took it but said: 'What do I do with this?'

'Just hold it to your ear and speak normally and someone will talk to you.'

Merisi lifted the phone to his ear, warily, and I was just set to snatch the phone back, suddenly anxious and mystified as to who was calling him, but Merisi had already started speaking. 'Yes, this is Michele,' he was saying. He listened to the caller for a least a minute without saying anything back, and then said: 'Yes, I'd like to. That will be most enjoyable. I'll see you later.' He handed the phone back to me.

'Who was that?' I asked.

'None of your business,' Merisi said, but with a smile.

'It is my business,' I said heatedly. 'Don't forget we are in a very bizarre situation here. You should not be here, in this century, and nobody must know you are here. I am your protector, your guardian, if you like.'

'But not my jailer, eh, Stefano.'

'I will be if I have to.'

'If you think you are strong enough,' Merisi said, still smiling.

'You know how clever we are in this century,' I warned him, not having a clue what I was talking about. 'I have ways and means of stopping you from doing anything stupid.'

'They haven't worked very well up until now, have they?'

'I haven't used them yet,' I said. 'Please, just let me know who that was and what you are up to?'

'If you must know, it was a friend of mine.'

'A friend?' I said. 'You haven't made any friends here.'

'I met my friend Silvio in the Riverside Tavern the other day.'

'How did he get my mobile phone number? You certainly don't know it.'

'I don't know what you mean by that. I told Silvio I was staying with you, with some miserable cold-hearted English bastard who only ever wants to work and not play. So Silvio has invited me to a night out with some of his Italian friends in Bedford tonight. And I'm going.'

'Oh, no you're not,' I said, emphatically. 'That's far too dangerous. Nobody must find out who you are and what is going on here. If you get drunk and start shooting off your mouth, it could get very tricky.'

'Oh, relax!' Merisi cried. 'I'm not going to say anything. Even if I did let something slip, who would believe that I'm an Italian painter who died four hundred years ago and has been resurrected by aliens? You didn't believe it until I forced you to.'

'Well, I'll go with you then.'

'No. I want to talk Italian, with fellow Italians, not with some mealy-mouthed Englishman listening to everything I say.'

'I have the ChronoTranslator ring. I can speak Italian as well.'

'They'll see through you in a second. It would be more dangerous than not coming with me at all.' I had to admit to myself that he had a point. 'Anyway,' Merisi continued, 'you will probably be off to Rome to interview someone tonight.'

'I haven't decided about that yet,' I said. 'Where are you going tonight?'

'Somewhere called the Juventus supporters club at the Coach and Horses. I don't know what all that means.'

'Juventus is a famous Italian football club and the Coach and Horses is a pub in the town centre.'

'Whatever,' Merisi said, indifferently.

'How will you get there?'

'You can get me one of those car things, what do they call them . . . taxis.'

I thought about this problem for a few seconds. Perhaps it wouldn't be too risky. Merisi seemed to be getting bored with our inquest. Perhaps it would settle him down to go out and tie one on for a change. 'Very well,' I agreed. 'I'll book you a taxi, there and back, but for Christ's sake don't get too pissed.'

'I won't, you English blasphemer.'

'Before I book your taxi, let's talk about one last painting, one of the most extraordinary you ever did.'

'Very well,' Merisi said, considerably cheered up by the thought of a night out with the boys. 'Which one?'

'Your painting of the god Bacchus,' I replied. 'It was rescued from the storerooms of the Uffizi Gallery in Florence, only about one hundred years ago, by the namesake of your friend Onorio, the art historian Roberto Longhi. He had the knowledge and insight to recognise this work for what it is, a stunning masterpiece.' (*Plate 22*).

'Thank you,' Merisi said. 'I had a lot of fun with that picture.'

'How do you mean?' I asked.

'Well, it was not commissioned by anyone. I did it as what you might call a commercial exercise. I was feeling at the height of my powers. I wanted to make it dazzling, erotic, shocking even, and pour every ounce of my skill into the face and figure of Bacchus, the fruit and flowers, and the still life. I knew it would be highly saleable. It was necessary, of course, to include some moral fable into the work, in this case the transience of love, youth and sexual allure. It worked! I sold it for a good sum as soon as I had finished it. Mario, however, was not so pleased.' Merisi began to laugh heartily at the memory.

'You mean Mario Minnitti,' I asked, seeing the resemblance to Merisi's friend.

'Yes!' Merisi cried delightedly. 'Haven't I made him pretty? All the bardassas in Rome were fluttering with excitement when they saw this picture. Poor Mario had many unwelcome invitations! He was disgusted with me, that I had made him into such a pretty boy! It was the first time I had seen him really angry with me.'

'Angry enough to want to kill you,' I asked. 'We know he was capable of it.'

'No, not Mario,' Merisi said. 'I was most entertained by his reaction. I "wound him up" for a long time afterwards.' He looked at his picture. 'It is an exceptional piece of work, even if I do say so myself.'

'It certainly is,' I agreed, wondering about Mario Minnitti's reaction to this work. Even allowing for Minnitti's allotted role as Merisi's guardian, any red-blooded heterosexual male would be appalled at being portrayed in such a manner as the Bacchus. I made a careful note on my list of suspects.

'Come on, Stefano, let's eat. We've done enough work, and I'm going out on the drizzle tonight.'

'I think the word the ChronoTranslator searched for is "razzle",' I said.

23

Despite my apparent acquiescense to Merisi's jaunt into Bedford, I had no intention of letting him loose on the unsuspecting citizens of my county town. To have argued with him, or insist that I go with him, would have ensured that he concocted some devious ruse to evade me. I had planned a devious ruse of my own. Unknown to Merisi, I had purchased another car. The Alfa Romeo was a complete write-off, so I had bought a more modest and inconspicuous vehicle, a second-hand blue Vauxhall Astra, which was small but nippy. I took the precaution of keeping it parked in a quiet side road about a hundred yards or so from my house, to prevent Merisi from trying his hand on the Queen's highway again. About half an hour after Merisi had left in his taxi, I walked down the road to my car and drove into Bedford at a leisurely pace. Bedford was only a ten minute drive away, even at that speed. I had decided to unexpectedly turn up at the meeting of the Juventus supporters club and present Merisi with a fait accompli. I parked the Astra in the Lurke Street multi-storey car park and walked to the Coach and Horses pub. It was a small Victorian pub near Bedford town centre. I had never been in the pub but I knew where it was. I went in to find there were only a few other customers in the pub. There were two couples eating a meal, the pub having a reputation for a limited but excellent menu, and two drinkers at the bar. I was not surprised by the paucity of customers as it was still fairly early in the evening. I guessed the Juventus supporters club meeting was being held in a separate room. The landlady, an attractive and smartly dressed woman in her thirties, welcomed me with a pleasant smile. 'Good evening,' she said. 'What can I get you?'

I said: 'I'm here for the Juventus supporters club meeting.'

The landlady looked at me with a blank expression. 'I don't know what you mean,' she said.

'I was told that there was going to be a group of Italians here tonight, you know, football supporters who support the Juventus team.'

'I don't know anything about it,' the landlady said. She turned to the landlord, who I supposed was her husband and who was serving a customer at the other end of the bar. 'Jack, is there a Juventus football club meeting planned for here tonight?'

'I bloody hope not,' Jack replied. 'English fans are bad enough. We don't want a bunch of Eyeties swigging chianti and chucking pasta around the place.' It was said with a smile to indicate that he was only joking. 'No,' he continued, 'not here. Sure you've got the right pub?'

'I was told the Coach and Horses in the town centre.'

'Well, this is the only Coach and Horses in the town centre,' Jack said, 'but there's definitely no meeting here. Who told you about it?'

'An Italian nutcase who is staying with me,' I replied.

'We've already had an Italian nutcase in here tonight,' the landlady said, chuckling. 'Left a few minutes ago. Asked me if I was a "courtesan" or something or other. So I asked what a courtesan was, and he said a whore, a prostitute. Asked if he could buy me for the evening! Well, Jack wasn't best pleased. Told this Italian that I was his wife and to watch what he was saying. The man apologised and had a glass of wine and then left.'

'Lucky for him that he did,' Jack said, 'or else I'd have thrown him out on his arse. Calling my wife a whore!'

'Oh, he was all right,' the landlady said. 'He'd got the wrong end of the stick or something. He was quite charming after that. I quite liked him.'

'Don't tell me,' I said, 'he was tall and well-built with long unruly black hair, big black eyes with big round eyebrows, a small black beard and moustache, faint white scars on his face, and he was dressed in a black suit with a light blue shirt.'

'That's right!' the landlady said. 'It must have been your friend. How did he get those scars?'

'He was beaten up outside a bar in Naples,' I said.

'Oh, my God!' the landlady gasped. 'Is he in the Mafia? Is he a criminal?'

'He was wanted for murder once,' I said, 'but it was all a long time ago. He is now a respectable painter and art historian.'

'Really?' the landlady said, intrigued by my teasing remarks. 'Perhaps I should have taken him up on his offer.' She looked at a husband with an arch smile as she said this.

'Might be a nice sideline for you,' Jack said. 'I've always fancied myself as a pimp.' His wife thumped him playfully on the arm. The two of them moved away to serve other customers.

A man at the bar, who looked like a respectable businessman enjoying a drink before he went home to his family, had been listening to this conversation. He moved towards me and said: 'That Italian chap you were talking about, that friend of yours, I met him in the gents. He asked me if I knew where he could pick up a whore. I told him to try down by the river, just

1. Ottavio Leoni: Portrait Drawing of Michelangelo Merisi da Caravaggio
Biblioteca Marucelliana, Florence

2. Supper at Emmaus *National Gallery, London*

3. The Ambassadors (by Hans Holbein)
National Gallery, London

5. Boy Bitten By A Lizard
National Gallery, London

4. Sick Bacchus
Borghese Gallery, Rome

6. Boy Peeling Fruit
Royal Collection, London,
HM Queen Elizabeth II

7. Boy With A Basket Of Fruit
Borghese Gallery., Rome

8. Gypsy Fortune Teller
Pinacoteca Capitolina, Rome

9. Cardsharps
Kimbell Art Musem,
Fort Worth

10. The Musicians a.k.a
The Concert Party
*Metropolitan Museum of Art,
New York*

12. Basket Of Fruit
Pinacoteca Ambrosiana, Milan

11. Lute Player
Hermitage, St Petersburg

13. Medusa
Uffizi, Florence

14. Ecstasy of St. Francis
Wadsworth Atheneum, Hartford

15. Conversion of the Magdalen
Institute of Arts, Detroit

16. Judith and Holofernes
National Gallery of Ancient Art, Rome

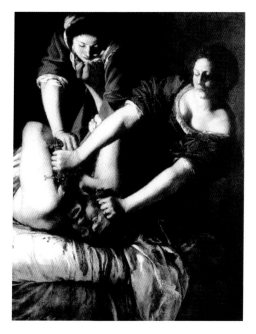

17. Judith Beheading Holofernes (by Artemisia Gentileschi)
Capodimonte Musuem, Naples

18. Fillide Melandroni (*Destroyed*)

20. Penitent Magdalen
Galleria Doria Pamphilj, Rome

19. St. Catherine of Alexandra
*Thyssen-Bornemisza Museum,
Madrid*

21. Rest on the Flight into Egypt
Galleria Doria Pamphilj, Rome

22. Bacchus
Uffizi, Florence

23. Martyrdom of St. Matthew
San Luigi dei Francesci Church, Rome

24. Calling of St. Matthew
San Luigi dei Francesci Church, Rome

25. Conversion of St Paul (first version)
Odescalchi Church, Rome

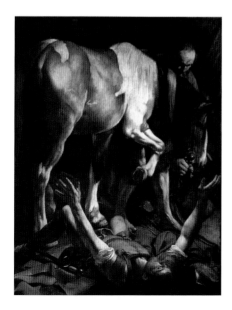

26. Conversion of St. Paul (second version)
Santa Maria del Popolo Church, Rome

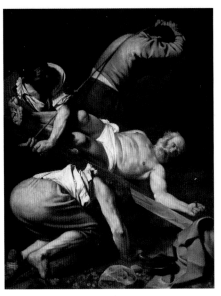

28. St. Matthew and the Angel
(first version) *Destroyed*

27. Crucifixion of St. Peter
Santa Maria del Popolo Church, Rome

29. St Matthew and the Angel
(second version)
San Luigi dei Francesi Church, Rome

30. Narcissus
National Gallery of Ancient Art, Rome

31. St John the Baptist
or Phrygian Shepherd
Capitoline Gallery, Rome

32. Victorious Cupid
State Museum, Berlin

33. David Contemplating
the Head of Goliath
(by Guido Reni)
Louvre, Paris

34. Maffeo Barberini
Private Collection, Florence

35. Arrest of Christ
National Gallery, Dublin

36. Doubting Thomas
Sanssouci Gallery, Potsdam

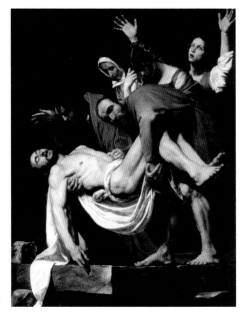

37. Entombment of Christ
Vatican Palace, Rome

38. Death of the Virgin
Louvre, Paris

39. St. John the Baptist
Nelson-Atkins Museum of Art, Kansas City

40. Divine Love Overcoming the
World, the Flesh and the Devil
(by Giovanni Baglione)
National Gallery of Ancient Art, Rome

41. Madonna of Loreto
San Agostino Church, Rome

42. St. Jerome
Borghese Gallery, Rome

43. Ecco Homo
Palazzo Rosso, Genoa

44. Madonna of the
Palafrenieri
*Borghese Gallery,
Rome*

45. St. Mary Magdalen in Ecstasy
Private Collection, Rome

46. Supper At Emmaus
(second version)
Brera, Milan

47. Seven Acts of Mercy
Pio Monte della Misericordia Church, Naples

48. Madonna of the Rosary
Kunsthistorisches Museum, Vienna

49. Flagellation of Christ
Capodimonte Museum, Naples

50. Alof de Wignacourt and his Page
Louvre, Paris

51. St. Jerome Writing (Malaspina),
Co-Cathedral of St. John, Valletta

52. Knight of Malta
(Antonio Martinelli)
Pitti, Florence

53. Sleeping Cupid
Pitti Florence

54. Beheading of St. John the Baptist
Co-Cathedral of St. John, Valletta

55. Burial of St. Lucy
Bellomo Palace Museum, Syracuse

56. Raising of Lazarus
Regional Museum, Messina

57. Adoration of the Shepherds
Regional Museum, Messina

58. Adoration with Saints Francis
and Lawrence
Stolen

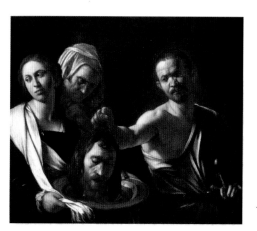

59. Salome with the Head of
John the Baptist
National Gallery, London

60. David with the Head of Goliath
Borghese Gallery, Rome

61. Crucifixion of Saint Andrew
Museum of Art, Cleveland

62. Martyrdom of
Saint Ursula
Commercial Bank of Italy

63. St. John the Baptist
Borghese Gallery, Rome

to get rid of him, so he might have gone that way. I don't like being talked to in the gents. Funny sort of chap.'

'Yes, he is,' I agreed, 'and I apologise for his behaviour, but you know what some of these foreigners are like. They don't know how to behave.'

'Tell me about it,' the businessman said. 'Enoch Powell was right forty years ago. Too many bloody foreigners in this country. Your friend is a painter I heard you say. My kitchen needs doing. Is he cheap? I'll give him cash in hand.'

I said: 'I very much doubt that you could afford my friend's type of painting, or even understand it.' I nodded and said thanks and left the pub, glad to get away from the bigoted businessman. I walked through the town towards the river, without any real hope of finding Merisi. I stopped on the town bridge, which was lit up son-et-lumiere fashion, and looked up and down the riverbank to see if I could spot Merisi anywhere. It was a still and clear Spring evening and the lights from the County Hotel and the pubs and restaurants along the river, reflecting in the water, made an attractive spectacle. I couldn't see Merisi but about a hundred yards downstream, towards the newly-refurbished road bridge about half a mile away, I noticed a group of young girls laughing and giggling at someone. Other passers-by, especially the women, were hurrying past to avoid the commotion and then looking back anxiously to make sure they were not being followed. Where there was a commotion like that going on, it had to be Merisi. I had suspected he was up to no good and I was glad that I had decided to tail him. I walked back off the bridge and on to the towpath and headed towards the commotion. As I approached nearer to the group of girls, I could see Merisi talking to them. He was swigging out of a bottle and looked as if he was offering them a drink. The girls were laughing and joking with him, or probably at him, but were keeping their distance from him, reassured by the supporting presence of each other but not taking too many chances. Before I could reach Merisi, a police car swept past me, blue light flashing silently, and stopped by the side of the group of girls. They ran away laughing as they saw the Jolly Greenfield Giant and Sergeant Caro get out of the police car. I stopped walking and hid behind one of the many trees that line the river bank. I could not make up my mind whether to go and interfere or stay out of it. Before I could decide, however, the police officers had made Merisi get into the car. The police car pulled away before I could do anything. I decided there was nothing to worry about. Merisi was in safe hands and off the streets. Bedford police station was well within walking distance. I could stroll to the police station and get Merisi away with as little fuss as possible, hopefully before he did or said anything revealing or incriminating about his presence in our modern world.

I went into Bedford police station. A constable was manning the reception desk, which was protected by thick security glass. Through the microphone speaker, I asked if I could speak to Sergeant Caro. The constable asked me to take a seat and wait. I sat down on one of the plastic visitor chairs while the constable phoned through to where the police officers worked. He put the phone down and, through the microphone, told me that Sergeant Caro was not in the station. I asked if P.C. Greenfield was available. The constable picked up the phone again and, after a few seconds, called over to me again and asked me what I wanted to see P.C. Greenfield about. I said it was about an Italian house guest of mine named Merisi who might have been arrested or was otherwise being held in the station. The constable relayed this information into the phone, listened to the reply, put the phone down and told me that P.C. Greenfield would come out to see me in a few minutes. About ten minutes later, the Jolly Greenfield Giant came out of the security door and into the reception area. 'Sorry to keep you waiting,' he apologised, as he lowered his huge frame on to a plastic chair beside me. 'You're inquiring about Mr. Merisi?'

'Yes,' I replied.

'How did you know that we had picked him up?'

'I was walking to meet him along by the river when you and Sergeant Caro bundled him into the car and did a Starsky and Hutch before I could reach you.'

'Oh, I see.'

'What was he doing?' I asked.

'Well, he was drinking alcohol in a public place, which is against the by-laws, and we had received phone calls from several distressed women that a drunken man had been accosting them on the towpath, so Sergeant Caro volunteered us to investigate.'

'Accosting them?' I queried. 'What was he doing to these women?'

'He wasn't touching them but apparently he was asking them if they were whores and, if they were, how much did they charge.'

'Christ!' I said, exasperated, 'what a fucking idiot! Has he been arrested? Can I see him?'

'I thought we were going to arrest him for drunk and disorderly or something but Sergeant Caro said he hadn't done any real harm and it wasn't worth the paperwork. We know who he is and that he's staying with you and won't be in the Bedford area much longer, so he wasn't charged. That's what the sergeant decided, anyway.'

'Do you agree with that decision?' I asked.

Greenfield looked down at me warily. 'She's the sergeant,' he said. Clearly, he did not agree.

'Well, can I see him. I can take him home for you if he's not stopping here.'

'You're too late,' Greenfield said. 'Sergeant Caro's already taken him home.'

'Back to my home?' I asked.

'Yes, where else?' Greenfield replied.

Where else indeed, I thought, but surely Sergeant Caro would not be so stupid as to take Merisi back to her place? I knew that she was hot for Merisi in a big way but I had warned her about him in no uncertain terms. 'Are you and Sergeant Caro off duty soon?' I asked Greenfield, conversationally.

Greenfield looked at his watch. It was just past eight o'clock. 'Another couple of hours,' he said.

'Is Sergeant Caro coming back to the station after she's taken my friend home?'

'No,' Greenfield said. 'She told me that she was going to make a tour of the village pubs, check up on any trouble, make sure their security is okay and so on.'

'Does she have to do that regularly?'

'No, never done it before, as far as I know.' He leaned towards me and said quietly: 'I like Sergeant Caro, I like working with her. She's a great lass and she's had a rough time of it, what with her ex-husband and all. I don't know what she's up to and I don't want to know. I know what you're trying to find out. Don't go stirring the shit for her.'

I thought, you're not quite as stupid as you seem, Greenfield, but I said: 'Don't worry, I've marked her card about Merisi and I won't do or say anything to drop her in it. I like her too.'

Greenfield patted my leg with his huge mitt. 'Good boy,' he said. 'Just as long as we're singing off the same hymn sheet.' He got up and disappeared back through the security door.

I left the police station and walked back through Bedford town centre to the multi-storey car park. The town was getting rowdier so I was relieved to be getting away from it. I would have loved to have asked P.C. Greenfield where Sergeant Caro lived but I knew he would not have told me. All I could do was drive back home and pray that Sergeant Caro had taken the sensible option and simply taken Merisi back to my home and dropped him off. But when I arrived home the house was empty and quiet. I looked around, even in the summerhouse, to make sure Merisi was not at home, but he was not. I went back to the living room, poured myself a large Scotch, and pondered what to do next. I looked in the telephone directory. There were four Caros in the Bedford area. I rang all four but none of them were Sergeant Caro or her relatives. There was very little else I could do, except wait. I switched on the television and that gave me the inspiration. I switched it off again and found the home number of my friend Joe, who had installed the television. I remembered that he did a lot of work for Bedford police station. He might know where

Sergeant Caro lived or might have her phone number. Joe answered the phone and I explained what I wanted but he was very wary of what I was asking. 'Why do you want to know where she lives?' Joe asked me. 'Why don't you just ring the nick or go and see her there?'

'It's personal, Joe. I don't want her bosses or colleagues to know.'

He chuckled. 'You fancy her, don't you?' he laughed. 'You're a bit old for her, aren't you?'

'No, I don't fancy her,' I said, 'but I know someone who might, and it might be trouble for her.'

'It's that mad Eyetie who's staying with you, isn't it?' said Joe, still amused by my predicament.

'No,' I lied, 'it's nothing to do with him either. Come on, Joe, this is urgent. I won't tell her that I got her phone number from you.'

'I haven't got her phone number at home here. I've got it at the shop. I can give it to you tomorrow.'

'What about her address? Where does she live?'

'Is this kosher?' Joe asked, still wary. 'I get a lot of work from the Bedford Bill. I don't want to queer my pitch.'

'Joe, it's kosher,' I promised him. 'I'm only trying to help the woman, I swear, and she could be in big trouble if I don't get to her tonight.'

'Somebody trying to kill her?'

'No, no, for fuck's sake. It's serious, but not that serious. Are you going to tell me or not?'

'All right, all right, keep your hair on. Oh, I forgot, you haven't got any left, have you? She lives in that big new block of flats out on the Putnoe road, what's it called . . . er.'

'Millennium House?'

'Yeah, that's it?'

'What number?'

'That's easy,' Joe said. 'Number 49. You know, like P.C. 49!' Joe chuckled heartily at his scintillating wit.

'Thanks Joe,' I said, 'I owe you one.'

'Just go and set fire to Dixon's for me,' he said. I put the phone down, grabbed my coat and rushed out to the Astra. I drove as fast as I legally could to Putnoe and parked outside Millennium House. I took the lift to the fifth floor and found number 49. I knocked politely and waited. There was no answer. Then I knocked harder. Still no-one came to the door. Finally, I banged on the door as loud as I could. A female voice said: 'Hold on, I'm coming.' The door opened, held by a strong security chain, and Sergeant Caro peered through the gap. I could see that she was dressed in a brightly-coloured silk kimono-style dressing gown. Her face fell when she saw it was me. 'What do you want?' she asked.

'Is Michele with you?'

'How did you find out where I live?' Caro asked.

'I followed you from Bedford nick,' I lied.

'Then you know damn well that Michele is with me,' Caro said, in a tone that dared me to argue with her.

'Can I come in?' I asked.

'No.'

'I warned you about Michele. Tell him to come out here and I'll take him home.'

'This is his home now,' Caro said firmly. 'What has all this got to do with you? He's a grown man. Michele can do what he likes.'

'Listen, sergeant,' I said, 'believe me when I tell you that Michele cannot do what he likes. He is my guest in this country and I am responsible for his welfare and safety. Michele is only using you. He'll dump you when it suits him.'

Merisi's voice from behind the door said: 'You've got a high opinion of me, Stefano. Thanks very much.'

Caro unlocked the security chain and let me into her apartment. It was sparsely, but tastefully, decorated. It was the apartment of someone whose work allowed them little time to relax or to spend too much effort on decoration. Merisi was standing naked but thankfully with a towel wrapped around his waist. His body was scarred, and very hairy, but well muscled. His hair was wet and slicked back. I could see why Sergeant Caro desired him. 'Come on, Michele. Get dressed and I'll take you back to my place.'

'Why should I?' he said, with a wry smile, relishing the awkward situation. 'I prefer it here, with Izzy.'

'Izzy?' I repeated.

'My name is Isabella,' said Sergeant Caro, embarrassed by her pet name.

'You know very well you cannot stay here, Michele,' I said. 'Don't do this to Sergeant . . . er, Isabella.'

'You are right, Stefano,' Merisi said. Then to Caro he explained: 'I will have to go with Stefano now but I will be back as soon as I can.' He kissed her lightly on the forehead. He went into the bedroom to get dressed. Caro stood there, with her arms folded, staring at me with an expression of resentment and detestation. We said nothing for a couple of minutes, then I couldn't stand the silence any longer.

'I haven't told anybody about this. Nobody will know. You won't get into any trouble. But this must stop now.' Caro carried on silently staring at me. I was relieved when Merisi, fully dressed, came out of the bedroom.

'Ciao, bambino,' he said to Caro, 'I will be back soon.' He kissed her again. He seemed as eager to get out of the apartment as I was. We walked out and Caro slammed the door behind us. In the elevator going down, Merisi put his arm around my shoulder and said: 'Thank you for rescuing me, Stefano.'

'Rescuing you!?' I exclaimed.

'I haven't had a fuck for four hundred years. That woman was wearing me out!'

We left the building and got into my car. 'New car, Stefano?' Merisi said, teasingly.

'Yes, and I'm hiding the fucking keys this time.' I drove out on to the road.

'Are you angry with me, Stefano?' Merisi asked, entertained by my foul mood.

'What the fuck did you think you were doing?' I shouted. 'Asking women if they are whores, getting arrested again, and then ending up in bed with a policewoman! You're not supposed to be in this century, Michele. You've got to keep a low profile. Let's just do what we have to do and get you back to wherever you have to go back to.'

'I think I'll go back to Izzy's room,' Merisi chuckled. 'I've never fucked a policeman before. They've fucked me several times. It was good to get my own back.'

'The word is policewoman,' I corrected him. 'Don't do this to Sergeant Caro. Don't ruin her life.'

'Oh, don't worry, Stefano. I got what I went out for.'

'Who made that phone call?' I asked.

'What phone call?'

'You know, the one inviting you to the Juventus supporters club meeting, or whatever it was?'

'That was someone called Silvio. I met him in that tavern. I paid him to make that call. I wanted to get out alone and get myself a woman without you lecturing me like a priest all the time.'

'We can get you a woman, if you're that desperate,' I said. 'But not Sergeant Caro, for fuck's sake. That's asking for trouble.'

'She is hot for me, no?'

'Yes, she is. But we cannot take the risk of anyone finding out who you really are. Who are you, anyway? A few hours ago, I was looking at a picture that you painted, the most tender scene of a mother and baby. The same man who painted that tender maternal scene then goes out, gets drunk, uses an unsuspecting woman like a whore to slake his lust. The same man who could paint a picture like the Penitent Magdalen!'

'Perhaps now I will paint the Penitent Isabella, eh, Stefano?'

Despite my anger, I had to smile. 'Don't go near her again,' I warned.

'I won't,' Merisi agreed. 'She is a nice fuck but a boring bitch. All I wanted to do was to pump my seed into her warm little box and get out for a drink. I won't go near her again.'

'Merisi,' I said, as I steered the car into my drive, 'you really are a piece of shit.'

24

Despicable and immoral behaviour had a heartening effect on Merisi. The next morning, as we settled down to work, he was in a cheerier mood than he had been since I first met him. As I was arranging my notebooks and textbooks on the coffee table in front of the living room fire, Merisi sat in his armchair contentedly sipping coffee and humming a tune which I did not recognise. 'Do you enjoy music, Michele?' I asked.

'Indeed I do,' Merisi replied. 'I have always enjoyed music and learned to enjoy it even more when I was surrounded by musicians at the palace of Cardinal Del Monte. You may not believe me but I am accomplished as a player of the guitar.'

I was aware that Merisi played the guitar but I did not admit it. 'When did you learn to play music?' I asked. 'As a child?'

'Yes. Costanza Colonna was kind enough to encourage my interest in music and I took instruction from a guitarist in the employ of the Colonna family. Although I say it myself, I learnt the basics more quickly than most pupils do and I thereafter improved my skill while playing for my own pleasure.'

'I would be interested to hear you play,' I said.

'I would be delighted to show you,' Merisi replied, 'but we have no guitar.'

'We can soon put that right,' I said. I went upstairs to my bedroom. Stored on top of a wardrobe was an acoustic guitar that I had owned ever since I was a teenager, when I had a brief flirtation with the most unsuccessful pop career in history. My dream of emulating Jimi Hendrix and Eric Clapton foundered on the inescapable fact that I had no musical talent. Occasionally, I would strum the guitar and, as it was an icon of my long-lost youth, I had always felt loathe to get rid of the instrument. It was covered with dust, so I took it down to the kitchen and cleaned it off with kitchen paper. Then I took it through to the living room. Merisi's face lit up with pleasure when he saw the guitar and he took it from me eagerly. 'You are always full of surprises,' he said, as he tried a few chords.

'Can you play either of the madrigals that you included in your paintings?' I asked.

'Which ones?'

'Perhaps the one in The Musicians, "You Know That I Love You",' I suggested.

'I can play it but I cannot sing it,' Merisi said. 'I am a poor singer.'

'Then just play it,' I said.

Merisi played a pleasant air. His technique was rusty but he confirmed that he was, indeed, an accomplished player.

'That was charming,' I said, truthfully.

'Do people still play the guitar today?' Merisi asked.

'The guitar is more popular now than it has ever been,' I told him. 'But now we have what are known as electric guitars which amplify the sound of the instrument. The electric guitar is mainly used in a fairly new form of music that is known as "pop" or "rock 'n' roll".'

'Can you play me some of this music?'

'I would love to be able to,' I said. 'I cannot, but I can let you hear an example. We can now make a recording of music played by other people and play it whenever we like.' I searched through my CD collection and found The Cream of Clapton. I put it into the player and told Merisi: 'This is a work by the greatest electric guitarist of modern times, a man named Eric Clapton, who is playing with a group that were called Cream. It's his live version of a musical form known as a blues, written by an American named Robert Johnson. You will never hear pop or rock music played any better than this. It's called Crossroads. Tell me what you think?' I started the track and watched Merisi's face with interest. He looked horrified as Clapton belted out the first few bars of the classic blues anthem, with Ginger Baker pounding the drums and Jack Bruce providing his usual inventive bass line. Soon Merisi was shouting: 'Stop, stop!'

'Don't you like it?' I asked, unable to suppress a smile.

'It is angry devil's music!' Merisi exclaimed.

'Many people today would agree with you,' I said.

'Is this the sort of music that people like today?'

'Millions do,' I replied. 'Millions more probably hate it. There are many, many other forms of modern music.'

'Music should be sweet and joyous and full of beauty,' Merisi said.

'You're right,' I agreed, 'and some other time I will play you some. I think you may prefer the work of an Austrian composer named Wolfgang Amadeus Mozart or German composers named Ludwig Beethoven and Johann Sebastian Bach. They worked a couple of centuries after you died.'

'Is all modern music composed by devils or northern heretics?'

'Not all,' I said. 'Just about the time you supposedly died, a composer named

Monteverdi, from your native country, invented a form of music known as opera and Italian composers have since composed many superb examples of the form. But let's get back to your life and work. That's what really interests me.'

'I have a deep interest in it myself,' Merisi smiled.

'I'd like to ask you about your two very important church commissions, the paintings that really launched your reputation as the most famous painter in Italy, starting with your commission for the Contarelli Chapel of the church of San Luigi dei Francesi.'

'Very well,' Merisi said. 'The church of San Luigi dei Francesi was just down the street from the Palazzo Madama, where I was living. It was the national church of the French in Rome. There were many French people living and working in Rome and this church was their spiritual centre. It had been bought several years before by a French cardinal named Matteo Contarelli and was dedicated to his namesake, Saint Matthew. The church was owned by the cardinal's heirs and was run by a council of leading citizens. The Contarelli chapel, within the church, had just been opened for the celebration of Mass and the council decided they wanted the chapel decorated with two scenes from the life of Saint Matthew. These scenes were to be Saint Matthew's martyrdom and his calling by Christ. Very wisely, the council chose me to paint these works.'

'Do you know why they chose you?' I asked. 'After all, you had acquired a good reputation as a painter but you had never been given such a big commission before. You were by no means the obvious choice. Your old friend the Cavaliere d'Arpino or Zuccaro or Annibale Carracci would have been more obvious choices at the time.'

'There had been many artists working on the church in previous years, including the Cavaliere, but there had been many problems. Despite my reputation as a scoundrel in other walks of life, my reputation as an artist who completed commissions on time was good. Perhaps they wanted a fresh approach.'

'Your rival and biographer Baglione suspected the hand of Cardinal Del Monte in getting you this commission.'

'That is undoubtedly correct,' Merisi smiled. 'I think the good cardinal used all his influence to win me the Contarelli Chapel contract. As did my agent Valentin who, as you know, was himself of French origin. I'm delighted to say that Baglione was extremely envious. He was eyeing this commission for himself but we snatched it from under his nose. I don't think he ever forgave me.' Merisi laughed and banged the arm of his chair several times, still relishing the memory of his rival's discomfiture. 'I was a very quick worker, you see. There was feverish excitement and anticipation in Rome about the forthcoming centenary jubilee in the year 1600. I signed the contract for the Contarelli

Chapel work only about six months prior to the jubilee, so the council were expecting fast work. There was an ambivalent attitude towards the French in Rome at that time. I think the church council wanted to put on a good show by the French, to improve their image and standing, in time for the jubilee.'

'Why was there an ambivalent attitude?' I asked.

'It was mainly because of the king of France, Henry IV,' Merisi replied. 'We have mentioned him before. He was an outstanding military leader, a dashing figure who for years, before and after he became king, supported the Protestant cause and inflicted grievous defeats on Catholic forces during the wars of religion. Then, in 1593 I think it was, he converted back to Roman Catholicism! While some accepted Henry's conversion as genuine, most believed it was a cynical and politically expedient ploy. I remember fierce arguments taking place in the taverns of Rome about this so-called conversion and, as you know, I was mixed-up in street fights against the French.'

'I'll bet you kept that quiet when the Contarelli Chapel commisssion was on offer,' I said.

'Of course I did! I couldn't care less whether King Henry's conversion to Catholicism was genuine or not but I was brought up in a Spanish province so, when it came to taking sides in a street fight, I sided with the Spanish faction. I'm proud to say that Spain carried on opposing King Henry of France even after this conversion. Anyway, a couple of years after Henry had announced this convenient change of religion, a ceremony of absolution was held in St. Peter's Square in Rome. I went to see the ceremony. All the spaces around the square and around the Vatican itself were taken. The crowd was huge. Henry himself did not attend but sent his representatives. In front of the pope and on behalf of King Henry, they abjured the heresies of Calvinism and received absolution from the Holy Father. The church of San Luigi dei Francesi, being the national church of the French, was naturally at the heart of the ceremonies to commemorate King Henry's conversion. Then, in 1598, came peace between France and Spain and the anticipation of the jubilee celebrations began. They chose me to prepare the Contarelli Chapel for the jubilee.'

'We know that you had many problems completing your commission but how did you feel when you were told that you had won the contract?'

'I was elated. I knew this was my big chance to show Rome, and the world, exactly what I could do. I knew that my dear friend, the Marchese Costanza Colonna Sforza and her son Muzio were coming to Rome for the jubilee celebrations. Her other son, my friend Fabrizio Sforza was already living in Rome. I was anxious to show them just how good an artist I was with this Contarelli chapel commission. Every artist dreamed of winning such a big commission, that's why Baglione was so jealous of me. But, as you rightly say

Stefano, if I had known what problems I was going to have, I would have thrown my brushes, and myself, in the River Tiber!'

'Okay, let's start with the Martyrdom of St. Matthew. (*Plate 23*). We believe that this work caused you the most trouble. We now have a technique, known as X-rays, that show you began with a completely different composition to the painting that is still in place today.'

'My pictures are still there?' Merisi said excitedly. 'Both of them?'

'Yes they are,' I said. 'They have not been moved since the day they were installed after you completed them.'

'That is very good to know,' Merisi said, with a broad grin. 'Yes, you are correct about the original composition. I first envisaged smaller figures in the foreground, set within a magnificent architectural surround, but I was not at all satisfied. It was formal, traditional, static. I wanted to inspire the viewer to feel dread, sympathy and terror at the moment of execution, not just admire a clever composition. So I abandoned this right-hand wall and turned my attention to the left-hand wall and the Calling of St. Matthew. (*Plate 24*). Here I felt more confident, more sure of what I wanted to do.'

'Can you remember who modelled for you?' I asked. 'I think I can recognise Mario Minnitti again. A Bolognese biographer named Malvasia thought that the youth with his back to the viewer was your friend Lionello Spada. Is that correct?'

'Yes. I had known Lionello for a couple of years by this time. He often visited my studio. He was very impressed and influenced by my work and we became close friends but I cannot remember whether it was him or Nicholas who posed for this youth.'

'You mean Nicholas Cordier, the French sculptor?'

'Yes, that's right. I recall that Nicholas was keen to be involved in the decoration of the French church, being French himself. I was pleased with the effect I had achieved in this painting.'

'About fifty years ago, an art historian named Valerio Mariani wrote about your Calling of Saint Matthew that "this revolutionary work marks the beginning of a new age in painting". I think he was right.'

Merisi smiled with pleasure. 'Thank you, Stefano. When I turned back to the Martyrdom, I knew that what I had already painted was completely wrong compared to the Calling. I devised a whole new composition, with bigger figures emerging from the darkness, in a radial form. Lionello certainly modelled for me as the executioner in the centre. I had immense difficulty getting the whole thing right. I had to paint the scene twice. I missed the deadline by several weeks and the pictures were not hung in the Contarelli Chapel until after the jubilee new year celebrations.'

'We believe that both pictures may have been exhibited at the Palazzo Madama before they were hung in the chapel. Is that true?' I asked.

'Yes, it is. Word of what I had achieved spread like wildfire through the Roman art world. The pictures were displayed at the palazzo and caused a sensation. On the strength of the Contarelli pictures I won the contract for a large altarpiece for a Sienese patron, thanks to my good friend and promoter Onorio Longhi. It was a large work, nearly nine feet high. Do you have a picture of it in your book?'

'Sadly, Michele, that work is now lost.'

'A great pity,' Merisi said, shaking his head. 'I put a lot of effort into that altarpiece, in order to build upon my newly-won reputation and success.'

'You very soon won another important commission, for the Cerasi chapel of the church of Santa Maria del Popolo. This was only two months after the Matthew pictures had been hung in the French church. How did you win the Cerasi contract?'

'By sheer talent, I suppose,' Merisi replied, smugly. 'Tiberio Cerasi, who commissioned the work, was Treasurer-General to the Holy Father. He wanted the best young painters in Rome to decorate his church and so he chose me to decorate the Cerasi chapel and my friend Annibale Carracci to paint the high altar. I think that Cerasi was intrigued to see if there was any rivalry between me and Annibale but we respected each other's work too much for that. The subjects I was given were the crucifixion of Saint Peter and the conversion of Saint Paul on the road to Damascus. Being the jubilee year, when the faith was being particularly celebrated, the two founding fathers of the Roman Church were especially revered and it was an honour to be chosen to depict them.'

'We know that your first versions of these paintings were rejected by the church,' I said. 'Why was that?'

Merisi shifted uncomfortably. 'I was hoping that you would not know about that. Yes, they were rejected, and it was entirely my own fault. Despite my success with the Contarelli pictures, I became seized with self-doubt. What if the success of my new style had been a fluke? Was I really good enough to introduce a radically new course of art? So, when it came to the Cerasi chapel pictures, I decided to play safe.'

'Your first version of the crucifixion of Saint Peter has been lost, but your first version of the conversion of Saint Paul is still in a gallery in Rome. It has puzzled art historians ever since but, from what you have just said, perhaps we can now understand why.' (*Plate 25*)

'Show it to me,' Merisi requested, and I passed him the book of his complete works to refresh his memory about one of his most unsatisfactory paintings. He shook his head in dismay. 'It is even worse than I remember it. It's the sort of crap that Baglione or Zuccaro might have painted. It's tame, timid, old-fashioned, stuffy, cluttered and dull. What was I thinking of?'

'Your patron was expecting a work in keeping with the dramatic impact of your Contarelli works, and you present him with this? No wonder it was rejected.'

'I cannot argue,' Merisi said, disconsolately. 'Annibale had already completed the altarpiece and had produced a masterful work. I admit that I was intimidated. I lost my vision and my courage. But the shock of rejection reassured me that I had been right to follow my own vision. So I reassessed what I had to do and I think the second version worked much more successfully.'

'Critics are still puzzled by the Conversion of Saint Paul picture,' I said. (*Plate 26*). 'The huge hindquarters of the horse dominates the picture and even in your own time this aspect of the composition was found to be puzzling. We have a record of a conversation between yourself and a prelate of Santa Maria.'

'What was said?'

'The prelate asked you: "Why have you put a horse in the middle and Saint Paul on the ground? Is the horse God?" and you replied: "No, but he stands in God's light!"'

Merisi chuckled. 'I vaguely remember that conversation. He was a bumptious little bastard, that prelate. Who was he to question my work?'

'Anyone who views any work of art that has been placed in the public arena has a right to question it,' I said.

Merisi looked at me keenly. 'You agree with the prelate, don't you? You don't like my version of Saint Paul's conversion.'

I pondered for a second whether to tell the truth but decided it would not damage our relationship too much if I did. 'No, I don't,' I answered.

'What about the crucifixion of Saint Peter?' Merisi asked. (*Plate 27*).

'That affects me in an entirely different way. It makes me want to step into the picture and stop what is happening. He is a lonely old man, stoically trying to face a brutal death in solitude, accompanied only by his persecutors and his own faith. I defy anybody to look at that picture and not be moved by it. I think it's an astonishing work.'

Merisi nodded. 'That is exactly the effect I intended. I'm glad you think that I've succeeded.'

'But you were not quite finished with the Contarelli chapel, were you?' I said. 'Let's clear that up before we move on.'

'Do you mean the altarpiece?' Merisi asked. I nodded. 'Well,' he continued, 'the church council had commissioned a sculpture of Saint Matthew with the angel from a Flemish sculptor, whose name I have forgotten, but this sculptor struggled with his work for years, literally, and when he finally presented it to the church council they were very disappointed with it as it was such a dull work. So they discarded the sculpture idea and decided to commission a painted altarpiece from me.'

'But the church didn't like your first version of Saint Matthew and the Angel, did they?' (*Plate 28*).

'No,' Merisi snorted. 'The dumb fuckers didn't understand what I was trying to do.'

'Maybe they did,' I said, 'but perhaps, even so, your image was too shocking for them.'

'What do you mean?' Merisi challenged.

'Well, you've made Saint Matthew look like a dolt,' I said. 'His lumpen body and bemused expression, together with his dirty feet sticking out at the viewer, are hardly saint-like or reverential.'

'All the disciples were working men,' Merisi protested, 'not effete cardinals and aristocrats.'

'And the angel figure is quite erotic. She leans across Matthew and touches his hand as if she is trying to seduce him.'

'She? She?' Merisi said emphatically. 'It is an angel. Angels are sexless!'

'Not this one, Michele. She almost gives me a hard-on just looking at her.'

Despite himself, Merisi could not help smiling. 'Perhaps you are right.'

'Your biographer, Giovanni Baglione, tells us that the picture pleased no-one.'

'Baglione should have been used to that,' Merisi shot back, 'because his pictures never pleased anyone.'

'And another biographer, Bellori, tells us that you were in despair over the rejection of the Saint Matthew.'

'Despair is too strong,' Merisi said. 'Great disappointment, yes. A blow to my professional pride, yes. But despair? No.'

'Anyway, your second version of Saint Matthew and the Angel was accepted and still hangs in the Contarelli chapel today.' (*Plate 29*).

'Good,' Merisi shrugged. 'I had lost interest. It's a bland work. Nicely painted but the only interest I had left in that work was to fulfil my contract. I was being offered much more interesting work.'

'Your commissions for these two churches had made you the talk and the toast of Rome,' I said. 'Did you enjoy all the attention?'

'Yes, for a time,' Merisi replied. 'It was very gratifying. Everybody who was anybody wanted to make my acquaintance. Cardinals and dukes, as well as other painters, poets, scultors and architects wanted to talk to me and find out my views on aesthetics. There were many poems written in honour of my paintings. If anyone wanted a portrait or an altarpiece, they wanted me do to it. All the success I had ever dreamed of had suddenly come true.'

'Your painting of Narcissus, one of your few works on a subject from classical mythology, seemed to fascinate the poets.' (*Plate 30*).

'Yes, it is what is known as a vanitas picture, a contemplation of youth and age and self-love and the transience of time. It certainly caught the intellectual fancy of the time.'

'Who modelled for it?'

'My friend Lionello Spada.'

'You seem to have become close to Spada about this time.'

'Yes. Lionello was a lively character. He was from Bologna. He was an average painter and an even worse poet, but his poetry was risque and satirical and amusing. We certainly became close friends at about this time.'

'So much so,' I ventured, 'that Spada earned the nickname of "the ape of Caravaggio".'

Merisi smiled. 'Yes, I was aware of that. Spada followed me everywhere. He was in awe of my painting and was always willing to model for me, which was useful because Mario Minnitti seemed to be keeping his distance from me, so Spada took his place. Lionello said that I would make him immortal by putting him in my work. I think he was right!'

'Many of your works from this time, curiously, seem to have been lost,' I said. 'We have references to several portraits and gallery pictures that have disappeared. It's a great pity.'

'Considering all the effort I put into them, it certainly is,' Merisi agreed.

'With the possible exception of Annibale Carracci, you were suddenly the most popular and fashionable painter in Rome. Was there a rivalry between you and Carracci?'

'Only a friendly and respectful rivalry. You see, Annibale was about ten years older than me. He had already become a famous painter in Bologna when he was invited to Rome to decorate the Palazzo Farnese, which was the grandest of all the Roman palazzi. He was a real painter, really talented, with an original artistic vision. Most of the other painters I knew were merely competent journeymen, but Annibale had the real gift. But he was a strange character.'

'In what way?' I asked.

'He was a very simple, very humble man. He was very uneasy in the company of popes, princes and cardinals. He much preferred the company of simple working men. In fact, he was very uneasy in any company. He would blush anxiously when in the company of important men and avoided their presence as much as he could. He was dirty and ill-dressed. He cared nothing for his personal appearance because his mind was always elsewhere, planning his latest artistic project. He worked like a dog but, like me, he never seemed to make any money, unlike pricks like Zuccaro or the Cavaliere d'Arpino, who could afford to build there own palazzi. Annibale's pupils adored him but he had a sharp tongue and, like me, he was violently jealous when other artists had a success . . . except when I did. And vice versa. I didn't begrudge him his success because he deserved it. He was a superb fresco painter. The first time I saw any of his work was just before I scored my successes with the church commissions. Annibale had painted an altarpiece of Saint Margaret for the church of Santa Caterina dei Funari. The colours were bright, the light beautifully rendered, the whole work suffused with a warm and tender humanity. I remember remarking to my companion, who I think was Spada, that I was happy that, during my time, I could see a real painter.'

'All that sounds too good to be true, coming from you,' I smiled.

'Oh, I still had some fun with Annibale,' Merisi said. 'His brother, Agostino, was a completely different character. Agostino was clean, well-dressed, erudite and worldly, and he loved the company of distinguished men and poets and painters. This used to infuriate Annibale, so when they were together I would delight in starting an argument between them. Annibale would call his brother an ingratiating intellectual snob and Agostino would counter by calling Annibale a stupid, dirty unkempt lackey. It was a lot of fun!'

'That's more like you,' I said. 'Before we stop for lunch, I want to talk about two of the sort of pictures that you produced at regular intervals that are so bold, so shocking that, even today, four hundred years later, in a much more lax moral and religious climate, they still seem almost pornographic. Today we call them Victorious Cupid and Saint John the Baptist.' I showed Merisi the two pictures in his complete works. 'These are two works that encouraged the idea that you had homosexual inclinations because they are so overtly homo-erotic. You must have used the same model for both paintings. Who was he?'

'This was my apprentice, Giovanni,' Merisi replied. He pointed to the picture now known as St. John the Baptist. 'This is not meant to be Saint John! This picture was commissioned by Ciriaco Mattei, who wanted a picture of Paris as a Phrygian shepherd!' (*Plate 31*).

'Okay,' I said, 'it's a picture that has caused disagreement among art historians in recent years.'

'Who decided that it was Saint John the Baptist?'

'I don't know,' I admitted. 'I suppose the presence of the ram led experts to believe that it was Saint John.'

'No. Both these paintings were inspired by Michelangelo's Ignudi and I was attempting to match the work of Carracci in these warm flesh tones.'

'What about the Victorious Cupid?' I asked. 'Is that a correct title?' (*Plate 32*).

'It will do,' Merisi said. 'The boy is meant to be Cupid, or Eros, as a representation of love, so a better title would be Amor Vincit Omnia.'

My ChronoTranslator could not manage a Latin translation so I had to ask Merisi what that title meant in English. 'Love Conquers All,' he replied. 'Eros is trampling all of Man's arts, sciences and military prowess. The power of love is mightier than all of them. This picture was commissioned by Vincenzo Giustiniani.' Merisi smiled. 'I have to admit that this image was probably not what the pious banker had in mind but he adored it. He kept it in his private salon at the Palazzo Giustiniani.'

'You have to admit, Michele, that such works would lead people to assume you were a bardassa yourself.'

'If they do not understand why and for whom these pictures were painted, then maybe so.'

'Was this apprentice, Giovanni, living with you?'

'Yes, he was. We were both together in the Palazzo Madama. He has an enticing face and body, don't you think. That's partly the reason I took him on as an apprentice, to use him as a model in such works as these. He was a sweet boy, full of fun, and eager to learn the trade. He never took any notice of my bad moods or my foul temper. He would always repay me with a mouthful of cheek and then run away before I could clout him. He knew how to cheer me up.'

'Are you quite sure you were not teaching him other things?' I suggested. 'He sounds like an interesting character. I think I might travel back to Rome and interview this apprentice of yours.'

'That will not be possible, Stefano.'

'Why not?'

'In 1601, the banks of the Tiber burst after weeks of heavy rain caused flooding. The water poured into the cellars of the Palazzo Madama where Giovanni was preparing some canvases for me. He was drowned. He was thirteen years old.'

I didn't know what to say for a few seconds. 'I'm very sorry, Michele. Of course, I didn't know that. But surely, these two paintings were completed after that sad event?'

'Yes, they were,' Merisi said. 'When it came to making these pictures, I used a stable lad from the Palazzo to model for the body but I put Giovanni's head on his shoulders. I saw Giovanni in my dreams for a long time after he drowned. I knew his face very well.'

It seemed an appropriate point to stop for lunch. Merisi, like Ben Gunn in Treasure Island, had developed a passion for Welsh rarebit, which is simply melted cheese on toast, and insisted we had it for lunch every day. I didn't mind as I was very fond of it myself, despite the calories it packed. Over lunch we tried to analyse the paintings we had talked about in the morning session but we could not pin down any clues in them that might lead us to the reason why Merisi had been murdered. Merisi was evasive and reticent about what we now know as the Victorious Cupid picture but whether he was hiding something or whether he was still sensitive about the death of his apprentice, Giovanni, I couldn't tell.

Settled back in our living room armchairs after lunch, I broached a subject that puzzled me. 'A year or so after the centenary jubilee celebrations, you had become the most talked about, the most fashionable, the most famous painter in Rome. Much of your success was thanks to the patronage of Cardinal Del Monte. You had a comfortable life with him at the Palazzo Madama. And yet you chose to leave Del Monte and the Palazzo Madama and move to the Palazzo Mattei. Can you explain the reasons for that?'

Merisi thought for a while, and then said: 'There were several reasons. As you know, I had established my studio in the cellars of the Palazzo Madama. After they had flooded and drowned my poor apprentice Giovanni, I found it difficult to face working there again.'

'That's entirely understandable,' I said.

'My good friend Prospero Orsi, who was doing such a good job on my behalf by singing my praises around Rome and securing many commissions for me, was in the service of the Mattei family. And Cardinal Vincenzo Giustiniani, who was an admirer of my work, urged me to make the move.'

'We know that Vincenzo Giustiniani was a friend of both Del Monte and Cardinal Girolamo Mattei,' I said. 'What reason did he give for urging you to move?'

'No particular reason. It was all rather vague. He suggested that I would be more free at the Palazzo Mattei, that it would give a new impetus to my creativity to be surrounded by new and different works of art.'

'As you say, that seems rather vague. You didn't feel stifled or stultified by working at the Palazzo Madama, did you?'

'No, not at all,' Merisi said. 'I was very contented there, except for the Tiber flood. I'm not sure why Vincenzo Giustiniani was urging me to move.'

'Vincenzo seems to have suddenly become very important in your life, both as a friend and a patron.'

'Yes,' Merisi agreed. 'He was completely bowled over by my new style of painting. Couldn't get enough of it.'

'Did Del Monte know that Giustiniani was urging you to move?'

'I don't think so,' Merisi answered. 'He asked me not to mention it to his friend Del Monte.'

'So how did Cardinal Del Monte react when you made the move?'

'He seemed surprised. He asked me to reconsider and stay with him. I explained that the death of Giovanni had upset me and that I felt I wanted to work somewhere else. He offered me a new studio location within his palazzo but I had decided the move to the Palazzo Mattei was better for me because of one very good reason.'

'What was that?' I asked.

'The Mattei family were considerably wealthier than Cardinal Del Monte. They could afford to pay higher prices for my work. Does that seem immoral to you?'

'No, it seems eminently sensible. Did Mario Minnitti also move to the Palazzo Mattei with you?'

'No. Del Monte had urged Mario to move with me, as a companion, but I think Mario had tired of both of us. He was certainly tired of me. He had met his future wife, she had gone back to their native Sicily and I think he was eager to move back there with her. I didn't mind. I was just as tired of him always hanging around me.'

'So Del Monte had to accept your decision but I would surmise that he was not best pleased?' I said.

'That is true,' Merisi agreed, 'but he was too much of a courteous gentleman to show his displeasure. I don't know whether he thought I was an ungrateful wretch but I was not his prisoner and, in the end, there was nothing he could do to stop me.'

'You said that the Mattei family were considerably wealthier than Del Monte. Did you think they would give you more lucrative commissions?'

'Yes, indeed,' Merisi replied. 'There were three Mattei brothers. Girolamo, who lived in the Palazzo Mattei, was not particularly interested in art, over and above what a cultured gentleman needed to be in those times, but his brothers Ciriaco and Asdrubale, who lived in an adjacent palazzo, were avid collectors, very wealthy, and very keen to obtain more of my work. Poor old Del Monte! I had found fame mainly thanks to him, and technically I was still in his service, but now he had been priced out of the market! He could no longer afford to buy any of my pictures!'

I made a note that, benevolent Christian gentleman or not, Del Monte must have felt peeved and aggrieved by that circumstance. 'Tell me about the Palazzo Mattei,' I said. 'Were you glad, afterwards, that you had moved there?'

'The palazzo had a fairly plain but elegant facade which had been frescoed by Zuccaro's older brother Taddeo. It overlooked the Piazza Mattei with its elegant fountain. The interior was sumptuous, especially the grand salon, which had a magnificent carved wooden ceiling. The palazzo had been decorated by a fashionable Flemish landscape painter, Paul Brill I think his name was, a couple of years before I moved there. Brill had covered the palazzo with hunting scenes, restful landscapes, and bucolic village scenes. The palazzo had an atmosphere quite different to most of the palazzi in Rome, which were mainly decorated with scenes from classical mythology. I was given a comfortable room and an airy studio. Yes, it was a good move for me.'

'You had now achieved everything that an aspiring young painter in Rome could have dreamed of,' I said. 'You had a comfortable room and studio in a magnificent palazzo, you had plenty of food and drink on the table, you had access to the art collections in the Palazzo Mattei and other palaces for you to study and enjoy, Prospero Orsi and Vincenzo Giustiniani were actively promoting your work, you had so many offers of commissions that you could pick and choose which ones you wanted to do, and you were about to begin work on what I believe were the greatest, most confident and most astonishingly skilful paintings of your entire career. And yet, from what we know, the rot is already beginning to set in . . . the serpent has already entered your Garden of Eden.'

'What do you mean?' Merisi said warily.

'With great success comes great envy on the part of others. Fellow artists who, in the past, might have helped and supported you, who were your friends, are now consumed with jealousy because of your success. And your reaction to that envy was to behave with increasing arrogance and insensitivity to your friends and fellow artists. At the very height of your triumph, your behaviour starts to become even more violent and capricious than it was before. You seemed determined to "get your own back" on fate, on a world that had treated you so cruelly up to now.'

'That is a harsh judgement, Stefano!' Merisi protested. 'I admit that I flaunted my success in the faces of some of my fellow artists who had considered me a boorish provincial nonentity. I rubbed their noses in it. I was careful not to upset my rich patrons. You have to admit that they kept on supporting and protecting me, even in the midst of the worst of my troubles.'

'Yes, that aspect intrigues me,' I said, looking at Merisi for a reaction. 'You have told me that you were careful to suck up to them but even that does not fully explain why rich and powerful men were so loyal to you. I think I will have to travel back to Rome and ask one of them.'

'Which one?' Merisi asked, unconcerned.

'Cardinal Del Monte,' I replied. 'I missed the good cardinal once but now it is time that I came face-to-face with this gentleman and find out what he really thought of his protege, Michelangelo Merisi da Caravaggio.'

25

Cardinal Del Monte's major-domo, Carlo, ushered me into the grand salone of the Palazzo Madama. It was a very spacious room, lavishly decorated with frescoes of mythological scenes and hung with tapestries, although some of the tapestries were worn with age. The salon was carpeted and filled with the heavy, dark, ornately carved Italian oak furniture that I was becoming used to seeing. At the far end of the room, two men were standing by a huge marble fireplace. The fire was unlit, it being a reasonably warm day in Rome. The two men were standing in front of an easel on which rested a painting. I surmised that it was one of Cardinal Del Monte's new acquisitions for his art collection. He looked up as I entered the room and walked towards me, hand outstretched, to greet me. I bowed and took his hand. He shook hands warmly with a firm and confident grip. 'Signor Maddano, welcome,' he said. 'I have been expecting a visit from you. In fact, I have tried to find you but you are an elusive character, as the good Doctor Mancini told me.' He smiled at me to show that he was not perturbed by my elusiveness.

'It's good of you to see me at such short notice, Your Eminence,' I replied.

Del Monte was just how I had imagined him to be, how everyone had described him. He was slim, tall and elegant. His movements were graceful. His hair was thinning and just beginning to turn grey. There was a sardonic twinkle in his eye. As with Pope Paul, his eyes betrayed a quick wit and penetrating intelligence; eyes that missed nothing. He was dressed in a plain but well-cut black robe, with a silver crucifix on a chain around his neck. His only affectation was a gold ring with a hefty ruby set in it. Like most men of the time, he sported a moustache and a small neatly trimmed beard. Now that I stood closer to him, he was not as tall as I had first thought. He was the sort of man who carried himself well, and kept himself in trim, so that he looked taller than he actually was. He said: 'Come and look at my new picture.'

We walked towards his other guest, who I recognised from the portrait engraving by Claude Mellan as Vincenzo Giustiniani. As befitted a wealthy and cultured banker, Vincenzo Giustiniani was dressed much more showily than Del

Monte, but still with exquisite taste, in blue silk. He was slightly taller than Del Monte, but thinner. His face had a pinched, strained look, but his expression was kindly. His hair was full, but high on his forehead, and cut fairly short so that it stood up spikily. His eyes were set wide apart above a thin Roman nose. A pointed beard and moustache, greyer than his hair, surrounded his thin lips. The whole combination gave the impression of an intellectual ascetic. 'Signor Maddano,' Del Monte said, 'may I introduce the distinguished banker, Signore Vincenzo Giustiniani, Cavaliere de Bassano.' I shook hands with Giustiniani. His handshake was drier and more limp than Del Monte's had been.

'An honour to meet you, sir,' I said. 'I had the pleasure of meeting your brother and his charming wife not so long ago.'

'So I understand,' Giustiniani said. He turned to Del Monte. 'No doubt Signor Maddano wishes to talk to you in private, so I will take my leave of you.'

I wanted to talk to Giustiniani as well, so I said: 'Please do not leave on my account, unless the cardinal wishes to talk to me alone. You know that I have come to talk about the painter Michelangelo Merisi da Caravaggio and his mysterious demise. You were both friends and patrons of him, so I would be only too pleased to talk to you both.'

'Excellent,' Del Monte said, almost with relief. 'Will you stay, Vincenzo?'

'If you wish Francesco . . . I mean Your Eminence.'

Del Monte waved his hand. 'Oh, don't bother with titles just because Signor Maddano is here. He knows that you are my very dear friend.' He turned to the painting on the easel. 'What do you think of this work?' he asked me. 'I have just acquired it after years of bargaining. It is David contemplating the Head of Goliath by Guido Reni. What do you think?' (*Plate 33*).

'I'm afraid I'm not qualified to judge,' I replied, 'but it looks a competent work.'

Del Monte looked at me appraisingly. 'Not qualified?' he said. 'Doctor Mancini told me that you were an artist, that you had worked with our friend Michele?'

I had stupidly put my foot in it and had to think of a way out quickly. 'Yes, but I'm afraid my abilities are poor compared with true artists such as Michele and Signor Reni here. I hesitate to pass judgement on such men.'

'You are too modest!' Del Monte cried heartily. 'Look at it carefully. Doesn't something look familiar in this work?' His eyes twinkled as he observed my reaction.

'I'm probably being fanciful,' I said, 'but the head of Goliath looks very much like Caravaggio.'

'Exactly!' Del Monte exclaimed with delight. 'Do you know Guido Reni?'

'No, sir,' I replied. 'I have not met him yet.'

'Then mark him down on your list of suspects. He and Caravaggio thoroughly detested each other. What do you think Michele would have made of this picture, quite apart from Reni's triumphant gesture with his head?'

Here, I was on more secure ground. 'Michele would have hated it,' I stated firmly.

'Yes, he would, wouldn't he,' Del Monte agreed, delighted with my response. 'Let me offer you some refreshment, Signor Maddano. Let's have a glass of wine and drink to Michele's memory.' I smiled and nodded, loathing the thought of having to drink some more of the sour and tasteless wine they seemed to enjoy in this century. Del Monte pulled a tasselled bell-rope hanging down by the fireplace and, when a servant appeared at the door, ordered a carafe of wine with three glasses. 'Let's sit down at the table.' He led us over to a small round table, with uncomfortable wooden chairs, and we sat down. I began by asking Del Monte how he had first noticed Merisi as a talented artist and how he had come to invite him to live in the Palazzo Madama. I knew the answers to these questions and everything that Del Monte told me confirmed what I already knew so, after the servant had brought the wine, I turned to Vincenzo Giustiniani, who had said nothing so far. 'When did you first meet Michele?' I asked him.

'It was here in the Palazzo Madama, thanks to Francesco. He was excited about this new young artist he had discovered and he invited me here to meet Michele and look at some of his work. I became equally excited by his talent.'

We spent the next hour swapping reminiscences and stories about Caravaggio and his extravagance and his strange behaviour. It was fascinating stuff but it was bringing me no nearer to finding the answers I needed about Michele's murder, so I turned the conversation back to my usual final tack. 'Gentlemen,' I said, 'you know that the Holy Father has given me his blessing to enquire into the circumstances of Michele's death. You were both very good friends and supporters of his and, if I may make so bold about my old friend, you were protected from his most bizarre behaviour by your rank and your wealth and the power of your patronage. Therefore, you are clearly not suspects in this sad affair but I have to ask you if you have any certain knowledge of who might have murdered, or attempted to murder, Michele?'

Del Monte was completely unfazed by this question, but Giustiniani looked uncomfortable. 'I'm afraid,' Del Monte said, 'that I can only echo what I suspect most people have told you. Michele made so many enemies, known and unknown, that it is impossible to say.' Del Monte shook his head sadly. 'So many fights, so much envy, so much hatred. The artist Baglione, of course, grew to hate Michele as much as anyone but it is hard to imagine him intriguing in murder. The same with Guido Reni. Michele came to hate Guido but Guido is such a gentle soul. The obvious suspects are the Tomassoni clan, relatives of the man Michele murdered. They would naturally seek revenge and they had the power and the lack of scruples to do so. Have you interviewed the Tomassoni family yet?'

'No,' I replied.

'Be very careful when you do,' Del Monte warned me. 'Even the Holy Father's blessing and protection may not keep you safe from those dogs of war.'

'I will be careful,' I said. 'Signor Giustiniani, have you any ideas?'

Giustiniani took a sip of wine. 'I can only say what my friend has just said. I have no certain knowledge.'

'Very well, gentlemen,' I said. 'Thank you for your time. Before I go, Your Eminence, I would like to ask one very great favour.'

'Name it,' Del Monte said.

'Michele often talked about your excellent collection of paintings. I wonder if you would permit me a view of your collection, especially any of Michele's works and your portrait gallery of famous and powerful men, if it is not too much time and trouble.'

'My dear sir,' Del Monte said, getting to his feet, 'nothing would give me greater pleasure. Vincenzo, would you like to accompany us.'

Giustiniani looked as if he was going to demur, so I said to him: 'I would consider it a great honour if you would accompany us. Your reputation as a man of taste and refinement is second to none and I would be delighted to hear your views.'

'In that case,' Giustiniani said, 'I would be glad to. It is always a pleasure to view Francesco's collection.' Flattery certainly does get you everywhere, I thought to myself.

We followed Del Monte across to a door next to the fireplace. He opened the door and I stepped through into a treasure house of works of art. The door opened into a wide and very long gallery room, of the sort that were so popular in Italy at that time, with windows all along one side to allow the maximum amount of light with which to see the paintings, engravings and sculptures. I wondered whether, in this century, they knew about the damaging effects of sunlight but I said nothing. As Del Monte led us down the gallery, both he and Giustiniani became more animated, discussing the works of art, laughing and arguing, so much so that I think they almost forgot I was there, which suited me fine. Then Del Monte said: 'Here are Michele's pictures.' There, right in front of me, in the place they were intended to hang, was a priceless group of Caravaggio's work. There was The Gypsy Fortune Teller, The Musicians, The Lute Player and Fillide Melandroni staring out at me as St. Catherine of Alexandria. Of all the astonishing sights I had seen since starting on this most bizarre of adventures, this was the most astonishing. To see all of Michele's paintings, all together in one place, was an almost overwhelming experience. Any one of these pictures, I thought, would be worth millions of pounds back in my time. But it wasn't about money. It was about genius.

I became aware that Del Monte was saying something to me and both men were looking at me curiously. 'I'm so sorry, Your Eminence,' I apologised. 'I am so overcome at the beauty of Michele's paintings that I quite forgot where I was.'

'Yes, I was merely asking you what you thought of them,' Del Monte said.

'I have seen copies of them, I have seen engravings of them and I have heard descriptions of them,' I said, 'but nothing could have prepared me for the beauty of such works. They are . . . magnificent.'

'He was a singularly talented man,' Giustiniani said, quietly.

'Forgive me for saying so,' I replied, 'but you do him an injustice. He is . . . was, a genius.'

'Perhaps you are right,' Giustiniani said, not at all put out by being corrected by the likes of me.

'At the far end here are my portraits,' Del Monte said. I didn't want to leave the Caravaggios but I had to follow him. Del Monte, with graceful gestures of his hand, began indicating each portrait. 'Pride of place, naturally, goes to this portrait of the Holy Father, Pope Paul. Here is my friend and patron, the Grand Duke Ferdinando Medici. And here are some of the crowned heads I have had the honour to meet, including your own King James here, I believe. Cordier told me that you were from Scotland, like King James.'

I couldn't remember whether I was supposed to be Scottish or from the Netherlands, so I hedged my bets. Whatever I was, I couldn't be English. 'My father was Scottish and my mother was a Hollander,' I said.

'Ah, quite so,' Del Monte said, looking puzzled.

To quickly change the subject, I asked: 'How is Monsieur Cordier?'

'Alas, he continues to decline, despite the efforts of Doctor Mancini.'

'I understand that you have been helping as well?' I said.

'With my potions, you mean? Yes, I have tried every concoction I can think of that might improve the poor man's condition, but nothing seems to revive him permanently. I pray for him daily.'

I adopted a suitably reverent pose, and then Giustiniani said, pointing to a portrait higher up on the wall: 'Who is this man, Francesco?'

'Which one?' Del Monte asked, looking up.

'This one, directly above Caravaggio's portrait of Cardinal Barberini.' (*Plate 34*). I knew that Cardinal Maffeo Barberini was soon to become Pope Urban VIII but, of course, my companions did not.

'Why, that is the French king, Henry. I'm sure you have seen that portrait before. I have told you, surely.'

'Yes, I'm sorry Francesco. I remember us joking that it is appropriate that King Henry appears to be sitting on Maffeo's head.' Then to me, Giustiniani said: 'It is an interesting portrait of the French king, don't you think, Signor Maddano?'

I pretended to study the portrait and then said: 'Yes, most interesting,' although I didn't think it was at all interesting, or even very accomplished.

Del Monte said: 'Well, Signor Maddano, what do you think of my collection?'

'It is exquisite,' I said. 'Thank you for allowing me to see it. I have taken up more than enough of your time. With your permission, I will take my leave.'

'Of course,' Del Monte said, and we followed him back through the gallery. I couldn't resist a farewell glance at Michele's paintings.

Back in the grand salone, Giustiniani said: 'I must go as well, Francesco. I will leave you to admire Signor Reni's enigmatic picture and I will show Signor Maddano the way out.'

'Perhaps, Signor Maddano, you would care for another glass of wine before you go,' Del Monte said.

'No thank you, Your Eminence. I've got a train to catch.' That is what I intended to say, stupidly, but fortunately the ChronoTranslator was programmed to suppress any modern phrases, or phrases inconsistent with the time, so it came out as a garbled cough.

We took our leave of Del Monte and Giustiniani escorted me out of the grand salone and down a flight of stairs, adorned with intricately carved balusters and newel post, and out into the bustling Roman street. 'As you know, Signor Maddano, the Palazzo Giustiniani is just across the road, so I will bid you farewell and wish you luck with your inquiries. It may be difficult for you. Circumstances, and the people involved in them, are often not as they seem.'

I wasn't going to let him get away with an enigmatic statement like that. 'If you have any information you wish to give me, Signor Giustiniani, then please do so. I would remind you that my inquiry has the blessing of the pope himself and you must tell me the truth on peril of your immortal soul.'

'I am aware of that,' he replied. 'I have no information to give you. I am merely suggesting that you look beyond the obvious.'

I looked at him severely, and said: 'What are you trying to tell me?'

He said: 'I am a wealthy banker. My family were rich before I became a banker. Now we are much, much wealthier than we were before. That is because I consider all possibilities, all options, before I make a decision.'

'You clearly have suspicions about somebody or something. You must tell me.'

'I do not have anything as strong as a suspicion about Michele's murder. But, if I were you, I would consider all possibilities, all indications that are shown to you, however absurd or unlikely they may seem.'

'Why were you so keen to persuade Michele to leave the Palazzo Madama here and move to the Palazzo Mattei?'

'Was I?' Giustiniani replied.

'That is what Michele himself told me once.'

'It was Michele's friend, Prospero Orsi, who urged him to move. The Mattei family are much wealthier than my poor friend Del Monte here. I thought it would be good for Michele to get away from here.' He indicated the palazzo behind us. 'Cardinal Del Monte is a charming gentleman but somewhat . . . suffocating.'

'Is that all?' I challenged him.

'And I wanted to get Michele well away from my brother's wife. They told you that Michele was besotted with Gerolama. Relationships can be very difficult, and very enlightening, can't they?'

'Signor Giustiniani, you are as inscrutable as an Oriental.'

'Thank you,' he replied, bowing slightly. 'Goodbye, Signor Maddano.' Before I could say anymore, Giustiniani had crossed the street and disappeared into the Palazzo Giustiniani. I thought, if you think you can shrug me off that easily, you've got another think coming, old son. I looked up and down the crowded street, looking for a suitably secluded place to operate the ChronoConverter, and then I noticed the church of San Luigi dei Francesi. I had just been viewing some of Merisi's exquisite easel paintings. I realised that I now had the opportunity to see his church paintings on the calling and the execution of Saint Matthew. It was late afternoon, the light was beginning to glow golden, and would be perfect for viewing Merisi's masterpieces. I could not resist. I headed towards the church.

I had timed my visit to perfection. The golden afternoon light flooded the interior of the church and made it breathtakingly beautiful. The light ignited the multi-coloured patterning of the marble columns, shone radiantly on the fresco paintings of scenes from the life of Saint Matthew, and burnished the gold leaf that set off the panels in the elaborate stucco ceiling. I stood there enjoying this exultant sight but the spell was broken by a voice behind me. Someone said: 'Can I help you at all?' I turned round to see a young prelate. He smiled benignly at me. I said: 'I'm a stranger in Rome. I wanted to say a prayer and perhaps view the paintings in the Contarelli chapel by Michelangelo Merisi da Caravaggio. I have heard that they are very good. And, of course, I would like to make a contribution to the upkeep of the church. Forgive me if it is not permitted. I am unfamiliar with Roman ways.'

'This is the house of God,' the prelate said. 'All are welcome here to worship the Lord. You are most welcome.' Thinking of the beggars who thronged the streets outside, I wondered how welcome I would have been if I were not dressed like a fine, wealthy gentleman. 'Please follow me. I will show you the chapel. Then I will leave you in peace to say your words to God.'

I followed the prelate into the church. We passed a pair of columns and came into view of two men standing at the entrance to what I guessed was the Contarelli chapel itself. The prelate confirmed my guess by saying: 'Through there is the Contarelli chapel. I don't know who those two men are. I didn't know they were in here. But they are armed with swords! This is outrageous.' The prelate walked over to the two men and said: 'Why are you wearing swords in this house of God. Shame on you!' As bouncers and bodyguards do to this day, the two big men looked at the prelate with disdain and said nothing. I began to edge away from this scene when the prelate pointed at me and said: 'This gentleman wishes to worship in the chapel. You must take off those swords or leave this church instantly.' I had to give the prelate ten out of ten for guts. I was ready to run for it. The prelate repeated that I wished to pray in the chapel and that the two men must remove their weapons. One of the men looked at me and then walked over to me. He was tall and sturdy, with a scowling and pugnacious face framed by straggling black hair and a black beard. His eyes were like jet black coal with a hint of fire burning in them. He, and his companion, were simply but expensively dressed. He looked familiar but I couldn't place him. He looked like a born troublemaker. 'Who are you?' he asked, brusquely.

Despite my apprehension, I was nettled by his preremptory arrogance. I said: 'Who are you, sir, to be asking who I am?'

The man looked me up and down, took in my expensive clothes and jewellery, and decided I might be important enough to be worth being polite to. 'My name is Fabrizio Sforza. That gentleman over there is my brother Muzio. This prelate here says you wish to worship in the Contarelli chapel?'

Fabrizio and Muzio Sforza! These were Costanza Colonna's two eldest sons. I was right about this man being a born troublemaker. Fabrizio Sforza had landed himself in trouble throughout his life, more so than Merisi ever did. I decided to be conciliatory in return. I bowed and said: 'I am honoured to meet you. My name is Stefano Maddano. I am visiting Rome with papal blessing to . . .'

When he heard my name, Fabrizio Sforza had taken a step backwards. 'Would you excuse me a moment, Signor Maddano?' Fabrizio went back to his brother and whispered something. Then the two of them went into the Contarelli chapel. I could hear them talking to someone but I couldn't make out what was being said. The young prelate was floundering about, wondering what to do, as no-one was taking the slightest notice of him. The discussion within the chapel was becoming more heated. Eventually, Fabrizio Sforza came back out of the Contarelli chapel and said to me: 'Signor Maddano, my mother is making an act of private worship in the chapel at the moment. She wishes to speak to you. Do you agree?'

'I would be honoured to make the Marchese's acquaintance,' I replied. Fabrizio Sforza was not at all surprised that I knew who his mother was. My fame was spreading. 'We know who you are and why you are in Rome. As you know, my mother was fond of Michelangelo Merisi. She is still grieving his death. Please try not to upset her or you will have to answer to me and my brother. We will be waiting outside.'

'Good,' I said. 'I may wish to speak with you afterwards. How well did you know Merisi?'

'We grew up together, Signor Maddano. He was a friend of my childhood and he was a friend of my adulthood. I sincerely hope that you discover the identity of the murderer, if Michele was murdered.'

'I believe he was,' I said. 'How well did your brother Muzio know Michele?'

Fabrizio turned and beckoned his brother to join us. Fabrizio said: 'Signor Maddano is asking how well we knew Michele. I was closer to him than you were, Muzio. Is that not so?'

Muzio Sforza nodded. 'I associated with Michele only rarely, even when we were children. I did not like him, as Fabrizio did, but I was civil to him for my mother's sake. I am a poet. We met occasionally at social or artistic gatherings. I had nothing to do with his death.' I looked at Muzio's dark scowling face, his long straggly black hair, and the jewelled hilt of a stiletto dagger stuck in his belt, and decided that seventeenth century poets were nothing like dear old John Betjeman.

I said: 'Please introduce me to your mother.' The Sforza brothers led me into the Contarelli chapel. I did not know whether to first look at Merisi's paintings or at the Marchese Costanza Colonna Sforza. With her sons standing next to me wearing swords and daggers, I decided to look at Costanza first. She was seated on a marble bench in front of the altar. She was dressed elegantly, but all in black. A black lace mantilla covered her hair. She looked up at me. I knew that she was well over fifty years old at this time. Her face was blandly neutral, neither pretty or plain, but her skin was good and her almond eyes were kindly. Her expression was careworn and worried. I said: 'Thank you for allowing me into the chapel, your ladyship. I did not know you would be here. I apologise for interrupting your worship.'

Fabrizio Sforza decided I could be trusted to be alone with his mother for a few minutes. He said to his mother: 'We'll be right outside.' It was said to Costanza but it was also a warning aimed at me.

The Marchese Costanza Colonna Sforza looked at me and said: 'Please sit down beside me. Forgive my sons, Signor Maddano. They are both of a fierce temperament and very protective of me. These are sad and difficult times for our family. I am grateful that my sons look after me. I knew you would be coming to see me sometime. Now is as good as any.'

'Perhaps better,' I said. 'After all, we are surrounded by Michele's paintings.'

She smiled sweetly and we both looked around at Merisi's magnificent masterpieces. Right in front of us was the painting that Michele had called bland and that I had not thought too much off. Bathed in the golden afternoon light, the orange colour of Matthew's robe and the white of the angel's robe looked stunning. To the left of us was the Calling of St. Matthew and to the right the terrifying Martyrdom of St. Matthew, all bathed in the light coming in through a hemispherical window high up on the marbled wall. Costanza said: 'Who would have believed that Michele would be capable of work such as this? I think back to that little boy in my palazzo in Milan, studying my collection of paintings, and carefully drawing in charcoal or at his little easel painting an apple with such care and concentration. I knew he had talent, but this surpasses anything I ever could have imagined.'

'Michele often told me of your kindness. He was very grateful for all your help.'

'Did you know him well?' Costanza asked.

'I can't say that I knew him well. I worked with him for only a short time. In Naples.'

'I don't remember you as an artist working there. Michele never mentioned your name.'

I had forgotten that Costanza also had a palazzo in Naples. 'I was only ever a humble assistant,' I said. 'I could never aspire to do work such as this.' I waved my hand at the paintings.

'So, you think Michele may have been . . . murdered,' Costanza asked, the last word sticking in her throat.

'I'm afraid it is possible,' I replied.

'Do you have any ideas about who did it?'

'Some ideas, yes, but proof or real evidence, no. But I am only halfway through my inquiries. Do you have any ideas?'

'Like you, I have many ideas. Poor Michele had many enemies. Many people wished him harm.'

'That is my problem,' I agreed. 'Perhaps it will become clearer as my inquiries proceed. For instance, I have not yet interviewed the Tomassoni family. They are the obvious suspects, killing Michele for revenge.'

Costanza shuddered, and tears welled up in her eyes. I mumbled an apology for my crass comment but Costanza waved it away. 'No,' she said, 'we must face facts, however painful they are. If you ever need any help or assistance with your inquiries, be assured that the Colonna family will help you. Don't be afraid to ask.'

'The Colonna family have been very protective of Michele throughout his life,' I said. 'I am aware of the arrangement whereby you paid the painter Mario Minnitti to watch over and protect Michele.'

Costanza looked at me. 'Mario Minnitti?' she repeated. 'I'm afraid I have no idea what arrangement you are referring to.'

'The Holy Father has commanded the truth from all witnesses who speak to me on the subject of Michele's life and death,' I reminded her.

'I swear by Almighty God that I have no knowledge of any such arrangement. Are you saying that this man Minnitti was being paid to protect Michele?'

'Yes, I am,' I said. I scrutinised Costanza's expression. She seemed genuinely bewildered. 'Forgive me, your ladyship, for asking another blunt question. You were particularly close to Michele but Michele was the son of one of your servants, Fermo Merisi. Your love and protection of him transcends what I would have expected of a noble lady towards the son of an employee.'

Costanza bowed her head for a second. 'You are wrong,' Costanza eventually replied, thankfully not as offended as I thought she might be by my question. 'Fermo Merisi was more than an employee. He was very kind to me when I needed a friend more than I have ever done in my life. After he died of the plague, the least I could do was to watch over Michele.' I noticed that Costanza made no mention of Fermo's other children, or his wife. Suddenly Costanza stood up and, out of courtesy, I scrambled to my feet as well. 'I suddenly feel fatigued, Signor Maddano. Perhaps we can meet again when your inquiries have made progress.'

'I will look forward to it,' I said.

'Then please excuse me for the time being.'

I bowed and watched her leave. Fabrizio stuck his head inside the chapel to make sure I was not pursuing her with a dagger or something. When I was sure that they had left the church, I sat down again in the Contarelli chapel and studied Merisi's paintings. It was very difficult to equate my crude house guest with the artist who had painted these scenes with such miraculous skill. It had been an interesting surprise to find Costanza Colonna Sforza and her sons here in the chapel. This encounter, together with the meeting with Cardinal Del Monte and Vincenzo Giustiniani, had given me much to ponder. I sat in the chapel, just thinking things over, for at least an hour. Then I peered out of the chapel. There was no-one else in the church so I ducked back into the Contarelli chapel, pressed the centre of the ChronoConverter and floated back to my own time.

26

I materialised in my bedroom. Apart from pale moonlight, the room was completely dark and I noticed that my bedside electric alarm clock was not illuminated. I tried to switch on the bedside lamp but the bulb did not light up. I tried to switch on the ceiling light with the same lack of result. There was a power cut but it was not a general power cut as the street lamps were on and I could see lights shining in houses further down the road. By the feeble moonlight I managed to change into modern clothes. I decided to look in Merisi's room. I guessed that, because of the darkness, he might have chosen to go to bed. I kept a torch in my bedside cabinet so I took it out, checked that it was working and went to Merisi's room. I quietly opened the door. I could just make out what looked like three tall metal objects standing in his room. I switched on the torch. Merisi was not in the room. I saw that the metal objects were photographers' tripod lamps. One of the lamps had toppled over and smashed the bedroom window. It looked as if the bulb had exploded because I could see shards of glass all over the carpet. What had Merisi been up to while I had been away time travelling? I backed out of the room and went downstairs. 'Michele!' I called out, to warn him that it was me. 'Are you at home? I'm back.' There was no reply. The entire house was in darkness. I went into the living room and saw that the patio door was open. There were items of clothing, male and female, strewn all over the floor. At that moment I saw a hooded figure standing outside in the garden. It was not Merisi because the figure was not tall enough. There had been a local problem with vandalism by hooligans and thefts by travellers so it looked like my home had been broken into and that I was the latest victim. I switched off the torch and went back into the hallway to pick up my tennis racket to use as a weapon. Then I quietly crept back into the living room. The hooded figure was still standing in the same place. I could hear laughter and shouting from further down my garden, so it seemed that there must be a gang of them. I pondered whether to call the police but it usually took several minutes, at least, for the police to drive out from Bedford, even if they were interested in my plight. I decided to handle the problem myself. I walked over to the open patio door and shouted: 'Oi, you!' then charged towards the hooded figure. The figure turned round and saw me rushing forward with the tennis racket raised above my head ready to strike. A female voice screamed in terror and, before I could stop myself, I crashed into the figure and we both went sprawling on to the lawn. 'Mister Maddan!' said my neighbour, Mrs. Chowdry. 'You scared me to death . . . again!'

'Mrs. Chowdry!' I exclaimed. 'What on earth are you doing in my garden dressed like that?'

'Dressed like what?' Mrs. Chowdry said. 'I don't know what you mean?' I switched on my torch and saw that Mrs. Chowdry, despite it being a reasonably warm evening, was wearing a padded anorak with the hood up. She said, sheepishly: 'I didn't want them to recognise me.'

'Didn't want who to recognise you?' I asked, as I helped Mrs. Chowdry to her feet.

'Mister Maddan,' she said indignantly, 'that house guest of yours has a woman here and they are both running around your garden stark naked!' From down the garden we could hear screams of laughter and sounds of splashing water. 'There you are,' Mrs. Chowdry said. 'They are skinny dipping in the river. I think they are both drunk.'

I was surprised that Mrs. Chowdry was familiar with the expression 'skinny dipping'. 'Well, I'm sorry,' I said, 'but I've been out and only just got home. I don't really . . .'

'I know you were out,' Mrs. Chowdry interrupted. 'I've been knocking on your door. Your front doorbell wasn't working and I couldn't see any lights on. At first, I thought you might have had burglars. And then I saw those two running around the garden without any clothes on. It's disgusting. They should be ashamed of themselves.'

Merisi and his companion, whoever she was, had seen the light of my torch and were walking towards us. Merisi was stark naked and his companion was cowering behind him to cover her own nakedness. Merisi was completely unabashed. 'Hey, signora,' he shouted to Mrs. Chowdry. 'You come for a closer look?' He began to gyrate his hips, causing his not inconsiderable equipment to swing from side to side.

Mrs. Chowdry looked on with horror and disgust. 'Mr. Maddan,' she said, 'you must call the police!'

'I think they are already here,' I replied, as the face of Sergeant Caro, sheepish and blearily drunk, peeked out from behind Merisi. 'Mrs. Chowdry, please go home. I'll put a stop to this.'

Mrs. Chowdry hesitated but then Merisi, holding his todger and with a lascivious satyr grin, started to move towards her. 'Disgraceful,' Mrs. Chowdry said, and stalked away back to her own house.

I turned to Merisi and Sergeant Caro and said: 'For Christ's sake stop playing Adam and Eve and come in and put your clothes on. And then you can tell me what you've been doing. I'll go and make us some coffee . . . if I can.' I left them in the living room to get dressed and went to look in the kitchen pantry where the fuse box was located. I was relieved to see that whatever Merisi and Caro had been up to had merely tripped the master switch. I switched it back on and the lights came on. I made three mugs of coffee and carried them into the living room. To my relief, they were both dressed. Sergeant Caro was slumped on the sofa, giggling and incoherent. Merisi was standing up, swigging bourbon from straight out of the bottle. I put the mugs on the coffee table and then closed the patio door.

'Ah, it's good to be alive . . . again,' Merisi said, patting his stomach.

I snatched the bottle of bourbon away from him and whispered: 'For God's sake be careful what you say! She's still a police officer!' I glanced at Sergeant Caro but she was on the verge of falling asleep. 'What were you doing up in your bedroom with all those lights?'

'Izzy was modelling for me,' Merisi replied, enthusiastically. 'I was experimenting with lighting effects.'

'Lighting effects?' I said. 'Why?'

Merisi lowered himself into an armchair and pointed up at the chandelier-style ceiling light. 'You take all this for granted, don't you,' he said. 'To me, it is miraculous. To be able to have light, any kind of light, exactly when you want it. Izzy brought those lights for us to play with. I was experimenting with different coloured lights and with different angles of lighting. You know my work. This is what I am famous for. I am fascinated by light.'

Again I glanced at Sergeant Caro but she had toppled over and was now fast asleep. I said quietly: 'Izzy must not find out who you really are. You must be careful.'

'Don't worry, Stefano. I am adept at lying to beautiful women. Did you talk to my friend Del Monte?'

'Yes,' I said, 'but I'll tell you about that tomorrow.' I had already decided that I would not mention to Merisi that Vincenzo Giustiniani had been with us, and especially not that I had unexpectedly met Costanza Colonna. 'What happened to put all the lights out?'

'I don't know,' Merisi answered. 'Izzy was laying on the bed. I was moving the lamps around and then one of them burst open with a bang. I threw it aside in fright, smashed the window, and all the lights went out.' The fuse box master switch had done its job correctly. 'So Izzy and I went out to the summerhouse with a couple of bottles and switched on that gas lamp that you keep out there. We had a few drinks, made love, and then decided to go swimming in the river.'

There was a look of deep satisfaction on Merisi's face at an evening well spent.

We both looked over at Sergeant Caro, snoring lightly on the sofa. 'Looks like she'll be spending the night here,' I said. Merisi nodded indifferently. 'Don't ruin her life, Michele. Don't lead her on.'

Merisi stretched his legs out and said: 'My dear friend, tonight was all her idea.'

27

Throughout the night I was entertained by the sound of Isabella Caro throwing up in my bathroom. I resolved to reinforce my warning about Merisi in the morning but, by the time Merisi and I had woken up, Caro had gone. Merisi came into the kitchen while I was finishing my breakfast.

'Isabella has left,' I said.

Merisi shrugged, seemingly unconcerned about her.

'In case you didn't notice, Izzy was very ill during the night.'

'I'm not surprised,' Merisi replied. He opened the door of the refrigerator, thrust his face inside to enjoy the reviving cold air, and then took out a carton of fresh orange juice.

'Aren't you concerned about her?' I asked.

'Why should I be?'

'You've seduced her, used her to slake your lust, put her in compromising positions, endangered her career, made her drunk and foolish. Is there a word in Italian for "conscience"?'

'Yes, there is,' Merisi replied. 'It is spelt "y-a-w-n".'

'On that subject, how did you sleep?'

'As well as Hypnos,' Merisi said, with satisfaction.

I didn't know what he meant but I couldn't be bothered to ask. I made him some breakfast and then we settled down in the living room to work. I said: 'We've established that, after completing your two church commissions, you had become the most talked about and fashionable painter in Rome. You were about to complete a series of easel paintings that show you were at the height of your confidence and the height of your powers as an artist. Let's begin with the picture that brought us together, your first version of the Supper At Emmaus, which is now in the National Gallery in London. As you know, I admire this picture of yours as much as any other painting I've ever seen. We know that Ciriaco Mattei, who commissioned this painting, paid you for it in January 1602, so presumably you painted it during the previous year?'

'I certainly started it in 1601,' Merisi replied. 'Ciriaco paid me 150 scudi for it, which was a lot more than I had previously been getting for a picture. I was very popular and much in demand as a painter so I could, at last, name my own price, within reason.'

'Your biographer and enemy, Giovanni Baglione, was of the opinion that Ciriaco Mattei was being overcharged for your paintings. He thought that your friend and promoter Prospero Orsi was duping Mattei into paying too much, what we now call "ripping him off"?'

Merisi snorted contemptuously. 'That's just pure jealousy on Baglione's part. Nobody would give Baglione as much as a bucket of warm piss for one of his paintings. He couldn't stand the thought that I had won those two big church commissions and that I was now a far more marketable artist than he was.'

'He wasn't the only one who was envious of your sudden fame, was he?'

'They all were!' Merisi said, with relish. 'Even my so-called friends. They were only too happy to be seen in my company but, behind my back, they were all bitterly jealous about my success.'

'Well, that's what we are trying to find out, whether one of them might have been bitter enough to want to do away with you when the chance came. I would imagine that most of your rival artists would look at the skill with which the Supper At Emmaus is painted and feel deep pangs of envy. There is a strong sense in this picture that you are "showing off", in the best sense. You are saying to the world "here I am, this is what I can do".

'You are absolutely right,' Merisi agreed.

'The still life in the foreground is a meraviglia.' Merisi smiled at my use of the Italian word for 'miracle'. 'We know that you once commented to Vincenzo Giustiniani that there is as much craftsmanship in a good painting of fruit and flowers as there is in a good painting of the human figure. Would you still agree with that analysis?'

'Yes, in terms of the figure,' Merisi replied. 'The supreme test for the artist is the human face. To achieve not only a likeness, but to show the inner soul of the subject, is the greatest triumph any artist can achieve. I think I succeeded well in that respect.'

'One day, Michele, I will show you the work of a man who I have already mentioned and who was much influenced by your work. He was born in Holland about the same time as you fled from Rome. He is the greatest portraitist of the inner soul in the history of art. His name was Rembrandt.'

'Uumm,' Merisi said dubiously. 'I will be interested to see his work. I doubt that it can be as good as mine.'

I smiled at him and raised my eyebrows. 'Care for a wager, Michele?'

'I bet only on card games,' Merisi said. 'Painting is not a fit subject for common wagers.' He looked at the sardonic smile on my face and said: 'Fuck off . . . you and this Rembrandt.'

'Did Ciriaco Mattei suggest any of the elements contained in the Supper At Emmaus,' I asked. 'Anything within the picture which might give us a clue?'

'No,' Merisi answered. 'He gave me the subject but also gave me a completely free hand otherwise. It was a fine opportunity to construct such a forceful and dramatic composition. There can be no hidden messages in it. I am still very pleased with this work.'

'So you should be,' I said. 'Let's move on to the picture now known as the Taking of Christ, or variously known as the Arrest of Christ or the Betrayal of Christ. (*Plate 35*), We know that this was also commissioned by Ciriaco Mattei, It's another strikingly dramatic and forceful work.'

'Yes, I only received 125 scudi for that one. It was about a year later. I was already going out of fashion.'

'Well, that was your own fault, but we'll come on to that later,' I said. 'This is a more moving work that the Supper At Emmaus. The anguished look on Christ's face and his interwoven fingers are superbly rendered. You couldn't resist including yourself in the picture, on the extreme right, holding the lamp.'

'Yes,' Merisi confirmed. 'I was young and handsome then, don't you think?'

I ignored his preening. 'Who modelled for the other figures? Can you remember?'

'As with the Supper At Emmaus, I employed some of the servants from the Palazzo Mattei. The bearded soldier standing in front of me, who modelled for Saint James in the Supper picture, was an old retainer working in the service of the Mattei.'

'What about the man who models for Judas Iscariot, the one betraying Christ with a kiss. He seems to have modelled for many figures in your paintings. Who was he?'

'Does it matter?'

'Any detail might be important to our inquiry.'

'Let me think,' Merisi prevaricated. 'He was a waiter and potman at the Tavern of the Turk.'

'Why did you use him as a model so often?'

'I was fascinated by his squashed-up face. He was always willing to earn an extra few scudi by modelling for me.'

'What was his name?'

'I cannot remember.'

'Oh, come on, Michele. I know it was four hundred years ago but you must be able to remember his name if he posed for you that often.'

'His first name was Gianfranco,' Merisi replied irritably. 'I cannot remember what his last name was. Perhaps I never knew it. He never said much and I knew little about him.'

'Okay. So did Ciriaco Mattei give you the subject and leave the rest up to you?'

'Yes, he did. I don't think there can be any hidden clues in that picture.'

'The third picture that was commissioned about this time by Ciriaco Mattei, as a gift for Cardinal Benedetto Giustiniani, or so we believe, is the Doubting Thomas. (*Plate 36*). This is another extraordinarily powerful and moving work. The image of Saint Thomas pushing his finger into the wound on Christ's side fascinated artists for generations afterwards. It's simultaneously intense yet tender. This picture was copied and imitated more than any other of your works. It is such a simple and yet monumentally composed picture that I doubt it has anything to offer in the way of clues to your murder. Would you agree?'

'Yes, because once again I was given the subject and it was left entirely up to me how I did it. It was another chance for me to show life as it is, with all its pain and anguish, and not as some twee and complacent tableau as this subject had usually been portrayed.'

'They are an extraordinary trio of works,' I said. We then talked for a long time about several pictures completed by Merisi at about this time, all of them regrettably now lost. There had been pictures of St. Sebastian, St. Jerome, St. Augustine, Mary Magdalene and Christ on the Mount of Olives, which is known from old black and while photographs but which was destroyed during the Second World War. Merisi could not remember enough details about these paintings, or was not willing to tell me, and we could not find anything that might have led us towards the identity of Merisi's murderer.

'Let's have some lunch,' I suggested, 'and then I want to talk about two of the most compelling religious pictures ever painted, both by your own fair hand, Michele. Just one thing though . . .'

'What's that?'

'We are going to have something else to eat other than cheese on flaming toast!'

I microwaved a couple of spaghetti bolognese ready meals for lunch but Merisi grizzled so much about the lack of cheese on toast that I decided not to change the menu in future. I was forced to agree with Merisi that melted Emmenthal cheese, on top of the local baker's thick bread, and topped with slices of onion, was much superior to microwave ready meals, even if it did play hell with the breath. Eventually we settled back down to work.

'In 1602,' I began, 'you won the commission for the altarpiece in a new chapel within the Oratorian church of Santa Maria in Vallicella.'

'Yes, I remember it well,' Merisi said. 'Santa Maria was probably the most fashionable and popular church in Rome at the time. It was another opportunity to show the world what I could do with a paintbrush. The church was set right in the heart of the rich business centre of Rome and surrounded by the palazzi of the aristocracy. Other chapels within this church had altarpieces by Alberti, Muziano and, I think, Barocci. Also a crucifixion, one of the few paintings by that sentimental dauber Scipione Pulzano that was any good. So I had a lot of competition, a lot to live up to and be compared with. I knew I had to achieve one of my best works.'

'You didn't have such a free hand as you had done with the Ciriaco Mattei easel pictures, did you?'

'No. The church wanted an Entombment of Christ (*Plate 37*) and they insisted on preliminary drawings or plans. As you know, I did not usually bother with preliminary drawings but I explained my plans through a few rough sketches and my composition was approved. My reputation, at that point, was so high that they were keen to employ me whatever I planned to do, within reason. I had studied versions of this subject by Raphael and Michelangelo, and even one by my old master, Peterzano, which was one of his better efforts. In my version I kept within the classic tradition of Roman art but in a much more naturalistic and realistic way.'

I said: 'The whole composition is a tour-de-force. The three figures in the foreground are wonderfully realised. The tenderness of Saint John, even though he is sticking his fingers into Christ's wound, the workmanlike strength of Nicodemus as he bears the weight of Christ's legs and looks out at us to draw us into the scene. Christ's body inspires awe and pity as any death does. The figure of Mary Cleophas in the background, flinging out her arms, is a bit too theatrical for my taste. But the figures of Christ's mother, in the nun's habit, and the weeping Mary Magdalen, are very touching. Can you remember who modelled for those two figures?'

'Once again, I seem to remember that they were servants from the Palazzo Mattei. The Virgin Mary certainly was. I remember her kindly face, her motherly compassion. But I don't agree with your comment about the figure of Mary Cleophas. I depicted her with those flung out arms in order to balance the composition.'

'But they tend to draw the eye away from where the focus should be, on the figure of Christ,' I objected.

'You are wrong,' Merisi said, becoming annoyed.

'If you think I am wrong, I am in good company,' I said, 'because Peter Paul Rubens made what is virtually a copy of your Entombment and left out the figure of Mary Cleophas. The composition is all the better for it. Let me show you.' In a reference book of art, I had found a picture of the Rubens Entombment shown by the side of Merisi's Entombment for comparison. I passed it across to Merisi.

'No, no,' Merisi said. 'This man's composition makes it look as if the entire group of figures are toppling over to the left. In my version, the figure of Mary Cleophas pulls the whole group together and balances them all up. Can't you see that, you ignorant heretic?'

'No, I prefer the Rubens,' I said.

'But the way he has painted his figures is rubbish compared with mine. All the feeling, sympathy and intensity has gone!'

'That, Michele, I cannot argue with,' I said, and that admission calmed Merisi down. We spent a few more minutes examining the Entombment for possible clues but, as usual, it was a fruitless effort. 'Let's move on to another altarpiece which is now considered one of your best works but, at the time, ended in bitterness and despair for you.'

'You are talking about the altarpiece for Santa Maria della Scala in Trastavere,' Merisi sighed.

'Yes. We now know it as the Death of the Virgin.' (*Plate 38*).

'That's right. It was ordered for the new altar of that church by Laerzio Cherubini, who lived near the church of San Luigi dei Francesi and who had been most impressed by my Saint Matthew pictures for that church. Cherubini was a successful and very wealthy lawyer and businessman who owned a lot of property in Rome. He was also a devout and public spirited man who did a lot of charitable work in Rome.'

'We believe that Cherubini's friend Vincenzo Giustiniani was instrumental in landing you this commission?'

'That is correct,' Merisi confirmed. 'Vincenzo was appointed to be the judge of the picture, when I had completed it, and to decide on a fair price. I was paid an advance of fifty scudi.'

'Unlike the church for which the Entombment was painted, Santa Maria della Scala was in the poorest working class area of Rome, wasn't it?'

'Yes, it was. It had been founded with the special purpose of giving refuge to married women who had been abused, beaten or impoverished by their husbands.'

'Perhaps that's why your protectress Costanza Colonna was a patroness and took such a keen interest in the church. Her marriage had not been happy.'

'Her marriage had not been happy to begin with,' Merisi said, 'but that is because she had been very young and unsure of herself. But I suppose that early experience gave her sympathy for these unfortunate married women. And she was a close friend of the Giustiniani family, who protected the church, so it was natural for Costanza to be interested.'

'You produced a stark and tragic version of the death, or transition, of the Virgin Mary. It was too stark and realistic for the church because they rejected the painting.'

Merisi brooded for a few seconds. 'I intended to show the moment just after the Virgin Mary has died. Christ and His angels have already taken Mary's soul to heaven. Christ's Apostles, who were miraculously transported to Mary's deathbed, have just been admitted to the room to view the body. It was meant to be a tender and sympathetic meditation on her death. Unfortunately, I made one big mistake . . .'

'What was that?' I asked.

'I opened my big mouth and let it be known that Fillide Melandroni had been the model for the Virgin Mary, so it became common knowledge that I had used a prostitute, a notorious courtesan, as the model for the Virgin Mary. The church officials were outraged by that knowledge and by the finished picture. When I first showed them this painting, they metaphorically flayed me alive. They said the figures were poor and dirty and even the Virgin Mary herself was poor, dirty and humble. She looked pregnant, with her hand on her belly. They knew I had used a known prostitute as a model. They said it was an affront to the dignity of the church and to the Holy Mother herself. I had intended to engender tears of sympathy in the viewer. Instead I engendered tears of anger in my patrons. But what did they think Mary was? She was a humble woman herself, not some pristine aristocrat! They missed the point completely.'

'I agree,' I said, 'but it didn't do your reputation any good to have this altarpiece rejected.'

'Vincenzo Giustiniani liked it,' Merisi protested. 'He deemed it was worth 280 scudi. That was a considerable sum.'

'Doctor Mancini liked it,' I commented, 'although even he said it lacked decorum.'

'What would an atheist whoremonger like Mancini know about art? He was too busy servicing half the women in Rome.'

'Peter Paul Rubens liked it,' I persisted. 'He recommended the picture to his master, the Duke of Mantua, and it was later sold to our King Charles and then to the French King Louis XIV. So what the friars of the church of Santa Maria della Scala could not abide was welcomed by dukes and princes across Europe.'

'Well, that fact proves the point that what I attempted to show was correct,' Merisi said.

'One last thing I want to ask you about the Death of the Virgin,' I said.

'What is it?'

'It was very unusual to include Mary Magdalene in this subject. Why did you do that?'

'It was unusual in the tradition of painting this subject,' Merisi agreed, 'but don't forget that the church of Santa Maria della Scala was associated with fallen women or married women in distress. Mary Magdalene is a role model of repentance for female sinners and women who have fallen because of their inability to control their lust. It seemed appropriate to include Mary Magdalene as a warning.'

'Did the church officials ask you to include Mary Magdalene?'

'I can't remember,' Merisi said. 'Perhaps not. I think it was my idea.'

'Am I right in assuming that Anna Bianchini was again the model for Mary Magdalene? I can see the same distinctive slope of her neck and back as she leans forward, the same red hair in the same style.'

'Yes,' Merisi said. 'It was Anna. I thought you would be going back in time to interview Fillide and Anna. Aren't you curious about them?'

'Very much so,' I replied, 'but I have good reason to leave those two ladies until later in your story.'

'Why is that?' Merisi asked.

'All in good time, Michele, all in good time. Now, let's talk about your second version of St. John the Baptist, (*Plate 39*) or rather your first version as you have now corrected us. The setting is unusual, being a natural background, with leaves and plants, instead of a . . .'

We were interrupted by the ringing of my front door bell. 'Hold on,' I said to Merisi. 'I'll just see who's at the door.' I went out to the front door and opened it. Outside were standing Mrs. Chowdry, Sergeant Caro and P.C. Greenfield.

It was P.C. Greenfield who began the conversation. He said to me: 'We've received a complaint from your neighbour about an incident that occurred last night.' I glanced at Sergeant Caro, who was standing to the side and a little behind the Jolly Greenfield Giant. Her face was ghostly pale and she slowly shook her head, her eyes pleading with me not to give her away. 'We'd like to speak to Mr. Merisi,' Greenfield said.

I wondered whether to say that Merisi was not here but then decided that this problem was not going to go away, so I replied: 'Could you hold on a minute? I'll see where he is.' I went back to the living room and quickly and quietly pushed the living room door shut so that the accusers could not hear what I whispered to Merisi. 'Sergeant Caro and Greenfield and my neighbour are here to complain about your antics last night. For God's sake don't lose your temper or say anything you don't have to. Let me do the talking, understand?' Merisi nodded and I stepped out into the hallway and beckoned to the group waiting at the front door. 'Please come through to the living room. Mr. Merisi is in here.'

P.C. Greenfield, followed by Mrs. Chowdry, and then Sergeant Caro entered the living room. Caro shot another pleading glance at Merisi. He did not react, just watched the trio shuffling around uncomfortably as I cleared away all my books and notes about the life and work of Michelangelo Merisi da Caravaggio as unobtrusively as I could. 'Would you like to sit down,' I said, indicating the sofa where Sergeant Caro had spent most of the night when not otherwise engaged in the bathroom. 'Are you comfortable, sergeant?' I asked, unable to resist exploiting her patent embarrassment as she sat down at the end of the sofa with Mrs. Chowdry at the other end and the Jolly Greenfield Giant perched like a lighthouse in between them.

P.C. Greenfield had been instructed to do the talking and he broached his task with relish. Looking at Merisi, whom he disliked intensely, he said: 'Your behaviour has come to the notice of the police on several occasions since you arrived to stay with Mr. Maddan. As you are a guest of Mr. Maddan's, and perhaps unfamiliar with the laws and customs of our country, we have allowed you considerable leeway. Now we understand from Mrs. Chowdry that you indecently exposed yourself to her last night while cavorting around the garden, naked, in the company of a woman.'

Sergeant Caro visibly shrank back into my sofa. I said: 'Signor Merisi comes from a part of Italy where such behaviour is not considered unusual or immoral. I have explained to him that, in this country, such conduct is completely unacceptable. He wishes to express his profound apologies to Mrs. Chowdry.'

'I should think so too,' Mrs. Chowdry said. 'Ever since he arrived I don't know what is going to happen next. Drunkenness, shouting, swearing, cars crashing into our garden. And last night, when I noticed that Mr. Maddan's lights were out and I saw two people running around his garden and went, out of a sense of civic responsibility, to see what was happening, this hooligan subjected me to the most filthy display of lewd behaviour.' She pointed at Merisi when she spoke the word 'hooligan'.

Before I could intervene again, Merisi scowled and said: 'You must have seen hundreds of cocks in your time, woman. Mine is very like any other.'

'You see, you see what he is like!' Mrs. Chowdry exclaimed. 'The only cock I have ever seen is my husband's!' She suddenly realised what she had said and blushed bright red.

I said to Greenfield: 'I accept and agree with what Mrs. Chowdry said. She was doing her civic duty and was trying to help me and I am very sorry that all this misunderstanding has occurred. It won't happen again.' I looked pointedly at Sergeant Caro, who was now almost turning green.

'There was no misunderstanding,' Mrs. Chowdry said. 'This man Merisi knew exactly what he was doing. He deliberately exposed himself to me.'

'We were having a swim!' Merisi shouted, 'and you had to come round and poke your nose in. It's the most exciting thing that's happened to you for years, you dried up old bag.'

'Shut up, Michele,' I said. 'Your attitude is not helping matters.' I turned to Mrs. Chowdry. 'Mr. Merisi has to stay here for another few days and then he will be gone forever. I will do my best to see that he doesn't disturb you again.'

'That's not good enough,' Mrs. Chowdry said. 'This time he must be taught a lesson. I want him arrested and charged with indecent exposure. I will not tolerate any more of this abuse.'

'Fuck me,' Merisi said, 'you're worse than my old landlady, Prudenzia Bruna.'

'And what did you do to her?' Mrs. Chowdry asked, sarcastically.

'She threw me out just because I hadn't paid my rent for three months, so I threw stones at her window and called her an old cunt.' The rest of us froze in horror at Merisi's statement. 'What?' he exclaimed, baffled by our reaction. 'It's true. You British can't keep your women under control!'

'Who was the woman you were with last night?' Greenfield asked Merisi.

'Just some tart I picked up in Bedford,' Merisi said. Sergeant Caro had turned from green to scarlet. 'I don't know what her name is.'

'Isn't there any way we can sort this out amicably?' I said to Mrs. Chowdry. 'If Mr. Merisi is arrested it will only delay the work we are doing together and then he will have to come back here to finish it. You will only be prolonging the agony.'

'No,' Mrs. Chowdry said, adamantly. 'This time, I want action. I demand that Mr. Merisi is charged. He has gotten away with this behaviour for too long.'

'I tend to agree,' P.C. Greenfield said. He looked at Sergeant Caro, as his superior officer, for confirmation and guidance. Sergeant Caro said to him: 'Could I talk to you outside?'

The two police officers stood up. Mrs. Chowdry said: 'You're not going to leave me here with this man, are you?'

'We'll be back in a few minutes,' Caro said, 'and Mr. Maddan is here to protect you.'

Judging by the look on her face, Mrs. Chowdry was clearly not impressed with the level of protection that I could offer and the three of us sat in silence, Mrs. Chowdry glaring at Merisi, until the officers returned. Sergeant Caro said: 'Mrs. Chowdry, Mr. Merisi here will be issued with an official caution about his behaviour but we don't think it will be helpful to arrest him. If it came to a court of law, it would be his word against yours.'

'But Mr. Maddan was there!' Mrs. Chowdry exclaimed. 'He saw what happened!'

I looked at Sergeant Caro, and then at Mrs. Chowdry. 'I didn't see a thing,' I said, slowly. 'It was very dark and I was sprawled on the floor.'

Mrs. Chowdry gasped. 'So, you wash your hands like Pontius Pilate! I thought you were a decent and honourable man, Mr. Maddan.' To Sergeant Caro she said: 'In that case you must find the cheap drunken little trollope who was cavorting about with Mr. Merisi.'

Sergeant Caro winced. 'I doubt very much whether she would incriminate herself, or anybody else.'

'Well, you could at least make an effort to find her. You could ask these two to give you a description of her.'

Merisi said: 'She had a lovely arse.'

Mrs. Chowdry spluttered and began to speak but Caro, again bright red, was ushering her out of the room. 'I'll take you back home, Mrs. Chowdry. There is no point you staying here.'

P.C. Greenfield waited until he heard the front door close. He looked at Merisi, his near seven feet frame towering over Merisi's armchair. 'So, you've got away with it again, you nasty dago bastard.' Merisi, angered, tried to get up but Greenfield pushed him back with a huge mitt. 'Don't try it with me, sunshine. I learned a few tricks in the England front row. There's nothing I'd like more than to rip your fucking head off. You stay away from Sergeant Caro in future. If I find out you've been seeing her again, you're going to have a nasty accident.' He turned to me. 'You keep this cunt in line, or the same goes for you.' Greenfield walked out of the living room. I didn't get up to see him out.

Merisi and I looked at each other. 'Well,' I said, 'you obviously have a rival for the affections of Sergeant Caro. Are you going to take his advice?'

'I have never seen a man that big before,' Merisi replied. 'They used to say I have a crazy brain but even I am not crazy enough to take on a man like that. He is welcome to little Izzy. I just feel sorry for her if he ever climbs on top of her.'

I retrieved my reference books to begin work again. 'Michele,' I said. 'As we have just seen, your genius as a painter is surpassed only by your genius for making enemies. You had become the most admired and talked about painter in Rome. Many artists, your enemies as well as your friends, were drawn to your new style of painting ... your realism, your naturalism, your use of chiaroscuro. And yet, as we have mentioned several times, your reaction to success was not magnanimous but belligerent. We have notes from your contemporaries that your arrogance and belligerence became the talk of Europe, not just of Rome or Italy. You became increasingly involved in street violence. A Dutchman named Van Mander mentions that you, quote "worked for two weeks and then sallied forth for two months together with a rapier at his side, going from one tennis court to another, always ready to argue or fight, so that he is impossible to get along with". You made bitter enemies of the older and more traditional artists with your arrogant and boastful remarks about their work. You attracted partisan and argumentative supporters but, if they came close to matching your achievements, you became resentful and envious of their success. Other painters came to fear you. You seemed to go out of your way to upset everybody.'

'What is your point?' Merisi asked, irritated by this recital.

'My point is why? And how are we ever going to find out who attempted to murder you when half the painters in Rome would have gladly stuck a knife in your back?'

'That is your job to find out,' Merisi shrugged.

'This Van Mander also left us an interesting comment about your attitude to your work. He said that you thought little of the works of other masters but, equally, you would not praise your own. He said that you believed that all art is nothing but a bagatelle or children's work, unless it is done after life, and that an artist could not do better than to follow nature. Would you agree with that?'

'Yes,' Merisi said. 'That is basically how I felt. I sometimes used to think that being a painter was no job for a man. I would have been happier as a soldier and a swordsman.'

'You not only attacked some fellow artists verbally but you attacked them physically. Soon after your paintings had been installed in the Contarelli chapel, you and Onorio Longhi attacked a painter named Marco Tullio.'

'They started it,' Merisi protested, like a recalcitrant schoolboy. 'He and Canonici started hurling insults at us.'

'This is Flavio Canonici, who was a guard at Castel Sant' Angelo?'

'Yes,' Merisi confirmed. 'Tullio was a friend of that old bastard Zuccaro. He had been with Zuccaro when they came to look at my Contarelli chapel works. Zuccaro had made some comment that he saw nothing in my work except an imitation of Giorgione! I had been incensed when I learned of this remark. It was deliberate provocation. So when Tullio and Canonici started hurling abuse at us in the street, what was I to do?'

'Your friend Longhi told the magistrate that you yourself were too weak from illness to take part in this brawl.'

Merisi chuckled. 'Onorio was lying to keep me out of trouble. He was a loyal friend. We weren't going to take insults from the likes of Tullio and Canonici so we knocked their heads together. Then the sbirri turned up and separated us before we could really teach them a lesson.'

'But you got your own back on Canonici a few months later, didn't you?'

'Yes,' Merisi said. 'We hated each other. We went at each other with drawn swords. I wounded him in the hand and was arrested again. I was forced to make a judicial peace with him to get myself out of trouble.'

'Well, Tullio and Canonici must be added to the ever-growing list of suspects,' I said. 'As, I suspect, should the name of Girolamo Spampa.'

'Who?' Merisi asked.

'Spampa made a complaint to a notary that you had attacked him outside a candlemaker's shop one evening. He said that you had crept up behind him and started to rain blows on his back with a cudgel. Attacking from behind, Michele. That was brave of you!'

'Ah, yes, I remember now,' Merisi said. 'That little fucker was merely a pupil at the Accademia di San Luca and yet he had dared to criticise my work. He was asking for for a beating.'

'And you would have given him a beating if a group of butchers hadn't come to see what all the commotion was about and scared you off.'

'They didn't scare me off. I drew my sword. Spampa tried to protect himself with a thick cloak so I cut it to pieces for him and then decided to make a judicious withdrawal.' Merisi smiled.

'The question I want you to answer, the same question that every historian who has ever studied your life wants answered, is why did you behave like that? A young student criticises your work. He was a nobody. So what? An older and more revered artist is not impressed with your work. So what? They had never created anything as brilliant as you had. Why risk everything you had gained with such violent behaviour?'

'It was a point of honour,' Merisi replied. 'In those days, one could not let such insults go unanswered without losing respect.'

'Many artists did,' I argued.

'If they wanted to act like pussy cats, that was up to them. No-one was going to disrespect Michelangelo Merisi in such a way!'

I consulted my reference books, to check my dates, and said: 'Forgive me if I dredge up unpleasant memories, Michele, but we are up to the year 1603. It is just a couple of short years since your resounding successes with the Contarelli chapel and Cerasi chapel commissions made you the most fashionable painter in Rome and yet, according to what we know, there is already a real sense that your star is on the wane. All this legal trouble, the fighting and feuding, seems to have caused the major new commissions to be withheld from you. Was that how it happened?'

Merisi was lost in thought for several seconds and then replied: 'Unpleasant memories indeed. These were strange and troublesome times, not only for me but for Rome itself. It was, as you say, 1603 and Camillo Borghese, who became Pope Paul and who you met on your time travels, was appointed Cardinal

Vicario. He was quick to reinforce the intimidating rules that Cardinal Rusticucci had set down for the production of religious art. So-called "indecent" altarpieces were proscribed. If you failed to obtain a licence for your work you could be fined or even imprisoned. Artists were ordered to submit preliminary drawings before starting work. As you can imagine, such strictures did not suit me at all. Patrons became afraid of me, afraid of my reputation for violent behaviour as well as my reputation for a shockingly new kind of painting. The commissions did, indeed, begin to dry up.'

'Your brushes with the law also seemed to become more frequent. We know of the incident when you threw a plate of hot artichokes into the face of a waiter named Carnacia at the Tavern of the Blackamoor. What was that all about?'

Merisi chuckled. 'I'm amazed that is still known. I vaguely remember this incident. That damn jackanapes Carnacia had handed me a plate of artichokes and I had simply asked him which ones were cooked in oil and which ones in butter. Do you know what that cheeky bastard said? He said: "Smell them and you will easily know"! Well, I wasn't about to take such insolence from a mere waiter, so I threw the artichokes back into his cocky face.'

'According to witnesses,' I said, 'you snatched a sword from one of your companions and made to strike Carnacia, and you shouted something like: "You damned cuckold, you think you are serving some damned bum".'

'That is not true,' Merisi protested. 'The words are true. I said something like that, but I did not threaten Carnacia with a sword. Anyway, it started a fight and I ended up being sued by Carnacia and a lot of the other patrons in the tavern. Didn't do them any good. Cardinal Del Monte made sure the charges were dropped. At least, I think it was Del Monte.'

'A few months later you and your friend Onorio Longhi, and some other friends, were imprisoned in the Tor di Nona for throwing stones at the police. And a month later, you were imprisoned again for using coarse language.'

'I had been carrying my sword and some pompous fucking corporal had asked me if I had a licence to carry a sword. I gave him my licence and I also gave him a mouthful of abuse. The fucker arrested me.' I looked at Merisi and, for once, he seemed abashed. 'It's a melancholy recital, isn't it,' he said.

I nodded. 'Very well. Tomorrow I want to talk about an artist whom you badly disrespected and who must be one of the prime suspects in the search for your attempted murderer.'

'Who is that?'

'Your biographer and bitter enemy, Giovanni Baglione.'

'God, do we have to talk about that bastard?'

'Of course we do,' I said.

'Are you going back to interview him?'

'Eventually,' I replied, 'but first, to fortify our resolve, we will take a trip into the great metropolis of Bedford and I will introduce you to the finest aspect of Italian genius, apart from the genius of you artists that is.'

'And what aspect is that?' Merisi asked.

'Food and drink,' I replied. 'I'm tired of cheese on toast and microwave meals. We deserve a treat. I will make an appointment at the best Italian restaurant in Bedford and, thanks to the large Italian population in Bedford, one of the best Italian restaurants outside of Italy. It's named after one of your illustrious predecessors. It is the Ristorante Raphael.'

'I hope the food is more satisfying than his painting was,' Merisi said.

28

That evening I found an empty parking space for the Vauxhall Astra just across the road from the Ristorante Raphael in Bedford. Miracles do happen sometimes. 'There it is,' I told Merisi. We looked at the inviting restaurant. The exterior was gaily decorated with hanging baskets of flowers. The three large windows, steamed up from the heat inside, bore gold leaf letters, formed in an arch, which announced that it was, indeed, the Ristorante Raphael. The diners inside were visible from where we sat and the restaurant was doing a brisk trade.

'It looks very nice,' Merisi said.

'It is very nice, Michele,' I agreed. 'Now, I don't want to sound like a father talking to a naughty child but I want you to promise me that you'll be on your best behaviour tonight.'

'What do you mean?' Merisi asked, with a touch of annoyance.

'You have a history of throwing dishes back in waiter's faces or starting fights in the taverns of Rome. Times have changed, Michele, as well as the country. If you dislike something, we can complain about it in a discreet and diplomatic way. Do you agree?'

'Yes, I understand,' Merisi said.

'And don't forget that you should not even be in this century, let alone here in Bedford. This restaurant is run by Italians and many of the patrons are Italian. If you get into a conversation with anyone, just be careful what you say. You can mention that you are an artist, visiting this country and staying with your friend Stefano Maddano, but don't start talking about how you hated Guido Reni or how you painted a portrait of the pope. They'll think you are a raving lunatic.'

'As you once did?' Merisi shot back.

'Yes, and it took a lot to persuade me otherwise. I'm still not sure I've not turned into a raving lunatic, let alone you. I'm not going to drink alcohol and I'll be keeping an eye and an ear on you. Do you understand?'

'Yes, daddy. How do I get this belt thing off me?'

I unlocked my safety belt and then pressed the button to unlock Merisi's seat belt. As I did so, I noticed a metallic glint from under his jacket. I had let him borrow one of my old suits, a smart dark blue pinstripe number and, together with a pale blue shirt and a tie, he looked very presentable. 'What have you got under your jacket?' I asked him.

'What do you mean?'

'I saw something metallic glinting under your jacket.'

'It's just the buckle on my belt. Come on, let's go and eat. I'm hungry.'

Merisi made to open the car door but I stopped him. 'You're not wearing a belt,' I said. 'Open your jacket and show me what you've got under there.'

Merisi sighed and opened his jacket. On his right hand side, sticking out of the top of his trouser band, was the ornate silver hilt of a dagger.

'Are you fucking crazy?' I shouted at him. 'I've just asked you to be on your best behaviour and you come out wearing a dagger? I've told you, this is Bedford in the 21st century, not Rome or Naples in the 17th century. Why are you wearing a dagger?'

'I don't feel dressed without it,' Merisi replied.

'Take it out,' I ordered. 'Let me see it.'

Merisi whipped out the dagger with a surprising speed which made me lean back in alarm. He held up the dagger. The thin stiletto blade was well over a foot long. I said: 'How on earth do you wear that without it showing?'

'A special sheath. It fits snugly down the leg, tied in place just above the knee. Nobody can see it. Nobody knows it's there. And when I need to use it quickly, out it comes.'

'What do you think might happen to us tonight?' I said. 'All we have to do is cross that road, eat a meal in a convivial atmpshere, come back across the road, and drive home. We are hardly likely to be attacked by a band of marauding banditti, are we?'

'You never know,' Merisi insisted. 'Bitter experience taught me to be ready for the unexpected at all times.'

'Look, Michele, I promise you such a weapon will not be needed tonight and, what is more, it is illegal to carry such a weapon. If your friend Sergeant Caro catches you wearing such a lethal object, she will have to arrest you. Give it to me.' Merisi reluctantly handed me the dagger. 'It's a beautifully made weapon,' I had to admit. 'Spanish?'

'Spanish, my arse,' Merisi said, contemptuously. 'Milanese, where the best swords and daggers in the world are made.'

'Used to be made,' I corrected him, and threw the dagger on to the back seat. 'Come on. Let's go and eat.'

Merisi looked longingly at the dagger but made no further protest. We climbed out, I locked the doors, and we crossed the road and went into the Ristorante Raphael. I have to admit that, after our rocky start to the evening,

Merisi was on his best form. He was delighted to be surrounded by genuine speakers of Italian as opposed to someone like me wearing a ChronoTranslator and talking in stilted Italian. The food was superb. I also wanted to introduce Merisi to some of the good modern Italian wines and show him how palatable they were compared to the sour wine that he and I had been drinking in 17th century Rome. I ordered a bottle of Montepulciano d'Abruzzo. I abandoned my intention of drinking no alcohol whatsoever. I decided that I could afford to drink one glass but the Montepulciano was so good that I stretched the limit to two. Then we went on to a top-class Chianti. I estimated that just one more glass, on top of a big meal, would not put me over the drink-driving limit. I could not resist just one more glass after that. We finished off with a bottle of Barolo. At first, I refused another glass, but Merisi did not have much trouble in persuading me to try just one glass of the Barolo. It was dark and plummy and full of tannin. Heavenly! I simply had to have just one more glass. After we had finished our meal and I had handed over my credit card to pay the bill, the proprietor brought us over a small glass of Strega on the house. Merisi was delighted to find out that the proprietor of the restaurant was a native of Milan and knew the small town of Caravaggio very well. Merisi, quite truthfully, told the proprietor that he had not visited his home town for many years since moving to Rome and the proprietor was happy to describe what it was like now, as well as what the city of Milan was like. The two men were still talking after the other patrons had left and the restaurant had closed for business. A bottle of Amaretto was opened and, before I knew what I was doing, I had consumed another couple of glasses. Finally, with hugs all around and promises of eternal friendship, we staggered out of the Ristorante Raphael at about one-thirty in the morning. The town of Bedford was very dark and quiet. We got into the car and I put the key into the ignition, and then took it out again. 'I can't drive,' I told Merisi.

'What do you mean, you can't drive?'

'I'm too pissed,' I said.

'What do we do then? Walk home?'

'Hold on, lemme think. Lemme think.'

'Let me drive,' Merisi offered, hopefully.

'You've got to be joking,' I replied. 'I don't want to end up in Ma Chowdry's fish pond.'

'You're in the car with me this time. You can show me what to do.'

'Bollocks,' I said. 'Lemme think. Can't drive, too far to walk, no buses. Taxi! I'll ring for a taxi.' I fumbled in my pockets for my mobile phone. 'Fuck. Left it at home.'

'You said you weren't going to drink alcohol,' Merisi accused me.

'Yeah, I know. Forgot, didn't I. Didn't mean to get this pissed. We'll have to walk to the station.'

'What station?'

'Railway station.'

'What's that?'

'You know, fucking railway. What do you Eyeties call them? I dunno. Pendolino.' Merisi looked at me helplessly. 'Oh, fuck me, you don't know what a railway is, do you? Sorry, my friend.' I took a deep breath. 'At the railway station are taxis. You know, motor cars like this one, of which we can hire to take us home.'

'Ah, I see,' Merisi said. 'How far is this railway station?'

'Not far. Maybe a mile or so. Come on.' I opened the car door and got out. I breathed deeply in the cool night air, trying to clear my head. 'Are you coming?' I called to Merisi, who was still in the car.

'I'm stuffed with food,' he said. 'Do we really have to walk a mile, however far that is.'

'No choice, my old friend. My fault, I admit. Shouldn't have let myself get so pissed. Come on, get out of the car.'

Merisi reluctantly climbed out. I said: 'This way.'

We headed off through the deserted streets of Bedford. First, we had to walk back through the town centre. I was hoping there might be a taxi for hire in the town centre but we couldn't find one. I could not use a phone box as I didn't have any change or a phone card. Merisi was following me, swearing softly in Italian. 'Not far now,' I said encouragingly. I turned down a street that I knew led to the general vicinity of the railway station. It was a narrow street with a high brick wall on one side and a deserted and derelict engineering works on the other.

Merisi put a hand on my shoulder to stop me. 'I don't like this,' he said.

'Wassa matter,' I said. 'What doncha like?'

'This narrow street. We could get bottled up down there. It's a perfect place to set a trap for us.'

'What the fuck are you talking about?' I said, swaying slightly. 'Who's going to set a trap for us ... the Wehrmacht, Murder Incorporated, an Apache raiding party, Genghis Khan with his Golden Horde sweeping in from the steppes of Asia ...'

'I don't know what you're talking about. But I don't like it.'

'Oh, come on, you great Italian wuss. I told you, this is Bedford, not fucking Naples.' I started walking briskly down the dimly-lit street. Merisi had no choice but to follow me. 'There you are,' I said to him, as we neared the end of the street. 'Nothing to worry about. Bedford is a civilised town.' At that precise moment we heard running footsteps behind us. We turned round to see two figures running at us. I just had time to shout: 'Muggers!' before one of the attackers barged right into me and knocked me flying into the brick wall. My head struck the wall first and I collapsed on to the pavement. I was dazed but still conscious and I could feel blood beginning to trickle down my face. Three more muggers appeared out of the shadows of the old factory across the road and ran towards us. I tried to get up but a mugger kicked me in the leg and I collapsed again. Merisi stood in front of me to protect me from further blows just as the muggers, all carrying knives, surrounded us. One of them shouted: 'Give us your money and mobile phones, quick. We've all got knives and we'll slit your fucking throats if you don't.'

Merisi, as calm as if he was at a church service, said: 'You call those knives? This is a knife.' In a blindingly fast movement he unsheathed the stiletto dagger from inside his jacket and, before the muggers were even aware of what was happening, had slashed the gang leader's parka wide open. All the muggers were momentarily transfixed by Merisi's glinting steel dagger as if they were cobras being charmed. Then one of them screamed: 'Fuck this!' and started running in the direction of the railway station. The rest of the gang also decided this was the wisest option and began to run after their colleague as fast as they could. Merisi set off in pursuit shouting: 'You want trouble, you cowardly fucking turds. I'll give you fucking trouble.' He did not pursue them for more than a few yards before he turned back to me. I was still flailing around trying to lift myself off the pavement. There was a huge grin across Merisi's face. He looked down at me and began laughing heartily. 'God, that was good fun!' Merisi said. 'Haven't enjoyed myself that much since about 1603.' He held up his stiletto dagger. 'It's a good job I didn't take your advice, you stupid Englishman. If I hadn't retrieved this from the back seat we'd both be lying down there with our throats cut. Let me look at your head.' Merisi knelt down and tried to assess the damage in what little light there was. 'You've got a lovely big bump just over your eye and a cut on your forehead, but it's not bad. You'll live.' He put his hands under my arms and lifted me up. I felt dizzy for a moment but it soon passed off.

'Okay, Crocodile Dundee,' I said. 'You were right and I was wrong.'

Merisi put his arm around my waist to support me and we staggered off towards Bedford railway station.

29

'How is your head this morning?' Merisi asked, as he entered the living room.

'The swelling has gone down,' I replied, 'but I still feel a little groggy.'

'It will take a day or two to get over a blow like that. I should know, I suffered enough of them back in Rome. I will get myself something to eat and make you a cup of coffee.'

Merisi was becoming domesticated, I thought, as he disappeared out to the kitchen. I was touched by his concern for me. When Merisi came back, carrying two mugs of coffee, I said: 'I can't remember whether I thanked you for saving my skin last night.'

'There is no need to thank me. We are friends, and friends watch out for each other.'

'You were right and I was wrong about taking protection with us,' I conceded.

Merisi settled into his armchair and said: 'For all the marvels in this modern world of yours, human nature does not change. There always were, and always will be, dangerous animals walking the streets disguised as human beings. I should know, I was once one of them. In your world, you have become used to being shielded from them but monsters will always be lurking in the terrible shadows.'

I nodded at Merisi's apt remark. 'On the subject of monsters,' I said, 'let's talk about one of our prime suspects, your biographer and enemy Giovanni Baglione and his henchman Tommaso Salini.'

'I would sooner talk about Beezlebub and Satan than that pair.'

'The strange thing about Baglione,' I said, 'was that he hated you and yet he copied your new style of painting.'

'Baglione had very little original imagination. He used to copy the style of the Cavaliere d'Arpino until I showed everybody how to paint properly and then Baglione began to imitate my style.'

'Such imitation usually infuriated you, didn't it?' I asked.

'Very much,' Merisi agreed. 'I had come up with a much better way of painting, a much clearer way of seeing things, which was a vivid, dramatic and realistic presentation of scenes from actual life. And then I found, when it became successful, that everyone was copying my new style and taking work and kudos that were rightfully mine. Of course it made me angry!'

'Tell me about Tommaso Salini. He was nicknamed Mao, wasn't he?'

'Yes. A most unattractive character,' Merisi replied. 'Why are you smiling?'

'It's just that, in recent years, we have had another unattractive character named Mao in our world and, believe me, he did much more harm than Tommaso Salini ever did.'

'Well, Salini was a despicable character. He was a poor painter himself and most of the other painters despised him for his sarcastic manner. Even Baglione spoke about Mao's sharp tongue and Mao followed Baglione around like a dog, agreeing with every pearl of wisdom that dropped from Baglione's lips. Mao was afraid of me, as a man and as a painter. Did you know that one of my flower paintings in Del Monte's collection somehow became attributed to Mao and that little turd did nothing to deny it, just went around letting everybody think what a fine painter he was! Just to prove that it was me who painted the flowers, I painted some more, even more skilfully and beautifully, and that stopped his arrogant bragging.'

'It may be one of those pictures that survives today,' I said, 'in the Ambrosiana Gallery in Milan. It's a beautiful work and is now considered to be one of the earliest and best examples of Italian still life.'

'You would expect nothing less of me,' Merisi answered, pompously.

'Anyway,' I said, 'it was one of Baglione's works that precipitated this libel trial that you were involved in. The picture survives today and we know it as Divine Love Overcoming the World, the Flesh and the Devil.' (*Plate 40*).

'Yes, that was the one,' Merisi said, bitterly. 'Not only was Baglione copying my style but he was attempting to better my own Victorious Love with this miserable travesty of a work. He was also taking on my friend Orazio Gentileschi who was exhibiting his picture of St. Michael the Archangel. Baglione actually hung his Divine Love opposite Orazio's St. Michael at the same exhibition. We were both incensed by Baglione's arrogance. He dedicated the picture to Cardinal Benedetto Giustiniani and the cardinal awarded Baglione the compliment of a gold chain. Gentileschi and I were beside ourselves with rage.'

'What was the significance of being given a gold chain?' I asked, knowing full well the answer.

'It was the ultimate compliment from a patron to an artist for an outstanding work of exceptional merit. It conferred status on the recipient. It even suggested noble or exalted rank. Every painter was ambitious to be awarded the gold chain. I had never been given one. I, whose work was the talk of Rome, of all Europe, who could paint a better picture with my cock that Baglione could with brushes, had to watch while that plagiarising cunt swaggered around Rome with that gold chain around his neck!' I was secretly amused by Merisi's four hundred-year-old seething resentment. After a few seconds, he calmed down again. 'Fortunately, Baglione's painting pleased very few other artists, except that little creep Mao. Gentileschi quite rightly told Baglione that the picture had many imperfections, not least that the figure of Divine Love should not have been of an older man wearing armour but of a young man completely nude. So Baglione did a second version of his picture, and do you know what the cheeky cunt included in this second version?'

'No,' I lied, again knowing full well what the answer was.

'He included a portrait of me, as the devil!' Merisi was almost spluttering with indignation.

'That is shocking,' I agreed, trying to keep a straight face.

'As far as I was concerned, Baglione had thrown down the gauntlet and I was more than ready to pick it up. My friends and I mocked Baglione's Divine Love mercilessly at every opportunity. Baglione had been driven mad with jealousy by my success and was attempting to claim the crown as the best painter in Rome. To make matters worse, Baglione had also just completed a Resurrection for the Gesù church, which was one of the foremost churches in Rome. It had been a commission that all the top painters had been eager to win. Just why the Jesuit General awarded the commission to a hack like Baglione is anyone's guess. To my intense joy, when Baglione unveiled his Resurrection, it was greeted with scorn by most of the painters who saw it. You will not be surprised to hear that I was the most virulent critic of them all. Baglione and I had come to hate each other with venom.'

'Shortly after the unveiling of Baglione's Resurrection,' I said, 'a scurrilous verse began circulating in Rome. This poem attacked Baglione and Mao in the most filthy and obscene language.'

Merisi looked at me shrewdly. 'Really,' he said. 'I never read it.'

'Never read it! You probably wrote it!'

'I have already stood trial for that,' Merisi smiled.

'Then allow me to read it to you,' I said.

'These poems have survived?' Merisi asked, genuinely surprised.

'Indeed they have, so don't play the innocent with me, Michele.'

'Then I would be delighted to hear them again.'

I recited: ' "Giovan Bagaglia, you are a know-nothing; Your pictures are mere daubs. I'll warrant that you will not earn so much as a brass farthing from them, not even enough cloth to make yourself a pair of breeches, so you'll have to go round with your arse in the air, so take your drawings and cartoons round to Andrea Pizzicarolo." Who was Andrea Pizzicarolo?'

'He was a grocer,' Merisi replied. 'Carry on reading this most entertaining work, Stefano.'

' "... or maybe wipe your bum with them, or stuff them up Mao's wife's cunt, so that he can't fuck her anymore with his great mule's prick. I'm sorry I can't join in all of this mindless praise, but you are quite unworthy of the chain you're wearing, and a disgrace to painting because, having seen the fathers, you now appear to practise with the sons." ' I looked at Merisi for his comments but he simply grinned at me. 'It's hardly up to the standard set by your great compatriot Dante is it?' I said.

'Dante did not have to put up with Baglione and Salini.'

'The second poem is not so filthy but is even more critical of Baglione as a painter while singing your praises to a nauseating extent. Do you want me to read the second poem?'

'No,' Merisi chuckled joyously. 'I remember it very well. Longhi and I had a lot of fun composing those verses.'

'Well, Baglione and Mao were so incensed by your insults that they sued you for libel.'

'Together with Longhi, Gentileschi and Trisegni, who had stupidly given Mao copies of the poems.'

'But you were the ringleader, weren't you?'

Merisi smiled. 'Perhaps,' he said.

'You, and the other defendants, were arrested and imprisoned in September 1603,' I said. 'We still have the transcripts of the trial. It seems to have been a muddled and confusing affair. The advocates acting for Baglione and Salini tried to prove that you and your friends wrote these scurrilous poems. You and the other defendants were intent on prevaricating, on muddying the waters, to prevent the truth from emerging. In fact, you metaphorically stabbed each other in the back to avoid being convicted.'

'Our tactics worked,' Merisi claimed. 'Trisegni pretended loss of memory and said that he could not remember from whom he had obtained copies of these poems. Gentileschi almost panicked, nearly giving the game away. Longhi was away from Rome so he avoided involvement.'

'Your testimony,' I said, 'was a masterpiece of prevarication, mind-changing, bet-hedging, nauseating sycophancy and downright arrogance.'

'You have summed it up very well, Stefano. I was pleased with my performance. In the end, nobody could prove what I had done or what I was thinking.'

We discussed the libel trial in detail, as much as Merisi could remember about it, and I made copious notes that I knew would be of immense value and interest to future art historians. All I had to do was make up some convincing cock-and-bull story as to how I came to discover such details! I said: 'It seems that, after a few days, the trial petered out through lack of definite evidence and you were released from prison.'

'That's right,' Merisi confirmed. 'I was, however, confined to my home on pain of being sent to the galleys.'

'Is it true that the French ambassador, Philip de Béthune, stood bail for you?'

'Yes.'

'Why him?' I asked.

'Why not him?'

'What I mean is, you had many other powerful and rich patrons and protectors. The Colonna family, for instance. Or Cardinal Del Monte. Why did the French ambassador step in.'

'Monsieur de Béthune had bought some of my works. He liked what I did. It is possible that such friends as the Colonna family or Del Monte did not wish to sully their reputations by getting involved in a sordid trial. But the French ambassador, being an outsider, had no such qualms. I suspect that Del Monte put him up to standing bail.'

I nodded. 'Your friend Onorio Longhi came back to Rome and proceeded to make matters worse, didn't he?'

Merisi smiled. 'When Longhi heard what had been going on, there was no containing his fierce temper. He followed Baglione and Salini to church one day, hurling insults at them on the way and then pulling faces at them as they attended Mass. As they left the church, Longhi threw a brick at Baglione and knocked him over! Baglione was armed with a dagger, so Longhi withdrew, armed himself with a sword, and waited for them. He chased Baglione and Salini with his sword and got himself arrested and imprisoned for his pains. What a madman!'

'You, meanwhile, were away from Rome, weren't you?'

'Yes. Cardinal Del Monte ordered me to go to the town of Tolentino, in the Marches, to do an altarpiece for a Capuchin church. He said that getting me out of the way would give time for the situation in Rome to cool off and calm down. So I duly obliged and created an altarpiece of the Blessed Isidoro Agricola. Whether it was because my blood was so hot, or for whatever reason, it is one of my best works.'

'I'm afraid it was one of your best works, Michele. Unfortunately, it has now been lost, but we know it was still in place during the eighteenth century because a guidebook described your work, passionately, as a most singular masterpiece.'

'A description I am unable to disagree with, Stefano.'

30

The ChronoConverter landed me in a dark and confined space. For a moment I was terrified that I had materialised in a place from which I could not escape. I was crouching and when I lifted my head it banged into something hard. I looked up and could see that I was in a space underneath a staircase. I cautiously looked out and saw that I was in the lobby of what looked to be an elegant and palatial building. On the right was a stained glass window but it depicted secular motifs based on the arts and sciences rather than religious motifs. Across the lobby was a pair of elaborately decorated wooden double doors topped with an exquisitely carved pediment depicting fruit and flowers. I could hear voices emanating from the room beyond the double doors. I stepped out from beneath the staircase and walked around to the double doors. The door to the street beyond was slightly ajar, affording me a glimpse of the passers-by outside. I guessed that the man I was seeking was working beyond the double doors so I pushed one open and looked inside. In front of me was an elegant salon. It was very long but narrow and high windows admitted plenty of light. The walls were hung with many framed canvases. It looked like there was some sort of art exhibition being set up and there were several artists busily preparing to hang their work. A man seated at a table just inside the door, who was writing in a ledger, looked up at me. He was dressed very simply in black, but the clothes were of good quality. He was tall and thin, clean shaven and with a large dome of a bald head. He exuded a quiet and scholarly air. I was dressed in my most impressive finery, a red velvet cap adorned with an ostrich feather, a red and gold silk doublet and pantaloons, fine red boots made out of the leather from a kid, a small dagger in my belt and a huge fake red ruby hung from an elegant and fake gold chain around my neck. The man at the table rose to his feet, always a welcome sign of deference, and said, in a very soft voice: 'Good day, sir. Welcome to the Accademia di San Luca. May I help you?'

'I have come to see the artist Giovanni Baglione. Someone told me that he would be here hanging his work today. Is that so?'

'Most certainly, sir. Cavaliere Baglione is further down the room, nearer the end. Signor Salini is helping him. May I take you down and introduce you?'

'You are most kind but I recognise Cavaliere Baglione. Please carry on with your work. I will go and see him, if that is permissible?'

'By all means,' the man said.

I now knew that I was in the most prestigious artistic academy in Rome, the Accademia di San Luca. I also knew that Baglione, much to Caravaggio's disgust and envy, had been made a Knight of the Order of Christ by Pope Paul in 1607. That had been during the time that Caravaggio had been in exile from Rome after killing Ranuccio Tomassoni. I also knew that Baglione's chief henchman, Tommaso Salini, known as Mao, had been expelled from the Accademia for some offence but I did not know what offence it was.

It is remarkable what a fine suit of clothes will do for you because some of the other artists broke off from preparing their pictures and actually bowed to me as I walked past. I inclined my head in acknowledgement in a most regal way. I recognised Giovanni Baglione from the portrait drawing by Ottavio Leoni. Baglione, like me, was dressed in a fine doublet, as befitted his status as a knighted artist. He wore the gold chain which had been awarded to him by Cardinal Benedetto Giustiniani, an award that had enraged Merisi with jealousy, as well as enraging many other artists. Baglione's hair was thin and wispy and he sported an upturned moustache and a little goatee beard. His eyes, as he watched me approaching, were sad and sleepy, almost bovine. 'Signor Baglione,' I said, as I approached nearer to him, 'I would like to talk to you, if it is a convenient time.'

Before Baglione could reply, and before I could get any closer, a small figure stepped in front of me to block my path. I could tell from his belligerent attitude, his pudgy and pasty face, his double chin, his perky hat with a feather in it, something he wore habitually, that this was Baglione's most ardent supporter and one of the most detested artists in Rome, Tommaso Salini, known as Mao. He said: 'Who are you? What do you want with the Cavaliere?'

I shot Salini my most disdainful glance and then ignored him. Over Salini's head, I said to Baglione, in a loud voice: 'My name is Stefano Maddano and I am investigating the circumstances of the death of the artist Caravaggio.' I became aware that, at the mention of the magical name Caravaggio, activity behind me had momentarily stopped. I looked around and saw that the three artists within earshot had indeed stopped what they were doing and were looking at me. Salini thrust out his hand and pushed me in the chest. 'The Cavaliere is busy preparing his work for the exhibition. He does not wish to talk about that Godless madman Caravaggio.'

I whipped out my dagger and held it to Salini's throat. 'If you ever lay a hand on me again,' I whispered, 'I'll slit your throat from ear to ear. Do you understand?' I was pleased with this move. With the help and guidance of Merisi, I had been practising my fast draw. Salini looked at me with pure hatred but withdrew his hand. Thus the seeds of many of my later troubles were sown! I should have gone on ignoring the little shit but, as the historical records showed, he was an obnoxious bastard without even trying to be. My aggressive response to Mao's bullying had drawn warm applause from the three artists behind me.

Baglione said to me: 'Your performance has found favour with the Unholy Trinity.'

'Who are those three?' I asked, looking behind me.

'On the left is Bartolomeo Manfredi. In the middle is Carlo Saraceni. And on the right is Orazio Borgianni.' The three artists had listened to Baglione's introduction and I bowed to them.

'I have heard of all of you,' I said. 'Caravaggio was the friend of all three of you, was he not?' I knew from my research that these three artists were profoundly influenced by the new style of painting introduced by Caravaggio and, eventually, had spread his influence all over Europe. Many works once attributed to Caravaggio are now attributed to Bartolomeo Manfredi, who copied Caravggio's style and subject matter particularly closely. All three of them were rivals of Baglione and Salini. The smallest man, but the most pugnacious, was Orazio Borgianni. He was short and balding, with a luxuriant upward-pointing moustache, like the one worn by Franz Hals's Laughing Cavalier, and he thrust out his barrel-shaped chest. 'You need look no further for Caravaggio's killer, Signor Maddano,' he said to me. 'Either one of those talentless bastards behind you could have done the deed.' This statement provoked a general shouting match between Salini and Borgianni. The tall scholarly man who was sitting at the door became aware of the commotion and was walking towards us. Before he could reach us, however, Baglione defused the situation by saying: 'Please calm down, gentlemen. I've been expecting a visit from Signor Maddano. I'm sure I can accommodate him about whatever he wishes to ask me.'

'What right has he to ask questions?' Salini challenged.

'As I understand it,' Baglione said, 'the Holy Father has given his blessing to Signor Maddano's inquiry.' To me he said: 'Please put your dagger away, sir. I will answer any questions you may ask me as honestly as I can.'

I said: 'I have the same questions for Signor Salini here so, if he will divest himself of that hostile attitude, perhaps we can kill two birds with one stone.'

Baglione smiled. 'What a quaint and apt expression! I have heard that you are not Italian. Perhaps we can learn something from each other.'

Salini glared at me and muttered: 'Cursed foreigners.'

'Stop it, Tommaso,' Baglione scolded. He shooed away the tall scholarly man, who returned to his table by the door and then, to me, he indicated his painting, which was leaning against the wall waiting to be hung. 'What do you think of my work, Signor Maddano?'

I pretended to critically examine Baglione's painting. It was a stiff and wooden version of David slaying the Philistine Samson. In direct contrast to the belligerent Salini, I found myself taking a liking to Baglione. He exuded a sort of avuncular and world-weary resignation. I wondered how he could stand the incessant company of the little shit Salini. So, although I did not think much of Baglione's painting, and to defuse any remaining tension, I paraphrased a clever response by the composer Mozart to the pedestrian work of his fellow composer Salieri I remembered from the film Amadeus. I said: 'Such a work confirms all that I have heard about you, Cavaliere. One looks at such a painting and says to oneself "only Baglione could have done this".'

Baglione smiled with pleasure, fortunately missing the double-meaning in my statement. 'Thank you, signor. I know that you were a friend of Caravaggio so I expected that you might have shared his contempt for my work.'

'Yes, I was a friend of Caravaggio, but being a friend does not mean that you always have to share their taste or opinion.' I looked pointedly at Salini. 'Or enjoy their company all the time.'

'Perhaps you shared his taste in young boys,' Salini sneered, 'or his taste for scurrilous and slanderous poetry.'

I said: 'I'm surprised to see you here at the Accademia di San Luca, Signor Salini. I understood that you had been ejected from this august company.'

Salini, deflated, said: 'I am here to help my friend, Cavaliere Baglione.'

'Come,' Baglione suggested, 'there are some chairs over here. Let's make ourselves comfortable while we talk.'

We moved away from the Unholy Trinity and towards the back of the room. We sat down on some plain wooden chairs. Baglione said: 'Those three did not know Caravaggio as well as I did. They all arrived in Rome long after Caravaggio and had little direct experience of his sarcastic tongue. They are all enamoured by his dramatic style but none of them can match Caravaggio's skill.'

'As I understand it,' I said, 'both yourself and Salini here were once enamoured by Caravaggio's new style.'

'To begin with, yes,' Baglione agreed. 'I think every artist in Rome was influenced by him to begin with. His paintings for the Contarelli chapel are a revelation, even though I coveted that commission myself.'

'I'm surprised by your attitude, Signor Baglione. Caravaggio treated you abominably, he detested you, and you detested him, and yet you praise his painting and copied his style.'

'When it comes to painting, Signor Maddano, I like to think that I can be objective and not influenced by my personal prejudices. Take Salini here . . . he has some talent, especially for painting fruit and flowers and such subjects, but his figure work lacks gravitas.' Salini, stung by this comment, shifted uneasily. 'Take Manfredi over there,' Baglione continued. 'He paints subjects that I consider lack dignity, such as soldiers drinking in taverns or gamblers or peasants. He is a good painter and some of his work is almost indistinguishable from that of Caravaggio. Artists who visit Rome from the Spanish Netherlands and France, who have little respect for the holy scriptures or classical mythology, are impressed by Caravaggio's work. Carlo Saraceni, whose work is being hung today, is a much more dignified artist. His sense of design and colour are excellent and he is equally adept at small landscapes with figures in them, all luminously painted, as he is with large altarpieces.'

'Didn't he paint the replacement for Caravaggio's Death of the Virgin when the church of Santa Maria della Scala rejected it a few years ago.'

'Indeed he did,' Baglione confirmed, 'but I have to say that I much preferred Caravaggio's work, which was most touching.'

'You are clearly a man of taste, discernment and insight, Signor Baglione,' I said, laying on the flattery with a trowel. 'What is your opinion of Orazio Borgianni?'

'As a person, very much like Caravaggio. He is nasty and aggressive. As an artist, he is the best of the Unholy Trinity. He is much the most versatile. He is equally adept at fresco, easel painting and etching. And his portraits are unsurpassed. If he could just control his demonic temperament and imagination, he would match Caravaggio himself.'

'These are fascinating insights,' I said. 'Have you ever considered setting down your opinions on paper?'

'You mean in the manner of Giorgio Vasari and his Lives of the Artists?'

'Yes, exactly so,' I said. 'I'm sure such a work would be of immense benefit and interest to generations to come.'

'An interesting suggestion, Signor Maddano,' Baglione said, genuinely pleased. 'Perhaps if I live to be an old man and am finished with painting, I might take up your suggestion. But perhaps you have come to arrest me for the slaying of Caravaggio.' He said it with the hint of a world-weary smile.

Salini, restless and irritated by all the talk about other artists, could not help intervening. 'That cunt Merisi deserved all he got. I wish I had done the deed myself. Did you read the things that he and his bumboy friends wrote about my wife in that poem?'

Despite my dislike of Salini, I had to admit that Michele's scurrilous poem about Baglione and Salini was crude, schoolboyish and unfunny. There had been no need to make such salacious comments about Salini's wife. 'I did read the poems and I agree that such comments about your wife were completely unnecessary. I fully understand why you and Signor Baglione here had to sue Caravaggio and his accomplices for libel. You were provoked beyond endurance by Caravaggio's behaviour. It seems that artistic rivalry tipped over into a nasty personal feud. I don't think there is any need for us to go over all these details again. I know what happened and you obviously know what happened. Clearly, however, such a confrontation could be considered a very strong motive for murdering Caravaggio. The Holy Father has given me his warrant to investigate the circumstances of Caravaggio's death and has enjoined anyone giving evidence to tell me the truth, in peril of their immortal soul. So now I ask both of you, did you have any involvement in the death of Caravaggio or do you have any knowledge of anyone who might have done so?'

Salini said: 'I've just said, I wish I had done it. I would have enjoyed to watch that bastard in his death throes.'

Baglione winced, and said to me: 'Tommaso is a braggart. He was afraid of Caravaggio and would not have had the courage to take him on face-to-face. He did not kill Caravaggio. We were nowhere near Porto Ercole on that day and we did not send anyone to accomplish the deed. I can provide ample proof of that claim if need be. Caravaggio made my life a misery, Signor Maddano, but his talent as an artist was supreme. Whatever he had done to me, I could not have willingly destroyed such a talent. It is a tragedy for Italian art that Caravaggio did not live longer. Although, had he done so, I would have much preferred him to stay in Naples.' Again, Baglione smiled in his world-weary way.

I had already reached the conclusion that neither of these men had had anything to do with Caravaggio's death, so I said: 'Thank you for your time, gentlemen. I will leave you to hang your work, which has left me . . . speechless.'

Baglione inclined his head in thanks. Salini glared at me and said: 'I don't like you, you foreign bastard. You were lucky today. You were protected by your fine clothes and your dagger and by three of Merisi's bumboys over there. I just hope that I meet you again. You will not be so lucky.'

'Signor Salini,' I said, 'I think that Caravaggio was wrong to claim in his poem that you have a prick like a mule because it seems to me that you are just one big prick all over.'

Salini rose from his chair to attack me but Baglione laid a restraining hand on him and told his companion, in no uncertain terms, to stop making a fool of himself.

'Good day to you, gentlemen,' I said, and walked out of the salon, pausing only to look at Carlo Saraceni's depiction of Christ destroying the temple, which was a much, much better work than Baglione's.

31

I materialised back in my bedroom and was greeted by the delicious aroma of Indian food. I changed into modern dress. It was early evening. As I walked downstairs I could hear that the television was on and that Merisi was talking to somebody. Merisi had a visitor and I could guess who it was. I silently opened the front door and then slammed it shut so that it would appear I had just entered the house by the traditional route. I called out: 'I'm back!' I went in to the living room. Merisi and Isabella Caro were sitting together on the sofa. The coffee table in front of them was covered with tubs of takeaway Indian food.

'Hey, Stefano!' Merisi asked. 'How was your trip?'

'It went well,' I replied. 'I'll tell you all about it tomorrow.' I was eager to tell Merisi how I had intimidated Mao Salini with my quick-draw dagger, as Merisi had taught me, but my story would have to wait. 'Good evening, sergeant.'

Isabella Caro looked embarrassed but she said: 'Why don't you call me Izzy instead of sergeant. I wanted to apologise for my behaviour. Michele said you would probably be back soon so I brought some food for you as well. As you can see, we're not drinking tonight.' She smiled ruefully. She was wearing a red blouse and a black leather skirt and she looked very attractive.

'No need for apologies, Izzy,' I said. 'I hope you two are not dropping rice on my carpet.' I said it with a smile.

Izzy dug Merisi in the ribs with her elbow. 'I told you we should have eaten in the kitchen.'

'Don't take any notice of Signor Grumpy over there,' Merisi teased. 'Go on, Stefano. Eat something. There's plenty of it. We're eating in here because I wanted to watch this play on the box that lies.'

'The box that lies!' I exclaimed, with a jocular tone, and looked at Izzy with an expression that said 'what can you do with him?' 'What a quaint Italian expression! You mean the television. What are you watching?'

Izzy said: 'It's some boring film. The Fall of the Roman Empire.'

'I know the one,' I said breezily. 'Alec Guinness and Sophia Loren.' I sat down in an armchair and selected a tub of chicken jalfrezi. 'One of the huge benefits about the fall of the British empire is that our former colonial subjects followed us back here and started all these convenient and tasty restaurants and takeaways.'

Merisi looked at me, puzzled. 'This is Indian food,' he said. 'You English have never ruled India. India is much bigger than England.'

'We British - that includes the Scots and the Welsh, as well as the English - certainly did rule India.' I looked at Izzy and smiled. 'The education system in modern Italy must be sadly lacking if Michele doesn't know that.' I emphasised the word 'modern' to warn Merisi not to say anything out of the context of our time.

'Very well, so the British once ruled India,' Merisi said, 'but the greatest empire the world has ever seen was the Roman empire.'

I looked at Izzy. She shrugged helplessly.

'You know very well, Michele, that the British empire was far, far larger than the Roman empire ever was and that, little more than one hundred years ago, the British ruled a quarter of the area of the entire world and a quarter of its entire population. This is delicious jalfrezi.'

Merisi threw down his fork. It bounced off the coffee table and on to the floor. 'You're a liar,' he accused me. 'Do you expect me to believe that a tiny, damp, shabby little island like yours, full of blue-veined, pasty, mealy-mouthed, la-di-da creatures could conquer a quarter of the world?'

'Well, we didn't exactly conquer it. Just sort of acquired it by various devious means. Izzy will confirm that I am telling you the truth.'

Merisi looked challengingly at Izzy. Izzy said: 'It's true, Michele, but it's all gone now.'

Merisi stood up angrily. 'You are both lying to me. It's impossible. If the empire has now gone it must mean that the oppressed colonial people fought back, just like the barbarians fought back against Rome and eventually defeated her. But you tell me that all they did was move to Britain and open restaurants. You are both mad and both liars.'

'Please sit down, Michele,' Izzy pleaded.

It must have been an excess of adrenaline from my confrontation with Mao Salini that caused me to act foolishly. 'Let me prove it to you,' I said. I stood up and, from my bookcase, took out a historical atlas of the world. It was a volume published just before the First World War. It was bound in leather with hand-tooled gold leaf lettering on the binding. I had bought it at an auction for £200 having not been able to resist it. I took it over to Merisi, who was still standing up, and first showed him a map of the Roman empire at its greatest extent. 'This was the Roman empire. Do you agree?'

'Yes,' Merisi nodded.

I turned the pages to a map of the British empire in 1900. 'All the areas coloured red were ruled by Britain. As you can see, it was much bigger than the Roman empire.'

Merisi took the atlas and examined the map. 'What is this?'

I looked to see where he was pointing. 'That is North America. Most of it is made up of two countries named Canada and the United States of America. The British ruled Canada and, for a time, a large chunk of America.'

Merisi nodded. 'What is this?'

Without considering that Isabella Caro was listening, I said: 'That is a new continent, unknown in your time, called Australia.'

Merisi hurled the book aside. 'You have invented this continent and drawn it in yourself to make a fool of me.'

I was furious with Merisi for treating my precious atlas like an old newspaper and went into a blind rage. 'Oh, sure,' I shouted, bending down to pick up my atlas, becoming even more annoyed with Merisi because his childish action had broken the spine, 'I drew in a continent that doesn't exist just in case some Eyetie painter who was born in the sixteenth century visited me and didn't believe that we British had a bigger empire than the Romans. I'm delighted to tell you and your Catholic dago friends that our empire was founded during the reign of that queen you and your compatriots hated so much.'

'You mean that bitch Elizabeth.'

'No,' I roared, 'I mean Her Gracious Majesty Queen Elizabeth. And if you don't like it, why don't you fuck off back to the seventeenth century and crawl back in your coffin.'

Whether it was the mental strain of the strange situation I was living through that made me say such a cruel thing, or for whatever reason, I immediately regretted my savage comment. It shocked both Merisi and I back to our senses. Simultaneously, we looked at Isabella Caro. She said: 'Don't worry. Michele has told me everything.'

'And what, exactly, has he told you?' I asked.

'That he is the artist Michelangelo Merisi, known as Caravaggio, and that he was brought back to life by an alien race and has travelled through time to find you so that you can both investigate how and why someone tried to murder him.'

I forced myself to laugh heartily. 'Oh, don't take any notice of that nonsense,' I said, in a light-hearted tone. 'It's just a private joke between us. Isn't it, Michele?'

'Izzy believes everything I have told her,' Merisi said. 'Unlike you, she trusts me and has faith in me. I have shown her the ChronoConverter and demonstrated how it works. She knows everything, Stefano.'

'Jesus Christ,' I said, truly shocked. 'I need a drink.' I opened the drinks cabinet and poured myself a large bourbon. To Izzy I said: 'At least you now understand why it is pointless to get involved with Michele. He cannot stay in this century for much longer.'

'What will happen to him then?' Izzy asked, pensively.

It was a question that had been troubling me almost from the start of this crazy venture. 'I don't know,' I replied. 'That will be for the Tralfamadorians to decide. He will probably be allowed to travel back to his own century but live out his life under an assumed identity. But I really don't know.'

'I am Michelangelo Merisi da Caravaggio, Knight of the Order of Saint John. I will not be anyone else.'

'That knighthood was stripped from you,' I reminded Merisi. I turned to Izzy. 'What are you going to do about all this? Are you going to report this to anyone?'

'No,' she replied. 'I have promised Michele that I will not breathe a word of this to anyone else. I make the same promise to you. I love Michele and I will not do or say anything that might cause him to be taken away from me.'

'Well, thank you for that promise,' I said, 'but you will have to lose Michele sooner or later.'

'We'll see,' Isabella Caro said. 'We'll see.'

32

The next day was warm and sunny. I decided that Merisi and I would work in the garden. I knew that Mrs. Chowdry was away visiting her daughter and grandchildren so there was no possibility that we could be overheard. We sat at my tacky garden table, which was made of white plastic but manufactured to appear as if it was made of intricate cast iron work. I was still miffed with Merisi, but more for his brutal treatment of my valuable atlas than for telling Isabella Caro the truth about himself. Even so, I asked him: 'Why did you have to tell her? I thought you cared nothing for her.'

'She is beginning . . . what is that expression you use? To get under my skin. Yes, that's it, get under my skin. There is nothing more flattering to a man, erotic even, than a woman who is totally devoted to him. Do you understand what I'm saying?'

'Yes, of course,' I replied, 'but it could lead to unforeseen complications. Is it wise to let yourself become attached to Isabella? And is it fair to allow her to become so attached to you when the likelihood is that you must part forever, and very soon.'

'Maybe not,' Merisi agreed, but said no more.

'Well, as long as the Tralfamadorian ChronoCouncil don't find out that . . .' Merisi was not listening to me. He was gazing up at a low-flying jet airliner going overhead. The airliner was in the orange livery of EasyJet and was probably heading for nearby Luton Airport.

'Are there really people sitting in that flying carriage?' Merisi asked me.

'Yes, truly. Even your illustrious predecessor, Leonardo da Vinci, dreamed of being able to fly.'

Merisi nodded. 'Yes he did, and of all the wondrous things I have seen in this century, this is the one that fascinates me most. People flying like birds in the sky. How many people travel in those things?'

'Usually about two or three hundred people but the largest airliners can carry about seven hundred passengers.'

'And how fast do they travel?'

'Usually about five or six hundred miles per hour.'

Merisi looked at me. 'You are lying to me again.'

'No, I swear it. In fact, we British once co-operated with the French in building an airliner that travelled at over one thousand miles per hour. It was known as the Concorde.'

'Now you are lying!' Merisi exclaimed. 'I can believe that one of those things can travel so fast but I can't believe that the British would co-operate with the French to build it! How did all this come about, this ability to fly like the birds?'

I attempted to give Merisi, as far as my limited knowledge would allow, a potted history of powered flight. I began with the Wright brothers, then went on to Bleriot, Alcock and Brown, Lindbergh, the invention of the jet engine, Chuck Yeager breaking the sound barrier, the rise of passenger air travel and even the manned landings on the Moon, which Merisi adamantly refused to believe, thinking I was making a fool of him. Being cynical about human nature, he was only too ready to believe, however, about the role of aircraft in the two twentieth century world wars and the catastrophic effect those wars had wreaked on humanity.

Merisi pondered all I had told him and then said: 'I would like to try this flying but I'm frightened. Is it dangerous?'

'Only very rarely,' I said. 'Statistically, it's the safest form of travel.'

At that moment Isabella Caro walked round the corner of the house and into the back garden. She was in uniform. 'Good morning, boys,' she greeted us cheerily. 'I heard your voices and thought you might be loafing about in the sunshine out here.'

'Izzy!' Merisi exclaimed, with genuine delight. 'This is an unexpected pleasure. What brings you here?'

'I came in my official capacity to see Mrs. Chowdry but she is not at home.'

'No,' I said, 'she is away visiting her family. Am I allowed to ask why you came to see my sorely-tested neighbour?'

'Certainly,' Caro replied. 'Michele dear, please hold out your hand.'

Merisi did as he was asked, albeit warily. Caro slapped him lightly on the wrist. 'That is an official formal caution, from Bedfordshire police, concerning your future behaviour. You are a bad, bad boy, Signor Merisi, and I love it.'

'Well,' Merisi said, 'it is certainly more pleasant dealing with the Bedfordshire police than with the old Roman sbirri!'

'That is what I came to tell Mrs. Chowdry, that you have been formally cautioned. I'm relieved she is not at home and I do not have to face her.'

'Sit down, Izzy,' Merisi invited her. 'Can you stay for a while?'

'For a few minutes. What were you two talking about?'

I said: 'I was explaining to Michele about the history of powered flight and about how aircraft work. Please tell Michele what Neil Armstrong did in 1969?'

'Didn't he have a number one hit with What A Wonderful World?'

'Not Louis Armstrong, sergeant. Neil Armstrong!'

Izzy smiled at me to show she was teasing. To Merisi she said: 'Neil Armstrong was the first human being to walk on the Moon.'

'There, Michele,' I said smugly, 'now do you believe me?'

'I believe everything that Izzy tells me,' Merisi replied. 'I have always been a fool for a pretty face. Would you like a cup of coffee, Izzy?'

'Yes, please,' Caro said, and Merisi went inside to the kitchen.

'Michele is becoming thoroughly domesticated,' I said. 'He'll make someone a lovely wife, one day.'

Caro was suddenly pensive. 'One day,' she repeated, wistfully. 'Do you really not know what will happen to Michele when all your inquiries are finished?'

'No, honestly I don't. The Tralfamadorians have not given me any clue about what will happen to him when we're finished.'

'Do you think they might kill him?'

Izzy's blunt words made me shudder but also made me realise I had not thought nearly enough about what was going to happen after our research project had ended. 'No, I don't think so,' I answered. 'They revere Caravaggio as a great artist on their planet, just as we do on this one. They spent an awful lot of effort and resources on keeping him alive and bringing him here but it would be unfair to Michele to just leave him alone in this century. He's learned a lot about how our world works but he would still be hopelessly lost without guidance, and I have no intention of letting him live with me for much longer.'

'What if he lived with me?' Izzy said, hesitantly.

'I have to be honest, I doubt whether the Tralfamadorians would allow it. It is too dangerous to the fabric of time. Michele was foolish to tell you the truth, even if it meant breaking your heart one day without you ever knowing why. In all probability, the Tralfamadorians will send Michele back to the seventeenth century but somewhere in Italy well away from Rome and his old haunts, to live out his life among people of his own kind and his own time.'

Izzy looked down and fiddled with a loose piece of plastic on the patio table. 'What if I went back to live in his century? Would they allow that?'

'That's even more dangerous. What if you went back with him and something happened to Michele? You would be just as lost in his century as he is in ours. Not to mention all the noxious diseases that might affect you if you went back with him.'

'You have been going back. Why haven't you caught the plague or whatever?'

'Because the Tralfamadorians gave me medication that affords temporary protection. I emphasise temporary. I have only been travelling back for short periods, no more than a few hours at most.'

Caro ripped off the piece of plastic and, in a very unladylike manner, said: 'Oh, bollocks.'

'I warned you not to get involved with him. My advice is to stop it, break it off, get away from him as soon as possible.'

At that moment, Sergeant Caro's colleagues in the Bedfordshire police surveillance helicopter flew past overhead, the roar of its engines drowning out further conversation for several seconds. Isabella Caro, with a thoughtful expression on her face, intently watched the helicopter disappearing until it was out of sight.

After Sergeant Caro had finished her coffee and departed, reluctantly, to carry on with her official duties, I said: 'Talking of high-flyers, Michele, as we have been, I'd like to ask you about an artist who became perhaps your most dangerous rival for the accolade of the best painter in Rome.'

'You mean Guido Reni?'

'Yes. Reni was a more serious contender for that title than even Annibale Carracci was. I would have enjoyed to go back in time and interview Signor Carracci but, as you very well know, he died before you supposedly did, so the ChronoLaws do not allow it.'

Merisi was thoughtful for several seconds. Then he said: 'Poor Annibale. He was a sensitive man and he was treated abominably. He fell into a deep depression. You have seen the pictures of the work he did on the Farnese Gallery. It was a merivaglia, a miracle and, arrogant as I am, I have no hesitation in admitting that I could not have matched Annibale's work. He was considered to be the best fresco painter since Raphael. And do you know how much Cardinal Farnese had paid him for all his work since he came to Rome? Five hundred scudi, that's all! Five hundred, including all the work on the Farnese Gallery! You will recall that I was paid 125 scudi for the small easel painting of the Supper at Emmaus alone. And that damned cardinal had sent this derisory fee to Annibale's room on a saucer! Annibale was already exhausted from the sheer amount of work he had been doing. Now he had been humiliated. He became gripped with melancholy and all the commissions he had been working on came to a halt. He never fully recovered. Annibale and I talked about how little we were paid compared to some other fashionable painters. Unimaginative daubers like the Cavaliere d'Arpino and Zuccaro could afford to buy their own palazzi. Annibale and I lived in one shabby room, ate our meals off a piece of canvas, drank out of wooden beakers, wore the same clothes until they fell to pieces. Other artists, with far less talent, grew rich.'

'One of whom,' I said, 'was Guido Reni.'

'Much as it pains me to say it but Reni was a fine painter. I remember that he had arrived in Rome, already with a high reputation from his work in Bologna, not long after I had scored my first big successes with the Contarelli and Cerasi chapel projects.'

'He seems to have been your opposite in almost every respect,' I said. 'According to his biographer, Reni was "patient, affable and polite, tractable and courteous". These are not terms that could be applied to you.'

'Go on, Englishman, have your little joke at my expense. Reni was also my opposite in that he was not intelligent, not learned, could hardly write his own name, and he preferred the company of simpletons, thus he would have enjoyed your company. Also, like the Cavaliere d'Arpino, he was anxious and endlessly worried that all his success might vanish overnight. He was very afraid of witchcraft and magic. Of course, I used this knowledge to play on his fears.'

'You are such a Christian gentleman,' I said sarcastically.

Merisi ignored my dig and said: 'I'm no bardassa but Reni was a startlingly good-looking man. He had an almost feminine beauty. He was fair-skinned, with rosy cheeks, clear blue eyes, and a finely chiselled nose. His figure was very well made. Women used to drool over him in his presence. Now, you would think that a man with that sort of effect on women would be fucking his brains out day and night.'

'Didn't he?' I asked.

'No!' Merisi exclaimed. 'He was petrified of women. He was not a bardassa, as far as I know, but as far as anyone else knew, he never went with a woman either. Whether he used his hand to satisfy himself is also anybody's guess. He was devoted to the Virgin Mary and that is what he was himself, all his life . . . a virgin. His only vice was playing cards. He earned a lot of money from his painting and lost most of it at the card table. He was a strange mixture of a man.'

'What about his painting? What did you think of that?'

'He was good,' Merisi replied, looking uncomfortable at having to admit the fact. 'His style was much more graceful and idealised than mine. He used colours, which again were lighter and brighter than mine, with refined skill and taste. Yes, he was a powerful and dangerous rival.'

'We know that the Cavaliere d'Arpino was becoming increasingly jealous of your success and reputation, and increasingly antagonistic towards you.' Merisi nodded in confirmation. 'The Cavaliere was attempting to form a sort of coalition of painters in order to wrest the leadership of the Roman art world away from you. Were you aware that the Cavaliere had written to Reni, during one of Reni's trips back to Bologna, encouraging Reni to hurry back to Rome to create opposition to you. D'Arpino considered you to be an enemy.'

Merisi looked genuinely surprised. 'I knew that d'Arpino was leading the opposition against me but I didn't know he was writing letters like that. Reni and I had rubbed along together without too much friction since he had arrived in Rome but, in 1604, the trouble really flared up.'

'We now think it was over the commission for a new church in Loreto, in the Marches. Is that correct?'

'Yes,' Merisi confirmed. 'The commission was to fresco a new sacristy for the basilica of the church of Santa Maria di Loreto. My good friend Lionello Spada was already working on frescoes for the church and for some reason, which none of us could properly fathom, Reni was called in to pass judgement on Lionello's work. Reni condemned Lionello's work and thereby completely dashed Lionello's hopes of securing the commission for the new sacristy. Lionello was beside himself with anger. We all thought that Reni had condemned Lionello's work so that he could win the commission himself, which is probably true, but the commission was finally awarded to Roncalli.'

'You mean Cristofero Roncalli?' I asked.

'Yes. Roncalli was an excellent fresco painter, much more experienced and established than either Lionello or Reni at that time, but it was all a mystery.'

'Your friend Baglione claims that you yourself was so enraged by Roncalli winning this commission that you had him beaten up because you wanted it for yourself.'

'What!' Merisi exclaimed. 'That's another one of Baglione's half-baked lies!'

'Baglione claims that you hired a Sicilian thug to beat up Roncalli,' I persisted.

'I didn't,' Merisi said, 'but Lionello did. I didn't want the commission. I didn't expect to be offered it. I was not known as a fresco painter. But Lionello had been desperate to win it. He thought that Roncalli had colluded with Reni to deprive him of the commission.'

'Are you sure that it was Lionello Spada who hired this Sicilian thug?'

'Yes, because I recommended this "Sicilian thug" as you call him.'

'Well, I suspect you knew all the violent low-lifes in Rome,' I said. 'What was the name of this Sicilian?'

'I have forgotten,' Merisi replied, unconvincingly, and changed the subject. 'That wasn't the end of the humiliation that Reni was heaping upon his fellow painters. It was now my turn. Later that year, I was approached to do an altarpiece of the crucifixion of Saint Peter for the church of the Tre Fontane. It was being awarded by the nephew of the pope, Cardinal Pietro Aldobrandini. The Cavaliere d'Arpino got wind of this approach and went to the cardinal and urged him to award the commission to Guido Reni instead, which is what happened. That cheeky cunt Reni even copied some features from my own version of the crucifixion of Saint Peter in the Cerasi chapel. Those two bastards didn't think I knew about there little conspiracy but I found out and from then on, as far as I was concerned, they were my mortal enemies. Lionello Spada and I plotted our revenge, usually when we were well in our cups. To add another grave insult to the injuries that Reni had already doled out to me, he painted a picture which he called David contemplating the Head of Goliath.'

'But I saw this painting!' I exclaimed, 'when I visited Cardinal Del Monte. It is now in his collection and he pointed out the similarity between yourself and the head of Goliath.'

'Exactly!' Merisi agreed, 'and there are many other messages contained within this scurrilous picture.'

'Really?' I said, intrigued. 'Let me fetch a reproduction of this painting and you can tell me what messages they are.' I went indoors, found Reni's painting in the History of World Art, and came out to lay the book in front of us on the garden table.

Merisi waved his hand over the picture. 'This painting was a direct attack on me and my pre-eminence in the Roman art world. Not just an attack on me but on my friends and supporters as well.'

'What do you mean?'

'Reni has imitated the lighting effects of my style. His David is wearing a red cap with a shocking pink feather in the cap. Not only is this symbolism suggesting that I am a bardassa but that this painting is a feather in Reni's cap. Look at David's insoucient and languid pose, as if he is suggesting that he has overthrown my leadership with ease.'

'Oh, come off it,' I objected. 'Surely you're reading too much into . . .'

'You think so?' Merisi spat back, becoming increasingly agitated. 'Such symbolism was common in the art world of my day. What has Reni placed David's foot on?'

'Well, a sword,' I replied.

'Exactly!' Merisi said again. 'And what is the Italian word for sword?'

'Spada . . . ,' I replied, suddenly grasping the significance of what Merisi was saying.

'Yes. My friend Lionello Spada. His surname means "sword". He used to sign his paintings with a sword motif. Reni is saying that he has destroyed Goliath, me, and trampled on my friend Spada. We have already established that he tricked us both out of commissions. That is what Reni thought he had done, destroyed us both as painters.'

'Could all this just be a coincidence?' I asked.

'No, of course not,' Merisi said, emphatically. 'Reni was mocking both of us. Look where he is resting his elbow.'

'On a broken column. So what?'

'What is the name of the family who supported me throughout my life more than any other?' Merisi asked.

'Well, the Colonna family,' I replied.

'And Colonna means, in English . . .?'

'Column,' I said. 'It means column.'

'My point is made,' Merisi said triumphantly. 'There is our murderer! The rogue who painted this picture! This is what the assassin who tried to murder me was referring to. Guido Reni did not like the thought of me returning to Rome. He wanted me out of the way, once and for all. Go back in time and tell Reni that Michelangelo Merisi da Caravaggio has returned from the grave and names him as the murderer.'

I was certainly excited by these revelations. Perhaps Merisi was right. Symbols hardly constituted proof but they were indications that merited a thorough interrogation of the saintly Signor Guido Reni. 'I think it's certainly worth interviewing Guido Reni,' I said, 'but we must not jump to conclusions.'

'Reni was a devious hypocrite,' Merisi said with a sneer of comtempt. 'Behind that courteous and affable mask was a selfish and scheming backstabber. I doubt whether Reni would tell you the truth or even deign to talk to you at all.'

I thought about the problem and then said: 'You mentioned that Reni was superstitious and mortally afraid of magic and witchcraft?'

'Yes,' Merisi replied.

'Then if our Tralfamadorian ChronoMasters will permit it,' I said, 'perhaps I can prepare a little "entertainment" that will loosen Signor Reni's tongue . . .'

33

I had contacted the Tralfamadorian ChronoCouncil to explain my plan and, to my surprise, it had been approved and the costume and other accoutrements I had asked for had been sent via the ChronoConverter sooner than I had expected. I had asked for a velvet costume that was all black in colour but lined with silver embroidery and with specially tailored sleeves. I put on the costume in my bedroom and studied my appearance in a full-length mirror. I had donned a new black wig with long, black, greasy-looking tresses that hung down my back. A false pointed beard and moustache emphasised my Satanic appearance. Around my neck hung an enormous silver cross bearing a sculpted figure of Christ being crucified. I knew that Guido Reni's one true vice was gambling at card games and, thanks to an old hobby of mine and to Bedfordshire Magic Circle, I possessed a pack of playing cards that could possibly cure Signor Reni of his gambling habit forever. I then contacted Guglielmo Pellegrino to make the specific arrangements for meeting Guido Reni.

As I was checking my costume in the full-length mirror, Merisi hesitantly peeped into my bedroom. 'Come in, Michele,' I invited.

'I do not wish to.'

'Why not? How do I look?'

'I know that under that costume is merely a paunchy and pasty Englishman but you frighten me.'

'Excellent!' I exclaimed. 'That is just the effect I intended.'

'You will burn in Hell for this.'

'That's just what my ex-wife told me once, only in her case it was a command and not a prediction.'

Because of the nature of my request to Guglielmo Pellegrino, I had to be ready when his call beckoned me and so I stayed in costume and practised my parlour tricks until I had perfected them. It was a little under three hours later that Pellegrino sent the signal and I immediately activated the ChronoConverter. I had expected to land outside one of the palazzi that Guido

Reni rented in Rome but I found myself outside the door of what looked like another artist's house and studio. It was late at night and very dark, all of which suited my purpose. I knocked on the door and waited a few minutes but there was no answer. I knocked again, louder, and heard a female voice shouting: 'Alright, alright, I'm coming!' The door opened and a tall, stout woman, dressed for bed in a nightgown and nightcap, stood holding up a small smoking oil lamp. The expression on her plump and sour face registered deep disapproval. Before I could speak, she said: 'Ha! Another drunken wastrel. You're too late! They've eaten all the food and no doubt drunk all the wine . . . and the beer. Who are you? I've never seen you before.'

'Forgive my intrusion, signora, but who's house is this?'

'It is the home and the studio of the distinguished artist Signor Zampieri. My husband is at home so don't try any funny business. What do you want?'

'I have come to see Signor Reni.'

'Why come here, at this time of night, to see Signor Marble? Why don't you go to his studio tomorrow?'

'I have to leave Rome early this morning,' I lied. 'It is imperative that I talk to Signor Reni before I go. I am on papal business.'

'Oh, come in then, although I doubt whether you'll get any sense out of them. Follow me.'

I followed the woman, her ample buttocks rising and falling beneath her nightdress as she walked, through a large and gloomy studio, occasionally catching glimpses of some huge canvas being prepared with a Biblical or mythological scene. At the far side of the studio was an open door. The room beyond was illuminated by candlelight. It looked perfect for the operation of my plan, if I needed to implement it. I could hear the sound of men laughing. The woman had entered the room and the laughter stopped as she loudly scolded the occupants for all the noise they were making. She then announced that there was a gentleman who had come to visit. She turned to me and beckoned me into the room. 'Here he is,' she announced. 'I told him all the food was gone. Keep the noise down and don't drink too much. You've got work to do tomorrow.' The woman left without any further acknowledgement of my existence.

The room looked like a large kitchen or scullery, with a huge unlit cooking range, pots and pans of many sizes hanging from the walls, cupboards full of crockery, and a bare tiled floor strewn with straw and sawdust. In the middle of the room was a large and roughly-made wooden table at which three men, not the two I had expected, were sitting. There was a three-pronged candelabra in the middle of the table, which was strewn with pewter plates, containing the leftovers of a meal, together with tankards, bottles and playing cards.

I recognised Guido Reni, with his upturned moustache, sitting on the far side of the table. He looked back at me, trying to appear nonchalant but his eyes betraying apprehension at my demonic appearance. Sitting at the left of the table was a young man, who appeared to be in his early twenties, looking at me with an amused grin and all the insou.ience of fearless youth. I noted that, unlike the two other men, this young one had laid his dagger on the table so that it was well to hand. I would need to watch him carefully. It was the other man, sitting at the right of the table, who rose to greet me, albeit without offering his hand to shake. I knew he must be Domenico Zampieri. Like Guido Reni, Zampieri was in his middle thirties but his beard and moustache were wispy and white, which made him look considerably older. He looked tired and old in comparison with the handsome, almost beautiful, Guido Reni. Having just met his wife, I was not surprised by Zampieri's careworn appearance. I knew that Zampieri and Reni had trained together in the Academy founded by the Carracci brothers in Bologna and that they were close friends. I knew also that Domenico Zampieri was better known as Domenichino. It was interesting to meet Domenichino but, as far as I knew, he had never had any sort of quarrel or rivalry with Caravaggio so my business tonight was not with him. Zampieri, too, looked bewildered by my sudden appearance. He said: 'I am Domenico Zampieri. This is my home and my studio.'

I gave a slight bow. 'I am honoured to be here, Signor Zampieri. I have seen many examples of your work. May I say that you are a very fine artist.'

Zampieri acknowledged my compliment with a bow and then sat down.

I said, in my best Vincent Price tones: 'Forgive me for intruding at such an hour, gentlemen, but it is necessary that I speak with Signor Reni as a matter of urgency.' Reni looked even more apprehensive after that statement. 'As you comprehend, I recognise Signor Reni. My name is Stefano Maddano and I am here in Rome, with papal authority, to investigate the murder of Michelangelo Merisi da Caravaggio.'

Guido Reni said: 'I have heard of your mission. I surmised that you would be visiting me, but not in these circumstances. You are not what I expected.'

Zampieri said: 'Please sit down, Signor Maddano. Would you like some ale . . . or wine, perhaps?'

'Thank you, no.' I said. 'I do not put the Devil in my mouth to steal my senses.'

The young man said: 'Please sit down, Signor. If you don't drink, perhaps you will care to make a fourth at cards?'

'Alas I cannot,' I replied, as I sat down. 'The Devil's books burst into flames at my touch. I would wish that they would do so for all men they lead astray.' I looked straight at Reni as I uttered this seemingly odd statement. As a conversation stopper it had worked brilliantly. I looked at the young man and said: 'I know Signor Reni and Signor Zampieri as distinguished and accomplished artists. Are you an artist as well?'

Zampieri said: 'Forgive my lack of manners, Signor Maddano. This young man is Antonio Carracci.'

'Carracci?' I repeated. 'You are related to Annibale and Agostino and Ludovico Carracci?'

'Yes,' the young man said. 'Annibale was my uncle and Agostino was my father.'

'Ah!' I said, 'then I know that you were born the wrong side of the blanket.'

Antonio, his face a sudden mask of fury, reached for his dagger but Guido Reni gripped his other arm and said: 'No, Antonio. I am sure that Signor Maddano did not mean any offence.'

'On the contrary,' I said, 'I mean every offence. The bastard son of a Venetian whore should mind his manners and not assume such arrogance and presumption in the company of his elders and betters.'

This time, Antonio could not be restrained. He went for his dagger but, before he could get to it, I had produced, as if by magic, a wheel lock pistol. I held it to his head. 'Calm down, young man,' I said, 'and show some respect.' Antonio was not to know that the pistol was a replica which could not fire bullets, but it was a cunningly disguised Taser and would have knocked the young man out with several hundred volts if I had pulled the trigger.

Domenichino remained quite calm during this scene despite the dramatic appearance of the pistol, which had been concealed up my specially tailored sleeve. 'Sit back, Antonio,' he said. 'This is my home and I do not want death to enter it. Signor Maddano is plainly a man of experience and respect, not one of the stupid young street urchins that you are accustomed to fighting.'

Guido Reni reached across and took Antonio's dagger and threw it away across the room. 'Let us deal with whatever business you want with me,' he said. 'Antonio is here in Rome to help me with the decoration of the Palazzo del Quirinale. He has inherited the talent of his father and uncle. Please do not kill him, Signor Maddano. I would hate to lose such a good assistant. It is not Antonio's fault that he was born . . . as he was.'

'Well spoken, Signor Reni,' I said, satisfied that I had thrown everyone off-balance by my provocative and aggressive behaviour, as was my original plan. I returned the Taser pistol to my sleeve and looked at Antonio. 'I admire very much the work of your uncle and your father. I know that Caravaggio also admired the work of your uncle. As Signor Reni rightly points out, the circumstances of your birth are not your fault but one must look for the Devil's handiwork everywhere.' I pointedly looked at the playing cards on the table. 'Now, Signor

Reni, I need to ask you about the death of Caravaggio. You have heard of my quest and you know that I have a papal warrant that enjoins every witness to tell me the truth on pain of his or her immortal soul. Do you understand?'

'I understand,' Reni replied, and took a swig from his tankard. I noticed that his hand was shaking slightly.

Zampieri asked me: 'Would you prefer it if Carracci and I left the room so that you can speak to Reni in privacy?'

'Thank you for offering,' I replied, 'but I would prefer it if you stayed, to witness and verify Signor Reni's answers to my questions.'

'Very well,' Zampieri agreed.

I looked at Guido Reni and said: 'Everything that I have heard about your appearance, Signor Reni, is confirmed as I look at you now. You are very handsome and well-made in every respect.' Reni looked uncomfortable but said nothing, so I continued. 'Why do you not consort with women?'

Antonio, on my left, could not help sniggering. 'He knows Zampieri's wife too well. She is enough to put any man off women for life.' Instead of being angry, Zampieri smiled indulgently.

Reni said, bristling with annoyance: 'What has my relationships with women got to do with the death of Caravaggio?'

'Perhaps you were jealous because he was more of a man than you, as well as being the more talented artist.'

'I was certainly not jealous of him as a man and I certainly do not think he was a more talented artist than me.'

'Why did you copy his style?'

'That was only for a short while. He had achieved some interesting effects. Then I tired of his dramatic tricks and returned to the truth.'

'Are you a homosexual?'

Reni threw up his arms in exasperation. 'I am dedicated to my work, Signor Maddano. I have dedicated my life to the Virgin Mary. I consort with neither men nor women.'

'Only with the Devil's children,' I said, indicating the playing cards.

Antonio Carracci pushed back his chair in frustration. 'You have no need to justify yourself to this man, Guido. He is a foreigner. He is here only to blacken your good name. He is here to put the blame on anyone he can find for the extinction of the life of that Godless wretch Caravaggio. He is trying to frighten you like a priest frightens a congregation with fears of eternal damnation.'

'Young man,' I said, 'I am here to find out the truth. I am doing God's work. I am seeking justice for Caravaggio. I have been given powers by a higher authority that you cannot begin to understand, so keep your own counsel and do not interfere again.'

'What powers?' Antonio snorted. 'Is that what you meant by the Devil's books bursting into flames if you touch them?'

'That is one of my powers, yes.'

'You mean these playing cards on the table here,' Antonio persisted, playing right into my hands. 'You expect us to believe that, if you picked up a playing card, it would burst into flames?'

'Yes,' I said. From up my sleeve, I was already palming one of my special Magic Circle playing cards in readiness.

'Why don't you show us?' Antonio said.

Zampieri said: 'Signor Maddano has no need to demonstrate. He is here on more important business.'

Guido Reni regarded me with distaste. 'I agree with Antonio. Signor Maddano is obviously a friend and supporter of the late unlamented Caravaggio. I am not going to answer your questions, signor. I do not trust you.'

'You are commanded by the Holy Father to tell me the truth. You must answer my questions truthfully or risk eternal damnation.'

'I will not lie to you because I am not going to reply to your offensive questioning.'

I ignored Reni's statement and asked him: 'I want you to tell me about your relationship with . . .'

'Don't tell him anything, Guido,' Antonio shouted. 'He is a fake!'

'I agree, Antonio,' Reni said. 'Take your impertinent questions and take your leave of us.'

'If you will not answer my questions,' I said, 'then you will answer to the Devil.' From the table, I picked up a genuine playing card, conjured it out of sight up my sleeve so that the swap was not apparent and passed the trick playing card swiftly over the candle flame. It burst into blue flames, a chemical reaction which produced no heat, and I held it in my hand while passing my other hand through the flames. It was a fake tarot card, bearing a picture of the devil, which I made sure was visible to Guido Reni as it burned. The flames died out as rapidly as they had appeared and nothing was left of the card. All three men were stunned by what they had seen. Reni was terrified and gripped the edge of the table in panic. Zampieri was wide-eyed in shock, as was Antonio. He picked up another playing card and passed it through the candle flame as he had seen me do. Nothing happened. He tried time and time again and then held the card in the flame for sufficient time for it to genuinely catch fire but had to throw it on the floor and stamp it out when the heat seared his hand.

'As I was saying, Signor Reni, I want you to tell me about your relationship with Giuseppe Cesari, now known as the Cavaliere d'Arpino.'

All resistance and dissimulation from Reni had disappeared. 'The Cavaliere and I were both envious of the success that Caravaggio was making,' Reni said, his face as white as a ghost. 'I was back working in Bologna but the Cavaliere wrote to me urging me to return and join him in opposing Caravaggio.'

'So it was a concerted effort to ruin the reputation and career of a fellow artist?'

'Yes,' Reni admitted.

Zampieri shook his head in disgust. 'I warned you not to get involved with anything like that,' he said. 'We are all trying to make good pictures. There is room enough for everyone.'

'Caravaggio was a bully and a loudmouth,' Reni protested, trying to defend his position. 'He disrespected my paintings.'

'Really?' I said. 'He respected your talent and, as far as I can ascertain, did nothing to harm you. You, on the contrary, did very much harm to Caravaggio's friend Lionello Spada.'

'In what way?' Reni asked, cautiously.

'You were called in to judge the work that Spada had done on the church of Santa Maria di Loreto in the Marches. Who decided that you should be the arbiter of his work?'

'The church commissioners . . . the council of the church.'

'Why you?'

'I am a fully trained and distinguished artist,' Reni bristled. 'Why not me?'

'It's very unusual for an artist to be called in to judge the work of a fellow artist. Who ordered the church council to invite you to judge Spada's work?'

'I cannot tell you,' Reni replied.

'Cannot . . . or will not?'

'Cannot,' Reni said. Then: 'It was a cardinal, a powerful cardinal, but I do not know which one. I swear it.'

'Very well,' I said, 'I accept your reply. Anyway, there had been a commission issued to fresco the new sacristy at Santa Maria di Loreto. You passed judgement that Spada's work was not adequate and so he had no chance of winning the commission.'

'It was not adequate,' Reni insisted.

'Others thought it was very adequate, including Caravaggio, who was enraged on his friend's behalf. Isn't it the truth, Signor Reni, that Spada could be the greatest painter that ever lived but, with you sitting as judge, he could never have hoped to have won the commission. Isn't it the truth that, as far as you are concerned, Signor Reni, anyone who was a friend and follower of Caravaggio could not possibly hope to win any favour from you?'

Reni looked at me. I expected a denial but he said: 'Yes, that is true. But I did not win the commission either. It was given to Cristofero Roncalli. And he was given a beating-up because of it, thanks to your friend Caravaggio.'

'Caravaggio had nothing to do with that attack,' I lied. 'It was instigated by Spada.' I omitted the fact that Caravaggio had provided Spada with the appropriate Sicilian thug to carry out the attack.

Reni shrugged. Antonio Carracci had been drinking steadily and was slipping down in his chair. He seemed to be losing interest in events that had taken place long before he had arrived in Rome. Domenico Zampieri looked grave and uncomfortable. He was a lifelong friend of Reni but disapproved of Reni's machinations.

I said to Reni: 'You and the Cavaliere d'Arpino now hatched a plot to deprive Caravaggio himself of an important commission. He was summoned by Cardinal Pietro Aldobrandini with a view to painting an altarpiece of Saint Peter for the church of the Tre Fontane here in Rome. Somehow, the Cavaliere got wind of the cardinal's approach and went to him and persuaded him to grant the commission to you instead of Caravaggio. That is true, is it not?'

'Yes,' Reni agreed, abashed by my knowledge. 'Did Caravaggio know of this?'

'Yes, he did. And he was very angry. He and Spada were plotting revenge on you. I think you have been lucky to remain unscathed from Caravaggio's vengeance. Perhaps that is why you had him murdered when you heard of his imminent return to Rome after being pardoned for slaying Tomassoni?'

'I had nothing to do with Caravaggio being murdered,' Reni protested. 'I did not think he knew how we had plotted to deprive him of the Tre Fontane commission. I am not a murderer or an accomplice.'

Zampieri sat back in his chair and folded his arms in disapproval of his friend's actions. He had drunk a lot of wine but he held his senses together well. He gave the impression of a man of honour and integrity and nothing I had read about him in the art histories gave me cause to doubt that impression. I was certain that he was not a man to get caught up in the Byzantine plots of his fellow artists and equally certain that he had had nothing to do with Caravaggio's death.

I carried on interrogating Reni. 'Not content, Signor Reni, with depriving both Caravaggio and Spada of lucrative commissions, you then proceeded to publicly insult them and crow about your ascendancy in the art world in a painting of David contemplating the head of Goliath.'

'What makes you think that that picture was an insult?'

'Caravaggio himself explained the significance of the symbolism to me. Your insoucient pose as you gaze at the head of Goliath, which is a portrait of Caravaggio. You have your foot on a sword, a reference that you have trampled

Lionello Spada underfoot, and you are leaning on a broken column, a clear allusion that you have overcome the influence of the Colonna family.'

Guido Reni smiled. 'I'm glad that Caravaggio understood my message.'

'Only too well, signor.'

Zampieri interjected: 'I'm aware that you are a foreigner, Signor Maddano, and perhaps unfamiliar with the petty rivalries of the Roman art world but the inclusion of such hidden messages within paintings is fairly common. I don't think you should ascribe any undue malevolence to this painting you have mentioned. My friend Guido, like Caravaggio himself, is an ambitious and prickly character and very sensitive to the imagined slights and jealousies of our art world. It does not make him a murderer.'

'Loyally spoken, Signor Zampieri,' I said. 'So, I am going to ask Signor Reni directly, in fear of endangering his immortal soul, whether he had anything to do with the death of Caravaggio or has knowledge of anyone who did?'

Reni had recovered his nerves and replied emphatically: 'No, Signor Maddano. I swear on my immortal soul, in front of God and these witnesses, that I had no hand in Caravaggio's death. Equally, however, I cannot say I am sorry about it.'

Zampieri was exasperated by Reni's final sentence. 'Guido did not murder Caravaggio, nor I, nor poor drunken Antonio over there. Can we please get back to our game of cards . . . if we can find another pack now that you have ruined the old pack.'

'Certainly,' I said. 'Perhaps you will be good enough to see me out. I would hate to disturb your good lady wife again.' Antonio Carracci sniggered at this new reference to Zampieri's wife. I held out my hand for Antonio to shake and said: 'Goodnight, Signor Carracci. It has been a pleasure to meet a member of such an important artistic family.'

Antonio looked at my hand and made no move to take it. He said: 'I have no wish to catch fire by shaking your hand, signor.'

I bowed to Guido Reni and followed Domenico Zampieri out of the room and back through his studio. At the front door I said: 'My apologies for spoiling your evening, Signor Zampieri.'

'It has been . . . interesting,' he replied, with an uncertain smile. 'You are an unusual person, an exotic foreigner, Signor Maddano, so let me emphasise that my friend Guido is a strange mixture of courtesy and arrogance. He is not very bright. He allows himself to become involved in things that an artist has no place in being involved in. But he is not capable of murder. I would hate to see him destroyed. He is a very fine painter. His work will be remembered long after mine is forgotten.'

I knew that Domenico Zampieri, known as Domenichino, had enjoyed a reputation as an artist second only to Raphael himself during the 17th and 18th centuries. That reputation had, effectively, been destroyed during the 19th century by the effete British art critic John Ruskin, whose taste had been believed to be infallible but who had a distaste for all Bolognese artists, including Guido Reni. 'I have seen your work, Signor Zampieri, in the Palazzo Farnese and elsewhere, and I have seen Reni's work. I am sure that you will both be remembered by future generations as great artists.'

'But not as great as your friend Michelangelo Merisi da Caravaggio?' Zampieri replied, with a twinkle in his kindly eye.

I smiled, shook Zampieri's hand, and slipped out into the Roman night. After I had returned home I stood in my bedroom and, for many minutes, mentally considered and examined the ramifications of my dramatic meeting with Guido Reni but once again I finally had to conclude that I had hit another brick wall. I believed Reni's protestations of innocence in the matter of Caravaggio's murder and I reluctantly crossed off his name from my list of suspects. I had allowed myself to become excited that the hidden messages in Reni's painting of David with the head of Goliath might have been the clues that Merisi's murderer had referred to so enigmatically. Upon reflection, however, I was forced to conclude that those messages were simply another example of the interminable, incomprehensible and – to modern sensibilities – frankly childish power plays in the Roman art world of the seventeenth century.

34

The next morning, over breakfast, I told Merisi about my dramatic encounter with Guido Reni. Merisi was genuinely amused and gratified by the effect of my magic tricks on his hated rival. He began to talk volubly about some of the other petty feuds prevalent in the enclosed word of Roman art in his century but, interesting as it was, I eventually managed to steer him away from that topic and back to the reason why we were working together. I made our morning coffee and we took our places in our fireside armchairs. I opened my notebook and Helen Langdon's biography of Caravaggio. 'I'd like to begin,' I said, 'by examining what I consider to be one of your most tender and moving pictures, the Madonna of Loreto.' (*Plate 41*).

'Ah, yes,' Merisi said. 'I was asked to do this altarpiece for the church of San' Agostino. The cult of the Madonna of Loreto was very popular at the time. Loreto is a small town in the Marches, to the east of Rome, which contained the holy house of the Virgin Mary. The house had flown to Loreto from the Holy Land sometime in about 1290 or thereabouts, and it was . . . what are you smiling about?'

'I'm sorry, Michele, but my ChronoTranslator must be faulty. I thought you said that the house of the Virgin Mary had flown to Loreto.'

'Yes, indeed it did. To escape damage from a war that was going on.'

Merisi's face was completely straight, so I said: 'Surely people didn't really believe that this house had actually flown from the Holy Land. It's a very unlikely story, to say the least!'

'Of course people believed it,' Merisi said, staring at me with a puzzled expression. 'God can do anything He likes. He made the house fly to safety.'

'Oh, come off it,' I protested. 'That's impossible!'

Merisi frowned and looked at me for several seconds. He said: 'You are sitting here in England, in the 21st century, talking to an Italian artist who died four hundred years ago. You now implicitly believe that I am Michelangelo Merisi da Caravaggio. You have told me yourself how human beings have learned to fly and you have proved to me that a human being has actually walked on the

Moon. And yet you cannot believe that the house of the Virgin Mary could fly from the Holy Land to Italy. You are very selective in your disbelief, aren't you?'

'My apologies, Michele,' I replied. 'I was brought up and educated in a cynical and faithless age. You are absolutely right. Please carry on.'

Merisi, mollified, said: 'You tell me what you like about my painting?'

'I very much like its warmth and sincerity,' I answered. 'It has those qualities perhaps more than any other of your works that we know about. The Madonna looks down at the pilgrims with genuine tenderness and love. And the two pilgrims return her look with warm and sincere adulation. It is such a welcoming and human work. Your work is always full of surprises, Michele. You are, I think, the most complex and surprising man I've ever known or heard about. Who modelled for the Madonna?'

'I cannot remember,' Merisi said, 'but I had someone in mind when I was painting the figure. Someone I once loved.'

'Can't you tell me who it was?'

'I won't tell you who it was,' Merisi said. 'It is of no consequence to our enquiries and I will not reveal all of my heart to you, or to anyone else.'

I could see it was no use to press him, for the time being, so I said: 'Well, it's another of your revolutionary paintings. Never before in the history of art had such humble pilgrims been put at the centre of an important altarpiece. Although you have been criticised, subsequently, for giving one of the pilgrims such dirty feet.'

'I was criticised during my lifetime,' Merisi laughed. 'You see, some people, perhaps most people, certainly in those days, could not bear to look at stark truth and reality when it came to matters of faith. That truth and reality is what I tried to express, always, in my work. What else would a humble pilgrim's feet be but dirty? It does not make one less pious or worthy to be dirty!'

I nodded in agreement. 'We know that this painting was a popular success with the so-called humble people who saw it during your lifetime. It is a work full of comfort and consolation. Unfortunately, however, an event took place that would have an adverse impact on your success and popularity.'

'What do you mean?'

'The death of Pope Clement.'

'Ah, yes,' Merisi said mournfully. 'That sad event was certainly unfortunate for me and for many other painters.'

'This was early in the year 1605?'

'Yes, that is correct. The French population of Rome were in despair and deep mourning over the death of the pope because their beloved Clement had absolved the king of France, Henry, from his mortal sin of supporting the heretics and had brought him back into the Catholic fold. But their despair turned to jubilation when, very unexpectedly, Alexander de Medici was elected as Pope Leo. Leo was very pro-French and had been elected mainly as the result of tireless diplomacy by the French ambassador, Philip de Béthune.'

'This was the same man who had secured your release from prison after the Baglione libel trial?'

'The very same,' Merisi confirmed. 'But then tragedy struck again because the new pope, Leo, died after barely a month in office. He had been very frail anyway. His death plunged Rome into total anarchy. It will be perhaps difficult to understand, in your modern democratic and structured society, just how important the office of the pope was in my country and in my century. Without a pope, all government, nearly all of the justice system and, of course, decisions on all spiritual matters were suspended. Prisoners were released from jail and riots between Spanish and French factions returned to the streets, each side hoping for a new pope who would favour their side. The election of the new pope turned into a scandalous farce and a schism threatened but, thanks to the wisdom of a few cardinals, a compromise candidate was elected. He was Pope Paul, whom you met earlier in your time travels.'

'Yes. From what I have read, he was politically neutral but, when it came to art, he did not favour your new naturalistic style.'

'Alas, that is so true, Stefano.' Merisi shook his head sadly. 'Pope Paul preferred the grandiose, classical style of my old rivals like Zuccaro, the Cavaliere d'Arpino and that arse-licker Guido Reni. Reni's style became popular with the pope and therefore with everyone. At the same time, the opinions of one cardinal, Agucchi, were becoming more prevalent in the Roman art world. He considered that I had abandoned beauty for dark naturalism. I prefer to say that I abandoned false hope for the truth, but that is by the way. I was out of favour and that was that. If it had not been for the good taste and support of the pope's nephew, Cardinal Scipione Borghese, I would have been completely out in the cold.'

'At the very same time that your new dark naturalism was falling out of favour, your pictures from around this time seem to be becoming even darker and more austere.'

'Which ones do you mean?' Merisi asked.

'Well, your studies of Saint Jerome, a thin old man with a skull as a memento mori on his writing desk, (*Plate 42*) and Saint Francis wearing a heavy frayed robe, and Saint John the Baptist as a young man, with rough and reddened hands, almost lost in darkness. (*Plate 39*). These are intensely melancholy pictures, Michele. Are they a reflection of your mood at this time?'

'Very much so,' Merisi replied. 'I had tired of being a courtier, always at the beck and call of a Del Monte or a Giustiniani or a Mattei. I rented a house in the Vicolo dei Santi Cecilia e Biagio. I could just about afford to be independent and I just had enough money coming in to employ a servant, Francesco, who was also my apprentice. I remember that Annibale Carracci felt the same way, that he wanted to be more independent, to paint subjects that truly interested him but poor Annibale took things to heart too much. His mind went and it took him a long time to recover. Yes, they were melancholy times.'

'We know something about your house,' I said. 'It was on a narrow street with the walls of the Palazzo Firenze just opposite.' Merisi nodded. 'And we know of some of the things you owned then. Poor things . . . a few pieces of cutlery and crockery, old and well-used furniture, a few clothes, a few books, a knife, a sword, a guitar and a violin. But your bed seems to have been more luxurious, with two columns attached, and a truckle bed for your servant underneath.'

Merisi smiled. 'Yes, the bed was comfortable. And I miss my guitar. That instrument gave me much consolation.'

'And yet you never included a guitar in any of your pictures,' I said, 'at least, the ones that survive. Why is that?'

'It's a good point,' Merisi conceded. 'I don't know. Probably because the guitar was too personal to me.' He shrugged. 'I don't know.'

'It seems like a rough and basic bachelor existence.'

'It was, and yet Guido Reni could afford to rent not one but two palazzi! And the Cavaliere d'Arpino, with his new-found popularity, could afford to buy his own palazzo on the Corso! Zuccaro's palace we already know about. And yet Carracci and I, far better painters than any of that trio, were living in poverty.'

'How did they do it?' I asked.

'Creeping, arse-licking, sucking up to anyone who had the power and the money. To these men, prestige and success were far more important than artistic truth.'

'You were living in the most crowded part of Rome and the streets were becoming increasingly dangerous.'

'Yes, there seemed to be more and more ruffians prowling the streets. More and more fights in the taverns.'

'Which, no doubt, you joined in enthusiastically?'

Merisi smiled. 'Sometimes,' he conceded, 'but I was, by now, well over thirty years of age and my appetite for street and tavern fighting was waning. I remember that there was a big riot between the French and Spanish factions on the Campo Marzio about this time. I refused to get involved. Just as well because many rioters were wounded badly, some killed. I had enough trouble from the Tomassoni clan.'

'Tomassoni?' I repeated. 'In what way?'

'They all lived literally just around the corner from me. Giovan Francesco Tomassoni was the caporione of the Campo Marzio, in charge of the local lay police force. His brothers, Alessandro and Ranuccio, helped him enforce the law with enthusiasm. They would swagger around their patch, armed to the teeth with swords and daggers, throwing their weight about and, of course, I was their prime target. After our clashes over Fillide Melandroni there was a lot of bad blood between Ranuccio Tomassoni and me. I wasn't about to let that jumped-up prick get the better of me. And Baglione became the caporione in the Castello district so, wherever I went, these arseholes were on my case . . . watching me, threatening me over any slight misdemeanour. They were just waiting for me to step out of line.'

'So, all the seeds of your later clash with Ranuccio Tomassoni were being sown at this time.'

'Yes. I suppose it had to end with one of us dead and, happily, it was that cunt and not me.'

'We know that you were running into various other difficulties with the law at this time. You were arrested for carrying arms without a permit and . . .'

'I had to carry arms!' Merisi protested. 'I had to protect myself from the Tomassoni clan, whatever the law said!'

'Okay, but a couple of months later you were thrown into the Tor di Nona prison again for attacking the house of Laura and Isabella della Vecchia.'

Merisi made a dismissive gesture. 'That was nothing. I had been fucking Isabella after she had done some modelling for me. Her mother Laura found out and started screaming in the street at me, saying that I was a pimp and a rapist or something or other. So I went round to her house and smashed a few windows and threw rocks at her front door.'

I looked at Merisi and shook my head. 'Couldn't you have just let it go?' I asked. 'I keep coming up against this dichotomy in your nature. The same man who could paint a picture as tender, as human and moving as the Madonna of Loreto, acts like a petulant child just because he has been confronted by an outraged mother. And there was much worse to come just a few days later.'

'Oh, fuck it,' Merisi said, getting up from his armchair. 'Let's go out and get drunk instead of sitting here raking up all these memories.' He stalked out of the room and, a few seconds later, I heard the front door slam. I knew why he had become so upset. He might have left the house but he didn't have any money and I didn't think he would go very far. I decided to let him cool off and I took the opportunity to study two paintings that Merisi had completed in 1605 for a client named Massimo Massimi. Both pictures, now known as Crowning with Thorns and Ecce Homo (*Plate 43*) were simple yet powerful depictions of Christ just before His crucifixion. I looked at them carefully but it was difficult to imagine that they contained any secret messages about why Merisi was murdered. I was only too conscious that I was continually groping for straws, although a thread of clues was, I considered, beginning to appear. I looked up to see Merisi, coatless, wandering around the garden. It was, very unusually, a frosty morning for so late in the Spring and the trees down by the river were rimed with white hoar frost, which Merisi seemed to find fascinating. I went out to the kitchen and made us another mug of coffee and took them back into the living room. I tapped on the window to attract Merisi's attention and held up a mug to offer him the lure of his favourite beverage. The ploy worked. He walked back to the house and I opened the patio door to let him in.

'The frost is beautiful, don't you think?' I said.

'Yes. We very rarely saw it in Rome. I would like to paint it one day.'

We sat down and I said: 'Something else that was very beautiful was Lena.'

I thought Merisi would bridle at the name but he remained relaxed. 'Yes,' he agreed, 'she was very beautiful.'

'Were you very much in love with her?' Merisi shrugged, unwilling to talk about it. I continued: 'There is nothing to be ashamed of in loving someone so much.'

'How do you know I was so much in love with Lena?' Merisi challenged me.

'Because Lena was the model for the Virgin Mary in the Madonna of Loreto. That is why you could create such a tender and beautiful image of her, because you were in love with her.'

'Fuck it. You have caught me in a trap again,' Merisi said, but with good humour. 'I admit it, I was very much in love with Maddalena.'

'Your own actions in viciously attacking your love rival also give you away, Michele. Please tell me about Lena.'

Merisi sighed and took a sip of coffee. 'The first time I ever saw Lena I became totally besotted by her dark beauty, her dark flashing eyes. I desperately wanted to paint her. But she was not a whore, as most of my female models were. She came from a poor but respectable family. I approached her family. Lena's mother reluctantly allowed Lena to model for me but the greedy old cow charged me a lot of money for the privilege. So Lena came to my house to model for me.'

'Did you sleep with her?'

'No, to my infinite regret, I did not. Lena was an honourable and virtuous girl. She had a suitor, a notary named Mariano da Pasqualone, who wished to marry Lena but Lena had rejected his suit because of his job, which cursed him with damnation.' I did not understand this comment but I did not want to interrupt. Merisi went on: 'Pasqualone found out that Lena was visiting my studio and assumed that we were having an affair. He went to Lena's mother and protested vehemently. He called me an "excommunicant and cursed man". I went looking for Pasqualone. My blood was on fire. Not only had he insulted me but he was a rival for a woman I loved. I came across him on the Piazza Navona and I immediately went after him with my knife. He was with someone else so I tried to hide my face with a black cloak I was wearing so that they could not identify me. I slashed the bastard three or four times. He went down, and then I ran away.'

'Oh, Michele,' I said, 'you have an amazing talent for destroying what you love through the wrong actions.'

Merisi looked crestfallen. 'You are right,' he admitted. 'I am not proud of this incident. Of course, Lena's mother refused to let her anywhere near me after this. A warrant was issued for my arrest so I cleared off to Genoa to let things cool off.'

'Why did you choose Genoa?' I asked.

'I didn't exactly choose it,' Merisi said, ruefully. 'Costanza Colonna got wind of my trouble with the law and ordered me to go to Genoa. The Doria family were powerful in Genoa and the Doria and Colonna families were connected by marriage. I think Costanza's niece was a Doria. Genoa was a good choice as a refuge. It was a rich city so, if I had had to stay there, I could have found plenty of commissions.'

'Talking of commissions,' I said, 'is it true that one of the Doria clan, Marcantonio, offered you 6,000 scudi to fresco his villa?'

'Yes, it is true,' Merisi said, uncomfortably. 'At first, I agreed.'

'I'm not surprised! Six thousand scudi is an enormous sum compared with what you had been earning!'

'But, eventually, I turned down the commission for two reasons.'

'What were they?' I asked.

'Firstly, I was very inexperienced in fresco work. I didn't want to accept such a commission and make such a poor job of it that I became the subject of ridicule from my fellow artists. Secondly, and more importantly, I had the chance to get back to Rome sooner than I thought. Back to Lena, to see if there was still a chance of getting back with her.'

'And was there?'

'No. Lena, not to mention her mother, had been appalled by my attack on Pasqualone. They refused to have anything to do with me. As you have rightly said, Stefano, my talent for destroying the things I love by the wrong actions is unsurpassed. I was a complete idiot.'

'It's about this time, just after you returned to Rome, that Cardinal Del Monte had to apologise for your behaviour, with a memorable phrase, to the Duke of Modena. Apparently, you owed the duke a picture and, because of all your troubles, you were late in delivering it.'

'Yes, that's right,' Merisi confirmed. 'What did the cardinal say about me?'

'He said you were "stravagantissimo", which translates into English as something like your "extravagant brain". In other words, you were a very odd person.'

Merisi laughed ruefully. 'Who am I to argue with the good cardinal?'

'Anyway, it was another cardinal, Scipione Borghese, who saved your skin, albeit at the cost of a humiliating apology to Pasqualone.'

'Yes,' Merisi said, 'it was, indeed, humiliating, but it allowed me to return to Rome. Scipione Borghese brokered a peace between Pasqualone and me at the price of my apology. It was signed and witnessed at the Palazzo di Quirinale. In gratitude, I gave Cardinal Borghese my painting of Saint Jerome. He was very pleased. He still liked my work even if nobody else did!'

'There is a very great English dramatist named William Shakespeare, who lived at the same time as you did, who once said: "When troubles come, they come not as single spies, but in battalions". Your troubles, self-inflicted as they were at this time, just keep on piling up. On the very day that you signed your peace with Pasqualone, your landlady, Prudenzia Bruna, legally sequestered all your goods and barred you from your house, which was next to hers. Apparently, you had not paid your rent for four months.'

'I had been exiled in Genoa for a few weeks!' Merisi protested. 'I had not been able to paint. I didn't have any commissions at all. I didn't have any money to pay the rent but that cow Bruna would not give me any leeway.'

'With your usual fine judgement and understanding, you went to Prudenzia Bruna's house and threw stones at her windows until you damaged her blinds. Then you went away and returned with some rowdy friends of yours, shouting insults at her and playing the guitar loudly in the street. So she took you to court again.'

'Yes,' Merisi agreed, curtly.

'Here you are in the autumn of 1605, having once been the most famous and successful painter in Rome, homeless, penniless, and now you manage to get yourself mysteriously wounded in another street fight.'

'Yes. What of it?'

'Fortunately for you, a lawyer friend named Andrea Ruffetti gave you shelter.'

'Yes. I was grateful to Ruffetti. I painted his portrait for no fee.'

'A notary visited you to inquire about your wounds and you offered the lame excuse that you had fallen down some stairs and wounded yourself with your own sword!'

'I didn't want that prod-nose knowing the truth of what had happened,' Merisi said.

'What was the truth, Michele?'

'I had had a run-in over Fillide with Ranuccio Tomassoni. He had got the better of me and wounded me in the neck and the ear.'

'Why didn't you tell the notary and have Tomassoni prosecuted?'

'Firstly, the embarrassment of people knowing that Tomassoni had got the better of me would have been unbearable. Secondly, I was saving my revenge for that bastard. I wanted him to have something more memorable than a legal prosecution. I wanted him to taste cold steel!'

I shook my head in frustration at hearing of yet another of these childish and egotistical confrontations of honour. 'And yet,' I continued, 'in the midst of all this misfortune, when you were at your lowest ebb since you first arrived in Rome, you had been given a commission that could have completely restored your fortunes, your reputation, everything. A commission for an altarpiece for the most important church, not just in Rome, but in all Christendom . . . St. Peter's.' (*Plate 44*).

Merisi nodded. 'It was for the altar of the Palafrenieri. They were the papal Company of Grooms. Their altar had been removed from the nave of their old church and re-sited to the right-hand transept of the basilica of St. Peter's. They wanted a replacement for their old altarpiece. The new one was to show Saint Anne, who was their patron saint, with the Virgin Mary and the infant Christ. Up until then I had been excluded from commissions for St. Peter's, an exclusion that had made me very resentful. Such commissions had gone to painters like Roncalli, Cigoli, Passignano and the like, but they were now all copying my style so the officials of the Palafrenieri decided, quite rightly, to employ the real thing rather than all these weak imitators.'

'Talking of weakness, and forgive me for saying so, but I think that for this, perhaps the most important commission you could hope to win, you produced a work that is one of the weakest and most unsatisfactory works that you ever painted.'

'Very well,' Merisi replied, angrily. 'You are a renowned art critic who never picked up a fucking paint brush in your life. Tell me where I went wrong?'

'The figures of the Virgin Mary and the infant Christ crushing the serpent are excellent but your depiction of Saint Anne is a disaster. You have made the mother of the Virgin Mary look like a witch, a hideous old crone. She stands there, stiff and awkward, dressed like a peasant.'

'Now you sound like Cardinal Agucchi!' Merisi protested. 'The mother of the Virgin Mary must have been a humble woman. Truth and naturalism were my whole ethos as a painter!'

'Couldn't you, just for this important picture for St. Peter's, have given the Palafrenieri what they wanted, a noble and spiritual portrait of their patron saint?'

'That is why I am a great artist and a great man while you are not,' Merisi said, petulantly. 'You would have done what everybody else was doing. You would have done what Zuccaro and Reni and d'Arpino and Roncalli and everybody else, except Carracci, would have given them; a nice sweet, sanitised, saintly lie!'

'Why did you make Christ so obviously . . . naked?' I persisted. 'It was bound to be seen as offensive, His willy pointing at the snake.'

'He is an infant!'

'He is the son of God! And, anyway, the whole composition is lumpen and static. I find it very unsatisfactory.'

'Well, fuck you,' Merisi said and, for a moment, I thought he was going to walk out on me again.

'The only satisfactory figure,' I resumed, after a few seconds, 'is the Virgin Mary. She is very beautiful. It is Lena again, isn't it?'

'Yes,' Merisi said, grudgingly. 'I had made a study of her for this very picture just before all the trouble with Pasqualone started. She posed for me in that low-cut dress. It drove me to distraction. I desired her so much but she always rejected my advances.'

'Well, she is clearly the only element in this picture that you were interested in.'

'That's not true,' Merisi protested. 'I did my best.'

'I don't think I believe you,' I said. 'You are not familiar with the modern science of psychology but it teaches that sometimes people can be more afraid of success than of failure. Too much success puts them under pressure to succeed again, to live up to expectations. This seems to be the case throughout your life.'

'Bullshit,' Merisi snorted.

'Perhaps. But at least I have uncovered two more suspects who may have been complicit in your attempted murder.'

'Who? Lena and Pasqualone?'

'Yes. I think I will have to pay them a visit through the ChronoConverter tonight, if Pellegrino can arrange it.'

'There is no need, Stefano. Pasqualone died before me.'

'Oh. How did he die?'

'I heard that he had made a journey, on business, to Venice, where he caught the plague. I was in exile away from Rome at this time. I suppose Lena must have been deeply upset by his death but I also know she married before my supposed death.'

'Well,' I said, 'it might still be worth visiting her. She might have been so upset at your vicious attack on Pasqualone that she sought revenge on you.'

'Lena was a gentle soul, a Christian and God-fearing girl. I consider it extremely unlikely that she would seek my death. And, as I said, she had married. Why should she risk any new-found happiness by trying to settle an old score with me?'

Merisi's comments persuaded me that travelling back in time to interview Maddalena would be fruitless, but I was disappointed. I had wanted to meet her out of sheer curiosity, to see what she was like, but I bowed to Merisi's opinion, untrustworthy as it was. 'That's enough for now,' I said. 'Let's have some lunch and then we will have to talk about the most famous incident in your life, and the family that probably most desired your death.'

'You know how to ruin my appetite,' Merisi answered, gloomily.

35

After lunch Merisi seemed unusually tense, as I had fully expected. He waited in his armchair, without speaking, and sipped his coffee meditatively. He knew that we were going to talk about the most famous and the most regrettable incident in the long and lamentable list of his misdemeanours. He was reluctant to do so.

'We have to talk about these events, Michele,' I said encouragingly.

Merisi nodded. 'I know.'

I looked at him and he gestured for me to go ahead. 'It was in late May, 1606. We know that, a few days earlier, you had had another run-in with your bitter enemy and love rival, Ranuccio Tomassoni. What was that about?'

'Fillide Melandroni,' Merisi replied, curtly.

'Was this incident caused by the fact that Fillide preferred Tomassoni to you?'

'What makes you think that?'

'Records that survive from this time. Comments from biographers and historians of the time. It suggests that Fillide preferred Tomassoni's company to yours.'

Merisi pursed his lips. He was breathing heavily. 'Yes. I have to admit it was true. That is why I was so angry, so determined to get revenge.'

'I know it's painful to discover that the woman you love prefers another man but injuring that man is the worst way to try to get her back.'

'Do you speak from experience?' Merisi challenged me.

'My experience is not being discussed here,' I replied prissily, but Merisi had caught me on a raw nerve. He could see it and he grinned at me sarcastically. He said: 'I was not trying to get Fillide back but, if I couldn't have her, I didn't want Tomassoni to have her.'

I said: 'From what we know, Tomassoni had had her many times.' I instantly regretted this crass remark.

Merisi pounced. 'Even you, a cold-blooded Englishman, knows how bad it feels to have your pride and your manhood diminished. It happened to you when your wife walked out. It is important for a man to know that he can make a woman happy. You try to wound me because you understand what it feels like to be wounded, so you strike out blindly and savagely, only you do it with your tongue, like a woman. I used a sword, like a man.'

'You are right, Michele. I apologise for my stupid and hurtful comment.' My apology was only half meant.

'Very well, it's forgotten, Stefano. Woman drive us men crazy until we don't know what we are doing. Some women don't understand the power they wield. Fillide did . . . only too well.'

'So you had had another argument with Ranuccio Tomassoni over Fillide?'

'Yes. On the evening in question, the bad blood that had been simmering between Tomassoni and me was more than ready to boil over. We had agreed to meet and settle things once and for all, at a tennis court near the Palazzo Firenze in the Via della Scrofa. As I walked to the tennis court with my friends, we had to pass the Tomassoni house. The Tomassoni clan saw us walk past. Ranuccio rushed to get his sword and they followed us to the tennis court.'

I said: 'We know that a Bolognese soldier named Petronio Toppa was waiting at the court to be your second. And we know that you were accompanied by Onorio Longhi and another friend. We don't know who this friend was. Can you tell me?'

'It was Lionello Spada,' Merisi answered.

'Ah, your friend Spada, the so-called "ape of Caravaggio". That is a surprise. Historians have surmised that it might have been Mario Minnitti or, perhaps, Prospero Orsi.'

'No,' Merisi said. 'Lionello detested Ranuccio Tomassoni even more than I did but he did not have the skill with a sword that I did. Or my hot temper.'

'Why did Spada detest Ranuccio so much? Was he also involved with Fillide?'

'No, not that I know of, but any enemy of mine was an enemy of Lionello's.'

I nodded. 'We know that Ranuccio was accompanied by his formidable brother, Giovan Francesco, and his two brothers-in-law. Can you confirm that?'

'Yes, that is correct.'

'You all arrived at the tennis court. What happened next?'

'The two factions had been hurling insults at each other and Tomassoni and I were more than ready to go at each other. We drew our swords and started fighting. Ranuccio was fairly skilled and fairly tough but, in fair fight, he was no match for me, although he gave me a hard time for quite a while. Eventually, though, he had had enough and tried to disengage. I was fighting mad and, made senseless by blood lust, I had a crazy idea that I would aim for his balls and castrate the fucker, if I could. Just as I thrust forward at his crotch, he lurched towards me again. My sword ran him through the stomach. He collapsed. His brother Giovan Francesco leapt in between us to protect Ranuccio. I was shocked by what had happened and had lowered my sword. Giovan Francesco came at me, enraged by what I had done to his brother. I defended myself and then Petronio Toppa came to my aid. Giovan Francesco was an altogether tougher customer than his brother. He was a soldier, experienced in battle as well as street fighting. He had wounded me in the head before Toppa could intervene but Toppa was just as tough as Giovan and the two of them ended up wounding each other badly.'

'What was Longhi and Spada doing while all this was going on?' I asked.

'I don't know exactly. They told me afterwards that they were holding off Ranuccio's brothers-in-law but I remembered that the two pairs were on opposite sides of the tennis court. I suspect that my friends didn't have the stomach for a fight.'

'I thought Onorio Longhi was always ready for a fight?'

'A street brawl, perhaps,' Merisi said. 'Throwing stones, shouting insults, fisticuffs in a tavern perhaps, but my feeling was that he and Spada were scared stiff of what was going on between me and Ranuccio.'

'Okay,' I said. 'Ranuccio was carried back to his house where he took confession and eventually died of his wounds.'

'Yes,' Merisi said. He looked at me pleadingly. 'I did not mean to kill him. I wanted to hurt him, to beat him. But not kill him. I had beaten him. He was pulling away. I should have stopped then but I wanted to wound him one more time and then he suddenly came towards me again. I could not stop the thrust of my sword. I felt it enter his body. I can still feel it to this day.'

'Easy, Michele,' I said, trying to reassure him. 'I'm not here to judge you.'

'No, but I will have to answer to God one day. I should have answered to Him four hundred years ago. Let's have a drink.'

It was still early afternoon but I could see that Merisi needed something to settle him down. I poured us a couple of bourbons, a large one for Merisi and a small one for me. Merisi took a large gulp and it did, indeed, calm him down. He said: 'Petronio Toppa, who may have saved my life, was badly wounded. He was taken to a barber and his wounds were treated. He had been deeply cut on his left arm and had stab wounds on his leg. Because of the severity of Toppa's bloody wounds I think the barber must have alerted the police because Toppa ended up in prison in the Tor di Nona. There was a hell of an uproar. Longhi fled back to his native Milan. I don't know where Spada went. The Tomassonis fled to Parma where they were under the protection of the Farnese family.'

'What about you? Where did you go?'

'Initially, Longhi and Spada got me to the Palazzo Giustiniani. They took me in for a while and then alerted the Palazzo Colonna where, luckily for me, Costanza Colonna was in residence. She had my wounds treated and I rested up for a few days and then she spirited me out of Rome and into Colonna territory in the Alban Hills.'

'Did you think of retreating to Milan?' I asked. 'After all, that was your home town and it was under the protection of the Colonna family.'

'No. I was too well known in Milan. Too many enemies there.'

I decided, at the risk of causing Merisi to walk out again, to suggest another possible cause of the vicious feud between Ranuccio Tomassoni and himself. 'You have told me,' I said, 'that this fight was over Fillide Melandroni, which is mostly true. How long had you been spreading gossip about Ranuccio's wife Lavinia?'

Merisi was surprised. For a moment I thought he was going to deny any such underhand behaviour but then he smiled. 'Bravo, Stefano,' he said. 'You are a clever bastard.'

'Not really,' I said, 'but you and Ranuccio had been sniping at each other for years. As far back as 1599 you had legally agreed not to attack Ranuccio, and vice versa. The way this trouble erupted on this murderous night in 1606 suggests that something out of the ordinary had happened between you two. The fact that Ranuccio's brother and brothers-in-law accompanied him to this fight suggests that there was a matter of family honour involved. I believe you found out that Ranuccio was being cuckolded by a man named Fabbio Romanino de Sanctis and you began to spread this gossip and taunted Ranuccio with it.'

Merisi drank another slug of bourbon. 'Lavinia had been constantly upset by Ranuccio's infidelities, particularly with Fillide. She fell in love with this man de Sanctis. They were having an affair behind Ranuccio's back. Lionello Spada found out about it and told me. This was like manna from heaven for me. Ranuccio being cuckolded! Of course I taunted him with the knowledge but he refused to believe me. He fancied himself as such a charmer, such a ladies man, that no man could be more attractive to his wife than he was, despite his affair with Fillide. The whole honour of the Tomassoni family was at stake. You are right, Stefano. My duel with Ranuccio Tomassoni was as much about family honour as it was about rivalry over a woman. Very clever, my friend.' He lifted his glass in salute.

'I didn't know for sure,' I said. 'I just put two and two together. After Ranuccio's death, Lavinia refused to take care of their daughter Plautilla, as did Plautilla's grandmother. And, with almost indecent haste, Lavinia married her lover, de Sanctis. With one thrust of your sword, you not only destroyed the life of Ranuccio Tomassoni but you made an orphan of Plautilla Tomassoni.'

'I did not know that,' Merisi said ruefully. 'Violence affects not only the victim but their loved ones as well. I acted shamefully. We all acted shamefully. I bitterly regret the whole business.'

'Well, you suffered the consequences, Michele. We know that the wheels of the legal process took a long time to turn and that, for a while, it looked as if the consequences of your actions would not be too serious. An inquiry was held and some of the participants, like Toppa, gave evidence. Your friend Longhi and Ranuccio's brothers-in-law were exiled from Rome for a few years. Spada disappeared. Giovan Francesco Tomassoni, as a close relative of the victim, was in the clear. But you, as the actual perpetrator of the killing, were the subject of the banda capitale.'

Merisi's eyes betrayed the pain of the memory as he looked at me. 'Do you know what was meant by the banda capitale?' he asked.

'You tell me,' I replied. 'I know it was an unusually harsh sentence.'

'Harsh!' Merisi echoed. 'The banda capitale meant that anyone, in any place, could legally take my life. Could legally kill me. I became a fugitive from Rome. My life was worth nothing. You know how many enemies I had made, how many people detested me. They must have been rubbing their hands with glee at a sentence like that.'

'Well,' I said, 'that is what we are doing here, attempting to find out which of them, if any, acted upon this sentence and tried to assassinate you. You fled from Rome into Colonna territory. Can you remember where you went?'

'Thanks to Costanza Colonna, who had arranged to smuggle me out of Rome, I found shelter in the small town of Zagarolo, up in the Alban Hills. I was protected by Prince Marzio Colonna, whose Palazzo Colonna was a huge impregnable fortress. I moved around between Zagarolo and Paliano and Palestrina so that no-one who was pursuing me could be exactly sure where I was at any given time. All these towns were in Colonna territory.'

'Extraordinarily,' I said, 'you were still painting pictures.'

'It was the one consolation that remained to me, as it had been throughout my life.'

'In both of your pictures from this time, your guilt and remorse are clear from the way you painted them.'

'Which ones do you mean?' Merisi asked. 'It was such a confusing time.' I showed him his Mary Magdalen (*Plate 45*) and his second version of the Supper at Emmaus, (*Plate 46*) the subject of the painting in the National Gallery that I had loved most of my life and which had brought us together. 'Ah, yes,' Merisi said. 'The Mary Magdalen reflects the way I felt at that time. Exhausted, weary, desolate, abandoned by God, betrayed by my own inner demons. I sent it back to Rome for Orsi to sell. I hoped that it would be seen as an expression of my remorse and might help my rehabilitation.'

'What about the Supper at Emmaus? Who was that for?'

'That was a gift for Prince Marzio Colonna, to thank him for protecting me. I used my first version of the subject as the basis for this one but, as you rightly point out, the mood is completely different. Gone is the cocky and confident young artist who was taking the art world by storm. This is the work of a repentant sinner, a man cast out into the wilderness, a man with blood on his hands, a man who has ruined lives. In Christ, we can perhaps attain forgiveness and redemption. In meekness and humility, perhaps we can forgive ourselves. I had committed a grave sin against God. Anyone who looks at this picture can see that and, I hope, see my anguish.'

'Michele,' I said, 'you know very well how I love your first version of the Supper at Emmaus, but this second version is a more profound picture. I can imagine you up in the Alban Hills, working alone, with this crushing weight of sin on your shoulders, and I find this work very moving. With this picture, you gave the world a priceless gift.'

Merisi grunted. 'It could not give back Ranuccio his life. Or Plautilla her father. It would have been a more valuable work of art not to have acted as I did in the first place.'

'We are all victims of our own personality, our own impulses. Ranuccio was as much to blame as you were.'

'Perhaps,' Merisi said, unconvinced.

'Anyway, there were people back in Rome who were quick to cash in on your misfortune,' I said.

'In what way?'

'The Palafrenieri at the Vatican sold your Madonna to Cardinal Scipione Borghese and made a handsome profit.'

'Good for them, the tasteless bastards.'

'Laerzio Cherubini cashed in on your new-found infamy by putting the Death of the Virgin on the market. Doctor Mancini tried to buy it for two hundred scudi but it was eventually bought by the Flemish painter Peter Paul Rubens, who admired it enormously, for his patron the Duke of Mantua.'

'So the flies were buzzing around the corpse,' Merisi smiled.

'Yes, indeed. And your old friend Giovanni Baglione was attacked and almost murdered by a young painter named Bodello. Baglione claimed that you and your supporters had hired this young assassin.'

'What!' Merisi exclaimed. 'Isn't that typical of Baglione. Everything was my fault. Was it my fault that he was a lousy painter? I bet he was overjoyed by my predicament.'

'Possibly so,' I conceded. 'What made you eventually leave the protection of Colonna territory?'

'I had hoped that I could very soon return to Rome but it became apparent that that would be impossible for a very long time. And then the imposition of the banda capitale made it extremely dangerous to be anywhere near Rome. I still wanted to continue my career, to paint pictures, so I decided to leave Colonna territory and move to Naples.'

I said: 'It's been a difficult day's work, Michele. Let's stop and relax for the rest of the day. I am going to call Pellegrino. I think it's high time that I talked to the delectable and dangerous Fillide Melandroni.'

'Delectable and dangerous are accurate words, Stefano. Remember them when you meet her. Like a queen spider, she lures men into her web and then sucks them dry. Even so, how I wish I could see her again.'

36

The ChronoConverter landed me in a dusty little alleyway which was stacked high with empty wooden barrels on either side. A mangy dog was cocking its leg against one of the barrels and was not at all concerned by my sudden appearance. I turned right and walked down to the end of the alley. It led me to a green field, dotted with Lombardy cypresses, on top of a hill which sloped gently down towards the centre of the city of Rome in the distance. It was a clear and warm day and I took a few minutes to savour the astonishing vista. The sun was right overhead, so it must have been around noon. The Italian sunlight danced off the white marble buildings and reflected off the gold crosses and cupolas that topped the churches of Rome. There were many couples and children walking and playing on the hill, enjoying the sunshine. I turned back reluctantly and walked to the other end of the alleyway. I looked out cautiously and knew that this must be the right place. It was the fashionable Via Paolina in the parish of Santa Maria del Popolo on the outskirts of Rome. It was an elegant avenue of two-storey houses, all constructed in different styles, but all designed with elegant Italian Renaissance symmetry. I had expected a quiet street but, to my surprise, there was much activity up and down the avenue, with wagons and carts jostling with horses and pedestrians of all sorts, from elegant ladies to the usual throng of crippled and deformed beggars. I found it difficult to accept the horrific spectacle of these destitute beggars. The better-off native Romans ignored them with equanimity. I walked down the avenue, trying to avoid the throng, until I found the house that Guglielmo Pellegrino had described to me, the house of Fillide Melandroni. I walked through an elegant archway let into the surrounding wall and knocked on the elaborately carved wooden front door. Large wooden tubs, containing cone-shaped shrubs, stood sentry either side of the door. The exterior of the house was plain but elegantly proportioned. The windows, with rounded tops on the ground floor but rectangular on the first floor, were adorned with exterior shutters which gave the house an idyllically rustic appearance. Fillide Melandroni's chosen profession had evidently done well for her. The front door was opened by a woman of about fifty years of age. I was familiar with how Fillide Melandroni looked, from the many portraits of her contained in Caravaggio's work, so I knew this woman was not her, even if she had been a lot younger, as Fillide was at this time. The woman took in my appearance. I had chosen a brighter and more colourful costume than I usually wore for time travelling. I was wearing a plum-coloured doublet and hose with a short chamois leather cloak and boots. My floppy velvet cap was of a deeper plum colour and adorned with a light blue feather. I had also added more 'bling' in the form of gold rings on my fingers and, worn around my neck, an elegant gold chain complete with an impressively large pigeon-blood ruby pendant. To protect my bling, I also wore a Spanish dagger, made from Toledo steel, with an elaborate Damascened handle. All in all, I made a pretty impressive showing . . . pretty being the apposite word.

I took off my cap and said: 'Good day, signora. I wonder if it is possible to speak to Signorina Melandroni?'

The woman looked a little flustered and said: 'I'm afraid Fillide has not woken up yet. Can I help you at all?'

'I'm afraid not. My business can only be with Signorina Melandroni. My name is Stefano Maddano. I am here in Rome, with the authority of the Holy Father, to investigate the unfortunate death of the painter known as Caravaggio.'

Invoking the name of the pope always did the trick. 'I am Fillide's aunt Petra,' the woman said. 'Won't you please come in and I will see if Fillide can receive you.'

I stepped into the house. The doorway led straight into a grand reception room. The room was well furnished but the furniture was not of the best quality compared with what I had seen in the palazzi I had visited. The floor was tiled, not carpeted, but was strewn with colourful rugs. The best feature of the room and stairs was undoubtedly the woodwork, which was very well made. At that moment a young man ambled into the room from the back of the house. He was physically disabled in some way. His limbs were bent and jerked pitifully with each step he took. His head and his eyes rolled incessantly and his front teeth protruded out of his mouth. He was completely bald, his head having been shaved clean. He was dressed plainly and simply and he was immediately fascinated by my outfit. He stopped in front of me and, without saying anything, started to feel the material of my doublet and then took hold of the ruby pendant. The woman slapped his hand away. 'I'm so sorry, signor,' Petra said. 'This is my nephew, Fillide's brother, Silvio. As you can see, he is one of God's mistakes. I apologise for him touching your clothes.'

'It's quite all right,' I said, and held out my hand. 'I'm very pleased to meet you, Silvio.'

Silvio stared at my hand, unused to such consideration. Aunt Petra said: 'Shake the gentleman's hand, Silvio.'

Silvio slowly advanced his hand, and then shook mine, which sent him into paroxysms of delight. 'How do you do?' he said, with difficulty because of his protruberant teeth, and a ribbon of drool fell down the front of his waistcoat. Aunt Petra clouted him on the back of his head with a painful smack. Silvio stood there chastened. Petra said: 'Make yourself useful, you idiot, and go and see if Fillide is awake yet. Tell her there is a gentleman sent by the Holy Father who wishes to speak to her.'

Silvio scuttled away up the staircase, which led to a balustraded balcony which ran all around the upper floor, with several doorways leading off to what I assumed were bedrooms. Before Silvio reached the top of the stairs, one of the bedroom doors opened and Fillide Melandroni emerged, still in her night attire, her hair tousled. She yawned lazily.

Aunt Petra called up to her: 'Fillide! Go and make yourself respectable. There is a gentleman from the Holy Father here to see you.'

Fillide Melandroni, far from being embarrassed by my presence, looked over the balustrade with interest. 'Good morning, signor,' she said, sleepily. 'You must be Signor Maddano.'

'Indeed I am,' I said.

'I've been expecting you,' Fillide said, and leaned over the balustrade so that I had a perfect view of the cleavage of her ample breasts.

'Fillide!' Aunt Petra cried. 'Go and get dressed properly!'

'Don't worry, auntie,' Fillide replied, coquettishly. 'Signor Maddano looks like a handsome man of the world. He knows full well what I do for a living and I'm sure that he has many times seen what I have to offer.'

'Well, really!' Aunt Petra said, shocked. 'That girl is incorrigible. I apologise for her forwardness, Signor Maddano.'

Fillide giggled. 'Oh, shut up, you old prude. Please give me a few minutes to get dressed, Signor Maddano, and then we can talk.' She turned to Silvio, who was standing at the top of the stairs, and her manner changed completely. 'Silvio, you stupid ape. Don't stand there goggling! Go and get Signor Maddano some refreshments, whatever he wants.' Fillide went back into her bedroom and closed the door. Silvio walked painfully back down the stairs and said to me: 'My sister is very pretty. What can I get you, sir?'

'It's very kind of you, Silvio, but I am perfectly refreshed.'

'Then I'll get back to the kitchen,' Silvio replied, and looked at Aunt Petra for her approval. Petra nodded and Silvio scuttled jerkily away.

'Would you like to sit down, Signor Maddano?' Aunt Petra asked. 'I'm sure Fillide will not keep you for long.' She indicated a cushioned armchair by the unlit fireplace. I thanked her and sat down.

'Please don't let me hold you up, signora,' I said. 'I'm sure you are very busy.'

'Thank you,' Aunt Petra replied. 'Please call me or Silvio if you need anything.' She hurried out to the kitchen, as relieved not to have to entertain me as I was relieved not to have to endure her vile presence. Several minutes later, Silvio came out of the kitchen carrying a tray. There was a plate of food and some sort of hot drink on the tray. He walked jerkily past me, showing considerable skill in keeping the tray level, and climbed up the stairs. He took the tray into Fillide's bedroom, came out again and walked back down the stairs. He stopped in front of me and said: 'Are you a prince or a cardinal?'

'No,' I smiled. 'What makes you think that?'

'You are dressed so finely, sir, with so many gold rings.'

I held up my hands to show Silvio the rings. They were all fakes, of course. Silvio examined them intently. I said: 'Are you happy living here, Silvio?'

'My sister bought this house for us all to live in. She is very kind. She is very pretty.'

'Yes, she is,' I agreed. 'Do you like Aunt Petra?'

Silvio was about to say something when Aunt Petra appeared at the kitchen door and barked: 'Silvio! Come here! Stop bothering the gentleman.' Silvio went back into the kitchen and a silence descended on the house. Fillide's 'few minutes' turned into almost an hour. At last, she emerged from her bedroom. She was fully-dressed in a low-cut flame-coloured taffeta dress. She called over the balustrade and said to me: 'I'm sorry to keep you waiting, Signor Maddano. If it doesn't shock you or Aunt Petra too much, perhaps you would like to come up to my room while I do my hair. We can talk in there.'

I walked up the stairs, along the balcony, and into the bedroom of Fillide Melandroni. I confess that my heart was beating faster than normal. I wasn't sure why except, of course, that she was an alluring woman. Fillide closed the door behind me. I was trapped, willingly, in her web. It was a large room and the air was scented with a heady perfume. The room was carpeted and furnished much more expensively that the downstairs part of the house. Fillide's bed, a large tester bed with richly embroidered hangings, dominated the room. The bed had been made and was covered with a light embroidered eiderdown. Through the windows on either side of the bed, I could look down into a small but pretty walled garden. Fillide said: 'We can talk in here without that bitch of an aunt or my idiot brother hearing what we are saying. You can sit on the bed.' She sat down at a dressing table. The large oval mirror on the dressing table looked very much like the one that Caravaggio had used in the Conversion of Mary Magdalen painting, for which Fillide had modelled.

'I thought this was your house?' I said.

'It is.'

'Then why, if you detest your aunt and brother so much, do you allow them to live here?'

'I promised our late mother that I would take care of Silvio. I let Aunt Petra do most of the work in looking after Silvio but she is in the pay of my beloved Giulio.'

'In the pay?' I repeated, puzzled. 'Do you mean in the pay of Giulio Strozzi?'

'Yes.'

'But he wishes to marry you, doesn't he?'

'Yes,' Fillide said. 'He is so hot for me, and has been for years, that he wishes to make an honest woman of me, despite the opposition of his family. Dear Giulio! I will become his wife. He will make me very happy.'

'You are very much in love with him, then?' I asked.

Fillide laughed loudly. 'I am completely indifferent to Giulio Strozzi, except for one thing.'

'What's that?'

'Why, the size of his purse! He is a very rich man.'

'Well, I must say you are very frank with me.'

Fillide turned away from her mirror and looked at me. 'I know all about you, Signor Maddano. You are a very clever and unusual man. I know that you have literally put the fear of God into many people during your enquiry into the death of poor Michele. The Holy Father has enjoined us all to tell you the truth and that is what I am doing. I have made a lot of money by lying, in both senses of the word, on my back, but I will not lie to you. Ask me what you like, Signor Maddano, and I will tell you the truth.' She turned back to her mirror.

I studied Fillide as she fiddled with her hair. She was, at this time, about thirty years old and in her prime as a desirable woman. Her figure was superb, her skin flawless, her hair shining. A hint of a sardonic smile played around her mouth, just as Caravaggio had captured it so accurately on canvas. But the feature that dominated was her melting, liquid dark eyes. They held such femininity, such sexual promise, and yet they were eyes that looked at the world without a trace of sentiment or self-delusion. Not hard eyes, not cynical eyes, but eyes that announced that Fillide Melandroni would not be fooled, or demeaned, or beaten down by anyone, from the highest cardinal down to the lowest street beggar. She was stunningly attractive in a blowsy Mae West-type way, although she was much more beautiful than the film star. What is more, she was fully aware of her effect on me and, I suspected, every man she met. Sitting on her bed, watching her prepare her hair and make-up, I was disturbed and pleased at the same time to feel myself becoming aroused. I was old enough to be her father. I tried to concentrate on business.

'Tell me why your Aunt Petra is in the pay of Giulio Strozzi?' I said.

'She doesn't know that I know. Giulio is so obsessed with me that he wants me all to himself. He is trying to make sure that I don't go back to my old life and so he pays Aunt Petra to report my activities and make sure I do not "entertain" any gentlemen.'

As if on cue, there was a rap on the door and Aunt Petra called out: 'Fillide! Is Signor Maddano in there with you? He has vanished.'

Fillide winked at me and opened the door. 'Yes, auntie,' she said. 'Here is Signor Maddano, still fully clothed, and very likely to remain so, unless he makes me a very good offer. He is keeping me company while I finish my toilet.'

'Really, Fillide,' Aunt Petra said, wringing her hands, 'I don't think it is seemly to entertain such a distinguished guest in your bedroom.'

'Signor Maddano is not that distinguished,' Fillide replied, looking at me archly. 'He is a foreigner, so he is probably not shocked by our loose ways. Furthermore, he is a man and probably quite excited by being alone with me in my bedroom.'

'That is what I'm afraid of,' Aunt Petra said.

'Don't fret, auntie, Signor Maddano's chastity is safe with me.'

'If you insist. But don't take too long.'

Fillide closed the door again. 'There you are,' she whispered. 'Your presence here will be reported to Giulio forthwith.'

'Do you still "entertain" gentleman callers?' I asked.

'Occasionally, when that cow is not around, but now I entertain for my own pleasure.'

'Aren't you concerned about losing Giulio Strozzi . . . and his big purse?'

'No,' Fillide snorted. 'He has been besotted with me for years, despite all the other men. I have him wrapped around my elegant little finger.' She held up the said finger and waggled it at me. She filled the gesture with sexual connotations. 'Are you rich, Signor Maddano? Do you wish to make me a better offer?'

'If I were a younger man, Fillide, I would be very tempted. May I call you Fillide?'

'You may, if I can call you . . . what is your name . . . Stefano.'

'You may,' I said. 'This house tells me that you have done very well out of your chosen profession, Fillide.'

'Do you disapprove?'

'Not at all. I admire you for beating the system.'

'What is "beating the system"?' Fillide asked, giggling.

'Well, doing better than a girl from your station in life would be expected to do. I believe you come from a so-called "humble" family. You were born in Siena, weren't you?'

'You are well informed, Stefano,' Fillide replied, regarding me with renewed interest. 'Yes, the family is from Siena. After my father died, my mother Cinzia moved Silvio and I here to Rome. Mother was in poor health. She knew I was a precocious girl, and pretty, so she encouraged me to become a courtesan.'

'Your own mother encouraged you to become a prostitute?' I said, shocked.

Fillide looked at me with reproach. 'Have you ever been poor, Signor Maddano? So poor that you literally do not know when the next meal will be coming. So poor that you have to live off scraps for days on end. And, on top of that, you are in poor health and you have to support an idiot son who can never amount to anything. That was the situation my mother was in. I possessed something that men would pay a great deal of money for and my mother knew it. She did what she had to do to survive. And she was right. So please remove that look of disgust from your face.'

'You are right to scold me, Fillide. I am not here to be your moral judge. I apologise.'

Fillide waved her hand at me. 'It is forgotten.'

'You were only thirteen years old when you and your friend Anna Bianchini were arrested and put in prison for being out on the streets after dark. Were you already selling yourself at that age?' This question had nothing to do with my search for Merisi's murderer, it was prurient interest on my part, but Fillide was not discomfited by the question.

'No,' she replied. 'That time we were arrested we were simply walking home to prepare a meal for my mother. She had been ill again and Anna was helping me to look after her. My mother had plans for me to sell myself to men but not as a common whore down the Ortaccio. The Ortaccio is the part of Rome where all the brothels are located, where the street girls work.'

'Yes, I know,' I said.

'I began working the Ortaccio without my mother knowing. She was intent on saving me until we could find a special "client". When I was sixteen years old, we found one.'

'This was Ulisse Masetti, was it not?' I asked, attempting to show Fillide that I knew a lot about her and that she better not lie to me.

'Yes, it was Ulisse Masetti,' she confirmed.

'How did you get to know him?' Fillide hesitated to reply, so I said: 'He was introduced to you by Ranuccio Tomassoni, wasn't he?'

'You are well informed, Stefano,' Fillide replied, seeming unsure of herself for the first time.

I decided to take a gamble on impressing her with another piece of personal knowledge which I could guess but could not be sure of. 'You were already sleeping with Ranuccio. He was your first real love.'

'Damn you,' Fillide spat. 'How do you know such things?'

'I have been given knowledge and powers that would be difficult for you to comprehend, Fillide. I am not here to censure or punish but just to learn the truth. Ulisse Masetti was a friend of Ranuccio and Ulisse was in the service of Cardinal Benedetto Giustiniani. Ranuccio knew that you were looking for a wealthy "protector", so he introduced you to Masetti. How would you describe your relationship with Ulisse Masetti?'

'It was . . . satisfactory, in a financial sense. He was a much older man, too fat, no good as a lover but I didn't care about that. He was generous and not too demanding. My mother and I, at last, had enough money to live comfortably and to look after Silvio.'

'Did you ever meet Cardinal Giustiniani's brother, the rich banker Vincenzo Giustiniani?'

'Why should I have done?' Fillide replied. 'Ulisse Masetti was working for Cardinal Giustiniani but that does not mean that I met any of that distinguished family. They would care nothing for a girl like me.'

'Then I wonder why Vincenzo Giustiniani owns so many portraits of you, some by our mutual friend Michelangelo Merisi da Caravaggio.'

'How should I know?' Fillide said angrily. 'You know what these men are like. They buy pictures of pretty women and pretty boys so that they can play with themselves in private. I modelled for Michele but I don't know what became of the pictures he made of me.'

For the first time, I knew Fillide was not telling me the truth. She was verbally dancing around my enquiry and trying not to answer directly. 'Look at me, Fillide,' I ordered. She did as I asked but she was pouting with annoyance. 'You made a great deal of money in a very short time out of being a courtesan. Look at this house we are sitting in. To afford to buy a house like this, in one of the most fashionable areas of Rome, for which a woman in your station in life also needs to buy a certificate of exemption, costs a lot of money. You bought this house when you were just twenty-two years old. Ulisse Masetti was comfortably off, but to make money like this you would need the favours of a very rich man. Vincenzo Giustiniani is one of the richest men in Rome. He owns many portraits of you. Was he one of your patrons?'

Fillide looked back at me steadily and said: 'Why to you think this Giustiniani paid for all this. Giulio Strozzi had come to Rome from Florence when I was seventeen. He is a nobleman and he has been besotted by me for years. He wishes to marry me. His family are totally against me. It would look better for Giulio if I am at least living at a comfortable station in life.'

'Fillide,' I insisted, 'you are not answering my question. Remember that the Holy Father has commanded that all witnesses who speak to me during my inquries must tell me the truth or imperil their immortal souls. Now, was

Vincenzo Giustiniani one of your clients and did he buy this house for you?' I ducked as Fillide threw her hairbrush at my head.

'Yes and yes,' she said. 'Damn you. Please don't tell Vincenzo that I have told you that.'

'I swear that Vincenzo Giustiniani will never know that you have revealed your secret.'

'Thank you,' Fillide said, still pouting.

'All this time that you were "entertaining" Ulisse Masetti and Vincenzo Giustiniani and Giulio Strozzi, you were still desperately in love with Ranuccio Tomassoni and you . . .'

'Stop right there, Signor Foreigner! What makes you think I was "desperately in love" with Ranuccio?'

'Fillide, Fillide!' I said, with mock exasperation. 'It is a matter of legal record. Ranuccio was having an affair with a woman named Prudenzia Zacchia. You attacked this woman with a knife, not once but twice. If you were not in love with Ranuccio Tomassoni, why should you react in that manner when you found out he was having an affair with Prudenzia Zacchia?'

'I wish you would not speak that bitch's name in my house,' Fillide replied, her dark eyes flashing with fury. 'Yes, Ranuccio was fucking her. I could not kill her but I wanted to mark that pretty face of hers with scars so that men would not look at her again.'

'So, to get your own back, you began an affair with one of Ranuccio's bitterest enemies, our friend Michele?'

'Yes . . . and I made sure that Ranuccio knew about it.'

'How and when did you first meet Michele?'

'It was while I was still seeing Ulisse Masetti but before Giulio arrived in Rome. I was picking up extra money by modelling for a young artist. He was a nice boy but, unfortunately for him, he fell in love with me. I would model for him and then we would make love. He was young and lusty and, after being pawed about by the fat Signor Masetti, it was nice to be with a young man of about my own age. But, as usual, this boy became obsessed with me and started to become a nuisance. He was a friend of Michele. Michele would sometimes visit his studio. I could see that Michele fancied me, not just as a woman but as a model. He was already making a reputation and was a much better painter than my young lover.'

'Who was this young artist lover of yours?' I asked. 'I may need to interview him sometime. If Michele stole you from him, he might have sought revenge.'

'His name was Lionello,' Fillide said. 'Lionello Spada.'

I was very excited but puzzled by this revelation. I tried not to show it. 'I have heard that name. He was a close friend of Michele's, wasn't he?'

'Yes, they were friends.'

'Did Michele know that you and Lionello were lovers?'

'No. Michele, with his customary arrogance, never considered the possibility that Lionello and I were lovers. I'm sure Lionello never told him.'

'And, after you and Michele had become lovers, did Lionello know about that?'

'Perhaps. I really don't know. I certainly never told Lionello. I always calculated that the less people knew about my activities, the more secure I would be.'

'Did you finish completely with Lionello when you went with Michele?'

'Yes, I had to in the end. Lionello was making such a nuisance of himself. Following me around, turning up at my door at all hours, telling me how much he loved me. I was bored with him. I ended up detesting him.'

'And you chose Michele as your lover simply to get your own back on Ranuccio Tomassoni?'

'That was one reason, yes. There was no-one in Rome that Ranuccio hated more than Michele. But Ranuccio was fucking that whore Zacchia, so I decided to teach him a lesson by sleeping with his worst enemy. But also, I truly admired Michele's work. His portraits of me are beautiful.'

'Indeed they are,' I said. 'Did Michele fall in love with you?'

'In his way, I think he did. But Michele was only ever out to benefit himself, which I didn't mind. I didn't want some besotted little boy like Lionello constantly making a nuisance of himself. By this time I had met Giulio Strozzi, who was making his intentions towards me very clear. He even commissioned Michele to paint my portrait, never suspecting that we were lovers. Michele knew how to keep his mouth shut when there was money to be made. So, I was stringing Strozzi along, as I still am, and Michele was stringing me along while he became the most famous painter in Rome. But we had a lot of fun. Michele sometimes became jealous but he was a man of the world. He relished the fact that he was cuckolding Ranuccio and that Ranuccio knew he was being cuckolded.'

I said: 'No wonder those two ended up hacking at each other with swords.'

Fillide shuddered and I apologised for my crude use of words. She said: 'I loved them both, in different ways, but you are right . . . Ranuccio was my real love, but he could never have given me the financial security I wanted, even if he could have kept his hands off other women, which he could not. Michele was a strange man, a difficult man. But I think I knew him as well as anyone. Behind all the shouting and the bluster and the violence he was like a lost little boy. Also, as you can see in his paintings, he had the deepest sympathy for humanity. Not human beings as individuals but the human condition. He suffered, more than most. But then he killed the man I loved most in all the world. I wept for Ranuccio, for days. Then I heard that Michele was dead and I wept for him too but not for days, just for an hour or two. My actions had caused both their deaths.' Fillide now began to weep again. I carried a finely-embroidered silk handkerchief in the pocket of my doublet. I pulled it out and offered it to Fillide. 'Thank you,' she said. 'I thought I had cried all I could. Talking to you has brought it all back.'

'I'm sorry I have to revive all these painful memories,' I apologised. Then we both looked up at each other as we heard a knocking on the front door. A few moments later, Aunt Petra called up the stairs: 'Fillide! Anna is here to see you!'

'Is that Anna Bianchini?' I asked.

'Yes.'

'Then I would like to meet her when we have finished here. I don't have many more questions for you.'

Fillide, still dabbing her eyes, opened her bedroom door and leant over the balcony. 'Anna,' she called out. 'Signor Maddano is here. We will not be much longer and then he would like to meet you. Go and talk to Silvio for a few minutes.' Fillide came back in and sat down in front of her mirror but left the door open.

I said: 'I would like to ask you about one of Michele's paintings which you posed for.'

'Which one?'

'You sat as Saint Catherine of Alexandria.'

'What about it?'

'Michele told me once that you never tried to influence whatever he was painting, except this one time, when you were insistent upon that pose with you stroking the blade of a sword with your finger. It is a most erotic image. Was that deliberate?'

Fillide giggled delightedly at the memory. 'Yes, it was deliberate. I was in a playful mood. That painting was commissioned by Cardinal Del Monte. Michele was very dubious about that pose. He was worried that the cardinal might reject his picture as obscene but I knew men, especially the good cardinal, better than Michele. Del Monte lapped it up. It is, as you say, most erotic. It was a message to Lionello Spada whose name, as you probably know, means "sword". I managed to persuade Michele in the way he liked best . . .' Fillide smiled at me in a way that was both lascivious, alluring and disturbing. She was quite a woman. 'Did Michele talk about me often?' she asked.

'Yes. He was very fond of you.'

'When did you know him?'

'In Naples,' I said, trotting out the old lie, 'just before the end.'

'And you think that he was murdered?' Fillide asked.

'It is possible,' I replied. 'Did you murder him?'

'No, of course not.'

'Was it Lionello Spada?'

'How should I know? Perhaps.'

'The Tomassoni family then.'

'They are certainly capable of such a brutal act. Have you spoken to them yet?'

'No,' I said. 'They are next on my list. Fillide, do you have any knowledge about anyone who was planning or attempting to murder Michele.'

'No,' Fillide sighed. 'I don't.'

'Very well. Let's go and meet your friend Anna Bianchini.'

We left Fillide's bedroom and walked downstairs. Anna Bianchini was sitting in the same chair that I had sat in while waiting for Fillide. She was short and running to plumpness but with a pleasantly attractive face and a good complexion. She was wearing a canary yellow dress trimmed with white lace. It set off her black hair very effectively. She was using a white paper fan to keep herself cool. 'Anna,' Fillide said, indicating to me, 'this is Signor Stefano Maddano. He is here to investigate the death of Michele.'

I looked at Anna Bianchini. 'Is that your natural hair colour, signorina.'

Anna Bianchini looked surprised. 'Yes. Why do you ask?'

'Have you ever dyed your hair or used anything to colour your hair?'

'Certainly not,' Anna replied indignantly.

'Not even to model for any of Caravaggio's paintings?'

'I never modelled for Merisi,' Anna replied. 'I didn't like the man at all. I could not understand what my friend Fillide here saw in him. He was dirty, and he smelled.'

'So you never posed for him at all?' I persisted.

'No, I hardly knew him. I met him only a few times and then only reluctantly.' Turning to Fillide, she said: 'I'm sorry to have to tell Signor Maddano all this, Filli, but you know how I felt about that man.'

Fillide said airily: 'It's of no consequence, Anna.' To me she said: 'Anna and I have been friends since we were children, when I first came to Rome. Such a friendship survives, and will always survive, the men in our lives. Anna thoroughly disapproved of Michele.'

'Enough to want to murder him?' I asked, pointedly.

Anna laughed, a very attractive throaty laugh, and playfully struck my arm with her fan. 'Don't be ridiculous, Signor Maddano. I couldn't care half a scudo about Merisi one way or another. He was nothing to do with me.'

Aunt Petra had come in from the kitchen, trying to listen to what was going on. I considered that I had found out as much as I was going to, and much more than I had expected. I said to Fillide: 'Would you mind if I had a word with Silvio, alone, before I take my leave?'

Aunt Petra said: 'I don't think that's a good idea.' I ignored her and carried on looking at Fillide. She said: 'Yes, if you think it would do any good, but you won't get any sense out of that clown. He's in the kitchen.'

I knew I should not be applying 21st century morality here in the 17th century but I could not bear to think of Silvio being ill-treated by his aunt and sister. There was very little I could do but it was worth a try. I went out into the kitchen where Silvio was sitting on a stool, rocking backwards and forwards and humming to himself, while he prepared some vegetables. When he noticed me standing there, he made to stand up. 'Don't get up, Silvio,' I said. I pulled off the three ornate rings that I was wearing on my fingers. The actual rings were real gold. The stones, two diamonds and a sapphire, were fakes but I doubted that anyone in the 17th century would be able to tell the difference. I took Silvio's hand and put the rings on his palm. 'Thank you for looking after me, Silvio. These are for you. I want you to put them in a secret place so that your sister and aunt can never find them. If you are ever in any trouble, or need help, they are yours to sell or barter with. Do you understand?'

Silvio was gazing at the rings in awe. 'For me?' he murmured.

'Yes, for you alone, Silvio. Go and hide them now, while I talk to your aunt and sister.' Silvio rocked back and forth a few times and then got up and limped out into the garden. I went back to rejoin the women. 'You are very blessed to have Silvio,' I announced cheerfully.

'Blessed?' Aunt Petra repeated. 'The boy is a monster.'

'A monster?' I repeated, acting as if I was confused. 'He is a special gift from God.'

'What do you mean?' Fillide asked me.

'Perhaps you have different customs here in Italy,' I said, 'but where I come from, people such as Silvio are regarded as a gift from God, to be cherished and cared for. If they are so cherished, they bring good luck and good fortune on the household and everyone in it. If they are ill-treated then doom, death and misfortune will result.'

Aunt Petra clutched her neck in dismay. 'Are you sure? Have you seen proof of this?'

'There is no doubt about it,' I said. 'I have given Silvio a gift and that means that God will smile upon me and some of this good fortune will rub off on me.'

'A gift?' Fillide said. 'What sort of gift?'

'That is between Silvio and I, and anyone who attempts to take away his gift will suffer the worst torments imaginable. I have seen it with my own eyes. Poor souls screaming for mercy, worse than the seventh circle of Hell. So, take care of Silvio and he will take care of you. I may wish to see you again, Fillide, and I will check that Silvio is being treated well. If not, the Holy Father shall hear of it. Thank you for your hospitality, ladies, I must be on my way.' I left them, literally opened mouth with astonishment, and stepped out into the dust of the street and the warm afternoon sun. It had been a most informative visit and I had much to think about.

37

It was very late at night, past two o'clock in the morning, when I materialised in my bedroom after returning from my interview with Fillide Melandroni. There were lights on downstairs. I felt I could not be bothered to change out of my seventeenth century clothing. I looked into Merisi's bedroom but he was not in there. I listened for conversation from downstairs but could not hear anything, so I went down. The lights were on in the living room but Merisi was not in there either. The kitchen light was on. I looked in and found Merisi sitting at the kitchen table with a large tub of Ben and Jerry's ice cream. He looked morose, and sober. 'Hello, Stefano,' he greeted me. 'You look very gallant. I'm sure dear Fillide was impressed by your manly figure. How was she?'

'Very playful. Very alluring,' I replied. 'More than can be said for that bitch of an aunt.'

'Aunt Petra? A fiend from hell. Did you meet brother Silvio?'

'Yes.'

'He should be outside with the animals. He is a freak.'

'Good God, Michele,' I said, in exasperation. 'Your century could learn much from mine about disability. Silvio is like he is through no fault of his own, just as you are and I am.' I sat down opposite Merisi.

'Have I earned a stern lecture about how compassionate you all are in this modern world? How many people did you say were killed, wounded and exterminated in your world wars?'

'No, I'm too tired to lecture you. I see I've created an ice cream addict, as well as a coffee, cheese on toast and bourbon addict. I'm surprised that you're still up.'

Merisi shoved another spoonful of chocolate chip into his mouth. When he had consumed it, he said: 'I couldn't sleep.'

'Why not?'

'I kept thinking of you with Fillide. Then Izzy came to see me. We made love on your sofa.'

'Too much information,' I said, making a mental note to buy more Vanish stain remover.

'Everything is going crazy, Stefano.' Merisi waved the spoon near his temple to emphasise how crazy everything was. 'You are visiting a woman I loved in the seventeenth century and I am falling in love with a woman from the 21st century. What am I doing here? What is happening to me? It's all crazy.'

'Why don't you have a drink? That usually knocks you out.'

'No, I wanted to think.'

'Have you reached any conclusions?'

'No. Except that I am beginning to dream. To hope.'

'What do you mean?' I asked.

'At first, when I came back to life, so to speak, it was enough just to be alive again. Strange, confusing, frightening even, but alive! Now I am beginning to dream of more than just being alive. Can I build a new life? Can I become an artist again? What do the Tralfamadorians have in store for me when all that we are doing is over?'

'I think I understand, Michele. You know as well as I do that I was dragged into all this, most unwillingly to start with. I cannot give you any answers . . . not honest ones. The Tralfamadorians are using me just as much as they are using you. They have not confided in me. I cannot help you. Except chemical help if you can't sleep.'

'What sort of chemical help?' Merisi asked.

'Sleeping pills.' I got up and went to the wall cabinet. I kept all my pain relievers, blood pressure medication and antiseptics on the top shelf. At the back of the shelf were the sleeping pills that I had been prescribed, and which I had used for a time, after my wife had left me. They were long past their 'use by' date but I thought they would not do any harm, even if they no longer had any effect. I placed the small brown plastic bottle in front of Merisi. 'As you are still awake, and before you take those sleeping pills, I want to ask you a couple of questions.'

'Very well,' Merisi agreed, off-handedly.

'Did you know that that Vincenzo Giustiniani was one of Fillide's clients?'

Merisi looked up at me, genuinely surprised. 'Are you serious?' he said. 'The ascetic Vincenzo was fucking Fillide?'

'Well enough to buy her that house up in the Via Paolina.'

Merisi whistled softly. 'No wonder Vincenzo was so keen to buy any painting that Fillide had modelled for, not only mine but by other painters as well.'

'Painters such as Lionello Spada?'

'Yes. Lionello used Fillide as a model. That's how I first met her, in his studio.'

'Did you know that Lionello was sleeping with Fillide?'

'Nonsense,' Merisi snorted. 'Fillide would not have wasted her time with a blushing boy like Lionello! Did Fillide tell you she was fucking Lionello?'

'Yes. Not only was she fucking him, as you so delicately put it, but Lionello was besotted with her. In love with her. Did you know that?'

'No, Stefano. Truly, I did not. I never suspected it. Fillide never told me and neither did Lionello. I thought I was merely borrowing his model, not his lover.'

'I believe you,' I said. 'Did Lionello know that you and Fillide had become lovers?'

Merisi shrugged his shoulders. 'I certainly never told him. Whether Fillide did, I don't know. I don't remember ever discussing it with Lionello or sensing that he resented me for such a situation. But that explains his hatred for Ranuccio Tomassoni, who he knew full well was fucking Fillide and who was Fillide's real love. I should have guessed that Lionello felt more than professional interest in Fillide at the time, but the thought never occurred to me. Truly.'

Once again, I accepted that Merisi was telling me the truth. I said: 'If Lionello had found out about you and Fillide, it gives him a powerful motive to want to murder you. Sexual jealousy, as you very well know, is a powerful incitement to violence and revenge.'

'It's possible,' Merisi admitted, 'but I never sensed any resentment or hostility from Lionello. Quite the contrary, he admired my work without reservation and always seemed glad to be in my company.'

'He could have been playing a deep and devious game, keeping his cards close to his chest, as you are with me, Michele.'

'What do you mean by that?' Merisi challenged me.

'Another woman of your acquaintance came to visit Fillide while I was there. Anna Bianchini.'

Merisi sat back in his chair and looked at me. 'So?'

'You told me that Anna modelled for you. You told me that you were sleeping with her. She told me that she detested you, that she had never modelled for you, and that she thought you were a dirty and smelly brute.'

'Dear Anna, always a kind word for everyone, the lying bitch.'

'You claim she was lying to me?' I asked.

'Of course she was!'

'You told me that you had used her as the model for the Penitent Magdalen and the Rest on the Flight to Egypt and in the Death of the Virgin. But Anna has black hair, not red, and she looks nothing like the model in those paintings.'

Merisi threw down his spoon in exasperation. 'It's called artistic licence, you ignorant heretic! Sometimes an artist uses a model to get the basic body shape correct, not simply to slavishly copy every physical feature of that model. I used

Anna to get the basic pose and then changed the colouring and some of her features to suit the needs of the picture.'

'I don't believe you,' I said. 'Anna well knew who I was, she knew that the pope had ordered her to tell me the truth, on peril of eternal damnation. She had no reason to lie to me. You, however, seem to be taking every opportunity to lie to me. You are not constrained by Pope Paul's warrant.'

I expected an explosion of temper from Merisi but he merely looked at me for a few seconds. 'Tell me,' he said, 'when Anna told you that she had not modelled for me and didn't like me and had not shared her favours with me, was Fillide listening?'

'Yes, she was,' I had to admit.

'There you are then,' Merisi said, with smug satisfaction. 'Fillide never knew that I was fucking Anna. You know what a temper Fillide had. She slashed the face of some whore that Ranuccio Tomassoni was fucking. Anna dare not admit the truth with Fillide, her best and oldest friend, listening.'

'Even at the risk of imperilling her place in the afterlife?'

'Anna was a whore! What sort of afterlife has she gone to? Anna would much sooner lie to you, and the Holy Father, than she would expose herself as a lying trollope and risk losing her best friend.'

'I still don't believe you,' I said, although now with less conviction.

Merisi looked at me steadily and said: 'I don't fucking care.' He picked up the bottle of sleeping pills and pretended to read the instructions on the label.

'Take two of those,' I said, 'and you'll sleep like a cardinal. But don't take more than two, or drink alcohol with them, or you won't wake up for a week.'

'Your century has a pill for every ailment,' Merisi said morosely. 'Do you also have a pill to cure hope?'

'Even we are not that clever yet,' I said.

38

The next morning Merisi slept late and woke refreshed after the ministrations of the sleeping pills. He was still miffed, however, about my late night questioning and was reluctant to knuckle down to work. I insisted that we should keep going.

'You are more of a fucking slave driver than a Turkish galley master,' he said wearily, as he sank into his armchair.

I ignored his chuntering and asked: 'What made you choose Naples as a refuge from Roman law?'

'Several reasons,' Merisi replied, with a sigh, 'the main one being that the Colonna family had close links with Naples and with Spain, the country that ruled Naples at that time. The city was the capital of the Kingdom of the Two Sicilies. The Colonnas were very powerful in Naples and they put me under their protection. Anyone or any group, however tough they were, would have thought twice about crossing the Colonnas by harming me. When I arrived in Naples I stayed at the Palazzo Colonna, which was an imposing building on the Via Toledo. Naples was a wealthy and vibrant city. It was, at that time, about three times bigger than Rome. There was plenty of work for a talented artist like me, even one being hunted for murder.'

'Naples has always been the most cosmopolitan city in Italy. It must have been an impressive place in your day.'

'Very much so,' Merisi agreed. 'It was a bustling port, with trading links throughout the Mediterranean, the sea having been made safe by the glorious victory over the Turks at the battle of Lepanto. The beauty of the bay had been celebrated since antiquity and, from the shores, the tightly-packed buildings rose up the hills, all surrounded and dominated by the city walls. The harbour teemed with merchant ships and Spanish galleys. As you rightly said, Naples was a cosmopolitan city, full of traders, diplomats, soldiers, courtiers, entrepreneurs and artists from all over Europe. It was forbidden to build outside of the city walls and the city had retained its ancient Greek grid plan with long, straight avenues. Because of the lack of building space, some buildings were constructed with four or five or even six storeys, so that they loomed over you wherever you walked. Of course, they were nothing like the enormously tall buildings that frightened me so much in London when I first saw them but, at the time, these high buildings in Naples were overpowering. The city was packed with many palaces and churches and monasteries and oratories. In fact, these buildings took up so much space that the common people were forced to live in cramped and tightly-packed houses. I had thought that Rome was cramped and noisy but it was calm and tranquil compared with Naples. The rich and powerful, as they always do, hid themselves away behind high walls in palaces of limitless luxury and comfort while the poor people crowded the streets in between. And I literally mean crowded. It was difficult to walk around, what with the press of people everywhere, and the carts and carriages constantly trying to find a way through the throng. Even seeking sanctuary in the churches was pointless because they were crowded with beggars and the very poor, the lazzaroni, as well as worshippers. It was a much more violent city than Rome. Vendettas and murders were commonplace so, to the Neapolitans, my crime did not seem to be so heinous. And, just before I arrived, there had been a terrible famine in the city, one of a series that had made life very arduous for the inhabitants. Nobody, apart from my fellow artists, was much interested in an itinerant painter like me, however notorious, on the run from Roman law. The place suited me very well. The taverns were excellent.'

I was fascinated by Merisi's description of Naples in the year 1606. 'I'll look forward to travelling back in time and seeing for myself,' I said.

'You had better be careful if you do. As I said, it was a much more violent and dangerous city than Rome, especially for an Englishman who is not "street-wise", as your modern expression has it!'

'I'll be careful.' I promised. 'We know that the artistic community in Naples were excited by your arrival, even if the general populace were not. Your reputation was high and your work well-known to many Neapolitan artists. It must have made a pleasant change for you to be popular with your fellow daubers.'

'Indeed it was,' Merisi agreed, not offended by my derogatory remark. 'Let me tell you, Stefano, that I had learned my lesson after killing Ranuccio Tomassoni. I had decided to keep my own counsel and let my painting do the talking for me. I had had enough trouble for one lifetime, so I tried to keep my mouth shut. The Neapolitan elite, although immensely wealthy, were not as sophisticated as Roman patrons such as Del Monte and Giustiniani. They were eager to commission works from me, this talented and notorious refugee from Rome, as soon as I arrived. I was offered a place at the studio of two Flemish painters, Abraham Vinck and Louis Finson, who were dealers as well. They were eager to handle my work and, if I had been inclined that way, other things of mine as well. Their studio was in the Carita, a district of narrow alleys filled with taverns, shops and prostitutes. I had comfortable lodgings and a good income. I accepted a commission from a wealthy merchant from Ragusa named Radulovich. It was for an altarpiece of the Madonna with the Christ child in her arms and surrounded by saints. I had finished it by the end of the year, it had paid me well, and it caused a sensation in Naples. I had well and truly arrived. Do you have a picture of my altarpiece? I would love to see it again.'

'Sadly, Michele, it has not survived. We have a record of your painting but nobody knows where it is now, even if it actually survives. Happily, however, your next work, which we now call the Seven Acts of Mercy, survives in all its glory.' (*Plate 47*).

'I think I know which one you mean, but that title is not the one by which it was known in my time.'

'No, it was originally called the Madonna della Misericordia or, in English, Our Lady of Mercy.'

'Ah, yes, for the high altar of the new church of Pio Monte della Misericordia. Now, that picture really did cause a sensation. Nothing as good as that had ever been painted in Naples.'

'Is there anything in this work that could relate to our search for your attempted murderer?' I asked.

I handed Merisi the book of his complete works. He studied his painting for several seconds and then said: 'No, I really don't think so. Most of the subject matter was suggested by a poet friend named Manso, but he was certainly not antipathetic to me. All the figures and allegorical motifs are derived from Biblical accounts.'

'Okay,' I said. 'We know that you were working on another altarpiece, the Madonna of the Rosary, (*Plate 48*) at about the same time as the Seven Acts of Mercy, but we don't know who commissioned the Madonna of the Rosary altarpiece. Can you remember who it was?'

'Yes, it was commissioned by the Colonna family, as suggested by the inclusion of that column on the left of the picture. As I have told you, "colonna" means "column" in English, and the Colonnas wanted this altarpiece for the Chapel of the Most Holy Rosary in San Domenico, where Marcantonio Colonna, Costanza's father and the hero of the battle of Lepanto, was buried. The cult of the rosary was popular at the time. It was believed that the prayers of the humble to the Madonna of the Rosary had caused winds favourable to the Christian fleet at the battle of Lepanto. You can see that there is a portrait of Marcantonio Colonna on the left of the picture.'

'And yet we know that this altarpiece was being sold on the open market not long after you had painted it and after you had left Naples. Was the picture rejected by the San Domenico church?'

'Effectively, yes,' Merisi said, somewhat disconsolately. 'It was an aristocratic church and they were uneasy about my depiction of the lazzaroni, the poor people. They had expected something more idealised but, as you very well know, that was never my style. The picture was never hung in the church. Don Maurizio Colonna, one of the patrons of the church, was in dire financial trouble and he took the opportunity to sell the painting as soon as my back was turned. It was a crafty move!'

'And again,' I said, 'given the subject, it doesn't seem likely that there are any hidden clues as to your murderer within this work. All your works from your time in Naples seem to be straightforward commissions on given subjects. As was your next surviving commission, the Flagellation of Christ for the de Franchis family.' (*Plate 49*).

'Yes, I was pleased with this work, and pleased with the fee I received for it!'

'It's a moving meditation on suffering,' I said, 'like so many of your works. Christ is depicted with immense skill. I don't think anyone with an ounce of humanity could look at His suffering under the scourge without being moved to pity by His plight. It's a very great work.'

'Thank you, Stefano.'

'Is there any significance, as far as our quest for your murderer is concerned, in the fact that Christ is tied to a column. Any reference here to the Colonna family?'

'No,' Merisi said firmly. 'It was purely an artistic device to show where Christ is being tied. I am not aware of any other significance.'

'Well, this series of works had revolutionised the Neapolitan art world. Your good friends Vinck and Finson were singing your praises and promoting your work. Finson was even making copies of your pictures that were being sold all over Europe. Your income had never been higher, your reputation had never been higher, you were secure and comfortable and yet, in the midst of all this praise, acclamation and money, having been in Naples for less than a year, you do something that has puzzled historians ever since.'

'And what is that?'

'You abandon all this and move to Malta! Why?'

'There was a very good reason, Stefano.'

'Okay, let's examine that reason tomorrow. As you are so reluctant to work today, I think I'll travel to Naples, if Pellegrino can arrange it, and talk to your good friends Vinck and Finson.'

39

Guglielmo Pellegrino experienced considerable difficulty in finding the correct ChronoCo-ordinates for my trip to Naples but, after a delay of a couple of days, I found myself materialising in a narrow alley. I was hidden from view by a stack of large crates. I stepped out into the main street and found, to my disappointment, that it was pouring with rain. I had hoped for a sunny day with a clear view of Naples bay and Vesuvius but the visibility was very limited. I knew I was high up in the city in the Carita district. A shallow river of muddy water was pouring down the street. Despite the weather, there was a frantic bustle of activity. Pedestrians, carts and carriages jostled for space on the narrow street. Tall four-storey buildings, unlike anything I had seen in Rome, loomed over me. The roofs were almost invisible because of the downpour. I decided that climbing up the street looked more promising than walking down the hill. My red and gold finery, the same outfit that I had worn to interview Baglione and Salini at the Accademia di San Luca, was soon drenched with rain. I had picked the right direction and I soon found myself looking into the small window of the studio and art dealership shared by the Flemish painters Abraham Vinck and Louis Finson. I could see artworks on display inside and I was preparing to enter the shop when an unloaded horse and cart came rattling down the hill. It hit one of the many potholes in the road and shot muddy water all over the back of my clothing. I reacted angrily and shouted at the disappearing driver: 'Be careful you fucking idiot!' In return, I received what I guessed was an obscene Neapolitan gesture. The door of the shop opened and a dapper little man said to me: 'Oh, you poor man. I saw that you were about to come in and I saw what that dreadful wagon driver did to you. Come inside and let me dry you off.'

'Very kind of you,' I muttered, and followed the little man into the shop. I looked around. The shop was crammed with framed paintings, many hung on the walls but the majority just stacked against the walls. A quick glance suggested that most of the paintings were Flemish in style and subject matter. There were pastoral scenes, interiors of inns and taverns and what must have been dozens of paintings of luscious fruit and flowers and of hanging game. If I could have spirited any one of them back to my own century it would have been worth many thousands of pounds. The dapper little man had disappeared into a back room but very soon reappeared holding a voluminous rough cloth. He bustled behind me, wiping the muddy water off my fine silk doublet. Another man emerged from the back room. He was taller, with a sour look on his dark and saturnine face, but he was elegantly dressed. He watched as the little man fussed over me mumbling something about 'these lovely clothes, such a shame.' The little man finished drying me off, and said: 'By the way, I'm Louis and this is my friend Abraham.' Abraham Vinck bowed slightly and tried to smile.

Louis, however, was off again. 'Oh, look, I've missed a bit!' He started dabbing at my backside with the cloth.

'For goodness sake stop fussing over the gentleman,' Abraham said, sourly.

'Hush,' Louis replied, 'and go and find a chair for our guest.'

Abraham Vinck returned with a spindly but finely crafted chair that hardly looked strong enough to bear my weight. I risked it and sat down. As Abraham moved away I caught a whiff of a musky scent.

'Now, sir, what can we do for you,' Louis Finson asked me, clapping his pudgy little hands in anticipation. He was as eager as a puppy to please me. 'Would you like a glass of wine to help you recover from your ordeal.'

Abraham's expression became even more sour. I said: 'Very kind, but no thank you. You must be the two distinguished artists that I have travelled from Rome to talk to.'

Abraham Vinck looked wary but Louis was beside himself. 'All the way from Rome!? To see us!?'

'If you are Louis Finson and Abraham Vinck, then yes.'

'We are completely at your service,' Louis gushed. 'I'm sorry the Neapolitan weather is so poor today. It is very unusual for it to rain like this. Abraham and I have lived here for about seven years and we've never seen anything like it, have we Abraham?'

Abraham said: 'I'm sure the gentleman has not travelled all the way from Rome to discuss the weather, Louis.'

Louis moved closer to me and whispered: 'He gets very moody when his painting is not going well. It's not going well today.' Louis made a face to show me how much he suffered from Abraham's moods. 'Are you interested in looking at these wonderful works of art. I'm sure we can find something to suit the taste of such an elegant gentleman as yourself.'

'Thank you,' I replied, 'but I am here to ask you about a painter, not to buy a painting.'

At the prospect of not being able to make a sale, Abraham lost interest in me and started to move away into the back room.

'A painter?' Louis said, puzzled. 'Which painter?'

'I believe he was a friend of both of you. Michelangelo Merisi da Caravaggio.'

Abraham Vinck stopped in his tracks. Louis Finson's eyes welled up with tears and he produced a silk handkerchief from up his sleeve to dab his eyes. I said: 'I'm sorry if the mention of his name upsets you. I am investigating the suspicious circumstances of Michele's death in Porto Ercole last year. I have the permission and authority of the Holy Father to make such inquiries.' From inside my doublet I took out the papal warrant and handed it to Louis. 'My name is Stefano Maddano. I was Michele's friend. I know that you two were good friends of Michele as well. You are not under suspicion in any way but you may be able to help me with a few facts about Michele's life in Naples.'

'Why do you think Michele's death is suspicious?' Louis asked, sniffing away a tear.

'There is good reason to believe that Michele was murdered.'

Louis broke down completely and sobbed into his handkerchief. 'Oh, no! Poor, poor, Michele,' he breathed. 'Abraham, go and bring us some wine.'

Abraham Vinck ignored his partner and said to me: 'Your accent tells me, Signor Maddano, that, like us, you are not Italian. Where are you from?'

Without thinking, I said: 'I'm English.' Then, realising what I had let slip, I said lamely: 'Please don't let anyone else know that.'

To my surprise, Abraham Vinck's attitude towards me changed completely. He came over to me, smiling broadly, offered his hand for me to shake and said: 'My dear sir, welcome to our home. It is an honour to meet a subject of the former great Queen Elizabeth. Your country is the best hope of our freedom from the Spanish yoke and the Catholic tyranny. I still remember the joy I felt when I heard the news that Lord Howard and Hawkins and the estimable Francis Drake had destroyed the Spanish invasion armada. I will go and fetch our best wine.'

Louis was looking at his friend with horror. 'Abraham!' he scolded. 'Be careful what you are saying! Signor Maddano might be a Spanish spy or informer. You will get us both locked away in the Castel Sant'Elmo!'

'Gentlemen, gentlemen,' I said. 'I am not here to talk about politics. My only interest is our mutual friend Caravaggio.'

Vinck said to me: 'Please come through to the back room. Let's take a glass of wine. Louis, bring Signor Maddano's chair through.'

I followed Vinck out into a small back room which was also crammed with framed canvases but which also served as an office. A large desk was piled high with record books and account books. Vinck had gone through to another room to fetch the wine. Louis Finson placed the spindly chair by the desk and ushered me to sit down. He arranged two more chairs around the desk. Vinck returned with a wooden tray which held a bottle of wine and three Venetian glasses with spiral stems and gold filigree decoration shot through the glass. He sat down, poured the wine, and we toasted each other's health. 'Now,' Abraham Vinck said, 'what can we tell you about Michele?'

I said: 'I understand that, when Michele first arrived in Naples, he had a profound impact on the Neapolitan art world. But . . .'

Before I could go on, Louis Finson had interjected. 'Profound impact is an understatement, Signor Maddano. We all knew he was coming, so we were excited before he actually arrived here. We knew of his reputation as an artist. Abraham and I had made a special journey to Rome, just to look at his work, didn't we Abraham?' Abraham nodded his head and was about to speak but Louis was off again. 'Well, I can't tell you what an effect he had on me, Signor Maddano. I stood in the Contarelli chapel and the Cerasi chapel and the tears were running down my face, weren't they Abraham? Genius, pure genius, Signor Maddano. And we saw a few other works by Michele. The Death of the Virgin. I was in tears again! So moving! And the Madonna of Loreto. So beautiful! So beautiful.' Louis had pulled out his handkerchief and was dabbing his eyes again.

I asked Abraham Vinck what he had thought of Caravaggio's work. 'A revelation, Signor Maddano,' he replied. 'Nothing as good as that had ever been seen in Naples. You can imagine what Louis and I thought when we heard he was coming to Naples.'

Finson said: 'We just had to meet him, as soon as he arrived here, didn't we Abraham? And we did! We offered him a place here in our studio. We are dealers as well, we could promote his work, so that persuaded him to come and stay with us.' Louis Finson's little hands were windmilling with excitement. 'Such a privilege, Signor Maddano. Such a privilege!'

I said: 'Let me be blunt, gentlemen. As much as I liked and respected Michele, he was sometimes a very difficult man to get along with. Didn't his fearsome reputation and the fact that he was on the run after killing a man give you any pause.'

'Not at all,' Louis said. 'He was a pussy cat, Signor Maddano. We took care of him. He was still shocked and humbled by what he had done to that poor man in Rome. He was under sentence of death, even here in Naples, the dreaded banda capitale. He was contrite and anxious. All he wanted to do was hide away and paint his masterpieces.'

Abraham Vinck looked at his partner coolly. 'I was concerned, Signor Maddano. Michele came to Naples because it offered the protection of the

Colonna family, who have a powerful influence in this city. But it is still a violent city. I was very worried that ruffians might break into our home to try to kill Michele.'

Louis shuddered. 'Michele told me he did not mean to kill that poor boy in Rome and I believed him. It was worth the risk to have a genius like Michele in our home. I used to watch him working for hours on end. He didn't know I was watching him. That brooding demeanour, those intense dark eyes staring at the canvas and then the brush starting to move and the most extraordinary images leaping off the surface. Do you know, Signor Maddano, that Michele did not even make preparatory drawings! Extraordinary! It was all there in his head and it just came out of his brain and on to that canvas almost perfectly formed.'

'You certainly wasted hours watching him,' Vinck said, petulantly. 'You hardly looked at me or my work while Michele was here, not to mention ignoring your own work.'

Louis looked at me with an expression that demonstrated his exasperation with his partner. 'I made many copies of Michele's work,' he explained. 'We sent them all over Europe to promote Michele's reputation.'

I said: 'Michele was prone to be annoyed when anyone copied his style. Didn't he mind that you were making copies of his work?'

'Bless you,' Louis smiled happily. 'Michele could not have been more pleased! Abraham and I were not rivals to Michele, you see. We were simply admirers and who does not enjoy a devoted admirer, Signor Maddano? We took care of Michele, made a fuss of him, soothed his feathers and found him lots of work.'

'Well,' I said, 'that is what I have come here to find out. Michele scored an enormous success in Naples and was making lots of money. He knew . . .'

Once again, Louis Finson could not resist interrupting me. 'After everyone had seen the Madonna della Misericordia,' he gushed, 'I mean all us artists, virtually every artist in Naples stopped what they were doing and started painting like Michele. Sellitto, Santafede, Carracciolo, Corenzio, not to mention we two here, we all changed our approach.'

I could not think which painting Finson was referring to until I realised that Madonna della Misericordia was the original title of Caravaggio's work now known as the Seven Acts of Mercy. He had painted it with the full intention that it would take the Neapolitan art world by storm and he had succeeded.

'This is what I am trying to discover,' I said. 'Michele had such an enormous success here in Naples, why did he . . .'

Louis Finson was about to interrupt again but Abraham Vinck put a restraining hand on his arm and said: 'Let our guest finish his sentence, Louis.'

'Of course,' Louis said, contritely. 'I apologise, Signor Maddano. Abraham thinks I talk too much.'

'Not at all,' I lied. 'Why did Michele suddenly leave for Malta and abandon all the success he was achieving here in Naples?'

Vinck and Finson looked at each other. Abraham Vinck said to his partner: 'We must tell Signor Maddano about our visitor. What harm can it do now?'

'If Michele was murdered, as Signor Maddano suspects, then we must do all in our power to help him catch the culprit,' Louis Finson agreed, soberly.

Vinck said: 'A compatriot of ours, a Flemish lawyer named Theodore Amayden, arrived one day from Rome. He talked to Michele in private. After Amayden left, Michele was like a changed man.'

'Suddenly, he couldn't wait to get away from us,' Louis Finson confirmed. 'Not away from us, but away from Naples. Malta, Malta, Malta, that's all we heard from him!'

I remembered the name Amayden from my researches but said nothing to my hosts. 'Do you know what this lawyer said to Michele?'

'No,' Vinck answered. 'Not specifically. But it was obvious that Amayden had promised that, if Michele left Naples and travelled to Malta, it would be hugely to his advantage. But what was actually said, we never knew, and Michele did not tell us.'

I said: 'Then I must go back to Rome and interview this lawyer . . . this Theodore Amayden.'

'There is no need to travel back to Rome,' Abraham Vinck said. 'Theodore now lives in Naples. Being Flemish himself, he found the large Flemish community here much to his liking and was delighted by the beautiful scenery around Naples.'

'Excellent,' I said. 'Can you tell me where he lives?'

'He has a quite charming villa not more than three or four streets away,' Louis said.

'If you give me directions,' I said, 'I will go to see Signor Amayden.'

'Would it be of service if I went to see Theodore and brought him back here?' Louis offered. 'Knowing Theodore, if a stranger just turned up out of the blue and asked to see him, he would not admit you. But I can always tempt Theodore out to look at some new paintings and then I could introduce you and assure him of your bona fides.'

'That would be most helpful,' I agreed, 'but it's pouring with rain. I couldn't ask you to get soaked just to make it more convenient for me.'

'Nonsense,' Louis said eagerly, standing up. He looked out through to the shop window. 'It's stopped raining now. The sun is coming out. I will go now and return with Theodore in a trice. Abraham will entertain you while I am gone.' Before I could protest further, Louis Finson had dashed out on his mission.

The thought of being 'entertained' by the saturnine Abraham Vinck and being subjected to his thoughts on the cruel Spanish rule in his home country and the magnificent part being played by England in securing its freedom did not appeal to me, so I asked if I could view some of the pictures stacked up against the wall. 'You don't have any of Michele's work still in your possession, do you?' I asked.

'Alas, no,' Vinck replied. In order to pass the time and avoid awkward conversation, I made an exaggerated play of examining each painting that Vinck showed me. I looked at every painting that was in the office and then we went out into the shop. We were looking at the last stack, and almost the last picture of all, when Vinck showed me a portrait of a young woman. I recognised her immediately as Fillide Melandroni. It was a superb portrait but certainly not painted in the style of Caravaggio. Whoever had painted it was a very talented artist. Fillide's jewellery and elaborate dress were painted with exquisite skill, and the artist had captured her bewitching and teasing expression.

'This is delightful,' I said to Vinck.

'It is! If only we could sell it,' he replied mournfully.

'I would have thought such an attractive and skilled work could be sold easily,' I said.

'If we knew who the subject of the portrait was, then perhaps so. But an anonymous Portrait of a Lady does not seem to be attractive to the Neapolitan cognoscenti.'

'But I know who she is,' I said.

'You do?' Vinck answered, in surprise. 'Who is she?'

'I cannot recall her name,' I lied, 'but I have met her a few times at social events in Rome. I would love to take this back to her as a gift. How did such a portrait come to be in your shop? Do you know who painted it?'

'Yes,' Vinck said. 'It was in a batch that we bought years ago from a compatriot of ours, a young artist who was apparently working in Rome at the time. I don't know what happened to him. I think he went back to the old country.'

'Can you remember his name?' I asked.

'Yes . . . Peter something,' Vinck pondered. 'Yes, that's it . . . Peter Paul Rubens.'

I nearly dropped the painting in shock. I was holding a portrait of Fillide Melandroni by Peter Paul Rubens, a work which would be completely unknown in my own century. I remembered that a painting by Rubens, his Massacre of the Innocents, had sold for £45 million just a few years before. That was a much larger painting, of course, but what I held in my hands must be worth several million pounds in the 21st century market. The young Rubens

354

had obviously availed himself of the services of Fillide Melandroni when he was working in Rome. Why he had not given her this portrait could never be known. I clutched the frame harder, to stop my hands from shaking, and casually asked: 'How much are you asking for this painting?'

'To you, Signor Maddano, as an Englishman and a friend of Michele, you can have it for nothing with my blessing.' I started to protest but Vinck held his hand up and said: 'I know Louis will agree with me. He loved Michele dearly, as I did. Please take this portrait, give it to the lady concerned, if you wish. If a painting cannot be sold, I would sooner have it out in the world giving pleasure than gathering mould in our shop.'

I thought: 'Give it to Fillide? Not bloody likely! This portrait is coming back to the 21st century with me!' It is not often, especially in the 21st century, that being English brings any respect or reward as far as foreigners are concerned and, as far as this particular arrogant Imperialist fascist stiff-upper-lipped haughty war-mongering how-d'ye-do Englishman was concerned, I was going to fill my boots with this one. I knew that if I carried the painting outside of the ChronoConverter chain it would age by four hundred years on the journey back and look entirely genuine. Rubens was a very prolific artist and it would not be at all strange if one of his unknown works turned up unexpectedly. I could hardly contain my excitement and I had almost forgotten why I was in 17th century Naples when Louis Finson walked back into the shop followed by a man who I knew must be the lawyer Theodore Amayden. I was still holding the Rubens portrait when Louis Finson said to me: 'Signor Maddano, may I introduce the distinguished lawyer Signor Theodore Amayden.' Amayden was an old man, I guessed about seventy years old, but he was tall, erect and dignified and his eyes suggested that he had lost none of his mental acuity. He was dressed all in black, as befitted his legal status, except for a white shirt with a wide embroidered collar. He was clean shaven and had a shock of white hair that flew in all directions like the proverbial mad professor. I returned Amayden's bow and put the Rubens back down on the stack, making a mental note not to forget it when I left. Finson continued talking to me: 'I have explained to Theodore your purpose in visiting Naples, your inquiry into the suspected murder of Michele, and your papal authority.'

'Well,' I demurred, 'papal authority is not strictly accurate. Papal approval would, perhaps, be a fairer summary.' To Amayden I said: 'Please understand, Signor Amayden, that I have no real legal authority either. The only legal power I have is to pass on any facts that I might discover about Michele's death to the appropriate official legal authorities. But even that course of action is not certain. My main purpose is to keep the promise I made to Michele himself that, if he died in suspicious circumstances, I would do my best to discover what had happened. He was a hunted and haunted man at the end. He knew that his life might end violently. You are certainly not under any suspicion yourself but, as I understand things, it was after your visit to Michele that he suddenly discovered a resolve to travel to Malta.'

Amayden regarded me suspiciously and considered my statement for several seconds. Then he said: 'I am sorry, Signor Maddano, but I cannot tell you anything. Whatever I may or may not have said to Michelangelo Merisi is covered by the confidentiality I owe to the client who hired me to deliver the message. Without his permission, I cannot tell you anything.'

Desperately trying to think of a convincing argument, I said: 'Is client confidentiality superior to the truth you owe to God and the Holy Father?'

'I am not of the Catholic faith,' Amayden replied, 'so I do not owe the Holy Father anything. As to God, the oath of confidentiality I make to a client is an oath to God.'

Louis Finson, listening to this exchange, was wringing his hands with anxiety. Abraham Vinck looked uncomfortable and put his hand on his partner's shoulders in an attempt to calm him down.

I said to Amayden: 'If my suspicions are correct, that Michelangelo Merisi was murdered, and that he left Naples for Malta and thence eventually to his death because of actions that you conspired in, doesn't that mean that you owe Merisi justice. I enjoin you to tell me the truth.'

'That is no argument at all,' Amayden replied. He turned to Vinck and Finson and asked: 'Would you mind if I talked to Signor Maddano alone, perhaps in your office?'

Louis Finson stared at us as if he was in a trance but Vinck said: 'Not at all, please carry on.'

I followed Amayden into the back room office. I sat down at the desk while Amayden closed the door but left it slightly ajar and positioned his chair so that he could be certain that Vinck and Finson were not eavesdropping outside. He sat down and said: 'Signor Maddano, I appreciate that you have travelled all the way from Rome to make these inquiries, but I really cannot tell you anything, except to give you a piece of advice.'

'Go ahead,' I said.

'My dear friend, the fragrant Louis Finson, tells me that you are English. Is that so?'

'Yes,' I admitted. 'Is that a problem?'

'Not for me,' Amayden replied. 'Unlike Abraham, I could not care less one way or another about England, or Italy for that matter. But I do care about my own skin. And so should you. My advice is to get out of Italy and back to England as soon as you can.'

'I have every intention of doing so,' I answered, truthfully.

'Good, because you are delving into things that are beyond your power to comprehend or to adjust. Seeking truth and justice for Merisi is a laudable aim but let me ask you a blunt question, Signor Maddano: Is it worth getting a blade run through your back in order to obtain justice for that arrogant braggart? That is what you are asking for. I have been told about the enquiries you have been making in Rome. You have ruffled many feathers and the squawking is getting louder and louder. Forget this futile quest and flee to England . . . as fast as you can.'

I considered that anyone who was genuinely not going to tell me anything would not have made such a teasing statement. I had formed the impression that Amayden desperately wanted to talk to me but was afraid to do so. I said: 'Can you tell me anything about the message that you delivered to Merisi? Surely it will not be breaking client confidentiality to tell me, in general terms, what were the contents of this message that prompted Merisi to precipitously leave increasing wealth and the felicitous care of Vinck and Finson to go and live in Malta.'

'As I have just indicated, Signor Maddano, this is a dangerous business. My client knew that Merisi's life was threatened if he remained in Naples. I see no harm in telling you that the message promised Merisi complete safety from his pursuers, guaranteed by the Knights of Saint John, and promised that all efforts would be made to obtain a knighthood for Merisi himself.'

'Yes, a knighthood was an honour that Michele desired above all else. So your client was a friend and protector to Merisi?'

Amayden considered whether to reply and then said: 'Yes, he was . . . and is.'

I remembered facts about Theodore Amayden from my researches and decided to try the ploy I had used before, culled from watching too many American and British television cop shows, and pretend that I knew something that I didn't in an attempt to make Amayden talk. I said: 'Signor Amayden, I have been waiting to ascertain how honest you would be with me but I have been less than honest with you, because I know that your client was Michele's friend and patron Cardinal Francesco Del Monte.'

I was gratified to see that Amayden was thunderstruck by my remark and his reply was far more vehement, and different, from what I had expected. 'You are mistaken, Signor Maddano. Sadly mistaken. I would not work for that hypocritical two-faced dog if he was the last client left in the world. He is a pander and a poisoner for that wretch Ferdinando de Medici and yet he parades his oh-so-pious frugality and simplicity around Rome with ostentatious reasonableness. He is like a cherry tree, Signor Maddano. Above the surface, the blossoms look very attractive and give delight. Under the shade of his branches he shelters artists and poets and sculptors. But under the surface, like the roots of the tree, Del Monte's tentacles snake out in all directions, covered in dirt and filth, to strangle and destroy all around him. And no-one, apart from a few such as I, know what is really going on in that cunning and calculating mind of his. Cardinal Del Monte was not a friend to Merisi. The man who sent me to visit Merisi knows, like me, what Del Monte is really like and was a true friend and supporter of Merisi. My client was attempting to get Merisi to safety.'

'Vincenzo Giustiniani,' I stated, in a tone that suggested that I was certain, although I was still making an educated guess.

'Very clever,' Amayden admitted. 'You have been playing with me, Signor Maddano. You are much better informed than I imagined you could be. I wish I knew how. Yes, Marchese Vincenzo Giustiniani, Cavaliere de Bassano, a man of incomparable virtue and merit. I have known him for over twenty years, Signor Maddano, and saw him virtually every day when in Rome. The world has never seen a greater intellect. He can discourse on all things, even the most recondite science. He is affable and erudite and completely honest. He admired the work of Caravaggio beyond reason. Of course, Vincenzo was protected from Merisi's odd humours because of his rank and wealth, but he thought Merisi the greatest artist he had ever known. I have been present when Merisi and Annibale Carracci were holding a stylistic debate with Vincenzo, and Vincenzo delighted in every second of it. Yes, Vincenzo asked me to travel here and persuade Merisi to go to Malta where he would be out of danger and be afforded every honour possible.'

'Did Vincenzo tell you why Merisi was in danger? Who was pursuing him?'

'No,' Amayden replied. 'I tell you truly, Signor Maddano, that Vincenzo never told me any details, only that Merisi was in danger and that forces were operating that were beyond the control of even an extremely wealthy and influential man such as himself. Vincenzo knows everything that goes on in Rome, in Italy and, quite possibly, the whole of Europe.'

'I have met Vincenzo Giustiniani once,' I said, vividly remembering Giustiniani's enigmatic behaviour. 'In fact, it was at the home of Cardinal Del Monte, the Palazzo Madama. I formed the impression that the Cardinal and Vincenzo were close friends.'

'That is just the impression that Vincenzo intends to convey,' Amayden said. 'As the old saying goes: "keep your friends close but your enemies even closer". Will you now return to Rome and interview Vincenzo?'

'Perhaps,' I said. 'I will have to consider my next course of action. I thank you for your frankness after I have placed you in a difficult situation, Signor Amayden. If I do see Vincenzo again I give you my word that I will not betray your trust. He need know nothing about this meeting.'

'I accept your word, Signor Maddano. Thank you. Now, if you have finished with me, the perfumed pair outside have promised me some fine new paintings to look at.'

We went back out into the shop where Louis and Abraham were ostentatiously busying themselves doing nothing in particular. I said: 'My business here is complete. Thank you for your hospitality, gentlemen. Michele spoke to me often in gratitude for your kindness towards him. It has been a pleasure to meet you.'

'Oh, do come back and see us again!' Louis Finson cried.

I bowed and went out into the street. I turned down the hill towards the alleyway where I could operate the ChronoConverter for my return journey. The sun was now shining strongly and, in the distance, I could see the vivid blue Mediterranean sea. I was tempted to walk down to the harbour but I had been given a lot to think about and wanted to get back home to ponder all that I had just learned from Amayden. I turned down the deserted alleyway, carefully looked around to make sure I was alone and hidden from view by the stacks of crates. I was just about to operate the ChronoConverter when I heard a thin, hysterical voice shouting: 'Signor Maddano! Signor Maddano!' I went back out to the mouth of the alleyway just as Louis Finson ran past me carrying a framed painting.

'Louis!' I shouted after him. 'I'm back here!'

Finson stopped and turned around and came running back to me. 'Oh, Signor Maddano! You nearly forgot your painting!'

I was shocked to realise that I had left behind the Rubens portrait of Fillide Melandroni. It was like realising you had left a winning National Lottery ticket in the pocket of your trousers after you had put them in the washing machine. I accepted the painting from Louis Finson and said: 'Are you sure that you do not want payment for this, Louis?'

'No, of course not. Abraham was right to give it to you. Just go and find justice for that poor boy Michele.'

'I'll do my best, Louis,' I promised, and clutched financial security for the rest of my life, in the shape of the Rubens portrait, to my fast-beating heart.

40

I floated back through time to my own bedroom. I was firmly clutching the Rubens portrait of Fillide Melandroni outside of my ChronoConverter chain so that, without the protection of the ChronoConverter, the painting and frame would age the requisite four hundred years and would pass any expert analysis as entirely genuine. As soon as I had materialised, I eagerly examined the picture. It was early evening and the light was still good. The wooden frame had certainly lost its pristine gold-painted condition and the oil paint of the portrait itself was still clean and bright but was affected by the network of fine cracks, known as craquelure, that can only be achieved by the passage of time. It was perfect. I gently laid the picture on the bed and changed into a T-shirt and Levi's, relieved to be once again free of the confining and over-elaborate fashions of the seventeenth century. I rummaged in the drawers of my divan bed and found a spare bedsheet. I carefully wrapped the Rubens portrait in the bedsheet and placed it in the back of my wardrobe, concealed by a large suitcase and other bric-a-brac. Nobody in the 21st century knew I was in possession of such a valuable object. I had no intention of mentioning to anybody, and certainly not to Merisi, that I was in possession of such a painting until I was ready to put it up for sale. I felt incredibly elated. All my money problems, for the rest of my life, were solved. I already had a Rubens worth millions, or several hundred thousands of pounds, and Merisi had promised to paint me his best work before he disappeared from my life. That painting would certainly be worth several millions of pounds. I would have to be very canny about how I put the two paintings on the market, probably through trustworthy intermediaries so that it was not apparent that two such rare works came from the same source, but I could work on that scheme later.

As I left my bedroom I could hear sounds of laughter coming from the direction of my back garden. I went into Merisi's room to look through the window and try to see what was going on. A long section of Mrs. Chowdry's trellis garden fence was lying on my lawn. The blue wisteria that once covered the fence was also spread across my lawn. Merisi was standing in front of the wreckage. He was talking to somebody in Mrs. Chowdry's garden. Whoever he was talking to was concealed by the remains of the tall trellis fence. Merisi was holding what looked to be a glass of champagne. My heart sank. What was that Italian maniac up to this time? Holding a rave party in my back garden? I rushed downstairs and out through the back door. As I approached Merisi I could see that he had a purple and yellow black eye and he was talking to Mr. and Mrs. Chowdry. 'Michele!' I called out. 'What have you been up to this time?' Then, as I approached nearer, I said to the Chowdrys: 'I'm so sorry. I'll pay for whatever damage my friend has caused.' To my surprise, the Chowdrys did not look the least bit perturbed. In fact, they were smiling and also holding glasses of champagne.

'Don't worry, old chap,' Mr. Chowdry said. 'Mr. Merisi was helping us to clear up the mess. Have a glass of champagne.' Perched on top of a wheelie bin was a tray holding glasses and a bottle of champagne.

'Who did this?' I asked. 'Who ripped the fence down?'

'I did,' Merisi said, 'I was in the . . .'

'Are you crazy?' I shouted. 'Haven't you caused enough trouble to my neighbours?'

'Take it easy, Mr. Maddan,' Mr. Chowdry said. 'Here.' He handed me a glass of champagne. 'We were saving this up for our fortieth wedding anniversary but this is a much more special occasion. If it had not been for Mr. Merisi, we might not have been having an anniversary celebration at all.'

Mrs. Chowdry was looking at Merisi with something like adoration. I was thoroughly confused. 'Would somebody please explain what has happened here?' I said.

Mrs. Chowdry said: 'Mr. Merisi saved my life this afternoon.'

'Thank you, signora, but that is an exaggeration,' Merisi said.

'I don't think so,' Mrs. Chowdry insisted. 'Those men was intent on doing me serious harm.'

'What men?' I asked.

'They are so-called "travellers", Mrs. Chowdry said. 'They are well-known troublemakers and inveterate racists. As you know, I am a magistrate and, a few months ago, I had occasion to sentence all three of them for petty larceny and drunk and disorderly offences. The fact that I am a "bloody foreigner" was enough excuse in their twisted minds to cause them to hurl the most filthy abuse and threats against me while I was still sitting on the bench. They had to be dragged out of the courtroom. Well, earlier today I was in my back room working on some papers. My husband was out on business. Suddenly the French doors were smashed in and these three travellers forced themselves into the house. As you can imagine, I screamed in shock. They were shouting the most vile obscenities at me and had just started to move towards me when suddenly

Mr. Merisi appeared and clouted one of them on the back of the head with a cricket bat. This attacker fell down unconscious but the other two turned on Mr. Merisi. They both lunged at Mr. Merisi and they all fell to the ground. They had quite a fight. Fortunately, Mr. Merisi is a much bigger and stronger man than the travellers and they eventually thought better of taking him on any further. Their companion regained consciousness and then caught Mr. Merisi by surprise and managed to punch him in the face. But all three of them had had enough by then and shoved Mr. Merisi out of the way and managed to escape. I'm sure they would have done me serious harm if Mr. Merisi had not intervened.'

I had noticed my old cricket bat laying on the Chowdry's lawn and wondered how it came to be there. Smiling, Mr. Chowdry said: 'Mr. Merisi played a superb innings . . . worthy of Sachin Tendulkar. I hear that his reverse sweep is a beautiful stroke to see!' Merisi, naturally, was baffled by these cricket references.

'But why is the fence strewn all over my lawn?' I asked.

Merisi said: 'I was in the summerhouse working when I heard glass smashing and Signora Chowdry screaming. I grabbed the first weapon I could lay hands on, that heavy wooden club you call a cricket bat, and looked over the fence. I could see these men attacking Signora Chowdry. I knew I did not have time to run around to the front and up the drive so I just ripped down this fence and jumped into her garden.'

'Mr. Merisi was incredibly brave,' Mrs. Chowdry said.

Merisi actually had the grace to blush. 'It was nothing, signora, I was used to trouble like that all the time in Rome. I remember . . .'

I interrupted before Merisi could say anything incriminating. To Mrs. Chowdry I said: 'What about these travellers? Aren't you afraid they might come back?'

'Oh, I reported all this to the police and they arrived very quickly. It probably helps that I am a magistrate. They took statements from Mr. Merisi and I and the three miscreants have been arrested already. They are safely in custody.'

The Chowdrys moved away to finish clearing the broken glass from off their patio. I turned to Merisi and said: 'Well, Michele, you are turning yourself into quite the hero, aren't you. First you save my skin from the muggers in Bedford, now you save Mrs. Chowdry from a gang of thugs.' I raised my glass of champagne. 'Congratulations.'

Merisi regarded me with a serious look. He said: 'Such actions are out of character for me but I hate to see anyone bullied and I have never allowed myself to be bullied, even if it meant I had to become a bully myself. I know that is a morally ambivalent thing to say. I hope that God will see that helping you and Signora Chowdry makes up, just a little, for the sin of killing Tomassoni.' Then he smiled: 'But you know how much I love a good fight.'

41

I handed Merisi a mug of coffee, settled myself in my armchair, and said: 'So why did you abandon a flourishing and prosperous career in Naples and move to Malta?'

Merisi took a sip of coffee and replied: 'Because I wanted to be made a Knight of the Order of St. John.'

'Why was that suddenly so important to you?'

'There was no "suddenly" about it,' Merisi said, almost angrily. 'All my life, like many young men at that time, I had dreamed of becoming a knight, especially a knight of Malta. I had always felt ashamed and belittled by my lowly status in life. I could create pictures, miraculous for their beauty, truth and intensity, and yet I still had to bow my head in front of rich and powerful men in order to survive. My belligerence, my love of swordplay, was all tied up with this dream of becoming someone better than I was . . . someone of higher rank, honour and status. When Giuseppe Cesari was created a knight by the pope and became the Cavaliere d'Arpino, it almost drove me mad with jealousy. To become a Knight of the Order of St. John would have elevated me above him, and above most of my friends and acquaintances.'

'But what made you think that you could obtain a knighthood in Malta?' I asked, holding back my knowledge of the secret visit that had been made to Merisi. 'After all, you were a fugitive from the law of Rome, branded as a murderer. Surely that would have made your being created a knight an insoluble problem?'

'Not necessarily,' Merisi replied. 'In the eyes of the knights of St. John, there were worse crimes than murder, depending upon the circumstances. The knights were known for awarding the accolade to men of honour and virtue, men who had excelled in their chosen field of endeavour, as I had in the field of painting.'

'Surely you would still have had a better chance of a papal knighthood back in Rome? There were already grave legal doubts about whether you had deliberately intended to murder Ranuccio Tomassoni. Rome was where you had made your reputation, where you had many powerful patrons, protectors and allies.'

'I would still have preferred a knighthood from Malta,' Merisi said. 'Perhaps it is difficult for an Englishman from this modern time to understand in what high respect the Knights of St. John were held. They had moved to Malta from Rhodes in the first half of the sixteenth century and, in 1565, had held off a terrible onslaught by the Turks under that devil Suleiman, known as the Magnificent. For months, the knights had suffered terrible hardships and privations but had defended Christian Europe with courage and dignity and, in the end, had driven off the Turkish hordes. Every young boy, every young man of my time would have been honoured to be a knight of Malta. And then, a few years later, at the decisive sea battle of Lepanto against the Turks, the Maltese galleys played a distinguished role in the battle. So, the knights themselves were held in the highest esteem, by popes and kings, as well as we humble mortals, and the island of Malta was seen as a shining Christian bulwark against the dark invading Turkish devils. I could not help myself, Stefano. I longed to be one of them and I had to take my chance in Malta. And another good reason was that I was much safer in Malta. Don't forget that I was the subject of a banda capitale. Anyone could kill me, and I knew the Tomassoni clan would be seeking revenge. In Naples, I had to be very careful. Despite the protection of the Colonna family I was still very vulnerable. In Malta, as a guest of the knights and under their protection, no-one would dare touch me.'

I had to admit the strength of Merisi's argument. 'As you say, Michele, a very good reason. You journeyed to Valetta in the summer of 1607. What was Malta like in those days?'

'Valletta was, back then, a newly-built city. After the Great Siege, the knights decided to build a new and impregnable capital city and the city was named after their leader and revered hero during the Great Siege, the Grand Master Jean de La Valette Morisot. It was a small city, built on a rocky promontory, but elegant and pleasing. It had been laid out on a grid plan, with long streets enlivened with small gardens and fountains. Of course, the whole city was surrounded by an enormous defensive wall but, within this wall, the city was delightful, with stone buildings of a warm and glowing colour.'

'Where did you stay in Valetta? Did you have a studio there?'

'No. I stayed in what was known as an Auberge. Each nation had its own Auberge. They were two-storey buildings built within the city, not cut off from the general populace, which made it very pleasant, and we were surrounded by shops and traders and taverns and women. My Auberge, the Italian, had a flat roof. We could sit out on the roof in the summer, getting drunk and calling out to the women to come up and see us. It was a convivial atmosphere.'

I asked: 'I thought the Knights of St. John were supposed to be a Christian monk-like order? You say you were all drinking and fornicating?'

Merisi laughed. 'In theory they were supposed to be meek and Christ-like and pure and virtuous, but try imposing that sort of morality on lusty young warriors from all around Europe. Impossible! A few years earlier, the Grand Master had attempted to rid Valletta of its loose and disorderly women. Well, the knights actually rebelled against that edict and the Grand Master had to back down. I have to say that I found most of the knights to be as arrogant and worldly, promiscuous and drunken, as ready for a brawl as most of the other soldiers I've known in my life. The knights didn't care to live like Christ, but they were more than ready to die for Him.'

'The Grand Master of the Knights of St. John, when you arrived, was a Frenchman named Alof de Wignacourt. Your portrait of him survives. He looks like a formidable man.'

'Indeed he was,' Merisi agreed. 'You know me, I'm not afraid of any man and I was not afraid of de Wignacourt but I was very careful not to cross him. He had arrived in Malta from Picardy just after the Great Siege. As with thousands of young European men, he had been inspired by the heroics of the Great Siege and had come to Malta determined to make his name in defence of Christianity. This he rapidly did. He became a Grand Hospitaller of France, Captain of the City of Valletta and, about five years before I arrived, became the Grand Master with a pledge to restore the Order to its former prestige and splendour. He was about sixty years old when I first met him. He was as tough as an ox. Not tall, but stocky and powerfully built. His hair was thin above a rough and suntanned soldier's face. He had a large nose, with a large wart on it, but heaven help you if you mentioned the wart or sought to make fun of him. In the year I arrived in Malta he was made a Prince of the Holy Roman Empire and thus gained the title of Serene Highness. And he ruled the Order like a prince. The palace of the Grand Master was a large, plain square building built around a courtyard and gardens. The palace was covered by appallingly bad frescoes by an artist named d'Aleccio. When I saw them, I wondered whether I could ingratiate myself further by replacing them with more accomplished work. Anyway, de Wignacourt spent a lot of his own money on the upkeep of the Order, as well as living lavishly in his palace. He had about a dozen servants looking after him and almost two hundred slaves. He was very well established.'

Mention of that heinous crime of slavery, especially perpetrated by a so-called Christian, was appalling to my 21st century sensibilities and I would have liked to have asked Merisi more about that aspect of de Wignacourt's life but I did not want to be distracted from our main purpose, so I simply said: 'Such a man must have been more powerful and influential than most cardinals or dukes, perhaps even more so than some princes and kings?'

'Yes, he certainly was. Not only was he the commander of a formidable body of fighting men, feared and respected throughout Christendom as well as the Moslem world, but young men from the most noble families in Europe courted him assiduously to be allowed into the Order. He knew everyone who was anyone in Europe, apart from you heretic Northerners.'

'We know that you had some very influential friends in Malta when you arrived,' I said.

'Who do you mean?' Merisi asked, warily.

'One of the Giustiniani clan, Marc'Aurelio, was on the island when you arrived, trying to offer de Wignacourt a property in which he could found an Italian division of the Order.'

'Ah, yes. I remember that he was there but I had little to do with him.'

I had no doubt that the presence of Marc'Aurelio Giustiniani, almost certainly sent by Vincenzo, had smoothed Merisi's reception. I said: 'You must have had more to do with Costanza Colonna's son, Fabrizio Sforza Colonna?' I had never told Merisi that I had already met Fabrizio once through our encounter in the Contarelli chapel where he and his brother Muzio were escorting their mother.

'Once again, I am impressed with what you know,' Merisi smiled. 'Fabrizio was an even more stormy and difficult character than I was, and had gotten into even more trouble with the law. Fabrizio had committed some serious crime in Rome but, because he was Costanza's son, the pope did not want him sent to prison, so he sent Fabrizio to Malta and entrusted his care to the knights. He was, for years, kept in a sort of open house arrest, officially in prison but allowed a great deal of freedom. Because of his noble blood, de Wignacourt, and a lot of powerful friends of the Colonna family, tried to clear his name and eventually the case against Fabrizio was deemed unproven and he was given his freedom. De Wignacourt insisted that Fabrizio stay with the Order and perform some service with them as recompense for the help and protection he had received. Fabrizio was made a General of the Galleys. I travelled with him, on his galley, from Naples to Malta. It was his first voyage in command.'

I had been waiting to hear if Merisi volunteered this information about Fabrizio Sforza but, as usual, I had had to winkle it out of him, so I wanted him to be uncertain of what I already knew in order to test his veracity. 'Was there anyone else of any importance travelling on this voyage?'

'Yes. There was Ippolito Malaspina, who was one of de Wignacourt's closest friends and advisers. Malaspina was another impressive man, famed for his courage. Unlike de Wignacourt, he had fought at both the Great Siege of Malta and in the battle of Lepanto. Malaspina had been living in Rome, at a palace in the Piazza Navona, near where I lived, attending the papal court, so I knew him fairly well. The Grand Master wanted him back in Malta, so he travelled back on the galleys with us.'

'With connections like these, Michele, it's not surprising that you were immediately accepted into the highest social circles of the Knights of St. John. We believe that, for obvious reasons, your first paintings in Malta were portraits of the Grand Master, de Wignacourt. Is that correct?'

'Yes, indeed. As you imply, I was eager to ingratiate myself with the Grand Master and my first two works were portraits of him, one showing him standing, attended by a page and dressed in full armour; the second seated, not wearing armour.'

'Do you remember who the page was who is carrying the Grand Master's helmet in the armoured portrait?'

'No, I cannot remember who he was,' Merisi answered.

'It may interest you to know that it is Nicholas de Pris Boissy. He became the Grand Prior of France in 1657.'

Merisi nodded appreciatively. 'I recall he was a cheeky monkey, which I tried to show.'

'Unfortunately,' I said, 'the seated portrait is now lost but the portrait of de Wignacourt in his black armour survives in all its glory.' (*Plate 50*).

'That is very gratifying,' Merisi said. 'I next made a portrait of Saint Jerome for Ippolito Malaspina. I included the Malaspina coat-of-arms in this portrait. Does that one survive?' (*Plate 51*).

'Yes, it does,' I replied, and showed Merisi a picture of the Malaspina St. Jerome. 'It's now housed in Valletta Cathedral.'

'A good place for it,' Merisi commented. 'I think my next work was a portrait of another of the Grand Master's close friends and confidantes, Fra Antonio Martelli. (*Plate 52*). Like Malaspina, Martelli had had a long and distinguished military career. He had fought with valour during the Great Siege and later, having recovered from a severe wound, had spent several years in the service of Ferdinando Medici, the Grand Duke of Tuscany.'

'Were the subjects of these portraits pleased with your work?'

'Very much so,' Merisi said, a tad smugly. 'Especially Martinelli. I thought that I might have made him look too old or too haggard but he was a down-to-earth man and he told me that his whole life of service and suffering was captured in my portrait.'

'A fine compliment,' I said. 'And these four works won you a precious award, we believe?'

'Yes,' Merisi replied, 'the Grand Master graciously awarded me the Cross of Malta for my efforts. Such an award was not easily won.'

'Even more importantly,' I said, 'the Grand Master himself now embarked on a quite extraordinary campaign to get you rehabilitated.'

'What was extraordinary about it?' Merisi asked, irritably.

'Forgive me for saying say so, Michele, but despite your eminence as an artist, there seemed to be very little else going for you. You did not come from a noble family, you were not a distinguished soldier, and you were not wealthy. So why was Grand Master de Wignacourt so keen to win your rehabilitation from the papal court? Why did he involve himself, personally, on your behalf when he was receiving requests for favours and preferment from noble families all over Europe, and especially when he knew you had been accused of murder in Rome? Homicide was a serious bar to ever becoming a Knight of St. John. De Wignacourt's efforts on your behalf seem completely out of proportion to your importance.'

Merisi scowled at me. 'Well, the ability to create great works of art might not seem of much importance to you but de Wignacourt was a man of taste and valour. He was keen to secure my services on a permanent basis.'

'That is still not a convincing reason,' I persisted. 'For instance, at the end of 1607, de Wignacourt wrote two letters to his ambassadors at the papal court in Rome. Those letters ardently, almost aggressively, pleaded your cause. He even wrote that he wanted to invoke, quote: "one single time" an ancient privilege to award you a knighthood "without the necessity of proofs". He goes on to say that he "passionately" desires to honour "a most virtuous person, of most honoured qualities and habits". Even your best friend, Michele, would not recognise you as "a most virtuous person of honoured qualities and habits"?'

'As I said,' Merisi replied, unconvincingly, 'de Wignacourt wanted me to remain in his service.'

'That's lame, Michele. The Grand Master could have snapped his fingers and had almost any accomplished painter in Europe at his court, most of them would have arrived with far less problems than you presented.'

'But I was the greatest painter in Europe at that time,' he protested.

'Many would argue with that judgement,' I said. 'I would not, but many would, especially at that time. The Grand Master even states, in his letter, that you will not be denied a knighthood because you had, in a brawl, committed a homicide. That is an extraordinary thing for the head of an Order, devoted to Christians virtues, to write.' Merisi made a dismissive gesture but said nothing, so I continued. 'Then, early in 1608, Grand Master de Wignacourt wrote to Pope Paul himself, begging for the authority, quote: "for one time only" to award a knighthood to yourself and another person. So, once again, a man who wields immense power and influence such as de Wignacourt is almost abasing himself in front of the pope, asking for a special privilege on your behalf. You, a lowly and humble painter from a small town in Lombardy!'

I thought Merisi would react angrily again but this time he was more thoughtful. 'I have to confess,' he admitted, 'that I am surprised by the efforts made on my behalf. I was not completely aware of them at the time.'

'Do you know who this second person was, for whom de Wignacourt was asking special papal dispensation to be made a knight?'

'It may have been the Conte de Brie, who was the illegitimate son of the Duc du Barry. Illegitimacy was a far more serious handicap to becoming a knight than was murder. I knew the Conte slightly and I remember that there was fierce opposition to him being admitted to the Order, even more so than there was to a "lowly and humble" painter like me becoming a knight.'

'Let's sidetrack for a minute and talk about one of your most puzzling works, one we now know as Sleeping Cupid.' I showed Merisi a picture of his work. 'What prompted you to paint such a subject, so at odds with your normal subject matter?' (*Plate 53*).

'Oh, that,' Merisi replied, dismissively. 'I painted that at the request of the Grand Master's secretary, a Florentine named Francesco dell'Antella. He suggested the subject and asked me to sign the picture on the back, which I did not normally do, just to prove that I had made the picture and so that he could brag to his dilettante friends that he possessed a genuine Caravaggio. He was pleased with it. I found him to be a strange man. I also painted for him an oval portrait of his master, de Wignacourt. We were both acting with shameless sycophancy!'

'Well, it worked,' I said, 'because we know that, in July 1608, you were received as a knight into the Order of St. John a year and a day after you had arrived in Malta.'

'Yes, that's right. Each novitiate had to spend a full year in service. I lived at the Italian Auberge near the city gate. My room was fairly spartan but the public rooms in the Auberge were luxurious and very comfortable. Most novitiates had to tend the sick in the hospital but I was allowed to forego this privilege in return for my paintings.'

'Just as well for the poor, unfortunate sick people,' I said. 'A more unlikely nurse than you is hard to imagine.'

Merisi smiled. 'Just for once, I agree with your estimate of my talents.'

'You had promptly been given papal authorisation to be received into the Order. It was clear that the grounds for this authorisation were because of your artistic genius.'

'Yes. It was the proudest day of my life,' Merisi said, wistfully. 'I was admitted to the Order as a Knight of Obedience, which was as much as I could have hoped for. Usually, that title suggested that the recipient had some claim to nobility, so it was an unusually high honour for a mere tradesman like me. Knight of Obedience was a subdivision of the noble class of the Knights of

Grace and, fortunately for me, did not entail taking vows of chastity, poverty and obedience, although we did swear to lead a life of Christian perfection and to carry out social works. I was also free, of course, to follow my profession. I remember the investiture ceremony as if it was yesterday. I kissed a white linen Cross and then received the habit of the Order, something I had always dreamed about. That was one in the eye for all my old rivals like Reni and d'Arpino and Zuccaro. I was now of a more exalted rank than they were.' Merisi grinned at me, full of self-satisfaction.

'Okay, let's talk about a work that added to your fame throughout Europe and which is, today, considered to be one of your greatest works. It was painted for the Oratory of the Co-Cathedral of St. John in Valletta and is known as the Beheading of St. John the Baptist. We believe that you began this work before you were actually admitted as a knight. Is that so?' (*Plate 54*).

'Yes. Normally a prospective knight had to pay a passagio, a large sum of money, in order to be admitted but this work was allowed to be part of my passagio. I also paid for the fitting out of a galley to fight against the Turks. That took every fucking scudi I had. Expensive business, becoming a knight in those days.'

'It still is in Britain today. If you liberally grease enough political palms today you can buy a knighthood or even a lordship, but let's not digress. We know that the Oratory of St. John was then used for several purposes, not just for religious services but for good works, as a training school for the novices and for criminal trials.'

'Yes, the Oratory was a newly-built rectangular building, plain on the outside and with a flat roof. The inside was also plain, cavernous and sombre. I was ordered to paint the execution of St. John to fill the wall at the east end. It was a big picture and I had to paint it in place.'

'It's a brutally realistic picture. If one simply looks at the painting in a book it appears to be a highly unusual composition but when one looks at it in the context of the Oratory, with the light flooding in from those high windows on the left, it succeeds dramatically. Since your time the Oratory has been redecorated in an ornate Baroque style but your painting still dominates the interior. As I have said, it made you the talk of Europe once more and artists travelled from many miles away to view it. Also, it seems to have been the only painting that you ever signed.'

'Yes,' Merisi said. 'By the time I had finished it, I had been made a knight and, in my pride, I wanted to sign it in a dramatic way, so I wrote "f. michel", meaning "Brother Michelangelo da Caravaggio" in the very centre, so that no-one in the future could be in any doubt that I had painted it and that I was a knight.'

'Did the Grand Master like your work?'

'Very much so. I calculated that its brutal honesty and simplicity would appeal to an old soldier like de Wignacourt and I was right. He rewarded me with a gold chain, which every artist coveted, and gave me two slaves.'

I should have asked Merisi about his two slaves. They might conceivably have been connected with his attempted murder but I was worried that our conversation might degenerate into a heated moral debate, so I said: 'Let's review what life was like for you at this period. One of your biographers, Bellori, comments that you lived in Malta, quote: "in dignity and abundance". You had achieved your lifelong dream, to become a knight. You had been awarded the Cross of Malta and the coveted gold chain. You had slaves and servants to attend your every whim. You were prosperous and able to enjoy life in a wealthy and cosmopolitan society. You were gaining commissions, two for Alof de Wignacourt that we know about but that are now lost, a Madgalen and a St. Jerome; and an Annunciation for Henry of Lorraine. Moreover, you must have been well on the way to a papal pardon for killing Ranuccio Tomassoni and you were completely safe from the vengeance of the Tomassoni clan or any other enemies. You had everything and then, in your own inimitable style, you threw it all away.' Merisi shifted awkwardly in his armchair but said nothing. 'You picked a fight with a Knight of Justice. Why?'

'He insulted me,' Merisi said, shortly. I waited for him to elaborate but he said no more.

'What did he say?' I asked.

'He said that I was a low dog, a mere painter, a known murderer, and not fit to be wearing the same cross as himself. He said I was a clown masquerading as a nobleman. So I drew my sword and attacked him.'

'What was this knight's name?'

'I don't remember,' Merisi said.

'Do you think he provoked you deliberately?'

'Perhaps.'

'Did this man draw his own sword?'

'No. He backed off and some of his friends approached me, threatening to draw their swords, so I withdrew.'

'But the damage had been done because to attack a brother knight, according to the laws of the Order, meant imprisonment.'

'Yes.'

'So you were taken to the formidable Castel Sant'Angelo and thrown into an underground cell, which was a bell-shaped hole cut into solid rock and about eleven feet deep.' Merisi said nothing, so I went on. 'You managed to escape from this cell. How did you do it?'

'I somehow managed to scrabble my way out,' Merisi replied.

'What about the prison guards?'

'I managed to evade them.'

'And you got out into the castle grounds?'

'Yes.'

'Weren't there any locked doors in the way?'

'No.'

'How did you scale the castle walls?'

'Luckily, I found a rope lying on the ground,' Merisi said. 'I managed to climb the castle wall and lower myself down the other side.'

'And there were no guards or sentries to impede your progress?'

'No.'

'Then you made your way to the harbour at St. Elmo.'

'Yes.'

'Where there were sentries posted, we believe?'

'I didn't see any.'

'And you found a felucca that was about to sail to Sicily?'

'Yes. I was lucky.'

'How did you pay for your passage? I presume you didn't have any money or identification or anything else, having just escaped from a prison cell?'

'Luckily, the master of the felucca was an old drinking friend of mine. I promised to pay him later.'

'And off you sailed to Sicily and freedom.'

'Yes, that's right.'

I laughed theatrically. 'Do you seriously expect me, or anyone else, to believe such an obvious pack of lies?'

'That's how it happened' Merisi said, off-handedly. I knew he was lying.

'All that we are attempting to find out is pointless if you lie to me like this, Michele. All this happened four hundred years ago. What's the point of covering it all up now?'

'That's how it happened,' he repeated stubbornly.

'You know perfectly well that I have the ability to travel back in time and establish the truth. Why don't you tell me the truth now and save me the trouble?'

'That's how it happened.'

'Very well,' I sighed. 'The laws of the Order of St. John stated that any knight leaving Malta without written permission would be deprived of his knighthood. You had now drawn your sword against a brother knight and left Malta without permission. Your knighthood was now forfeit. Everything you had worked for, every advantage you had gained, was now lost. Who helped you to escape?'

'No-one,' Merisi replied. 'I escaped as I have told you.'

'So why did the Order set up a criminal commission to investigate how you had managed this extraordinary escape which even Houdini would have been proud of?'

'Who is Houdini? Did he escape as well?'

'Many times,' I said, 'but he doesn't concern us. The commission could not establish how you had escaped but you had certainly breached the laws of the Order and, in December 1608, a public assembly of senior knights gathered in the Oratory of St. John, the very place in which you had painted your Beheading of St. John, to strip you of your knighthood. So, as one of your greatest works loomed over them, these knights voted unanimously to deprive you of your knighthood and, in a very graphic and memorable phrase, you were expelled from the Order of St. John, quote: "thrust forth like a rotten and foetid limb".'

I had learned that Merisi controlled the external expression of his emotions very well but mention of the hated phrase with which he had been expelled from his knighthood had a visible effect on him. We sat without talking for quite a while. Then I said: 'Why don't you just tell me?'

'I will not,' Merisi said, firmly.

'Very well,' I shrugged. 'You stepped off this felucca and on to Sicilian soil. You were still a branded murderer, under the threat of the banda capitale. Not only had you lost the protection of the Knights of St. John, you were now being actively pursued by them as well. No Greek tragic dramatist would have dared to write a story that heaped on you the misfortunes that you had heaped upon yourself.'

Merisi smiled at me bleakly, and still said nothing.

42

The heavy wooden door of the Oratory of Saint John closed behind me. The sound echoed through the building. The man I had come to interview, who was kneeling at the altar at the far end, rose slowly and painfully on to his feet, having to hold on to one of the wooden pews which ran down the length of the Oratory to assist his ascent. Behind him, Caravaggio's great masterpiece of the beheading of Saint John loomed out of the gathering gloom. There was nobody else in the building. My heart was beating rapidly. I was transfixed by my friend Merisi's incredible painting and nervous about having to interview the man who now turned to confront me. He was a stocky and powerfully-built man and I knew that he was now over sixty years of age. He was balding and sun-tanned, with a large wart to the right of his nose, and his eyes, which had seen death many times, were calm but hard. He looked exactly like Caravaggio's portrait. The white cross of St. John stood out brilliantly on his long black tunic. This was his Serene Highness Alof de Wignacourt, Prince of the Holy Roman Empire, Grand Master of the Knights of Saint John. 'Who are you?' he challenged me, not at all afraid. 'How dare you interrupt my communion with God?'

I knew I must not be disrespectful to this man but I must not be intimidated either. I replied: 'My name is Stefano Maddano.'

De Wignacourt pursed his lips. 'I have heard of you. You have powerful friends. How did you get in here, past all the guards?'

'Quite easily, Your Highness. As easily as one of your knights once escaped from here.'

He turned to gaze at Caravaggio's masterpiece. 'You mean the ungrateful wretch who painted this work.' He waved his hand at the huge canvas, which covered the entire east end of the Oratory.

'That's correct,' I replied. 'You have heard of me, so you must know of the quest I have been undertaking.'

'You speak French very well,' de Wignacourt said, 'but you are not French?'

I had been given a new ChronoTranslator ring so that I could converse with de Wignacourt in his native language. It had been thought that this might sweeten his attitude towards me. 'No, sir, I am not French.'

'Then what are you, Signor Maddano. Who are you? I knew you would come here eventually. I wished to be prepared. I caused extensive enquiries to be made about you, all fruitless. You seem to have appeared out of nowhere. Nobody knows of you before you turned up in Rome a few weeks ago. And now you have magically evaded all my knights and have suddenly appeared in my Oratory. Do you intend to harm me?'

'Not in any way,' I replied. 'You are a great man, a courageous soldier, a servant of God, and a protector of the Christian faith. All I want is a few minutes of your time . . . and the truth. Besides, I am unarmed, and I doubt very much whether you would allow me to harm you. I am a man of letters, not a man of the sword.'

'Very well,' de Wignacourt conceded. 'You are not going to tell me who you really are, but you speak well enough. If you wish to ask me about Michelangelo Merisi da Caravaggio, what better place than this? Shall we sit down.' De Wignacourt beckoned me over and I took the pew next to him, by his side. 'Have you seen this painting before?' he asked me.

We both looked at the brutal and uncompromising image which dominated the Oratory. 'I have heard about it,' I replied, 'but to actually see it is . . . overwhelming.'

'That is the effect it has on most of the novices who enter this building for the first time. I enjoy watching their faces when they first enter. Only a painter of genius could have created such a work. If only Merisi had not been such a madman. But, if he had not, he would not have been such a powerful artist.'

'Did you like him?' I asked.

'He interested me very much. While he painted my portrait he would explain to me his theories of art and the creative impulse. He would become very animated. His brain was very cultured and perceptive, as well as being confused and angry. Then he would suddenly remember where he was, what he was doing and who he was talking to. I was protected from his strange humours by my rank. I was impressed by his artistic sincerity, his refusal to compromise. I didn't understand what he was trying to say much of the time. I am not an intellectual, just a simple soldier.'

I smiled to myself at de Wignacourt's disingenuity. Only a man of the highest courage, subtle diplomatic skills, energetic organisational ability and Machiavellian ruthlessness could have risen to the position that he now occupied. A simple soldier he was not. I asked him bluntly: 'Why did you make such strenuous efforts to obtain a knighthood for Merisi?'

'You come to the point boldly, Monsieur Maddano. We both agree that Merisi was a painter of genius. Such skill and talent should be rewarded. I was eager for Merisi to come here to Malta and work for us, for the greater glory of the Knights of Saint John.'

'That is no doubt part of the reason,' I said, 'but, according to what I have found out, your efforts on Merisi's part are little short of incredible. He might have been a genius but he was still a humble painter, little more than a tradesman. Not only that, he was a known troublemaker, a murderer on the run with the death sentence of the banda capitale hanging over his head. And yet you aggressively lobbied the papal court in Rome to allow you to give Merisi his knighthood, even invoking an ancient privilege, quote: "one single time" to grant Merisi a knighthood "without the necessity of proofs". Your Highness, you have noblemen, dukes, princes even, all over Europe, currying your favour, desperate for their sons to be admitted as a Knight of Saint John. Why did you make such efforts for Merisi?'

I could see that de Wignacourt was not best pleased by my questioning but he answered mildly enough. 'My congratulations. I have heard that you are very well informed and that your sources are reliable. The reasons for granting Merisi a knighthood are as I have just told you.'

'Are you aware that my inquiries have been given the personal approval of the Holy Father himself, who has enjoined all who give evidence to me to tell the truth, on peril of their immortal souls?'

'Is that supposed to impress me or intimidate me, Monsieuer Maddano? I will tell you the truth as I see fit, for the benefit of God and of the order of the Knights of Saint John. I long ago commended my soul to God's safe keeping. If I do wrong and He rejects me, then it is to Him I will answer, not to this pope and his greasy nephew.'

'Were you influenced by Costanza Colonna Sforza, Marchese di Caravaggio on Merisi's behalf? After all, you were very helpful to the Marchese's son, Fabrizio.'

'I was indeed helpful to Fabrizio,' de Wignacourt agreed, 'but that has nothing to do with Merisi. I say again, the reasons are as I have told you.'

'Were you paid by the Giustiniani family to make Merisi a knight?'

'Enough!' de Wignacourt roared, and banged his palm down on the arm of the pew. 'Now you insult my honour and integrity.'

'Perhaps your distinguished colleague, the Prior of Messina, Fra Antonio Martelli had some influence on your decision. After all, he was in the service of Ferdinando de Medici, Grand Duke of Tuscany, for many years. So is Cardinal Francesco Del Monte, who was one of Merisi's most ardent patrons and supporters.'

I expected another explosion of temper but de Wignacourt simply looked at me. 'You are impudent and impertinent but you press home your attack with courage. I will say no more on this matter. The reason for Merisi's admittance as a knight is as I have told you, to reward an artist of genius.'

De Wignacourt was made of sterner stuff than most of the people I had interrogated. The only thing to do was change tack. 'Very well, let me ask you about the quarrel that Merisi had with this Knight of Justice, the quarrel that caused him to be thrown into prison. Can you tell me who this knight was?'

'No,' de Wignacourt answered firmly.

'Do you know exactly what this quarrel was all about?'

'Merisi took exception to some remarks that the knight had made. Apparently, the knight had been talking to another artist some time before. This artist had been telling the knight all about Merisi. Remembering this other artist's remarks, this knight met Merisi and then made some insulting remark about Merisi's mother and derided Merisi as a mere tradesman and a murderer, not fit to be wearing the Cross of Saint John. You know what Merisi was like. He rose to the bait, struck his fellow knight with his hand and made to draw his sword. Such behaviour is strictly forbidden by the laws of the Order.'

'You say that this Knight of Justice had been talking to an artist some time before? Was this artist a colleague of Merisi, or known to Merisi?'

'I am not sure,' de Wignacourt replied. 'This painter had been recommended to my colleague, Ippolito Malaspina, who had recently been working in Rome, as a fine painter of frescoes and he had just arrived on the island to start work on the redecoration of my palace.'

'Can you tell me who had recommended this painter to Malaspina?'

'I see no harm in doing so. It was Cardinal Del Monte.'

'And what was the name of this painter?' I asked, hardly daring to draw breath.

'Let me see,' de Wignacourt pondered. 'I cannot recall his name but he signs his work curiously, with a picture of a little sword.'

'Spada,' I almost cried out. 'Lionello Spada.'

'Yes, that's it.'

'Lionello Spada was here in Malta at the same time as Merisi?'

'Yes. Is that significant?'

'Perhaps,' I lied, knowing that it could be hugely significant. 'You said Spada was decorating the Grand Master's Palace?'

'Yes. After Merisi had been imprisoned in the Castel Sant'Angelo, this man Spada apparently visited the prison and pleaded for Merisi to be released. Spada made up some lame story about needing Merisi's help on the fresco work in my palace but I have since found out that Merisi hardly ever worked in fresco and would have been of very little help to Spada, so Spada was obviously trying to find an excuse to get his friend released.'

The fact that Spada had been here in Malta at the same time as Merisi was a stunning piece of news. I was not sure whether the fact that Spada was in Malta decorating the Grand Master's Palace at the same time that Merisi was on the island was known to modern art historians. If it was, I had missed finding it during my researches. The news that one of Merisi's staunchest friends and supporters was on the scene perhaps explained how easily Merisi had been able to escape from such a secure and forbidding prison as the Castel Sant'Angelo. 'I have to ask you a blunt question, Your Highness. Did you allow Merisi to escape from the Castel Sant'Angelo?'

'By no means,' de Wignacourt replied, emphatically. 'I wanted Merisi to stay under my protection. The incident with his fellow knight was not particularly serious. I could have sorted it out without Merisi being stripped of his knighthood. But after he had escaped and fled to Sicily there was nothing I could do to save him.'

'Do you think Merisi could have escaped without outside help?'

'It is impossible,' de Wignacourt answered. 'Someone certainly helped him to escape. I have evidence that the prison guards were bribed. As you know, there was a court of enquiry set up afterwards to investigate the whole incident, but no firm evidence could be found.'

'Did you authorise any pursuit of Merisi?'

'No. He had chosen his course of action. He was no longer worth the bother. His knighthood was stripped away from him and, as a fugitive murderer with the banda capitale hanging over him, he was no longer under our protection. That was punishment enough.'

'Do you have any evidence that points to whoever helped Merisi escape?'

'No. None,' de Wignacourt replied. 'Perhaps it was this man Spada?'

'I think, Your Highness, that that is entirely likely.'

'In that case, I hope I have been of some help to you. If you find out that this man Spada helped Merisi escape, please let me know.'

I had no doubt that Spada's life, having caused the humiliation of the Knights of Saint John, would not be worth a plugged nickel, as the Americans say, if it was proved that he did. They would go after him. I gazed at Caravaggio's Beheading of St. John while I considered my next question. The interior of the Oratory was very plain, with a barrel-shaped ceiling and rows of pews down each side. It had not been until the 19th century that the interior had been transformed into an ornate faux-Baroque palace. I preferred what I was seeing now, with the plain walls and the great painting dominating the church. I couldn't think of anything else that I should ask de Wignacourt, at least, nothing to which he was likely to give me a honest answer, so I said: 'Thank you for your time, Your Highness. I have been honoured to meet you and you have been most helpful. With your permission, I will now take my leave.'

De Wignacourt levered himself out of his seat, slowly and painfully again, and accompanied me to the door. We went out into the brilliant Maltese sunshine. The knights who were escorting and guarding de Wignacourt were startled to see me emerge from the Oratory with him. They reached for their swords but de Wignacourt raised his hand to allay their fears. He turned to me and said: 'Go with God, and I wish you success with your quest. Everyone, even the Devil and Michelangelo Merisi, deserves justice.'

43

I returned home to find Merisi sitting in a garden chair on the patio and enjoying the afternoon sunshine. There was a tall glass of orange juice, complete with ice cubes, on the patio table. Merisi was certainly learning about the comforts of modern living. It looked so inviting that I poured myself the same, but with the addition of a slug of vodka, and joined Merisi on the patio.

'Stefano!' he cried cheerily. 'Welcome home. How was the Grand Master?'

'Impressive,' I said. 'And imposing. But not nearly as imposing as your painting of the Beheading of Saint John.'

'You went into the Oratory especially to see it?'

'I met the Grand Master in there. It was . . . quite an experience.'

'One of my best works, eh, Stefano.'

'There is no other artist, before or since, who could have conjured such a shocking and powerful image, which so perfectly fits its intended location. My congratulations, Michele. What are you reading?'

'I have borrowed your History of World Art. I hope you don't mind?'

'Not at all. Just don't throw it aside and break the spine.'

Merisi looked sheepish. 'I won't. I'm sorry I damaged your atlas.'

'Not at all, old boy,' I replied. 'You are not the first person to be upset by the extent of the British empire.'

Merisi ignored my barbed comment and said: 'By the way, you were correct about this man Rembrandt.'

'In what way?'

'His portraits are better than mine. The later ones at least.'

'That's quite an admission, coming from you.'

Merisi shrugged. 'I have made some notes.' He indicated some sheets of paper on the patio table. 'My opinions and judgement of my fellow painters since I "died" and up until now.'

Intrigued, I picked up the papers but I found it difficult to read Merisi's large and jagged characters. 'What does this say?' I pointed to the first sentence.

'It says that I am disappointed with the standard of Italian art since my day.'

'Why is that?'

'This man Canaletto and this man Guardi. Technically accomplished, pretty views of Venice. Probably made them a lot of money but they express nothing about the human soul.'

'Is that what you think painting should be?'

'Yes, of course. To paint for any other reason is to decorate, not to create.'

'What do you think of your near contemporary, Peter Paul Rubens?' I asked, trying to suppress a smile at the thought of my Rubens portrait hidden away upstairs.

'Very talented, very versatile, but he was more interested in fame and money than art. I prefer the work of his pupil, Van Dyck.'

'What about the Dutch painters?' I asked.

'I very much admire their landscape work, van Ruisdael and Hobbema and the like. It was not considered a major discipline in my day but the Dutch have produced some very skilled work.'

'Vermeer is very popular today. Like you, he was forgotten for many years. What do you think of him?'

'Again, as a technician, I have seen none better. But his work is too still and lifeless for my taste. Young girls reading letters or pouring milk, what's that all about? I much prefer his contemporary, Pieter de Hooch. His work is skilled, touching and full of life and humanity.'

'For once we agree on something, Michele. His work has been overshadowed by Vermeer but I, like you, prefer de Hooch. What about Spanish art? Your influence was felt more deeply in Spain than perhaps anywhere else, apart from Italy itself.'

'Yes, we have talked already of this man Velasquez. A great artist but he had to sell his soul and his talent to the Spanish royal family or he might have been as great as me. Zurbaran, Murillo, very talented but, for me, it has to be Goya. His work could be light and charming or dark and disturbing. He pours his soul on to the canvas and illuminates the human condition.'

'French artists were influenced by your work,' I said, 'especially Georges de la Tour. He copied your chiaroscuro effects.'

'Yes, and overdid them, from what I can see. Boucher and Watteau, it makes me sick to look at their work, but Chardin had a charming style. The later French artists were better . . . Courbet, Delacroix, Gericault and particularly Jacques-Louis David. I'm very impressed by him. And Ingres, a superb draughtsman.'

'I hardly dare ask this, Michele, but what about the British painters of this time?'

Merisi laughed heartily. 'British artists! Surely that is a contradiction in terms!' He looked at me and said: 'I'm teasing you, my friend. You had some excellent portraitists in Reynolds, Gainsborough, Raeburn and so on. The best of them was Hogarth. I don't understand some of his other work, but his portraits are so full of character and humanity as to almost compare with Rembrandt. This so-called Pre-Raphaelite movement was interesting. They were technically accomplished but it all looks stilted and overdone, like tropical hothouse blooms. But the real glory of British art seems to me to be in landscape. John Constable seems to lead on to everything that these so-called Impressionists achieved much later. But your real star has to be this man Turner.'

'I didn't think you'd like his style,' I said, genuinely surprised.

'I used to dream of one day painting light in such a manner,' Merisi said, wistfully. 'Turner, and all your other watercolour painters, such as Thomas Girtin, had the chance to paint light effects in such a manner and took their chance well. I am most impressed with them.'

'Well, they did, as you say, have a profound influence on the most important artistic movement since your Baroque days, the Impressionist movement. It was mainly led by French painters. What do you think of them?' I expected a barrage of contempt but I was completely wrong.

'They took painting to the place it should truly be,' Merisi said. 'I would have loved to have been a part of this revolution. To have been able to create effects inspired by nature, of subjects chosen by me, and not ordered by some rich cardinal.'

Merisi's comments made me realise that, to our modern eyes, the Impressionist style had become almost a cliche, but a true artist like Merisi, to whom it was unknown, was seeing it in a completely fresh and original way. 'Which of the Impressionists do you like most?' I asked.

'I particularly like the work of these men Degas and Manet,' he replied. 'Cezanne and Renoir I am not so sure of but they achieved some interesting effects.'

'What do you think of the Dutchman, Vincent Van Gogh?'

'He seems to me extraordinary,' Merisi said. 'It says in your book that he was a much troubled man, that he committed suicide. That internal agony comes through on the canvas. Even his still life of a simple chair vibrates with intense life. An extraordinary technique.'

'We're now up to the 20th century,' I said. 'Anybody impress you since then?'

'I have to say, Stefano, that I begin not to undertand what is going on. This Cubism . . . I'm not sure I understand what they are trying to achieve.'

'It's main proponent, Pablo Picasso, is considered the greatest artist of the 20th century.'

'Yes, there are many examples of his work in this book. It leaves me cold, and baffled. There are many artists mentioned here who seem to have achieved some interesting effects . . . Gustav Klimt, Edvard Munch, Chagall. This Surrealist movement is interesting, especially this Spanish man Dali. He was obviously a very gifted technician but he seems to have squandered his talent on some very strange images. The only painter I can see here whose work I really like and understand is someone named Hopper. But I accept that the fault is in my understanding, rather than the work of these men. After these men, however, painting seems to have completely lost its purpose. It simply becomes blobs of colour, odd patterns, depictions of everyday objects, splashes, whirls, contours . . . even a canvas painted all over in the same colour! What meaning is there in that? What light does it shine on the human condition? What is it trying to say? Does no-one paint like me any more?'

'Believe me, Michele, there is no-one living today who can paint like you. Since the advent of that technique called photography, which I have explained to you, representative art, in its highest form and especially painting in oils, has gradually been dying. Painting in water colours is still popular but more as a hobby than a high art form. Proper representative oil painting is not taught, oil painters are not trained as in your day and such skill with mere brushes and oil paint is frowned upon by the so-called cognoscenti and regarded as old-fashioned and unnecessary. Our modern taste runs to bisected sheep pickled in formaldehyde and elephant dung wrapped in tinsel.'

'That is very sad to hear,' Merisi said, mournfully.

'Anyway, why are you suddenly taking an interest in the history of art?'

'Apart from sheer curiosity,' Merisi replied, 'I want to know what sort of competition I might face when I revive my career.' I remained silent, so Merisi continued: 'Yes, I know that the Tralfamadorians might not let me stay in this century. But if they do, I want to be prepared.'

Fascinating as our conversation had been up until now, I did not want to get into any uncomfortable speculation about Merisi's future. So, to change the subject, I asked: 'If you've finished with researches into the history of modern art, do you feel like discussing your time in Sicily?'

Merisi closed his book and laid it on the patio table. 'Yes, let's get it over with,' he said. 'I expect Grand Master Alof de Wignacourt is still very displeased with me for escaping from his dungeon.'

'Very much so,' I agreed, but decided to say no more. De Wignacourt's revelation about the presence of Lionello Spada on Malta at the same time as Merisi had given me a lot to think about. Once again, Merisi had failed to mention such an important nugget of information but I decided not to confront him with this knowledge until I was ready. All I said was: 'I'll get us another drink.'

44

I took a sip of my Harvey Wallbanger and opened Helen Langdon's biography of my companion, Michelangelo Merisi da Caravaggio, who was sitting opposite me and contentedly enjoying his orange juice and the rare English sunshine. I said: 'After your precipitous flight from Malta, you disembarked at Syracuse in Sicily. Sicily, just like Naples and your home area of Caravaggio and Milan in Lombardy, was under Spanish rule.'

'Yes,' Merisi said. 'Costanza Colonna's ancestor, Marcantonio Colonna, the hero of the battle of Lepanto, had been appointed Viceroy of Sicily only a few years after I was born, so Colonna influence was very strong in Sicily.'

'Did you feel relatively safe in Sicily because of that?'

'No, I didn't feel safe at all. The Colonna protection helped but it was not all-embracing as the protection of the Knights of St. John had been on Malta. The banda capitale was still in place, any number of enemies, particularly the Tomassoni clan, could have found me and killed me at any time. And I believed that the Knights of St. John would be looking for me as well. I felt like a hunted animal.'

'Sicily, at that time, seems to have been similar to most of Italy. It was a picturesque and fertile island, rich in grain, fruit, olives, wine and so on, and yet there had been a devastating famine just before you arrived. Once again, we know of wealthy cities like Syracuse, Messina and Palermo, where the rich people lived in isolated and guarded luxury while the streets were crowded with the poor, the homeless, the beggars and the vagabonds.'

'Yes, that's right,' Merisi confirmed. 'The island was constantly under threat of attack from the heathen Turks and huge amounts of money had to be spent on fortifications and defences. And yet those three major cities that you mentioned were vying with each other to display their wealth and power by building grandiose new churches and civic buildings.'

'And again, your high reputation as an artist opened many doors for you despite the fact that you were being hunted as a murderer and was a fugitive from the Knights of St. John?'

'Yes,' Merisi smiled, 'it was very odd. The Sicilian patrons seemed not to care what crimes I might have committed in the past. I was still considered to be the best painter in Italy, very much better than any artist working in Sicily, and they were almost literally fighting each other to buy a picture from my hand.'

'But once again, as in the past, all this success seemed to bring out your worst behaviour. We know that you were enraged by any criticism of your work, you were insulting and abusive to local Sicilian artists, and that you were erratic, restless, and almost deranged in your behaviour.'

'I can't argue with that assessment,' Merisi said, mournfully. 'I felt like a hunted animal, constantly threatened. You try living in fear of being assassinated day and night and see how rational your behaviour would be. I always wore a dagger by day and slept with it by my side at night.'

'I'm not criticising you, Michele, just trying to get to the truth. It's no wonder, in these circumstances, that your pictures took on a new sense of darkness and depth that express the frailty of human life.'

'It was a very difficult time,' Merisi agreed.

'But one happy circumstance in Syracuse was that you were reunited with your old friend Mario Minnitti.'

'Yes. Mario had become tired of the excesses of life in Rome, especially my excesses, and had returned to Sicily where he had built a successful career and a large studio. Like me, however, Mario had committed a homicide soon after his arrival back in Sicily and had had to seek sanctuary in a monastery. I don't know what it was all about but the family of the murdered man were seeking Mario's blood in revenge. Eventually he sorted out his problems and gained the protection of the authorities and thereafter built up a flourishing studio. His pictures were light and colourful and pleasing. He had no pretensions to be a great artist. He would sketch his compositions and leave his apprentices to paint them in, with Mario simply applying the finishing touches, and perhaps not even bothering with that if he considered that the apprentices had done a good enough job. Mario enjoyed his success. He lived well, wore elegant clothes, and was happy. I am still not sure whether Mario was completely pleased about my arrival in Syracuse but he extended every kindness to me. He even lobbied the Senate of the city to give me work, calling me the greatest artist now living. He meant it whole-heartedly. He was very generous to me.'

'At this time you completed your altarpiece depicting the Burial of Saint Lucy.' (*Plate 55*).

'Yes. Mario persuaded the Senate to give me this commission, and he even helped me paint the background and one or two of the figures. Saint Lucy was a local saint, therefore very popular in Syracuse. Her church was built outside the city walls and was being restored by the local Senate. I wanted very much to paint this subject. It was very personal to me.'

'Really? Why is that?' I asked.

'Because Lucy was the name of my mother. I had not behaved well when she had died, many years before, and I wanted to make amends by including her namesake in this altarpiece as a tribute to her loving care of me.'

'Once again, Michele, you produced a work that moves the heart to pity for the human condition.'

'Yes, I was pleased with it. The huge bulk of the gravediggers, representing the overwhelming power of the Roman empire, frame the tiny body of Saint Lucy, who would not recant her Christianity despite grievous tortures. I was behaving strangely at the this time but I had learned a lot about human suffering and the support of a loving family would have been very consoling, but I had lost my parents, alienated by brothers and sisters, rejected and abandoned my friends, and never married. The only mother I had left was a painted image. But I think my real mother would have been pleased with my work.'

'I'm sure she would, Michele,' I said, touched by Merisi's unusual openness and sincerity. 'Your painting is not in a good condition today, but much effort has been made to restore and preserve it.' We discussed whether there could be any concealed messages in this altarpiece, especially if included by Mario Minnitti but, once again, could find nothing conclusive. 'Your Saint Lucy altarpiece became very popular and was copied many times. You had found success very swiftly and, just as swiftly, as usual, you left it all behind and moved to Messina. Why was that?' I could see Merisi's mind working and wondering how much to tell me before he answered.

'Mario's wife resented my presence in her house and, as sometimes had happened in Rome, I found Mario's constant attention cloying. So, despite his kindness and generosity, I made an excuse and went to Messina. It was a big and attractive city with a population about the same as Rome. It had a busy harbour and was hemmed in by mountains but the streets were wide and straight and there were many fine and elegant buildings. There was a flourishing local school of artists, plenty of work for everyone and, once again, they were fascinated to meet me and observe my working methods. My predecessor artist from my home town, Polidoro da Caravaggio, had worked in Messina about eighty years before. His Adoration of the Shepherds was very much admired by the local artists, so the name Caravaggio was known and respected long before I made my name.'

'You immediately won a commission for a chapel in the church of the Padri Crociferi from a rich Genoese merchant named Lazzari.'

'That's right,' Merisi said. 'This man Lazzari was excited by my sudden arrival and was determined to get a picture out of me. He asked for a conventional work, a Madonna with Saint John, but I persuaded him to let me do the Raising of Lazarus (*Plate 56*) as a play on his own name Lazzari. He paid me one thousand scudi for that picture. I had never seen such an amount of money before! I asked the local hospital for a room to work in. They gave me their best room. Once again, I had fallen on my feet.'

'Is it true,' I asked, 'as the biographer Susinno claims, that you employed some workmen as models and forced them to hold a real decomposing corpse as the model for the figure of Lazarus?'

Merisi chuckled merrily. 'Of course not!' he replied. 'I was working in secret and I put that story about so that I would not be interrupted by constant visitors. One of the workmen modelled for Lazarus and held himself stiffly, like a corpse, but he was very much alive.'

'That's a relief,' I said truthfully. 'When your picture was first unveiled, it caused quite a stir, didn't it?'

'I caused quite a stir,' Merisi answered. 'I made the mistake of inviting a group of local artists to be present at the unveiling, as well as the usual local dignitaries, and some of these artists could not resist the temptation to make some criticisms of my work. They thought they would promote their own taste and knowledge at the expense of the great Caravaggio. I lost my temper with them. You know how much I detest criticism. I slashed the canvas to ribbons in front of them and told Lazzari that I would do another version, which I did. The second version proved to be more acceptable to the local cognoscenti and the Senate immediately offered me another commission, for an Adoration of the Shepherds.' (*Plate 57*).

'Yes,' I said, 'but before we move on to that work, I'd like to ask you about an intriguing quote by you, one of the very few of your quotes that have survived the ages, as recorded by Susinno.'

'Very well,' Merisi agreed.

'It seems that you entered the church of the Madonna del Piero and was offered holy water to wash away venial sin. You replied: "I don't need it, since all my sins are mortal". Do you remember this incident?'

'I have to confess that I don't,' Merisi said. 'It sounds like something I would say. Perhaps I was drunk at the time.'

'You would enter a church in a state of intoxication?'

'Yes. It would seem a small sin compared with some of my others.'

I smiled and agreed. 'Let's talk about your Adoration of the Shepherds. We know that it was for the church of a Capuchin monastery outside of the city, near a small hamlet.'

'Yes,' Merisi said. 'I cannot remember the name of this hamlet but the Capuchins had a strong presence in Messina and this church was very popular with the common people. I decided to do an entirely conventional work, which was to be placed above the high altar.'

'Some critics have called it a bleak work but I find its simple, dignified and sincere tenderness very compelling. I like it a lot.'

'Thank you,' Merisi said. 'And there was something else about this work that I liked very much.'

'What's that?'

'I was paid another one thousand scudi for it. I had more money than I had ever had before!'

'We know that you also completed some other works in Messina that are, sadly, now lost.'

'Do you know which ones?' Merisi asked.

'You completed a Saint Jerome Writing for the same church as the Adoration. That is lost. And we know that a wealthy nobleman commissioned four works from you on the Passion of Christ. Did you complete this commission?'

'Only one of them, as I recall, of Christ carrying the Cross.'

'It's a great pity that you didn't finish them all because we know that this nobleman gave you free rein to paint these subjects as you saw fit and you were to be paid "as much as is fitting for this painter who has a crazy brain". His words, not mine, Michele. Why didn't you complete this lucrative commission?'

Merisi hesitated for a second and then said: 'I decided to move to Palermo.'

'What on earth for?' I asked. 'Once again you were comfortably off in a wealthy city and winning all the commissions you could handle. Why move? Was it to do with this incident with the school teacher?'

'You know about that?' Merisi said, suddenly alert.

'Yes, the biographer Susinno says . . .'

'What does he know about anything?' Merisi interrupted, dismissively.

'Well, Susinno claims that you fell into the habit of following this teacher and his pupils down to the arsenal, where galleys were built and where the pupils would play together. After this had happened several times, the teacher confronted you and asked why you were hanging around the pupils.'

'He accused me of being a bardassa, a pervert. I became so angry with him that I punched him in the head.'

'It sounds like he was only trying to protect his pupils. This behaviour seems out of character and very odd, even for you. What were you doing?'

'Nothing!' Merisi protested. 'I was simply observing the movements and behaviour of the boys for one of my paintings.'

'Which one?' I asked. 'On what subject?'

'I cannot remember.'

'Did you ever complete this picture?'

'I cannot remember,' Merisi said, stubbornly. 'Are you accusing me of having an unnatural interest in these boys?'

'Did you? It was four hundred years ago, Michele. I am not going to call the police and have you arrested for it!'

'You know that I was not interested in boys, in a sexual sense, but the playfulness of these children fascinated me. I simply enjoyed watching them play. There was nothing more to it than that.' Merisi looked at me challengingly, expecting me to interrogate him again. I was not at all convinced by his explanation, and I made a note of it, but I knew Merisi was not going to tell me any more.

'So you moved to Palermo which, I believe, was an even more beautiful city than Syracuse and Messina.'

'Yes, it was,' Merisi said. 'The city was built on a plain, which spread down to the sea, with mountains in the background. Its citizens boasted that it was one of the grandest and most modern cities in Europe. It had the usual massive fortifications, especially down at the harbour, but its streets were wide and spacious, with gardens and fountains and many imposing buildings. As usual, there was much poverty and hardship for the poor people despite those imposing facades.'

'We know of only one work that you completed while in Palermo, your Adoration of the Shepherds with Saints Lawrence and Francis.' (*Plate 58*).

'Yes, that was an altarpiece for the Oratory of St. Lawrence.'

'Once again you produced a work that is more conventional and lyrical than most of your pictures. It's unchallenging, almost sweet. I'm not sure whether your patrons would be relieved or disappointed by its conventiality!'

'They seemed pleased enough,' Merisi said, unconvincingly.

'Your stay in Palermo was very short and by the autumn of 1609 you had returned to Naples. Your biographers comment upon your circumstances and behaviour at this point. Baglione says that your enemies were hot on your heels, that's why you returned to Naples. Bellori says basically the same thing, that fear hunted you from place to place, that you no longer felt safe in Sicily and so you fled to Naples.'

'That is partly true,' Merisi agreed, 'but I had been exiled from Rome for nearly three years, and three years was the customary term of exile. I knew that many of my powerful patrons in Rome had actively been trying to get me rehabilitated and pardoned by the pope. The Archbishop of Palermo was a member of the Doria family. That family had always supported me. The archbishop advised me that I should try to move back nearer to Rome. The Giustiniani family also had close links in Palermo and they sent me the same message. I was desperate to get back to Rome. However rich and beautiful these other cities were, no matter how much work I had obtained in them, they were not Rome. Rome, for an artist, is where you had to be. So I went back to Naples as the first step back home.'

'You were welcomed home to Naples by Costanza Colonna, the Marchesa di Caravaggio, who was staying at her Palazzo Cellamare nearby at Chaia.'

'Yes. Once again, Costanza was very kind to me. Word of my return to Naples soon spread and I was inundated by offers of work, from the Church, from noble families, from the Spanish Viceregent, and even Cardinal Scipione Borghese, the nephew of the pope, so I guessed that a pardon must be on its way very soon. And Chaia was such a beautiful place that it was good for my soul to spend some time there. It was the most beautiful bay that you have ever seen. Many noble families had built villa retreats there, so there were gardens wherever you looked, and figs and vines and cedars growing in abundance, all giving off their heavenly scent. The Palazzo Cellamare itself was idyllic. It was only a few minutes walk from the Palazzo Colonna, and it was set in terraced gardens which were decorated with marble fountains, and its walls were covered with frescoes. It was a delightful place and, for a short while at least, I felt happy and optimistic about the future. And then my enemies caught up with me.'

'This was the attack outside the Osteria del Cerriglio,' I said. 'This is clearly an extremely important incident in relation to our search for your murderers. Do you feel able to talk about it?'

'Oh, yes,' Merisi said, 'the little I can remember about it that is. The Osteria del Cerriglio was the best tavern in Naples. Indeed it was celebrated throughout Europe. It consisted of two very large rooms, supported by arches, with a courtyard and a fountain and a terrace outside. The downstairs walls were covered with proverbs celebrating the joys of wine, women and food. Upstairs, many whores plied their trade. What with this, and the fact that the tavern attracted poets, artists, writers and other creative people from all over Naples, you can see that it was my kind of place.'

'So how did this attack take place? I asked.

'I cannot remember much about it,' Merisi replied. 'It was late at night and I had had too much to drink, as usual, and I walked out into the darkness. Then, before I was even aware of anyone near me, I was given a blow on the head. It knocked me down but I kept my senses. I went for my dagger but it was wrested away from me. I could not tell whether there were three or four men attacking me. At least three. They were kicking me and slashing at my face with knives. You can still the scars, faintly, to this day.' Merisi pointed to his face. 'I was trying to protect myself but I thought my time had come. I became unconscious and, from what I heard later, my attackers must have been disturbed or frightened off in some way, otherwise I would surely have been killed. The next thing I remember was waking up in the Palazzo Cellamare, with a hangover from my drinking and in hellish pain from my wounds. Costanza had brought a doctor to the palace to tend my wounds, otherwise I should have been more badly disfigured than I was. He gave me a draught of something or other to ease the pain.'

'You have no idea who these assailants were, or who had sent them?'

'No. No idea.'

'Did you hear them say anything? Did they say each other's names, anything like that?'

'No. The attack was carried out in silence, I could not see their faces, or even what sort of clothes they were wearing. Believe me, I racked my brains for clues to see if I could remember anything about them or find out who they were. I wanted to take my revenge with cold steel. But, to this day, I have no idea who they were.'

I was disappointed that we could not glean any clues from this savage attack. The sun was going down and I felt we had done enough work. 'We'll leave it there for today,' I told Merisi. 'We'll have something to eat and then I have to arrange my next time travel trip with Guglielmo Pellegrino.'

'Who are you going to see this time?' Merisi asked.

'I don't know if I should tell you,' I answered. 'You might become jealous. I'm going for a night out with the boys, at the Tavern of the Turk.'

45

The ChronoConverter landed me in a small but well-furnished room. It was evening. Heavy brocaded curtains were drawn across the windows. I could feel thick pile carpet beneath my feet. There was a cheerful fire burning in the grate and light from the candles in wall sconces twinkled merrily on ormolu furniture. The door opened and a man entered the room. I was happy to see that he was very tall, well over six feet, and powerfully built. He was also very good-looking, in an Errol Flynn sort of way, and his fine 17th century costume of green and gold silk complemented his long wavy chestnut hair and Van Dyck beard. He was wearing a rapier with a gold basket handle. He cut a very impressive figure. This was not a man to be trifled with. He seemed ideal for the role he had imposed upon himself and ideal as my guardian for the night's work.

I announced the password: 'Live long and prosper!'

'You too, Stefano,' the man said drily, 'but there is no need for the passwords. I doubt if there is anyone else travelling through time and arriving in my house tonight. It is a pleasure to meet you at last. I am Guglielmo Pellegrino. Or, at least, that is the name I have to use in this century. I will not tell you my real name. It's better if we maintain our disguises as far as we are able.'

I shook his hand and said: 'I'm very pleased to meet you. You have looked after me very well. If this room is anything to go by, you have a pleasant lifestyle here.'

Pellegrino looked around the room. 'Yes, I try to live as comfortably as possible within the parameters allowed to me in this century. This is a fascinating city and a fascinating time to be living in but sometimes, I must admit, I do long for more sophisticated modern comforts.'

'Well, I am trying my best to ensure that your sacrifices have not been in vain. That's why I requested this little jaunt tonight.'

Pellegrino frowned. 'This "little jaunt", as you call it, might be a lot more difficult and dangerous than you anticipate. We will be meeting some strange and volatile men tonight. Are you sure that this meeting is really necessary?'

'I believe so,' I replied. 'These three men are arguably Caravaggio's closest friends in Rome. They were involved in his most desperate and disreputable incidents. I want to see what they know. I want to get them drunk and I want to "rattle their cages" a little, to see if they spill any beans.'

'You might find that it's blood, not beans, that are spilt. That is why I insisted on accompanying you. It would be far too dangerous for you to meet these men without me.' Pellegrino unsheathed a few inches of his rapier. 'I know how to use this sword,' he said. 'I see you are wearing a dagger. Are you also carrying the Taser pistol?'

'Yes'. I was wearing the same specially tailored outfit that I had worn to meet Guido Reni, but without the long greasy wig, so I demonstrated my dexterity to Pellegrino. The pistol suddenly appeared in my hand, conjured from up my sleeve.

Pellegrino was not over-impressed. 'That may prove to be a useful trick,' he commented. 'Very well, if you insist on continuing with this foolhardy project then we better get on with it. The three men should be waiting for us in the Tavern of the Turk. Are you ready?'

'Yes,' I replied. I followed Pellegrino out of the room, down a flight of stairs, through his studio and out into the Roman night. The streets were thronged with people, many carrying torches, some already staggering drunk, with gangs of youths shouting obscenities and laughing at the deformed and disabled beggars, who were still trying to ply their trade. I could not see any women. The respectable women were no doubt safely at home behind closed doors and the disreputable ones were plying their trade down at the Ortaccio.

'It's not far,' Pellegrino said. 'Stay close to me.' It was an order I was happy to comply with. We walked about half a mile through narrow streets and then emerged out into a piazza. Pellegrino pointed to a large two-storey building on the other side of the square. 'That is the Tavern of the Turk,' he said. I could see people going in an out and there was a small throng of patrons standing outside drinking and enjoying the passing show. I could see many people moving about inside. It certainly appeared to be a popular watering hole.

'So, that is where Caravaggio used to drink and eat regularly?' I asked, fascinated to see his 'local'.

'Yes. This one, and the Tavern of the Blackamoor were his favourites. I chose this one for our meeting because it is slightly more salubrious than the Blackamoor. Come on, let's go over.' We walked across the piazza and I was reassured to see the riff-raff treating Pellegrino with respect. I surmised that he was well-known in the area and his size would make anyone think twice before incurring his wrath. We entered the tavern and my nostrils were assailed by strong smells, not all unpleasant. It was a combination of wood smoke from the fireplaces, candle smoke from the candleabras and wall sconces, the aroma of cooking food and the musty smell of wine and ale. Unlike a British pub, there did not seem to be a bar as such. There were wooden tables, some round, some long and rectangular, with groups of drinkers and diners gathered around them. Waiters carried trays, which were laden with plates, tankards and flagons, to the seated customers. The floor was tiled and covered with straw and sawdust. The roof was supported by decorated stone pillars that rose up to equally strong decorated supporting beams in the ceiling. Some drinkers were standing up and leaning on the stone pillars. The place was packed.

Pellegrino said: 'Our guests should be waiting upstairs. It will be slightly less crowded up there and I have reserved a table in the window alcove, which should give us a bit more privacy to talk.'

I followed Pellegrino up a crude but strongly-made staircase. I suspected the original staircase had been more elegant and probably wrecked in a brawl. The upper floor was, as Pellegrino had said, less crowded and better appointed with better-made tables and furniture.

Pellegrino indicated a table at the window overlooking the piazza. 'I see Prospero Orsi and Onorio Longhi but it looks like Spada has not arrived. Come on, I'll introduce you.'

We walked across to the table. The two artists sitting at the table regarded me with cool indifference. 'Gentlemen,' Pellegrino said, 'allow me to introduce Signor Stefano Maddano, who is inquiring into the circumstances surrounding the death of our mutual friend Michele. He has interviewed me at my home already and, as we agreed, he is here to ask you a few questions.' He indicated the man on the left first. 'This is Prospero Orsi and this is Onorio Longhi.'

Neither man offered to shake my hand, so Pellegrino and I sat down at the table with them. I could distinguish the two men from their descriptions in the historical records but, of course, I could not allow them to know that. Prospero Orsi was a small man, with a wispy black beard, and he regarded me pleasantly enough. Onorio Longhi was a bigger man, and was clearly well into his cups. He was dressed in his habitual black velvet which showed off his blond hair and beard to best effect. His watery eyes were suspicious and defensive. As I had planned, I wanted to get them drunk and "rattle their cages" and perhaps get a response they had not intended to give. I decided to stamp my authority right away. 'Where is Lionello Spada?' I asked. 'He is supposed to be here as well.'

Orsi said: 'He is over there, talking to the waiter Carnacia.'

'Carnacia?' I repeated. 'Isn't he the waiter who Merisi attacked with hot artichokes?'

'How do you know about that?' Longhi challenged me, and I made a mental note to be a bit more careful in revealing what I knew.

'You will be surprised what I know about Michele, Signor Longhi,' I replied. 'As you know I am inquiring, with papal blessing, into the suspicious circumstances of Michele's death and I am determined to ferret out the person or persons responsible for such a foul deed.'

'You are convinced that Michele was murdered?' Longhi asked.

'I am almost fully convinced.'

'Why are you so interested in Michele?' Longhi persisted. 'He never mentioned your name. We were his closest friends for years. Why have you taken it upon yourself to be his avenger?'

'I seek no vengeance, Signor Longhi, just facts and, perhaps, justice. Signor Pellegrino, would you be so kind as to ask Signor Spada to join us. I have many questions to ask and I do not intend to repeat myself.'

I expected Pellegrino to get up and fetch Spada but he called across in a booming voice: 'Hey, Spada, get over here! Don't keep our guest waiting. And ask that lazy bastard Carnacia to bring us our food and drinks.'

Spada raised his hand in acknowledgement and finished saying something to Carnacia. Then Carnacia eyed us balefully and shouted: 'What do you want to drink?'

'Wine and ale for all of us,' Pellegrino replied, 'and plenty of it.'

Spada walked over and, unlike the other two, offered his hand. I shook it and he sat down next to me at the end of the table. He had a pleasant, open face and a friendly smile. He looked to be in his mid-thirties, while the other two men were several years older.

'What were you saying to that scumbag Carnacia?' Longhi asked Spada.

'I was complaining about a meal I had here the other evening,' Spada replied. 'It was not cooked properly.'

I said: 'Poor Signor Carnacia always seems to be on the receiving end of complaints from you artists.'

'Poor Signor Carnacia!' Longhi snorted.

The artists swapped not very funny anecdotes about Carnacia and other waiters until Carnacia himself appeared and walked over to our table with a tray loaded with drinks. He said to me: 'Ale or wine, sir?'

I had not been impressed by the wine I had tasted here in the seventeenth century, so I replied: 'Ale. Thank you.' Carnacia placed a tankard of ale in front of me and then put the rest of the drinks in the middle of the table.

'Hey, Carnacia,' Longhi said. 'How come he gets special service, with his own fine pewter tankard, and we get the tin and the wood?'

Carnacia replied: 'Because he is a gentleman, a dignitary, on the business of the Holy Father. He is not a low artist like you. And, despite the fact that is a friend of that unlamented swine Merisi, he deserves the best service.'

'I see you have recovered from your artichoke wounds,' I said to Carnacia. 'Perhaps you sought your revenge on Merisi, a man you clearly despise, by murdering him.'

'Yes,' Carnacia replied, 'I despised him all right, the ill-mannered brute, but I didn't attack him.'

'Because you were shit scared of him,' Longhi said. 'Fuck off, you little twerp, and keep the drinks coming.'

Carnacia began to stomp away angrily but I called him back and asked: 'Is Gianfranco working tonight?'

'Gianfranco? I do not know any Gianfranco,' Carnacia replied.

'He is a waiter and potman here at the tavern.'

'I know everyone who works here, signor. There is no Gianfranco here.'

'Perhaps he no longer works here. He certainly worked here nine or ten years ago. How long have you worked here, Carnacia?'

'More than twenty years, signor. There has been no-one named Gianfranco who has worked here in my time.'

'Very well,' I said. 'Thank you.' Carnacia walked away and I turned to the four artists surrounding me. 'Do any of you recall a waiter named Gianfranco who used to work here and who modelled for Michele?' They all shook their heads. 'He appeared in Michele's Betrayal of Christ,' I persisted, 'and later in his Flagellation of Christ. He has a squashed-up, evil-looking face, like a satyr. You must have seen him or know who he is?'

'Yes, I remember this man,' Spada said. 'but I have no idea who he is or what his name is.'

Orsi said: 'Like Lionello, I know who you mean but I don't know who he is.'

Once again, Merisi had lied to me and left me with a mystery to solve. There was no more I could do about it for the moment so I took a sip of ale. I was pleasantly surprised to find it very palatable, with an almost spicy taste. 'Very well, gentlemen, let's get down to business. You all know why I am here. All three of you were close friends and supporters of Merisi, so you are not directly under suspicion, but you were all involved in schemes or incidents with Michele that upset other people, people who might have sought to take revenge on Michele. Let me start with you, Signor Spada . . .'

'Call me Lionello.'

'Very well, Lionello. You were such a close friend and supporter of Michele that you have earned the nickname of "scimmia del Caravaggio", the "ape of Caravaggio". Does that bother you?'

Spada looked uncomfortable and Longhi said: 'Spada apes the style of every artist, the talentless bastard.'

Spada ignored Longhi and said: 'I admired Michele's painting without reservation. Unlike myself, and every other so-called painter sitting around this table, Michele was a genius, a truly great painter. To me, he was the equal of da Vinci, Michelangelo Buonarotti, Raphael and Titian.'

Longhi made a girly sound and said: 'Sounds like you were in love with him, Lionello my dear. Did you kiss him goodnight as well?'

Spada merely smiled. 'Michele was a good friend. He took my side over that business in the Marches, when that bastard Guido Reni ruined my chances of a good commission.'

I asked: 'That was the commission that was eventually awarded to Cristofero Roncalli?'

'Yes. Michele was very sympathetic.'

'And, with Michele's help, you had Roncalli attacked and beaten up?'

Longhi laughed with delight. 'Oh, do tell us more, Signor Maddano! Little Lionello Spada had Roncalli beaten up?'

'Yes,' I said. 'Michele knew of a Sicilian thug who was willing to undertake the attack and recommended him to Lionello.'

'Little Lionello wouldn't have the guts to do it himself,' Longhi crowed. 'Ooh, Lionello, aren't you a naughty little artist.'

I turned to Longhi and said: 'I wouldn't crow too loudly, Signor Longhi. I may know something about you that is not to your credit.' Longhi stared at me with a sullen expression, and I turned back to Spada. 'I believe, Lionello, that you enjoy, and are very adept, at writing satirical and sarcastic verse. Is that so?'

It was Longhi who answered: 'That's right, Signor Maddano. One of his poems reads: "Little Lionello, kisses every arse, loves Merisi's best of all, what a fucking farce!" Longhi laughed delightedly at his impromptu invention.

I asked Spada: 'Did you help Merisi write those scurrilous verses about the painter Baglione?'

'No, it wasn't me,' Spada denied. 'I was apprenticed to Baglione. I respected him. I would not have written such stuff about him.'

'No wonder you're such a crappy painter,' Longhi said, 'being apprenticed to Baglione.'

Spada replied: 'I realise I am not a great painter, poet and architect like you, Onorio, but then neither are you.'

'Oh, very clever, little Lionello.'

'Let me ask you directly, Lionello,' I said. 'Have you any knowledge of anyone who was plotting or planning or arranging to have Michele murdered?'

'No, I don't have any actual knowledge, but it must have been the Tomassoni clan. They had the strongest reason of all for wanting Michele dead.'

'Well,' I said, 'you were there when Michele killed Ranuccio Tomassoni, so I suppose you would say that.'

There was a shocked silence around the table. Spada sat with his head bowed. Orsi looked puzzled. Longhi, for once, was silent. 'Nothing to say, Signor Longhi,' I challenged him. 'After all, you were there at the slaying as well. And, from what Michele told me, both you and Spada took the trouble to stay clear of any actual danger.'

'Wait a minute,' Prospero Orsi said to Spada. 'You were there when Michele killed Tomassoni?' Spada nodded. Orsi said: 'You have never breathed a word of this to me.'

'Or anyone else,' Spada admitted. 'I didn't want anyone to know. By great good fortune I had steered clear of being incriminated or being called as a witness. My compliments to you, Signor Maddano. It is clear that Michele trusted you implicitly if he told you that.'

'As I said when I arrived, you all may be surprised at what I know. For instance, Lionello, isn't it true that you were very happy to see one love rival, Ranuccio Tomassoni, killed and another love rival, our friend Michele, exiled and out of the way for doing the killing?'

Spada sat, with head bowed, and said nothing, so Longhi asked: 'Love rival? What are you talking about, Signor Maddano?'

'Signor Spada here,' I said, 'was besotted with the model and courtesan Fillide Melandroni.'

'Fillide!' Longhi exclaimed. 'She would not be interested in a boy like Spada!'

'On the contrary, Signor Longhi, Lionello and Fillide conducted a torrid affair for several months.'

Longhi, such is twisted male morality, regarded Spada with new respect. Spada said: 'That was a long time ago. It is all over and forgotten now.'

'Still,' I said, 'it must have given you satisfaction that two men whom Fillide preferred to you were suddenly out of the way.'

'I did not murder Michele,' Spada replied. 'I did not know that Michele was making love to Fillide.'

'Then you are more stupid than you look,' Longhi commented.

Carnacia had returned to the table. He asked me if I wanted another tankard of ale. I was surprised to find myself somewhat light-headed already, but I said 'yes' and he placed another pewter tankard in front of me and then checked the rest of the drinks.

Orsi waited until Carnacia was out of earshot, and said to Spada: 'You are very good at keeping a secret, Lionello. I have never suspected that you were fucking Fillide or that you were there when Michele did for Ranuccio Tomassoni. You devious bastard!'

I said: 'Well now, Signor Orsi, you are not bad at keeping a secret yourself.'

'What do you mean?' Orsi challenged me.

'Would you like me to tell your fellow painters here how you and Michele and Bernadino Cesari took your revenge on Federico Zuccaro by breaking into his palazzo?'

Prospero Orsi literally went pale and took a large gulp out of his wine goblet. 'Michele told you about that?' he asked.

Longhi chortled gleefully. 'Why, little Prosperino! You were part of that mad adventure against the distinguished Signor Zuccaro? It was the talk of the art world at the time, Signor Maddano, but nobody ever found out who was responsible . . . until now. Your name "Orsi" means "bear" but you are really quite the little tiger, aren't you!'

I said to Orsi: 'As a result of that ill-judged attack, you fell out with your friend and employer Giuseppe Cesari, now the Cavaliere d'Arpino. He found out that you and Michele and his own brother Bernardino had taken part in this criminal escapade and he was terrified that any repercussions would seriously damage his reputation and livelihood. Isn't that so?'

'Yes,' Orsi confirmed, reluctantly. 'You know, or probably know, what an old woman Cesari can be. His reaction really infuriated me. After all, we had tried to disable Zuccaro for his sake as well as ours, so that we could all be involved in the most important commission in Rome at the time.'

Longhi snorted. 'Three of you, and you couldn't get the better of an old man like Zuccaro!'

Orsi was used to Longhi's barbs and ignored him. 'I lost patience with Cesari and fell out with him.'

'So you decided to leave Cesari's studio,' I said, 'and you encouraged Michele to leave as well.'

'Yes. As you know, Michele had been injured and fell into a fever and was desperately ill for a long time. Cesari would not have taken Michele back anyway.'

'You became a tireless advocate and salesman for Michele's work, didn't you, Signor Orsi?'

'Yes. I considered Michele to be a great painter. I wanted to promote his work.'

'And make some money for yourself by so doing. Isn't that the truth?'

Orsi bristled for a second and then shrugged equably. 'I wanted to do both. What's wrong with wanting to make something for oneself?'

'Nothing,' I admitted, 'but, through your promotion of Michele you prized many commissions away from other artists and, together with Michele's aggressive temperament, bitterly upset a lot of your fellow painters.'

'So what?' Orsi challenged. 'It's a cut-throat world out there. Grab what you can and fuck the others.'

'And that is why you encouraged Michele to leave the service of Cardinal Del Monte, who had been so helpful to Michele, and move to the Palazzo Mattei where your brother Aurelio was in service. The Mattei family were considerably wealthier than Del Monte, Michele's reputation was on the rise, he was able to charge considerably higher prices for his work and you, naturally, a not very talented painter of grotesques, was able to profit considerably from your cut of the fees.'

Orsi tried to contain his anger with me. 'So what,' he said. 'I made money out of Michele but I genuinely do think he was a great painter and I didn't fucking well murder him. I didn't kill the goose who was laying the golden egg for me.'

'Do you know who did murder Michele?'

'I agree with Spada here. The Tomassoni clan are the obvious suspects. It would be natural for them to seek revenge.'

Onorio Longhi looked at Orsi and said: 'I didn't realise you were such a crafty fucker. Congratulations, my friend.'

'Signor Longhi,' I said, 'I must now turn my attention to you.'

'Ask away, foreigner, I have nothing to hide.'

Carnacia had returned and had placed another tankard of ale in front of me. I was feeling quite drunk, the alien smells and sensations I was experiencing were making me feel disorientated. I determined not to drink any more, and then found myself taking a swig anyway. Onorio Longhi was looking at me with hostility and, thanks to the ale, I was ready to take him on. 'Michele told me a lot about you, Signor Longhi. He told me you were a staunch and generous friend but your aggressive, satirical and liti . . . litigin . . . litiginous nature appalled even him at times.' I was uncomfortably aware that I was now slurring my words, even when I managed to remember what word I intended to say. Guglielmo Pellegrino was looking at me with concern. I took a deep breath and tried to pull my wits together. 'Michele told me that you were a cultured and erudite man, a fine architect, a moderate painter and a crappy poet. What d'ye think of that?' I took another gulp of ale.

Pellegrino said to Longhi: 'I think what Stefano means is that he appreciates that you were a good friend to Michele and that these playful insults were part and parcel of your friendship. Is that not so, Stefano.' He gave me a warning stare and, under the table, kicked my foot.

'Yes,' I said. 'Thank you, Mister Spock.' Fortunately the ChronoTranslator turned the name into 'misty pox'. 'I mean, thank you, Gluglielmo. Glug, glug, glug, just like this ale.' I took another gulp. 'You were a good friend to Michele but you were involved in the two most serious legal events of his life, the libel trial about Baglosi, no Bagleon, no Baglaci . . .'

'Baglione,' Longhi said, helpfully.

'That's it, Baglione, and the murder of Randolph Tomasetti . . .'

'Ranuccio Tomassoni,' Pellegrino corrected me, and leant over to whisper in my ear. 'Keep your voice down about Tomassoni, for Christ's sake. There may be some of his henchmen here tonight. And don't drink any more.'

I patted his arm and said: 'Don't worry, my friend.' I took another drink. Pellegrino looked away in disgust. 'How is your good lady wife, Caterina?' I asked Longhi.

'What do you know of my wife?' Longhi asked, belligerently.

'Easy, man,' I said. 'Caravaggio told me that you had commissioned him to paint her portrait. He said she was a lovely lady. Too good for you!' I found myself sniggering at my own comment and I was beginning to see two of everything. I was used to drinking so either this seventeenth century ale was particularly strong, which I doubted, or there was something wrong with me. I wondered if all this time travel might have affected my metabolism.

Longhi was about to rise from his chair but Pellegrino put a restraining hand on his arm. 'Take no notice of him, Onorio. He is a foreigner and not used to drinking, particularly our good Roman ale.' He turned to me and said: 'Finish your questions, Stefano, and then I'll take you home to let you sleep it off.'

'Good, excellent,' I said. 'Anyway . . . Signor Longhi, you were with Michele when he got into all this trouble but you always seemed to be away from Rome when the . . . when the shit hits the fan.'

This time the ChronoTranslator translated the last four words verbatim and Longhi stared at me, puzzled: 'What the fuck do you mean?'

What did I mean? My brain, befuddled with alcohol, struggled to remember what point I was trying to make. 'What I mean is, Signor Longhi, that you were away from Rome while the libel trial was taking place, you legged it out of Rome after the Tomasso-what's-it killing and, from what Michele told me, you and Spada here stayed clear of any danger when the sword fight with Tom-a-what's-it and his mates was going on. Sounds like you ran your mate Caravaggio into trouble and then left him in the dicky dirt when the rozzers came to feel your collars.' I was aware myself that the ChronoTranslator was translating my words as gibberish, but Spada and Longhi understood enough to know that I was accusing them of cowardice. I went to take another drink but Pellegrino snatched the tankard away.

This time, Longhi could not be restrained. 'You foreign bastard,' he said, rising from his chair and unsheathing his dagger. 'I'll show you who's a coward.'

'You cannot harm me,' I shouted, 'I am protected by the pope. Here is the warrant authorising me to question . . .' In my panic I had forgotten that my doublet was laced-up and, in desperately pulling it open to find the warrant, the gold-looking ChronoConverter chain had become clearly visible.

At that moment, luckily for me, a squeaky voice behind me said: 'What's all this? A meeting of the Michelangelo Merisi appreciation society falling out with each other?'

I turned around to see the pudgy face and the diminutive but threatening figure of the artist Tommaso Salini. He was backed up by five of his friends. They were all very drunk and all laughing at us. Pellegrino whispered in my ear. 'Cover up that chain.'

'Whispering sweet nothings in your lover's ear, Pellegrino?' Salini said. 'How touching.'

'Fuck off, Mao, you little cunt,' Pellegrino said. 'And take those apes with you.'

'Apes?' Salini repeated. 'Surely there is only one ape here, little Lionello Spada here, the ape of Caravaggio!'

'Shut your mouth, Mao,' Spada said.

'And what about Signor Maddano here?' Salini continued. 'My friend Baglione and I merited a special visit from the Holy Father's representative. And yet when it comes to Merisi's old bumboys, here he is drinking with them in a most convivial way! What a charming scene you all make. Have you asked them if they killed Merisi, Signor Maddano?'

Attempting to maintain my dignity, I burbled in rely: 'I am conducting my inquiries in a fair and impartial manner, Signor Saltino.'

Onorio Longhi, already standing up ready to attack me, picked up his tankard of ale and hurled it at Salini. He scored a direct hit on Salini's head and the ale soaked his dapper little hat. The ale-soaked feather drooped and fell over Salini's face. We all laughed, except Pellegrino, at Salini's discomfiture.

'Come on,' Salini said to his friends. 'Let's go and drink downstairs. There's a nasty smell of conspiracy up here.' They trooped off downstairs.

'Time to leave, my friend,' Pellegrino said to me, quietly.

'But I haven't finished questioning . . .'

'You're doing no good here. You are very drunk, God knows why. Salini's thugs noticed your gold chain. We are in a great deal of danger. We have to get out of here and back to my house.' Pellegrino stood up and said to the three artists: 'Please forgive Signor Maddano for any offence he has caused. He is not used to the drink and has been taken ill. I will take him back to my place and let him sleep it off.'

'I'm not that drunk,' I protested. I stood up and my legs buckled under me. I sat down heavily in the straw with my legs folded under me. My pratfall defused the angry tension around the table. Longhi sat back down and sheathed his dagger. 'Bloody stupid foreigners,' he muttered.

Pellegrino took me under the arms and lifted me up. 'Hold on to me,' he said. He put his arms around me and we headed for the stairs.

'Goo'night, gennelman,' I said to the three artists as we lurched away.

One of the other drinkers shouted: 'Taking your new boyfriend home, Pellegrino? I hope for his sake that he's on top of you tonight, you big bastard!'

'Sorry,' I said to Pellegrino. 'Didn't mean . . . get so pissed. Can't understand . . . what.' We stumbled down the stairs, to the general amusement of the lower floor patrons, and out of the door. The cooler air out on the piazza cleared my head a little. We stopped and I took several deep breaths.

'Salini's gang are over there watching us,' Pellegrino said. 'They must have seen your ChronoConverter chain. They will naturally think something like that is valuable. We could be in trouble if they follow us. Have you got your pistol handy?' I produced the pistol from my sleeve and waved it at Pellegrino. 'All right, put it away again.' He looked around the piazza. 'I can't see any police patrols that might help us. They're never around when you need them.'

'Just like back home,' I said. 'Never see a copper . . . swan around in cars . . . plenty of speed cameras though.'

'Shut up, for God's sake,' Pellegrino said. 'Come on, we'll start walking and see if they follow us. Can you walk properly?'

'Yesh, don't worry about me.' The effects of the cool night air were wearing off and I felt more drunk that I had ever done in my life. Pellegrino walked off, I staggered behind him and began to sing. 'Show me the way to go home. I'm tired and I want to go to sleep . . .'

'Keep quiet,' Pellegrino warned me. 'Remember where you are.'

'Yesh, in Rome,' I mumbled. 'Eternal city, all roads lead to it, when in Rome, do as the . . .'

'God in heaven,' Pellegrino said. 'Why did the ChronoCouncil pick you for a job like this. Can't even take your drink.'

'I'll have you know, Mister Gluglielmi, that I was once . . .'

'They're following us,' Pellegrino interrupted.

'Who are?'

'Salini and his gang of thugs, you idiot. Who do you think I mean? When we get to the other side of the piazza, we'll run for it.' He looked sideways at me, saw me wobbling along on rubber legs, and said: 'No, that plan won't work. Once we get into those narrow streets, we'll be sitting ducks. We'll have to make a stand and try to frighten them off. We are well armed and they know it. Men like these act like hyenas. If they scent fear or weakness they will be all over us.'

'Right, lesh make a stand like the Alamo or Rorke's what's-it,' I agreed.

We reached the other side of the piazza and stood at the mouth of a narrow street that was enclosed by the high walls of a palazzo on either side. We stopped and turned to face our pursuers, who were now only about fifty yards behind. As we did so, we heard running footsteps from the street behind us. 'Damn!'

Pellegrino swore. 'Some of them must have doubled back. They're coming up behind us. Arm yourself!'

I was trying to look both ways at once, utterly terrified despite being anaesthetised by alcohol. I pulled out my dagger but it tumbled out of my hand and into the gutter. Salini's gang were moving in from both directions but Pellegrino was brandishing his rapier and fear of that weapon in the hands of the big man was keeping them at bay. He said: 'Pick up that dagger and get your pistol out. That might scare them off.'

I bent down to retrieve my dagger but lost my balance completely and went crashing down into the gutter.

'Holy Mother of God,' Pellegrino swore, exasperated by my incompetence. 'Get your pistol out, quickly!'

I attempted to stand up while I was fumbling the pistol from out of my sleeve. I straightened up, with the pistol in hand, but caught my foot on a cobble, fell into Pellegrino and accidentally pulled the trigger. A blue flash of several hundred volts pierced his body. He screamed in agony and then fell backwards unconscious. The rapier fell out of his hand and rattled along the cobble stones. Shocked by what I had done, and anxious that my seventeenth century attackers should not get hold of such an incongruous weapon, I stuffed the pistol back up my conjurer's sleeve. The ruffians coming across the piazza were nearest so I turned and tried to run down the narrow street but as soon as I had entered the shadows they were on me like a pack of wolves from both sides. One punch in the face and I was down. They grabbed my hands and pulled the showy gold rings from my fingers but, thankfully, did not notice the thin gold ChronoTranslator ring. But now they were going for the ChronoConverter chain. In the back of my drink-sodden brain I knew that, without it, I would be stranded in the seventeenth century. I dimly wondered whether Pellegrino was wearing his ChronoConverter chain. Three of Salini's hyenas were scavenging his inert body while the rest concentrated on me. They were now ripping open my doublet and grabbing at the ChronoConverter chain. 'No,' I shouted. 'Don't take. . .sentimental value. . .my old dad gave. . .' I was answered by a boot in the face and the chain was pulled off over my head. I tried to grab it back, shouting: 'You fucking Eyetie fuckers. Give it back!' Having taken my valuables, they decided to have their sport with me. As their boots started flying at my body I managed to roll into a foetal position and put my arms over my head to protect my face. As I slipped into unconsciousness, I glimpsed another group of men running towards us. They were carrying torches, waving swords and shouting at my attackers, who ran off back across the piazza. The men with torches ran right past me, except for one man who stopped and looked down at me. He was a big man and he carried a sword which looked more like a cutlass. He leaned over me and, to my surprise, he said: 'Good evening, Signor Maddano. I've been waiting to talk you.'

'Who are you?' I croaked.

As the black veils of unconsciousness overtook me, I just had time to register his name as he said: 'My name is Giovan Francesco Tomassoni.'

46

I slept fitfully and dreamed of tankards of ale and running men and swords and torches and the walls of great palazzi pressing in on me. I heard a voice crying out in my sleep and woke up in darkness and realised the voice was mine, only to fall asleep again immediately. When I awoke properly it was light again. I was naked and I was lying in a narrow and uncomfortable bed in a shabby little room which contained no other furniture except a chair over which my clothes had been folded. I was covered by a white sheet which was discoloured and did not smell too clean. The pillows under my head were not pillows but embroidered cushions of some kind. My head ached with a venom I had never experienced before and the vision in my right eye was blurred. I felt the eye and discovered, to my relief, that my vision was blurred simply because the eye was badly swollen. I tried to sit up but a shooting pain in my ribcage made me stop. I heard a female voice say: 'Don't try to move. You have been badly injured.'

I turned my head to see who she was and, at that moment, she pressed a damp cloth on to my forehead. The coolness was soothing and reviving. 'Where am I?' I asked.

'You are safe in the house of Giovan Francesco Tomassoni,' the woman replied.

'Oh God,' I groaned. 'Am I under arrest?'

The woman smiled gently. 'No, of course not,' she replied. 'You are the victim, the one who was attacked. Giovan and his men are, at this moment, out searching for your attackers. They asked me to take care of you while they are gone.'

'Who are you?' I croaked.

'My name is Lavinia de Sanctis. Would you like a drink of water?'

'That would be most welcome, signora.' With gentle tenderness, Lavinia de Sanctis supported my head while I drank a flask of water. She was a very beautiful woman despite the fact that her facial skin had been ravaged by what must have been smallpox. Her raven black hair had been cut and styled shorter than was fashionable for most women of her age and class during this century.

She was dressed simply, as befitted her nursing duties, but I could see that her clothes were well made. She regarded me with a kindly expression but there was also a hardness in her eyes.

She asked: 'How did you know I was married?'

'I'm sorry,' I replied. 'I don't understand what you mean?'

'You called me "signora", not "signorina". I have taken my rings off so that I do not scratch you further, yet you know that I am a married woman.'

'I know that you have married again after once being the wife of Ranuccio Tomassoni.'

'Yes,' Lavinia replied, calmly. 'Your friend Caravaggio, for whom you are so keen to obtain justice, killed my husband.'

I didn't know how to reply until, stupidly, I asked: 'Are you going to kill me?'

'Don't be ridiculous. You did not kill Ranuccio. Somebody was going to kill Ranuccio one day. I am surprised it didn't happen sooner than it did. I would have done so myself if I had had the courage.' She applied the cold compress to my forehead. I suddenly realised that my wig was not on my head. I felt my face and the false beard and moustache were also gone. Lavinia was amused by my discomfiture. 'I can understand you wearing a wig,' she said, 'because you are old and bald. But why do you wear a false beard and moustache?' She rubbed my chin. It was not an unpleasant sensation. 'You have plenty of bristles. Why don't you grow your own beard and moustache, like a man?'

'Where I come from, it is a vain affectation for men to wear such things. Evidently it is not a custom that is practised in Italy.' Then, to change the subject, I asked: 'From what you just said, am I to understand that you hated Ranuccio?'

'Yes,' Lavinia replied. 'I came to hate him. I loved him once, as so many women did. Then this happened' – she indicated the smallpox marks – 'and he came near me no more. Then I found out more and more about his infidelities, his pimping, his drinking and his cruelty. He was a bully. He picked on your friend Caravaggio but Caravaggio was not a man to be picked on. He stood up to Ranuccio for years and Ranuccio baited him whenever he could. They were in love with the same woman. At least, Caravaggio was in love with her. Ranuccio was just using her to make money . . . pimping for her.' I knew this was Fillide Melandroni but I said nothing. 'It was inevitable that one day they would cross swords, literally. My beloved Ranuccio came off worst. From what Giovan has told me, Caravaggio did not intend to kill Ranuccio. No, Signor Maddano, I bear no malice towards you, or towards your dead friend, but perhaps he deserved to die as much as Ranuccio.'

'Why did you abandon your daughter Plautilla?' I asked.

Lavinia was silent for a few seconds and then her eyes welled up with tears. 'Damn you,' she whispered. 'You think I am a monster. You are thinking: "what sort of woman can abandon her own child?"'. Every time I looked at Plautilla, I saw Ranuccio. My husband is a good and kind man, but he did not want Plautilla. The Tomassoni family take care of her, see to her education and will give her a safe upbringing until she can find a husband of her own. It is the best way for everybody.'

'I am not fit to judge you, Lavinia. I can understand your reasons. I am surprised that you are still so closely connected to the Tomassoni family. Weren't they upset or bitter that you and your husband rejected Plautilla and that you married again so soon after Ranuccio's death?'

'No,' Lavinia answered. 'But you must ask Giovan about that.'

'I certainly intend to.'

'You must rest again,' Lavinia ordered. 'I will make you some broth to rebuild your strength. I can hear Giovan returning. He will want to speak to you.'

'You are very kind, Lavinia. Thank you.' She gave me a brief smile and left the room. I knew that my ChronoConverter chain had been stolen by Salini's ruffians but I did not know whether the wheel lock pistol with the Taser facility had been taken. The Tralfamadorian ChronoCouncil had given me special permission to take it into the seventeenth century and for such a powerful and incongruous weapon to get into the wrong hands would have very serious repercussions. I was not too concerned about the loss of my ChronoConverter as Pellegrino had another one and nobody from this century could operate it. It would remain inert, even if the lid of the hexagonal pendant was lifted. All that would be seen were tiny jewels. No, I was not concerned about the ChronoConverter but I was desperately worried about the pistol. Once again, I tried to get up off the bed but the pain was too much and I sank back on to the cushions. Trying to ignore the pain from the broken ribs, the headache, and the other bruises and contusions I had sustained in the attack, I frantically considered my best course of action. I decided that the less legal fuss was caused and the sooner I could get back to my own century, the better. Merisi would be wondering where I had got to and, bearing in mind his track record, he would probably demolish my house if I left him alone too long.

About an hour later, Lavinia returned with a bowl of beef broth and a flagon of wine. I could not raise the spoon to my lips because of the pain in my ribs, so Lavinia spoon fed me. It was not an unpleasant experience but I had not felt so helpless since I was a baby. I was stuck in an alien century, in an alien country, unable to move or defend myself, and imprisoned in the house of the brother of the man whom my known friend, Michelangelo Merisi da Caravaggio, had slain in a sword fight. I could only surmise, with dread, what Giovan Francesco Tomassoni and his family had in store for me. Lavinia finished feeding me with the broth and helped me drink a little wine. It was not vintage wine but it was reviving. I felt a little better and stronger and I thanked Lavinia. She had not said anything while spoon feeding me. Now she said: 'Giovan and his men are eating. He will be up to see you soon.' She left the room and I lay thinking over all the possibilities I could imagine. I again decided to say nothing of what I knew about my attackers. I did not want them to go to prison, where I could not get to them, or dispose of the ChronoConverter in fear of arrest or discovery. I didn't know what Pellegrino might tell Tomassoni but I hoped he had come to the same conclusions.

I had almost dozed off when I heard boots on the stairs. Giovan Francesco Tomassoni put his head round the door. 'How do you feel?' he asked.

'Awful,' I replied. 'Weak and in a lot of pain.' I played the sympathy card in the hope Giovan might take pity and let me off whatever hook he was planning to impale me on.

'Do you feel strong enough to answer some questions about last night?'

'Yes . . . just about,' I said feebly.

He came into the room, saw the chair with my clothes folded on it, took the clothes off and tossed them on to the bed. I held my breath in terror that he would discover the Taser wheel lock pistol but, if it was still up the trick sleeve, he did not notice it. Giovan was a tall man, heavily built, and looked every inch the soldier he had once been. He was weatherbeaten, with long hair, turning to grey already although he was about the same age as me. He was wearing a brown leather coat with long cavalry boots. He was not wearing a sword but there was a sheathed dagger hanging from a broad black leather belt around his waist. He pulled up the chair next to the bed and sat down. 'We have been out looking for the men who attacked you and Pellegrino but we have had no luck. I have made inquiries at the Tavern of the Turk but they could not tell me anything. I have also been to talk to your drinking companions, Orsi, Longhi and Spada but they do not know who the attackers were. Apparently you were very drunk and Pellegrino was helping you back to his home. Is that correct?'

'Yes, I drank too much ale.'

Giovan grunted, unimpressed by my unmanly failure to hold my drink. 'Pellegrino does not know who the attackers were either. He was unconscious when we found him but he did not seem to be wounded or bruised in any way. He told us that he passed out from too much drink. That surprises me. I have been drinking with him often and he can usually keep his head. Do you know what happened to him?'

'No, I can't tell you. I was on the floor being kicked around until you and your men frightened them off. Did you catch any of them?'

'No,' Giovan said disgustedly. 'They bolted down the narrow alleys like sewer rats. What did they steal from you?'

'A couple of gold rings, that's all,' I said.

Giovan regarded me suspiciously. 'No money?'

'No, I wasn't carrying any. Pellegrino was taking care of that.'

'Yes, he told us that his purse was stolen. Did they take anything else?'

'No,' I replied, fully expecting him to brand me as a liar, but he said nothing. 'What about Pellegrino?' I asked. 'Did he lose anything else?'

'No, just the money.'

'So what happens now?' I asked.

'There's nothing else we can do except ask around some more and hope that we can find somebody who knows something about who attacked you, in the same way that you are asking questions about who might have murdered your friend Michelangelo Merisi.' Giovan Tomassoni's black eyes stared at me but, whether it was wishful thinking or not, I could not see any malice in them. 'We will talk about that later, when you are stronger. I have sent for a doctor to examine your wounds. I looked at you myself while you were unconscious. I have been in many battles, many fights, and I've seen many wounds. Yours are not serious, except for your ribs. They need binding up properly.'

At that moment we heard more footsteps coming upstairs. Guglielmo Pellegrino came into the room. He nodded to Giovan Tomassoni. They were not bosom buddies. Pellegrino said to Tomassoni: 'Is it all right if I talk to my friend Maddano here?'

'Go ahead,' Giovan replied, getting to his feet. 'I've no doubt you two have a lot to talk about. I cannot get your property back or bring your assailants to justice unless you tell me the truth.'

'There is nothing more we can tell you,' Pellegrino said. 'I thank you for your efforts.' Tomassoni regarded us both with distaste and left the room.

Pellegrino took Tomassoni's place on the chair and said: 'We'll talk in English in case they try to listen at the door. This is a total fucking mess you've landed us in.'

'Me?' I protested. 'I didn't know that Mao and his men were . . .'

Pellegrino put his finger to his lips to shut me up. 'I hope you haven't told Tomassoni who attacked us.'

'No. The main thing is to get my ChronoConverter back and if our attackers are banged up in prison there is less chance of getting hold of it.'

'Good. At least you are showing a bit of sense.'

'Hold on,' I said, stung by Pellegrino's contempt. 'It wasn't all my fault.'

'Most of it was,' Pellegrino spat back. 'I didn't like the idea of this meeting in the Tavern of the Turk in the first place, but you insisted on it. Then you go and get yourself blithering drunk and then knock me out with your Taser pistol! A brilliant piece of work, Signor Maddano!'

'Okay, I fucked up. While we are on the subject, pass me my clothes. If the Taser is still there you can smuggle it out of this house for me.'

'I hope it is for your sake,' Pellegrino said. 'If that has gotten into the wrong hands in the wrong century we will be in deep shit with the ChronoCouncil.'

I felt the sleeves of my specially tailored doublet and, to my intense relief, found the pistol. I handed it to Pellegrino, who unlaced his doublet and secured the pistol on his right side, held by his leather belt and concealed under his arm. 'Well, that's another fiasco avoided anyway,' he said sourly.

'Look, things are not too bad,' I said, 'but I have to get back to my time as soon as possible. Merisi has been left there on his own. You know what he is like, he could get himself into all sorts of trouble if I'm not there to stop him. As soon as I can get up, and as soon as Tomassoni let's me go, you can take me back to your house and I'll use your ChronoConverter to get back home. I can leave you to find my ChronoConverter in your own good time . . . no pun intended.'

'You've worked it all out, haven't you?' Pellegrino said, sarcastically. 'Simple, isn't it . . . you scuttle back to your own century and leave me to clear up the mess. Except, you're not going anywhere, and neither am I.'

'What do you mean?' I asked, with a sense of doom at Pellegrino's comments.

'While I was unconscious, thanks to your drunken antics, you-know-who's men broke into my house and ransacked it, knowing I was lying spark out on the cobbles. They've taken all my valuables, my money, and my ChronoConverter.'

A wave of shock caused my ribs to throb with pain. 'You mean, you haven't got your ChronoConverter either?'

'That's exactly what I mean.'

'Christ, I'm stuck in the seventeenth century, with Merisi all alone in my house. This is a disaster. You'll have to go and see you-know-who and get back our ChronoConverters somehow.'

'I've already been to see him,' Pellegrino replied. 'The little bastard refused to help. I cajoled him, threatened him, told him that the ChronoConverters were made out of an unusual but valueless metal. He knows that are not made of gold or silver. They are much too light for that. Actually they are made from a ChronoAlloy that is probably the rarest alloy in the universe.'

'Did you offer to buy them back?'

'What with?' Pellegrino said. 'I've got no money left.'

'But if our friend now thinks the ChronoConverters are valueless, he or his friends might just destroy them. Nice work, Guglielmo.'

'No, he won't destroy them. They have some value as decorative objects. And he now knows that they are valuable to us. I told him they were tokens of rank and privilege in your country, that is why we were eager to get them back. If he thinks he can get more money from us rather than merely selling them as trinkets, he will keep hold of them for a time.'

'Well,' I said, 'you will have to raise some money somehow. Steal it if you have to. We must get those ChronoConverters back.'

Pellegrino looked away in embarrassment. 'He wants two thousand scudi for them. Two thousand each.'

'Then you'll have to find it!' I insisted.

'Do you realise how much money that is?' Pellegrino protested. 'I am posing in this century as a humble artist, a not very good or very successful one. I have no powerful or wealthy friends. Neither do you. I don't know how I can raise such a sum.'

'Like I said, you'll have to steal it.'

'Have you ever been inside the Tor di Nona prison? I'm not going to end up in there. I couldn't take it. Despite having lived in this century for a long time, I am not completely inured to it. I'm still used to modern comforts. I'm not a tough bastard like our friend Merisi.'

'So you're just giving up?'

'No, of course not. But what can I do? Have you got any ideas?' I had to admit that I had not. 'Then we are completely stymied for now,' Pellegrino said. He stood up. 'I'll keep trying. I'll think of something. As soon as you can move, if Tomassoni let's you out, come back to my house. If we cannot get the ChronoConverters back then eventually the ChronoCouncil will realise something is wrong and launch a rescue mission.'

'They might assume we are dead and not bother. And where does that leave Merisi. And my family and friends back home. I will have simply vanished. What will they think?'

Pellegrino shrugged and smiled. 'It is not all bad in this century. I will teach you how to mix paints. You can be my apprentice.'

'Apprentice, bollocks,' I said. 'I'll get those ChronoConverters back . . . somehow.'

'Rest easy, then. I'll talk to Tomassoni. He cannot keep you here for long. You have done nothing wrong.'

'I wish I was confident about that. It seems to me that it's easy to make people disappear in this century. And Tomassoni is a man with balls enough to make me disappear.'

'Try not to worry,' Pellegrino said lamely, and left the room.

I was left stunned and frantic with worry by this turn of events. How could I get hold of enough money to buy back the ChronoConverters? If I approached someone wealthy enough to lend me two or four thousand scudi, such as Vincenzo Giustiniani or even Cardinal Del Monte, what security could I give them? What could I tell them to justify asking for such a sum? Despite the intense worry of it, I was also very exhausted and I fell into a doze.

I slept fitfully for what must have been several hours. Every so often I was awakened by a commotion downstairs, doors slamming, people talking and coming and going. Every time I heard footsteps on the stairs I dreaded the appearance of Giovan Tomassoni coming to pronounce my doom. My headache became worse and my ribcage pounded with pain. I had never felt so ill in my life. Lavinia brought me wine, water and broth, which I could hardly keep down, but I fought off nausea, fearing that the strain of vomiting might finish me off. It was late afternoon when I heard voices downstairs and then footsteps, heavy and male, coming up the stairs. The door opened and, to my intense relief, there stood the small smiling figure of the Pan-like Doctor Giulio Mancini. As usual, he was dressed foppishly in what I was certain was the latest Roman fashion. He radiated confidence, good humour, kindness and energy, and his mere presence had a tonic effect on me that all Lavinia's ministrations had failed to achieve. He said: 'Well, well, well, Signor Maddano. I know you are a strange and elusive character but the last place I expected to meet you again was in the house of Giovan Francesco Tomassoni.'

Renewed hope flooded through my aching body. 'Doctor Mancini! I am overjoyed to see you. Now you know that I am here, you cannot let the Tomassoni family murder me.'

Mancini laughed. 'Hush, man. You are under my care now. Do you think they would have sent for me if they intended to kill you? They might give you a rough time in other ways but your mortal existence is safe . . . for the time being.' Mancini found my cowardly discomfiture most amusing. 'You look awful,' he said, examining my puffed up eye and bodily lacerations. 'They look clean enough. I understand your ribs may be broken?'

'Yes, that's right. My ribs ache furiously but, if anything, my headache is worse. Have you got any aspirin . . . I mean, anything to help.'

Mancini put a cool palm on my forehead. 'I understand that you got yourself very drunk last night?'

'Unfortunately, yes.'

'Do you drink regularly? Are you used to alcohol?'

'Yes.'

'What were you drinking, and how much?'

'I had about three pints, I mean tankards of ale.'

'That is not enough to get you roaring drunk if you are used to alcohol. Let me smell your breath.'

'What?' I objected. 'Why do you want to smell my breath?'

Mancini put his face near to my mouth. 'Just do it, man. Breathe heavily into my nose.' I did as he requested, fearing a swift and disgusted withdrawal, but Mancini was intrigued by the contents of my stomach and lungs. He stood up again and said: 'Just as I thought.'

'What?'

'You were drugged last night. With sorcerer's root to be precise.'

'Drugged?' I repeated. 'You mean like a Mickey Finn?' The ChronoTranslator, thankfully, translated Micky Finn as unintelligible gobbledegook.

'I don't understand what you just said, but you were given a concoction based on sorcerer's root in your drink and that is what made you behave as you did, not the ale. It is fairly common practise in the drinking dens of Rome when someone wants to disable an opponent or make someone an easy target for robbery. Who were you with last night?'

'What is sorcerer's root?' I asked, avoiding Mancini's question about my drinking companions.

'You have a knowledge of medicine. You must know what it is.' Mancini caught my expression of bemusement and went on: 'How would you know it? Satan's apple, perhaps? Mandragora?'

'Mandrake,' I said. 'The root of the Mandrake plant.'

'Exactly!' Mancini confirmed. 'It causes blurred vision, confusion and hallucinations. Have you passed urine or a stool since you have been cooped up here?'

'No,' I answered. 'Why do you ask?'

'Mandragora also causes constipation and dehydration.'

While pondering this unusual lack of bodily secretions I suddenly realised that Mancini was my only chance of extricating myself from captivity in the seventeenth century. I decided to trust him completely and ask him to help me. I remembered something about him that would certainly tempt him to help me and I would tell him the truth as much as was possible. I beckoned to him to come closer so that I could whisper. 'Doctor Mancini,' I whispered, 'I am in a great deal of trouble, far and away more serious than any dispute I might have with the Tomassoni family. I want to tell you all about it but you must not repeat this to Tomassoni or his men.'

Mancini looked at me, puzzled. 'You are under papal protection, surely?'

'This is something that even the Holy Father cannot help me with. But you can, and I will swear on all that is holy that you will be handsomely rewarded.'

'You know that I do not believe in holiness and all that nonsense. I will help you because you have helped me, because you are a guest in our country, and because you are a friend. A strange friend, I grant you, but a friend nevertheless. And you were a good friend to Michelangelo Merisi. Calm yourself. First I must treat your injuries.' Mancini rummaged in his medical bag and drew out a phial of green liquid. 'Drink that,' he ordered, 'it will nullify the effects of the mandragora and ease your headache.' I did as I was told and then Mancini carefully and methodically palpated my chest and ribs. He put his ear to my chest and listened to my heart. 'You will live to be an old man, my friend, but you have two broken ribs and I must bind up your chest securely to make sure they do not move and that they mend themselves properly. Then we will talk about your problem.' Mancini helped me sit up straight as far as I was able. He produced a large roll of linen bandage from his medical bag and quickly and expertly swathed my aching ribs with sturdy support. I sat back on my cushions and realised that my headache had diminished as well. I said: 'All that I have heard about you as an excellent physician is true.'

'Well, let us hope that I am as adept at curing whatever else ails you.' Mancini glanced out of the door and then sat down beside my bed. 'There is no-one outside the door. Tell me quickly what happened to you last night and what you need?'

I told Mancini everything that had happened in the Tavern of the Turk, including the fact that Lionello Spada had been talking to Carnacia when Pellegrino and I had arrived. 'Carnacia knows who I am,' I said. 'He detested Michele and would have been perfectly placed to drug my drink. Or Spada might have paid him to do it.'

'Why should Spada have wanted you drugged?' Manicini asked. 'He was one of Michele's closest friends and, as far as I know, an amiable soul. And, if he had paid Carnacia to drug your drink, would he have been so open about talking to him in public, in front of you?'

'I suppose not,' I admitted. 'Onorio Longhi was the most hostile towards me. It could have been him.'

'Longhi is hostile to everyone except a few, such as Michele, and he was a closer friend to Michele than even Spada was.'

'Perhaps it will have to remain a mystery,' I said, not actually caring who might have drugged me. I had to get one, or both, of the ChronoConverters back. I told Mancini about being confronted by Tommaso 'Mao' Salini in the Tavern of the Turk and how Salini's gang had assaulted Pellegrino and then gone on to ransack Pellegrino's house. Then I fabricated a few lies to explain the importance of the ChronoConverter chains. 'They are not made of gold, or any valuable metal, but they are made of a light metal, common where I come from but of little value. These chains are of no intrinsic value to Salini or whichever of his gang are in possession of them. But, in terms of rank, prestige and honour, these chains are of infinite value to me. If I go back to my country and have to admit I have lost my chain, for whatever reason, then I will be ruined socially and financially. So, you see, I will pay anything to get them back but I am stuck here in Rome and unable to come up with the ransom that Salini wants.'

'And how much does Salini want?' Mancini asked.

'Two thousand scudi for each chain.'

Mancini whistled thoughtfully. 'That's a lot of money. Why did Pellegrino have one of these chains?'

Thinking quickly, I lied: 'Because he once performed a great service for me and my country, details of which must remain a secret.'

Mancini was not convinced. 'Then there is more to Guglielmo Pellegrino than meets the eye,' he said. 'I have always found him a dull fellow. The women fall for his looks and his clothes and his tall manly figure but he is a bad painter and a poor talker. It is like he is always keeping a secret, always holding something back. What you have just told me perhaps explains a lot about him. You want his chain back as well?'

'If possible,' I confirmed.

'So we are talking about four thousand scudi.'

'Yes. Can you do it?'

'I can raise that amount of money. But, tell me, what do I get out of all this and, more importantly, how can I trust you not to disappear without paying me back?'

'As to the second part of your question, doctor, all I can give you is my promise as a gentleman.' Mancini snorted with derision but said nothing. 'As to the first part, I want to ask you a question about your work as a doctor.'

'Very well,' Mancini agreed.

'Do any of your male patients complain that they can no longer satisfy their wives or mistresses because they are ... too soft ... down there?'

'Yes,' Mancini agreed cautiously. 'Many of them, after a certain age, do.'

'I can give you a drug that guarantees an erection as hard as Toledo steel. Would that be of value to you?'

'Value?' Mancini exclaimed. 'I would pay a fortune for such a drug myself. I already find my own powers are not as enthusiastic as they used to be. Are you sure there is such a drug?'

'I swear it, doctor,' I replied, and made a mental note to bring back a few boxes of Viagra, suitably disguised, when I next visited the seventeenth century. 'And that is not all. You once asked me if I owned any works by our late lamented friend Michelangelo Merisi da Caravaggio, and I told you I did not. I lied to you. I am in possession of two of his finest paintings. If you help me out of this situation I am in, they are yours.'

This time, Mancini's eyes lit up with greed. I knew he was an avid collector and the prospect of owning two paintings by the greatest artist he had ever known was irresistible. I knew I had him hooked. All I had to do was persuade Michele to actually paint them when I returned home. If Mancini did get me out of this scrape, I fully intended to keep my promises to him. I asked: 'Can we make a deal, Doctor Mancini?'

Mancini pondered for several seconds. 'Tommaso Salini is a nasty and dangerous little bastard. He will need careful handling. But I am more nasty and dangerous than he is, when I have a mind to be. And I have powerful friends. I will agree to help you, Stefano, but be aware . . . if you fail to keep your end of this bargain and try to return to your own country, I will have you hunted down. I will make lying here with a throbbing head and two aching ribs seem like paradise compared with what I will do to you. Do you understand?'

I looked at Mancini and had no doubt that he would carry out his threat. 'I understand, doctor. I swear again that I will keep my end of this bargain. The only other thing I would ask of you is to act as swiftly as you can before Mao Salini and his henchmen decide to dispose of my property.'

'I agree,' Mancini said, and offered his hand. I shook his hand and said: 'What do I owe you for today's treatment?'

He stood up and smiled at me. 'You keep your word and get me the Caravaggio paintings and today's treatment is free. Farewell . . . for now, Signor Maddano.'

After Doctor Mancini had left, I felt intensely relieved. There were still many things that could go wrong but at least I had found a lifeline and taken some definite action to retrieve the ChronoConverters. My headache had abated considerably and my ribs also felt much better now that they were being supported by the good doctor's bandages. Lavinia brought me some more food and drink, which this time I managed to eat with something approaching enjoyment. The room was growing dark as evening deepened into night. 'Would you like a candle?' Lavinia asked me.

'No, thank you,' I replied. The moonlight was strong enough to illuminate the room.

'Giovan will be coming up to see you soon.'

'I look forward to it,' I said, genuinely not worried about Tomassoni now that Doctor Giulio Mancini was on my side. I laid back in my bed and dozed off again. When I awoke again I was startled to see a shadowy figure standing over the bed. The moonlight was slanting into the room, just like one of Caravaggio's paintings, and I could see that the figure was Giovan Francesco Tomassoni. To my surprise, he was holding a flagon of wine and two pewter goblets. He said: 'It's time for a drink, Signor Maddano. And it's time to talk about your friend

Merisi and my brother Ranuccio.' Giovan placed the two goblets on the window sill and poured wine into both of them. He was dressed the same as he had been that morning except I could not see a dagger or sword anywhere on his person. He quite rightly considered he would not need a weapon to protect himself against an injured and enfeebled cissy like me. Even though I no longer feared for my life, I felt a dread about having to talk to the man whose brother had been killed by Merisi. He carried the goblets back to my bed and handed one to me. 'Take it,' he urged. 'I promise you it is not drugged.' I said nothing, not daring to say anything incriminating. 'How do you feel now?' Giovan asked.

'Much better. Thank you for sending for Doctor Mancini.'

'He owed me a favour,' Giovan said, but did not elaborate. He sat down on the chair. 'You are trying to find out who may have murdered your friend Michelangelo Merisi?'

'Yes. I'm not absolutely sure that he was murdered but there are good reasons to believe so.'

'You have the blessing of the Holy Father for this inquiry?'

'Yes, I do,' I replied, glad that Tomassoni was aware that I had such papal blessing.

Tomassoni took a sip of wine. I did the same and was pleasantly surprised to find that it tasted considerably better than most of the wine I had been offered in seventeenth century Rome. It tasted like sherry so I was not surprised when Tomassoni said: 'I brought this wine back from Spain. It is better than Roman wine. Most Roman wine tastes like horse piss.'

'I agree,' I said. 'What were you doing in Spain?'

'Killing Frenchmen,' Tomassoni replied, 'in the wars of religion.'

'Oh,' I said lamely.

'I was a soldier for many years. Are you afraid of me?'

'I am . . . apprehensive,' I admitted.

'Your friend Merisi killed my brother. Now you are looking for justice for Merisi. What about justice for my brother?'

'I wouldn't say that I'm looking for justice for Merisi,' I blathered. 'I'm just looking for the truth about how he died. I promised him that I would. He knew he was a hunted man. I have no power to punish whoever was responsible. Merisi paid dearly for killing Ranuccio. Believe me, it made him a changed man . . . a remorseful man. It led to his death.'

'All that may be true, but it does not bring back my brother. And whatever you find out about Merisi's death can be passed to the authorities. They have the power to punish whoever was responsible, so don't tell me that your inquiry is a simple search for truth. It could lead to terrible consequences for whoever was responsible for his death.' I nodded in agreement, afraid to say too much. In the evening gloom of the room it was hard to discern the expression on Tomassoni's face, to discern what he might have been thinking. 'I respect your loyalty to Merisi,' he continued. 'I am a soldier. Loyalty to one's comrades is vital to a soldier. Do you think that I murdered your friend Merisi?'

Summoning up my courage, I replied: 'You and your family have the best reason I have found for wanting Merisi dead. Did you kill him?'

Tomassoni didn't answer my question, but said: 'As you know, I was there at the tennis court when Merisi killed my brother. After Merisi had struck the fatal blow, I intervened between them to stop Merisi inflicting more harm on my brother. I wanted to kill Merisi then. But I saw the look on his face. Merisi was horrified by what he had done. I could see from his expression that Merisi did not intend to kill Ranuccio, so I just held him off to protect Ranuccio from further harm. If I had wanted to kill Merisi, I could have done so then.'

'Perhaps you were afraid of the law. Afraid of the consequences. So you waited for a better opportunity, when nobody could prove it was you. You waited until Merisi was coming out of an inn in Naples, so drunk he could hardly stand up, or until he was prostrate in a bed in Porto Ercole.'

'No, Signor Maddano, I know nothing of what you are saying. I would not have been afraid of killing Merisi at the time. The law would have supported me. To watch my own brother being slain, and then to have slain his slayer in grief and rage, would have been strong mitigating circumstances. Anyway, I was not thinking like that at the time. Have you ever been in a battle or a war, Signor Maddano? Have you ever killed a man?'

'No.' I replied. 'I have never seen anyone being killed.'

'Then you should know that, apart from a few crazy headed maniacs, there is no-one more loath to take another human life than a soldier who has seen far too much killing already. I did not kill Merisi on the tennis court. Me and my family sought no revenge on Merisi afterwards. Do you know why?'

'No, tell me,' I invited.

'Because Ranuccio, God bless his soul and forgive me for saying so, asked for all he got from Merisi.'

'Lavinia said very much the same thing,' I said. 'Why should I believe you?'

'It is a hard thing to say that your brother, your own flesh and blood, was a worthless leech. Ranuccio was a good-looking boy. He had that immoral charm that women find so attractive for reasons known only to their sex. He preyed on women. He was a pimp. He used them, without regret, for his own ends. He used everybody for his own ends. He was a strong boy, he knew how to use his fists and his sword. He was a bully and a spoiled brat who had to get his own way. Most of his victims gave in and avoided Ranuccio. But, as you know, Merisi was not a man to back away from a fight. Ranuccio had baited Merisi for years on end. I warned Ranuccio time and time again that Merisi was a crazy man and that if Ranuccio carried on, it would end in bloodshed. Also, Merisi had powerful friends because of his skill as a painter. But Ranuccio didn't listen to me. I kept him under control when I was here in Rome but I was away at the wars too often and so this feud between Ranuccio and Merisi simmered away. It might have fizzled out . . . except for one person.'

'Fillide Melandroni,' I said.

Tomassoni got up and refilled our goblets. 'Fillide Melandroni,' he repeated, standing at the window, illuminated by the moonlight. His face was wistful. 'If Merisi and Ranuccio were not primed for trouble already, that woman coming between them was the fuse that caused the explosion.' He brought our drinks over and sat down again. It was difficult not to be convinced by Giovan Tomassoni. He had that strong but quiet dignity that many military officers in my own time seemed to possess. The discipline and self-control needed to face death on a regular basis seems to imbue them with a seriousness of purpose, the realisation that life is not a trivial affair to be frittered away on frivolous nonsense. He went on: 'Fillide Melandroni is a she-devil. Not that she entirely intends to be, but that is the effect she has on some men . . . on most men. So, here we had the eternal triangle. Fillide Melandroni was in love with Ranuccio. Ranuccio enjoyed fucking her but could not care less about her and would pimp for her. Merisi was in love with Fillide but Fillide cared little for Merisi. Merisi knew how badly Ranuccio was treating Fillide and that fuelled his hatred of Ranuccio. Then Ranuccio's wife Lavinia fell in love with this man de Sanctis and they began an affair. Merisi found out about this affair and taunted Ranuccio with the knowledge. I tried to persuade Ranuccio time and time again to stay away from Merisi, to take no notice of his taunts, but he would not listen. Here we had two proud, crazy, violent, self-centred men, driven mad with sexual jealousy. How is such a situation going to end? Only one way, in death for one or another. In this case, it was both. Ranuccio first, killed by Merisi's sword. Merisi next, exiled from Rome, a hunted man, his fortunes spiralling down until he collapses on a malaria-ridden beach in Porto Ercole. It has the inevitability of a Greek tragedy. Except, I swear to you, Signor Maddano, on my immortal soul, that Merisi's death was not caused in any way by my revenge or that of my family. What is being said about us in Rome, what we are being accused of, is entirely untrue. Can you accept my word on that?'

I made myself remain silent for several seconds, to give the impression that I was in deep thought, but I had already made up my mind. I believed Tomassoni but, even if I had not, I would have said I did, just to get out of his house. 'I accept what you are saying, Signor Tomassoni. I am convinced because you have accepted Lavinia back into your family, which I doubt you would have done if Ranuccio had been blameless. I accept that you could have killed Merisi on the tennis court, if you had wanted to. I believe you because of your courtesy and kindness in bringing me to your own house so that I could recover from being attacked, for which I thank you. I will now make sure that everyone knows that you have been eliminated as suspects in the death of Merisi and that your name is completely cleared.' I had no intention of doing anything of the kind but I was desperate to get out of Tomassoni's house, even if it was only as far as up the street as Pellegrino's house.

'Good,' Tomassoni said. 'I'm glad that we have reached an understanding. I know there is much about last night's attack that you haven't told me, but that is up to you. I have done my best to apprehend the perpetrators. You are welcome to stay in my home until you recover sufficiently to move to wherever you are staying.'

'Most kind of you Signor Tomassoni. I drink to your health.' We finished our wine in companionable silence. The day was ending with considerably more hope and reassurance than it had begun with. Tomassoni said: 'I'll leave you to get some sleep. Lavinia is staying the night with us. She is in the next room if you need any help.' He took my goblet, collected his flagon of wine, and left me in peace. I almost immediately fell into a deep sleep, still exhausted by my injuries and the stress of my situation. I was very anxious about the ChronoConverters but I thought that if anyone was resourceful and ruthless enough to retrieve them from the obnoxious Mao Salini, it was Doctor Giulio Mancini.

My faith was not misplaced. I was awoken in the morning by someone shaking my shoulder. It was Mancini himself. Lavinia was standing behind him with a pitcher of hot water and a bowl. Mancini said to me: 'Good morning, my friend. I thought I would pay you an early call to check on your progress.' He turned to Lavinia and said: 'Thank you, signora. I will make sure the patient washes himself properly.' Lavinia set down the pitcher and wash bowl on the window sill and left the room. Mancini silently pushed the door closed and, from his voluminous medical bag, produced two ChronoConverter chains. 'Are these what you have been anxiously seeking?' he asked.

'Yes. God bless you, Doctor Mancini. You have saved my life.'

'Saving life is my occupation,' he smiled, 'but I do not believe in God.'

'Then Aesculapius bless you.'

'Much more appropriate.'

'Did you have any trouble retrieving them?'

'It needed a little persuasion,' Mancini said, with a thin smile, 'but Tommaso Salini will think twice before arguing with me in future.'

The relief at seeing the ChronoConverters was almost overwhelming. I reached out to take them but Mancini held them back. 'Remember our agreement,' he warned me.

'Help me get up and get dressed and get out of here,' I said. 'I will not forget my promise. You will soon be the proud possessor of two paintings by Caravaggio and a hard-on that Priapus himself would be proud of.' Although it was still very painful, I managed to get out of bed and was pleased to discover that the pain was eased by standing up. With Mancini's help, I managed to get dressed. When we were ready to leave, Mancini hid the ChronoConverters in his medical bag and followed me downstairs. I ignored the discomfort and pretended that I was perfectly fit to move around again. I said my goodbyes and thanks to Lavinia and Giovan Francesco Tomassoni. As soon as we were outside and out of sight, Mancini supported me while I hobbled to the house of Guglielmo Pellegrino. Pellegrino was almost as relieved as I was to see the ChronoConverter chains returned. As soon as Doctor Mancini had left, I explained to Pellegrino how I had managed to get the chains back and, as soon as I could decently take my leave, floated back to my own century.

I had never been so glad to see my own bedroom again. It was sometime during the day. I just managed to put on a modern shirt over my bandages but I did not bother to try to change out of my seventeenth century pantaloons. I walked painfully down the stairs. The house looked to be intact but it was ominously quiet. I looked into the kitchen. No damage in there. Then I went into the living room. Merisi was sitting comfortably in his armchair, reading a book.

'Stefano!' he exclaimed. 'I've been reading some more of your History of World Art book.'

'Are you all right?' I asked him.

'I'm fine,' Merisi said. 'Why shouldn't I be?'

'Don't you want to know where I've been?'

'Where have you been?' Merisi asked, not bothering to look up from his book.

'Oh, getting pissed and drugged with your friends Orsi, Longhi and Spada. Getting beaten up and robbed by Tommaso Salini and his gang, breaking two ribs, being captured and imprisoned by Giovan Tomassoni, nearly getting stranded forever in the wrong century.'

'Sounds like a normal night back in dear old Rome. You're just a soft modern Englishman. I knew you would get yourself into serious trouble one day, back in my time,' Merisi said, still not looking up. 'This man Goya was very good, wasn't he?'

'Never mind Goya,' I said. 'Get off your arse and get painting. I owe Doctor Mancini two of your finest works or, next time I go back to Rome in 1611, I'm dead meat.'

47

I had been disappointed that Merisi could not remember anything about the attack outside the Osteria del Cerriglio and that we could not find any clues from this savage event but I was determined to complete our research. I knew that Merisi had been lying to me, or at best withholding knowledge, throughout our research so far. It was a fact which I found very discouraging and demoralising. I had been convinced by Giovan Francesco Tomassoni's denial that he had anything to do with Merisi's murder. My inquiries were now at a very late stage. I could see a thread of evidence, nothing more than a remote possibility, running through Merisi's life but that thread was as insubstantial as a wisp of smoke. There were several prime suspects, most particularly Lionello Spada, but I could not pin anyone down. I was hoping against hope that something, anything, might yet turn up to give me a clue to the answers I was looking for. So, yet again, Merisi and I settled into our armchairs and resumed our search. I lowered myself gingerly into my chair. I had visited my own doctor to get my broken ribs properly strapped up with modern equipment and they felt much more comfortable but still very sore. Merisi was delighted by my puffy black eye and general beaten-up appearance. I ignored his little jokes and said: 'You seemed to recover from the attack outside the Osteria del Cerriglio very well because, during the next few months, you produced an astonishing amount of work for someone who had been wounded so badly as to come near to death.'

'Yes,' Merisi replied. 'The excellent care that Costanza provided for me and the comfort of her beautiful Palazzo Cellamare helped me to recover very quickly. I was still hopeful and optimistic of a swift return to Rome. I had nothing else to do during my convalescence so I plunged myself into my work.'

'During this time you created some works of astonishing power and simplicity, almost a brand new style of painting.'

'Many of these pictures were intended as gifts to placate people I had upset, or to curry favour with those I needed to help me obtain a papal pardon. For instance, I did Salome with the Head of John the Baptist (*Plate 59*) and sent it to Alof de Wignacourt. I was symbolically offering my head on a plate to him, begging him for his mercy and my rehabilitation as a knight. I did a David with the Head of Goliath (*Plate 60*) and sent it to Cardinal Scipione Borghese, the pope's nephew, who obviously had great influence with Pope Paul. Once again, I was symbolically offering him my head in penance for my sins. The head of Goliath is a self-portrait, just so that my meaning would be clear.'

'I'm sure it was,' I said. 'These are such simply composed yet powerful paintings that they could not be ignored.'

'That was my intention, to show these influential men just what they were missing by my exile.'

'We know of another three works that you completed at this time, now unfortunately missing, for the Dominican church of Santa Anna dei Lombardi. Still with us, thankfully, is your Crucifixion of Saint Andrew.' (*Plate 61*).

'Yes, that one was commissioned by the Viceroy of Naples. I remember that he was very pleased with it.'

'So he should have been,' I said, 'for its a quite extraordinary depiction of someone close to death. Anyone who can look at your depiction of Saint Andrew on the cross and not feel sympathy for his suffering, and therefore for the suffering of the whole human race, cannot have a heart, let alone a soul.'

'Why, Stefano,' Merisi teased me, 'it's not like you to talk so passionately about one of my works. What happened to that English "stiff upper lip"?'

'I'm a human being first and an Englishman only a poor second.'

'Well said, Stefano!'

'Another of your powerful late works is the Martyrdom of Saint Ursula. (*Plate 62*). A not altogether successful picture, I have to say.'

'Don't get too carried away by your new-found skill as an art critic,' Merisi said, smiling. 'That picture was painted for Marcantonio Doria. It was painted in honour of Marcantonio's stepdaughter, who had become a nun and taken the name of Sister Ursula.'

'I see that you again included a self-portrait, on the right of this picture, very similar to the one you included in the Taking of Christ.'

'Yes. Once again I was trying to remind people that I was still alive and working. After the attack outside the Osteria del Cerriglio, a rumour had spread that I was already dead.'

'We are not sure which was the last picture you ever completed at this time. Was it your rather melancholy portrait of Saint John the Baptist?' (*Plate 63*).

'Yes, it was,' Merisi confirmed. 'That was another bribe for Cardinal Scipione

Borghese. He had been pleased with my gift of David with the Head of Goliath and he decided to squeeze another picture out of me before my return to Rome knowing that, after my rehabilitation, he would have to join a very long queue of patrons who wanted me to work for them.'

We spent a few minutes examining and considering all these paintings in connection with our search for Merisi's murderer but again, very disappointingly, we could find nothing that advanced our quest.

I said: 'You were still living and recuperating with Costanza Colonna at the Palazzo Cellamare when you suddenly departed for Rome. What made you do that?'

'A messenger arrived from the papal court in Rome. It was a letter from Cardinal Ferdinando Gonzaga. It bought me the news that the pope had graciously decided to grant me a pardon for my crime and it also enclosed a safe conduct pass authorised by the cardinal himself. I was in such a frenzy to return to Rome that I wasted no time at all. I immediately packed up the few belongings I possessed, collected a few of my newly-completed pictures as gifts for His Holiness and Cardinal Gonzaga and Scipione Borghese, and anyone else who had supported my cause, left some pictures with Costanza, and boarded the first felucca out of Chaia bound for Rome.'

'What did Costanza think of this precipitous farewell?' I asked.

'Oh, she tried to stop me,' Merisi replied. 'She tried to persuade me that there was no need to hurry back to Rome and that I should stay with her and make sure that I had fully recovered from my wounds.'

'I must say that Costanza's suggestion sounds eminently sensible. You were secure and comfortable and you were doing very good work. Why were you in such a fret to get back to Rome?'

'You know what I am like, Stefano, arrogant and impulsive. I had been away from Rome for about four years. All my rivals had made important advances in their careers. Rivals like Guido Reni, Cavaliere d'Arpino, Roncalli and Barocci and men like that. The only one I truly admired as an artist, Annibale Carracci, was already dead, driven mad by the parsimony of the Farnese family. Yes, Costanza's palace at Chaia was safe and comfortable but the only place I truly felt alive was in the studios and taverns of Rome. It was my true home. I just had to get back to her as soon as I could.'

'Did you tell anyone else that you were returning to Rome? Or did you send word to Rome that you were coming back?'

'No. I just packed up and left.'

'What about this felucca?' I asked. 'Did you hire one or was it a regular service or whatever?'

'It was a regular service from Naples to Rome, stopping at different places on the way to load and unload passengers and cargo, but the itinerary was usually the same. I just boarded and paid for my passage like any other passenger.'

'We know that the felucca stopped at a port named Palo and that you were arrested there. What was that all about?'

'Palo was a tiny place, just a fortress with one or two houses around it. We had stopped there and the captain of the fortress came on board, with some of his men, and said that they were looking for an escaped fugitive. When they found out that I was the famous painter Michelangelo Merisi da Caravaggio, wanted for murder in Rome, they arrested me. Of course, I protested and showed them the safe conduct pass from Cardinal Gonzaga and his letter saying that I was about to be pardoned. It made no difference. The captain said he would have to check these credentials with Rome and, in the meantime, he would take me into custody. So they dragged me off the felucca and took me to a cell in the fortress. I argued and argued and, as you can imagine, I kicked up a terrible commotion. All my possessions, including my pictures, had been left on the felucca, but I did have all my money with me, concealed in a hidden purse. It was a large amount and all the money I had in the world. I offered this captain a bribe to let me go. When he found out how much money I had, he demanded all of it in exchange for my freedom. In the end, I had no choice. I gave him the lot and he released me. If I had had my dagger I would have slit the bastard's throat. They let me out of the fortress and I went down to the quay but the felucca had gone.'

I said: 'You were in quite a fix, I can see that. Why did you decide to follow the felucca to Porto Ercole? You could have walked to Rome from Palo.'

Merisi laughed derisively. 'It sounds so easy, doesn't it? Sitting here in a comfortable armchair in a warm sunny room in England. I had no money left to buy any sort of food, drink or transport. If I headed for Rome, the chances are I would have had my throat cut by any one of the bands of brigands that infested the area. But if I stayed on the coast and followed the felucca I would avoid the brigands and have a better chance of recovering my property, especially my pictures and my sword. I knew there were a couple of fishing villages on the way where I could possibly cadge or steal some food or drink.'

'But we know that the coast was malarial in your day,' I said. 'Didn't that worry you? After all, it was midsummer. It must have been very hot.'

'Yes, of course it worried me. I knew it was a risk. I knew there were mosquitoes everywhere. I knew I would be moving away from Rome. But imagine if I had headed for Rome and turned up penniless, starving, bedraggled, with no property and no pictures to offer the cardinals. Everyone would have thought "same old Caravaggio". I wanted to arrive in Rome with more style.'

'It was about sixty miles from Palo to Porto Ercole. That would take a couple of days to walk in the best of conditions. Surely you must have thought that you had little chance of catching up with the felucca?'

Merisi shrugged, tiring of explaining his reasoning. 'I made my decision. I hoped that the captain of the felucca might have put my property ashore in Porto Ercole, in safe-keeping with someone. I was desperate and panicked. Perhaps it was the wrong decision.'

'It must have been a very ardous journey from Palo to Porto Ercole. What was it like?'

'It was a nightmare. I was very hungry, desperately thirsty and I was constantly bitten by the mosquitoes. By the time I arrived in Porto Ercole I was in a state of complete exhaustion and I knew that a fever was starting within me. Porto Ercole was another small fortress town. It was built on a spit of land and connected to the mainland by a causeway. It was a desolate place, surrounded by the sea on one side and dark looming mountains and forts on the other side. When I finally arrived there, I just had the strength left to get to the harbour master's office. Of course, the felucca had already left but they had left something for me . . . one picture. One picture! Why hadn't they left the rest of my property? I'll never know. The shock and disappointment was too much for me. I collapsed and I was taken off to the local infirmary. I was very ill but I was not dying. Then happened these extraordinary events, which we have been inquiring into, when someone attempted to murder me. Do you still not have any idea who it was who tried to kill me?'

'I have many ideas, Michele,' I confessed, 'but still no concrete evidence.'

'What can we do now?' Merisi asked. 'We have explored my life, my pictures, my friends, my enemies, my family, my lovers. What else can we do?'

'How far have you got with those paintings for Doctor Mancini?'

'I have completed one,' Merisi replied. 'A basket of fruit of flowers. I took the fruit from your kitchen and the flowers from your garden. Are you going back to Rome to see Mancini?'

'No,' I said. 'Mancini will have to go without his pictures. I need to complete my research into the final days of your life. With your permission I want to take your painting as a gift.'

'A gift for who?' Merisi asked.

'Your friend the Marchesa Costanza Colonna. Would you mind if I gave her your picture, to sweeten her reception of me?'

'Nothing would give me greater pleasure, Stefano. I only wish, with all my heart, that I could go back and give it to her myself.'

48

The door knocker on the main door of the Palazzo Cellamare was made out of bronze and shaped like a letter 's' entwined around a column. It announced to the world that this was a Colonna Sforza residence. I knocked loudly. I waited two or three minutes but the door did not open. I knocked again, even louder, but still the door did not open. I was about to knock again when I heard the sound of bolts being drawn back. The door opened slowly and a face peered out of the gap. 'Good morning,' I began, 'I have an appointment with . . . Gianfranco!' I had recognised the unmistakeable impish squashed-up face that peeked out as Gianfranco, the man whom Caravaggio had frequently used as a model over the years and who was supposedly a waiter at the Tavern of the Turk. I remembered that his face had first appeared in about 1602 in such works as the Betrayal of Christ and had appeared frequently in Caravaggio's works since then, including one of his final works, Salome with the Head of Saint John the Baptist, which was housed in the National Gallery in London, right next to the Supper At Emmaus.

The impish servant looked at me in puzzlement. 'My name is Fillipo, sir, not Gianfranco. I am the Marchesa's major-domo.'

'I thought you were a waiter at the Tavern of the Turk in Rome.'

'I beg your pardon, sir, but I don't know what you are talking about.'

I was still bemused by this sudden and unexpected apparition. 'Haven't you ever been a waiter at the Tavern of the Turk in Rome?'

'No, sir. With respect, I have no knowledge of what you are talking about.'

After a few seconds thought I decided to drop the subject until later. 'Very well,' I said. 'My name is Stefano Maddano. I have an appointment with the Marchesa.' I could not help noticing that Fillipo had looked at me curiously, but warily, when I announced my name, a look that was unbecoming of a servant towards a supposed distinguished visitor like me. I was still trying to consider the ramifications and implications of this sudden revelation. Merisi had told me that the model's name was Gianfranco and that he had been a waiter at the Tavern of the Turk, yet here he was named Fillipo and was Costanza Colonna's major-domo, a fact that must have been known to Merisi. Once again, Merisi had deliberately concealed a potentially important fact.

I was carrying Merisi's still life painting under my arm. It was wrapped in brown silk and bound with a yellow ribbon. Fillipo looked at it pointedly. I said: 'It is a gift, a painting, for the Marchesa. Don't worry, Fillipo, it is not a weapon and I am not armed.' It was true. I had decided not to carry any weapons for this visit. I had also discarded all the bling of rings and gold chains and dressed in a dignified manner in a simple but elegant royal blue doublet over a white shirt with the large floppy lace collar of the type that was so popular during the early seventeenth century.

'Please come in, sir,' Fillipo said. I stepped out of the hot Neapolitan sun into the cool shade of the entrance hall to the Palazzo Cellamare.

Gianfranco was a short man. His upper body was broad-shouldered and powerfully built but his legs were bowed to an alarming degree. His hair was still cut short, as in the Caravaggio paintings, but it was now almost completely grey, as was his full beard and moustache. His ears stuck out and his eyes were piggy and narrowly set above a pug nose. His hands were twisted and contorted by the advanced stages of arthritis. He looked like an evil Satyr. I took him to be about seventy years old but, because he looked so tired and ill, that could have been an over-estimate. 'The Marchesa is taking the sun on the terrace. Please follow me, sir,' he said, and he opened a side door and scuttled away, his breathing already becoming laboured.

'Fillipo!' I called, following him through the door and into a service corridor. 'Please wait a moment. I would like to ask you a few questions.'

We had already reached a doorway to the kitchen of the palazzo. Fillipo stopped and turned around. He looked extremely reluctant to talk to me.

I asked: 'How long have you worked for the Marchesa?'

Fillipo hesitated but then said: 'I have had the honour to be in the service of the Marchesa all my life.'

'Do you know the reason why I am visiting your mistress today?'

'I am merely a servant,' Fillipo replied. 'It is no concern of mine.'

'With respect, Fillipo, that is not what I asked you. Do you know the reason why I am here today?'

'Yes, sir.'

'You must have known Michelangelo Merisi, known as Caravaggio, very well. You modelled for him on several occasions over the years.'

'Yes, sir.'

I looked at Fillipo, expecting him to say more, but he remained silent. I asked: 'How long had you known Michelangelo?'

Fillipo, disrespectfully ignoring my question, turned away from me and started walking again. Over his shoulder he said: 'Please follow me, sir. We must not keep the Marchesa waiting.'

I followed Fillipo through the spacious kitchen of the palazzo, wondering why he was taking a distinguished visitor like me through the tradesmen's route. The cooks and kitchen maids looked at me curiously as I hurried to catch up with Fillipo. He led me through a large storeroom and then we suddenly emerged on to the terrace of the palazzo. The scene that lay before me was so breathtakingly beautiful that I had to stop and drink it in.

Fillipo became aware that I had stopped, so he also stopped and looked round at me. 'Is anything wrong, sir?' he asked.

'Quite the contrary,' I replied. 'I don't think I have ever seen such a beautiful place in my life. Do you mind if I just look at it for a few seconds?'

'Please, sir, I do not wish to keep the Marchesa waiting.'

'Fillipo,' I ordered firmly, 'lash yourself to the mast and calm down. My appointment with the Marchesa was not for a definite time and she does not even know that I'm here yet, so we are not keeping her waiting. I know you do not wish to talk to me and such reluctance betrays the fact that you know something you do not wish to tell me. So, wait a few moments while I enjoy the view.' Fillipo said nothing more but waited uncomfortably, shifting from foot to foot.

I could see for miles around the bay. The sea and the sky were so blue that it was difficult to see where they met. A warm breeze was blowing and gently stirred the myriad cedar trees, vines, fig trees and flowers that surrounded the palazzo and which also grew below us on the terraced garden. In the distance were blue-green mountains with other villas and palazzi nestling at their feet, as far around the bay as the neighbouring village of Posilippo. Fishing boats bobbed jauntily out in the bay. Below us, the terraced gardens fell away right down to the beach. There were fountains and statues dotted everywhere. High walls, covered in frescoes, were strategically placed to provide shade, and small terrazo patios, equipped with marble benches, were also strategically placed to provide resting places. I had never seen anywhere in my modern world to compare with it for loveliness.

Fillipo was still shifting around on his feet but I could see that it was not from impatience but because he had difficulty standing for any length of time. I asked him: 'You said you have been in the service of the Marchesa all your life?'

'Yes, sir.'

'Then you knew her when she was a girl?'

'Yes, sir,' Fillipo replied, very uncomfortable with my questioning. Then, to my surprise, he asked tentatively: 'You are the gentleman from Rome who is looking into the death of Signor Merisi?'

'Yes, I am.'

Fillipo's rheumy and piggy old eyes looked at me pleadingly. 'The Marchesa is a great lady, sir. A good lady. I am devoted to her, as was Signor Merisi. She was deeply upset by Signor Merisi's death.'

'Don't worry,' I replied. 'No harm will come to the Marchesa from my inquiry. I will be as gentle as I can be. I just want to find out a few facts about Signor Merisi's last days. You must have known Michele when he was a boy?'

'Indeed I did, sir. He frequently used to visit the Palazzo Colonna in Milan. He was a strange boy, quiet and intense. Even then, he seemed to be driven by some inner demons. I didn't know him well. At that time I was just a servant, one among many, so he ignored me, but he was not rude and naughty as the Marchesa's sons could be. Forgive me, sir, I am speaking out of turn.'

'Not at all, Fillipo. There is nothing that you can say to me that will shock me or scandalise me or that will be used against you. I swear it in the name of Christ. The Holy Father has decreed that all persons giving evidence to me about Michele's death must tell the truth, so I would like to ask you a few more questions before I go to meet the Marchesa. Now, when did you . . .'

'Forgive me for interrupting, Signor Maddano. I am aware of what the Holy Father has decreed but I will not answer any further questions until I have obtained the advice and permission of the Marchesa do to so. I will not talk about her or her family behind her back, sir. I hope my reply has not offended you.'

'On the contrary, Fillipo, your loyalty does you credit, not to mention your good sense. Please take me to the Marchesa.'

'It is quite a long way down, sir,' Fillipo said mournfully, looking at the terrace steps with apprehension. They descended steeply down for what must have been about two hundred feet. 'I am not as young as I was and I may be slow.'

'Take your time, Fillipo. I am only too happy to enjoy this view as we descend.'

Fillipo took the first step. He had to half twist his body as he lowered himself in order to allow for his bowed and arthritic legs. He breathing became laboured. I guessed, from the blue tinge of his lips, that he also had a bad heart. We had descended no more than twenty steps when Fillipo stumbled and fell. He landed on his knees and managed to break his fall by thrusting out his arthritic hands. The pain of his landing made him gasp and wince. His eyes welled with tears, more from embarrassment and shame than from the pain. I grabbed hold of him under his armpits to pull him up. 'No, no,' he protested, 'I cannot allow a gentlemen such as yourself to take such trouble for me.'

I ignored Fillipo's protests and pulled him to his feet. Fortunately, the accident had occurred on one of the small terrazo patios with a marble bench provided. I sat Fillipo on the bench and sat down beside him. He held his face in his hands and rocked backwards and forwards. 'Oh, the shame,' he moaned. 'I'm so sorry, sir. What will her ladyship think of me when you tell her? I'm ashamed to behave so in front of a fine gentleman such as yourself.'

I gently pulled Fillipo's hands away from his face and said: 'Look at me, Fillipo.' He did as I told him. 'First of all, I have no intention of telling her ladyship. The only thing that matters to me is that you are all right and haven't broken any bones or anything. Despite my appearances, I am not a gentleman myself. I was born in humble circumstances. I am the son of humble parents. I have been in service to other people, albeit differently to you, all my life. We are comrades and brothers, Fillipo, so stop worrying. And call me Stefano, not Signor Maddano.'

Fillipo stared at me, scarcely comprehending what he was hearing. I could not tell whether he thought I was mad or whether I was setting a trap for him. He insisted: 'I still have to ask the Marchesa for permission to talk to you.'

'I fully accept that, Fillipo. Don't worry. We'll rest here awhile until you get your strength back.' Fillipo carried on staring at me for several seconds, completely unused to such consideration from a member of the 'upper classes', but then he accepted that I genuinely meant what I said. I could sense him relaxing. He closed his eyes and rested. I looked out at the sea lapping up to the beach far below. Now that I had a few minutes to think, I should have realised that Merisi had not been telling me the truth about the man sitting next to me. Fillipo had modelled for paintings completed in Rome as early as about 1602 and for paintings completed in Naples as late as a few months, or even weeks, before Merisi's 'death' in Porto Ercole in 1610. As Costanza Colonna's major-domo he would, naturally, have been with her in whichever of her palazzi in Milan, Rome or Naples that she was living in. If he had been, as Merisi had told me, simply a waiter in a tavern in Rome, he would not have been available to model for Merisi in Naples. Also, Fillipo's saturnine visage did not appear in any of the paintings that Merisi had completed in Malta or Sicily. Looking back, it seemed obvious that Fillipo must have been travelling around to some of the places where Merisi had been staying. Hindsight is a wonderful gift.

I heard some sort of commotion up near the palazzo. There was an exchange of loud voices and then I heard someone running towards the terrace. A tall man came bounding down the steps and stopped short as he saw Fillipo and I peacefully resting on our marble bench. It was Fabrizio Sforza. He walked up to Fillipo, who still had his eyes closed, and kicked him in the shin. Fillipo woke up with a start and looked up at Fabrizio. Fabrizio said: 'Get up, you lazy piece of shit.' A look of pure hatred crossed Fillipo's face but he struggled to get to his feet. I put my hand on his arm to hold him back.

'Good morning, Fabrizio,' I said, deliberately using an informal form of address in order to annoy Costanza's arrogant son. Fabrizio knew full well who I was after our meeting outside the Contarelli chapel in Rome.

Fabrizio ignored me and snarled at Fillipo: 'What are you doing sitting down, you idle old bastard? What are we paying you for?'

Fillipo could not answer back, but I could. 'I ordered this man to sit down with me. He was eager to show me to your mother but I wanted to enjoy this magnificent view before I disturbed her ladyship. He was only doing what I told him to do.'

Fabrizio turned his attention to me. 'I have just heard that you were back, you damnable snooper. Thank God I have arrived in time to warn my mother about your impertinent prying.'

'Why, Fabrizio,' I taunted him, 'it sounds as if you are worried that I might discover something about you. Is there anything you wish to tell me?'

'Yes,' Fabrizio replied, 'I wish to tell you to roast in hell.' He turned to Fillipo. 'As for you, I will deal with you later, you useless cripple.'

I said: 'You are a brave man, Signor Sforza, when you are taking on an elderly servant who cannot defend himself. If you cause this man any harm, or punish him in any way, for simply obeying the instructions I, as a guest, gave to him, then I will personally make sure that you suffer in return. This I swear on the Holy Cross.' My courage was reinforced by the fact that, as a guest at the palazzo, on a mission with the blessing of Pope Paul, Fabrizio Sforza would not dare to lay a hand on me.

Fabrizio regarded me with a look of pure malice but simply hissed: 'Do not keep my mother waiting much longer.' He bounded off down the terrace steps.

I said to Fillipo: 'I do not like that man. He is, as they say in my country, a "nasty piece of work". I know that he committed some grave crime back in 1602, for which he was exiled to Malta, but I don't know what it was. Do you know anything about that?'

Fillipo, energised by anger and adrenalin, replied without regard to my supposed status. 'I have suffered that man's cruelty, ill-temper and insults since he was a child. I have kept silent, for the sake of the Marchesa, whom I love dearly. I will stay silent no longer. As you have seen, I am not long for this world. My heart is weak, my body fails. I can see that you are a man of humanity, a man of fairness, and I thank you for protecting me. The Holy Father, through you, has ordered that the truth be told. I will now tell you the truth about Fabrizio Sforza, our friend Michele, and my beloved daughter Gabriella.'

'Very well,' I said. 'Take all the time you need.' I felt very excited that, at last, I might be about to hear the solution to the mystery of Merisi's murder. Fillipo had appeared in several pictures by Merisi. This could be what the murderer had meant in his enigmatic comment about the answer being in the pictures. Merisi had been involved in whatever incident Fillipo was about to tell me about. This could be the breakthrough I had been waiting for.

'I had known Michele all his life,' Fillipo began. 'As I have said, I was merely a servant but Michele always treated me with respect or, at worst, benign indifference, unlike that bastard Fabrizio, who is the spawn of the Devil. Anyway, Michele and I didn't have much to do with each other until after Michele had moved to Rome and become a famous painter. His paintings for the Contarelli chapel and the Cerasi chapel had made him the most talked about painter in Rome. One day, Michele visited the Palazzo Colonna to pay his respects to the Marchesa. He saw me and asked if I would model for a painting he was doing. It was going to depict the betrayal of Christ. Michele told me that he had always been fascinated by my face and had always wanted to paint a portrait of me. Well, you can understand that I was flattered. Here was the little boy I had once known, now the most famous painter in Italy, asking if he could paint my picture. I asked the Marchesa's permission and, being the kind person she is, she agreed to allow me to sit. I went to visit Michele's studio. He was living in the Palazzo Mattei at the time. My daughter Gabriella came with me. She was working as one of her ladyship's maids at the Palazzo Colonna. She was fascinated by the prospect of actually meeting the famous painter Michelangelo Merisi da Caravaggio. Gabriella is not married. I love her dearly but she is a pious and God-fearing woman and I feared she would become an old maid. She was about the same age as Michele. They took to each other straight away, but just as friends, you understand. You know what a fierce temper Michele had, but Gabriella was then a good-humoured and high-spirited girl. She teased him and flirted with him and Michele enjoyed every minute of it. I knew of Michele's reputation with women but my Gabriella was a good girl, a pure girl. She would never have allowed any inappropriate advances but Michele always treated Gabriella with courtesy and respect. Whenever he visited the Palazzo Colonna, he would seek her out to enjoy a few minutes of her company. He even used her as a model for one of his Contarelli chapel works, of Saint Matthew and the Angel.'

'Do you know whether that was the first version of that painting, or the second?' I interjected.

'The first version,' Gianfranco confirmed. 'Gabriella, I have to say, is no beauty. I'm afraid that she has inherited some of my features. She has a sweet face but she still looks like a child, even though she was about thirty years old at this time. Gabriella, as a pious girl, was pleased to be portrayed as an angel. There was no impropriety between Gabriella and Michele but they were warming to each other. I very much hoped that it might lead to marriage, despite Michele's peculiar ways. Gabriella certainly had a beneficial effect on Michele. Then that bastard Fabrizio ruined Gabriella's life.' Gianfranco had to stop talking for a few seconds, the pain of bad memories causing a catch in his voice.

'What happened?' I encouraged him, gently.

'Gabriella was found in one of the upstairs rooms in the Palazzo Colonna. She had been raped. For many weeks, I did not know who was responsible. There were many enquiries but the truth was covered up. The crime was blamed on an unidentified servant but I sensed that something was going on behind the scenes, and I was right. Our lords and masters treat servants as if we are dumb and blind idiots but we look and listen and we eventually found out the truth. The culprit must have been Fabrizio Sforza. It was the latest in a long series of crimes committed by that bastard. The Marchesa's attitude towards me changed. She hardly dared to look me in the face. When Fabrizio was suddenly banished to Malta, to the care of the Knights of Saint John, I knew that the Marchesa had finally tired of her son's evil ways and it convinced me that Fabrizio Sforza was responsible for the violation of my daughter. It changed Gabriella completely. She became silent and withdrawn. In the end, she decided to take the veil, to enter a nunnery. I have lost my daughter and her comfort in my old age. The Marchesa arranged for Gabriella to enter the nunnery and then, not long afterwards, she promoted me to be her major-domo, a much more comfortable and well-paid position. Why me? I am reliable and well-educated but so were several of her servants. Was it because of guilt over her son's crime? I think so. I know Fabrizio raped my daughter, but I cannot prove it. He is protected by his powerful family and friends. There has been no way I could avenge the violation of my daughter . . . until now, perhaps.' Fillipo looked at me expectantly.

'It all seems to fit,' I agreed, intrigued by this story, but unable to see that it had anything to do with Merisi's murder. 'How did Michele take the news of Gabriella's rape and her decision to take the veil?'

'As usual with him, he withdrew inside himself but I could see that he was deeply upset. It was soon after Gabriella's death that his behaviour began to become more and more aggressive and capricious. That was not entirely owing to what had happened to Gabriella but it was another reason for his cynical bad temper. He was always well behaved towards me. We always liked each other. He continued to use me as a model, whenever he needed to. He paid me very well, more than was necessary. It was his way of consoling me for the loss of my daughter. But no amount of money can console for such a tragic waste of a life.'

'As I understand it,' I said, 'Fabrizio and Michele have always been friends. Did you ever share your suspicions with Michele about Fabrizio being the man who had raped your daughter?'

'No, never,' Gianfranco answered emphatically. 'I knew that if Michele had ever found out about Fabrizio, it is quite likely that he would have committed murder a lot earlier than he actually did.'

'Did Fabrizio know of Michele's warm relationship with Gabriella?'

'No. At least, not that I know of,' Fillipo replied.

'And you never subsequently observed any friction or hostility between the two?'

'No. Fabrizio was always friendly and solicitous towards Michele. When he heard that Michele had returned from Sicily to stay with the Marchesa here at the Palazzo Cellamare, he journeyed from Rome to be with Michele. The night that Michele suffered the beating outside the Osteria del Cerriglio, he had asked Fabrizio to accompany him to the tavern but Fabrizio had made other plans and went out before Michele did. Fabrizio said afterwards that he felt bad that he had not gone with Michele that night and had not been there to help and protect Michele. Fabrizio joined the Marchesa in trying to talk Michele out of travelling back to Rome so suddenly after receiving the papal pardon, that fateful journey that led to Michele's death. No, I have to say, despite my personal feelings towards Fabrizio, that he was a good friend to Michele.'

I said: 'I am truly sorry to hear about what happened to your daughter but thank you for telling me about all this, Fillipo. I am now ready to meet the Marchesa.'

With difficulty, Fillipo got to his feet and stood, breathing heavily: 'Soon my beloved Gabriella will be weeping over my grave. I pray for it every day, God forgive me. Come, Stefano, I must take you to the Marchesa, or else she will find herself a new major-domo.'

I stood up. 'Why don't you return to the palazzo?' I suggested. 'I can surely find the Marchesa on my own.'

'Out of the question,' Fillipo replied. 'It would be unseemly and I would be failing in my duty, and I don't want to give that bastard Fabrizio any such satisfaction.'

'Come along then,' I smiled, 'but hold on to my arm until we are in sight of the Marchesa.'

Fillipo hesitated but then took my arm. We walked down a winding path lined with scented bushes of some kind. Fillipo still had difficulty keeping his balance, despite my support, and I wondered how he would manage the arduous climb back up. Eventually, the bushes opened out and there was a large terrazo patio below us. I could see Costanza Colonna sitting in a chair. A large red and white striped awning had been erected to provide her with shade. There was a set of long shallow steps at her feet, leading down to another part of the garden. I could see Fabrizio sprawled nonchalantly on the steps at the

Marchesa's feet. Fillipo let go of my arm. Fabrizio heard us approaching and leapt to his feet. He watched us move towards him but said nothing. The Marchesa also watched our arrival calmly. Fillipo bowed as low as his aching back would allow and said: 'Signor Maddano, your ladyship.'

'Thank you, Fillipo' Costanza said. Fillipo moved off to begin his arduous climb back up the hill.

I bowed to the Marchesa and said: 'Thank you for agreeing to see me at such short notice, your ladyship. It is an honour to meet you again.'

Costanza inclined her head in acknowledgment and said: 'This is my son Fabrizio. You may remember meeting him in Rome.'

I bowed to Fabrizio and he bowed back, making sure not to bow quite as low as I did in order to establish his superior status. Trying to keep a sarcastic tone out of my voice, I said: 'I'm honoured to meet you again, signor.'

Fabrizio said: 'My mother tells me that you are still inquiring into Michelangelo's death. Why do you want to talk to my mother again? She had nothing to do with it. Why come here dredging up unhappy memories for her?'

'Hush, Fabrizio,' the Marchesa said. 'Signor Maddano is not here to apportion blame or to upset me. I am happy to talk to him about Michele's last days here.'

'Indeed, your ladyship,' I said. 'I just need to know what Michele's life was like here in those last few weeks before he . . . before he left for Rome.' I turned to Fabrizio, who was scowling darkly at me. 'Did you know Michele very well?' I asked him.

'What are you?' he asked. 'Some damn policeman? Why should I answer your questions?'

'Apart from the fact that the Holy Father has given me his blessing to make these inquiries, I would expect it as a common courtesy from a gentleman of rank such as yourself.'

Fabrizio, furious at my reply, automatically reached for his dagger and then realised he was not wearing one. Costanza said mildly to him: 'Please calm down, Fabrizio.' To me she said: 'As you can see, Signor Maddano, my son Fabrizio and Michele had a lot in common . . . a crazy brain and a fiery temper.'

I knew that Fabrizio, over the years, had managed to get himself into even more trouble than Merisi had done. His life had been full of unexplained crimes and extreme reversals of fortune until he had been effectively exiled to Malta under the protection of Alof de Wignacourt and the Knights of Saint John at the behest of the Colonna family. It was to save him from himself. Fillipo had just given me one of the reasons why. I repeated my question: 'Did you know Michele very well?'

Fabrizio, still fuming, was not going to answer but the Marchesa said, with sudden and surprising authority: 'Fabrizio! Answer Signor Maddano's question!'

'No, signor,' he spat out. 'I did not know Michelangelo very well but I knew him fairly well. We have been friends, of a sort, all our lives.'

'You were both together on Malta for a time,' I said. 'Surely you got to know him better then?'

'A little,' Fabrizio conceded. 'But we were never close. We had little in common.'

'Except a talent for causing trouble,' Costanza observed, drily. 'Fabrizio, find Signor Maddano a seat so that he can sit by me while we talk.'

Fabrizio looked at the painting I was carrying. It was a small painting, about eighteen inches wide and twelve inches deep. It had been placed on a stretcher and wrapped in silk. 'What is that?' Fabrizio demanded, pointing at the picture.

'It is a gift for her ladyship,' I replied. 'It is not a weapon of any kind.'

Fabrizio reluctantly went off in search of a seat. Costanza said: 'Do you wish to ask Fabrizio any more questions?'

'No, your ladyship, not at this point. I don't wish to enrage him any more.'

Costanza smiled. 'Like Michele, he is consumed with hot-blooded aggression but, just as Michele was, he is devoted to me.'

I tried not to smile as Fabrizio returned carrying a marble bench. It was a small bench but very heavy. Sweating from the exertion, he placed the bench down next to his mother. Costanza said: 'Thank you, Fabrizio. I wish to talk to Signor Maddano alone. You can go now.'

'I'm not leaving you alone with him,' Fabrizio said, vehemently.

Costanza sighed. 'I have met Signor Maddano before. I have made inquiries about him. I know him to be an honourable and trustworthy man. He is not here to harm me or upset me. I want to tell him about Michele's last days with me. Please go, Fabrizio.' Fabrizio hesitated, but then stalked off up the terraced path towards the palazzo.

'Fabrizio!' I called after him.

He turned around. 'What?'

'Will you be staying in the palazzo for the next few hours?'

'What has that got to do with you?'

Costanza interrupted and said: 'Fabrizio is staying to take lunch with me.'

'Am I?' Fabrizio said, with mock surprise.

'Good,' I said. 'I may need to talk to you again before I leave.' Fabrizio turned on his heel and stalked off again without a word.

Costanza invited: 'Now, Signor Maddano, please sit down. What do you want to ask me?'

I sat down on the heavy marble bench and began: 'I'd like to ask you about Michele's life here at the Palazzo Cellamare after that dreadful assault at the Osteria del Cerriglio. He suffered terrible wounds but, thanks to your care, he recovered from that assault more quickly than could be expected.'

'Yes,' Costanza replied, her face betraying her sadness at the horrific memories. 'That was in the October of the year before he . . . before he died.'

'This is such a beautiful place,' I said, indicating the scenery all around me, 'that it must have helped his recovery enormously.'

'I think it did,' Costanza agreed. 'I like to think that Michele achieved some happiness here and was as content, for a while, as a person of his temperament could be.'

'I believe that Michele did an astonishing amount of work here after he had recuperated. Is that so?'

'Yes. I was amazed at how swiftly he returned to his painting. After the attack, there had been rumours that Michele was already dead but then the news got back to Rome that he was alive and painting again. There were emissaries from the wealthy and the cardinals and the nobility of Rome arriving almost every day with commissions for paintings. Michele was still the most famous and sought after painter in Italy. He worked with an intense ferocity that I had never seen before, as if he was making up for lost time or, perhaps, sensing that he did not have long to live. Of course, the light here is perfect for an artist but his paintings were so dark, as if they reflected the darkness within him. He worked outside most of the time. I watched him working as often as I could. I don't think it would be blasphemous to say that it looked as if God was working within him. He worked with such speed and precision that it seemed to me... miraculous. It made me happy, Signor Maddano, just to have Michele with me, and to be able to look after him and watch him work. I was as content as I have ever been in my life. And then, the next year, everything seemed to go wrong, as quickly as it possibly could do.'

I was looking at Costanza as she was speaking and the strain was increasingly apparent. It was clear that, underneath that aristocratic bearing, was a soul at breaking point. Costanza was about sixty years old but looked older. When I had last met her in Rome, in the Contarelli chapel, her head had been covered with a mantilla. Here, in Chaia, she was bareheaded and I could see that her hair was golden red. It was still thick and arranged in an elaborate style. As far as I could tell, it was her natural hair colour and there was not a grey hair to be seen. She was still an impressive and beautiful woman. I asked, as gently as I could: 'It must have caused you much anguish when Michele suddenly left you to return to Rome?'

Costanza looked down at her hands, which were folded in her lap. Her lower lip trembled slightly but she regained her self-possession and replied: 'Only two months before, I had lost someone I loved dearly. I was still grieving for him. Then a messenger arrived from Cardinal Gonzaga with a pardon for Michele. As soon as Michele received it, he wanted to be gone from me and back to Rome. With all my heart, I didn't want to lose him.'

'You must have tried to talk Michele out of such a precipitous move?'

'Yes, of course. I asked what the great hurry was? He seemed happy here at Chaia. He was being offered more work than he could handle. He was fully recovered from his injuries. He had perfect working conditions. And yet all he could talk about was getting back to Rome. I couldn't understand it.'

'Who else knew of Michele's plans to return to Rome?'

'He didn't tell anyone, apart from me. And there was no plan at all. One morning, I found Michele all ready to leave. He had packed his belongings and was taking a few of his paintings. He said he was taking the felucca back to Rome that very morning. I begged him to stay but he simply would not listen to any argument. Before I knew it, he was gone.'

'So no-one else knew of his intention to return to Rome that very morning?'

'No, they could not possibly have done. Even the servants could not have known. They knew that Michele was preparing to leave but they were not told where he was going.' As I pondered this information, Costanza asked me: 'What happened to Michele on that last journey?'

'Do you really wish to know, your ladyship? It was not pleasant. It may be upsetting for you.'

'I want to know, Signor Maddano,' Costanza insisted. 'Please tell me.'

I related how Michele had boarded the felucca but had then been detained at Palo, how he had bought himself out of prison but was too late to reboard the felucca and had to make that last fateful and terrible journey on foot along sixty miles of hostile and malarial coast until he had arrived at Porto Ercole. Costanza listened with fortitude but she was deeply affected by this knowledge. 'When he arrived in Porto Ercole,' I said, 'Michele was very ill, but I don't believe that he was dying.'

'Then you still believe that Michele was murdered?' Costanza asked.

'Yes, I do.'

'Do you know who by?'

'No, your ladyship. I have not been able to establish for certain who did it, although I have some ideas.' Costanza nodded, not trusting herself to speak. I picked up Merisi's still-life painting. 'I have brought you a gift, your ladyship.'

'Who is it from?' Costanza asked.

'It is from Michele himself. Something he wanted you to have as a token of his love and gratitude.'

Costanza looked at the gift for a few seconds and then asked: 'Why is it in your possession?'

'Michele painted it for you as a gift when I knew him in Naples. He left it with me after his sudden dash to Malta.'

I handed the silk wrapped painting to Costanza. She laid it in her lap and gently and slowly untied the ribbon and folded back the silk to reveal the picture. The Marchesa Costanza Colonna Sforza gazed at the luminous and perfectly painted still-life of fruit and flowers. Her self-possession broke down. She bowed her head and held the edge of the painting to her lips and kissed it as the tears flowed down her face and dropped onto the small canvas panel.

Moved by Costanza's grief I looked at the distinctive arch of her neck, and the swirls of her golden red hair, and I knew that my hunch had been correct. I said: 'It's time for you to tell me the whole truth, your ladyship. When did Michele first find out that you were his real mother?'

49

After I had returned from my visit to the Marchese Costanza Colonna Sforza, Merisi sensed that my attitude towards him had changed radically. I was incredibly angry but I was determined not to lose my temper and I kept my behaviour towards him icily polite but distant. He was no fool. He knew that I had discovered something that he should have told me right at the beginning. At first, he tried asking me how Costanza was, how had the meeting gone and what did I think of Costanza? He was not aware that I had previously met Costanza in the Contarelli chapel. I simply told him that the meeting had gone well, that I had to do a lot more research in my reference books and on the internet, and make two or three more short time travel journeys back to the seventeenth century. In the end, Merisi gave up asking and mooched around the house brooding about what was in store for him. It took me another several days to find out all that I needed to know and then, one morning when Merisi came into the kitchen for breakfast and coffee, I announced to him: 'Today is the day.'

'What do you mean?' he asked.

'Today is the day when I tell you about what was really going on during your previous life and about who murdered you.'

Merisi sat down at the kitchen table and sipped his coffee thoughtfully. 'I see,' he said, eventually. 'You are angry with me.' I made no reply, just looked at him, so he went on: 'I planned to see Izzy today.'

'You are seeing no-one,' I replied, 'except me. Have your breakfast, and then we must talk.'

Merisi shrugged. 'Very well.' Then he asked: 'Can I talk to Izzy on your telephone device? Tell her not to come over?'

'Yes,' I agreed. 'Use the telephone in my office. Judging by the size of the telephone bills I've been getting, you know how to use it anyway. Do it now and then have something to eat. We have a lot to get through today.' Merisi made no move, so I said: 'Don't fight me, Michele. Go and call Izzy now.'

This time Merisi got up and went out to my office. He talked to Isabella

Caro for several minutes and then came back into the kitchen. 'Isabella is not pleased,' he said petulantly. 'She has arranged a day off especially to see me.'

'Tough,' I said, and left him to his breakfast while I went upstairs for a shower.

An hour later we were sitting in our customary armchairs, facing each other, as tense as duellists, across the fireplace. My notes and reference books were arranged on the coffee table. I picked up my notes and pretended to study them for a few minutes. I could sense that Merisi was only just keeping his temper in check, so I began: 'Why didn't you tell me, right at the start of our inquiries, that Costanza Colonna was your real mother?'

The bad temper seemed to drain out of Merisi as he faced the inevitable. 'I wanted to protect her,' he answered. I waited for him to say more but he remained silent.

'To protect her from what?' I asked.

'To protect her from you,' Merisi replied, 'and from these strange aliens who brought me back to life. To protect her from the judgement and condemnation of history.'

'Why should I and the Tralfamadorians and history condemn her?'

'Because she cheated on her husband, gave herself to some unknown seducer, and gave birth to a bastard son. She disgraced herself, her family and her rank. I did not want anybody to know that she was my mother. I spent most of my previous life protecting her from such public disgrace. I hoped that I could prevent you from finding out as well, so that the secret should remain where it should be, in her grave and, when the time comes, in mine.'

'Are you so ashamed of her?'

'No,' Merisi said, contemptuous of my inference. 'I loved her with all my heart. And she loved me. I caused her much pain, much heartache, because of my peculiar temperament. The least I could do in return was to protect her from public knowledge of her fall.'

I looked at the anguish in Merisi's expression and my anger dissipated. 'You judge her too harshly yourself. She was a young girl when you were conceived, very unhappy in her marriage, confused, frightened, vulnerable to any seducer who professed his love for her. Illegitimacy is not regarded as such as a sin as it used to be. In fact, it is not regarded as a sin at all. I think history will regard your mother as what she was, a kind and compassionate lady whose subsequent life of love and service more than made up for an adolescent mistake.' Merisi grunted, unconvinced. 'Another small thing,' I continued, 'is that she gave birth to, and loved and supported the greatest Italian painter of the seventeenth century. You could not have achieved what you did achieve without her protection and encouragement. That is no mean epitaph for any human being.'

'Perhaps you are correct,' Merisi said grudgingly. 'Do you know who my real father was?'

'We will be coming to that later,' I replied. 'If you had told me that Costanza was your real mother right at the beginning, it would have saved me a lot of worry and effort, not to mention saving me from a beating by Mao Salini's thugs.'

'I'm sorry for your beating,' Merisi said, 'but I am still not sorry for not telling you about Costanza. I also owed silence to the woman with whom I spent my childhood and whom I did call mother, Lucia Aratori.'

'I understand, Michele,' I said. 'Your filial loyalty does you credit. Do you want me to tell you the circumstances of your conception and birth, or would you rather not know?'

'It's a good question, Stefano. Does it reflect badly on my mother, either of them, or on my father, either of them?'

'No, not at all,' I replied.

'In that case, tell me all. It is time I faced the whole truth.'

'Very well,' I began. 'In 1567, Costanza Colonna had married Francesco Sforza and became the Marchesa Costanza Colonna Sforza di Caravaggio, a grand title for a girl who was only twelve years old. Poor Costanza was very unhappy in this marriage. She even wrote to her father, the hero of the battle of Lepanto, Marcantonio Colonna, saying: "If you do not free me from this house and husband I shall kill myself, and I care little if I lose my soul with my life".'

'How do you know that my mother wrote such words so long ago?' Merisi interjected.

'The letter still exists, Michele. It is a matter of historical record.' Merisi grunted and indicated to me to continue. 'Despite this unhappiness, the marriage produced a son, your half-brother Muzio Sforza, about two years after Francesco and Costanza were married. It seems that Costanza was still not reconciled to her husband and she was still unhappy. She found a sympathetic friend and comforter in someone who worked in the employ of the Sforza family, your father, or the man you thought of as your father, Fermo Merisi. Fermo, as you well know, was a kind and generous man. He had lost his first wife and one of his daughters. Fermo knew all about sadness and suffering and loss. Costanza found comfort and consolation with Fermo, albeit strictly within the bounds of propriety and of their respective ranks in life.'

'So Fermo was not my father?' Merisi asked, anxiously.

'No, he was not,' I replied. 'Fermo was, of course, much older than Costanza. There was no impropriety between them. Fermo's love for Costanza – and I believe they did love each other in a fashion – was strictly paternal.'

'Then who was my father?'

'Patience, Michele. You kept me in the dark about Costanza. Now it is your turn to be kept in the dark about your father.'

Merisi made a gesture of disgust. 'Ah, you enjoy torturing me, Englishman. You are from a cruel race.'

'Believe me, Michele, the wait will be worth it. Now, despite the birth of her son, Muzio, Costanza was still unhappy in her marriage. It was announced that the French king, Charles the Ninth, was to marry the princess Elizabeth of Austria in Paris on November 26th, 1570. Costanza expressed a desire to visit Paris to attend the wedding. After a family discussion, it was agreed that a change of scene and a chance to travel might help to settle the unhappy Costanza. Fermo Merisi also wished to visit Paris, in his official capacity as magister of the Sforza family. He wanted to buy furniture, tapestries and sculptures with which to decorate the Sforza palazzo in Milan. Paris was then, as it is now and as it has been for centuries, a centre for the production and sale of fine furniture and works of art.'

'What has this history lesson got to do with me or Costanza?' Merisi asked, restlessly.

I ignored him and carried on. 'It was seen as a perfect plan to allow Costanza to visit Paris in the care of the trusted family employee Fermo Merisi. It was hoped that it would give Costanza a chance to grow up and to reconcile herself to her own marriage, even if it did mean leaving her infant son Muzio behind in Milan. Costanza was excited by the thought of this trip, especially as it meant getting away from her husband and family. She would be looked after by her trusted friend Fermo plus, of course, a band of heavily armed soldiers. So Costanza and Fermo duly travelled to Paris. Costanza attended the wedding of King Charles and Princess Elizabeth and, to give Fermo time to purchase the decorative objects he needed, they spent Christmas in Paris. During the Christmas festivities, Costanza met your father.'

'Who was he?' Merisi asked again.

Again I ignored him and carried on with my narrative. 'He was a young man of seventeen years, only a year or two older than Costanza. He was handsome, confident, and, later in life, he became famous, or notorious, as a great seducer. Also, he was already a military hero, a dashing soldier whose exploits had enthralled the whole of Europe. At the battle of Arnay-le-Duc, six months before, when he was just sixteen years old, he had led a cavalry charge and, in the months following, proved himself to be a capable and courageous soldier. Costanza fell in love with him with an uncontrollable passion. All her life she loved your real father with a passion. You were conceived sometime in the New Year of 1571 and born nine months later. Costanza's husband, Francesco Sforza, knew that the child could not be his son. Possibly he and Costanza had not had relations since the birth of their son Muzio. I don't know. It was bad enough that Costanza had given birth to another man's child but, even worse, your father was a Frenchman and a Protestant. The Colonna and Sforza families were staunch supporters of the Roman Catholic faith, and staunch supporters of Spain, a country battling against the Protestant heresy. Your father was a bitter enemy, at that time, of both Spain and Catholicism. Costanza could not be allowed to keep her love child. All knowledge of the birth of her child, yourself, and knowledge of who the father was had to be kept as secret as possible.'

Merisi could not contain himself any longer. 'Englishman, if you do not tell me who my father was, right this second, I swear I will strangle you with my bare hands.'

'Your father,' I said, 'was Henry, Prince de Béarn, later known as Henry of Navarre, and later still as King Henry IV of France.'

Merisi stared at me, literally open-mouthed with astonishment. 'You are quite sure of this?' he breathed.

'Your mother, Costanza Colonna herself, told me.'

'I knew it,' Merisi cried unexpectedly, and thumped the arm of the armchair. 'I always suspected I was of aristocratic birth but now you tell me I was of royal birth!'

'Albeit the wrong side of the blanket, yes you are.'

Merisi could not contain himself. He stood up and paced up and down my living room. 'So all the while I was having to take orders from cardinals and dukes, and suffering the arrogance of low-born pompous talentless asses such as Zuccaro and the Cavaliere d'Arpino, I was the son of a king!'

'A future king, yes,' I confirmed.

'You take my breath away, Stefano. Did you suspect any of this?'

'No. I certainly did not expect to find that Henry was your father but it had crossed my mind that Costanza might be your mother. I have said before that I found it peculiar that an aristocratic lady should take such a lifelong interest in the son of a humble employee and this revelation answers many puzzling conundrums about your life.'

'How did Francesco Sforza react to the news that he had been cuckolded by Henry of Navarre? How did Francesco even know who the father was?'

'Costanza told him. She had fallen deeply in love with Henry and, with the naïveity of youth, was determined to leave Francesco and be with Henry. It was quite impossible of course, even if Henry had wanted it, which he did not. What to Costanza was the love of her life was to Henry just another sexual conquest and no more. Francesco Sforza was not a cruel man but his first instinct was to have you killed.'

Merisi resumed his seat in the armchair, shocked by this news. 'Why didn't he do so?'

'Because Fermo Merisi, who knew all about Costanza's affair with Henry, proposed a solution. Fermo, as you well know, was a widower but he was courting Lucia Aratori. Fermo proposed that he and Lucia took you, Costanza's illegitimate child, and raised you as their own son. Francesco Sforza eventually agreed to this plan, as did Costanza, with great reluctance of course, but as a much more preferable course of action than having to bear the death of her child by the man she loved. Costanza knew Fermo to be a man of trustworthiness, kindness and honesty and would make an excellent surrogate father for you. Lucia Aratori came from a minor aristocratic family and was a woman of good reputation. She would make a good surrogate mother. I have to tell you that she was never happy with having to take you as her son but no doubt the Sforza family made it well worth her while to marry Fermo. That is why Francesco Sforza paid them the honour of being a guest at their wedding, which took place the same year you were born, 1571.'

'All this explains so much,' Merisi said, trying to absorb everything that I was telling him. 'I loved my father, or who I thought was my father, without reservation. If I had been his own son, he could not have been a better father. When he died of the plague, and my grandfather on the same day, something changed inside me forever. I suppose, after that, I was always terrified of loss, whether it was honour, reputation, money, status, love . . . I don't know. I have loved several women but never allowed them to get too close to me, let alone marrying them, for fear of losing them. Perhaps that is why I became more bitter and resentful when other artists tried to copy my style. I was afraid of losing whatever success I had achieved. And I always sensed that my mother, Lucia that is, resented me and favoured her younger children which, I presume, were really her own.'

'Yes, they were,' I said.

'But she always looked after me, even when times were hard and money short after my father, I mean Fermo, died. She just could not bring herself to show me much affection.'

'I suspect that Lucia Aratori never knew the truth about who your real parents were,' I said. 'After Fermo died, Francesco Sforza did little to support Lucia and her children. Costanza helped in whatever ways she could but had to do so secretly until her husband Francesco died in 1580. By then, Costanza had had five more legitimate children but she supported Lucia as well as she could, although Costanza had accepted that she had to be a secret benefactor and that Lucia should never know the truth about your parentage. Lucia herself died in 1589, never knowing who you really were.'

Merisi, understandably pensive, was lost in thought for a few seconds. 'I always felt much closer to Costanza than I did to Lucia, the woman who I thought was my real mother. Now I know why. You remember that I was in prison in Milan when I heard news of Lucia's death?'

'Yes,' I said.

'And you remember how angry and upset my brother Giovan Battista was because of my cool reaction to news of her death?'

'Yes. He had visited you in prison to tell you and all you could say was that you were now free to sell your inheritance and go to Rome and be an artist.'

'That's right. Well, I was in prison because I had wounded that French bastard Dufre in a fight, God rot his soul. He somehow knew that I was Costanza's illegitimate son. He did not say so in so many words but taunted me by saying that I was the bastard son of a Colonna whore, or something like that. You know me, Stefano. I could not bear such abuse and I cut the bastard up. I did not believe what Dufre had said but I suspect, in the back of my mind, I knew there could be some truth in it. I wanted Costanza to be my mother. Not only did I love her more than Lucia but I wanted to be the son of an aristocratic lady. I did not want to be just a lowly commoner. I wanted to believe it but I was ashamed of such thoughts as well. That is why I reacted so coolly when Giovan informed me of Lucia's death.'

'And that is why,' I said, 'you denied that Giovan Battista himself was your brother when he came to visit you at the Palazzo Madama. By that time, you well knew who your real mother was and wanted nothing to do with the brother of your childhood, even though you did not know who your real father was.'

'Yes. I was full of conceit and arrogance at that time. It was a despicable way to treat Giovan.'

'When I met him, I suspected he was not your real brother. You two were so unalike, in looks, colouring, temperament, physique, that it was impossible to believe that you emanated from the same loins. By the way, have you ever suffered from gout?'

'Gout?' Merisi echoed. 'No, never. You have asked me this question before. What has gout to do with any of this?'

'Your father and grandfather suffered from it and your brother was suffering from it when I met him. Gout is a hereditary condition, that is why you have never suffered from it, because you inherited different genes.' Merisi was complelely perplexed by my reference to genes, so I said dismissively: 'It's of no consequence. Forget what I said. We were talking about your physical dissimilarity to Giovan Battista.'

Merisi nodded. 'I always looked much more like Costanza's other sons,

Muzio and Fabrizio, than Giovan. I was much more like them in temperament as well.'

'Did you have much to do with Muzio and Fabrizio when you were young?' I asked.

'No, not really. They are . . . were, both fiery characters. Muzio was a poet, a cultured man. I did not get to know Fabrizio very well until later on in life. He was more of a troublemaker than I ever was.'

'So I understand,' I agreed, 'but we're getting a bit ahead of ourselves. Costanza knew that you had artistic talent and arranged for you to be an apprentice with Simone Peterzano. Her hope and expectation was that you would learn your trade and have a happy and comfortable existence as a competent painter in Milan or one of the other towns in Lombardy. Of course, Costanza's expectations foundered on the fact that you were not only drivingly ambitious but prodigiously talented. She never expected that you would one day become the most famous painter in all of Italy. In all of Europe in fact. Combined with your strange and extravagant behaviour, there was no chance that you would remain a humble and anonymous artisan in the provincial backwaters of Lombardy. So, when you finally announced to Costanza that you were moving to Rome to be a great artist, she ensured that you travelled safely with her as part of your entourage and, once you had arrived in Rome, made sure that you had a guardian angel to watch over you.'

'What do you mean by that?' Merisi asked, warily.

'Let's have a break for coffee,' I suggested. 'And then I'll tell you about one of your closest friends.'

'You enjoy to tease me, Englishman. But, because of the coffee, I forgive you.'

'Most generous, your highness,' I teased him again as I went out to make the coffee.

I returned with two mugs of coffee. Merisi had been working things out because he said: 'You are now going to tell me about Mario, aren't you?'

'Yes. How did you guess?'

'I remember you travelling back in time to interview him. He was my first friend in Rome. He always acted like my guardian angel. It does not take genius to guess.'

I said: 'I'm sure you do not know why Mario became your first friend in Rome.'

'I'm sure you are going to tell me,' Merisi answered.

'Mario Minnitti became your friend because he was being paid to be your friend and protector.'

'Paid!' Merisi exclaimed. 'By whom?'

'By Costanza Colonna, indirectly. At that time, only a very few people knew who your real parents were, but such knowledge, if it had become widespread, could have endangered your life, especially as your real father had become the king of France a couple of years before you moved to Rome. Costanza had been hoping that you would settle down as a provincial artist in Milan or somewhere near Colonna territory where it would be easier to protect you, but you stymied that plan by your determination to live and work in Rome.'

'Who or what did I need protecting from?' Merisi asked.

'From religious fanatics. Your real father, Henry IV of France, was widely detested by Roman Catholics because he had spilled so much Catholic blood in his support of the Protestant cause, most of it Spanish blood. Your real mother, the Marchesa Costanza Colonna Sforza had most of her estates in Spanish territory and owed allegiance to Spain. It was imperative to her that knowledge of your real father remained as secret as possible because not only your life, but hers as well, could have been in grave danger. Henry IV's subsequent recantation of Protestantism and acceptance back into the Roman Catholic Church was widely seen as a cynical ploy and inflamed feelings against him even more. He was hated by certain fanatics on both sides of the religious divide. As his bastard son, your life was certainly at risk. So, Costanza could not protect you in Rome in an overt way, so she did the best she could by forcing Mario Minnitti to watch over you and report on your movements and way of life.'

Merisi was clearly bewildered. He asked: 'How did she find Mario? And how did she persuade him to perform this task?'

'She found Mario because of the network of patronage and protection that watched over you all your life. She approached a family who were neighbours and close friends in Rome, who already knew the secret of your parentage because of their immense wealth and widespread network of contacts and influence, and who she knew she could trust implicitly. One younger member of that family, who was already wealthy, with a deep interest in art and with close links to Sicily, knew that Mario was just the man for the job.'

'You must mean Vincenzo Giustiniani,' Merisi said excitedly.

'Exactly,' I confirmed. 'As you know, Mario had murdered a love rival back in Sicily. He was in desperate danger of revenge from the murdered rival's family. He was a man who could look after himself, not afraid of danger, handy with a sword and a dagger and also a talented painter. An enforced move to Rome, which he planned anyway, would remove him from danger of vengeance and, as a young painter, it would be entirely natural for him to befriend another young painter, newly arrived in Rome from the provinces, with no reputation as yet . . . that is, you.'

'Now I know why Mario was always hanging around me,' Merisi said thoughtfully. 'I couldn't get rid of him however hard I tried. Even when I painted him as a pretty boy bardassa, which always enraged him, or insulted him in front of our friends, I could never get rid of him.'

'You never could have done,' I said, 'until the time came that even his paymaster realised that you were so famous, or notorious, that Mario could do nothing to protect you, mainly from yourself. But his life was in danger if he had withdrawn from his allotted task without their permission.'

'Why was his life in danger?' Merisi asked. 'He was being paid, wasn't he?'

'Yes, Mario was being paid, and paid well but, as extra insurance to ensure that he would perform his duties, he had been threatened with execution if he abandoned you without their permission.'

'You keep saying "their" permission?' Merisi queried. 'Don't you mean Costanza's permission?'

'Costanza had instigated this arrangement but she, and Vincenzo Giustiniani, had to put the operation of the Mario plan into the hands of men who were tough and ruthless enough to enforce Mario's compliance.' I explained to Merisi how Mario had been visited in his prison cell in Sicily by the hooded man who had offered him the deal, which was go to Rome and protect Merisi, earning money and working as an artist in complete safety, or remain in Sicily and be the victim of a vengeance killing. 'That hooded man was none other than Alof de Wignacourt, Knight of St. John. This was about ten years before he actually became Grand Master of the order. It was the Knights of St. John who were ensuring that Mario stuck to his task.'

Merisi whistled in surprise. 'Did de Wignacourt know who I really was?'

'Not at that time. As you know, de Wignacourt was French and your real father, the French king, at the behest of your mother, had ordered de Wignacourt to assist in this matter without knowing the real reason. Such assistance did no harm to de Wignacourt's career.'

'And to think,' Merisi smiled. 'I used to side with the Spanish faction during the street riots against the French in Rome. All the while I was fighting my own side!'

'Yes, you were,' I agreed. 'In fact, all through our inquiries I kept coming up against this French influence. It occurs time and time again in your life, as we'll see as the story unfolds. I couldn't make sense of it until I realised that Costanza must be your real mother and made her tell me who your real father was.'

'That's a good point,' Merisi said. 'How did you realise that Costanza was my real mother? Did she volunteer that information?'

'No.'

'Well, how then?'

'I'll come to that later,' I smiled. 'For now, let's get back to Mario. He became your faithful and unshakeable companion because he had no other choice. He posed for you as a bardassa. He forced the Cavaliere d'Arpino at knifepoint to let you leave his studio when you were wounded and feverish after that disastrous attack on Zuccaro. He took you to the hospital, thus saving your life. Mario was in mortal fear that you might die and his life would be taken because of it. Even when his future wife, Rafaella, begged Mario to leave Rome and return to Sicily with her, Mario would not, could not budge.'

Merisi nodded but said nothing about his relationship with Rafaella. I did not say any more either. We would be returning to the lovely Rafaella later in the conversation.

I said: 'Into your life emerges the shadowy figure of the French art dealer, Valentin or, as he chose to call himself in Rome, Costantino Spata. The French connection again, you see!'

'What of it?' Merisi protested. 'Valentin did not like my work at all to begin with. I approached him time and time again and he turned me down.'

'But then he had a sudden change of heart, didn't he? You were living at the Palazzo Mattei for a short time. Valentin visited you and commissioned two paintings, the ones we now know as The Gypsy Fortune Teller and The Cardsharps. You always wondered why Valentin suddenly changed his mind about your work.'

'Yes, it seemed odd to me that he had rejected me for months and then suddenly decided that my work had merit after all. Are you saying that Valentin was asked or ordered to commission these paintings?'

'Yes, Michele, that's precisely what happened. You were struggling to make a name for yourself as an artist. You did not have a settled or comfortable place to live. Your guardian angels, Costanza Colonna and the French court, decided that it would be desirable to have you living in a much more comfortable and safer environment in the palazzo of a powerful cardinal who was known to be pro-French.'

'You clearly mean my good friend Cardinal Francesco Maria Del Monte,' Merisi said.

'The very same. The two pictures that Valentin commissioned from you were commissioned by Del Monte himself.'

'You mean that Del Monte approached Valentin first and asked him to commission those two pictures, which Valentin did, and then Del Monte pretended to see them in Valentin's shop window and then bought them?'

'Yes, Michele. That is what happened.'

'But why go through all that charade. Why didn't Del Monte commission those pictures directly from me. Or just simply invite me to go and live at the Palazzo Madama without all this subterfuge?'

'To do so directly like that would have looked odd. Del Monte had a reputation as a man of good taste. He invited only the best poets, painters and sculptors to live and work at the Palazzo Madama at his expense. To have commissioned work from an artist with little reputation, or to have invited you to live with him without good reason, would have looked odd or suspicious, and that is the very thing everyone was so anxious to avoid. It had to look entirely natural that Del Monte would invite an exciting new artist to live at his palazzo because he had seen and admired the new artist's work in Valentin's shop. Of course, what the instigators of this plan did not allow for, and which was an added bonus for Del Monte, was that you produced two works which revolutionised Roman art overnight, two masterpieces of genre painting. The plan had worked perfectly. No-one thought it at all odd that Del Monte took you under his wing. In fact, his friends were green with envy . . . one in particular.'

'Who was that?' Merisi asked.

'Vincenzo Giustiniani. As soon as Vincenzo saw those two pictures, he became your most devoted admirer and most avid collector and, as we shall see, a better friend than you can ever have realised.'

'Why is that?' Merisi asked, unable to restrain his curiosity.

'We will come back to Vincenzo soon,' I said, 'but first I have to tell you some harsh facts about the saintly Cardinal Del Monte.'

Merisi was almost angry with me. 'I knew you could not wait to blacken that man's reputation,' he accused. 'You disliked him when you met him and couldn't wait to denigrate him.'

'On the contrary,' I said, 'I found him a charming man and very personable. That was one of his weapons.'

'Weapons? What are you talking about? What do you mean?' Merisi shifted restlessly in his armchair.

'Cardinal Francesco Maria Del Monte was what is known today as a double agent,' I said.

'You'll have to explain what that means,' Merisi insisted.

'Del Monte was a very clever and subtle operator. He pretended, all his life, to be pro-French when, all the time, he was working for Spain.'

'Nonsense,' Merisi said, vehemently. 'You are making things up!'

'Me?' I said, taking mock offence. 'I didn't make up these facts. I was told of Del Monte's dual character by a Flemish lawyer named Almayden.'

'What would a Flemish lawyer know about Cardinal Del Monte?' Merisi spat back.

'Because Almayden was working for Vincenzo Giustiniani, and Vincenzo knew the truth about Del Monte.'

'What!?' Merisi exclaimed, becoming even more agitated. 'Vincenzo Giustiniani and Del Monte were the best of friends. Such an idea is complete nonsense.'

'As the old saying goes, Michele, keep your friends close but your enemies closer. Vincenzo knew all about Del Monte's real motives. It was in Vincenzo's interest to remain friendly with Del Monte, to keep an eye on what Del Monte was up to. I suspect that the two men genuinely enjoyed each other's company, but Vincenzo had no illusions about Del Monte.'

'Did this Flemish lawyer tell you all this?'

'No,' I replied, 'Vincenzo Giustiniani himself told me. The first time I met Vincenzo, in the Palazzo Madama with Del Monte present, when we were looking at Del Monte's portrait gallery, he deliberately directed my attention to a new portrait of your father, King Henry IV of France. I was too stupid to notice the physical resemblance between you and your father. Obviously, Vincenzo did not know that I had travelled back in time to investigate your murder. He had to be extremely careful about giving me clues. He tried to point me in the right direction but I didn't pick up on it. I can't be too hard on myself because the fact that you are the bastard son of the king of France is pretty outlandish.'

'I wish you would stop saying "bastard" son,' Merisi requested. 'Do you think Del Monte knew who my father really was?'

'I don't think he did,' I said. 'He knew you were Costanza Colonna's illegitimate son but not that King Henry was your father. I think the French were anxious to keep that knowledge away from Del Monte because they did not entirely trust him.'

'What makes you think that?' Merisi asked.

'Do you remember your friend Nicholas Cordier, the French sculptor?'

'Of course. His room was next to mine at the Palazzo Madama. We never became close friends but we were on affable terms. What about him?'

'Cordier had been working in France for the Duke of Lorraine. Cordier sadly lost his wife. Despite this unhappy event, Cordier wanted to remain in France in the service of the Duke, who was a kindly and generous employer. Cardinal Del Monte admired Cordier's work and invited him to move to Rome and live at the Palazzo Madama. Cordier did not want to move to Italy. The Duke of Lorraine did not want to lose Cordier. But Cordier was ordered to go to live with Del Monte and the Duke was ordered, by higher powers, not to interfere. It was the perfect opportunity for the French court to plant a mole in the Palazzo Madama, because Del Monte himself had asked Cordier to go.'

'Hold on,' Merisi stopped me. 'My ChronoTranslator must have translated incorrectly. I thought you said "mole". What has a little furry burrowing creature got to do with this?'

I could not help smiling at Merisi's helpless expression. 'A mole, in a modern sense, is a spy planted in an organisation who pretends to work for that organisation but who is really working for a rival organisation. Just as Del Monte himself was pretending to be working for the French side while all the time working for the Spanish side.'

'I see,' Merisi said. 'So Cordier had been ordered to spy on Del Monte.'

'Yes. To keep an eye on what Del Monte was up to, as far as a humble sculptor was able, and report back to the French court. Cordier did not like his new job or his new life and yearned to return to France. It was not to be. Poor Cordier died at the Palazzo Madama after a long and debilitating illness.'

'I thought you were going to tell me that Del Monte found out that Cordier was a spy and had Cordier murdered.'

'On the contrary,' I said. 'I believe Del Monte tried all the herbal potions he knew to try to save Cordier's life. Del Monte was not to know it but any effort would have been futile. I'm not certain but, from my researches, I believe Cordier was suffering from oculopharyngeal muscular dystrophy. It affects the muscles of the eyelids and the throat which causes progressive inability to swallow. The sufferer gradually starves to death, or did in your day. None of Del Monte's herbal potions could have saved Cordier.'

Merisi shook his head in genuine sadness. 'Poor Nicholas.' he murmured. 'Exiled from his native land and condemned to die a slow, painful death.' Merisi thought for several seconds and then said: 'I still cannot accept what you are saying about Del Monte. You said that the French court encouraged Del Monte to commission those two paintings from Valentin in order to make it look like a valid reason to invite me live at the Palazzo Madama. If the French court did not fully trust Del Monte, why did they want me to go and live at his palazzo?'

'It's a good question, Michele, one I have asked myself. Cordier was one reason. He was already in place and, like Mario Minnitti, he was ordered to keep an eye on you. Mario himself was also invited to live at the Palazzo Madama. Although Del Monte was suspected of being a ruthless poisoner, it was probably considered that he would not try anything against you. Del Monte did not know who your real father was.'

'There you go again,' Merisi protested, 'accusing the cardinal of being a "ruthless poisoner"!'

I ignored Merisi's point and said: 'Another factor keeping you safe was your own talent. Del Monte genuinely admired your work, almost as much as Vincenzo Giustiniani did. He would not have wantonly destroyed such a talent unless he had a very good reason.'

'Why poisoner?' Merisi persisted.

'You know very well yourself that Del Monte was fascinated by the pharmaceutical effects of plants and herbs. He experimented endlessly at his laboratory at the Villa Ludovisi, which you and Mario decorated. He knew all about the toxic effects of many different substances, as well as their curative effects. He took young Fabio Colonna under his wing and Fabio became one of the great herbalists of his age. If anyone knew how to poison someone, it was Del Monte.'

'Yes, but just because he had the knowledge and ability, that doesn't mean he put it into practise! He didn't make any secret of his interest.'

'Of course he didn't make it a secret,' I cried, trying to convince Merisi. 'Secrecy usually implies guilt or culpability. Keeping it out in the open makes it look entirely harmless, as if he was doing all of this simply for the benefit of mankind.'

'You have a foul and cynical mind, Stefano. I still believe Cardinal Del Monte was working for the benefit of mankind. Can you prove he was not?'

'I can't prove that he poisoned anyone, but some deaths were mighty convenient and benefitted Del Monte greatly.'

'If you mean the deaths of the Grand Duke of Tuscany and his wife on the same day, which allowed Del Monte's patron Ferdinando Medici to become the new Grand Duke, we have already talked about that. I have told you that it was not at all unusual, in those plague-ridden days, for family members to be carried off by the Grim Reaper at the same time. My own father and grandfather, or the two men I thought were my father and grandfather, were carried off on the same day. Are you going to tell me that they also were poisoned by Del Monte?'

'It had crossed my mind,' I smiled, 'but that was long before Del Monte knew you existed. No, I cannot prove that the Grand Duke and his wife were victims of foul play. As you say, such events were common. But, by the same token, such deaths would not arose much suspicion.'

'Such calumny was pointed at poor Del Monte even in my own day,' Merisi said disgustedly. 'What you have failed to take into account was that the new Grand Duke, Del Monte's patron, was fervently pro-French. He lent a huge sum of money to King Henry. Why should Del Monte, if he was against the French, have gotten rid of the old Grand Duke only to let an even more pro-French Grand Duke take over?'

'Our American friends have a charming expression when it comes to power and politics. They say that it is better to have an opponent inside the tent pissing out that outside the tent pissing in. If Del Monte poisoned the previous Grand Duke, and the new Grand Duke knew that Del Monte had helped him into that position of power, then the new Grand Duke would not only be eternally grateful but Del Monte would have a hold over him. He could perhaps, very subtly and discreetly, modify and suppress some of the Grand Duke's pro-French schemes.'

'I don't understand much of what you are saying about pissing, but I see your point. It's still a bit thin. Have you any other examples of the good cardinal's ruthless perfidy?'

'Perhaps,' I answered. 'What about Pope Leo XI?'

'What about him?'

'Pope Clement, who was pro-French, had died. The anti-French faction had thus got rid of one enemy but, to their horror, and thanks to the tireless diplomacy of the French ambassador, Philip de Béthune, another pro-French pope, Leo XI, was elected in his place. Fortunately for the anti-French, Pope Leo keeled over and died barely two months later. Del Monte, as an ostensibly pro-French cardinal was in Leo's circle. Perhaps Del Monte dropped a few drops of something noxious in the pontiff's bedtime cocoa one evening?'

'Rubbish!' Merisi cried. 'Pope Leo was of the Medici family, related to Del Monte's patron Ferdinando, Grand Duke of Tuscany.'

I smiled at Merisi. 'That fact would have placed Del Monte above suspicion. Who better to get rid of the awkward Pope Leo and let in our friend Pope Paul V who, if not actually pro-Spanish, was at least neutral.'

Merisi flapped his hand at me in contempt. 'You are making up fairy tales,' he said.

'Maybe,' I replied. 'Maybe not. In any case, when did good Cardinal Del Monte inform you that you were the illegitimate son of Costanza Colonna?'

My question caught Merisi by surprise. He didn't answer for a few seconds. 'What makes you think that it was Del Monte who told me that?'

'It is obvious that your attitude changes not long after you have gone to live in the Palazzo Madama. Nicholas Cordier told me that, when you were deep in your cups, you would brag about being of noble birth. Cordier didn't believe you and your other friends would laugh at such pretensions. In the morning, when you were sober, you would deny ever saying such things. You knew you had to keep quiet. This prickly and defensive attitude to your perceived lowly birth, this gut-wrenching envy you had of anyone of higher social status, it all started after you had moved into the Palazzo Madama.'

'Perhaps, but what makes you think that it was Del Monte who told me?'

'You once made a comment that he told you the truth when others did not. He told you because it gave him a hold over you. You owed him a debt of gratitude. You shared a precious secret. He had ensnared you in his devious web of deceit.'

'Fuck you,' Merisi said, angrily.

'Do you deny that it was Del Monte who told you?' I pressed him.

'Fuck you,' Merisi said again. 'I cannot deny it. It's true. Del Monte told me that I was the bastard son of a titled lady. Are you determined to take everything away from me, every shred of respect I have for anyone? I loved that man like a father and now you tell me he was a two-faced hypocritical murderer.'

I have to admit that my comments had caused Merisi genuine pain and I regretted it, although I had no choice. 'We've done enough for this morning,' I suggested. 'Let's stop for lunch. Cheese on toast?'

'Fuck your cheese on toast.'

'It might be a bit hot for that. I'll put a poached egg on top. Come on, Michele.'

'And some of that Worsesisterdister sauce?'

'Worcestershire sauce as well, I promise,' I said. I had finally learned how to cheer up my Baroque house guest.

I prepared our lunch and we sat at the kitchen table in silence for many minutes. Merisi was deep in thought and I did not want to disturb his contemplation with idle chit-chat. We ate our food and I made the coffee. As I was pouring coffee into our mugs, Merisi suddenly said: 'How did you find out that Costanza was my real mother?'

I said: 'Why don't we finish our lunch and then get back to work?'

'No,' Merisi insisted. 'Tell me now. Please.'

I considered his request for a few seconds and could see no harm in telling him right away. I put the coffee mugs on the kitchen table and sat down again. 'During our examination of your paintings, there were two that seemed particularly interesting in our search for clues. They seemed to be crammed with symbolism, much more so than most of your other works. These two paintings have always been kept together since you painted them and, although art historians have not been able to establish for whom they were painted, I think I can make a good guess.'

'Which two do you mean?' Merisi asked, taking a sip of coffee.

'I mean the two now known as the Penitent or Repentant Magdalen and The Rest on the Flight to Egypt.' Merisi allowed me an ironic smile. 'I'm right, aren't I,' I said.

'You tell me why?' Merisi challenged me.

'You threw me off the scent because you told me that the model for Mary Magdalen and then the Virgin Mary was Anna Bianchini. What you didn't know, because I didn't tell you, is that I met Anna Bianchini in Fillide Melandroni's house. You let me believe, by not contradicting me, that you were in love with Anna, or at least infatuated with her, but that was not true. Not only were you not in love with Anna, you hardly had anything to do with her, despite her being Fillide's best friend, because Anna Bianchini couldn't stand the sight of you.'

'She was a girl of little taste,' Merisi smiled.

'Perhaps,' I said, 'but she looked nothing like the model in the two pictures we are talking about. Also, Anna had black hair, not beautiful chestnut red hair, like the girl in the paintings.'

'You are correct, Stefano.'

'So, I came to know that this girl in these two paintings was not Anna Bianchini, but I did not know that the girl was Costanza Colonna, despite the fact that I had already met Costanza before I visited her at the Palazzo Cellamare.'

Merisi looked at me in genuine surprise. 'When did you meet Costanza before?'

'It was quite by accident. I had been to the Palazzo Madama and when I came out I decided to go and see your Saint Matthew paintings in the Contarelli chapel. Costanza was making a private act of worship, protected by her sons Muzio and Fabrizio.'

'Did you talk to Costanza?'

'Yes, briefly. I did not see her hair because it was covered by her mantilla, otherwise I might have twigged earlier.'

'Twigged? You mean a small branch?'

'No, I mean realised, guessed, understood.'

'These ChronoTranslators need improvement,' Merisi grumbled.

'If only we could have improved the trust and communication between us, Michele. You see how we have been playing cat and mouse games with each other?'

'Cat and mouse games I do understand,' Merisi said. 'Neither of us asked to be put in this situation. It's those bloody nosey aliens from Tralfamadore.'

I shrugged, unwilling to get into any further arguments about our mutual level of co-operation. 'Soon after Cardinal Del Monte had informed you that you were the illegitimate son of Costanza Colonna, you were commissioned to paint two pictures. As I have already told you, these two pictures have been kept together since they were painted and are now housed in the same art gallery in Rome. You were obviously thinking about Costanza, perhaps brooding on this wonderful yet disturbing news that she was your mother. In these two pictures, you took the opportunity to send messages to your own real mother, messages that she could hardly fail to understand but that anybody else was most unlikely to understand. The first one you painted was The Rest on the Flight to Egypt and it was intended to tell Costanza that you knew that you were her son and how much you loved her. The composition of this painting always seemed odd to me until I understood what you were doing. The figure of the angel completely separates the Virgin Mary from her husband, Saint Joseph. Just like Mary, Costanza had borne a child fathered by someone who was not her husband, hence the separation. Over Joseph's shoulder looms the eye of a donkey, much larger than it needs to be for artistic purposes. In Italian legend, the donkey was given a cross to bear on its back because a donkey had carried Christ into Jerusalem. The cross you had to bear was that you were separated from your own mother, Costanza, but you would always keep an eye on her. And the image of the Virgin Mary cuddling the infant Christ is full of tenderness. You were yearning to be held in your own mother's arms in the same way. The Virgin Mary is Costanza, complete with her lovely chestnut red hair and that distinctive arc of the nape of her neck. She didn't actually model for this painting, did she?'

'No, of course not,' Merisi answered. 'Fillide modelled for the body and I gave her Costanza's head and neck.'

'It is very unusual in the art of your time, if not unique, for the Virgin Mary to be portrayed with red hair, so the real audience you intended for this picture could hardly fail to realise that it was meant for her. And, of course, the angel is singing a motet entitled "How Beautiful Thou Art". The message to your mother could hardly be clearer.'

'Very clever, Stefano,' Merisi said, trying to be sarcastic but rattled by my exposition. 'What about the Penitent Magdalen?'

'The Rest of the Flight to Egypt had been a message of love and devotion to your newly-found mother. The Penitent Magdalen was an expression of your regret at her fall from grace and, perhaps, an expression to her of your regret that you had been denied your true birthright. The model for Mary Magdalen is Costanza again, so clearly the message is again intended for her. If her physical appearance were not clear enough, that unusual pattern just above the hem of her dress is the clincher. There has been much speculation about what it could signify, such as an urn or a bowl and so on, but I believe it is meant to be a stylised version of the capital at the top of a column. The family name Colonna means column. Again, you have made it abundantly clear who is the intended recipient of the message. Mary Magdalen was rich, beautiful and sensual, just like Costanza. Mary Magdalen, just like Costanza, renounced the vanities of the world to lead a solitary and spiritual life. Costanza never remarried after the death of her husband Francesco in 1580. She was still a relatively young and attractive woman, still desirable if for nothing else than her money, but she never remarried and she devoted herself to good works. The symbolism of the Magdalen's personal effects that are scattered beside her on the floor is crystal clear. The wine represents blood, as it represents the blood of Christ in the sacraments, but this shows that Costanza and yourself are of the same blood. Gold traditionally represents nobility and purity, the purity which Costanza had cast off through her affair with Prince Henry. Pearls are traditionally used to symbolise femininity, perfection, marriage and social order, all of which have been cast off by Costanza because of her reckless adultery. Pearls strung together represent social order and ancestral lineage. The Magdalen's pearl necklace had been broken and cast aside, perhaps how you felt because of Costanza's actions. Can you deny that all this is true?'

Merisi was reluctant to answer for a few seconds. 'You read too much into these things.'

'Do you deny that my interpretation is correct?' I persisted.

'What is the point of confirming or denying? Will it change anything now?'

'No, but am I right?'

'Yes,' Merisi snapped. 'Who do you think these paintings were commissioned by? Cardinal Del Monte?'

'No. I believe they were probably commissioned by Vincenzo Giustiniani and he probably encouraged you to include such symbolism as a message to Costanza that you at last knew the truth.'

'Why shouldn't Giustiniani just tell Costanza the truth directly, or encourage me to do so?'

'That was not Vincenzo's way. When I met him, I told him that he was as inscrutable as an Oriental. He took that as a compliment. I believe that Vincenzo found out that Del Monte had told you the truth about Costanza. Vincenzo probably knew it anyway. You do not become an immensely rich banker without a wide network of contacts and information and without being subtle and devious. To outfox his close friend Del Monte, Vincenzo had to be very subtle. When I was viewing Del Monte's art collection with Vincenzo, he casually drew my attention to a portrait of your father, King Henry. I stupidly did not realise the significance at the time but, looking back, the physical resemblances between you and your father were strong. When I talked to Vincenzo outside the Palazzo Madama, he tried to verbally point me in the right direction but he never said anything directly. That was Vincenzo's chosen method of operation then, if anything went wrong, nothing would rebound on him and he could deny everything. I would bet that Del Monte never saw the two pictures that we have been talking about, did he?'

'No, he did not. You are very clever, Stefano. Vincenzo did commission these paintings and he specifically asked me to keep them private. He told me that these paintings would be seen only by himself and selected family and friends. He paid me very well.'

'Vincenzo and Costanza were close friends. The Palazzo Giustiniani was next door to the Palazzo Colonna. These paintings were Vincenzo's way of warning Costanza that you knew that she was your real mother, without implicating himself by actually telling her directly. And, of course, he had secured two masterpieces by the hand of the artist whose work he admired above any other. A very clever and devious man was Vincenzo Giustiniani. Of course, you were not quite finished with including Costanza in your pictures, were you?'

'I suppose you mean the Death of the Virgin?' Merisi sighed.

'Yes. Such an apt subject in relation to Costanza, and there she is again, in the foreground of the picture, with that lovely red hair and distinctively-shaped neck, weeping over the death of the Virgin. Traditionally, it was very unusual to include Mary Magdalen in a painting of the death of the Virgin Mary but you couldn't resist the temptation, could you?'

'No, I could not. All of what you have said is true but you still have not told me how you knew that it was Costanza in these pictures. You say that she did not admit as much, so how did you come to realise?'

'It was you yourself, indirectly, that made me realise. When I visited Costanza at the Palazzo Cellamare, I took your still life painting with me. We had talked about your last days with her at the Palazzo Cellamare and Costanza had held back her feelings with restraint and dignity, as befits a noble lady. But when she unwrapped your painting and looked at it, she could restrain herself no longer. She wept, her head bent over your picture, to reveal that distinctively shaped neck and, of course, her chestnut red hair. There could be no mistake. I still did not know for certain but when I asked her if she was your real mother, she could not deny it. Also, she was still grieving for the love of her life, your father Henry IV, who, as you know, had been assassinated by a Catholic madman named Ravaillac just a couple of months before your own death.'

'Yes,' Merisi nodded mournfully. 'I had been puzzled why Costanza had seemed so upset by the news of Henry's death. Now, of course, I know perfectly well why.'

I nodded respectfully myself and then said: 'Come on, let's go back into the living room and get comfortable in our armchairs. There is still a lot to talk about.'

I got up but Merisi did not move. He asked: 'So, does all we have been talking about explain that enigmatic comment by the man who murdered me in Porto Ercole?'

'Which comment?'

'He said something like "the why is in the paintings . . . you should have been more careful". Are these the paintings he was talking about?'

'If only things were that simple, Michele. Come on, let's go and get comfortable.' We returned to the living room and settled into our armchairs. 'Let me just clear up one small mystery. I have already told you that your friend Lionello Spada was one of Fillide Melandroni's lovers. Her much wealthier lover, Vincenzo Giustiniani, knew all about Spada. Vincenzo was jealous of

Spada's youthful ardour. That is why Spada was thrown off the commission to fresco the basilica of the church of Santa Maria di Loreto in the Marches.'

'You mean that was Vincenzo's doing?'

'Through the power of his brother, Cardinal Benedetto Giustiniani, who appointed Guido Reni to judge Spada's work, with orders to find it inadequate however good it was.'

'So it was just an act of spite by a jealous lover?' Merisi said. 'That doesn't sound like Vincenzo Giustiniani at all.'

'People act in crazy and illogical ways through sexual jealousy. You, above all people, should know that.'

Merisi smiled. 'You are right,' he said, ruefully. 'And the commission for this church was given to the neutral and oh-so-respectable Cristofero Roncalli.'

'That's correct. And you and Spada arranged to give him a severe beating at the hands of your hired Sicilan thug as his reward.'

Merisi was genuinely repentant at the thought of this despicable act. 'Truly, I will have to answer to God one day for my wickedness.'

'We'll all have to do that, Michele,' I said. 'In the meantime, let's return to your career, which was just about to take off in a big way thanks to the commission for the Saint Matthew paintings in the Contarelli chapel of the church of San Luigi dei Francesi. As you know, this was the national church of the French in Rome. Your real father, King Henry IV of France, had recently been accepted back into the Roman Catholic fold. He knew of his illegitimate son's burgeoning reputation as a painter. The centenary jubilee was taking place in a few short months. When it came to painting, you were known to be a fast and reliable worker. Who better than yourself to complete this commission? So, the orders went out from the French court and, thanks to the relentless lobbying of Cardinal Del Monte and the art dealer Valentin, you were awarded the commission. Their reward, and that of the church, was a set of paintings that quite simply revolutionised European art and rank among the greatest masterpieces ever painted.'

'You are making me blush with such praise,' Merisi said, inordinately pleased with my compliments.

'Well, don't preen yourself too much, my friend, because we both know that your strange attitude to success meant that your life was going to spiral out of control in a few short years. But, at this time, you painted some of your best and most confident works. Your first version of The Supper At Emmaus, which I have always admired without reservation, the extraordinary depiction of Bacchus, which amazingly was stored unnoticed in the Uffizi Gallery in Florence for years, and the tauntingly erotic Victorious Cupid, or Love Conquers All, for our old friend Vincenzo Giustiniani.'

Merisi smiled. 'I remember that Vincenzo subtly suggested to me that he wanted something erotic. I think I gave him more than he had bargained for.'

'You certainly did. Vincenzo Giustiniani has gone down in history as a devout and rather austere man but there was certainly a hidden undercurrent of sexual passion in his life which he managed to keep well hidden. This must have been about the time that Vincenzo encouraged you to move away from the scrutiny of Cardinal Del Monte at the Palazzo Madama and move back to the Palazzo Mattei?'

'Yes, it was. I have already told you that I was puzzled by Vincenzo's suggestion. I was devoted to Cardinal Del Monte but I eventually accepted that it would be a sensible move to go to the Palazzo Mattei, especially as I could earn considerably more money from the wealthy Mattei brothers. Now that you have explained about Cardinal Del Monte's real motives, I understand why Vincenzo urged me to move away.'

'We have discussed the way your career moved after this time, gradually downhill, featuring the infamous libel trial which Baglione and Mao Salini brought against you and your friends. It's interesting to note that your release from prison was secured by the French ambassador, Philip de Béthune, standing bail for you. I always thought it odd that a distinguished figure such as the French ambassador should concern himself with releasing a trouble-making artist from prison, albeit one as talented as you were. Now we know what very powerful French allies you had, it is no longer surprising at all. Little of relevance regarding our quest for your murderer takes place for the next two or three years after the libel trial. You carry on working, with your talent as a painter surpassed only by your talent for attracting trouble. And the biggest trouble of all is what we have to discuss next.'

Merisi shook his head ruefully. 'You have a real talent yourself, Stefano. For ruining my day.'

'You certainly ruined Ranuccio Tomassoni's day, back in May 1606. The fight between you two had been boiling up for years and yet it never spilled over into real violence until you began spreading malicious gossip about Ranuccio's wife, Lavinia, and her affair with Fabbio Romanino de Sanctis.'

'It wasn't malicious. It was true!' Merisi protested.

'It was true,' I agreed, 'but it was malicious of you to spread such gossip.'

'Ranuccio Tomassoni and his family had been taunting me and causing me trouble for years. I was prepared to use all the ammunition I had against Ranuccio Tomassoni.'

'And who gave you that ammunition,' I asked.

'What do you mean?'

'Who told you about Lavinia Tomassoni's affair with de Sanctis?'

'Let me think,' Merisi said. 'It was Lionello. Lionello Spada. He hated Ranuccio as much as I did. Perhaps more.'

'Yes, and you once told me that you didn't understand why Spada hated Ranuccio so much. Now you know that it was because he was having, or had had, a passionate affair with Fillide Melandroni. Spada couldn't let go and was insanely jealous of Fillide's relationship with Ranuccio. Fillide herself had tired of Spada's attentions long before. Forgive me for having to tell you this, Michele, but Fillide was also trying to distance herself from you. And, despite her continuing passion for Ranuccio Tomassoni, she knew that any relationship with him was ultimately going to be fruitless. Fillide had major players like Giulio Strozzi and, especially, Vincenzo Giustiniani, supporting her. She no longer needed to model for impecunious artists like you and Spada or be used by a faithless pimp like Ranuccio. But Ranuccio, who had found out about his wife's affair with de Sanctis, made a big mistake. He told Fillide, probably in a drunken rage, about his affair. Fillide saw a golden opportunity to get rid of some, or perhaps all, of the unwanted men in her life without incriminating herself. She knew that you were unaware of her former relationship with Spada. She also knew, beyond doubt, that Spada would pass on this gossip about Lavinia Tomassoni's affair to you. She knew, beyond doubt, that you would use such gossip to taunt Ranuccio. So, Fillide told Spada about Lavinia's affair, Spada told you, you spread it all over Rome, Ranuccio became angered and humiliated beyond endurance, you two fought each other at the tennis court, and Fillide's plan worked better than even she could have dreamed. Spada disappeared from Rome, Ranuccio was dead, you were exiled from Rome forever, problem solved. Fillide had severed all her unwanted attachments with one brilliant strategy.' I waited for an angry reaction from Merisi but none came.

After a few seconds, he said: 'So Fillide was using all of us against each other?'

'I'm afraid so.'

'That fucking heartless bitch.'

'Well, in Fillide's defence, I don't think she dreamed that her plan would end up with Ranuccio dead. Perhaps she wanted you two in prison for a few months or years.'

'Perhaps,' Merisi sighed, 'but I doubt that Fillide lost any sleep over this outcome.'

'Lionello Spada was perhaps not unhappy with the outcome either,' I said, carefully.

Merisi shook his head in despair. 'I see what you are saying. He hoped to get Fillide back and with me and Ranuccio out of the way, he thought he had a much better chance?'

'That's correct, Michele.'

'Fuck,' he breathed. 'They all played me like a fish. What a fool I was.'

'It's interesting to note that, after the fight, Spada and Longhi took you to the Palazzo Giustiniani for protection and for your wounds to be tended. Not to Del Monte at the Palazzo Madama or to the Palazzo Mattei. Costanza Colonna was informed of your plight and you were whisked out of Rome into the safety of Colonna territory. You must have thought at the time that your biggest danger was the revenge of the Tomassoni clan but, as I have explained to you, the Tomassoni clan sought no revenge. They knew what Ranuccio was like. You felt like a hunted man but probably your only danger at that time was from some disgruntled enemy killing you under the protection of the dreaded sentence of the banda capitale. Thus you were relatively safe to eventually move to Naples where you wisely kept your head down and restarted your artistic career in a blaze of glory.'

'God was watching me,' Merisi said mournfully. 'That was punishment enough.'

I nodded. 'What do you want to eat tonight?'

Merisi, lost in thought, was momentarily confused by my abrupt change of subject. 'Anything you like,' he replied absent-mindedly. 'I'm not hungry.'

'I'll ring for a pizza,' I said, and rang Garibaldi's Pizza Place for a couple of twelve inchers with tomatoes, pepperoni, mushrooms and green peppers, with a side order of garlic bread and hot wings. I felt like celebrating because my work was nearly done. 'Back to Naples,' I continued, putting away my mobile phone. 'Your arrival in Naples had caused a sensation and you were safely esconced with Vinck and Finson, or so you must have thought. You still feared the vengeance of the Tomassoni clan but, unknown to you, far more powerful forces were beginning to stir against you, and Vincenzo Giustiniani knew all about them.'

'What powerful forces do you mean?' Merisi asked.

'Because of your Europe-wide fame, or should I say notoriety, not only as a great painter but now as a condemned murderer, it was inevitable that the secret of your parentage was gradually becoming known to more and more people. If you had remained as an anonymous provincial artist, perhaps no-one would have ever found out or even cared. Your father King Henry's perceived cynical conversion back to the Roman Catholic fold had enraged both Protestants and Catholics for years. As his son, albeit illegitimate, your existence could prove a threat to many different factions, perhaps even to your father, King Henry, himself. As your self-appointed guardian angel, Vincenzo Giustiniani decided to act to get you somewhere safer than the city of Naples. The solution was very obvious ... Malta. The island was a closed and very secure sanctuary, guarded by the formidable Knights of St. John, who were under the command of a Frenchman, Alof de Wignacourt. De Wignacourt already knew, or could safely be trusted, with the secret of your parentage. And Vincenzo knew that the one thing you coveted more than artistic fame was a title of nobility. He knew that the one thing that might persuade you to abandon a lucrative career in Naples was the promise that you would be made a Knight of St. John. So, to sweeten de Wignacourt, Vincenzo dispatched one of the Giustiniani clan, Marc'Aurelio, to Malta to offer de Wignacourt a considerable property at Venosa, in the Kingdom of Naples, for the founding of a command by the Italian division of the Knights. Perhaps some more subtle pressure was applied to de Wignacourt by his fellow countrymen and erstwhile monarch at the French court. Whatever the reasons, de Wignacourt agreed to accept you in Malta and Vincenzo's trusted friend and lawyer Theodore Almayden was sent to see you in Naples and offer you the deal. I suspect that you needed little persuasion.'

'You are right, Stefano. I was tremendously excited by Almayden's offer. I did not know that Giustiniani was behind all this but Almayden presented me with enough bona fides to persuade me that the offer was genuine. I wanted it to be genuine. As you have said, the one thing I wanted more than artistic success was a noble title to shove up the arse of all those rivals who had spent years belittling me all the while they were copying my style. I was more than happy to take my chances in Malta.'

'So, leaving Vinck and Finson bereft, you sailed to Malta on a galley commanded by Costanza's son, and your half-brother, Fabrizio Sforza.'

'That's correct, Stefano. Of course, Fabrizio had no idea that I was also Costanza's son, but we got along famously. Fabrizio was a lively character and he treated me very well.'

'When you arrived in Malta, you were immediately granted access to the highest echelons of Maltese society, thanks to your high-ranking connections which, as you now know, were even higher than you imagined them to be. We have examined how the Grand Master Alof de Wignacourt made such strenuous efforts with the papal court in order to award you your knighthood. We now know the reasons why he made such an effort. You were awarded your knighthood and then, in your usual inimitable manner, proceeded to throw it all away by picking a fight with a Knight of Justice and getting yourself thrown into prison. Are you going to tell me who this Knight of Justice was?'

Merisi hesitated, but then said: 'You have probably found out who it was anyway.'

'I might have done,' I replied.

'Then let's stop playing silly games. You know very well that it was Marco Malaspina, son of the great hero Ippolito Malaspina.'

I nodded. 'I did not know that but thanks for telling me. I suspected it might have been somebody like that.'

Merisi threw up his hands in exasperation. 'You have tricked me again, Stefano. Why did you suspect somebody like Marco?'

'Because his father, Ippolito, had been living in Rome, near the Piazza Navona where you lived, and had been involved with the papal court. When he saw you travelling on the same galley, he knew very well who you were. I don't know who Ippolito Malaspina was secretly working for, if he was working for anyone, but I suspect a man with his military reputation might have been horrified that a mere painter like yourself was going to be elevated to a Knight of Obedience.'

'But I painted a Saint Jerome for Malaspina, complete with his family coat-of-arms,' Merisi protested. 'He seemed friendly enough towards me.'

'Well, as I say, I am only guessing but these are shark-infested waters we are talking about, Michele. Who was working for whom, and how many people knew the secret of your parentage, I can only surmise but someone put Marco Malaspina up to picking a fight with you. Someone wanted you to be ruined.'

'I walked right into a trap,' Merisi sighed.

'I'm afraid so. But, fortunately for you, you had a friend who helped you escape from your cell in the Castel Sant'Angelo.'

'What makes you so sure that somebody helped me?'

'Come off it, Michele,' I said. 'We've been through all this. You could not have escaped from a bell-shaped underground cell, over castle walls, avoiding all the guards, and then down to the harbour, once again managing to avoid all patrols and guards, without help. And what you conveniently omitted to tell me in our previous examination of this incredible stunt was the identity of the friend who helped you.'

'And who was that?' Merisi asked me, challengingly.

'It was your good friend Lionello Spada, who just happened to be in Malta decorating the Grand Master's Palace.'

Merisi chuckled. 'I'm afraid you have tripped over your own cleverness this time, Stefano, because it was not little Lionello who helped me escape. Oh, he tried to persuade de Wignacourt to set me free but even the Grand Master could not break his own rules.'

'Who did help you then?' I asked, allowing Merisi his small revenge.

'It was Fabrizio.'

'Fabrizio Sforza?'

'Yes, my good friend and unknown half-brother, Costanza's son, could not stand to see me cooped up in a prison cell, even if only for his mother's sake. Of course, he did not know that I was his half-brother but he knew that his mother was very fond of me and springing me from prison was an adventure after his own heart. He got me out and away on a felucca to Sicily.'

'That's very interesting,' I said. 'Why didn't you tell me this before?'

'I was trying to keep Costanza out of all this.'

'Why didn't you tell me that Lionello Spada was in Malta at the same time as yourself?'

Merisi shrugged. 'I didn't think it was relevant or important.'

'Did you know that Ippolito Malaspina had recommended Lionello Spada for the work on the Grand Master's Palace?'

'No, I did not,' Merisi admitted.

'And do you know who recommended Spada to Ippolito Malaspina?'

'No.'

'Your good friend Cardinal Del Monte.'

'What of it?'

'Don't you see? Your enemies, and those of your real father, did not want you safely confined in a cell in Malta. In Malta, under the protection of the Knights of Saint John, you were invulnerable. They wanted you to be expelled from Malta. Marco Malaspina was encouraged to insult you and pick a fight with you. Del Monte wanted a trusted friend of yours like Spada in Malta to keep an eye on you. Spada was not aware of Del Monte's real purpose or his devious machinations. As it was, Fabrizio Sforza did the job for your enemies by helping you escape from the Castel Sant'Angelo.'

'Hmm. As you truly said, Stefano, these were shark-infested waters.'

'You arrived in Sicily and were given help and shelter by your old friend Mario Minnitti. You've already told me that Mario's wife, Rafaella, was unhappy about you living in her house and you soon tired of Mario's constant attention, so you moved on. At this time, you really did feel like a hunted man and your behaviour became increasingly erratic. You still feared the vengeance of the Tomassoni clan and you also feared that the Knights of Saint John were hunting you for dishonouring their order. You were still working but there were some very odd incidents, such as slashing your first version of your Raising of Lazarus picture because of local criticism, and your vicious attack on the schoolteacher in Palermo who was concerned about the attention you were paying to his pupils.'

'We have been over this,' Merisi said, irritably.

'And through Vincenzo Giustiniani,' I continued, ignoring Merisi's interruption, 'who had close contacts in Palermo, you received word that a papal pardon for the murder of Tomassoni was imminent and advised you to move back to Naples. He and Costanza made sure that you moved into the protection of the Palazzo Cellamare. Of course, you being you, you could not resist an occasional night out on the town, and that allowed your enemies to catch up with you outside the Osteria del Cerriglio. You were fortunate to survive such a savage beating.' Merisi touched the pale whitened remains of the scars on his face, but he said nothing. I looked at my watch. 'The pizza will be here soon but there is time to complete my report to you. There is little left to say. You stayed with your mother Costanza at the Palazzo Cellamare for several months but the lure of Rome was too strong and you made a precipitous departure. Costanza begged you to stay with her. She knew your life was in mortal danger. She could not, dare not, tell you who your real father was. King Henry IV of France had been assassinated by a deranged Catholic named Ravaillac in May. The secret of your real parentage was by now known to many people who were antipathetic towards you. Costanza knew that if you returned to Rome, you would probably not survive very long. I think that Costanza intended to one day tell you the exact truth about your father but you pre-empted her decision by very suddenly departing for Rome on that last fateful journey. But your murderer was on your heels. You nearly avoided him but then made his task easy by falling ill and being confined to hospital in Porto Ercole. Here, your murderer, disguised by a monk's cowl so you could not recognise you, struck you down.'

'Who was it?' Merisi asked anxiously.

'All in good time, Michele. Let's just go over what your murderer said to you.' I consulted my notes to get it right. 'He lifted up your head and gave you something to drink from a cup. Then he made this seemingly odd statement. He said: "This will ease all your problems. It is something you have always coveted, as all you artists do." This statement puzzled me for a long time. I tried to think about something all artists of your era coveted, and then I had an inspiration. What your murderer gave you to drink was a potion made from the laburnum plant. All the symptoms you described to me after you had drunk this potion are symptoms of laburnum poisoning. Such a potion would probably not be enough to kill a fit and healthy man but in your weak and feverish condition it certainly would have finished you off if the Tralfamadorians had not rescued you.'

'I still don't understand what this means,' Merisi said. 'All artists do not covet being poisoned?'

'No. This was your murderer's little joke because in Italian, as well as in English, the traditional name for the laburnum is golden chain. All you artists used to covet the award of a real golden chain to reward a particularly fine piece of work.'

'That is the poorest joke I have ever heard,' Merisi said. 'Are you now going to tell me who this murderer was?'

'I'm afraid, Michele, that is was your old friend Mario Minnitti.'

'Mario!' Merisi exclaimed. 'Are you sure?'

'Yes, I am.'

'But why did he do it? He spent years protecting me. He welcomed me to his house in Sicily and helped me get work. I cannot believe this.'

'Just before you nearly expired, Michele, you asked him who he was and why he was doing this to you. Mario answered: "For love, Michele! It is done for love! You know very well who I am, and the why is in the paintings, but you will never know! You should have been more careful!"' Mario always detested the way you used to portray him in those early paintings, making him look like a bardassa, a pretty boy, to be the butt of your jokes and of your friends.'

'Surely that was not enough for him to want to kill me,' Merisi exclaimed.

'No,' I replied. 'As Mario himself told you, it was all done for love. Mario loved his wife Rafaella passionately. After they had married, Mario found out that you and Rafaella had been lovers back in Rome. Mario was deeply upset, but even that was not enough for him to want to kill you, and he did not want to lose Rafaella. Then he discovered that Rafaella had borne you a son. She had discovered that you had made her pregnant. That is why she returned to Sicily while Mario was stuck in Rome, still under orders to be your guardian angel. Rafaella gave birth to your son and, knowing that Mario must never know, had the boy put in the care of relatives in Palermo. It broke her heart but it was the only thing to be done. That time in Palermo, when you kept going down to the harbour to watch the schoolboys playing, you were not studying them for a painting, as you told me, you were watching your son.'

Merisi did not say anything for several seconds. 'Congratulations, Stefano. I was certain that you would not find out anything about Rafaella and me, and certainly not about our son. Do you know anything about my boy . . . how he lived, what he did in life, anything like that?'

'I'm sorry, Michele, but it is all lost in the mists of time. Today, there is nothing known about your son.'

'Like so much about my miserable life, that is a great pity. So, Mario found out all this and tried to put an end to me?'

'Yes. Despite his Sicilian temper, he truly loved Rafaella and did not want to lose her, so he kept his counsel and bided his time. He followed you to Naples and waited for his opportunity. He had been saving the laburnum poison for years, ever since you and he completed the fresco at Cardinal Del Monte's Villa Ludovisi. That is where the cardinal conducted his plant experiments and Mario must have stolen the poison from there.'

'You have solved the mystery, Stefano. Well done. I am sorry it was my old friend who wished me such harm but I can see that I had done him much harm. It was a sorry affair all round.'

My front door bell rang and I got up to leave Merisi to mull over all that I had told him. I opened the front door and was glad to see the delivery boy from Garibaldi's Pizza Place with our dinner. I paid him and took the food into the living room and placed it on the coffee table. 'We'll eat in here tonight,' I decided. 'I'll get some plates and napkins.'

'I am not so hungry,' Merisi said, 'but I could do with a drink.'

'A good idea, Michele. Let's celebrate the completion of our quest. Pour us a couple of bourbons.'

I fetched the plates and tucked into the pizza and garlic bread. Merisi did not touch the food. I suppose the shock of hearing that your best friend tried to murder you does take the edge off the appetite. Merisi sat nursing his drink in silence for a long time. Eventually he nibbled on a piece of garlic bread but soon put it down unfinished. From time to time he looked at me. I ate my fill and Merisi poured us another drink. I was beginning to feel quite light-headed from the bourbon and from the relief of knowing that our quest had been concluded. Merisi must have been feeling the same, because he suddenly said: 'It's been quite an experience, Stefano, all this. You have been allowed to meet people and see things that you should never have seen, and the same for me. There is much in my life that I regret and that I would do differently if I had the chance. I cannot help wondering what will happen to me now.'

'I truly don't know, Michele. The Tralfamadorians have not confided in me. Would you prefer to go back to your own century or to stay in this one?'

Merisi sipped his drink thoughtfully. I was surprised to find my eyes were becoming heavy and I felt very relaxed. Merisi answered: 'I think I would like to remain in this century. It is much more comfortable. I would like to make a new life, a fresh start.'

'I'll help you in any way I can, Michele. I'm sure the Tralfamadorians will not harm you and it will surely be easier for them simply to let you carry on living in this century if that is what you desire. Let's have another drink.'

Merisi got up to refresh our glasses. I nearly fell asleep but was woken up by the clink of glass on the coffee table. Merisi said: 'You look tired, Stefano, but before you nod off, I would like to thank you for looking after me and for solving many mysteries that perplexed me during my previous life. My arrival here caused you much difficulty. I know you think little of me as a human being but you have stuck to your task and I thank you for it.'

I raised my glass to Merisi and said: 'On the contrary Michele, it is I, and every other human being on this planet who should be thanking you, for showing us who we are through your work.'

'I know that you admire my work,' Merisi said, 'but you have never exactly told me why?'

I was fighting off an almost overwhelming urge to fall off to sleep but I wanted to answer Merisi's question before I took a nap, so I stirred myself. 'Michele,' I said, 'There have certainly been many painters who were better human beings, although to examine your life as we have done is to understand why you are as you are. There have been many better painters than you in terms of technical skill. But what is the purpose of painting, of art? Is it to produce pretty pictures with which to decorate the walls of a house or a gallery? Such work has a place but it's not great art. If somebody were to ask me what is like to be human, in all its many forms . . . love, sex, joy, hate, anguish, suffering and death, I would say to them simply, go and look at the works of Michelangelo Merisi da Caravaggio and you will understand it all. I could not send them to any other artist who ever lived and make that claim. Your achievement is astonishing. On behalf of all humanity, Michele, I thank you.'

The last thing I remember before sleep overwhelmed me was Merisi smiling with pleasure. 'Sleep well, Stefano,' he said. 'Sleep well.'

50

I dreamt that I was in a deep, dark cavern and ice-cold water was dripping from the roof of the cavern and on to my forehead. The dripping became so irritating that I wanted to wake up. My mind forced me back into consciousness and I realised that my head was lying on something softer than rock but that it was still painfully uncomfortable. The water was still dripping on to my forehead. My feet were above my head and resting on something soft. A hand from somewhere gave me several stinging slaps on my face, which made me very angry. I tried to get up but somehow I could not. My healing ribs ached from the pain of my awkward position. I was now almost fully awake and could see that I was not in a cavern but in my own living room. My head was lying on the carpet and my legs were resting above me on the sofa. A tall, powerfully-built man was standing over me. 'Wake up, Steve,' he shouted, and slapped me on the face again.

He made to slap me again but I caught his arm. 'Alright, alright,' I shouted back. 'Who the fuck are you?'

'That's better,' the man said, ignoring my question. 'Let's get you up and on to the sofa.' He stood behind me, grabbed me under my arms and lifted me off the floor and into a sitting position on my sofa. A wave of nausea hit me and I had to breathe heavily to keep it down. My head and ribs ached abominably and my mouth felt and tasted as if twenty stray dogs had been sleeping in it.

The man sat down opposite me in one of my armchairs and looked at me intently. Once again I asked him: 'Who the fuck are you?' Through the pain and discomfort of a disastrous hangover, I realised that I was speaking English. The last thing that I remembered was talking to Merisi in Italian. I looked for the ChronoTranslator ring but it had been taken off my finger.

'I have taken back your ChronoTranslator,' the man said. He spoke perfect unaccented English. 'Don't you recognise me yet?'

The man was dressed in a normal modern suit and tie. His hair was cut short, in a modern style, but he did look familiar. 'Pellegrino,' I finally realised. 'What are you doing here?'

'You really can't take your drink, can you, Steve?' he said merrily. 'I've come to find out where Merisi is.'

'He was here a few minutes ago,' I replied. 'We were just talking.'

'He's been missing for nearly a day,' Pellegrino said. 'He has taken off the ChronoTranslator ring. We have been tracking both of you through your ChronoTranslator rings. Merisi's showed us that he hadn't moved an inch for nearly a day and yours showed only the slightest movement for the same time period. We knew something must be badly wrong.'

'Nearly a day?' I repeated, thoroughly confused. 'What day is it?'

'Wednesday, the 17th,' Pellegrino replied.

'What time is it?'

'Six o'clock.'

'Why are you waking me up this early?'

'It's six o'clock in the evening.'

'In the evening,' I repeated. 'The last thing I remember was talking to Merisi. It was about eight o'clock on Tuesday evening. I had just finished telling him all about my findings. We were having a drink and then I suddenly felt tired and . . . bingo. You mean I've been lying here asleep for nearly a day?'

'Looks like it,' Pellegrino said, still amused at my predicament. 'I think you've been Mickey Finned again. You really aren't any good at this lark, are you?'

'Hold on,' I said. 'I've got to pee.' I raised myself up from the sofa, fighting off a slight dizziness, and stumbled upstairs to the bathroom. I splashed my face with cold water several times, which made my head clearer. I went into Merisi's bedroom and looked in the wardrobe and chest of drawers. His clothes and personal belongings were all gone. A horrifying thought struck me. I went into my bedroom and looked into my wardrobe. I was afraid that Merisi might have taken my suitcase to pack his belongings. I was relieved to see my suitcase still in place in the wardrobe and the edge of the wrapped frame of the Rubens portrait behind it, hidden by all the other junk I had piled in front of it. If Merisi had done a runner, at least he had not taken the Rubens. I congratulated myself for not telling Merisi about it. My wallet was lying on the bedside table. All the banknotes had been stolen but the credit cards were still there, as were my car keys. I went back downstairs and into my office. Sure enough, the spare cash that I kept in my desk drawer was missing. I was not too upset. Merisi was welcome to the cash because I had a Rubens! I went into the kitchen and poured myself a large tumbler of orange juice. I drunk it down in one go and that eliminated most of the stray dog taste. I put the kettle on and called out to Pellegrino: 'Do you want a cup of tea or coffee?'

Pellegrino did not answer but, instead, came out of the living room and into the kitchen. His eyes were alight with anticipation. 'Tea or coffee?' he said to himself. 'I love both of them and, being stuck in seventeenth century Rome, I haven't drunk either for years. We don't have them on Tralfamadore either. God, it's good to be back on 21st century Earth!'

'Well, which one do you want?' I asked. Pellegrino was in an agony of indecision, so I said: 'Fuck it, I'm making a pot of tea. Then you can have as much tea or coffee as you like. Sit down while I take a packet of Alka Seltzer.' I looked in the kitchen cupboard for the Alka Seltzer and saw that my bottle of sleeping pills was in the front of the cupboard. Most of them were missing. 'That's how he did it!' I said aloud as the realisation hit me.

'Who did what?' Pellegrino asked.

'Merisi,' I said. 'He put sleeping pills in my whisky. That crazy Eyetie bastard could have killed me.'

'You were pretty far down,' Pellegrino admitted. 'Took me a long time to wake you up. I was just considering whether to call an ambulance when you came round. How do you feel now?'

'Fucking awful,' I said, 'but I'll live. Merisi's clothes and belongings are all gone. He's stolen all my cash, so he clearly has no intention of coming back here.' I made the tea, poured out two big, sweet, steaming mugs, gave one to Pellegrino, and sat down at the kitchen table. 'Why are you here?' I asked him. 'Is it just because Merisi has disappeared?'

Pellegrino was actually savouring the aroma of the tea before he tasted it. His lust for the taste was almost pornographic. He took a sip and almost had an orgasm. 'Oh, that is so good,' he breathed. He took another gulp and again started making groaning sounds of ecstasy. Eventually he calmed down and said: 'Thanks to you, I had to get out of Rome anyway.'

'Why "thanks to me"? What did I do?'

'Giulio Mancini was hopping mad because you reneged on your deal to give him two Caravaggios and a box of Viagra in exchange for getting our ChronoConverter chains back. Mancini had made some sort of deal with Mao Salini and his gang, and with the Tomassoni clan, which he cannot fulfil, so he put the blame on me. I've had Doctor Mancini and Salini's ruffians and Tomassoni's street soldiers all out looking for my blood. And you landed me in all that trouble because you got yourself pissed and then knocked me out with the Taser. Anyway, I made it look as if I had fled Rome and . . . here I am. Fortunately, my task there was finished anyway.'

'Wait a minute,' I protested. 'You know I was Mickey Finned with mandrake in the Tavern of the Turk! I wasn't that pissed. That was hardly my fault.'

Pellegrino shrugged. 'I always thought you were the wrong person for this job. You made heavy weather of a simple task, got me and a lot of other people into a lot of trouble, and it took you far too long to find the solutions to what we wanted to know. But it provided hours of entertainment for the folks back home, so that's all that matters.'

I slammed down my mug in anger and tea splashed on to the table. I reached for the kitchen towel and mopped it up. 'You ungrateful bastard,' I roared. 'I was pitched into all this with hardly any choice. I told your President Azumah that I was the wrong person and that I didn't want to do it. I've risked my life several times travelling backwards and forwards in time and then you . . .' I stopped when I realised what Pellegrino had said. 'Hold on,' I continued. 'You don't know that I've found any solutions yet! And what do you mean about providing entertainment for the folks back home? If you mean Tralfamadore, I haven't presented my report to the ChronoCouncil yet. I haven't even prepared my final report.'

Pellegrino chuckled. 'We don't need your final report. We've been monitoring and recording everything that you and Merisi have been doing since you started. Your ChronoTranslator ring is also a ChronoTransmitter. Everything that you and Merisi have done and said while wearing your ChronoTranslator rings has been transmitted back to Tralfamadore and broadcast by radio to the planet, live and as it happened.'

'Everything?' I repeated, desperately wondering whether I had said or done anything horrendously embarrassing or stupid. Yes, I concluded with a sinking feeling, there were many things.

'Oh, don't worry,' Pellegrino said cheerily. 'You might be interested to know that "Quest for Caravaggio's Killer" has been the highest-rated show in Tralfamadorian history. You were a superstar on Tralfamadore before you began. You are now a megastar.'

'Thanks,' I said. 'Do I get a share of the profits and repeat fees?'

'No. You have a Rubens up in your wardrobe and a Caravaggio out in your summerhouse. That's payment enough for your efforts. Personally, I think you're a megaprick, not a megastar. Can I have a coffee now?'

'Make it yourself,' I said, thoroughly piqued at Pellegrino's attitude. My headache had subsided but my brain was spinning with questions. 'I take it that you've searched through all my belongings, if you know where I've stashed the Rubens.'

'Yes, I noticed the frame when I was rifling through your wardrobe. We knew, of course, that that Flemish nancy boy had given you the Rubens portrait of Fillide Melandroni. You will be allowed to keep it as a reward for your efforts. I have taken back your ChronoConverter chain, your ChronoTranslator ring, the Taser pistol, the DVD from President Azumah, and all those fancy clothes. Merisi left all his devices behind as well. They have all been sent back to Tralfamadore, so no more time travel for you . . . or Merisi.' Pellegrino got up and found the jar of coffee, made himself a mug, and returned to the table. He didn't offer me one, the bastard. He started to make the same orgasmic sounds as when he was drinking the tea.

'So I don't need to make a report because all of Tralfamadore has been listening to everything that Merisi and I have been doing and saying since all this began?'

'That's correct,' Pellegrino confirmed. 'They've heard it all.'

'Including everything that I said to Merisi last night?'

'Yes. Including the lie you told.'

'I didn't know what plans you had for Merisi. How could I burden him with the complete truth if you were going to let him live out his natural life, either here or back in the seventeenth century?'

'We understand,' Pellegrino nodded. 'Your compassion does you justice.'

'What did you intend to do with Merisi?'

Pellegrino ignored my question and said: 'Where has he gone?'

'How should I know?'

'You became close friends. Perhaps he confided his plans to you?'

'We are not close friends. I don't know if Merisi ever had any close friends. If I had known what he was up to, he would not have needed to knock me out with my own sleeping pills.'

Pellegrino grunted. 'You two could have concocted an elaborate set-up to fool us.'

'Oh, fuck off,' I said. 'You're a worse investigator that I am.'

'We think he may have gone off with that policewoman.'

'Sergeant Caro? It's more than likely. Have you checked?'

'I haven't been able to,' Pellegrino admitted. 'I travelled directly from the seventeenth century to your house. I cannot drive a car. I wouldn't know where to go even if I did. I don't know how to use a telephone or a computer.'

'So you're not such a clever bastard as you think you are?' I goaded him. I took out my mobile phone. Then another thought struck me. 'If the Tralfamadorians were able to track us and record whatever we were doing, were we really stuck in the seventeenth century when Salini and his gang stole our ChronoConverter chains?'

'Yes, we were,' Pellegrino said. 'We could be tracked and recorded but, without those chains, they could not have got us out of the seventeenth century.'

'So my deal with Doctor Mancini saved us from a life of medieval squalor?'

'Well, it wasn't that bad in the seventeenth century, but yes it did. It was a real cliffhanger back on Tralfamadore when all that was going on. President Azumah declared a planetary holiday so that everyone could listen in without interruption.'

'That's what I live for,' I said, 'to entertain a bunch of aliens with the sound of my bowel movements.' I dialled the number for Bedford police station and asked to speak to P.C. Greenfield. It took a few minutes but he eventually came on the line. 'Steve Maddan here,' I said. 'Is there anything you want to tell me about Sergeant Caro?'

'I was going to ask you the same question later on today,' Greenfield said.

'What's happened? Can you tell me?'

'She hadn't reported for duty for two days, so I went round to her flat. Her front door was unlocked and open. Most of her clothes and personal belongings were gone. We checked her bank accounts. All her money had been withdrawn and the accounts closed. She's definitely done a bunk. She's gone off with that crazy Dago house guest of yours, hasn't she?'

'If you mean Signor Merisi, yes, it looks like she has. He has disappeared as well. That's too much of a coincidence for them both to disappear at the same time and not be together. If you find out where they have gone, can you let me know?'

Greenfield did not reply for a few seconds. 'I might,' he said, 'but we are not going to waste too much time finding her. She has obviously gone off voluntarily with that Dago bastard, so no crime has been committed. Stupid cow . . . she's thrown away a good career and a good life for a no-good foreign wastrel.'

'Love makes us do silly things, constable.'

'Yeah, tell me about it,' Greenfield said, and put the phone down.

'Yes,' I told Pellegrino. 'Isabella Caro has disappeared as well, so they must have gone off together.'

'Italy would be a good bet,' Pellegrino surmised thoughtfully.

'They could have caught a flight out of Luton Airport and landed in Italy before you even woke me up.'

'What about passports?'

'I'm sure Izzy must have had a passport. And, being a police sergeant, I'm sure she would be resourceful enough to obtain whatever documents they might need.'

'Hmm,' Pellegrino grunted. 'Not much point me trying to find them. I don't know how things work in this 21st century world. I don't suppose you would . . .'

'No fucking chance,' I said emphatically. 'What did the Tralfamadorians have planned for Merisi now that this is all over?'

Pellegrino looked uneasy. He said: 'He was to be returned to the exact moment in time and place when he was supposed to have died and he would be allowed to die. He would not even have been aware that he had lived again.'

'Then don't you see,' I said, 'that he was always meant to escape and never go back to Porto Ercole. Caravaggio's body was never found, so this is how it is meant to be.'

'Perhaps,' Pellegrino conceded, 'but the ChronoCouncil are not going to be pleased that a loose cannon like Merisi has been set free in the 21st century to disrupt the fabric of time.'

'What harm can he do?' I said. 'If he claims to be the Baroque painter Caravaggio come back to life, he'll just be written off as a nutcase.'

'He convinced you that he was.'

'No,' I said. 'The only thing that convinced me was that DVD-type thing with the message from President Azumah, and then, of course, the time travelling. Without those to back up his claim, nobody will believe him.'

'You might be right,' Pellegrino conceded, 'but what about his skill as a painter? Nobody living today has got anything like his talent as an artist. If he begins to paint again, it will be obvious that he is somebody extraordinary.'

'Well, he always was somebody extraordinary, even in his own century. And, as I once told him myself, even if he does produce some paintings in the style of Caravaggio, it doesn't prove that he is Caravaggio. Expert forgers like Van Meegeren and Tom Keating have proved that some modern artists have the skill to reproduce old masters. I hope he does find fame again. If he can help to drag art, or what is considered to be meaningful art, kicking and screaming away from the likes of Damian Hirst and his pickled sheep or Tracy Emin and her soiled bedclothes or Gilbert and George with their ludicrous posing, and back to the creation of works that require genuine talent, that touch the human soul, and leave us better and more aware as human beings for seeing them, then I say "long live Caravaggio". He will live forever, you know, far beyond the power of ordinary mortals like us to prevent it.'

Pellegrino regarded me with amusement. 'He really got to you, didn't he?'

'He got to me forty years ago, when I first saw his work in the National Gallery in London. I didn't care then, and I don't care now, about any of his faults as a human being. Like listening to a Beethoven symphony, or reading a novel by Dostoyevsky, or watching a play by William Shakespeare, looking at the works of Caravaggio shows us what we are, why we are and ultimately, makes us better than we are, if we truly open our hearts and our minds. He is one of that very small band of human beings whose genius has made human life profoundly worthwhile for the rest of us.'

'Perhaps you're not such an idiot as I thought,' Pellegrino admitted. 'I don't suppose there is any point in asking you to let us know if you ever find out where Merisi is hiding.'

'None whatsoever,' I replied. 'I wish him and Isabella Caro a long and happy life together, away from all the voyeurs on the planet Tralfamadore.'

'Very well,' Pellegrino said, standing up. 'I now have to make the dangerous journey through time to Tralfamadore and make a personal report to President Azumah and the ChronoCouncil. I will have to report your current intransigent attitude to them.'

'I'm trembling in my boots,' I said. I also stood up. I was beginning to feel a lot better and I could feel my appetite returning. I wanted to get rid of Pellegrino so that I could freshen up by taking a shower and changing my clothes and then have some belated breakfast.

'Do you mind staying here in the kitchen for a minute or two?' Pellegrino asked. 'As you know, the ChronoConverter does not work, without a lot of difficulty, if another human being is present. I will take off in your living room.'

'Be my guest,' I replied. 'Here, take these with you. Despite your lack of respect for my abilities as an investigator, you were a great help to me, and you allowed me to see spectacular things and fascinating people from the seventeenth century that I should never have been allowed by time to see.' I took a carrier bag and filled it with tea bags and a large unopened jar of coffee. 'That'll keep your caffeine buzz going on Tralfamadore for a few weeks.' Pellegrino eagerly accepted the bag. We shook hands and wished each other good luck. I waited a few minutes and then looked into the living room to make sure that Pellegrino had disappeared and was well on his way back to Tralfamadore.

I went upstairs and took a long shower. As I stood with the water, as hot as I could bear, streaming down my head and body, I was feeling very pleased with myself. Okay, I felt like shit at that particular moment, and I was pissed off with Merisi for knocking me out and stealing my money, but I had to accept that he had made the right decision to flee from the Tralfamadorians. All my money worries, such as they were, had vanished. After the Rubens and the Caravaggio in the summerhouse had been sold, the world was not only my oyster but a whole bucketful of Whitstable oysters. I stepped out of the shower, dried myself off, and walked naked into my bedroom to put on fresh clothes. I opened the underwear drawer in my chest of drawers. It was empty apart from one pair of boxers. I opened the sock drawer. That was also empty apart from one pair of hideous tartan socks that had been given to me as a Christmas present. Even Merisi had better taste than to steal them. He had taken everything else. I went to the wardrobe to find a shirt and trousers and realised that a couple of suits and a few shirts were missing as well. I put on a green polo shirt and a pair of Levis. I couldn't resist having another look at my Rubens portrait. I moved the large suitcase and the other junk out of the way and took out the painting. I carefully unwrapped the protective bedsheet and saw, to my abject horror, that there was only an empty frame inside. That chiselling Eyetie scumsucker had taken my Rubens as well. He and Isabella knew very well that I could not report the theft to the police, even if they had known where to look for the culprits. How would I have explained the presence of a priceless Rubens portrait stuck in the back of my wardrobe? I took out the frame and turned it around to find a folded note stuck on the frame with Blu-Tack. I took it off the frame and sat down on the bed to read it. It was written in English in Merisi's almost indecipherably jagged and slanted characters. It read: 'Dear Stefano, My apologies for stealing your Rubens. He was not a bad painter but there is a far better portrait waiting for you in the summerhouse. Isabella and I needed something to set us up when we get to where we are going and your Rubens is perfect (I have not told Isabella that it is a portrait of dear Fillide). We will send you your share when we sell it. I will miss your cheese on toast. Ciao, Michele.'

I screwed up the note and hurled it on to the floor. I relieved my disappointment with a stream of obscenities directed at my departed house guest. Perhaps he would honour his promise to send me my share of the profits after the Rubens had been sold but, knowing human nature as well as Merisi's nature, I thought that that was about as likely as a politician ever telling the truth. I consoled myself with the thought that a genuine portrait by Caravaggio was awaiting me in the summerhouse and I was seized with curiosity to see it. The trouble was that Merisi had just painted it, with modern materials on modern canvas or wood, so it would be impossible to pass off as a genuine Caravaggio, but I might be able, after a time, to age it sufficiently to pass it off as by an unknown artist in the style of Caravaggio, in which case it could still be worth several thousands of pounds.

I went downstairs and out to the summerhouse. It was evening but the light was still good enough to see properly. I opened the summerhouse door with a feeling of great excitement and anticipation. Merisi's easel was still standing upright and there was a piece of sacking covering a painting on the easel. I gently lifted the sacking and saw that it was, indeed, a portrait from the hand of the master, and it was a portrait of me. I removed the sacking and threw it aside. As Merisi had stated in his note, it was a better portrait than the Rubens. Merisi had captured the essence of my character with a finesse that Rembrandt himself would have been proud of. It was a work of the highest skill. It was also completely worthless because, as Merisi's final joke, he had portrayed me in modern dress, in a jacket and tie, complete with a ballpoint pen sticking out of my breast pocket and holding a mobile phone in my hand. It was a work of genius, and completely worthless on the open market. I pulled up an old stool and sat down. My headache was returning and my stomach was churning. I had come out of all of this with nothing. No financial reward whatsoever. All I had was a headful of amazing memories and a portrait that I could hang on my wall but never mention to anyone that it was a genuine Caravaggio. I almost wished that I had not lied to Merisi during our final conversation. But, even if I had known that he had stolen my Rubens and left me with nothing except a worthless masterpiece, how could I have told Merisi that his own beloved mother had effectively caused his death. Mario Minnitti had not murdered Caravaggio. Two months before Caravaggio died, his real father, King Henry IV of France, had been assassinated by a deranged Roman Catholic named Ravaillac. It was becoming more and more well-known that Caravaggio was King Henry's illegitimate son. After Henry was assassinated, Costanza Colonna grieved for her lost royal lover, the true love of her life. Costanza Colonna knew full well that, away from the protection of the Knights of Saint John on Malta, or away from the secure grounds of the Palazzo Cellamare in Chaia, it was only a matter of time before the assassins caught up with Caravaggio. They had nearly succeeded outside the Osteria di Cerriglio in 1609. After talking to Costanza, and her major-domo Fillipo, the identity of Caravaggio's attempted murderer was obvious, although I did not tell them so. It could only have been one person. What Costanza did not know was that the attack outside the Osteria di Cerriglio had been arranged by her son Fabrizio Sforza. Caravaggio had invited Fabrizio to go with him to the tavern that night but Fabrizio had claimed to have made other plans. Only Fabrizio knew that Caravaggio was visiting the tavern on that night. Only he could have arranged to have a gang of assassins in place when Caravaggio emerged, drunk, from the tavern. The planned brutal assassination had failed to finish off Caravaggio only because the attackers were disturbed and had to flee. A few months later, only Costanza, her major-domo Fillipo, and Fabrizio Sforza knew that Caravaggio had suddenly left Chaia for Rome on the felucca. Nobody else could have known where Caravaggio was going and certainly not the false culprit Mario Minnitti, who was still living happily in Sicily, unaware that his beloved wife Rafaella had once borne a son fathered by Caravaggio. When Caravaggio left so precipitously for Rome, Costanza Colonna immediately despatched Fabrizio to ride to the next port of call in Palo with orders for the captain of the fortress to detain Caravaggio so that she could make one last desperate attempt to get him back to the safety of the Palazzo Cellamare. Caravaggio had been detained but what Costanza and Fabrizio did not know was that Caravaggio was carrying so much money and could then bribe his way out of prison. Fabrizio came back to the prison at Palo and found that Caravaggio had got away. Fabrizio made frantic enquiries in the area and discovered, by a process of elimination, that Caravaggio was making for Porto Ercole. Fabrizio rode to Porto Ercole and was waiting there when Caravaggio arrived. He found out that Caravaggio was desperately ill and had been taken to the local infirmary. Everything else that I had told Merisi about the mysterious stranger who had forced him to drink the golden chain poison was true, except it was Fabrizio Sforza, not Mario Minnitti. Just one word had told me that the putative assassin was not an artist himself. He had said: "This will ease all your problems. It is something you have always coveted, as all you artists do." The phrase: '. . . as all YOU artist's do' clearly indicated that the assassin was not an artist himself.

Why had Fabrizio tried to murder his half-brother? Fabrizio always knew that his mother Costanza loved her son Michele more than she had loved him. Fabrizio was a tempestuous and cruel character. When he had found out that Caravaggio was his illegitimate half-brother, and the son of a king to boot, his jealousy and hatred was intense, but he was shrewd enough not to show it to either Caravaggio or his mother. Caravaggio was a threat to Fabrizio's position and inheritance. Fabrizio well knew that Caravaggio had been very fond of Fillipo's daughter, Gabriella, and that is why he had violated her, as an act of sheer petulant revenge. As only a mother knows how, Costanza could not help loving Fabrizio but even she could see what a worthless and cruel person he was and that is why, exasperated by his catalogue of crimes and especially by the rape of Gabriella, she finally banished him to the care of the Knights of Saint John on Malta. So Fabrizio's cruel rape of Gabriella had backfired because his banishment to Malta meant that he could do nothing to harm Caravaggio for the time being. Several years later, Caravaggio played right into Fabrizio's hands when he travelled to Malta on Fabrizio's own galley. Fabrizio could not believe his luck. But still Fabrizio could not harm Caravaggio while he was under the protection of the Knights of Saint John. He had to get Caravaggio away from Malta somehow. Knowing all about Caravaggio's volcanic temper, he encouraged Marco Malaspina to insult Caravaggio, knowing full well that Caravaggio would respond with aggression and end up in a cell in the Castel Saint Elmo. Fabrizio was only too willing to help Caravaggio to escape from Malta because then Caravaggio would be at his mercy, or at the mercy of any other assassin while the dreaded sentence of banda capitale was in force. Fabrizio was content to take his time. Eventually, he heard that Caravaggio had returned to his mother's Palazzo Cellamare in Naples. Fabrizio moved to Naples and waited for his chance. Finally, the perfect opportunity to get rid of Caravaggio, without any suspicion falling on himself, presented itself in Porto Ercole.

Perhaps Costanza loved Caravaggio more than her other sons because she had not been able to raise him and take care of him, and was overwhelmed with guilt and regret. Caravaggio had included what were effectively portraits of Costanza in three different paintings, The Rest on the Flight to Egypt, Penitent Magdalen and Death of the Virgin. Today, we can look in a reference book and see them all together. Fabrizio, in his time, could not simply look in a book. All three pictures were painted for different patrons. Only Fabrizio, as the son of the Marchesa Costanza Colonna, or someone of equally noble birth, had an entrée to all the great palazzi or churches where the three different paintings were kept. He was outraged that Caravaggio had portrayed his mother like that, not knowing, at that time, that Caravaggio was also Costanza's son. Costanza Colonna herself had given Fabrizio the golden chain poison, obtained from Cardinal Del Monte, and told Fabrizio to find Caravaggio on that last fateful journey and told Fabrizio that if he found Caravaggio suffering, as he had after the attack outside the Osteria di Cerriglio, that Fabrizio was to administer the poison and put Caravaggio out of his misery as an act of mercy. When Fabrizio found out that Caravaggio was desperately ill in the infirmary in Porto Ercole, he knew it was a perfect opportunity to get rid of his hated half-brother without any suspicion falling on himself. It would be assumed that Caravaggio had simply died of the effects of a fever picked up on his last terrible journey.

How could I have told Caravaggio that he had been murdered by his own brother with a poisonous potion provided by his own mother? I could not burden Merisi with that knowledge. He would have had to live with it for the rest of his life. To me, all these events were dusty subjects in reference books, but Merisi had actually lived them. He had really loved and cared for Costanza Colonna and, perhaps, Fabrizio as well. Better that he never knew.

I sat in the summerhouse, in the warmth of the evening, with the sun slanting through the windows in an effect that would have pleased Merisi, and studied his portrait of me, his last joke at my expense. For weeks he had irritated me, enraged me, inconvenienced me, robbed me, and been a real pain in the arse, but I found myself missing him already. As Caravaggio himself had shown us with the genius of his work, that is human nature in all its manifold perversity.

Author's Coda . . . the true story of Caravaggio

The quotation on the title page records the astonishment felt in Naples at the power and drama of Caravaggio's work on the art world of the city where, fleeing from Roman justice, Caravaggio had arrived to take up his career again. Such astonishment was eventually felt throughout Europe. What this tormented and dislikeable genius had achieved was not just a new art, but a new vision which has radically affected the course of painting and other visual mediums to this day. It has been claimed that modern art begins with Caravaggio and it is difficult to disagree with that assessment. In between bouts of drunken violence, Caravaggio obsessively committed to canvas, without bothering with preparatory drawings, works of emotional power arguably unsurpassed by any painter before or since. The aggression and prickly sensitivity of Caravaggio's personality is undeniable but there was not the coldly arrogant cruelty of, for instance, that other genius, the sculptor Bernini, who ordered the face of his wayward mistress Costanza to be slashed to ribbons with a razor.

On the surface Caravaggio was a thoroughly despicable character but to look at his works of such tenderness as the Madonna of Loreto, the frank sensuality of his portrait of Fillide Melandroni as St. Catherine, the sympathy for human suffering as expressed on the face of Saint Andrew as he hangs dying on the Cross, or his moving penance for his sin of murder as expressed in David with the Head of Goliath, in which the severed head is a portrait of Caravaggio himself, is to feel that the wellsprings of humanity, in the best sense of that word, ran deep in Caravaggio's persona and the angry lashings out recorded throughout his life were driven more by a sense of insecurity, and perhaps inferiority, rather than from an inherently sadistic nature.

'That Terrible Shadowing' is, of course, a fantasy but it was prompted by my fascination with Caravaggio's life and work and with the compelling idea of what it might be like to meet and talk to him. Within the story known facts about Caravaggio's life, and that of his contemporaries, have been woven into the narrative as they actually happened. Incidents that might appear to be unlikely inventions, such as Caravaggio's denial and rejection of his own brother, or the trial for the scabrous libelling of Giovanni Baglione, or the slaying of Ranuccio Tomassoni, or the Houdini-like escape from a dungeon in Malta, or the mysterious disappearance of Caravaggio's body after his staggering trek along a baking fever-ridden coast, are all true. Only where facts are not known have incidents been invented to enliven and progress the narrative. Caravaggio was not murdered, as far as we know, but he might easily have been. The ultimate secret of Caravaggio's background is an invention, but an invention which fits all historical facts and could have been entirely possible.

Having tampered with the story of Caravaggio in such a way, however, I am anxious that the true story of his life and work should not be traduced by this work of semi-fiction, although I hope that this entertainment will prompt in every reader an interest in this amazing character. If any reader wishes to find out the true story of Caravaggio, and the febrile world of 17th century Roman art, then I recommend 'Caravaggio: A Life' by the art historian and educator Helen Langdon, to whom this book is jointly dedicated. Helen Langdon's biography is beautifully and clearly written, is as exciting as any novel, and is packed with scholarship and fascinating insights about this most complex and gifted man. Let me make it absolutely clear that any errors of fact in 'That Terrible Shadowing' are my fault and not Helen Langdon's. Without her work, my efforts would have been much more difficult and a lot less interesting, and I thank her heartily.